EMPYRION

An epic SF fantasy in two
The Search for Fierra
The Siege of Dome

Sent on special assignment to the new colony of
Empyrion, ten light years from earth, Orion Treet and
his companions find themselves enmeshed in deadly
conflict between two civilizations dramatically opposed.

Can the free and perfect world of Fierra escape
annihilation?

Treet, with a handful of rebels, stands alone against
the evil might of Dome, as events move inexorably
towards a world-shaking climax.

STEPHEN LAWHEAD is the author of some fourteen
outstanding fantasy and science-fiction novels, including
the *Song of Albion* trilogy (Lion), *The Dragon King
Saga* (Lion), *The Pendragon Cycle* (Lion), *Byzantium*
(HarperCollins) and *The Celtic Crusades* trilogy
(HarperCollins). Sales of his books have reached
over two million copies worldwide.

Lawhead, an American, currently lives with his wife
in Austria.

Other titles by Stephen Lawhead:

EMPYRION

The Search for Fierra
The Siege of Dome

STEPHEN LAWHEAD

A LION BOOK

Copyright © 1985 and 1986 Author, Author LLC

The author asserts the moral right
to be identified as the author of this work

A Lion Book
an imprint of
Lion Hudson plc
Mayfield House, 256 Banbury Road,
Oxford OX2 7DH, England
www.lionhudson.com
ISBN 0 7459 1872 7

First published by Crossway Books
A division of Good News Publishers
Westchester, Illinois 60153, USA

First UK edition 1986, in two volumes
Combined-volume edition 1990
10 9 8

All rights reserved

A catalogue record for this book is available
from the British Library

Printed and bound in Great Britain by
Cox and Wyman Ltd, Reading

Stephen Lawhead's website address is:
www.stephenlawhead.com

And though the last lights off the black West went
  Oh, morning, at the brown brink Eastward,
      Springs—
Because the Holy Ghost over the bent
World broods with warm breast and ah! bright
  Wings.

G. M. Hopkins, God's Grandeur

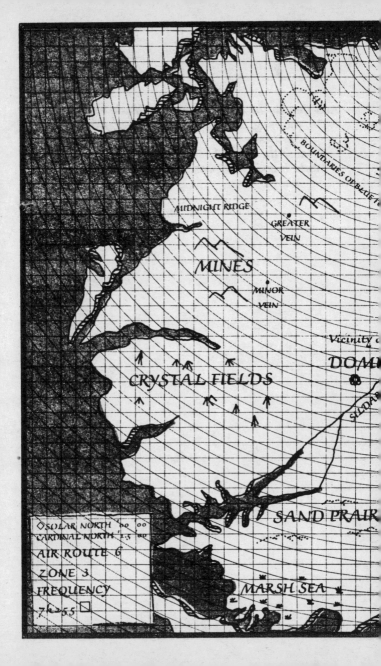

BOOK ONE

The Search for Fierra

PRELUDE

V1: [Static] We're down! And it's beautifull Wonderfull

V2: It's heaven! It really is.

V1: All probe data confirms observational analysis. Geoscience Officer Tovardy will dispatch a brief preliminary report.

V2: Okay—

V1: Keep it short, Ben.

V2: Right—just the highlights. Atmosphere is thin, but friendly—high oxygen and nitrogen content; other gas ratios well within normal tolerances—except for minute levels of rardon ionization in the inert sectors. No idea at present what effect that will have on freebreathing; we'll check that out. Weather—there's no weather to speak of here! It's Hawaii everyday. No observed cyclonic disturbances; projected climatic variation: negligible. Flora and fauna? This is a fairly complex environment. It's going to take time to sort everything out properly. At present no known pathogenic lifeforms identified. No sentient life either, for that matter. Like I said, the place is an absolute paradise! That's it for now. Full report to follow.

TEN SECONDS SILENCE

V1: Okay, let's take a look . . . How long ago did this happen?

V3: Three minutes maybe . . . not more.

V1: Ground control, we've got a situation here. We're not sure . . . [static—two seconds] . . . event monitors have picked up electromagnetic disturbances that could indicate . . . [static—four seconds]—anomaly in singularity region. Don't know what it means. We'll stay on it at this end. Next dispatch will be at our regularly scheduled time. This is Empyrion Colony Com—[static—five seconds]

END OF TRANSCRIPT

*T*he body staring up through the translucent green of the nutrient bath might have been dead. It floated beneath the surface, open-eyed, its face becalmed, a snaking nimbus of dark hair spreading like a black halo: a saint embalmed in emerald amber.

Presently a small bubble formed on the rim of one nostril, puffed up bigger, and broke free, spiraling to the surface. Plick! This was followed by another slightly larger bubble, which also spun up to the surface of the bath, drifted momentarily, and burst. Plick!

A whole fountain of bubbles erupted and boiled up, and in the center, rising with them, the head of Orion Tiberias Treet, sputtering and inhaling great draughts of air, like a whale breeching after a long nap on the ocean floor.

Two broad hands came up, dashing liquid from two dark eyes, pushing ropy strands of hair aside. Treet snatched up a watch from the rim of the white marble bath and held it before his face. "Six minutes!" he shouted triumphantly. "A new record."

"I'm impressed."

Treet glanced up quickly and saw a stranger sitting on the edge of the bath opposite him. The stranger had a needle gun aimed at his throat, and, contrary to his word, did not seem at all impressed with the new submergence record. Besides himself and the gunman, there was not another person in the public bath.

"What do you want?" Treet asked, the skin at his throat tingling beneath the aim of the needle gun.

"I have what I want: you," replied the gunman. Cool menace clipped his words efficiently. "Get out of the soup and get dressed."

Orion Treet glared dully at the slim needle gun in his abductor's hand as he rose slowly from the bath, took up the fluffy white bath towel the attendant had given him upon entering, and began drying his limbs and torso with exaggerated care in order to give himself a moment to think. By the time he was fully dressed he had concluded that it was probably no use trying to talk his way out of whatever it was this stranger with the gun wanted to do with him—he looked like a man who was used to having his way, and was not overly shy about how he got it.

"You have been a problem, Treet," the man was saying. "I don't like problems. In my line of work, problems cost me money, and you've cost me plenty. It's over now, so you might as well relax and put that brain of yours in neutral for a while. I don't want you taxing yourself over how to get away this time. Just stand easy, do as you're told, and you'll likely live that much longer. You like living, don't you, Treet?"

Treet had to admit that he did indeed like living; it was, after all, one of the things that made life so worthwhile. But he did not share this observation with the man training the needle gun on his jugular. Instead, he just glared and tried to look dutifully irritated.

The man took a short step closer. The gun did not waver. "I almost had you in Cairo, and then again in Addis Ababa, Cologne, Zurich, Salzburg, Milan, Tokyo, and San Francisco. I've got to hand it to you, you're a shrewdy. I don't know when I've enjoyed myself more, but it's over."

"As long as it's over," replied Treet evenly, "maybe you won't mind telling me why you've been trailing me all this time. What do you want?" He had known since Zurich that he was being followed, but was unsure why, though several possibilities sprang to mind. Still, he felt entitled to an explanation. Wasn't that a victim's prerogative?

"I don't mind telling you at all, scumbag. There are some people who want to talk to you. They seem quite anxious, in fact. Personally I don't give a rat's hind end. I'd just as soon drop you where you stand."

At least this meant the man would not kill him outright. But who were the people so desperate for conversation? Treet ran down a list of former employers, angry innkeepers, outraged restauranteurs, and offended debtors of various sorts, but the effort proved futile. He could not come up with anyone who would go to this amount of trouble to reach him. "So?"

"So, bright boy, we lockstep it to the nearest teleterm. I'm going to report in. Keep your hands where I can see them; turn around slowly and move. Outside there's a terminal directly to the right. If you so much as deviate one millimeter from the course, you're dead. Understand?"

Treet understood. They turned and marched from the spa and out into the main corridor of Houston International Skyport. Travelers, not a few of them free-state refugees by the tattered look of them, jammed hip to thigh, swept along the moving walkway before them, and Treet entertained the notion of jumping on the conveyor and worming himself into the crowd—a trick he had used in Salzburg. He started to turn his head, but felt the needle gun's sharp nose in the small of his back.

"Try it, slime ball. Let's see how you look with a cyanide tattoo." The voice behind him was disconcertingly close.

"Don't get your hopes up." Treet saw the triangular sign with the distinctive blue lightning bolt on a white oval screen and stopped in front of the booth. Passengers sliding by on the walkway ignored the two men as they squeezed into the booth together.

The gunman jammed a card into the slot above the keypad, and the screen flicked on. A line of blue numbers appeared in the upper right hand corner of the oval screen. Treet watched as his captor entered an alfanumeric code; the screen blanked. Instantly another code came up in the center of the screen. With one hand the man typed in two words: GOT HIM.

For a moment nothing happened. Then as Treet watched, hoping for some clue to the identity of the person or persons on the other end of the linkup, the words HOLD FOR PICKUP appeared below the gunman's entry. With that, the gunman tapped a key, the screen cleared, and his card ejected from the slot. "Okay, move it."

"Where to?"

"Heliport Six." The man jerked the gun upward toward Treet's chin. "Let's take our time, shall we? There's no hurry, and I wouldn't want you to get overheated."

They exited the booth and shunned the peoplemover, walking instead to a bank of escalators. They jumped on an escalator labeled TO HELIPORT SIX and rode up three levels to the rooftop. Through the tinted bubble, the sky glowed dark green-gray and the sun shone a nauseating chartreuse. Radiating out from the bubble were at least a dozen landing platforms on the end of walkway tubes. Helicopters sat on two or three platforms, their rotors spinning idly.

"Number three platform," the gunman whispered in Treet's ear. He underscored his words with another nudge from the needle gun. When they reached the tube entrance, the gunman shoved Treet into a sculptured foam chair and said, "Sit."

Treet sat, his hands atop his knees, his knees beneath his chin. "Who's coming to pick me up?"

"You'll see soon enough."

"How much are they paying you?"

"Trying to figure out how much you're worth? Forget it—you're not worth that much."

"I'll pay you more." Treet thought he saw a glimmer of interest flit across the man's pinched features.

"How much more?"

"How much are they paying you?"

"Thirty-five thousand in metal, plus expenses. I have a lot of expenses." The man with the gun watched him slyly. "Well?"

"I'll give you forty thousand." Treet tried to sound as if that were in some way possible.

"You lying filth! I ought to drill you for jollies."

Treet shrugged. "If you don't want to be reasonable—"

"What makes you think I'd let you go for any amount of money? You pus suckers are all alike."

"You won't let me go?"

"Never. I'd kill you first, and that's a fact."

"Why? I've never done anything to you."

"Principle. How far do you think I'd get in this business if my clients couldn't trust me to deliver the goods? Besides, you've made me look very bad in front of a very influential client. I don't like that—bad for business."

"You've got me now, don't you?"

"I've got you all right. But I lost a double bonus along the way."

Treet could tell he was getting nowhere and decided to wait and take his chances with whoever showed up on landing pad number three. He slumped back in his chair and tried to think who might value his company at thirty-five thousand plus expenses—and in precious metals, yet. He was still trying to produce a name when he heard the muffled sound of approaching rotors.

"On your feet, grunt-face." The gunman held his weapon

level and pointed down the tube to where the helicopter was dropping onto the pad at the other end. "After you."

Treet got slowly to his feet and shambled down the tube, watching as the copter's sidehatch opened and two men, dressed in dark blue paramilitary uniforms, scrambled out. They came to stand on either side of the tube exit and waited. Outside, the air was warm and rather humid. As Treet stepped from the tube, a hot wind from the helicopter's twin jets hit him in the face. The uniformed men grabbed his arms and led him forward without a word.

A third man inside the copter held the hatch open. Treet turned. "I guess this is good-bye," he told the gunman.

"This is good-bye all right." The gunman raised the needle gun, and his finger pressed the flat trigger.

Treet cringed away from the impact as a little puff of vapor issued from the sharp muzzle. He did not feel a thing. Was the gun unloaded after all?

He glanced down and saw a tiny needle sticking out of his stomach, its red cap pulsating, pumping poison into him. His hands reached for the dart, plucked it out, and threw it before his guards could stop him. Momentarily free, he turned and dived away from the helicopter, hit the rubber surface of the landing pad, rolled to his feet, staggered once, and fell backward with arms outstretched, his head bouncing off the pad on impact. Treet stared upward at the clear blue Texas sky as his eyesight dimmed and the leering faces above him diffused and disappeared.

17

T W O

Waves crashed in his head and his stomach heaved, as with the ocean's swell. Somewhere nearby someone was moaning, and Treet wished they would shut up—until he realized it was him. Well, perhaps moaning was called for, then.

After several long minutes, the ocean effect subsided and he battled his eyelids open. But the light hurt his head, so he closed his eyes again and listened instead. The moaning—his moaning—had stopped, and silence lay thick and artificial. A synthetic silence, he decided, as if the quiet had been manufactured in some way and layered over the noise that was going on all around him just to prevent him from hearing it.

He sniffed the air and smelled the heavily filtered, oxygen-enhanced stuff typical of a sealed building. Wherever they had brought him, it was at least up to code. But that could be any relatively modern structure anywhere in the Northern Hemisphere. Nevertheless, he guessed there was a good chance he was still in Houston. The copter—had there been a copter?—yes, he remembered something about a helicopter—had come from somewhere close to the skyport. No more than four or five minutes away.

Of course, they could have taken him anywhere after that. He had no idea how long he had been out. A few hours, most likely; less than a day. His stomach gurgled, reminding him he had not eaten in quite a while. Orion, he thought, you've really done it this time.

Close on this thought came a question: *what* had he done? He still didn't know. If he hadn't tried to escape, he would have found out by now. No, that pinhead gunman had shot him *before* he had tried to escape. At least the needle hadn't carried the promised dose of cyanide. His hand went to the spot on his stomach where the dart had stuck him. The wound, though tiny, throbbed mightily and was inflamed.

18

He was still taking physical inventory when he heard the sigh of a door opening automatically. "Up and at 'em, tiger," called a cheery female voice. "They're waiting for you upstairs." She gave the word *upstairs* a subtle rising inflection—as if Upstairs was the name of a foreign territory not altogether friendly to the interests of the sovereign state of Texas.

Treet kept his eyes closed and feigned sleep. The ruse did not work. "I've been monitoring you on my video, Mr. Treet. I know you're awake, although you probably feel a little rocky. The best thing is to be up and moving around. The drug will leave your system that much quicker."

Whoever owned that dreadfully cheerful voice was now standing directly over him. He could hear her breathing down on him, and then felt a cool touch on his forehead. He opened his eyes to see a rather severely pretty redhead looking down at him. She wore the white-and-blue shift of a nurse. "Temperature and blood pressure normal," the nurse announced, withdrawing her hand from his head.

"Where am I?" Treet made a move to get up, and his stomach rolled dangerously. The nurse expertly slipped her arm under his shoulders and levered him into a sitting position.

"All will be explained, Mr. Treet. I'm to see that you are up and around as soon as possible."

"And nothing else. Is that it?"

"I wouldn't want to spoil the surprise now, would I?" She gave him a quick professional smile. "Swing your legs over the edge and try to stand."

Treet did as he was told. He had a feeling that the boys in the blue uniforms were hunkered nearby, ready to pounce on him if he needed pouncing on again. He decided to go along peacefully for the moment. Keeping his options open was how he described it to himself.

Leaning on the nurse's arm, Treet managed to stagger, like a sailor making landfall after a long storm-tossed voyage, across to the door of the small, single-bed infirmary. The door slid open once again and admitted them to a brightly lit foyer done up in pleasant greens with blue and yellow foam chairs clustered around the cylindrical screen of a holovision: a doctor's waiting room.

"You're doing very well," said the nurse amiably. "I won't be a moment. Walk around if you like." She ducked behind a counter and into a cubbyhole. Treet heard her voice speaking low—into a teleterm, he guessed—saying, "He's ready, Mr. Varro. Yes, I will. You're welcome."

Varro? Varlo? He didn't know anyone named Varlo. The name did not connect. At the opposite end of the waiting room was a window. Treet walked over nonchalantly, pulled the green curtain aside, and peeked out. He looked down several stories into a square courtyard. Blank windows from four facing walls stared into the same courtyard, and none of them gave any clue to where he was. The sky, what he could see of it, was cloudless and greenish with a tint of orange.

"Mr. Treet?" The nurse called him pleasantly. "Your escort is here."

He turned to see another blue uniform approaching—a different blue uniform than the one worn by the men in the helicopter. Theirs had been dark blue with flashy yellow insignias on the upper arms. This man wore lighter blue, with a white collar and a black belt around the middle. Attached to the belt was a flat brown pouch which, Treet supposed, contained a needle gun or stunner of some sort.

The man beckoned to Treet with a jerk of his head. Treet joined him, fell into step, and was conveyed down a wide, low, vacant corridor, across a pentagonal lobby, and finally down another, shorter corridor to a waiting elevator. The elevator was open; they stepped in, and the guard pressed a button. The doors slid closed, and the elevator rose. There was, Treet noticed, only one button on the panel, marked OPEN/CLOSED. Which meant that the elevator was designed to be run from somewhere else. From upstairs, Treet guessed.

As the elevator rose, Treet weighed the advantages of striking up a conversation with his guard. Since no one else he'd met this day—if it *was* still this day—seemed inclined to enlighten him as to the nature of his predicament, he doubted whether a holstered elevator attendant would be the one to start giving away free information. So he stood and gazed at a point on the ceiling just over the elevator doors and waited to find out what sort of fate would greet him on the other side.

The elevator ride was longer than he guessed it would be. But finally the doors slid back to reveal a lushly carpeted receiving room of goodly size. Live plants in beaten brass pots lined softly glowing walls. Airy hangings of fabric and metal dangled from the ceiling, which slanted upward just slightly. From somewhere the sound of water splashing in a fountain-pool reached Treet's ears.

The guard lifted a hand like a doorman and ushered his passenger out of the elevator. Treet stepped out onto the cream-colored carpet. The elevator door closed behind him, and he was left alone. He stood waiting for something to happen, but nothing did or seemed about to, so he began looking around.

Large wooden doors—black teak, floor to ceiling, ridiculously expensive—stood on either side of the room. Neither door had any markings. Straight ahead were equally large double doors, but these were studded with gold or brass and were painted bright colors. Closer, he could see that the colors formed a design: two winged men, one on each door, faced one another with outstretched arms—one arm shoulder-high and the other raised over their heads. The images had long hair, braided into a single braid down their backs. They wore long robes or gowns, flowing as if in the wind; the robes were marked with spiral designs and symbols in red, blue, violet, and gold. The men's wings were gold, with long, broad feathers spreading out behind them the length of their bodies. Their faces were in profile—straight, angular faces with large, dark eyes. Upon their chests they wore some kind of copper-colored amulet on a chain; the amulet was in the shape of a symbol or a letter from some alphabet Treet did not recognize. Between the winged men and above them a very round and rosy sun cast down golden rays that wiggled like snakes. The sun was divided equally, one half on each door, and its wriggling rays slanted down across the surfaces of both doors, which Treet could now see were bound in leather.

"You're awake sooner than expected." The voice behind Treet did not take him completely by surprise. This had been a day for people sneaking up behind him, and he had come to expect it.

Treet turned to see a stiff, round-headed man approaching with hands folded behind his back. A fringe of short-cropped gray hair accented the roundness of his head, as did full cheeks that were thickening to jowl. The head perched on a short neck over sloping shoulders and overlooked a sturdy, short-limbed body.

"I see you appreciate fine things." The man smiled, glanced at the handsome doors with the approval and detachment of a museum curator, and then offered his hand. "I am Varro, and I am pleased to meet the famous Orion Treet."

Treet did not know whether he should shake the man's hand or throttle him, but considered that he would gain nothing by being belligerent, so took it, though a little less cordially than he might have under ordinary circumstances. Varro evidently sensed the restraint and responded, "I *do* most heartily apologize for the misunderstanding at the airport."

"Misunderstanding? Was that what it was?" Treet pulled a face that was meant to convey concern, and also anger under civilized restraint. His tone, however, was bewilderment.

"I am afraid so." Varro shook his head, as if deeply regretting what had taken place. He stepped close to Treet and took his arm, leading him a few steps aside to a nook. One wall of the two-walled cranny was glass; another was flat slabs of irregular stone down which a pleasant cascade of water trickled into a pool somewhere below them. "Please sit down, Mr. Treet. I'd like a word with you before we go in."

Treet glanced out the window and saw that they were atop the building. Green forested hills stretched out into blue misty distance. There was not a single sign of Houston, or any other city—at least not from this view. Treet sat down on a polished wood bench facing an opposite bench on which Varro settled himself. "I'd like a word with you too, Mr. Varro. The first one being why—why have you people been following me?"

Varro smiled again, showing very small fine white teeth. "Nothing sinister, Mr. Treet, I assure you. Perhaps I'd better explain."

"Perhaps you'd better. No one else seems inclined to, and I'm becoming testy. I get that way when abused."

"It isn't what you're thinking."

"I'm not thinking anything. I haven't done anything—as far as I know. Have I?"

"We're not the militia, Mr. Treet. But I'm not aware that you have done anything you ought to worry about. We don't particularly care one way or another. It is none of our concern."

"You're just concerned with drugging innocent citizens and kidnapping them in broad daylight." Treet looked down at his sore stomach and rubbed it distractedly.

"Please, I am sorry for that unfortunate incident. As I have said, it was a misunderstanding. The man responsible has been

22

severely . . . ah, reprimanded." Treet wondered what the clown at the airport had suffered for popping him with the needle. Varro did not give him time to wonder for long, but continued. "Now then," brushing all unpleasantness behind him, "I assume you have heard of Cynetics Corporation?"

"I've heard of it," replied Treet coolly. Who hadn't? It was one of the six or eight largest multinationals on the planet. Maybe *the* largest, for all anybody knew. Corporation law prevented anyone—especially the government, as long as a company paid its tribute—from finding out just how big it really was. But Cynetics holdings were thought to include whole countries, several independent corporate states, and not a few colonies. "What does Cynetics want with me?. I take it we're on Cynetics property somewhere?"

"Yes, Mr. Treet, we are. North American headquarters just outside Houston." Varro glanced back at the leather-bound doors quickly. "I'll try to explain briefly. We haven't much time. I wanted to speak to you first before we went in. We can talk at length after we have seen him."

"Him?"

"Chairman Neviss." Varro spoke as though Treet should have known instinctively who he meant.

"Oh," Treet said. Ordinarily he would have been honored by a private interview with one of the most powerful men in the known universe, but today the prospect did not exactly send a thrill through his viscera. Under the circumstances, he felt he was being extremely magnanimous to even consider an interview.

"He is intent on seeing you, Mr. Treet. He is convinced you are the man for a special assignment he has in mind."

"Which is?"

Varro made an impatient movement with his hand. "I'll let him tell you about it. What I want you to understand is that he is not at all well. Please, I am asking your cooperation. Do not excite him or cause him anguish in any way."

"How would I do that?"

"By refusing him."

"You mean I'm supposed to agree in advance to whatever he wants? What's the point of even going in there?"

"No, no. Nothing like that. I just meant—well, if you like what he offers, accept by all means. If not, just tell him you will require time to think it over. He'll understand that. He won't like it, but he'll understand it. However," Varro brightened once more, "I think you will find his proposal attractive."

"I'll play along." Treet shrugged. Why not? He had nothing to lose.

"Good. I knew I could trust you. Shall we?" Varro got up and moved off toward the painted doors, and Treet followed him. This time, as they approached the threshold the panels swung inward on silent hinges, and the two men entered a gallery decorated with pottery and alabaster carvings displayed on metallic pedestals, each with a light shining down upon it from the ceiling as in a museum. All of the pieces were pre-Columbian Aztec. It was an impressive collection.

At the end of the gallery another set of doors opened to reveal a young woman, dressed incongruously in a long white robe—much like the two winged men on the outer doors. Her hair was jet, like her eyes, and bound in a single braid down her back. Her skin was light bronze and porcelain smooth, her cheekbones high, her lips dark. She was easily the most beautiful woman Treet had seen in a very long time. He could not help staring.

"Miss Yarden Talazac," said Varro, "his executive administrator."

She offered Treet her hand and said demurely, "Welcome. I'm glad to know you, Mr. Treet. This way, if you please."

"My pleasure," replied Treet sincerely. For the pleasure of being in this radiant creature's company, Treet was willing to forgive whatever grievances he had been nursing to this point. Even his punctured stomach did not feel so bad anymore.

The stunning Miss Talazac conducted them into a cavernous domed room whose ceiling was dark and winking with artificial starlight like the ceiling of a planetarium. There were no windows, but at intervals around the circumference of the dome lighted niches contained statuary.

Before them, on a dais served by a long sloping ramp next to a very large and old-fashioned wooden chair, stood a smoking brazier on a tripod. The smoke was scented—like flowers, but delicate and airy, not oppressive. Treet felt as if his senses sharpened upon entering the room and wondered whether the incense had anything to do with that impression.

In the oversize chair facing him sat a man whose age could not be determined. This, Treet assumed, was Chairman Neviss.

Though his very ordinary features were expressionless, he appeared alert, and Treet thought something like mirth played at the edges of the full, fleshy lips—as if the Chief Officer of Cynetics were enjoying some amusing private observation.

"Chairman, may I present Mr. Orion Treet." It was Miss Talazac who spoke rather than Varro.

Slowly, almost painfully, the Chairman rose and, with a condescending nod of his head, diffidently offered his hand to Treet. Treet approached the dais and accepted the handshake. The grasp was dry and cool, and Treet felt bones beneath the flesh of the palm. "I'm glad you're here, Mr. Treet. I have been looking forward to this meeting with some anticipation."

Treet did not know what to say, so mumbled something about being honored and privileged to find himself in such exalted company.

"Please be seated, gentlemen." The Chairman indicated chairs, and Treet twisted his head to see that chairs had appeared where there had been no chairs before. Varro, no doubt, had produced them. Miss Talazac, on the other hand, had disappeared.

Treet sat down and rested his arms easily on the armrests. Now that he was here, he suddenly felt very nervous, very intense—almost excited. What was this all about? Why the intrigue? What did they want?

Chairman Neviss looked at him dryly, and then his mouth opened in a wide grin. "Orion Treet," he said, shaking his head, "this is indeed a pleasure."

"I'm honored, sir."

"Do you know that I have been following your writings for thirty years? From the beginning, in fact. You have a style, sir. Lucid. Astute. I like that; it shows a clear-thinking mind. Your grasp of the interconnected events of history is simply astounding. I envy you your abilities, sir—and there is not much in this world that I do envy."

It took Treet some moments to realize that it was indeed himself that the Chairman was talking about—he always had that reaction to praise. "Thank you, sir," he muttered.

"No. Thank *you*, Orion Treet. I have learned a great deal from you. I respect you as a man of keen intellect and sensitivity. Also a man to be trusted. Rare these days to find that, I'm sorry to say. Very rare, sir."

Treet wondered whether the Chairman knew that his honored guest had been pursued across three continents and then abducted by a contract nab artist in order to make this cozy meeting possible. Likely not—though he might be interested to know. Treet decided not to play that card just yet.

"I can't think, however," Chairman Neviss continued, "that writing monographs on history—excellent though they are—would offer much of a living for you."

True, true. No one had much use for history anymore; the present was enigma enough. And though his work was on laser-file with every major library in the world, as well as available through several global datanet services, his royalties from sub-scriber fees were barely enough to cover necessities. "I manage," Treet allowed.

"I'm sure you do. But I am in a position to help you, Mr. Treet. I have a proposition I think you will want to consider."

"I'm always willing to listen."

"Of course." The Chairman's smile flashed again, but this time it had a forced appearance. They were getting down to business.

"Empyrion, Mr. Treet. Ever heard of it?"

"Yes, of course. From Ptolemy's theory of the five heavens. The fifth and highest heaven, the empyrean, is a realm of pure, elemental fire. The home of God and His angels."

Chairman Neviss nodded as he listened, obviously enjoying the recitation. When Treet finished, the Chairman said, "It is also our newest colony—a planet in the Epsilon Eridani system."

At first this remark did not register with Treet. He did not believe he had heard correctly. Then, when he saw that no one was laughing, he figured the "illness" Varro had mentioned was mental. Now the warning made sense.

The Chairman leaned forward and said, "You perhaps did not hear me correctly." A response was necessary.

"But that . . . that," Treet stammered, "would be the first extrasystem colony. Epsilon Eridani is more than . . . what?—ten light-years from earth. It's—" Don't get him riled up, he remem-bered. He'd been about to say something that could upset a man of unstable bearing.

"Impossible? Was that the word you were looking for?" The Chairman seemed to be taking this in good humor. "I always say that a secret is no good unless you can tell someone, eh Varro?"

"Yes, Chairman." Varro, too, was smiling at Treet, apparently enjoying his befuddlement.

The Chairman raised his hand in an open gesture. "Now you know, Mr. Treet. I won't trouble you with a recitation of the details, although with a mind like yours, I'm sure you would find them fascinating. Only myself and a select number of Cynetics board members know of Empyrion's existence."

"Why tell me?" He did not mean the question to sound so terse. It just came out that way.

"The proposition I have in mind has to do with this colony. I want your help in solving a problem there."

Treet's next question was just as terse as the one preceding it: "Why me?"

From nowhere the Chairman's beautiful administrator appeared and handed him a laserfile reader. Chairman Neviss held it in his hands while it spooled information across its black screen, then began reading what he saw there: "Orion Tiberias Treet . . . son of Magellan Treet, noted historian and astronomer . . . conceived *in vitro* at Spofford Natal and engineered by Haldane Krenk on December 30, 2123 . . . graduated from Blackburn Academy in April, 2149 . . . received your first degree in anthropology from Nevada Polytechnic in March, 2160 . . . second degree in history from the Sorbonne in June, 2167 . . . third degree in journalism from Brandenburg Institute in August, 2172 . . . joined the staff of the *Smithsonian,* rose through the ranks and, as a result of an unfortunate dispute over editorial philosophy, left as editor-in-chief in May, 2200 . . . became food critic for Beacon Broadcast System, and quit in 2216 . . . taught philosophy at the University of Calgary until 2245 when the school was closed due to failing enrollment . . . have spent the last thirty-two years traveling and writing—mostly about history."

Here the Chairman paused and looked up. "Our information, as you can see, is quite extensive. I could go on, but you get the idea."

Treet nodded, although such information was readily available from any of several sources if someone cared to spend the time assembling it—which apparently they did. It still did not answer his question, but he let it go.

"In short, you are the man for this special assignment. I want you to go to Empyrion, Mr. Treet. I want you to study the place and write about it. I want you to find out all about it—how it's developing economically, culturally, philosophically. And I want you to send back reports, Mr. Treet."

Although stated quite reasonably, the idea struck Treet as preposterous. He had to suppress an astonished laugh. "You want me to *write* for you?" he asked incredulously. "That's why you have had me followed, drugged, and brought here?"

The Chairman made a deprecatory gesture. "Varro has informed me of the unfortunate incident at the airport—an overzealous agent who will no doubt think twice before exceeding himself next time. He was to have simply contacted you and persuaded you to accompany him here. I gather he had considerable trouble locating you and lost his patience."

"He thought I was some kind of criminal," scoffed Treet softly.

The Chairman glanced quickly at Varro, who shifted his eyes uneasily. "He was mistaken. A misunderstanding, as I said." The Chairman coughed suddenly, a deep, wracking cough that rumbled in his chest with a hollow sound. This brought on a fit of coughing which doubled the Chairman in his seat. Varro stood and started forward, but his boss held up a hand. "No, I'm all right; but I must rest now. Please, Mr. Treet, you are to be my guest this evening. I have requested a private apartment to be prepared for you. The building service will supply you with anything you need, and there is a very good restaurant on the nineteenth floor."

Varro got up from his chair and gave Treet a look which indicated that he was to follow. Treet rose reluctantly, still vaguely unsatisfied by the answers he had received to his questions. "Thank you, Chairman Neviss, I'm sure I will be quite comfortable."

"And think about my proposition. I've instructed Varro to answer any other questions you may have. He will also attend to any contractual arrangements which you may agree on." He smiled briefly, and Treet saw that his eyes had gone a little glassy—from pain?

"I will give it most careful consideration, Chairman. Thank you."

Treet was hustled from the old man's presence so quickly he felt as if the coughing spasm had been staged—a prearranged signal to bring the meeting to a close. But he said nothing as they left the domed room and walked back through the gallery.

Once outside, when both sets of doors had closed securely behind them, Treet turned, put a hand on Varro's arm, and spun the round-headed man around to face him. "Okay, Varro, what's this all about?"

THREE

Feet propped on a handsome and no doubt costly antique walnut table, hands atop his head, reclining in a comfortable, well-made, and also excruciatingly expensive leather couch, Treet ignored the holovision before him and instead replayed his conversation with Varro a few hours earlier. It played no better this time than it had originally. "Something is not right," he said aloud. He often spoke to himself; some of his best thinking was done aloud.

What he was thinking now was not some of his best. Try as he might, he could not come to any substantial conclusion about what it was that Cynetics was up to and why it should involve him.

"The Chairman has read your work; he respects your talent and ability. He'd like to see you on our team," Varro had told him when they had settled in the round-headed man's office—more an apartment or luxury suite than an office.

"Whatever the Chairman wants, the Chairman gets—is that it?"

"Something like that." Varro put on a wry smile. "You've met him. You see how he is. He's explained to you his reasons for wanting you."

"Yes, he explained. But why don't I believe him?"

"What is it that you find so difficult to believe?"

"That I should have been hauled in here like a wanted man, for one thing."

"But you *are* a wanted man, Mr. Treet. Chairman Neviss wants you."

"Your *agent*," he said the word with some contempt, "told me he was being paid thirty-five thousand in metal for finding me. Isn't that a lot of money to arrange a simple job interview?"

Varro simply shook his head. "No, it isn't. Not when you're the Chairman of Cynetics Corporation. Chairman Neviss is a man who is used to—"

"Used to getting what he wants—so everybody keeps telling me." What Treet wanted was to grab the smarmy man and pummel him. He forced the lid back down on his anger and tried a new approach. "For another thing, I find this proposal highly suspect. It was all I could do to keep from laughing in His Highness's Royal Face, if you care to know the truth."

"What exactly is your difficulty?" Varro blinked back at him; his round gray eyes held genuine puzzlement.

"Don't let's be coy, all right?"

"I don't see a problem, Mr. Treet. Perhaps if you'd elaborate—"

"Certainly I'll elaborate. Setting aside the fact that it is well nigh impossible to even get to Epsilon Eridani from here, it would be equally impossible to keep an extrasystem colony a secret. Why keep an achievement of that magnitude secret in the first place? And then there is the problem of wanting me to go there to write about it. Why me in particular? You must have dozens, hundreds, a thousand people equally or better qualified for such an assignment already on payroll. Why bring in an outsider? Why do it at all? If you want to know about Empyrion, why not go there yourself and find out? Better still, why send anyone? Why not have someone who is already there write back to you? Shall I continue?"

Varro laced his fingers beneath his chin and nodded slightly. "That is quite enough. I'm beginning to see it from your point of view, I think. Yes, looking at it that way it might seem rather odd."

"Odd? Oh, I wouldn't say odd. It's raving lunacy!"

"But you do not fully appreciate our situation here." Varro continued as if Treet's outburst had not occurred. "What you have been told is true. Cynetics has, as you know, several extraterrestrial colonies. Mining is an important part of our business. Empyrion is a colony like any other—it just happens to be on a rather more distant planet."

"One that just happens to be in another star system."

"Undoubtedly Chairman Neviss would prefer to visit Empyrion himself, but that is out of the question. As Chairman, he must remain here where his services are most needed. And then there is the matter of his health. He is simply not well enough to make the trip."

"What's wrong with him? He didn't look all that ill to me. And if he is, why isn't he in a hospital?"

"I am not at liberty to discuss his medical condition with

you. But he *is* being cared for, around the clock. The entire floor below this one is a private hospital. Small, but one of the best in the country, I'm told."

"All for him?"

"He is the principal recipient of its services, yes. But anyone may use it. Any Cynetics employee."

"What about the secrecy?"

Varro leaned forward in an attitude of perfect candor. "Have you any idea of the legalities involved in creating a colony?"

"I imagine there is a certain amount of red tape," Treet allowed.

"Mountains of it. Not just here in the United States, but in every other nation and paranation as well. Colonies are considered free states under international law—countries in their own right. We lose a certain amount of control as soon as the colonial charter is ratified in the League Internationale."

"You create a colony, finance it, and then give it its freedom. So? That's the cost of doing business, isn't it?"

"Of course. But an extrasystem colony would be an entirely different matter. First of all, there would have to be scientific studies carried out by the Leln and when they were through tramping around, trying to determine whether we had any right to be there, it would go to debate in the House of Nations, and then new legislation would have to be written, voted, enacted, and so on. Decades would pass before we saw a charter, Mr. Treet. If ever."

Treet had nothing to say to this. He had simply never thought about it before.

"Now then, suppose *you* were in a position to establish such a colony, what would you do?"

"I don't know."

"I think you do. You are an intelligent and practical man; you would choose the path of least resistance."

"And form an illegal colony?"

"Not illegal, Mr. Treet. Extralegal. There are no laws to govern this situation; they do not exist as yet."

Treet granted the point, then asked what had been uppermost in his mind all along. "But how do you get there? Even traveling at the speed of light—which we'll never get anywhere close to—it would take over ten years just to reach Epsilon Eridani."

"What would you say if I told you the trip could be made in slightly less than twelve weeks?"

Treet did not let his jaw drop, though he felt like it. "Are you telling me you have a vehicle that can travel faster than lightspeed?"

Varro smiled broadly. "I don't believe anyone has suggested that at all, though we are working on it. No, we have discovered something quite different."

"But you're not at liberty to tell me what it is, am I right?"

"If I told you and you declined the Chairman's offer, I'm afraid that would put us at something of a disadvantage."

Something told Treet that Cynetics was seldom at even the slightest disadvantage. "I see."

"Let's just say that it might be possible to make the distance between points a good deal shorter."

Treet ran his hands through his hair and rubbed them over his face. He didn't know what to think. There were theories that such a thing as telescoping space might be possible under certain circumstances—black holes, for example. Anyway, no one had ever gotten close enough to a black hole to find out exactly what did happen, nor was anyone likely to in the near or distant future.

Still, suppose what Varro was telling him was absolutely true. What then? "Are you saying that this whole scheme is merely the whim of an eccentric, wealthy old man?"

"I wouldn't use just those words, but yes, that's the sense of it. But don't give me your answer just now. Think it over; sleep on it. We'll talk again in the morning."

Varro showed Treet out and led him to the private elevator. The uniformed attendant was there waiting for him. "Enjoy your evening, Mr. Treet. I'll be looking forward to seeing you again."

As he sat in his luxury apartment, thinking about all that had taken place in the last twelve (or however many) hours, it occurred to Treet that he could make no sense of the situation because he had not eaten in at least that long. His brain cells were shrieking for nourishment.

He rose, somewhat dizzily, and made his way to the window that formed a wall of his apartment. He was somewhere in the middle of the building, judging from the height as he had estimated it from the top story (if Neviss' floor had in fact been the top story). A violet twilight, thick with faintly luminous haze, trailed across the landscape—mostly hills dense with short round trees: live oak and mesquite. Away toward the east (he presumed it was the east since he could not see the sunset at all), the faint glimmer of lights smudged the horizon. There was not enough to be seen from his vantage to tell if they were the distant lights of Houston or someplace else.

Treet gazed out upon the scene as the twilight deepened. The sky had clouded up during the latter part of the afternoon, and these clouds hung as if they were steel wool, rusted in spots and suspended on wires from an iron firmament. He looked on until he realized that he was staring but no longer attending to what he was seeing; his eyes were simply open to the view with nothing taken in.

He turned, put his shoes back on, and left the apartment, feeling the key in his pocket on his way out. Oh well, he thought, walking back to the private chauffeured elevator along a quiet, deserted, and well-lit corridor, if nothing else, he would have a good meal and a free night's lodging out of the deal. What could be so bad about that?

FOUR

"*I* am so glad you could join us, Mr. Treet. I do hope you will come back again very soon." The *maitre d'* placed the silver coffee urn on a warming cradle, tilted his head, and nodded as he backed away from the table. "Enjoy your dessert."

Glazed strawberries the size of hen's eggs swam in thick, sweetened cream in a chilled bowl on a silver tray before him. Spoon in hand, he stared thoughtfully at the luscious extravagance, but he was not thinking about the strawberries. He was instead puzzling over something that had been going on all during his meal: a polite but incessant stream of diners had made their way to his table to introduce themselves to him and make his acquaintance as if he were a holovision celebrity.

How did they all know his name? Was he so conspicuous that every Cynetics employee—he supposed that the thirty or so other diners in the restaurant were all Cynetics employees—knew who he was on sight?

Obviously they had been told of his arrival and instructed to greet him. But why? Was it really *that* important to the Chairman that he feel welcome? He imagined an order that may have been issued:

Executive Memo
To: All Cynetics Division Heads
Re: Arrival of Orion Treet

All employees using the restaurant facility this evening are instructed to extend every cordiality to Mr. Orion Treet, who is visiting at the special request of Chairman Neviss. Anyone found not in compliance with this directive will be terminated immediately with total forfeiture of all company benefits.

Varro

The thing that bothered Treet about all this, besides the interruption of one of the best meals he had eaten in nearly three years—not counting that dinner with the uranium heiress in Baghdad eighteen months ago—the thing that needled him most was that the lavish attention he was receiving was all out of proportion with the proposed assignment. In his mind Treet had begun calling it the *supposed* assignment; he felt that uncertain about it.

Treet spooned thick white cream over the ruby berries, sliced one in half with his spoon, and slipped it into his mouth as he turned the problem over in his mind, letting out a little sigh of pleasure as the strawberry burst on his tongue. The easy answer was that, as Varro had suggested, Chairman Neviss was an extremely—no, make that *unimaginably*—powerful man who was accustomed to having his slightest whim satisfied instantly and in spades.

He wanted Treet, and Treet he would have at whatever cost. The expense did not matter; it was not a factor. Money itself had no meaning to a man like Chairman Neviss. He wanted what he wanted; the money simply made it happen. For some quirky reason—perhaps all those spoony history articles he had written over the years to finance his wanderings and keep his brain from ossifying—Treet had struck the Chairman's fancy; so here he was.

Treet ate another strawberry and, with eyes half closed in gastronomic ecstasy, decided that perhaps he was being unduly moronic not to take the Chairman's proposal at face value. Besides, here was a chance to make some money. How much money? A seriously large amount of money; a sum quite radically excessive in the extreme. More, at any rate, than he was prepared to imagine on the spur of the moment.

For the first time since being surprised in the public bath at Houston International, Treet began to relax and warm to the idea that there may be something to this enterprise after all.

He was basking in this sunny notion when he heard an inviting female voice utter in a throaty whisper, "I hope I'm not disturbing you, Mr. Treet."

"Uh—Oh!" His eyelids flew open. "No, not at all." The woman standing next to him bent slightly at the waist as she slid onto the edge of the empty chair to his right.

"They *are* delicious, aren't they." She indicated the bowl of strawberries, now half full.

"An unparalleled pleasure . . . Miss, ah—"

"My name is Dannielle." She held out a slim, long-fingered hand and smiled. "I always have them with a nice Pouilly-Fuisse. It's a wonderful combination."

The girl was stunning. "I am happy to meet you, Dannielle. I much prefer a Rheinpfalz myself."

She glanced around the table. "But you're not drinking wine tonight?"

"No, just coffee. I wanted a clear head to think."

"Is that what you were going to do tonight? Think?" Dannielle folded her hands under her chin and gazed at him from beneath dark lashes.

Treet felt a sudden emptiness in his stomach, or a lightness in his head—he couldn't decide which. But he knew what the feeling meant. He heard himself reply, "Yes . . . think. That is, unless something more sociable turned up." He made a show of looking around the room. "I don't see your table. Were you with someone?"

"No, I was alone." She smiled languidly. "Until just a moment ago."

"In that case I insist you join me."

"Only if you order wine."

"Of course." Treet had only to look up and the *maitre d'* was there. "We'd like a bottle of Pouilly-Fuisse," he said, and then added, "One of your best please."

When he turned back to his unexpected companion, she had settled herself in her seat and had drawn it closer. Her perfume—something light and provocative—drifted to him, and he spent the next few moments trying to think of a suitably uncorny compliment he might pay her. Dannielle merely smiled and gazed at him with her liquid green eyes and rubbed a shapely hand up the smooth bare skin of an equally shapely arm.

"I understand you are something of a traveler," Danielle said. "I've always wanted to travel."

"It's what I do best," replied Treet. "When I'm not thinking."

"Oh, I bet there are *lots* of other things you do very well, Mr. Treet."

"Please, my friends call me Rion."

"Rion, then. I'm told you are a writer. What do you write?"

"History mostly. And the odd travel piece. The trouble is that the market for travel and history has all but dried up.

People have no use for history, and why read about travel when it is so easy to do? There's no place on Earth a tourist can't get to in less than four hours these days. But tell me something, Dannielle . . ."

"Yes?" She leaned closer, and he caught another enchanting whiff of her scent.

"Is everyone here at Cynetics so deliriously charming to all visitors, or is it just me?"

She lowered her head and favored him with that throaty whisper once again. "Haven't you heard? It's Be Kind To Visiting Dignitaries Day—an official Cynetics holiday."

"I was beginning to wonder. And I am a visiting dignitary I take it?"

"The only one I've seen all day."

"How is that you all know who I am?" The banter had gone out of his voice. He really wanted to know.

The girl was saved from having to answer by the appearance of the sommelier with a bottle of wine in his hand. Without a word he produced the bottle for Treet's inspection and began peeling the seal preparatory to uncorking. Dannielle reached over, took Treet's hand, and rose gracefully from the table.

"Steward, we'd like this sent to Mr. Treet's apartment," she said, then tugged Treet to his feet. "We'll enjoy it all the more." She laughed and took his arm, guiding him willingly from the restaurant.

At Treet's door he fumbled for his code key while Danielle, having pulled his free arm around her waist, nuzzled the side of his neck. The empty, light-headed feeling was back in force. Treet felt adrenalin pumping into him furiously as he jammed the plastic key into the lock.

They tumbled into the semidarkened room in full embrace. Dannielle's mouth found his, and she pressed herself full-length against him. Treet returned the kiss with every ounce of sincerity in him, devoting himself to it exclusively.

"Ahem."

A polite cough from a darkened corner of the room brought Treet's head around. Still holding Dannielle, he turned partway toward the sound. A shape emerged from shadow. "Varro!"

The round-headed man stepped apologetically forward. "I *am* sorry to interrupt, Mr. Treet."

Danielle turned and glanced at Varro, and Treet thought he saw a sign pass between them. She stepped away, saying, "I see that you two have business."

"No," protested Treet. "I don't—"

She planted a kiss on his cheek. "Maybe I'll see you tomorrow."

Treet found himself staring in stunned disbelief at the closing apartment door. He turned and faced Varro unhappily. "We were going to have a drink," he explained, and then wondered why he was explaining.

"Of course," sniffed Varro sympathetically. "I am sorry, but something's come up. We must talk."

"It couldn't wait until tomorrow?" Treet whined, still reeling from his loss.

"No, I am afraid it couldn't wait. Please, sit down." Varro seated himself in the leather armchair, so Treet took the couch.

"Whatever it is, it better be good."

"I promise you won't be bored."

FIVE

Treet drained his glass in a gulp and poured another before plunging the bottle back into the ice bucket. The wine spread its mellow warmth through him from his stomach outward to the extremities. Varro's glass sat on the table between them, untouched.

"So, what you're telling me is that I have to make up my mind right now. In that case, the answer is no—I won't do it." Treet swilled the Pouilly-Fuisse around in his long-stemmed glass for a moment, and then added, "Not for any amount of money."

Varro frowned mildly—more from concern than from any apparent unhappiness. Treet noted the frown. It, like all of Varro's movements, gestures, and expressions, was finely-tuned and rehearsed. Did the man spend his spare time posing in front of his mirror in order to get such precise effects? Were each of his actions so perfectly controlled?

"I don't think you should dismiss our proposition quite so hastily, Mr. Treet. I'll admit that this probably seems a little sudden to you, and that you'd no doubt rather have some time to think things over—"

"A week or two would be nice. I could straighten out my affairs, settle some old accounts, tie up a few loose ends."

"Then the idea of accepting our proposal is not entirely out of the question."

Varro was one slippery negotiator, but they were now heading in the direction Treet wanted to go—toward money. "Well, not entirely out of the question, I suppose."

"Then it's really a question of time—in this case, time to make up your mind."

"You might say that," allowed Treet. "Call it peace of mind."

"Yes, peace of mind. How much is your peace of mind worth to you, Mr. Treet?"

"Frankly, Varro, I don't know. I've never had to price it

before. As a man of some principle, however, I'd have to say that it doesn't come cheaply."

"No, I'm certain that it doesn't, Mr. Treet." Varro pressed his hands together and touched his index fingers to his lips. "I want you to understand that this is as awkward for me as it is for you."

"So you've said." Treet doubted that anything was ever awkward for Varro.

"But let me tell you, Mr. Treet, that in tracking you down we found that your prospects are . . . shall we say, minimal? Isn't it true that you have been dodging bill collectors of one type or another for several years now?"

Damn the man! Varro knew about his dismal financial prospects—that would bring the price down somewhat. Treet parried the thrust as best he could. "Occupational hazard." Treet shrugged. "Writers get behind occasionally. Slump seasons, and all that. So what?"

"What if I could guarantee that you'd never have to dodge another bill collector or suffer another slump season the rest of your life? Would that change your mind?"

"Perhaps. But I'd have to see the guarantee." Treet swallowed another sip of wine, eyeing the bottle carefully. Should he order another one? The first had arrived almost the instant Danielle left and was now nearly empty. He dismissed the idea: negotiating the deal of a lifetime while piffled on fine wine was not exactly in his own best interest. He placed his glass on the table, saying, "Why don't you just come right out and tell me what kind of terms we're talking about here?"

"Very well." Varro leaned forward slightly. "One million dollars in any currency you prefer. One third paid to you upon signature of a standard Cynetics service contract, one third paid to you upon completion of your assignment."

"And the remaining third?" Treet felt like pinching himself—a million dollars! Since the Currency Revaluation Act a few years ago, a million dollars was worth something again.

"The remaining third will be placed in an interest-bearing trust account in your name, payable upon your return."

· "I see. And if for some wild reason I fail to return, you keep the money, is that it?"

"Not at all. Let's just say that it is an incentive for the swift completion of your assignment and a speedy return. In any case, you can designate a beneficiary."

Treet stared across the antique table at Varro. Was he telling the truth? There was absolutely no way to tell; the man's face gave away nothing. Treet decided to see how far he could push it. "No," he said softly. He let silence grow between them.

Varro only nodded. "You have another figure more to your liking, Mr. Treet?"

"Three million," he said slowly, watching Varro carefully. He saw no flinch, not even the slightest blink at the enormity of the figure, so he continued. "Plus a million in trust."

Varro got up from his chair and headed for the door. Treet felt panic skid crazily over him. He'd misjudged the situation and had insulted Varro by naming such a ridiculous figure; now Varro was leaving, and he'd be thrown out by security guards any minute. His mind spun as he frantically tried to think of something that would bring Varro back to the table. But before he could speak, Varro paused at the door and said, "I hope you understand, Mr. Treet, that since time is short, I have instructed the contract to be prepared." The door opened, and a man held out a long white envelope. Varro took the envelope and came back to the table. He sat down and snapped the seal on the envelope, drawing out a pale yellow document, "I need only fill in the amount agreed upon, and—with your signature, of course—this contract is binding." He handed the sheaf of paper to Treet.

"Ordinarily my agent would handle all this," Treet mumbled, taking the document. For several minutes he silently scanned the contract, reading all the pertinent clauses and sub-clauses—especially those having to do with forfeiture of payment for breach of contract. All in all, it was a fairly simple, straightforward agreement; Treet had read far more obtuse and difficult publishing contracts. But then, he reminded himself, Chairman Neviss was not interested in actually publishing the material, merely reading it. Besides, Cynetics probably had a flock of sharp-beaked legal eagles who did nothing but slice, dice, and fricassee fools who thought they could waltz through a loophole in one of their contracts.

"I think you'll see that all is in order, Mr. Treet," Varro said after a suitable time. "Will you sign now?"

"Yes, it's all in order. You've thought of everything." Treet handed the contract back. "Fill in the amounts and I'll sign."

Varro already had a pen in his hand. "Three million upon

signing—" He scratched on the pale yellow paper. "Three million on completion of your assignment, and two million in trust."

"That's eight million!" Treet couldn't help shouting. Had Varro lost his senses?

"Yes, I am aware of that, Mr. Treet," Varro explained. "I have been instructed by Chairman Neviss to double any figure we agree upon as a demonstration of our goodwill—also, as a token of the Chairman's high regard for your abilities. He is very pleased that you are undertaking this assignment for him."

Treet swallowed hard. Eight million dollars! It was a blooming miracle! He stared open-mouthed at Varro, who looked up from his writing. "Was there something you wished to say, Mr. Treet?"

"N-no," Treet said, licking his lips. "It's fine. Everything's fine."

"Good. Now then, if you will sign here—" Varro slid the contract toward him and placed the pen in his hand.

After only a brief pause to remember who he was, Treet managed to scrawl his full name. Dazed, he stared at the signature on the document and at the figures Varro had neatly inscribed. Eight million!

"We're almost finished," said Varro. He flipped to the last page of the contract and pulled a piece of tape from the paper, revealing two shiny squares of about six centimeters each side by side. Varro pressed his thumb firmly in the middle of one of the squares, and then initialed the box. "Your turn, Mr. Treet."

Treet pressed his thumb onto the second shiny box and saw that when he removed it, the film had recorded a precise duplicate of his thumbprint. He looked up at Varro and said, "Now what?"

Varro folded up the contract and stuffed it back into the envelope. He glanced at his watch and rose quickly. "It is nearly time to go, Mr. Treet. We'll have to hurry, I'm afraid."

"What? Hold on!"

"Please, as I have explained, time is short."

"Yes, but I thought . . . you mean I'm leaving tonight?"

"Right now. You're boarding within the hour."

Treet sat stubbornly. "But—"

Varro looked at him sharply. "I assumed you understood. That's why I came here this evening."

"You don't give a guy much of a chance to enjoy his good

fortune. When do I get my money, by the way?"

"It will be waiting for you at the shuttle. Shall we?" Varro gestured toward the door.

"I haven't packed or anything. I'll need—"

"I don't recall that you arrived with any luggage. Did you?"

"No," Treet admitted, remembering the way he had been shanghaied in the skyport. Not that it much mattered—he was, after all, wearing his entire wardrobe. "No luggage."

"Just as I thought. Therefore, I've taken the liberty of arranging for suitable kit and clothing to be provided. You'll find everything waiting for you aboard the shuttle." The round-headed man glanced quickly at his watch again. "Now, we really must be going."

Treet stood up and looked around the apartment one last time as if he were being evicted from his childhood home. Then he shrugged, picked up the bottle of wine and his glass, and followed Varro out.

reet expected a quick flight back to the skyport and a lengthy preboarding passenger check which would culminate in a seat aboard a commercial shuttle to one of the orbiting transfer stations where he'd join a Cynetics transport heading secretly for Epsilon Eridani.

Instead, he and Varro took a long elevator ride down—so far down that he imagined the bottom had dropped out of the elevator shaft—eventually arriving at a subterranean tunnel where two men in standard Cynetics uniforms awaited them in an electric six-wheeler. Stepping from the elevator the moment the doors slid open, they climbed into the cart and were off, humming along the wide, low corridor whose illuminated walls cast bright white light over them.

The driver kept his foot to the floor the entire trip, and Treet, with the bottle between his knees, held onto the passenger handgrips and watched the smooth, featureless interior slide by. He felt like a bullet traveling through an endless gun barrel. No one said a word; both attendants kept their eyes straight ahead, and Varro seemed preoccupied with thoughts of his own. Twice he glanced at his watch, and then returned his gaze to the tunnel ahead.

At last the cart slowed as it rounded a slight curve and came to a gateway—a squatty set of burnished metal doors, guarded by a tollbooth arrangement and two more uniformed men who carried unconcealed stunners on their hips. Varro waved and one of the guards hurried forward with a press plate, which Varro took, pressing his hand flat to its black surface.

Instantly the right-hand door slid open just wide enough to admit the six-wheeler. With a jerk, the driver bolted through the gap and they entered another corridor, slightly larger than the first. This tunnel wound around a tight corner and unexpectedly opened into a gigantic cavern of a room.

Treet blinked in surprise as the cart rounded the last turn

and sped into the enormous chamber. Lights—red, yellow, blue—burned down like varicolored suns from a ceiling seventy-five meters above, forming great pools of light on the vast plain of the floor. Across this plain they raced, gliding in and out of the pools of light. First red, then blue, then yellow—plunging through light and shadow like minidays and nights until at last they came to a slope-sided metal bank which rose up from the floor.

Around this bank swarmed several score men and women—each dressed in orange one-piece uniforms. They were, Treet noticed, entering and emerging from the bank by way of numerous passages cut into the face. Some of these workers pushed airskids loaded with duralum cargo carriers, while others dashed here and there with mobiterms in their hands.

The driver parked the cart in a recharging stall near one of the passages, and Varro turned, saying, "Here we are, Mr. Treet. And not a moment too soon. Shall we?"

Treet got out of the cart, handed his bottle to the driver, and followed Varro through the passage. On the other side, glittering in a bath of white light, looking like a dragonfly poised for flight, a shuttlecraft stood on its stilt legs. The vehicle was smaller than a commercial craft by more than half, Treet estimated; but it was far more graceful and streamlined than the stubby, rotund taxis of the airlines.

The heatcones of two large engines swelled the skin of the craft on the underside near the center, then flared gracefully along the belly to end in a bulge at the rear of the vessel. Thin, knifelike wings slashed out from grooves along the upper back. Once in space, the wings would be retracted and solar panels affixed in their place. Along the side and beneath the wings, lettered in bright sky blue, was the shuttle's name: *Zephyros*. An escalator ramp joined the main hatch, which was open.

"Some boat," remarked Treet, but Varro was already striding toward the ramp, across a tangle of cables and hoses snaking to the shuttle from every direction. At the ramp Varro turned and waited for Treet, allowing him to mount the moving stairs ahead of him—less from courtesy, Treet decided, than from caution. Varro did not want to take any chances that Treet would get cold feet at the last minute and bolt.

As the escalator took them up into the belly of the gleaming, silver shuttle, Treet gazed all around him at the hurried activity below. Controlled chaos, he thought. They're obviously pushing a tight schedule. Why the rush?

The interior of the shuttle was divided into compartments of various sizes, and along one bulkhead a row of staterooms. "I think this first one's yours, Mr. Treet." Varro pressed a button, and a door folded back.

Treet dipped his head and stepped into a small room with curving walls. In the center of the room, dominating it, sat a wide couch, flat, with a panel at one side. It looked like a slightly more generous version of a dentist's chair. There was a closet of sorts next to the door; in a corner across from the couch, a small holovision with a few dozen cartridges on its carousel; opposite the closet, a sanitary stall; diagonally across another corner, a desk with terminal, screen, and chair all molded from a single piece of white plastic; directly above the couch overhead, a tiny oval window.

"I am certain these will fit, Mr. Treet," Varro said, dipping into the closet. He brought out a new singleton in light green with darker green boots and sleeves—the latest style. "Your measurements were taken while you were sleeping off the effects of the drug."

"Oh?" Treet cocked an eye. "Pretty sure of yourselves, weren't you? How did you know I would accept your offer?"

"Chairman Neviss is a remarkable judge of character, Mr. Treet. He is also a man who doesn't—"

"Doesn't like to lose. Yeah, I know."

"What I was about to say was that he doesn't mind spending a little money in order to smoothe things out. Speaking of which—" Varro reached into the closet and turned, hefting a bulging, zippered bag which he tossed to Treet. "Your stipend, Mr. Treet."

Treet caught the silver bag and tugged the zipper down. Inside were notes, banded and stacked. He withdrew a stack. "Five hundred thousand!"

"In platinum notes of twenty-five thousand. There are six bundles—three million dollars. As agreed?"

"As agreed." Treet breathed an inward sigh of relief. Up to this very moment he had doubted he would ever see the money. Now he realized that he had been told the truth. Crazy as it sounded, it was the truth.

Just then a man with a gold, long-billed flight cap stuck his head in the door. "Oh, Captain Crocker," said Varro. "Come in, I'll introduce you to your passenger. This is Orion Treet."

The man, tall, loosely knit, blond-haired, and slightly sunburned, ducked easily into the compartment. He wore the easy, breezy manner of the old-style Texas natives, and a generous portion of the legendary cowboy charisma as well. "So this is the VIP we're taking up tonight!" The Captain smiled and offered his hand. Treet zipped the bag shut and tucked it under his arm, extending his hand to grip that of the Captain's. "Welcome aboard the *Zephyros,* Mr. Treet."

"Thanks. You fly this route often, I take it?" asked Treet.

"Have you ever been in space before, Mr. Treet?"

"This is my first time, although I've done a fair amount of suborbital travel."

"It's exactly the same. We're going to have a good trip, so don't you worry 'bout a thing." He turned to Varro, smiled, and said, "Well, I've got a flight check in progress, so I best get back to business." He touched the bill of his cap and disappeared.

"Captain Crocker is Chairman Neviss' personal pilot, so I'm certain you'll be in good hands," said Varro. "And now I'll leave you to get settled." He brought up his watch once more. "You're scheduled to lift off in three minutes."

Outside a klaxon sounded, and the lights switched from white to red. Hoses were disconnected and retracted as the orange-suited army scurried for safety. Treet followed Varro back to the hatch. "We're looking forward to hearing from you soon, Mr. Treet. I think you'll find this a most extraordinary assignment."

"I'm looking forward to it," Treet said somewhat mechanically, then realized that with three million dollars in platinum certificates tucked under his arm he actually *was* looking forward to it. "You can tell Chairman Neviss that I won't disappoint him."

"Good. I'll tell him. Good-bye, Mr. Treet." Varro offered his hand, and Treet took it. "Bon voyage!"

"Thanks." Treet watched the back of Varro's round head as the slump-shouldered man rode the escalator down. A man in orange, standing on a platform beneath the moving stairs, drove the stairway back. Treet watched his last tie with the earth disappear, and then turned back to examine the interior of the shuttle.

"Two minutes, Mr. Treet." Crocker's voice sounded from a

hidden speaker overhead. Treet guessed that Cocker was in the cockpit already warming the engines, or whatever pilots did in the last seconds of preflight. "You'll want to get strapped in now. Think you'll need some help?"

"I can manage. Thanks just the same." Treet, back in his compartment, glanced at the console next to the couch and saw that a red button had lit up. He punched it and with the buzz of electric motors, the bed tilted up and scrunched in the middle, forming itself into a lounge chair. Pouches opened in the sides of the couch, and Treet drew out a single strap which he fastened across his hips as he lay back.

"Ninety seconds, Mr. Treet. All set?"

"Ready!" He clasped the zippered bag between his hands over his stomach and lay back in the chair as if basking in the bright sun of his incredible fortune. Who could have imagined that before this day was over he would be a millionaire! And who could have foreseen that this fledgling millionaire would be winging his way to a distant star system to write about a secret corporation colony!

The thrum of rocket engines seeped up through the floor-plates, sounding like the distant rumbling of an earthquake. Treet felt the deep sonorous vibration in his diaphragm, and realized simultaneously that he had not the slightest idea how the shuttle would escape the underground chamber. The thought made him frown.

"Thirty seconds, Mr. Treet." The Captain's calm voice fell from above. "Would you like to watch the liftoff?"

"Uh, sure—if it's no trouble."

"No trouble at all. I'll switch on the holovision."

A second later the holoscreen blipped on and Treet, swiveling his chair with the aid of a button on the armrest, saw a view of the cavern ceiling opening to a sky pitch-dark, devoid of moon or stars.

"Some cloud cover, as you can see. But all things considered, a pretty good night for flying. Fifteen seconds," Crocker's voice intoned. "I'll be a tad busy for the next few minutes. I'll talk to you when we've locked in our trajectory. Until then, relax and leave everything to me."

Treet felt the shuttle tremble and sensed slight movement around him. The holovision revealed that the ship had angled up—the floor beneath them had become a steep incline to give them a straight shot away. The thrum of the engines became a boom and then, with only the merest suggestion of a bump, the craft rose from the floor.

He watched the holoscreen and saw the cavern slide away slowly. Then they cleared the ceiling—the lights, now pointing skyward, flashed momentarily—and he glimpsed dark landscape spreading out around them. Treet felt himself grow heavy in the chair, sinking down into the cushioned material as the shuttle took on speed.

Faster and faster the ship climbed. There was nothing to see; the screen showed a dark, formless expanse of empty sky. Gravity pressed him down with a heavy hand. His eyesight darkened, as if the light in the compartment had dimmed, and his limbs became sluggish and lethargic. It took too much effort to shift his arms. Suddenly tired, he closed thick eyelids and allowed sleep to descend upon him.

Treet awoke—seconds, minutes, hours later, he couldn't tell which—to see through the oval window above him a slice of bright-spangled starfield. He sat for a moment without moving, then, feeling strangely light and buoyant, lifted his hand to open the catch on the seatbelt. The hand flew up and tugged him away from the chair. They were in orbit.

He retrieved his floating moneybag, stuffed it into a drawer under the seat of his couch, unbuckled his belt, and let himself drift up over the chair, then kicked off toward the door. Treet learned next why the walls of his stateroom were covered with a spongy padding, for he had misjudged the angle of his flight and piled into the doorframe. The door, evidently pressure-sensitive, folded back automatically, and he grappled his way through the opening and into the main compartment where he collided with someone just emerging from the cubicle next to his.

The body was male and pear-shaped, with hips slightly wider than shoulders. An overlarge fuzzy head, sporting jug ears, wobbled on a thin-pencil neck as the stranger richocheted toward the nearest bulkhead. "Hey!" he cried. "Watch it!"

"Sorry!" Treet said. "You okay? I don't quite have the knack of this yet."

His fellow passenger raised his arm and spun around like a diver making a slow-motion pirouette. "It's easy, once you learn how. Zero-G is a blast!" The man smiled. His glasses flashed in the light, and Treet realized that he was, despite the antique metal-framed glasses, much younger than he looked—half Treet's age at least. "You're overcompensating, that's all. Just take it easy."

Treet tucked his legs under him and pushed off, using about half as much muscle power as he thought he should. He drifted closer to the stranger and extended his hand. "Thanks. I see what you mean. My name is Orion Treet."

"Asquith Pizzle, here. Glad to meet you, Treet. By the time this flight is over zero-G will be second nature to you."

"Oh, I don't expect I'll get the chance to become an expert."

"Of course you will. After all there's really nothing else to do for the next twelve weeks." The young man drew his lips back in a goofy, toothsome grin which made him look like a bookish gnome.

"Twelve weeks? I'm getting off at the transfer station in a couple of hours. I—" Treet stopped. "What's the matter?"

Pizzle looked at him quizzically. "Are you sure you're on the right bird?"

"Of course! This is a Cynetics shuttle heading for rendezvous with a corporation transport." Treet's voice sounded thin in his ears.

"This is no shuttle, Treet. This *is* the transport. We're on our way."

SEVEN

"You're joking!" Treet glanced around him. The jerk of his head sent him gliding off at an angle to Pizzle. A ripple of panic fluttered his stomach. "We're going in *this?*"

"Righto mundo! This is a transport. Scaled down, of course—by about sixty times."

"But . . . I . . . thought . . ."

"Not to worry. Crocker is a champ. He could fly a washtub to Mars if it had hydrodrive. He'll get us to Empyrion with starch in our shorts."

"You're going too?" Treet's mind flip-flopped. Surprise made his voice whine. "I mean—I assumed I was alone." On second thought, there was no reason for that assumption. Varro had not mentioned any other passengers, but then again, he hadn't said there weren't any others. "Is anyone else aboard?"

"One other. I don't know who. He's in his compartment, and I haven't seen him. Then there's Crocker, of course."

The irrational fear ebbed away as Treet got used to the idea of traveling into deep space in such a small and apparently crowded craft. He wondered what else Varro had neglected to mention. "I, uh—got a little nervous just then. See, I was under the impression that we'd dock and transfer to a regular Cynetics transport. I guess not, huh?"

Pizzle shook his head. "Nope. This is it. Hey, but this is one elegant vehicle—a Grafschoen carbon-tempered titanium hull with twin sealed Rolls-Bendix plasma engines. There's not a better-made ship anywhere—you can bet your biscuits on that."

"You an engineer?" asked Treet. Pizzle shook his head again. "A physicist?" Another shake, ears wobbling. "What then?"

"I'm a TIA man." Pizzle grinned proudly.

"What's that?"

"Trend and impact analyst."

"You're an accountant?" Treet asked incredulously.

52

Pizzle's face fell a fraction. "Not exactly. TIA is more than statistics and balance sheets." He brightened again. "My branch is social integration of economic operants: SIE for short."

"Oh." Treet still had not the slightest idea what Pizzle was talking about—something to do with marketing, he figured. "I see."

To break the silence that followed, Treet asked, "How come you wear glasses?"

"You mean instead of corneal implants or permatacts?" Pizzle placed a thumb to the bridge of his nose and shoved his steel frames back into place. "Nostalgia. These belonged to Z. Z. Papoon—one of my favorite authors. We have the same astigmatism."

"Z. Z. Papoon? I don't believe I've ever heard the name."

"He wrote a long time ago—futuristic fantasy mostly. Marvelous characters: Beeno the Beast-Stalker—that was one of his. People tell me I look like somebody from one of his books, so I guess it's only right I should have his glasses."

"Only right."

"Why did they pick you?" Pizzle asked.

"Sorry?" Treet bobbed in the air, drifting off to one side.

"Here, kick your legs together like in the water—that'll straighten you out. I meant, what's your specialty, Treet? How'd you convince them to give you one of their precious berths aboard this tin cricket?"

"Oh, I'm a writer mostly. History is my specialty, but I also do the odd travel piece. I guess the Chairman liked one of my articles, so here I am."

"You must be some writer. Ever write any science fiction?"

"Strictly nonfiction."

Pizzle looked incredulous. "I had to fight to get on here. I was one of five hundred applicants. They narrowed it down to a hundred a week ago, and this morning I was chosen."

"You don't say. I was more like kidnapped." Pizzle acted interested, so Treet went on to elaborate the details of his day, leaving out the part about the eight million dollars. "But tell me, Pizzle," he said when he had finished, "what's your assignment on Empyrion? You mind my asking?"

"Not at all. It's long-range forecasting. Specifically, to prepare probability studies on the effects of high-production vibramining on the social and environmental infrastructures of the Empyrion colony." Pizzle made a gesture as if to say it was all in a day's work, then said, "Are you hungry? I could eat a brick. Let's get some breakfast."

Pizzle gathered himself into a ball and then whirled his arms; he tumbled end over end slowly toward the nearest bulkhead where he kicked off toward a console overhead. He grabbed the padded handring on the consol's pedestal and pulled himself around.

"Yo, Crocker!" he said, punching a button.

"What's on your mind?" Crocker's voice answered from a speaker somewhere below them. The ceiling had temporarily become the floor.

"We're hungry."

"I could use a bite myself."

"How about giving us a little thrust? It's a putch trying to eat in zero-G."

"We're scheduled for a little OA and A burn in about thirty minutes. I could give you some now and take it off the other end."

"Thanks. I'll get the coffee perking." Pizzle shoved away from the pedestal and spun in the air. "Follow me," he called to Treet. "The galley is this way."

Treet slouched in a basket-shaped foam chair, gum-soled boots propped on the edge of a retractable table, sipping black, pungent Tasmanian coffee. Both he and Pizzle were listening to the Captain explain the intricacies of space navigation.

Crocker had joined them earlier, wolfed down some eggs and a few slices of Texas ham, and now sat puffing on a very long, green aromatic panatela, saying, "Of course, ground control computers handle all the really tricky maneuvers. Our on-board system is nothing to sneeze at, though. We've installed the Cynetics Cyclops in place of the usual Hewlett StarNav equipment. That bugger is nearly a hundred times faster and smarter than anything commercially available. It's made solely for LeIn's peacekeeping forces." He smiled broadly. "But we got a special deal."

"Why such a powerful computer," asked Treet idly, "if ground control can handle everything?"

"Just plain good backup," shrugged Crocker, his sunburned face creasing in a conspiratorial wink. Then he leaned

54

forward and said, "Thing is, nobody really knows what happens when you get that close to the event horizon. And once inside the wormhole, we're on our own."

Treet blinked back at him. Had he heard right? "Wormhole, did you say?" He exchanged a bewildered look with Pizzle.

"Uh-oh." Crocker nodded slowly, took the cigar out of his mouth, and tapped the ash off into an empty mug. "Ol' Horatio has stepped in it again. I thought you fellas knew."

"Are you saying we're reaching Empyrion via wormhole?" asked Pizzle, visibly awed at the prospect.

"Well, let's just say we don't have provisions for a fifty-year trip, so we're taking a shortcut."

"Fan-super-tastic!" Pizzle rocked back in his chair, beaming. Crocker smiled broadly.

"I'm glad you're both so delighted," said Treet sourly. "Just what in blue-eyed blazes is a wormhole exactly?"

"Well, it's—nobody knows what it is *exactly*, but—" began Crocker.

"Let me tell him," offered Pizzle cutting in. "It's like a tunnel in space, only elastic, sort of . . . " His voice trailed off when he saw that Treet was frowning. "A hole in the space-time fabric, you know?"

"Something like a black hole, you mean?" Treet felt that sinking feeling in the pit of his stomach again. What had he gotten himself into? "Are we talking about a black hole?"

"Yes, sort of," said Pizzle. "Um . . . but not exactly. They're distant cousins, maybe."

"What kind of answer is that?" Treet kept his temper down, barely.

"It's a phenomenon on the level of a black hole," said Crocker. "Very difficult to describe."

"Apparently," puffed Treet indignantly. "Am I supposed to believe that we're going to fly through some *phenomenon* to get to the colony? Like diving through a hole in a wedge of Swiss cheese?"

"That's it!" Pizzle nodded vigorously. "But more like pinching Jello. Say you had a block of Jello—that's space, see?" His hands described a large cube. "You pinch it in the middle and push the two opposite sides together—collapse the center, see?" He brought his index fingers together through the imaginary Jello. "Well, the distance you have to travel decreases the more you pinch, see?"

"And since in space," added Crocker, "distance and time are one and the same thing . . . *Voila!* Decrease distance and you decrease time, see?"

Treet was silent for some moments, looking from one to the other of them and back again, a dark frown lowering his brow and pulling his mouth down. "I see," he said finally, "but I don't like it."

"Take it easy," Crocker soothed. "It's perfectly safe."

"How do you know? You just said nobody knows what happens inside a wormhole."

"Our best guess it that you just pop on through—like riding a trolley through a tunnel. Only you've carved about forty or fifty years off your travel time."

"I don't believe this," said Treet softly. "Both of you are crazy. You can let me off right here. I'll walk back."

"Look," said Pizzle, "it'll be all right. There's a book I can call up for you that'll tell you all about wormholes—what there is to tell, that is."

A chime sounded over the speaker system. "Back to the bridge," said Crocker, jumping up, obviously glad for an excuse to leave. "You read that book, Treet, and we'll talk again later."

Treet watched the pilot pull himself hand-over-hand up the wall toward the cockpit. Even at one-quarter gravity, Treet doubted he could have managed the feat. Feeling Pizzle's eyes on him, he turned and glared at the gnome. "Well?"

"Nothing. I was just thinking that it's going to be a long trip. We might as well be friends." He paused, waiting for Treet to say something polite, like: *Oh, of course, let's by all means be the very best of chums.* When Treet said nothing, he continued. "You play Empires?"

"No," Treet said coldly. "I detest games of chance."

"Oh, there's no chance involved—all intellect. It's a lot like chess, only bigger and more subtle." He grinned his snaggle-toothed impish grin again. "I'll teach you. How about it?"

Treet shrugged, getting up. "Some other lifetime perhaps. If you'd call up that book for me, I'd appreciate it." He turned and bounded from the table, leaving Pizzle to clean up.

"That slime devil Varro," Treet muttered, "better have a wonderful explanation for all this, or there's going to be a mutiny!"

EIGHT

"*I am* sorry, Mr. Treet, but as I have already explained, Mr. Varro is in Maracaibo for at least three weeks. He cannot be reached due to the recent severance of diplomatic relations. No calls are being transmitted between Venezuela and League countries."

Treet felt his temper rising dangerously. He wanted to reach through the screen and shake the smug young lady on the other side. "Then I must have a word with Chairman Neviss. It concerns a matter of utmost importance. Life and death," he added. "Please, you must let me speak to him."

"Mr. Treet, you know I would like to help you. I cannot. No one may speak to the Chairman without clearance."

"Get me clearance!"

"I would love to arrange for clearance, Mr. Treet, as soon as you give me your personal identification code. As you refuse—"

"Refuse! I don't *have* a code, dammit!"

"Anger won't help you, Mr. Treet. Perhaps you would like to call back when you have calmed down."

"Wait, don't hang up. Look, there must be someone there who can authorize clearance without a PI code—"

"Only Mr. Varro—"

"Besides him. Who else? There must be some other way."

"Well," the young lady paused, "I could have Chief of Security do a PSP on you—that's a Personnel Security Probe. Upon completion of the PSP you would be issued a personal identification code, but—"

"Do it."

"But—"

"But nothing. Just do it."

"Mr. Treet, it takes six weeks to do a thorough PSP."

"Grrr!" Treet growled and slammed his fist down on the EOT button on the console, ending the transmission. Instantly he regretted the move. There were still several things he wanted to say to the officious young witch on the other end.

Due to sunspot interference, it had taken him the better part of thirty-four hours to get a call through to Cynetics. All that time the *Zephyros* streaked ever closer to rendezvous with the wormhole, and with every passing hour the possibility of turning back diminished even further.

Not that there had ever been much chance of turning back in the first place. But Treet had at least hoped to scorch Varro with a few well-chosen words. Apparently even that was impossible. He had begun to think that Varro had caused the sunspots in order to avoid being contacted. And as far as Treet was concerned, the story about Varro's trip to Maracaibo was an out-and-out lie. The scumbag just didn't want to talk to him. It was the oldest tactic in the executive manual: don't call us, we'll call you.

Treet sat with clenched fists and teeth, grimacing at the empty screen. He knew now that he had been tricked, and that Varro also knew that he knew and was therefore avoiding him. That more than anything else angered him: the impotence of playing the dupe.

He shoved back his chair, gliding halfway across the room with the force of his movement. They were under thrust most of the time now, flying perpendicular to the orbital plane of Earth—that was as much as he had been able to get from Crocker about their route—and the acceleration created a comfortable one-half G, which allowed them near-normal conditions.

He was still sitting in the center of his compartment when he heard a muffled thump—a sound he had come to recognize as someone knocking on the padding around his door. "What do you want?" he hollered.

"Can I come in?" Pizzle yelled back.

"No!"

The door folded back regardless. "Sorry, Treet. I feel silly talking to closed doors. Let me in, okay?"

"It seems I can't keep you out!"

"Look, I brought you something."

Treet still stared at the blank computer screen across the room. "What is it?"

"It's that book I told you about. Some of it, that is. I only printed up the pertinent chapters. Here, take it."

"Go away. I'm not in the mood."

Pizzle put the book on the bed and took a seat there himself. "I was wondering if you've seen our fellow passenger yet."

"No, I haven't. So what?" Treet turned and looked at his guest for the first time.

"Well, I haven't either. And it's going on two days now. Don't you think that's strange?"

"Not particularly. He probably just wants to avoid having to play that stupid game with you."

"You said you *liked* Empires. You almost won last time."

"I lied. Besides, you let me almost win just so I will keep playing with you, which I won't."

"Two days though. That's a long time. One of us should have seen him."

"Did you ask Crocker?"

Pizzle nodded. "Sure. He said he didn't know who it was, but that he wasn't concerned and furthermore it was none of my business."

"There you are. It's none of your business."

"But two whole days, Treet. What if something happened to him? Maybe he had a heart attack on liftoff or something like that."

Treet thought about this. "What do you want me to do about it?"

"Be a spy with me. Help me find out who it is."

For a moment Treet considered this. "It *does* seem a trifle strange, as you say. But then," he added grumpily, "it wouldn't be the first strange thing about this trip."

"Like what?" Pizzle sat cross-legged on the bed, elbow on knee, resting his receding chin in his hand.

Treet got to his feet. "You really want to know? Okay. First, there's the supposedly oh-so-secret nature of this trip. Only I find out from you in casual conversation that you were one of five hundred applicants. Seems like everybody and his mother knows about this colony but me. Secondly, how come I've never heard of this wormhole business? I'm an intelligent person; I've been around a long time, and I've never heard mention of the alleged phenomenon. Thirdly, why were they so anxious to get me aboard this crate? The ink wasn't even dry on the line when I was hustled aboard. Why the big hurry? And why won't Crocker tell me anything? What more is there I'm not supposed to know? Shall I go on?"

Pizzle shrugged. "You're making more of this than there is, really. I can explain everything."

"Go ahead; be my guest. I wish you would."

"Well, the mission *is* secret. Sure, they took applications, but that's standard for any transfer situation. I knew only that there was a hefty pay bonus and a promotion for going. I'd been looking for a way out of the Northwestern Hemisphere Division for over a year and when the chance came up, I grabbed it."

"Even though you didn't know where you were going or what your assignment would be?"

"Didn't matter to me. Anything was better than NH under Oberman, not to mention there were at least seven guys ahead of me in line for promotion. I'd have been eighty-five before I joined senior staff!"

"Still, you knew about it. Varro told me it was a secret."

"It was for me too, up until the time I boarded the *Zephyros*. There was a confidential packet waiting for me in my cabin: length of trip, our destination, my assignment, that sort of thing. I'd never heard of Empyrion Colony either, until after I read my packet."

"What about wormholes?"

"Sure, I know about them. The concept has been around a long time. I'm surprised you haven't heard of them, really. But then again, they're not exactly common knowledge. In fact, they were entirely a mathematic speculation until Cynetics discovered one lurking on the rim of our solar system. On second thought, maybe you wouldn't have heard of them unless you read astrophysics abstracts or professional journals."

"How did you get so chummy with them then?"

"I read old SF novels." Pizzle's close-set eyes gleamed impishly.

"Sci-fi, huh?"

"Speculative fiction, if you please. There were some great books written about wormhole travel just before the turn of the century. Great stuff! *Timeslip* is a classic. My favorite, though, is *Pyramid on the Thames*."

"Okay, so I'm out of touch," Treet sniffed. "Now, why the big hurry to get me on board? Was that so I wouldn't change my mind?"

"Well, if you know anything about wormholes at all—"

"Which I don't."

"—you'd know that one of the major theories is that they are not a constant event."

"Meaning?"

"They come and go. They change. They move around. One might appear one place for a while and then disappear, only to reappear somewhere else. They're sort of elastic, like I said. Where a black hole is a fixed phenomenon, wormholes—displacement tubes or dilation tunnels, as they're sometimes called—are more unpredictable."

"Therefore?"

"Therefore, you have to move when there's one open or you miss your chance. Obviously—"

"Cynetics found out the wormhole was open now and didn't want to lose the opportunity."

"Righto mundo! Who knows when it might come again." Pizzle took off his glasses and polished them on his shirt.

"You just said they move around."

"Relatively speaking. As far as anyone knows, they usually occur in the same general vicinity of space. Whatever kind of force or disturbance creates a wormhole operates in a localized region—you know, like a whirlpool in a river. It swirls around, opens, and closes, sometimes deeper, sometimes shallower, stronger one time, weaker another, and so on. That's how it is."

"And we're going to dive through the eye of this whirlpool."

"Banzai!"

Treet gazed balefully at Pizzle, his brow wrinkled in thought. "Granting for the moment that what you say is true—which I intend to check out thoroughly—but say that it's true, just how did the first transport know that they'd reach Epsilon Eridani by jumping through this wormhole? How could they know that?"

"My guess is they didn't."

"Great heavens! You mean they dove in blind?"

Pizzle shrugged lightly. "It was a colony ship, remember. They were outfitted to start a colony, which they were intent on doing anyway, so what difference would it make where? They were pioneers. Someone had to be the first."

"But how do we know they made it?"

"You've got me there," Pizzle admitted. "Ask Crocker; maybe he knows something."

"We could be diving into . . . well, *anything*. Or nothing. There might be a sun at the other end and we'd burn up, or maybe an asteroid field and we'll be smashed to cosmic dust. What happens if the wormhole closes while we're still inside? What then?"

"Look, what do you want from a bookworm? Nobody has ever done this before, so we'll just have to wait and find out."

"Wrong. The first transport found out, didn't they?" Treet huffed. "Well, where are they now?"

Treet sat hunched on a folding stool in the crowded cockpit of the *Zephyros*. Pizzle sat next to him with his elbows on his knees, trying to take up less space. Crocker swiveled in his captain's chair, twirling his hat in his hand. After their discussion, Treet and Pizzle had gone directly to the Captain to find out what he knew of the fate of the first colonists.

"Epsilon Eridani," Cocker said, "is an extensive system. We know that it has at least thirteen planets in the OLZ—that's Optimum Life Zone."

"How do you know that? How do you know that the colony ship even reached Epsilon Eridani, let alone started a colony?"

"We had communication, of course. I have read all the transcripts myself. There were three communications received— one month apart for the first three months, Earth-time. The first one came when the ship reached the system—we know that they got through the wormhole without any problems. The second was sent when they identified Empyrion—that's what they named it—and decided to settle there. The third and last came when they had finished their survey of the planet and had started raising the environment dome."

"And then?"

"Nothing after that."

"What happened?"

"The wormhole closed. No more signals could be sent through the conduit, so to speak."

"No doubt they're still sending signals," offered Pizzle, "but without the wormhole it takes a whole lot longer. We just haven't received them yet."

"Maybe the signals stopped because they all *died!*"

"Possible," Crocker allowed, "but highly improbable."

"But why? You said anything could happen. Anything!"

"Theoretically yes. But you have to figure that once they reached the planet they knew what to expect. Colony ships are prepared for the unknown. Empyrion is uninhabited by any thinking creatures, and has little second-order animal life—certainly nothing to worry about. The probes would also have verified atmosphere, weather patterns, and climatic trends. There were no surprises there."

"Microorganisms, viruses, bacteria—what about those? Maybe they got down there and succumbed to a killing virus."

"Maybe, but I don't think so. They would not have disembarked until the environment dome was raised and the air and ground beneath it sterilized. Only then would they have actually set foot on the soil."

Treet remained silent. He had exhausted all his objections for the moment. He looked around at Pizzle, who sat nodding. "It's just like the IASA colonization manual recommends."

"Right by the book. All contingencies foreseen."

Crocker looked at Treet's unhappy face. "Look, it's going to be all right. Believe me. I read the transcripts. By all reports the planet is an absolute paradise. You'll love it. When we get there you'll see what I mean. An absolute paradise." Crocker spun in his huge, padded chair as an electronic chime sounded. "Now if you two will excuse me," he said, "I've got a little housekeeping to do."

Treet stood. "Thanks, I feel so much better," he said without meaning it. "See you later."

Pizzle rose and followed Treet out of the cockpit. They clambered into the connecting gangway and through the forechamber along to the passenger compartments. At Pizzle's door they paused, and Pizzle yawned. "I'm going to get some sleep. Maybe you'd better, too. It might be a long night."

Treet glanced up quickly. "Huh?"

"We're spying tonight, remember? You said if I went with you to talk to Crocker, you'd help me spy tonight. Well, I went with you, didn't I?"

"But you were on his side. You were supposed to be on mine."

"His side? There were no sides. You had some questions and we got answers. What more do you want?"

Pizzle had him there: what more did he want? Why was he

still not satisfied? "All right," Treet agreed reluctantly. "I'll help you spy." He turned and went into his stateroom.

"Good," called Pizzle after him. "I'll come and get you when I'm ready." He watched Treet disappear into his room and the door sigh shut behind him. "Loosen up," he called. "You'll live longer."

NINE

*P*izzle's idea of spying was to hide in some cramped place and wait long hours for the quarry to show up. He reasoned that unless separate supplies had been stocked in the mysterious stranger's cabin, which he doubted, then the man must eat when the others were sleeping. So far he had seen no evidence that anyone had been surreptitiously using the galley, but then as long as the person cleaned up after himself, there was no way anyone could tell.

So Treet and Pizzle crouched in a cramped cubbyhole for dry stores, waiting—an eternity it seemed to Treet—for the stranger to materialize. The galley lights had been turned off so they could observe the mysterious stranger without themselves being observed, and they had been taking turns watching. It was Treet's turn to put his eye to the crack in the partition, and he was ready to call it quits.

"I don't see why you need me at all," complained Treet, not for the first time. "This is a big waste of time."

"I need you to verify the sighting."

"You make it sound like we're waiting for a UFO." He craned his neck around and saw the metal rims of Pizzle's glasses glint in the dim light. "Phew! It's stuffy in here. I'm getting out before I'm hunchbacked for life."

"Shh! Quiet, will you? If anybody *was* out there, you'd have scared him off by now."

"Whoever it is is probably fast asleep in bed, and that's where we should be. Look, why can't you rig up a few motion detectors or proximity switches or something. Anyone messing around in the galley would trip the alarm and you could come running with your little Panasonic holocamera and catch them flatfooted in the act."

"Yeah, and get nothing for my trouble but pictures of you or Crocker sneaking food from cold service while I'm trying to sleep.

"Why is this so important to you, anyway?" Treet asked. "This guy just likes his privacy. So what? *I* should be so lucky."

"It isn't natural, that's why. And I'm curious—that in itself is enough reason for me."

"Well, I'm not that curious. I don't know why I agreed to this lunatic scheme of yours anyway. I'd feel silly if I wasn't so sore." Treet shifted his weight and banged his head against a shelf. "Ow! That's it—I'm getting out of here."

With that he pushed aside the partition and climbed out. "You coming?"

Pizzle glanced at his watch. "Might as well. Time's nearly up anyway." He crawled out of the cubbyhole on his hands and knees. "If he was coming tonight, he'd have been here by now."

Treet walked back to his compartment and Pizzle followed, pausing at the entrance to the stranger's quarters to press his ear against the door. Treet cast a disparaging look back at him; Pizzle shrugged and shuffled along to his room. "G'night, Treet."

Treet stood on the threshold of his compartment with the door open. When he heard Pizzle's door close, he tiptoed back to the stranger's compartment and listened. He heard nothing, so pressed his ear against the door. He was about to turn away when, to his surprise, the door folded back and he stood staring into two jet-black eyes. The eyes—set in an exquisite, bronze-colored face which was surrounded by a fall of shining black hair—regarded him coolly. His first impression was that he'd seen that face before, but in a very different context.

"Miss Talazac!" he said, recovering himself. "I didn't recognize you without your braid."

"Mr. Treet," she replied crisply, "is this one of your perverse habits—listening outside people's doors?"

"Not at all." Treet received the strong impression that she had expected him to be there. "I was just . . . well, curious. We wondered about you—I mean, about the person inside. We hadn't seen anyone, and it's been several days. We thought something might have happened to you."

"You need not have concerned yourself. I am, as you see, quite all right. If you will excuse me—" She made a move to pass by him, and Treet stepped back.

"I'm sorry if I disturbed you," he said, more for something to say than from any real regret.

She turned and faced him, holding his eyes with her own, her face expressionless. Treet felt ridiculous, as if he were floundering in shallow water. He wanted to look away, but her eyes held his and he could only stare back blankly. "I'm sorry," he murmured and the spell was broken.

She turned from him without a word and moved silently off along the gangway toward the galley. Treet watched her slender figure glide away. He realized his scalp was tingling all over and his palms were sweating.

He thought to himself: There goes one weird lady . . . or a vision.

Treet did not see her again for five weeks. What she did in her compartment, how she avoided all the others, and why he could but wonder, and did often. Why did she hole up like that? Why did she refuse to join the others? Certainly it was not because she feared them—the only woman on a ship full of men, that sort of nonsense. No, whatever the reason, it wasn't fear. Treet's manly intuition told him that Yarden Talazac would be more than a match for any male.

He did not tell Pizzle about the midnight meeting. Somehow he knew that Talazac would not want him to mention it. At the same time he felt silly carrying around his secret—especially since Pizzle continually nagged him to rejoin his espionage program. Treet refused, knowing somehow that she would not be caught again. Actually, he decided, she had not been caught at all. She had revealed herself to him alone; it was of her choosing.

But why? Why him? Why in that way?

Treet wondered about these things in idle moments, and he attempted to fix her face in his mind but could not. Every time he tried to remember what she looked like, he drew a blank. All he saw on his mental screen was a stock representation of a human face—vaguely Asiatic, or perhaps Polynesian, no distinct features, just a sketch. This both puzzled and frustrated him. Why could he not remember what she looked like?

He told himself that, after all, he'd only met her twice, and then fleetingly. But he also reminded himself that he had no difficulty remembering faces of people he'd met just as briefly: the Cynetics nurse who had helped him up when he awoke from the drug, the elevator attendant, the driver of the cart—all of them he could see in his mind's eye as clearly as if they stood before him.

But, Yarden . . . all he had of her was an impression: smooth, honey-colored skin, a deep darkness that was eyes or hair, slim, molded limbs, and a sense that she floated rather than walked. That was all.

Trying to remember her became something of an obsession with Treet. And when he wasn't wracking his brain in the futile attempt to conjure up a picture of the phantom woman, he thought about their meeting and tried to recall every word and nuance that had passed between them that night, to understand the meaning behind it. In this he was largely unsuccessful too. Despite his efforts, and long hours musing on it, he could discover no hidden purpose or explanation. Pure chance, it would seem. And yet, was it?

Treet was reasonably certain that very few things happened by chance where the mysterious Miss Talazac was concerned.

Another mystery occupied him as well—the mystery of wormhole travel. In the second week of the flight he had picked up Pizzle's book and begun reading, tentatively at first because the book began at the seventh chapter—Pizzle hadn't printed up the whole thing—and much of the terminology was astrophysics jargon. Clearly Belthausen's *Interstellar Travel Theory* was a book written for a select group of academics. There were, Treet decided, probably not more than seventy people in the whole world who could fully appreciate what Belthausen was getting at. That Pizzle should apparently be one of them surprised him.

But with little else to do besides eat and sleep and play Empires with the gnomish Pizzle, Treet made reading Belthausen a religious duty—struggling mightily with the interminable paragraphs made up of awkward sentences running on for pages freighting words whose meanings could only be guessed at or approximated in context and then only on second or third reading.

Belthausen was no William Shakespeare, but he seemed to know what he was talking about. Treet sensed as he read that the man grasped whole realms of possibility and feasibility that heretofore had been only hinted at, if considered at all. If he labored to bring his ideas into clear focus—and the signs of monumental labor were everywhere visible in his ungainly book, at least to the professional eye of another writer—it indicated that these were fresh ideas, concepts born of deep insight and creativity whose birth had cost the author something. He might not have been the Bard, but he wasn't chipped beef either.

So with increasing admiration, Treet slogged along, feeling like a foot soldier trudging under full field pack, following a commander whose orders he could scarcely comprehend. Along the way he also learned something about wormholes—among other things.

And what he learned disturbed him utterly.

Treet lay on his couch with the printout of Belthausen's book propped on his pillow while he sat cross-legged, tearing open rubbery capsules of dermal nutrient he'd found in his sanitary stall and smearing the viscid green emollient into his skin. It wasn't a proper nutrient bath, but considering he was several million miles from the nearest public spa, the little capsules were the next best thing.

So, smoothing the sticky substance over his face and chest and arms, he read, for the fourth or fifth time, a passage about time distortion in connection with wormholes—one of the more disturbing sections of the book for Treet—when he became aware that his scalp was tingling again. He stopped reading and tried to think where he had experienced that sensation before. With a start he remembered: Yarden!

At the same instant he glanced up and there she stood, framed in the open door of his compartment. He jumped up, opened his mouth to speak, but could not. What does one say to a vision?

"Mr. Treet," she said, less a greeting than the recitation of a known fact. "May I come in?"

For a moment Treet could only stare at her. Then he realized he had been addressed and asked a question. "Y-yes! Please come in. I wasn't expecting anyone. I . . . would you like to sit down?" He whirled around and picked up the foam chair at the terminal desk

"Thank you, no. I sit entirely too much as it is. I imagine we all do."

"Yes." He stared at her, trying to fix her face firmly in his mind this time.

"Mr. Treet, I won't keep you from your reading. This will only take a moment." She glanced around the compartment, which in six weeks Treet had managed to make look like the dayroom of an asylum for the criminally untidy.

With her standing there, he suddenly became aware of just how shabby the place looked. "I've been meaning to do some cleaning."

"It doesn't matter. I wanted to speak to you."

He waited. She looked at him curiously, full in the face, expectantly, as if there were some formal response he must make before she could continue. "Yes!" he said at last.

"Are you a sympath, Mr. Treet?"

It was a simple question, and Treet had heard the word before, knew what it meant, but her use of it caught him unawares, and for a moment its meaning evaded him. "A sympath?"

"Remote intelligence receptor. Surely, you are familiar—"

"Oh, yes! Yes, I know what it means. It's just that I didn't expect you to ask me that, of all things." He made an awkward gesture and realized he still had the foam chair before him. He put it down, saying, "No, I'm not a sympath. I've never had the training. Or the inclination for that matter. Why?"

She went on looking at him in that intense, engaging way and then said finally, "Some people are natural adepts and do not know it, Mr. Treet. You could be one of them." She said this last as if it were a challenge or an indictment, he couldn't decide which.

"I think I'd know, wouldn't I?" He smiled, trying to break through some of the high seriousness of the young woman. She seemed not to notice, but nodded slightly to herself as she backed away a slow step.

"Look, don't go," he said quickly. "It's a little . . . I mean, I'd like to get to know you a little better."

But she was already in the gangway. "No, Mr. Treet," her voice called back as she disappeared again, "perhaps you *wouldn't* know."

TEN

Orion Treet now had two things to be deeply disturbed about: wormhole time distortion, and the suggestion—no, the *insinuation*—that he was a sympath without his knowing it. About the former he had every right to be upset, but why the latter should bother him, he couldn't say. Except for the simple fact that he was a man who arranged his life like one of his essays: direct, uncluttered, balanced.

The insane expedition, as he now considered it, removed what little balance he had achieved of late. It had certainly eliminated the delicate equilibrium between penury and pelf (although the three million dollars stashed away in his flight kit had theoretically removed penury from the picture, his startling new wealth had yet to produce any tangible effects for him). Then there was the wormhole: how was it possible to find meaningful direction when at any moment *anything* might happen? The wormhole loomed as a monstrous, undulating question mark on his personal horizon, throwing unforeseen kinks in his ability to direct his fate. And Yarden Talazac's strange insinuation that he might be an unknowing sympath—in fact, her very presence—had cluttered his life with odd, irreconcilable thoughts and emotions, questions without answers, mysteries without clues.

As before, he said nothing of Yarden's visit to him. And though he wondered what it meant—as he wondered about what their first midnight meeting meant—he did not let on to Pizzle that he knew anything about the passenger in the adjoining stateroom. This silence had its price, for Pizzle was about to stampede him around the bend with his continual badgering: "Let's try to sneak into the ventilator shaft," or "I'll watch tonight, you watch tomorrow night," or "We could rig up a camera with a motion detector to photograph the gangway at night."

Instead, Treet deflected Pizzle's obsession toward a subject of more consequence, at least in his own mind.

"You've read Belthausen," Treet said as they sat knee-to-knee over Pizzle's Empires console, the flat green grid glowing between them. "What do you think of his time distortion theory?"

Pizzle's rims flashed as he glanced up. "It's a sound theory; no question about it. But then he starts off in pretty safe territory. I mean, distort space and you distort time—that much is elementary."

"Fine, it's elementary. But doesn't it concern you just a little? We're blasting away into the unknown, and both you and Crocker act as if we're on a holiday excursion to Pismo Beach. Doesn't the prospect of time displacement frighten you at all?"

Pizzle shook his head slowly. "I can't say as it does." He shrugged. "It's all the same in the end, isn't it?"

"What's all the same?"

"This—space travel. It's always into the unknown, right? And as far as time displacement, what difference does it make?"

"Why, an enormous difference!" Treet exploded in exasperation. "A carking great pile of a difference!"

"How?" Pizzle blinked mildly back at him.

"What?"

"How? How does it make a difference? You can't tell me that whether I arrive today, tomorrow, or a week ago last Thursday is going to make a molecule of difference—not to me, not to the colonists, not to anybody else, including you." He jabbed a button on the console. "It's your move. Careful, I've got your coastal lowlands mined."

As much as he hated to admit it, there *was* a microgram of cockeyed logic in what Pizzle said. In essence, it wouldn't make much difference *when* they arrived since their arrival had no field of external objectification, to use Belthausen's unwieldy term—that is, no exact temporal frame of reference.

Their normal frame of reference, Earth's time, would have no bearing on Empyrion time, and no real meaning either, since the two were not contiguous. Any problems posed by a time differential were largely illusory—in the sense that any such problems were merely due to the perception of the individual observer.

Except in the area of communication with Earth. Passing

signals back and forth through a space-time displacement tube—another term for wormhole—did complicate matters somewhat, as Cynetics had already discovered. Once into the tube, the signals became subject to whatever quirky laws governed the thing. Time shifts could occur, and probably did, although there was also the distinct possibility signals could pass through virtually unaffected, like arrows through a wind tunnel.

"What about parallel time channels?" asked Treet, intent on pursuing the discussion as far as possible. "Your move."

"Boy, you *have* been reading that book, eh?" Pizzle lowered his head over the grid. "Just captured one of your frontier base camps. Your turn." He looked up again. "Okay, what about them?"

"Well, suppose we come out of the wormhole and there's no colony because we've entered a parallel time channel? A channel, let's say, where a colony ship never arrived. We can't reach them because they're on another channel, and there's no way to change channels. What do we do then?"

"First of all, parallel time channels are merely an obscure mathematical possibility at this point." Pizzle held up his hand as Treet started to object. "But let's say that by some incredible circumstance we *did* end up in a parallel time channel."

Treet nodded. "Let's say."

"I imagine Crocker would simply turn right around and we'd go back the way we came. What's so terrible about that?"

Treet hadn't thought of that. Of course—they could just go back. Whatever happened, they could just turn around and hightail it back to Earth. Here he had been upset about persistent time distortions—static futures, variable pasts, parallel time channels, and all the rest—and Pizzle's unshakeable common sense had cut through all that with the modest wisdom of a weekend traveler: if we don't like the hotel, we'll pack up and go home.

With something approaching admiration, Treet gazed at his partner across the green grid screen. That scruffy, over-large head had a brain in it, and a good one. What other talents did Pizzle possess?

"Your capitol is in flames, and your escape routes are cut off," Pizzle was saying. "Unless you have a secret escape plan, your only chance is surrender. That's the game!"

"Wait! What was that?"

"Your empire is ashes."

"No, I mean—listen!" Treet cocked his head to one side, and the sound came again. "What's that?"

"That's just an acceleration signal." Pizzle cleared the screen. "Want to play another game?"

"No." Treet got up. "I want to find out what that signal is."

"I told you—" Before Pizzle could finish, the chiming signal changed, becoming louder, more insistent.

"Come on," said Treet. He entered the gangway and turned toward the cockpit. By the time he reached the flight deck, the signal had become an alarm, a blaring, raucous buzz. Treet tumbled into the cockpit and Pizzle after him. "Is this it? Is it happening?"

Crocker sat frozen over the navigator's instrument panel, his long-billed cap lowered over an orange oval screen. Yellow numbers flashed on the screen, changing to red as he watched. Without looking up he said, "I . . . don't know yet . . ."

Treet glanced around at the instrument panel. Several buttons were flashing red, and at least two screens spelled out the word WARNING! in crimson letters across their faces. Fear tugged his muscles taut, but Treet forced himself to remain calm.

Pizzle, standing beside him, whispered, "Could be a meteor field the vipath beam's picked up."

This was meant, no doubt, as a reassurance, but Treet's mind flashed the image of a million moon-sized chunks of rock hurtling into their tiny fragile craft, smashing it into a smoking tangle of twisted space junk.

"Sweet Julius!" said Crocker, spinning around to face them. "This is it, boys. Event horizon."

"The wormhole?" said Pizzle. "So soon?"

"We're still six weeks away," added Treet lamely.

The pilot shook his head, spinning back to his instruments. "Evidently we're in its backyard, and it's coming to meet us."

"Coming to meet us?" Treet stepped behind the Captain's chair and peered over his shoulder. "What do you mean?"

"Two A.U. and closing fast," he shot back over his shoulder.

"How fast?"

"You'd better get strapped in."

"How fast?" Treet demanded, gripping the chair with both hands.

"At the rate of one hundred thousand myms per second. Get back to your compartment and get strapped in—now! Both of you. Get going."

Treet backed away, reluctant to turn his eyes from the flashing screens. He felt Pizzle's hand on his arm, pulling him away. "Let's go. I switched on the holoscreens—we won't miss a thing."

They dashed back to their rooms, their feet barely making contact with the deck. Pizzle ducked into his compartment, grinning. "See you on the other end!"

"I sincerely hope so," muttered Treet, throwing himself onto the couch. His hand smacked the console, and the couch angled into flight attitude. He drew the seatbelt over him, and safety harness too, for good measure. He lay back and closed his eyes, trying to compose himself for whatever would happen next, and thought—what about Yarden!

Unhooking the belt and harness, Treet leaped from the couch and dove for the gangway. He reached Yarden's door a split second later and pounded it with both fists. "Yarden! Can you hear me? Open up! It's happening! The wormhole—we're going in! Did you hear? Open up!"

There was no answer. Likely she could not hear him. He pounded harder on the padded surface. "Yarden, open up! It's Treet!"

"Treet!" The overhead speaker barked at him. "Get back in your harness! She'll be all right. Move it!"

"Crocker, she doesn't know!"

"She *knows!*"

"But—"

"Get back in your harness, Treet!"

With a backward glance at Yarden Talazac's sealed door, Treet hurried to his room and rebelted. He had just snapped the harness buckle closed when the holoscreen before him pulsed with a bright light. Then the cabin lights dimmed, and Treet found himself staring into the mouth of the wormhole.

E L E V E N

The wormhole, as viewed through the 3-D projection of the holovision, appeared as a quivery purple spot in the center of the screen, expanding rapidly, blotting out the light of stars around its spreading rim. It glowed, according to Belthausen, because of something called Cerenkov radiation, which Treet did not pretend to understand. It had to do with the rotation of the Schwarzchild discontinuity exceeding the speed of light, the mechanisms of which Treet also failed to grasp.

He watched with dread fascination as the thing drew swiftly closer. Swelling. Turning.

The wormhole filled the screen, the glowing singularity so violet that needles of pain pierced the retinas. We must be at the very edge of it, thought Treet. We're going in!

Crocker's voice shouted over the sound system. "Brace yourselves! We're . . . one . . . two . . . three . . . NOW!"

Nothing happened.

This is it? wondered Treet.

Treet closed his eyes, expecting to feel something—a shudder through the ship, a spinning sensation, violent rocking motion, the collapse of the known universe—anything.

He felt nothing.

Then the first gravity waves hit the *Zephyros*. Treet experienced a heavy tug in his gut; his eyesight dimmed as blood drained from his head. He was weightless an instant later, and then squashed into his flight couch by a monster sandbag flung onto his chest. A split-second later he was floating in zero-G, lighter than air; the very next instant his bones were changed to lead. Gravity rippled over him. His stomach wriggled; his heart lurched against his ribs.

The disturbing effect subsided gradually. He opened his eyes and looked at the holoscreen and still saw the sharp purple, but something else as well. In the center of the screen a bright white dot of light shone like a single sun, very far away. The light at the end of the tunnel, thought Treet. Not so bad after all.

The white spot of sun grew slightly larger, though it gave the appearance of moving in the same direction as the ship, so that apparently the end of the wormhole receded as they approached. Still, the fact that it was getting bigger, however slightly, meant that they were traveling at a faster rate and would overtake it eventually.

Treet lay motionless and watched the screen, wondering whether the gravity waves would commence again, or whether they had entered the theorized gravity-free core of the displacement tube. Aside from the queasy anticipation, he felt just the same as before. If anything, shooting the wormhole was a big anticlimax, about as exciting as—what was it Crocker had called it?—riding a trolley through a tunnel.

By slow degrees, the spot of light in the center of the screen blossomed and Treet saw that it was not a disk, but rather a ring, hollow in the center—a donut of light. The donut continued to grow larger as the ship came closer and eventually swallowed the craft as it entered the hole in the center.

Instantly upon entering the donut of light, the holovision flared white. When the screen cleared, Treet was peering into an endless tube of soft blue-white light. It was like flying through a fluorescing neon tube.

Occasionally streaks of light—red, violet, deep blue, and green—flashed by them, disappearing in a lazy spiral down the tube. As Treet watched the brightly-colored streaks, it dawned on him that the walls of the tunnel were moving. In fact, they were woven of trillions of microscopic light particles spiraling along the inner walls of the tunnel around them.

The significance of this stunned him when he finally realized what it meant. That they were overtaking the tiny streaks meant that the *Zephyros* must be moving at a rate faster than the speed of light! Or very nearly. The larger colored streaks shooting past them—like artillery tracer bullets burning through the night—must be ultrafast particles of some sort: tachyons or accelerated photon bundles, somehow sped up by the phenomenon of the wormhole.

Faster than light? Could it be? Belthausen's book had described the possibility of light beams being caught in the wormhole, being bent and distorted—though the significance of this now eluded Treet—but he recalled nothing specific about the possibility of a vehicle traveling beyond lightspeed. That was supposed to be plainly impossible for a number of very good scientific reasons. But then, so were giant wormholes.

Treet could not take his eyes off the screen; he watched it greedily, studying the image before him. The walls of the tunnel undulated slowly, he noticed, bending like a tube flexed by the wind. Yet, the ship stayed on a perfect course through the exact center of the wormhole.

He heard a sound emerge from the speakers overhead. It sounded like Crocker's voice, but something was wrong. The words were garbled—chopped up, mixed together, and overlaid so that what came out of the speakers had the sound patterns of a voice, but none of the recognizable features of speech.

Something's wrong with Crocker! thought Treet. I've got to get to him. He fumbled at the harness buckle and jumped up. Treet's brain squirmed inside his skull. He saw his hands moving to lift himself off the couch as his legs swung over the edge, but the movement seemed to take forever.

He watched in horror as his hands smeared before his eyes, elongating, stretching as if made of rubber. He turned his head and his room smeared too, the objects blurring together, fusing, becoming a solid mass of shifting color.

Treet held his head completely still, and presently the room snapped back to its original shape, as if nothing had happened. Sitting on the edge of the couch, he waved his hand in the air. Again it smeared and stretched before his eyes, but he stopped the motion and held his hand steady, keeping his eyes on it. Treet discovered that the smear was actually made up of an infinity of frozen images, like individual frames of movie film fanning before his eyes—movie frames with the sequence out of order so that some of the frames showed his hand already stopped while others showed it as not having moved, or somewhere in between.

The effect made him nauseous. He closed his eyes and lay back. Above him the speaker buzzed again. He heard some urgency in the tone, but could not make out a single word; they were all clipped and jumbled and running over one another. The sequence was all confused. Something's wrong! he thought again. He's calling for help.

Treet struggled to his feet and the room shifted crazily, swerving and bending out of shape. He felt the couch behind his legs, closed his eyes, and staggered toward the open door and into the gangway. Holding his head very still, he glanced up the gangway, closed his eyes, and began walking toward the cockpit.

As long as I keep my eyes closed, I'm all right, he thought, feeling along the bulkhead as he went. He passed Pizzle's door and moved on, fumbling like a blind man. He reached the cockpit and entered, leaned against the padded doorframe for support, and allowed himself a quick look around. All was as before. Crocker sat in his command chair, strapped in, watching the screens, a look of immense satisfaction on his face. Sensing someone behind him, Crocker turned and Treet saw a most hideous sight—Crocker's head swerved in the air, his features losing solidity and blending together as if liquefied. Eyes ran together; hair and skin mingled; teeth, lips, and nostrils melted into one another. He appeared to Treet to be dissolving before his eyes.

The Captain spoke. His words tumbled out of his mouth helter-skelter, an unintelligible mish-mash of syllables.

Treet cringed back from the monstrous sight, and the movement caused the cockpit to spin and smudge crazily. The flight deck buckled beneath his feet and he fell back, unbalanced by the illusion of motion. In the same instant Treet felt the queasy, watery sensation of nausea wash through him. His stomach heaved, emptying its warm contents over the front of his singleton.

He slumped to the floor, eyes closed, stomach and brain quaking as darkness swam out of the bulkheads to engulf him.

"I told you to stay strapped in, Treet." The voice was Crocker's. "You okay?"

"Huh?" Treet turned toward the sound and raised his head. "What happened?"

"We reached wormhole terminus, and you fouled yourself."

Treet raised a hand to his chest and felt the sticky wetness there. The stench of vomit made his stomach roll again. He swallowed hard, tasting bile in his throat. "I thought you were in trouble."

"I was trying to tell you that terminus was coming up." Crocker knelt over him, a hand on his shoulder. "Okay now?"

79

"I think so. Motion sickness. I—how long have I been out?"

"Out?" Crocker lifted his hand. "You weren't out. Maybe just a second."

"It was terrible. I saw . . . you looked like a monster."

"You don't look so chipper yourself. Can you get up?"

"Sure." Treet placed his hands flat on the floor and pushed up on all fours.

"Woo! Who puked?" Pizzle came striding into the cockpit.

"Treet got a little seasick. He's okay now."

"Wow! Look at that! It's beautiful!" Pizzle dashed by him, and Treet lifted his head to see what had caused the outburst.

On the mainscreen before them the brilliant white ball of a sun blazed in the upper left, with several hundred other bright spots of stars salted in a sable field. In the center of the picture was the sight that had evoked Pizzle's ecstatic response: a brilliant green globe, wonderfully round and smooth, wrapped in a near-invisible veil of shimmering blue which thickened to a sparse dotting of puffy white clouds nearer the surface of the planet.

"Empyrion." The men's heads jerked around to see Yarden Talazac standing in the doorway behind them, her eyes too on the screen. "Realm of the gods."

"Miss Talazac!" exclaimed Pizzle in a hushed voice. "It was *you*—" He hesitated and faltered.

She glanced at Pizzle once quickly—as though to silence him—as she entered the room, and then turned her attention back to the screen. Pizzle appeared slightly embarrassed, then shrank away from her as she came to stand with them.

For a long time nobody spoke. They merely gazed at the slowly turning world before them on the screen, each wondering what they would find waiting for them down there. Finally a chime sounded on the instrument board, and Crocker moved to his chair.

"Well, we're twelve hours to orbit entry." Crocker spoke softly, almost reverently.

"How long to landing?" asked Treet.

"Depends on what the scanners find. We'll have to locate the colony before going down, but we'll start broadcasting on the spectrum right away. If they're listening—and they surely are—we'll get directions and landing instructions and go right on in. Maybe eighteen hours. No more than twenty-four."

"Great!" cried Pizzle, fairly dancing in place. "I can't wait! This is going to be ultrafantastic!"

"Let's just hope we're up to it," said Treet, and then wondered immediately why he had said it. Certainly he felt every bit as excited about what lay before them as Pizzle.

"My thoughts exactly, Mr. Treet," said Yarden, stepping up beside him. "You must have read my mind."

TWELVE

"*T*his is the sixth pass, Captain, and still nothing on scan—what's the problem?" Treet stood beside Pizzle, who leaned against the Cyclops housing looking bored. Behind them a great green expanse filled the mainscreen as *Zephyros'* cameras scoured the landmasses beneath them, searching for the colony.

"The problem—for the tenth time—is that we can't raise them on the radio. We're having to do a visual which is like . . ."

"Like looking for a quark in a quagmire," offered Pizzle.

"Why don't they answer the transmission?"

"I don't know why. We'll just have to be sure to ask them, won't we?" said Crocker, impatience lending him sarcasm. The last twelve hours had produced nothing but headaches; fatigue slumped his shoulders. "Look, this is going to be a long wait. Why don't you two go and get some sleep while you can. I'll call you if—*when* I find something."

"Good idea," offered Pizzle. "Come on, Treet. Let's leave the Captain to fly his ship. We're just getting in the way."

"Okay, but you'll call us—"

"I'll *call* you!"

They filed out of the instrument-jammed cockpit and along the gangway, pausing at Pizzle's compartment. "He's right about getting some rest, you know. We may not get much of a chance later."

"What do you mean?" Treet heard something in the words and spun on his heel to face Pizzle.

The close-set eyes darted away quickly. "Oh, nothing—just that, you know, it's likely to be somewhat hectic down there. First visitors from home and all."

"That's not it!" Treet took a step closer, confronting Pizzle. "Tell me what you meant."

"That's all I meant. I swear." He turned to go into his room.

"You meant that something's the matter down there. Admit it."

"Nothing's the matter." Pizzle yawned and shuffled into his compartment. "You'll see; nothing's the matter."

"Then why don't they answer the signal?" Treet shouted at his disappearing figure. The door slid shut, cutting off Pizzle's reply.

Three meals, four games of Empires, sixteen hours, and nine revolutions later, Crocker called them all back to the bridge. Treet fairly flew down the gangway with Pizzle close on his heels. Yarden came behind them at a more stately pace. Crocker, haggard and showing two days stubble on his jaw, sat hunched over the Cyclops keypad, a pile of silver mylex printout tape curling around his chair.

"Well, boys and girls, I think I've found them." His tone was less than certain.

The others remained silent, waiting for the pilot to continue. When he saw that no one had anything to say, he went on. "Don't everyone jump up and down at once! I said we've located the colony."

"You didn't sound any too overjoyed yourself," replied Treet. "What's wrong?"

Crocker bent over the keypad again, tapped a key, and then slumped back in the chair, rubbing his face with his hands. "I don't know. There's something screwy down there, that's for sure. I wish I could figure it out." He reached down and grabbed a handful of the mylex printout. "Look at this! I've run every scan and probe in my very fat manual, and I can't figure it."

Pizzle took off his glasses and rubbed the lenses on his shirt. "You might as well go whole-hog," he said, "and tell us what you know."

"It's pretty complicated, but the long and short of it is that every time I get a steady fix on the colony, it shifts. Rather, I get two readings—first one place, then somewhere else again." Crocker's words met with blank stares. "Here's a map—" He tapped a key and a green-and-gold landmass appeared on one of Cyclops' three screens. There were two red dots marked on the map—one in the center, near what appeared to be a blue, winding thread of a river, and another red dot in the lower right quadrant, nearer a tawny gold coast.

"Not much to go on," remarked Treet.

"We're still too high for a more detailed picture, and we don't have a snooper pack, but it'll give you the general idea. Of the three major continental land areas on the planet, this is the largest." Stabbing a finger at the red spot in the center of the map, Crocker said, "I get a fairly strong reading here—in the neighborhood of point zero eight seven nine, which ought to indicate a settlement of considerable size. Trouble is, the methane signature isn't what it should be—hardly anything at all. Over here, though, I get a reading of point zero six six two, with a good healthy methane signature."

"What's that mean exactly?" asked Treet.

"Two colonies," said Yarden. Crocker looked at her and nodded slowly.

"Yeah, two colonies. See, it took me a long time to separate the two because I didn't want to accept the readings. But that's what it looks like—two colonies. One nearly as big as the other."

"How is that possible?" asked Pizzle. "That would mean the first colony would have had to double in size in less than five years. That can't be right."

"I don't see anything so odd about it at all," said Treet. "It's probably natives."

"I thought of that too, but the transcripts of the landing party don't say anything about an extensive native population. Besides, they wouldn't have chosen this planet in the first place if there had been sentient humanoids down there—that would violate the IASA charter."

"Maybe they're not humanoid," said Pizzle. "Maybe it's a mob of long-horned blue kangaroos."

"That would have to be a sizable mob," replied Crocker flatly. "It's a density of point ninety-nine per square meter. Herds and such tend to be less dense—I looked it up. Strong LFR, too—that's life force reading—above 85 percent. It's the same reading you get from a well-populated city." He looked at Yarden, who was staring at the mainscreen where Empyrion turned slowly on its axis as they flew over its smooth terrain. "She said it: two colonies."

Treet rubbed his neck with his hand. "So why don't we just fly on down for a closer look? I don't see the problem."

"I wish it were that easy," said Crocker. "No, we're going to have to choose a landing site and take our chances."

Treet's features convulsed in a furious frown. "Take our chances! What is this? A game? Is that what it is? Roll the dice and see what comes up?"

Crocker glared at him. "I wouldn't say that. The colony *is* down there."

"Is it? You're sure, are you?" Treet fumed, getting red in the face. "Then why don't they answer our signals?"

"Obviously radio failure of some kind." Pizzle darted a look from one to the other of the two men.

"Radio failure, he says! They could have as easily gotten eaten by that swarm of blue-horned kangaroos or whatever. Shall we go down and make it dessert?"

Crocker waved aside the comment. "You're overreacting."

"Tell me I'm overreacting when you're simmering in your own sauce on a bed of hot coals."

"I'm sure there's a rational explanation," offered Pizzle.

"I'd like to hear it!" Treet demanded.

"We have weapons, Treet," intoned Crocker.

"We do? Well, why didn't you say so before?"

"Last resort, dire emergency, and all that. But yes, we have weapons. Does that make you feel better?"

Treet hated to admit that it did. "Somewhat," he replied grudgingly.

"Good. At last. Well," Crocker stood slowly and stretched, "it's agreed then, right? We go down on the next flyover and head for the larger blip." He pointed to the glowing red dot in the center of the computer screen, then glanced at Yarden Talazac.

Treet saw the look and wondered at it.

Yarden nodded once sharply. "I agree, Captain." She turned back to the screen.

Treet watched her for a moment; he felt a queer, uneasy sensation at the thought that somehow *she* was controlling this decision. Maybe she was. "How soon?"

Crocker consulted an instrument. "We're coming up on the continental landmass in thirty minutes. We'll start our descent in about fifteen. Actual landing won't take but a few minutes."

"And then?"

Captain Crocker stared at Treet levelly. "And then, Mr. Treet, we shall see what we shall see."

• • • • • •

What they saw, streaking through the atmosphere like a meteor, was a turquoise world, blue-green with vegetation, water, and sky. As the *Zephyros* sped closer, its wings folded back into knife-thin stubs, the landscape rolled out before them, puckered like a rumpled tablecloth, and laced through with blue-white water. Their descent brought them over a rugged range of jagged mountains, a flat expanse of plains, and the sinuous waves of a desert of stark white dunes which faded into an earthy brown, then changed once more to pastel blue-green as they rocketed across the shallow valley of a wide silver river.

Treet, strapped to his flight couch, watched the holoscreen. Although the land seemed fair and inviting, it was empty. He did not see any signs of life: no animals or birds of any description—no sign that the planet supported anything but plants—and possibly insects; there were sure to be insects.

As the land rolled by beneath him, Treet realized that he was seeing a world no one had ever seen before—except the colonists, and perhaps not even them. Here was a virginal world, rich and ripe, ready for the hand of a husband, a world offering a fresh start for those who would make their homes upon her.

Such was the mood the alien landscape cast over Treet. His heart stirred to the sight of endless miles of verdure and fresh, clean water under sparkling blue skies. No dark cities with hanging shrouds of foul air; no yawning ore pits scarring the earth; no highways or fences tying it down; no stinking, festering hellholes filled with humanity's untouchables. No war. No disease. No famine. No want.

Here was a new beginning, a dream worth fighting for—perhaps even dying for.

Treet wondered at his response to this place. He had traveled far and wide, had seen grand vistas and beautiful landscapes many times before. Some had moved him, it was true, but none like this; none as much as Empyrion. Why? Landscape was just landscape, one hill or river pretty much like another in the final analysis. And yet . . . this place *was* different. He could feel the difference, though he could not name it.

Perhaps it was the absence of mankind here and all that represented: a free, unspoiled, perfect world. A paradise which had not cast out its keeper. An Eden where no serpent slithered.

A realm of beauty, yes, but of beauty which was as much promise as physical presence.

The overhead speaker clicked as Crocker opened a circuit. "What a place!" he said in awed tones. Then came a long pause, after which he added, "We're coming up on the colony now. ETA two minutes. I'm feathering in the drag engines."

At that moment Treet heard a hissing sound like sand blowing over glass. The straps tugged at his chest as the *Zephyros* responded to the increased drag by slowing. They were skimming over the landscape now, wings extended to offer maximum lift. The picture on the screen tilted slightly and then righted itself, and Treet saw a ridge rising up across a valley. The ship flashed over the valley, climbing slightly.

"And here it is, lady and gentlemen," said Crocker, all business again. He might have been a bus driver casually announcing the termination of his route.

"Where? I don't see it." The voice was Pizzle's, but it spoke Treet's thoughts as well.

"The lower center of your screen," returned Crocker. "You'll see it . . . now!"

Leaning forward as far as his restraining straps would allow, Treet saw a dull, metallic-looking mound growing in the center of the screen near the bottom. "We'll make a reconnaissance pass," said Crocker, and the picture tilted sharply. The grayish mound dipped from the screen, and Treet saw a sky of intense blue above a turquoise horizon.

"Sensors report no radio or electromagnetic activity below. I've got a strong LFR confirmed." Crocker read off his instruments. "We are shedding altitude. Our second pass will be closer."

Again the picture tilted, and the horizon slanted up. Treet glimpsed a bit of white sunlight through the tiny oval window above him. On the screen the landscpe showed pastel green and barren rounded hills and flat places all around, with brown bluffs above a river in the far distance.

"I've got a visual," said Crocker. "The landing area is clear. I'm going to put her down."

Treet swallowed with a dry mouth; he heard a loud drumming sound and realized that his heart was thumping in his ears. His fingers dug into the fabric of the couch. This is it! he thought. We're landing!

The rumble and jolt of the engines suprised him, but he did not take his eyes from the screen for an instant. The picture shook momentarily, steadied, and then the horizon began flattening out as they came down vertically.

"Forty-two hundred," said Crocker. "Coming down nicely. Thirty-five. Very good." Another rumble rocked the ship. "A little more thrust; that's right. Good. Twenty-eight hundred. Slowing. Twenty-six . . ."

Where is it? wondered Treet, straining forward in his seat, eyes frozen on the screen. I don't see the colony! Where is it?

The holoscreen showed a panoramic view of a blue-green field of tall grasslike plants where wind sent waves rolling like breakers across the plain. The wind was exhaust from *Zephyros'* jets as the ship lowered itself from the sky. The picture spun and Treet got a glimpse of something rounded and glittering, rising up nearby—the mound he had seen moments before. The ship came around, and the object slid away.

With a soft, cushioned bounce like an elevator coming to a stop, the *Zephyros* touched down. "Happy landing, folks," announced Crocker. "Welcome to Empyrion."

THIRTEEN

"**I**s this really necessary?" asked Pizzle, grimacing with distaste. "I mean, really? We already know that the air is breathable—there's more oxygen in it than Earth's!"

"Just put it on, will you, and stop stalling," ordered Crocker. "It's by the book or not at all."

"But . . . the colonists breathe it, for crying out loud—"

"Shut up and do it, Pizzle. You're holding things up." Treet glared nastily at the balking Pizzle. "What are you afraid of?"

Grumbling, Pizzle lifted the massive helmet over his head and brought the neck seal down on the tabs. Crocker flipped the catches and checked to make sure it had sealed.

"Okay, we're all set. Everyone ready?" Crocker looked at each of the passengers in turn, waiting for a nod. "Let me hear you."

"All set," said Treet. His legs trembled with anticipation, and he thought, This is it! We're going out; we're really going out there! Mingled with this expectation was a distinct undercurrent of fear: the unkown. What lay on the other side of that hatch? Heaven? Hell?

"Ready," said Pizzle. He glanced nervously around at the others.

"I'm ready," said Yarden, her graceful form wrapped in a bulky, shapeless, red atmosphere suit like the others.

"Okay, I read you loud and clear. Let's go." The Captain reached out and tapped a code into the switchplate next to the outer hatch. There was a muffled whoosh and the hatch withdrew, swung outward, and slid away to the side. A stairstep ladder unfolded below the hatch, and Crocker stepped into the open hatchway. "One at a time. Follow me."

Crocker stepped over the threshold, turned, and backed down the steps, holding the handrail. Pizzle looked at Treet and gestured to the ladder.

"No, you go next," replied Treet. "I'll go after Miss Talazac."

Pizzle shifted his gaze to Yarden, nodded silently, and stepped into the hatchway. He disappeared, the top of his helmet sinking from sight as he went down.

"Your turn," said Treet, turning to Yarden.

"Thank you," she replied, turning crisply and descending without hesitation.

What is it with her? wondered Treet. He sighed and then stepped to the hatchway, turned, and lowered himself onto the first step, counting the steps as he went down.

When he reached the bottom he turned, expecting to see the others waiting for him. There was no one. A twinge of fear flitted over him. He spun around quickly, scanning the perimeter.

Then he saw them, at the rear of the ship behind one of the stilt legs. With instant relief Treet ducked beneath the heatcone of an engine and walked under the belly of the ship to join the others, who stood motionless, their back to him, apparently engrossed in something. Treet could not see what it was. The suit radios were silent; no one said a word.

Treet stepped from under the obscuring edge of an engine shield and came to stand beside Crocker. Only then did he see what the others were seeing: an enormous sparkling wall of glass shot through with veins of black swept up from the landing platform. Beyond this wall rose bank upon bulging bank of crystalline domes and cupolas, billowing one on top of another beyond counting.

Treet raised his eyes higher and higher still. The many-domed mound rose like a great multifaceted mountain of crystal. Here and there spars poked through the domes, trailing thick, dark cables which gave the appearance of lifting the mass like cathedral spires or the poles of a circus tent. Up and up like foothills climbing to the summit, the bright domes swelled—all sizes jumbled together, gleaming in the sunlight like wonderful, gigantic soap bubbles dropped from the sky—some big enough to cover a building or two, others, larger by many times, able to enclose a small city with room for a few suburbs.

The glistening mountain stretched away for kilometers on either hand, and wherever the eye rested, the glimmer of bright transparency winked back. Empyrion stood an enchanted crystal mountain whose top reached shimmering into the clear blue sky.

"Impossible!" said Treet, his voice hushed in awe. "I can't believe it."

"Incredible," agreed Pizzle. "It's unimaginable! How could they build this . . . this bubble city in so short a time? It isn't possible."

"Look at this," said Crocker. The three turned to look where he pointed. His gloved hand extended toward the ground. They saw the platform beneath their feet littered with small rocks and pebbles, bits of glass, warped fibersteel plates, and something that looked like crinkled pink moss growing in thickly scattered patches over the structure. "This landing field doesn't get much use, I'd say." He swiveled around and took in the broad expanse of the platform. "It looks like it's been abandoned for years . . . decades."

"The colony isn't that old," put in Pizzle.

"I know." Crocker turned back to the others. "I can't explain it."

"Maybe this isn't the colony," replied Treet simply, then shuddered to think what he had just said. Not the colony? Then who. . . ?

"It is the colony." Yarden spoke with such certainty that the men pivoted toward her. She stood stock-still with her arms pressed to her sides.

"What is it, Yarden?" asked Crocker. "What are you getting?"

Just then she stiffened and pointed at the wall directly before them about a kilometer away. "They are coming to meet us," she said, but the words were flat, no happiness or excitement in them, but rather something darker, almost sinister.

Treet saw a portion of the wall raise up and a dark shape emerge, followed by another and then a third. These came rapidly toward them on clouds of dust, filling the air with a ringing whine as they drew nearer.

Closer, the travelers could make out men standing in these strange vehicles—men dressed as they were, in atmosphere suits, dark and close fitting, however, and made of a material that shone with a faint luster. A helmet with black faceplate obscured their faces, making them appear monstrous and malevolent.

"I don't like this," said Treet. "They don't look too happy to see us. Where are the weapons?"

"We probably surprised them," suggested Pizzle. "No prior radio contact—they probably wonder who we are."

"Shh! They can probably hear you too," snapped Crocker. "Let me handle this." He stepped forward. "Yarden? Anything?"

The young woman was silent for a moment, then shrugged. "There is something there, but . . . it's blocked. I can't read it."

Now the first vehicle swept up, slowing only minimally as it approached. Men stood in the rear of the machine, darkened faceplates turned toward them. One man, a driver, stood ahead of the others, holding controls in both hands. Then the thing swung sideways, and Treet saw two wheels beneath its smooth belly throwing up dust. Another two-wheeler swung around to the other side and the third parked between them, somewhat closer than the other two.

The two groups watched each other. No one moved.

With a shock Treet recognized the snub-snouted barrels of weapons in the hands of the dark-suited colonists. "They're armed!" he whispered harshly.

"Shh!" Crocker hissed. "I'll do the talking."

With that, the pilot stepped forward slowly, raising his right hand in the classic greeting. "Brothers," he said, his voice confident, controlled, "we're glad to see you . . ." He hesitated as there was no answer, no sign of recognition from the other side. One hand went to his forearm panel to make an adjustment. "Wide-band broadcast," he said to himself, then continued boldly, "We've come from Earth." No response. "From Earth."

At this a harsh, guttural growl issued from one of the colonists—more a bark than a voice.

It was difficult to tell which one had shouted, but Treet saw a figure in the center two-wheeler jerk his hand upward and the men around him disembarked, stepping from the vehicle to advance cautiously toward them, weapons at the ready.

"Tell them we're friendly," Treet said urgently. "Tell them, Crocker!"

"We're *friends*. We've come from Earth," repeated the Captain, to no avail.

The line of men stopped just short of the travelers, and the man who had given the signal approached. He stepped closer and examined each of them carefully, his dark faceplate reflecting sunlight like the shell of a beetle.

"What is this?" Treet addressed the man. "What's going on? Why don't you speak to us?"

The man appeared not to have heard, but went on with his inspection, moving to Pizzle, Talazac, and Crocker in turn. The colonist stepped back a pace and looked at them, as if trying to decide what to do next. Clearly their presence here posed some kind of problem for the colonists. Treet sensed that a decision was being made and that the next few moments were critical. He had to break through to them, but how?

"We're from Cynetics," Treet said, speaking out suddenly. The colonist and his men jerked their attention to Treet. "Cynetics," he said again, repeating the word distinctly.

At the word, a garbled mutter broke out among the colonists. Treet heard it in his helmet as a gibber of voices talking over one another with subdued excitement, whereupon one voice cut through the others with a shout, and there was silence again.

The colonist raised his hand and pointed at Treet and said something, his low voice buzzing. Two men stepped forward quickly and grabbed Treet by the arms.

"Hey! Let me go!" cried Treet. "Hey!"

"Stop!" shouted Crocker, dashing up.

"Help!" Treet struggled in the grasp of the colonists, but they hauled him bodily along. "Shoot them!"

Behind him he heard the sounds of a scuffle: short breaths, grunts, and curses—presumably from Crocker and Pizzle; a gabble of thick, unintelligible syllables, from the colonists.

The fight sounds halted abruptly. In order to see behind him, Treet had to turn his whole upper torso around, which was difficult, pinioned as he was between the two who were dragging him toward the center two-wheeler. When they paused at the vehicle to shove him in, Treet managed to twist around. He saw two bodies lying on the platform, and the third—Yarden?— being dragged to one of the other two-wheelers.

"Crocker!" he screamed. "Pizzle! Talazac!"

There was no reply. He felt hands on him, hoisting him up into the two-wheeler, and he was tumbled in headfirst. Then they were speeding back to the wall and into the crystal mountain beyond.

FOURTEEN

"Where is this one going?" A Nilokerus guard stepped into the corridor, halting the suspension bed maneuvered by a second-order physician.

The physician stopped abruptly, turned stiffly toward the guard, and held up a packet with a violet Threl seal. "He's for the Saecaraz. Jamrog's initiative. He wants to keep an eye on this one personally."

The guard stepped close to the floating bed and peered curiously down into the face of the man lying there. "Is he the one that called on Cynetics?"

"No. I hear that one's to remain with the Supreme Director in Threl High Chambers. This is one of the others."

"Looks harmless enough." The guard shrugged and stepped aside, and the physician shoved the body-bearing bed away once more. They had traveled no more than ten paces when the guard turned his head to his shoulder and whispered, "The prisoner is on the way, Subdirector Fertig."

A click sounded in the folds of the guard's clothing as the circuit opened. "Acknowledged. Report to Fairweather level in Tanais sector for reassignment."

"At once." The shoulder mike clicked off, and the guard spun on his heel and hurried along the deserted terrace toward his new destination, muttering, "This is news! I'll get a round for this tonight. Maybe two!"

Orion Treet was awake, and his head felt stuffed with oatmeal. A small spot on his upper arm ached, as if he'd been burned with a lighted cigar just below the shoulder. Or branded.

Branded? The thought caused him to sit bolt upright on the suspension bed. He sprang up too quickly, the bed dipped, and Treet rolled onto the floor. Black spots of dizziness pinwheeled before his eyes. Presently the spots faded and, still sprawled on the floor, he looked cautiously at his right arm where he saw only a thin scratch and a tiny red bruise. He rubbed the spot for a moment as he studied his cell.

It was a small, pie-shaped room with a ceiling that curved upward, toward some apex beyond—a section of a dome. The ceiling was translucent and glowed light green, softly tinting the bare walls of the cell. The doorway, narrow, but with strangely rounded posts and a lancet arch, stood open. There was no door, and a further door glimpsed beyond a connecting room was open too. Either the colonists had no use for doors, or they had a more efficient way of sealing rooms.

Treet guessed the latter: a barrier field of some sort.

This inspection done, Treet turned his attention to the rest of the room. He saw a black-and-silver bundle on a shelf which jutted out from the wall. Since it was the only other object in the room besides the suspension bed—and since he was naked and beginning to feel foolish sitting on the floor—Treet decided to investigate.

Pushing himself up slowly—so as not to start the black spots dancing again—he moved toward the shelf, stealing a glance through the open doorway as he went. He was alone; no one appeared in either doorway, nor could he see anyone in the room beyond.

Taking the bundle from the shelf, Treet shook out the folds to reveal a lightweight robe of a material that looked and felt like silk. The robe—short, with a large V-shaped hole for his head—was black with silver diagonal stripes. A second garment fell out of the first—a pair of coarse, baggy black leotards with molded synthetic rubber soles sewn into the feet. There was no undergarment, but, not feeling at all choosy, he pulled on the leotard and drew it over his legs; the high wasteband came all the way up to his solar plexus.

Next he slipped the flimsy, long-sleeved robe over his head. The garment reached midcalf, but once the two broad silver bands dangling from his waist were wrapped around and tied at his side, creating a sash, the hemline rose to just above his kneecaps.

The clothes were remarkably comfortable—more so than the singleton he always wore. The fine quality of the robe, and the silky sensation against his skin, made him feel like a Chinese emperor. He smoothed the folds beneath his hands and, with nothing else to do, sat down once again on the edge of the bed to wait, replaying in his mind all that he could remember of the scuffle on the landing field.

He had disembarked and was immediately met by three vehicles carrying colonists. An attempt at communication had been made, at which point he had been attacked. Treet remembered being buffeted around somewhat—a sore thigh and ribs told him he had taken a blow or two—and then dragged toward one of the vehicles. At some point after being hauled aboard, his memory went blank.

Then he had awakened in this cell. He could remember nothing else after that, and only isolated patches from before. He remembered his conversation with Varro and meeting Neviss; he remembered eating a fine meal, but not what he ate; remembered a satchel full of money, now gone; and before that being hauled from a public bath at Houston International at gunpoint. Only snatches—a jigsaw puzzle with lots of pieces missing, islands of clarity surrounded by seas of featureless confusion.

But there should be more, he told himself. What about the others?

Certainly there had been others—he could hardly have come here alone. There had to have been a transport, and *someone* would have had to fly it.

I did not come alone, he thought. There *were* others, *had* to be others. Why can't I remember them?

—

The room in which Yarden Talazac found herself was faintly reminiscent of her childhood home. There was no ceiling, but the soft, shifting light, filtering in from high above, sending faint ripples of dappled shadow across smooth white walls, reminded her of the seaside villa of her father. Her room had been adjacent to the inner courtyard and open to the sky. She had always loved the feeling of freedom the room inspired, and at twilight, when the plexidome was raised for the night above the courtyard, stars shone down upon her bed.

But this room was not in her father's house. Somewhere else then. Where? She could not say. She had the feeling, though, that she had come from very far away to this place. How she had come, and why, she did not know.

At the same time, she felt that she had always been here—in this room, sitting on the bed, watching the shadow shapes drift like clouds over the wall. That could not be, she knew. There must be a life outside this room, but . . .

Thinking about it made her tired. She yawned and lay back against the pillows she had piled in the middle of the bed. She closed her eyes and gave herself to the cozy warmth of sleep, feeling safe and secure: a child in her father's home once again.

The moment he opened his eyes, Pizzle reached out to release his safety harness. It was gone. He pulled back his hand and wondered what had made him do that. Even as he tried to think about it, the thought evaporated.

For a moment he had the impression that he would remember something very important, that if he only concentrated hard enough it would come to him. But concentration eluded him; random thoughts drifted in and out of his head, and he forgot why he was concentrating in the first place.

He yawned, slid out of bed, and stretched, pulling his arms over his head and bending at the waist. It felt good to stretch; he'd been sleeping too long.

Pizzle slipped his yos over his head and tightened the sash at his side, blousing up the folds properly so that the hem reached midthigh. He stopped and looked at his hands. Where had he learned to arrange a yos?

Hadn't he always known? Wasn't it a thing everyone knew?

For a moment he experienced a strange sense of reversed deja vu—of doing for the first time things he had been doing all his life.

Oh well, it was probably nothing. Nothing at all.

FIFTEEN

Sirin Rohee, Supreme Director of the Threl, stared around the ring at his grim companions. Worry stretched his normally pouty expression into a deep, oppressive frown. Everyone in the darkened, heavily-draped room felt the full weight of that frown; it was like gravity—pulling all attention toward itself.

At last he spoke. His voice warbled slightly, a clue to his advancing age; but his hands were steady as he clasped his ceremonial bhuj. "The threat, though very great, has been averted, Directors. We have managed to isolate the intruders, and amnesiants have been administered."

"There was no trouble?" Kavan asked, averting his eyes briefly. The Supreme Director waved the bhuj to his left; the polished blade flashed in the light.

"None," replied Hladik. "They were but a small force; our own Invisibles subdued them easily."

"Weapons?" Cejka spoke in a raw whisper.

Hladik regarded him frankly from beneath his heavy brows and answered, "We found no weapons."

"But," added Rohee quickly, "there is no doubt that the intent of their mission was to discredit our security. Therefore, you will describe weapons of undetermined origin. Our official statement will be that we have, owing to tireless vigilance, thwarted a plot by Fieri spies."

Tvrdy, the sly, practical Director of Tanais, leaned forward in his seat, cleared his throat, and said, "What of this vehicle of theirs? I understand the spies possessed a spacecraft."

Saecaraz Subdirector Jamrog answered without waiting for a nod from his superior. "Obviously the vehicle must have been a decoy."

"Oh?" said Tvrdy. "I had not heard this." He glanced at Cejka, and then continued. "What would be the use of a decoy?"

"Deception," said Jamrog. "The Fieri are deviously clever.

They hope to make us believe that they have achieved space travel. We know this is impossible."

"Should not this decoy craft be mentioned in our statement? The people are certain to hear about it."

"You will make no mention of the decoy craft. It does not exist."

"Where is it now?" asked Tvrdy. "I would like to have it studied. It may be that it hides some clues to Fieri magic."

"It has been removed," Jamrog replied tightly.

"Yes. So I would expect. And where is it being kept? I wish to send Tanais magicians to study it."

"You will be notified when that becomes possible," said Jamrog.

"I see. And what prevents me from seeing it now?"

"I say when—" began Jamrog angrily.

Hladik, Director of Nilokerus, raised a hand and cut him off. "You will see the vehicle in due time, Tvrdy. I realize both you and Jamrog will have keen interest in the craft—even though it is but an elaborate toy. However, the Supreme Director asked me to make absolutely certain the machine poses no security threat."

"Of course." Tvrdy smiled. "I was merely curious, you understand." He nodded toward Jamrog. "I am sorry if my request upset you."

Piipo, the long-faced, taciturn Director of Hyrgo Hage, twisted uncomfortably in his seat and spoke up. "Supreme Director, if I may return to other matters, you said the spies have been isolated. Am I to believe they are being held in the reorientation section?"

"Allow me, Supreme Director," said Hladik as the Threl leader glanced toward him. "The force was small—only four. Since their presence was certain to be discovered by the Dhogs if they were placed in adjustment cells, I thought it best that they be introduced unobtrusively into suitable Hages. Of course they will remain under close surveillance until the effect of the psi-lobe is rendered permanent."

"You don't think they would pose an even greater threat loose among the populace? They could conceivably make contact with Dhogs who are sure to recognize them."

"Of course," replied Hladik equably, "such a thing is possible. But in their present condition they would be in no position to help their comrades." The Nilokerus leader smiled broadly.

"Besides, as I have said, their movements will be monitored very closely. Any attempt to contact the Fieri underground within Empyrion would compromise their organization. We would strike instantly and crush them once and for all."

Supreme Director Rohee raised the bhuj and rapped the gold-plated staff sharply on the floor. "The session is at an end, Directors. You will assure your Hagemen that we have dealt our treacherous enemies a decisive blow; we are now very close to smashing their network and ridding Empyrion of their hated presence forever."

With that he stood slowly, supported by Jamrog who held his elbow, turned, and shuffled from the circular chamber. The seven remaining Threl watched him go in silence.

As the others filed past, led away by their waiting guides, Trvdy stepped from the procession and walked to the terrace rim. He put his hands on the smooth surface of the breastwork and looked out over the Hage. The undulating arcs of a thousand terrace rims, falling away in sweeping stairsteps on every side, descending to teeming tangles of warrens and cells below, met his gaze.

There was much that had not been said in session about this so-called invasion of spies. What were the spies doing *outside* the dome? Why were they not simply terminated upon capture—standard policy for Fieri agents and Dhogs? Why had their spacecraft been hidden? Why was there no preliminary report from Saecaraz magicians? Which Hages had been selected for hiding the alleged spies?

"You look but do not see," remarked a withered voice behind him. Tvrdy nodded and turned to meet Cejka.

"I see too much that I do not like. But you are a Rumon; you must see even more than I." Tvrdy leaned against the terrace rim once again, turning so that a lipreader would not be able to observe their speech. Cejka joined him, and both men gazed out over the man-made hills and valleys of the colony's interior.

"I see that Jamrog and his puppet Hladik have been busy obscuring the facts. But one thing is clear—there is much they are not telling about these alleged Fieri spies. Therefore, they are afraid."

"Where are they, do you think?"

"I don't know, but I will find out. Rumon rumor messengers are already at work, and our agents have been alerted; you can be sure we will find out very soon."

"And then?"

"And then we will talk. Kavan, you, and I—also Piipo, if he will come."

"You trust him?"

"Yes. We have had opportunity for much informal discussion of late. He may not join us, but he will not betray us. He can be trusted."

"What of Dey? Should we try him?"

Cejka groaned. "The Chryse are in bed with the Saecaraz. We have lost Dey, I am afraid. No matter. Hyrgo is more important anyway, and it's true they have no love for Jamrog. Eee!" Cejka shuddered. "The prospect of Jamrog as Supreme Director . . . it's abhorrent . . . unthinkable!"

Tvrdy nodded absently. "I wonder if it could be true . . . do you think? Could the intruders really be Travelers?"

Cejka's shoulders lifted in a shrug. "Who knows? Stranger things are possible, I suppose. Though I think we will find that the Fieri are perhaps becoming unusually bold—that is more likely."

"I have heard that one of them invoked the ancient name . . . Cynetics." Tvrdy glanced sharply at his friend.

"Yes, very puzzling. I don't know what to make of it. It is said the Dhogs still worship Cynetics." He shrugged. "Well, we will find out—a Rumon always finds out." Cejka looked around him; across the terrace several people were milling aimlessly. He leaned close to Tvrdy and said, "We had better leave now. We are beginning to attract attention. I think I recognize one of Hladik's so-called Invisibles over there."

"Yes. Well, contact me as soon as you find out the intruders' whereabouts. We must work quickly if we want to save the information; otherwise the psilobe will destroy it."

"Of course," said Cejka, moving off along the rim, signaling for his guides to lead him away. "I'll contact you as soon as we have found them."

Trvdy remained gazing out over the colony's terraces for a time—until his own guides approached to lead him back to Tanais Hage.

SIXTEEN

"**W**here are you from, Hageman?" The man working beside him straightened, pushing back the brown hood to reveal a thin face twitching with curiosity.

"What?" Pizzle straightened too, feeling sharp stabs of pain in his lower back. They had been working for hours in the stinking muck, raking the thickened crust over to let the air get at the still-wet sludge beneath. "Ow!" He dropped his rake and rubbed his back.

"I've not seen you here before," the man said. "You're new to the Hage?"

Pizzle stared blankly at his co-worker. Other brown-hooded workers gathered around, staring and mumbling, eyes bright with questions. They waited for him to say something. He dragged a sleeve across his forehead, wondering what to say to them.

Fields of dun-colored sludge, arranged in rice-paddy style—in terraces, one above another—surrounded him on every side. Above, so high above as to form a sparkling, crystalline sky, the dome stretched its inconceivable canopoy over them, its dark-veined facets glinting as the sun struck their surface. How many times had he watched the glimmer of sunrays play across the planes of the dome?

All his life apparently.

"He makes no answer, Nendl. Why?" asked a worker, poking the man next to him. "Too proud to work the night soil?"

This caused a murmur among the others. Some nodded and others remained leaning on their wide rakes, staring at him, trying to make up their minds about him. Nendl shrugged and said, "It makes no difference. He wears the brown hood of the Jamuna. Wherever he comes from, he is one of us now. We will accept him and his pride." The thin-faced man took up his rake once more. "This field must be finished before allotment. I would not have the priests angry with us—my stomach suffers enough."

Pizzle watched this exchange and, strangely, understood what had taken place, though the words spoken were unfamiliar. Not a foreign language, exactly—the cadence and sound patterns he understood. But the words themselves were blurred, just slightly twisted so that clarity remained elusive.

He pondered this as the others turned away and went back to work, then stopped to retrieve his rake, pulling its handle from the mire and wiping his hands on his rump. He drew the tool over the crusted muck, thinking, trying to remember what had happened to him.

He had awakened after a sleep—long or short he could not tell—and had dressed himself. A red-hooded man had come for him then, and after a long journey through many winding tunnels he had been handed over to a man in a yos like his own, black with a brown hood and a wide brown stripe at the hem. He had been led out from the small, featureless room, through a low tunnel that curved as it went down. They had emerged from the tunnel onto tiers of fields. A rake had been pushed into his hand, and he had followed the other workers out into the field.

At first the acrid fumes rising from the fields of sludge had almost choked him. But he had gradually become numb to the stench, and as he watched the others he remembered what to do with the rake in his hands. Then he had fallen into the rhythm of raking, walking, raking, walking . . .

That was all he could remember. Had he always lived among the Jamuna? Where had that word come from? Oh yes, Nendl had said it. The Jamuna, yes.

Thinking about these things, the effort to remember, made his head hurt. Remembering is important, a voice deep inside told him. Yes, perhaps. Perhaps remembering was important, but it was hard work and it hurt. Forgetting was painless, and it was easier—easier to let the fuzziness that wrapped his mind in its gentle fog take away all memory.

The plaza was surrounded on three sides by brightly-colored stalls, and on the fourth by a low, ridgelike hump of grass. Beyond the plaza, stacked terraces rose up on every side, their broad, curving arcs stepping away into the distance to tower above the tall, finger-thin trees ringing the square.

Vendors hovered around the stalls, hawking their merchandise to anyone who wandered near. And although the plaza was filled with people—wandering aimlessly in groups of three or more, or sitting in clusters on the pavement—no one seemed interested in buying. All just looked politely and moved on.

Yarden, watching the thronging plaza from her place on the grassy ridge, wondered what the vendors sold in their stalls. Why did no one stop to buy? She turned to the young man sitting next to her, and asked, "Bela, will you take me down there?" She nodded toward the stalls.

Languid, long-limbed Bela, his hands clasped behind his head, raised himself up just enough to see where she meant. "Down there? Why?"

"I want to see what they sell. Take me please."

"Take you? You're free to go. You don't need my permission."

"Director Luks said—"

"*Sub*director Luks is an old mother. The Chryse go where they will and do what they please—that's how art is made. Luks and his kind will never understand." He cocked a round blue eye at her. "But you want to go?"

"Yes." Yarden bobbed her head.

"All right." Bela stood up and began ambling down toward the plaza. At the foot of the mound he paused and called back to the others, a group of fifteen or so, still gathered on the grass. "Give me a few minutes at the stalls and then come down. We'll do *Rain and Wind* for the crowds before allotment."

"Rain and wind?" Yarden asked as they walked across the saw-tooth-patterned bricks to the stalls. The speech of the people around her still sometimes confused her, but comprehension was fast returning. How could she ever have forgotten?

"It's a simple mime." He glanced at her puckered brow. "Don't worry. Just watch what we do and imitate. Nothing to it."

"Oh." Yarden accepted his reassurance and shifted her attention to the stalls. There were several of them directly ahead; tentlike structures all in different colors: red, blue, gold, violet and some in bold stripes and splotches. Each stall was open in the front and the merchandise arrayed on low shelves within.

The merchants stood wheedling before their stalls, trying to convince indifferent browsers to step inside for a closer look at their wares.

The first stall they came to offered bowls of various sizes, some ornamented and others plain. Yarden looked at the bowls quickly and then went on to the next stall, where she saw miniature tables covered with highly-polished disks arranged in formal designs. The objects seemed familiar, though she could not remember their use.

"Bela, what are they?" she whispered.

"Those? Tuebla pieces."

"A game?"

"Very good! You see?—it's all coming back. You'll be teaching *me* soon."

The vendor made a move to join them, waving his arms as if to pull them inside. Bela shook his head and pushed her along.

The next stall, blue with bright yellow splotches like sunspots, offered lengths of cloth in various colors and designs. A woman in a black yos with the sky-blue hood and single diagonal blue stripe of the Bolbe stepped up beside Yarden. "You like my cloth—I can tell. A Chryse knows good craft, seh? Here—" She lifted a length and handed it to Yarden. "Feel the quality of it. Much better than you get in allotment. You see?"

Yarden felt the cool, satiny smoothness as she ran her hands over the folds of scarlet cloth. "It's very nice," she agreed.

"Do you sew? Of course, you do—you're Chryse, after all. You could make a nice Hage robe. With your dark hair—beautiful! Or if you like . . ." The woman leaned close, whispered, "I know someone who would sew anything you wished. Very reasonable, too. Needs the work—she's trying to become a tailor."

Confusion swept over Yarden; the woman's voice became a buzz in her ears. She stared at the deep red cloth in her hands and at the vendor, feeling lost and unable to think clearly.

Bela, who had been watching the interaction closely, saw her distress and stepped in. "Can't you see that she's been in reorientation? Leave her alone!"

The woman's eyes darted from one to the other of them.

"Please," said Yarden, coming to herself again. "I—it's all right." She turned to the vendor. "I like the cloth. How much?"

Bela nodded to the woman, who withdrew a slender pen-shaped probe from the folds of her yos. "Normally fifty shares—" She glanced quickly at Bela, who shook his head, and then added, "But I think thirty would be enough."

"I'll take it," said Yarden.

The woman stepped close. "You've made a very good choice." She placed a hand on Yarden's arm and raised the probe.

Yarden saw the probe come close, its point glowing bright red. "No!" She jerked her arm from the woman's grasp and backed away.

"She just wants to read your poak, Yarden," explained Bela. "Remember? It won't hurt you."

The woman smiled. "Exactly right. I just need to see your poak for a moment. The stylus won't hurt you."

Muscles rigid, Yarden allowed the woman to raise the sleeve of her yos. The stylus came up, shining in the woman's hand, and the glowing point brushed the brown skin of Yarden's upper arm. The place where the instrument touched tingled for an instant, but that was all. She relaxed.

"You try to cheat me?" the vendor suddenly yelled, her voice becoming shrill. People strolling by the stalls turned to look.

"What's wrong?" asked Bela. "Be quiet!"

"She buys the cloth for thirty, but she has only ten shares in her poak!" She turned the blunt end of the stylus toward him so that he could read it. "What am I supposed to do for the rest?"

"Be quiet will you? A Chryse does not cheat Bolbe vendors. Here—" He held up his sleeve. "Take thirty from me. I'll buy it for her."

The woman wasted no time placing the probe against Bela's arm, saying, "It's very good cloth. It will look lovely on your Hagemate."

"Yes, yes," snapped Bela impatiently. "You remember your manners—it could be *you* who is taken for reorientation next time. I should report you to your priests for discourtesy."

"No, I'm sorry. I didn't mean anything." The cloth merchant whirled around and reached into a bundle and brought out a long, silver ribbon. "Here, a gift for you. For your beautiful hair."

Yarden accepted the gift silently. Bela took her arm and steered her from the stall to join the other members of the troupe who were now assembling in the center of the plaza. "A hair ribbon, seh? Very nice."

Yarden folded the bundle of scarlet cloth over her arm. "Thank you, Bela. I—"

He cut her off, saying, "Those phat-eating drones of Luks!—they release you with only ten shares. Their heads are full of night soil! How do they expect a person to live on only ten shares?"

"I will pay you back," Yarden offered.

"Forget it. I wanted to do it. Besides," he gave her a broad smile and an exaggerated wink, "maybe you will wear your new Hage robe for me when you finish it, seh?" He laughed. Yarden smiled too and realized that she was very deep in Bela's debt— just how deep she was only beginning to discover.

SEVENTEEN

He knew that he was being watched. Constantly. But in two—or was it three?—days of captivity, he had not seen a single guard, and none of the people he *had* seen impressed Orion Treet. All were drably dressed and mouse shy. They watched him warily when they came into his cell—the barrier field across the door erased any doubt that he was indeed a prisoner and not a guest—and left with relief visible on their silent faces. He spoke to them, but they did not answer, nor did they seem to understand what he said. Their eyes remained dull; the spark that ignited intelligence failed to catch.

His food, brought once a day and left in bowls, though satisfying enough, was bland—vegetables, mostly raw, without seasonings or spices: daikon, yucca, chayote, adzuki beans, nori, and a cheesy substance that looked like tofu. No meat of any kind.

The water, in a wide-mouthed jug, tasted flat and quite stale, with that metallic flavor water takes on when left standing overnight in an open container. Treet drank it anyway when he got thirsty enough.

Dull fare and stale water aside, the simple fact that he recognized most of the food he was offered gave him a tremendous psychological boost. At least his diet was not against him; here was a common bond, however tenuous, with Earth.

Between feedings he sat on the bed, walked around the pie-shaped room swinging his arms, did a few light exercises to keep the blood flowing, and sang rude songs at the top of his lungs. All this failed, however, to keep him at the peak of mental alertness. Treet was used to a more stimulating existence, and wondered whether he could last any length of time in solitary confinement without losing his mind altogether.

Therefore, he made the most of every opportunity to express his fundamental dissatisfaction with the terms of his confinement. Every time a visitor came into his cell—usually a food bearer, or the dingy little woman who brought clean bedding and fluffed up the rumpled bed every day—Treet did his best to strike up a conversation. Never did he get a word out of any of them.

Obviously, he thought, they had been instructed not to communicate with the foreign devil. That could well be—he sensed a certain fear when any of them entered his presence. He wondered what they had been told about him.

Treet was sitting on his bed, munching a crunchy slice of jicama root, when the incessant insect buzz of the door's barrier field cut out—a signal that someone was coming to see him. It was still too early for food service, and the maid had been in to change the sheets hours ago. This was something else then. Treet's pulse quickened.

Presently he heard footsteps in the adjoining room, and two men stepped into his cell. For a moment the two men merely looked at him, but from their long, unguarded glances Treet guessed that they were of a different order than the serving people he had met thus far. He returned their frank stares with one he hoped was equally frank, and remained sitting on the bed.

Both men were wearing the black kimonos they all wore, but these had white sleeves and red hoods. From the way they stood—hands loosely at their sides, feet wide apart—Treet guessed they were prepared for anything. No doubt they had weapons concealed in the folds of their clothing.

Treet had no thought of escape. Where would he run to? His only hope was that he might be allowed to make contact with someone in a position to help him. There had, he felt, been a monstrous misunderstanding at the landing field—to put it mildly. If he could only make someone understand that he was simply a traveler who had come in peace with greetings from their friends back on Earth, Treet was certain the difficulty could be cleared up straightaway.

What he did not care to admit—although it was a thought seldom long from his mind—was that something had obviously happened to the colony. Something very wrong.

The guard nearest him said something in an authoritarian tone of voice. Treet recognized some of the words, but they were changed subtly—as if the language had undergone a shift, though a shift toward or away from what, he couldn't say. The words were smudged and blurred, slurred and warped in unexpected ways, although still vaguely recognizable.

As Treet made no move to get up or answer, the man repeated himself, raising his voice. It came to Treet then what his visitor's speech was like: it was like listening to a foreigner trying to speak your mother tongue. A few words came out nearly right, others did not; the sounds were all stretched and puckered.

Treet addressed the men, keeping his tone flat and even, though his heart beat a tattoo in his throat. "I am Orion Treet. There has been a mistake. I mean no one any harm. Please believe that. I am unarmed, and I wish to talk to your superior."

The two men looked at each other. One shrugged—it was such a human gesture that Treet knew they shared some kind of common ancestry. But what had happened to these people?

"Come." The red-hood nearest him gestured toward the door.

Treet understood both word and gesture perfectly. He slid off the bed, stood, and walked toward the doorway. The second red-hood stopped him with a hand placed against his chest, waved a wand over him front and back—a weapons detector of some kind, guessed Treet—and then led the way through the narrow doorway and the connecting room beyond. Treet followed, and the other man came along a few paces behind.

Tanais Director Tvrdy reclined in a suspension bed which undulated in slow ripples to the soft music drifting into his sleep chamber. Though his eyes were closed and his hands lay folded over his chest, he was far from sleep. He was waiting and piecing together a plan by which he meant to visit the captive intruder being held somewhere in the stacked mazes of Saecaraz Hage.

This bit of information had come to him earlier in the day. It confirmed what he had already guessed—that Supreme Director Rohee had not, as he intimated in session, placed all of the intruders in Hage: one had been kept. And this one Tvrdy meant to interview personally.

The Rumon rumor messengers had done their work well. Thanks to Cejka's network of informants, he now knew the whereabouts of the other three intruders as well. One had been placed among the Jamuna, another with the Nilokerus, and the third with the Chryse. The Jamuna and Chryse captives had actually been spotted in public.

Jamrog was wasting no time in covering up the affair. But why cover it up at all? What was there about these intruders that demanded these unprecedented measures? Who were they? Why were they being hidden in Hage? Why run such a risk? Why not simply destroy the spies? Why announce their presence to the Threl and then refuse to allow anyone else to talk to them? Why? Why? Why?

Tvrdy meant to find out.

"Director . . ." Pradim, the Tanais Director's guide, stepped quietly into the sleep chamber, his fingers weaving the air.

"I am not asleep," replied Tvrdy, getting up. "What is it?"

"A message—" Pradim turned his empty eye-sockets upon his master.

"And is the messenger still here?"

"Yes. Shall I bring her?"

"No, have her wait in the quiet room. I wish to question her."

The guide departed silently as the Tanais leader drew on a shimmering green Hage robe, then stepped over to a terminal set in the wall. "Systems check," he said softly. "Quiet room."

The screen instantly flicked on, presenting a schematic of the quiet room's webwork of anti-eavesdropping sensors. All were working and none showed signs of tampering. A second later the screen went blank, and Tvrdy strode out of the room.

The messenger was sitting on a cushion in the quiet room's pit. She jumped up and gave a quick, stiff-armed bow. "Cejka sends his greetings," she said.

This was a code phrase which meant that Cejka wished a full report of the proceedings. "You may give my regards to your Director," replied Tvrdy. This meant that Tvrdy intended to contact Cejka personally. Tanais Director joined the messenger in the pit and lowered himself to a cushion. "You may sit."

"I am hearing many interesting things from Saecaraz section . . ." the woman began, glancing around quickly.

"This is a quiet room," offered Tvrdy. "We can speak freely." The woman relaxed; a hand went to her hood and drew it back. She was young and sharp-eyed. No doubt one of Cejka's best. "You have located the intruder within Saecaraz?"

"Yes. I have not seen him, but I talked with the old mother who changes the bedding. He is deep in Threl High Chambers—on a level called Greenways. This, I am told, is near the Supreme Director's personal quarters."

111

"So! Just as I suspected!" Tvrdy rubbed his hands together very slowly. "Now then, how is the prisoner held?"

"Unidor."

"No chemical restraints?"

"Possible, but unlikely. The prisoner has been observed walking about his cell; he talks to the food bearers—although they have all been instructed to refrain from speaking to him. He also—" She hesitated.

"Yes? Tell me."

"He *sings*, Director."

"Does he indeed?"

"Several of the Saecaraz have heard him when they bring his food. They all talk about it."

"And what have they been told of his identity?" Tvrdy leaned forward, listening intently. He was getting good information from this messenger.

"They have been told that he is a close relative of one of the Threl leader's Hagemates, and has rejected reorientation, thus suffering regrettable mental trauma."

"I see. And do they believe this?"

The messenger shrugged. "They ask no questions."

"Has the prisoner been moved?"

"No."

"Visited?"

"No, but he is under continuous remote surveillance."

"As I would expect." Director Tvrdy nodded to himself. "I have only one more question. In your opinion, would it be possible to steal the prisoner or meet with him?"

The young woman blinked, taken aback to have her opinion asked. But she answered without hesitation. "No, it is not possible to remove the prisoner from his cell without alerting the Nilokerus—there are two at all times in the room adjoining. It may be possible to visit him briefly, if disguise were used effectively and the guards distracted."

The Tanais leader stood abruptly. "Well done, Rumon! I will see to it that one hundred shares are added to your allotment from now on."

"It is not necessary—" The woman rose quickly, replacing the hood as she stood.

"We reward our people, messenger. You have performed a difficult and dangerous assignment. Accept a leader's gratitude."

"Thank you, Director."

In a moment the messenger was gone. Tvrdy sat deep in thought until his guide entered the room. "Does the Director wish anything?"

"Yes, Pradim, contact Cejka at once. I will meet him in Hage—designation seven-six." At once Tvrdy rose and stripped off his robe. He moved to a cabinet standing against a wall, pressed the lockplate with his thumb, removing a blue-hooded yos from the drawer as it slid out, and began donning his disguise.

EIGHTEEN

Treet stood before a flinty old man who watched him carefully with hooded eyes. He had a sharp beak of a nose, and the wattles beneath his chin wobbled when he moved his head. Across his lap the old man held a stubby, curved broadknife affixed to a long ornamental handle—obviously a symbol of some official function. Judging from the extreme deference paid him by the guards—who had retired to a far corner—Treet guessed the old geezer was a high mucky-muck of Empyrion leadership.

The room also betokened high status: a great, round cylinder with a ceiling that arched dramatically overhead. Dark, richly patterned hangings draped the walls all around, and the ceiling as well, so the effect was that of entering a sultan's tent.

The sultan himself had been waiting for him on his throne—a tall, high-backed chair mounted on a raised pedestal. Treet had been led to stand before this seat, in a circle embossed on the floor. The moment he had stepped into the circle, the faint telltale whizz of the barrier field told him he was a prisoner once more.

The old man spoke. "I am Sirin Rohee, Supreme Director of the Threl and all Empyrion." He paused and nodded toward Treet encouragingly. "Do you understand?"

Treet heard several words he thought he recognized; but with the old man's wavering voice coming through the faint distortion of the barrier field, he could not be certain. Still, he assumed he had been addressed in some kind of introduction, so offered one of his own, speaking up loudly. "I am Orion Treet. I am a traveler. I have come from Cynetics."

Treet pronounced the last word distinctly, hoping for some effect. The last time he'd uttered that word, it had caused a considerable sensation. This time, however, the consequence was more subdued than at the landing field; the old man—Rohee, was that a name he'd heard among the barely intelligible

114

syllables?—merely nodded knowingly and pursed his lips as if he'd expected just that sort of response.

The guards—the two who had brought him and two others who were waiting in the chamber with the old leader—were slightly more demonstrative, murmuring loudly to themselves. Treet kept his attention on Rohee and tried to look both impressive and nonthreatening at the same time. The effort taxed his limited repertoire of facial expressions.

"Why have you come?" Rohee asked simply.

Treet blinked in mild surprises: he'd gotten all of that speech. By concentrating on the pattern of the speech rather than the words themselves, he could apparently understand simple sentences. He tried to couch his reply in simple words of single syllables. "I have been sent."

Rohee looked puzzled. He lifted the broad blade in his hands and gestured toward a guard. The man departed silently, returning only moments later with three others. These were dressed in silver-striped kimonos like Treet's, but each had a large silver medallion that looked like a two-pronged, wavy lightning bolt on a thick chain around his neck. They stared at Treet openly as they approached, then acknowledged their leader with a quick, stiff-armed bow. The three stopped at a point midway between the throne and the prisoner.

Interpreters? wondered Treet. The three looked more like judges. Or inquisitors.

Supreme Director Rohee flashed the curving blade at the foremost of the three. He turned toward Treet and asked in slow, deliberate tones, as one would address a child, "What do you know of the Fieri?"

The last word threw Treet. He shrugged and replied, "I do not understand."

The three looked at one another. "Fieri," the first one repeated. "Tell us."

"I can tell you nothing." Amazing! thought Treet. It wasn't so difficult to talk to these people once you caught the knack. Emboldened by success, he added, "I am a traveler. I have been sent here by Cynetics."

Again the word caused a slight sensation. The three inquisitors grew round-eyed and stared at one another. They put their heads together in conference and mumbled. Rohee looked on, a smile faintly spreading his lips. There was a quality in his expression Treet couldn't quite name—what was it?

While the inquisitors debated the implications of his last utterance, Treet studied the Empryion leader in an attempt at unraveling that enigmatic smile. He was still trying to decipher it when he was addressed again.

"Speak to us of Cynetics," said the first inquisitor. No doubt he was the official spokesman of the group. Treet noticed that when the man spoke, he seemed to be consciously forming his mouth around the words.

Treet spread his hands—what could he tell them that they didn't already know? "What do you want—" He halted as the implications of the statement jolted him. They didn't know about Cynetics! At least, they didn't know it in the same way that he did, and they were testing him.

Trouble was, *he* didn't remember precisely either; it belonged to that hazy confusion on the other side of that mental fog blank. Wanting nothing more than to be left alone to ponder this bit of information, Treet frowned at the inquisitors, who were waiting for an answer. He sensed that to disappoint them would make things much more difficult for himself in the days to come.

"I can tell you," began Treet importantly, relying solely on bluff and instinct, "that Cynetics is very great, very powerful— more powerful than ordinary men can imagine." Treet did not know if they were getting all of this, but he continued, liking the way his speech sounded. "Cynetics commands whole nations and rules the lives of millions. There is no other as great as Cynetics."

There, thought Treet, let them puzzle over that. He had intentionally—instinctively?—invoked the storyteller's tone of high pomp and consequence. The dodge appeared to be working, for the three inquisitors stared awestricken.

He glanced quickly at Rohee—the man's enigmatic smile had increased; he was positively beaming. Instantly the riddle was solved: the old coot was proud of his prize! He is pleased that I have stumped the experts, thought Treet; he was hoping I'd astound them, and I did.

From that moment, Treet placed his hopes of survival on the old fossil. He smiled back at the Empyrion leader as much as to say, *See, we are alike, you and I; we should be friends.*

• • • • • •

Nendl waited patiently, resting on one of the many mushroom-shaped projections ringing the open-air booth. Pizzle sat next to him, dimly aware of what was going on, yet anxious because he could not remember more clearly. They waited as, one by one, their fellow workers—Hagemen, Nendl called them—approached the booth.

"It's allotment," Nendl explained. "You'll remember."

When all the others had gone forward and hurried off again, Nendl rose and went to the booth. Pizzle followed. The men in the booth wore brown-hooded yoses like his own, but each had a large bronze medal across his chest: a double-ended arrow bent into an ellipse. The medal hung from a heavy chain around their necks, and Pizzle understood upon seeing the symbol that these were Jamuna priests.

"Yes?" asked a priest, looking up. Before Nendl could answer a second priest said, "Allotment is over."

"This one is new to our Hage," explained Nendl.

The priests frowned. One of them bent over a terminal and asked, "Name?"

Nendl nudged Pizzle, who stared for a moment, terror rising in him. *My name! What's my name?*

"Well?" snapped the priest. "How do you expect to claim your shares if you don't give us your name?"

"He has recently undergone reorientation," explained Nendl. "He has not perhaps been issued a new name."

"I see," grumped the priest. He nodded to one of the others. "What do you have there?"

The second priest gazed into a glowing screen, tapped a few keys, and then answered, "There are no new reassignments in the records."

"Erased most likely," replied the first priest. "Come back next allotment and we will see."

"Please," said Nendl quietly, "he cannot wait until next allotment. How can he live without his shares? How can he work?"

The first priest frowned even more deeply. "All right, all right. Put him down as—"

"Pizzle!"

The priests looked at him. "What did you say?" asked the first.

"My name is Pizzle . . . I think."

"Pizol?" The priest stared into the screen and shook his head slowly. "Nothing under that name."

"Enter it," commanded the first priest, and the other did as he was told. "We'll give him standard shares for a first-order gleaner."

Pizzle thought this sounded fair enough. He nodded, but Nendl protested gently. "He's worked very hard—he's one of my order, not a wastehandler."

The priest glared. "You challenge our authority?"

"You know what is best, Hage priest. I merely point out that he is a good worker because I know that you are fair. It is well-known that the priests of Jamuna Hage reward hard work generously."

"True enough," agreed the priest. "I will make this a lesson to you," he said to Pizzle. "Your allotment is fifty shares."

"Thank you, Hage priest," said Nendl, nudging Pizzle with his elbow.

"Thank you," Pizzle repeated. The priest picked up a glowing stylus and took Pizzle by the arm, raising his sleeve. He rubbed the point of the stylus over the skin of his upper arm.

"There, tell your Hagemen of the generosity of Jamuna priests. We take care of our own."

"Of course, Hage priest," replied Nendl as they backed away quickly. The priests grunted and began closing up the booth.

Nendl led them back along the wide, brick-paved walkway. Odd, flat-topped trees lined this winding boulevard; here and there the mouths of tunnels opened, and stairs led down to the other levels. Once out of sight of the booth, Nendl said, "Not bad, Pizol. They gave you two days' shares. Don't think that will happen again, though. The Jamuna Hage priests are fair enough as priests go, but they are priests all the same, and not often given to extravagance—unless it is their own poak."

"Fifty shares," said Pizzle. "You must help me, Nendl."

The thin-faced man stopped and faced him, placing strong, callused hands on Pizzle's shoulders. "We are Hagemen, are we not? You ask my help, and I will give it. You have fifty shares, and I have twenty-five from today's work. If we put them together, we can eat well tonight. What do you say?"

"I am very hungry, Nendl."

"So am I. Then it is settled. We'll put our shares together

118

and eat like Directors! I have no Hagemate at present, so you can stay with me. My kraam is not so big, but there is room for you if you do not mind sharing a bed. Later, when you have been in Hage a year, you can petition the priests for a kraam of your own. If one becomes available before that—so much the better."

Off they went, Nendl leading the way, fatigue suddenly forgotten. He led Pizzle down one of the nearby tunnels, and they emerged on a lower level where tiny shops, amassed in tiers and joined by flying walkways, lined the broad, circuitous avenue. Crowds of people—almost all of them dressed in Jamuna brown—pushed along the avenue and swamped the walkways. The din of voices rang from the ribs of the roof far above: vendors haggling over prices, patrons whining and wheedling, people arguing—arguing and doing business nonetheless.

"Ah, the Jamuna markets. No Hage has a more lively marketplace, I'm told. Let's go collect our dole and then—" He smiled broadly, revealing crooked teeth. "Then we will begin!"

They hurried through moving knots of people toward a yellow-topped kiosk standing in the middle of the avenue. The waves of shoppers broke around it, passing on either side. "Here it is," said Nendl. "Good, we won't have to wait. Come on."

He pushed Pizzle up to the kiosk. "Dole," said Nendl.

"Name?" asked a fat, bored clerk in the green-and-yellow yos of the Hyrgo.

"Nendl," the Jamuna replied. "And Pizol."

The clerk consulted a screen. "I have you, but not him." He reached down and placed a parcel on the ledge of the kiosk.

Nendl took up the cloth-wrapped parcel and replied, "He's been in reorientation. Check with the priests if you don't believe me."

The clerk grunted and placed another package on the ledge. "There. I believe you."

Pizzle took the package, and Nendl pulled him away. "What's inside?" he asked.

"Some coffee, a little tofu, a bonaito or maybe a jicama, flatbread if we are lucky. That's all. But we can buy the rest. Here—a cheese shop!" Nendl elbowed his way into the press at the entrance to the cheese shop. "What kind today?" he asked.

A Jamuna next to him replied, "What difference? It all tastes the same."

"White and red," said someone close by. "And they are gouging as usual—three shares per kil."

"Could be worse," sighed Nendl. When his turn came, he ordered half a kil of each, stuffing them inside his yos. He pushed Pizol up to the vendor, who brushed his arm with a poak reader.

They moved on along the avenue, Pizzle's head swiveling as he went, trying to take it all in. Everywhere he looked, people crowded and hurried. "Is it always like this?" he wondered aloud.

"Only after allotment. We have come late, but it's just as well. The stocks are holding up, and the crowds aren't so bad." Nendl dived into another throng surrounding a meat shop. He came back holding two small, plump, birdlike carcasses. He handed one to Pizzle and tucked the other into his yos.

"What is it?" Pizzle looked at the naked pink flesh.

"Cheken. A delicacy, believe me."

"Chee-ken," repeated Pizzle, nodding. "I remember chee-ken."

"Good! It's coming back!" Nendl pulled him away again, and they continued on down the avenue. "Now to the bake stall. I think there is a second-order bake stall further down. They are said to supply the Directors' tables. We'll see."

Pizzle walked as one in a dream, marveling at all he saw, the strangeness of it, and yet the eerie familiarity. He had been here before, seen these things, walked this avenue . . . why couldn't he remember?

Sitting in Nendl's kraam before a small brazier filled with black fuel pellets, the disjointed carcasses of the two chekens sizzling on the glowing coals, Pizzle listened to his host describe his life.

"You would do well to listen to an old man," said Nendl. "I may not be a Hage magician, but I know much and have seen much more."

"You're not old, Nendl."

"Old enough! But listen, I don't know what you did to deserve your punishment—your reorientation—and you don't have to tell me. I don't care. Probably it was nothing anyway. The stinking Invisibles, called such because of their cunning and stealth, watch everyone; and what they can't see, they imagine. It's all the same to them—they're scum."

"Scum," Pizzle repeated. "But you're not. You're not scum, Nendl; you're my friend." Pizzle's head felt mushy from the sweet liquor he was drinking freely. He felt light and airy, like a cloud expanding from its center. He beamed at his host proudly. "You helped me."

"I helped you, yes. Do you know why?" He leaned close even though there was not another soul in the filthy, cramped dwelling.

Pizzle leaned toward him. "Why?"

"Because I *know* someone."

"Oh!" Pizzle nodded, much impressed. "You know someone."

"Someone important. He said I was to watch for you and help you if I could. He said you would be coming. So I watched for you, and when you came I helped you."

"Thank you, Nendl."

"Shh!" Nendl cautioned. "They can hear everything. They can see through walls." He too had been nursing from the souile flask liberally and felt like talking. "But I don't care. I know someone. I am protected. If I have any trouble, I have someplace to go. I will be safe."

Pizzle nodded, his head wobbling loosely. "The cheken smells good. I'm hungry."

"It's just about done." Nendl reached over and flipped a few pieces over. "Have some more cheese." He offered a chunk to Pizzle and bit off one for himself. He gazed at his guest thoughtfully and said, "You know what the rumor messengers are saying about you?"

"No." Pizzle put the cheese in his mouth and chewed.

"I have heard rumors of Fieri spies," said Nendl, winking. "Spies."

"Do you know anything about them?"

Pizzle shook his head slowly.

Nendl reached into the brazier and gingerly handed him a piece of cheken. "Eat! It's good." He picked out a piece for himself and licked his fingers. "Directors don't eat any better than this!"

"It's good," echoed Pizzle happily. The sound of chewing and lip smacking overcame conversation for a few minutes.

When they had finished the first two pieces and were well

into a third, Nendl raised his head and looked at his guest thoughtfully. "If you were a Fieri, I know you wouldn't tell me—would you?"

Pizzle considered this and then shrugged. "I don't know. Am I a Fieri?"

Nendl went sly; his eyes narrowed. "You might be. Then again you might not. I don't expect you'd tell me if I didn't tell you something." He thought for a moment. "I will tell you something, Pizol. Would you like that? I'll tell you something, and then you tell me something. What do you say to that?"

Pizzle nodded readily. "I'd like that. You tell me something, and I'll tell you something."

"A secret," added Nendl.

"Yes, a secret."

The Jamuna recycler leaned close and lowered his voice to a whisper. "Nendl is my Hagename. I'll tell you my private name, but you must promise never to tell anyone else—especially a priest or magician. Swear it?"

"I swear."

"Trabant take your soul?"

Pizzle nodded, eyes growing wide.

With a quick sidewards glance, Nendl put his forehead close to Pizzle's. "My private name is Urkal." He smiled grimly and sat back.

"Urkal."

"Shh! Never repeat it! If a lipreader saw it, he would tell a priest—or worse, an Invisible—and they'd have power over me. If I didn't do what they told me, they'd curse me and I'd be without a guide through the Twin Houses; I would never become immortal." He looked eagerly at his guest. "Now it's your turn. Tell me your secret."

Pizzle's face scrunched up in thought. What secret could he tell his host? He didn't have any that he knew about. "Ahh," he said at last. "My name is . . . Asquith." How had that come to him?

Disappointment rearranged Nendl's features in a scowl. "Askwith," he replied flatly. That wasn't the secret he wanted to hear. "Is that a Fieri name?" he asked, thinking himself very smart.

"I don't know. Is it?"

"I have never heard it before—it must be. That means *you* are a Fieri," he deduced with satisfaction.

"If you say I am. Is that good?"

"Bad, more like. Fieri are hated here."

"Why?"

"I don't know. Some say they are trying to destroy us; others say other things. Who knows? The Directors know. Ahh, but I know someone too. Someone who will help me if trouble comes. I'm safe. You're safe too—as long as you stay with me." He took a long swig on the souile flask and passed it to Pizzle. "Drink! And eat—we have more cheken!" He took another piece from the brazier, licked his fingers, and smiled contentedly. "It's been a very good day, Hageman Pizol. A very good day."

NINETEEN

Yarden sat in a corner by herself, watching the others. They chattered to one another and laughed as they watched a holovision program calling out the names of the Hagemen they recognized. Bela's kraam, a flattened oval room with a low, gently rippled ceiling, lit with soft amber dish-shaped lights set in smooth, buff-colored walls, was warm and stuffy with so many people in it—ten others besides Bela and herself. But no one else seemed to mind. They lolled on overlarge silken cushions on the floor, bodies intertwined casually, dipping fruit from a large red bowl, and laughing.

"Among the Chryse, Bela's kraam is well-known," he had boasted to her with a wink as they walked along an arching aerial walkway far above terraced green fields and small, dome-shaped dwellings—one of Empyrion's preserves, Bela had told her, though what was preserved below she could not tell. "Tonight will be all laughter. You'll see."

Laughter yes, but Yarden did not share in it. After she had been introduced, she had quietly edged away to her cushion in the corner where she was content just to observe the others, as they were content to ignore her. She suspected that her presence was perceived as an intrusion—at least by the other women. She was a stranger, and therefore a potential rival for the men's attention.

So she sat alone, schooling herself on the manners of her new friends, watching them for clues to custom and behavior, alert to the nuances of speech and action that revealed the inner person. Outwardly passive—all but immobile—inwardly her mind whirled with activity: searching, sorting, cataloging, storing each minute observation and detail of her surroundings. This felt right; it was something that belonged to her, that she recognized as her own. At the same time, this intense mental activity puzzled her. Where did I learn this? she wondered. Haven't I always lived here?

No doubt her feelings of vagueness, of forgetting, had to do with the *reorientation* Bela spoke of. Whatever that was, it stood like a barrier between her present and her past, blocking out all memory on the other side. Yet, at odd moments now and then, she caught glimpses of another life—intimations that there had been a life on the other side of the barrier much different than the one she now knew.

"You are lost, cherimoya," said a voice above her.

Yarden looked up to see Bela standing over her. "I am just a little tired," she replied. Yes, tired—so many new things to observe and comprehend exhausts one's soul.

"Come then. Bed with me," he said, offering his hand. He smiled. "I am tired too."

Yarden caught the implication of his words, but was not alarmed by it. "Where do you sleep?" The kraam, as far as she could see, was but a single large room.

Bela laughed. "Wherever I like; it makes no difference."

"Do you all sleep together?"

"Sometimes." He shrugged. "Tonight I want to sleep with you."

The directness of his approach confused her; perhaps she misunderstood. "For pleasure?"

"Yes." Bela sank down beside her, grinning. "What else?"

Yarden peered back at him, not quite sure what her response should be. Certainly Bela was an attractive man; she could see that he would likely be a sensitive lover. She felt herself drawn to him, yet repulsed at the same time. At any rate, she doubted whether she could make love in a room full of strangers.

She was saved from having to make an answer by a clamor which arose across the room. "Bela!" someone shouted. "Bela! Dera is here with the flash!"

Bela looked away. A tall, flame-haired woman with large dark eyes and a shimmering yos that matched the color of her hair stood in the doorway. "Dera, my delight!" Bela called, jumping up. "What have you brought for us?"

She came to him, stepping over the knot of people on the floor in front of the holoscreen. Yarden watched as the two exchanged a lingering kiss. The woman's long fingers played in Bela's dark curls.

When they separated, Dera reached into the folds of her yos and drew out a black bag. Bela took the bag and hefted it, then opened it and put his nose in. "Ohh!" He rolled his eyes. "For this you will be made immortal."

Others had gathered around, grabbing at the bag. "Share it, Bela. What are you waiting for?"

"Patience!" He lifted the bag away from them. "You will have yours. Dera has brought enough to soak a priest."

He turned to Yarden, knelt, and held out the bag. "You first. You have been longest without it."

Yarden reached into the bag and withdrew several flat, dark pellets the size of beans. They were highly polished and slightly oily to the touch. "What is it?"

"Flash," said a curly-headed man in a brilliant, flower-printed yos. They all watched Yarden, smiling encouragingly. "Go ahead, you'll soon remember." The others laughed, and the man snatched the bag away. Attention now turned to the flash-bag as it was passed quickly around.

Yarden gazed at the lozenges in her hand. They had a faint aroma, like roasted nuts. She glanced up to see Bela still watching her. "Flash?" she asked.

"It has other names," he said, taking one of the pellets. "Each Hage has its own. The Hyrgo call it bliss beans, and among the Bolbe it is known as third hand. Don't ask me why, but that's what they call it."

"What does it do?"

"Here, I'll show you." He placed the seed between his front teeth and, tilting his head back slightly, bit down hard. The seed cracked, and a thick syrup oozed out. He closed his eyes and sucked his lips shut, and in a moment his features softened. When he looked at Yarden again, his eyes were muzzy and unfocused.

"Try it," he said, then laughed with sudden giddiness, rolling on his back. Instantly Dera was on top of him, a seed between her teeth. She bit it and then kissed him, sharing the syrup between the two of them. They came up laughing moments later, and then rolled into another embrace.

Yarden looked around her. The man in the flower-print yos was giggling loudly as he twirled around, his arms outstretched. Someone put a seed in his mouth and he bit it, then fell full-length backwards onto two women who were caressing each other. They broke apart, laughing, and began pulling off his yos.

Others were cuddled together, working each other out of

their clothes, naked limbs writhing. Music had begun playing: a light, drifty sound like wind in the trees or water slipping over stone in a tide pool.

Yarden put a seed in her mouth and bit down hard. The syrup splashed onto her tongue, and she tasted smoked honey. With the taste came a rush of pure pleasure—a flash which burst over her and then ebbed away, taking all thought, all tension, all desire with it. Her first thought was, "More! I need more!"

She quickly popped another seed in her mouth, bit, and felt time coiling around her like a silken rope. Her mind reeled in the sheer joy of flowing forever through endless time, flowing like music, rich and many-toned and deep as an ocean.

A picture floated up into her mind of a vast, limitless sea of gold and green. She saw herself floating beneath gentle waves, sinking, drifting. The water was warm; the current tugged her along past long ribbons of undulating seaweed. Down and down and down.

Yarden began to cry; tears rolled over her lashes to splash down her cheeks. The picture, she knew, was from her other life—the life she could not remember anymore. She felt that other life slipping further away beyond her reach. The tears fell heavy with strong, sweet sorrow. She took another seed in her mouth and let the waves carry her away.

Director Hladik rode the lift down toward Cavern level, the lowest level of Nilokerus section. Slanting bands of light flickered over his face, each marking a terrace or kraam level. Four levels above Cavern, he slowed the liftplate's descent, dropping the last two levels at quarter-speed and braking hard as Cavern came up. It took quick reflexes and an utter disregard for safety, but Hladik enjoyed overriding the automatic controls.

Hladik felt the momentary tug of gravity in his stomach and stepped through the capsule door, striding out into a rock-cut chamber before the lift had come to a complete stop. "Fertig!" he shouted, his voice echoing back from the empty spaces.

He waited, then marched across the chamber to the entrance of a tunnel, switching off the unidor at the console pedestal before the tunnel entrance. Lights blinked on as he stepped in, faint green lights at foot level illuminating the tunnel floor. Along the sides, a red light above each one, cell doors yawned, their unidors opaqued.

At the end of the tunnel, the Nilokerus Director halted before a rock wall. He reached into the folds of his yos and produced a sonic key, pressed it, and waited. From behind the wall came the sound of muffled hydraulics, and the wall tilted up and away. He ducked under the receding wall and entered the hidden room.

A guard in the white and red of the Nilokerus snapped to attention, giving a quick, stiff-armed bow, eyes to the floor. "Where's Fertig?" Hladik demanded, barely acknowledging the salute with an impatient wave of his hand.

"Subdirector Fertig is with the prisoner," the guard replied.

"Have the physicians been summoned?"

"Yes, Hage Leader. They are with him as well."

Hladik nodded, and the guard stepped aside. He pressed his sonic key, and the portion of the wall behind the guard rolled outward. Stepping over a puddle of water, he slipped through the opening quickly.

"Director Hladik, I—" began Fertig, glancing up as his superior entered.

"Will he live?" Hladik asked, moving to the side of a suspension bed. He looked down at the gray-faced body in the bed.

"It is too early to tell," replied Fertig uneasily.

Hladik turned on him with a fierce scowl. The Subdirector swallowed hard and added, "We may have lost him, Hage Leader."

"Does Jamrog know?"

"No, he has not been notified." The Subdirector glanced uncertainly at his superior. "Do you wish it?"

"I do not!" Hladik snapped. "I will deal with this personally."

A physician, a heavy-shouldered woman with short, white hair and sharp blue eyes, mumbled something and Hladik glowered at her, saying, "Speak up, Ernina. I didn't hear you."

The woman frowned, her lips creased in wrinkles of sharp disapproval. "I merely wondered how long you will persist in killing your prisoners and then expecting us to revive the corpses?"

Few people dared speak to a Director so frankly, and ordinarily Hladik would have had the offender removed for reorientation without a second thought. But he just glared at the flinty physician across the bed; hers was a mind much too valuable to throw away lightly. Still, it didn't do to allow first- and second-order Hagemen to hear her address him like a wastehandler.

"You question my directives, physician?" he growled.

"Not at all, Hage Leader," she replied. Her tone mocked him. "I merely point out that if you wish us to save your sorry experiments, you must give us more to work with. This—" She gestured helplessly toward the body before her. "This wretch is almost beyond hope—even for me."

"But he can be saved?" asked Hladik. He glanced down at the body; the man's straw-colored hair was matted and tangled, his eyes and cheeks sunken, his jaw slack. If he still breathed, there was no outward indication.

Ernina, a sixth-order physician, the best of the Nilokerus, shrugged. "We will see. But I warn you, Haldik, one day soon you will go too far in this conditioning of yours and there will be nothing left to save."

Hladik accepted the warning; it was sincere. But for the benefit of the others looking on, he replied, "Perhaps reorientation is not so unpleasant as we might suppose. Would you care to find out for yourself, physician?"

She tossed off the warning with a shrug. "Hmph!" Then she turned to the other physicians gathered around her. "Have you taken root? Remove him. We can do nothing in this dank tomb. Get him started on the aura equalizer, and one of you go take an offering to the Hage priest for a healing benefice of ten clear days. Tell him we must have no astral interference for at least ten days. Make certain he understands. Tell him the directive comes from Hage Leader Hladik—that ought to get his attention."

Hladik nodded sourly as the physicians pushed the bed away. Ernina stood with her hands on her wide hips, her blue eyes snapping.

The Director grumbled, "Out with it. What else is bothering you?"

"When will you learn that you cannot carve human flesh to fit your ridiculous power schemes? The mind-body exists in a tenuous balance. Upset that balance and the entire astral entity is threatened." She gazed at Hladik unflinchingly. "I know you think me a prattling old mother, but mark me well, Hladik: Cynetics will be served. Your tinkering will weaken us all."

"Bah!" Nilokerus Director made a face and dismissed her with a quick gesture. "Just make certain this prisoner survives—that's all I care about. I want twice-a-day reports until he recovers. Understood?"

Ernina inclined her head stiffly. "Of course, Hage Leader. When have I ever disobeyed you?" She smiled in grim satisfaction and swept past him with a swish of her red-hooded yos.

Hladik watched her go. "One day, woman," he muttered, "you'll go too far."

TWENTY

In a kraam on the Sunwalk level in the Bolbe section of Empyrion, Tvrdy, Cejka, and Piipo—each dressed in the blue-hooded yoses of the Bolbe—debated the wisdom of trying to contact the Fieri spies. They had been talking for nearly two hours, but were now getting to the heart of the matter.

"You oppose the plan, Piipo," said Tvrdy, careful to keep his voice even. "Yet, you do not put forth a plan of your own."

"Don't judge me hastily," replied Piipo, his small, close-set eyes flashing across the table. "I have my own reasons for urging caution."

"We're all for caution," said Tvrdy, "but—"

Cejka cut in. "You have information?"

Piipo nodded slowly.

"What have you heard? Tell us."

The Hyrgo Hage Director's eyes flicked from one to the other of his co-conspirators. He hesitated, weighing, making up his mind.

"Tell us now!"

"Wait, Tvrdy," cautioned Cejka. "Give him time." To Piipo he added, "It isn't our way to pressure anyone, and we do not use threats, but time is short. If you have any information that can help us, then tell us. Whether or not you join the Cabal, we—"

Piipo held up his hand, palm outward. "I understand. If I hesitate, it is only because my reply will bind Hyrgo Hage to a course of action which could mean our ruin, not to mention the destruction of the work of six centuries."

Tvrdy nodded solemnly, "You remind us of the seriousness of our task. I thank you for that. And I hasten to assure you that we would not like to see another Purge. But our work is ruined if Jamrog gains Threl leadership."

"I agree," said Piipo, "or I would not have come."

"We respect your discretion," offered Cejka.

131

"Flattery is not necessary, Rumon. We know each other well enough, I think; we can dispense with formalities." Piipo took a deep breath. He had made up his mind. "I will join the Cabal. I have seen enough; it is time to act."

Tvrdy smiled broadly. Cejka slapped the table in approval. "I wish we had brought some souile to celebrate this moment," he said, grinning.

"We will save that for Jamrog's defeat." Piipo's eyes narrowed, and he leaned forward. "You said time was short. I'll tell you what I know. A Hyrgo administrator of the dole encountered one of the Fieri spies when he came for his food allotment."

"Where? Jamuna Hage?"

"You know this already?" Piipo looked at Tvrdy in surprise.

"Only that the spies have been located," replied Cejka. "We know that those placed with Jamuna and Chryse have been seen in public. The Chryse is a woman; therefore, it must have been the Jamuna your dole administrator encountered."

"I see. But I can supply a name, and it shouldn't be too difficult to discover where he can be found."

"Oh?" Tvrdy perked up.

Piipo smiled. "We have our methods, too. Actually, it was luck. He approached the dole kiosk in Jamuna Hage—Market level—in the company of a recycler. His name was given as Pizol. There was no record, of course, but his Hageman vouched for him."

"His Hageman's name?"

"Nendl, a third-order recycler."

Tvrdy and Cejka looked at each other. "This Nendl may be one of our agents," replied Cejka. "Jamuna is Covol's section; he will know."

"I will have a Tanais priest look up the kraam coordinates," suggested Tvrdy. "And then we'll go get him."

"Too risky. We must first discover whether this Nendl is under surveillance by Invisibles," said Cejka. "Better to have one of my rumor messengers make inquiries at the fields, follow them if necessary. We'll find out that way."

"That will take more time."

"It can't be helped," said Cejka. "We must make certain before we move."

Just then a Rumon guide disguised like his master in a

Bolbe yos stepped into the room. "Director, the occupant of the kraam is returning."

"Detain him until we're clear," ordered Cejka. He turned to the others. "Leave this to me. And don't worry—we will have the Jamuna captured and hidden before Jamrog discovers he's gone."

All three rose and placed their clenched fists over their hearts in a Cabalist's pledge of secrecy.

Treet had spent the day back in his cell. Whatever had happened at his inquisition—he thought he'd made a few points with the old leader, but apparently not enough—he was still a prisoner. So far nothing had changed.

Nevertheless, he hoped that Rohee—was that his name?—had been intrigued enough with him that he would want to keep him around a bit longer. Treet didn't trust the inquisitors; they looked suspicious and nasty—as if they suspected the worst of everything and everyone all the time. Perhaps they did. Treet had decided that everyone in Empyrion was suspicious; as a group, they were the most skeptical people he'd ever met.

This brought him back to the thought that had occupied him since he'd returned to the cell: what happened to these people? What made them like this?

Treet tried putting himself in their kimonos, and still came up short of a satisfactory explanation. Yes, visitors from outer space were prime candidates for careful scrutiny, at least until their motives were known. He agreed that arrest and confinement were prudent measures when strangers in spacecraft showed up on your doorstep. In fact, human nature being what it was, he allowed that he had gotten off lightly. They could easily have blasted him first and sorted out the details later.

But these weren't *aliens*, dammit! These were Earthmen like himself who a little over fifty-three months ago had come to colonize this planet!

It didn't make sense. They should have been out on that landing platform waving handkerchiefs and throwing flowers. They should have called a holiday and given feasts in his honor. They should have begged him for news of Earth and showered him with gifts large and small.

Instead, they treated him like a criminal—and a dangerous criminal at that. It just didn't make sense.

Less than five years separated them from Earth. How could a society change so radically in so short a time? All he saw—their dress, their speech, their impossible city—everything about them pointed to a far older society.

There were two possible explanations. Either the colonists had encountered an alien civilization resulting in some unknown consequence, or . . . time distortion.

His scalp prickled, tingling with the sensation of closing in on the answer to a mystery. Yes, he was close. Very close. The mist that lay between him and the lost pieces of his scattered memory shifted and rolled as if driven by a fresh wind.

Concentrate! he told himself. Thinking made his head hurt. Ignore the pain and concentrate. This is important.

He squeezed his eyes shut and brought the full force of his attention to bear on lifting the veil that obscured his past. Think! You can almost see it. Concentrate! His temples began to throb. The pain surged in intensity. Treet cradled his head in his hands and forced himself to remember. Think! You can remember if you try!

The harder he tried, the more agonizing was his torment. But Treet gritted his teeth and kept at it. Sweat rolled in rivulets from his brow and down his neck. The pain was a red welt in his brain, a burning cancer that swelled and bloated, feeding on his effort.

But the effort paid off. He began to glimpse dimly familiar shapes lurking behind the thick, gauzy curtain. The fog thinned in spots and solid objects emerged, their outlines made sharp by the grinding in his head: a tall, slat-sided Texan with a pilot's cap . . . a smirking gnome in antique glasses . . . a dark-haired goddess, remote and mysterious.

Treet's head snapped up. Crocker . . . Pizzle . . . Talazac—the names tumbled into his consciousness. "I've done it!" he shouted. "I've seen them. I remember."

Now other names, details, and images emerged, one on top of another, thick and fast.

Belthausen . . . *Interstellar Travel Theory* . . . time distortion . . . wormholes . . . *Zephyros* . . . It all came flooding back at once. Oblivious to the drumming ache in his brain, he jumped up and began pacing his cell.

In another few minutes he had it all sorted out; and although a few of the details were still indistinct, he knew that his friends must be hidden somewhere within the colony, perhaps close by. He knew, too, beyond a doubt that in traveling through the wormhole they had undergone a serious time shift.

One or another of Belthausen's time distortion theories had been proved. But Treet felt none of the elation of the scientist riding the crest of a breakthrough discovery.

He shook his throbbing head; the effort at remembering sent fiery daggers stabbing into his cerebral cortex. He felt as if his brain were swelling inside his skull, threatening to burst its bony shell. Did it really matter *which* theory explained what had happened? Whether they had crossed over into a parallel time channel, or traveled through compressed time, or experienced some other bizarre phenomenon, functionally it was all the same.

The Empyrion they had discovered was not the Empyrion they had set out to find. That much was clear. Less clear was what, if anything, he could do about it. Here was a problem that would keep his poor palpitating brain occupied for some time to come.

TWENTY
ONE

On the Starwatch level of Nilokerus Hage, Empyrion physicians maintained a cluster of chambers beneath the heavy-corded webwork of the dome. In daylight, the sun shone through the translucent panes, warming the healing chambers with bright, white light. At night, the panes became transparent, and the stars shone through with crystal clarity. The physicians believed that light was a prime healing agent, sunlight being more intense and moonlight more subtle, but both essential in balancing a patient's aura.

Ernina, physician of the highest order—higher than any physician had ever obtained since records had been kept; high enough that if physicians had a Hage she would be a Director—held the status of a magician among her Hagemen. Her ways were certainly just as mysterious, and her knowledge of the healing arts just as far-reaching. Among the populace it was whispered that Ernina had come by her vast knowledge by communing with the oversouls of dead physicians from before the Purge.

But Ernina cared nothing about the orders or Hage stent. As she swept through the Starwatch complex, overseeing the care of patients, participating in the finer manipulations of body and aura when need arose, and teaching, always teaching her brood of eager followers, there was room in her mind for only one thought: healing. At night she worked alone in her large, many-roomed kraam—not communing with departed oversouls, but poring over ancient texts, searching into the wisdom of the old ones, probing ever further into the mysteries of healing.

Now, as dawn reached into the night sky, graying the black star canopy at the horizon, Ernina closed the book before her and rubbed her eyes. The cracked plastic binding creaked, reminding her of her own weary joints, which were beginning to declare their age. Black words on white pages still spooled before her eyes—old words, words whose meanings had been lost long ago.

Once again the sadness she sometimes felt upon rising from a night of reading came upon her. For one could not read very far into the ancients' books without understanding that a great change had taken place, a falling of almost unimaginable proportions. In these books were mysteries within mysteries. "What have we lost?" she murmured to herself. "What have we become?"

She rose, pressing a hand to the small of her back as she straightened, and went into the chamber adjoining her kraam. A single bed floated in the center of the room, the gleaming apparatus of an aura equalizer suspended above the sleeping patient. The acetic scent of ozone reached her nostrils. She sighed. The equipment is getting so old, and we cannot repair it forever. The magicians are slow, and each time a piece comes back, it comes back changed. They will not admit it, she thought, but they are losing their craft. Empyrion is running down, falling apart—you can see it everywhere you look.

Ernina reached up and flicked off the equalizer. Silence reclaimed the room, accented by the ticking of hot crystals inside the equalizer's housing. She shoved the machine back and stood over the patient, placing a hand on his forehead.

The man's skin was hot to the touch, but not, she thought, as hot as the day before. The sleep drug gave him some relief, though he must awaken soon and eat if he was to regain his strength. At least his aura had stabilized. The dangerous flares of red and yellow in his electromagnetic envelope had diminished considerably, and the blue and green had deepened and spread. He was out of danger now—for the moment, at least.

She smoothed his tangled hair back, allowing her hand to rest gently on the crown of his head. It was a womanly touch, as well as a healer's. Touch, she knew, was a healing agent, and in some could be made very powerful. But there was something about the man before her that made her want to cradle him, enfold him.

What did that imbecilic fool of a Director *do* to these people? The destruction caused by his *conditioning* was often permanent; many patients never recovered. And those were just the ones she saw, the ones Hladik wanted to save. What of those he did not bother to send to her? How many others died that she did not know of?

She shivered at the thought. "I don't know," she muttered. "I don't *want* to know."

A soft moaning whisper escaped the man's lips. Ernina let her hand slide to the base of his neck and felt the pulse there. It was not strong, but it was regular and even. She nodded to herself, thinking, Yes, at least this one will live.

His eyelids lifted, drawn up slowly, and he stared upward with cloudy eyes. Ernina bent over him, focusing the entire force of her healing energy upon him. "Who are you?" she asked. She waited a few moments for the question to sink in, and then asked again. "Who . . . are . . . you?"

The patient closed his eyes and sank back into unconsciousness. Ernina shook out the filmy body covering, and noticed for the first time since examining him a small round scar on his upper arm. It was an old scar, barely visible, just a faint white disk-shaped impression. She brushed the mark with her fingertips. Odd, she thought, I've never seen one of those before, and I've seen many scars.

She stepped to the opposite side of the bed and pulled back the cover. On the patient's right arm was a familiar mark—the narrow red scratch made by the insertion of the poak. That was one scar she had seen often enough. But what was it doing on a grown man? The poak was given to infants at the time of their Hage assignment, never to adults. There was no need.

On a hunch, Ernina went to a nearby equipment cabinet and took out a poak reader and placed it against the bruise. LED circuits flashed the number ten. Ten shares.

Just as I guessed, she thought. A very low number. This man had recently received a poak implant. Why? Unless he'd never received the poak as a child. How could that be? *Everyone* received the poak.

Her intuition screamed at her: He is not one of us!

An outsider then. But how?

There could only be one explanation: he was a Fieri.

Ernina stared at the man. If she could believe her eyes and her finely-tuned intuition, here before her lay a genuine, in-the-flesh Fieri—not a creature of myth, not a phantom of legend and speculation, but a skin, bones, blood, and sinew man! The Fieri were *real!*

The implications of her discovery collided with her awareness. She stepped slowly away from the bed, a dazed expression on her face.

Thoughts came spinning past her in dizzy flight—snatches of folklore from her childhood, shreds of rumor passed on among Hagemen. It was all true then—all the old myths of a separate race, once part of themselves, who had been cast out in times beyond remembering. A fair people, wise and strong, powerful magicians whose machine lore rivaled Cynetics. And there were those among them, the Dhogs—the shadow people, nonbeings who haunted the Old Section—who secretly revered their memory, handing down the old stories by word of mouth all these many hundreds of years—they knew the truth! Here was a discovery equal to any she had made in her lifetime.

And to think that the Threl mercilessly persecuted the Dhogs and killed them or consigned them to reorientation cells whenever they were discovered. Why? It made no sense, unless . . . unless the Threl knew, too, that the Fieri existed. Knew and feared the knowledge, feared it enough to destroy anyone who might share it—why else torture those who believed? The cold-blooded inhumanity of it astounded her.

I should have guessed long ago, Ernina thought. I have closed my eyes to this all my life. I have kept myself above the repulsive politics of the Directorate, and I have paid the price. I who prize knowledge so highly have wrapped myself in ignorance.

The man in the bed stirred. Ernina approached again and replaced the thin coverlet. "You must revive," she whispered to him. "We have much work to do, you and I."

Treet was awakened by a presence beside his bed. Pink-white light tinted the sky; the section of dome above him had not yet become translucent. He rolled over slowly and peeped an eye open. A young man stood a pace away, apparently waiting for him to wake up.

"What do you want?" Treet's sleep-clouded voice sounded suitably gruff.

The youth, dressed in the standard black-and-silver striped short kimono, opened his mouth, then closed it, as if he had forgotten what he had come to say.

"Get out then," said Treet. "I don't like people standing over me while I sleep." He rolled over again. "Come back when you remember what you came for."

"Supreme Director—" began the guide.

Treet's head whipped around, and he sat up. "He wants to

see me?" He threw his legs over the edge of the bed, smoothed a hand through his ruffled hair, and noticed for the first time that the youth was blind. Empty holes stared where his eyes should be. "Um . . . okay. Let's go."

The guide led him out of the room and through a long, sinuous tunnel-like corridor—red tiled ceilings, gray stone-flagged floors. Amber lights, shining from half-mood recepta-cles set flush in the wall near the floor, illuminated their passage as they wound further and further into the convoluted heart of Threl High Chambers. Broken tiles lay scattered over the floor; blank squares dotted the ceiling and walls; here and there a light had gone out. The place reeked of disuse, and made Treet think of a long-deserted subway station.

Treet padded after the guide, wondering how the blind youth managed to find his way so easily. Practice, he guessed. As they moved along, Treet began wishing he had not been quite so hasty. He should have spent a moment or two at the sanitary stall—he smelled like a buffalo, and his face itched from the healthy growth of beard taking over his face.

Did these people shave? wondered Treet as they walked along. Did they bathe? So far all of the men he'd met sported smooth, beardless faces. None of them smelled like he did, either. He guesed that he was being kept away from such things as razors and bathing paraphernalia—perhaps in the interest of safety for all concerned.

Still, his skin felt tight and dry—like wearing a parchment bodystocking. It had been too long since his last nutrient bath; the capsules aboard the *Zephyros* didn't count. I could use a good soak, thought Treet. I could use some red meat, too. Come to think of it, I could use a lot of things I probably won't get any time soon.

For the first time since arriving on Empyrion, Treet felt like himself. He enjoyed the feeling. The ache in his head had van-ished with sleep, taking with it the fog barrier that had blocked his thoughts. Now, aside from a few minor details—such as what had happened out there on the landing field—he remem-bered everything clearly and without pain. Furthermore, last night he had worked out a plan to ingratiate himself to the Supreme Director and win his confidence.

The guide entered a darkened, crumbling doorway and stopped. Treet remained standing in the corridor and realized that the guide had disappeared. He waited. In a moment the guide emerged and motioned Treet to follow him. Treet stepped into the darkness and felt himself turning—the floor was moving with him on it. Then the movement stopped, the light came up, and they were standing in a vestibule which opened onto a larger room.

Treet stepped into the room. It was, like all the rooms he'd seen so far, asymetrically round with a ceiling that sloped like a portion of the interior of a much larger tent. Sunlight, now a little stronger, had clouded the panes of the dome above, so soft white light shone over everything.

The room was formally arranged with many pieces of furniture of sleek, exacting design: clever cantilevered chairs, several elegant tables large and small, a free-standing cabinet with many shelves holding odd art objects, a strange, oblong chest or trunk made of a woven material, a mound of silken cushions in one corner, and something that looked for all the world like an ordinary holovision screen, surrounded by a ring of cushions, standing in the middle of the floor. The place could have used a good dusting.

"Do you like your new kraam?" The voice came from a cabinet in the center of the room.

As Treet watched, Supreme Director Rohee emerged from behind the cabinet. "My new . . . krawm?"

The Director waved a hand to indicate the room. "Kraam," he repeated, accenting the syllables separately. "It is yours."

"It is?" Treet asked dumbly.

He had expected the audience to be much the same as their meeting of yesterday—conducted with official pomp from behind a barrier field, with guards and inquisitors in attendance. He had expected anything but to be offered his own plush apartment.

The old man smiled, his eyes disappearing into crinkled folds of skin, his jowls bulging. "We will sit." He led Treet to the cushions and pulled one from the mound, sinking down onto it with a sigh.

"Where are your guards?" Treet glanced back over his shoulder and sat down cross-legged.

"We will not need them anymore. I have made up my mind about you, Traveler." He smiled again, lips pressed firmly together. "You can be trusted."

Treet did not know what to say. This turnabout was blowing holes in his plan of ingratiation, but the effect was better than he could have hoped for.

"Can you understand what I am saying to you, Traveler?"

"I understand." Treet nodded. Yes, his facility for languages had served him well. He now caught nearly every word spoken to him—it was, after all, merely a mutated dialect of old reliable International English.

"Good! Good!" Rohee seemed very pleased with this information. "We can talk freely then."

"I hope so," replied Treet, taking the opportunity to launch into his prepared speech. "I mean no one any harm. I do not wish my presence here to cause anyone alarm. I have come to help you."

"Help me?" the Supreme Director asked. "How would you help me?"

"It appears to me that Cynetics is no longer remembered in Empyrion." Rohee's flinch told him his hunch was true. Treet continued boldly, "Cynetics is very powerful. Cynetics will help those who help me in my mission."

"What sort of mission, Traveler?" The old man cocked his head to one side. His fine white hair had been brushed until it shined. His quick eyes watched intently.

"To learn why your people have forgotten," he said, stretching the nature of his assignment slightly. Under the circumstances he didn't think Chairman Neviss would mind. He paused and then delivered his next revelation. "My friends will tell you—we all have similar missions."

Rohee gave away nothing by his expression. He merely peered back at Treet with a benign smile and remained silent.

Treet continued. "Yes, I remember my friends. I didn't at first, but I do now. In fact, I remember everything."

TWENTY
TWO

According to Bela, the Chryse were second only to the Saecaraz in Hage stent. This was important, he maintained; it meant that artists and sensitives could finally assume the exalted position they rightly deserved. It meant that the long years of austerity were over—as anyone could see by allotment. Now even musicians and storytellers, Chyrse of the lowest order, regularly received meat in the dole.

Yarden listened attentively as the troupe walked the teeming byways of Hyrgo Hage, with its multi-layered terraces all growing green, the smell of rich damp soil thick in the air. She liked hearing Bela talk; he had such a high opinion of himself and of all Chryse that it made her feel important. She suspected that Bela liked hearing himself talk too; he enjoyed the sound of his own modulated tones.

"The Nilokerus do not like this," he was saying, "since we've advanced over them. No one likes to lose stent." He shrugged, his lanky shoulders lifting under the ample yos. Today they were all dressed in the same sea colors of deep blue-green, head to toe, their hands and faces painted blue, their hair dyed or covered with close-fitting caps of the same color. Today they were playing *Ocean* for the Hyrgo and Saecaraz. "The Nilokerus should just be glad they're still above the rest; they value themselves overmuch."

Yarden nodded, not quite understanding this, but taking it in all the same. The effects of the flash still lingered. Her head felt soft and mushy, slightly detached from her body, which felt, not unpleasantly, lethargic, wrapped in a drowsy, cottony numbness that dulled physical sensation. She was happy just to walk and listen and not think—thinking had become such an exhausting chore lately she preferred letting her mind wander aimlessly. It was easier.

"It's pretty here," she observed. "It smells like . . ." Her voice trailed off. Strange, she had nothing to compare it with. "I like it here."

One of the other troupe members who had been walking close behind moved up beside them. "Wait until you taste their food! Everyone knows they save the best for themselves. Whenever we play the Hyrgo we eat like priests."

"True enough, Woiwik," replied Bela. To Yarden he said, "If we do well today, we'll be given gifts of food—it's a tradition with the Hyrgo. They are so proud of their abilities they always try to impress us."

"They impress *me!*" admitted Woiwik, rubbing his stomach and rolling his eyes.

"You're too easily impressed," Bela snorted. "The Hyrgo think that if they give away food they can improve their stent." He chuckled. "They don't know it doesn't work that way."

"And we'll never tell them," laughed Woiwik. "They're *growers!* Even their magicians—just growers all the same."

"Someone has to grow the food," said Yarden. "They work hard—harder than we do. I don't see what's so funny about that."

Both men looked at her askance. Woiwik opened his mouth to challenge her, but Bela warned him off with a glance and said, "It isn't the work. We all know they work hard. But their craft is not subtle; there is no art in it. Without art, life is . . . well, life is not life. Seh?"

"Maybe *she* was a Hyrgo," muttered Woiwik. "Before—"

"Hagemen!" Bela turned and shouted. "Let us play so well today that we will embarrass the Hyrgo if they don't send us away groaning with pleasure."

This exhortation brought a shout of acclaim from the troupe, which this day numbered forty because the nature of the play required that two troupes merge. They continued on to a place where the lower terraces met to form a wide quadrangle. The troupe stopped here to wait for their audience to assemble.

"How will they know to come?" asked Yarden.

"When they see that we are here, they will come," explained Bela. "Also, a Hyrgo always stops at midday to eat a meal, and they always eat together."

"That's why we always choose this time and this place to perform for the Hyrgo," Woiwik put in, looking pleased with himself. "We don't mind coming down here in deep Hage if it means better gifts."

Yarden nodded absently and raised her eyes skyward. The dome glittered faintly from far above—so high individual cords and panes could not be made out. It was a blank white shell, an enormous curving bowl above all, glowing with sunlight. The tallest of the narrow trees grew upward toward it, but did not begin to reach. Wide, flat terraces—fields with dwelling clusters interspersed—rose like stair-step mountains on all sides; the topmost layers formed plateaus crowned with orchards.

As she looked around her, Yarden saw figures moving in the landscape. As Bela had predicted, the Hyrgo had seen the troupe from afar and were coming down to meet them, calling to their Hagemen to leave their work and follow. In minutes the lower terrace rims began filling with Hyrgo Hagemen young and old, dangling their feet over the rimwall or squatting on their haunches below it. All were quiet and orderly, their faces radiating anticipation. Here and there a mud-stained smile welcomed the troupe, but for the most part the Hyrgo looked on in silent expectation.

When a sizable crowd had assembled, Bela motioned to some of the troupe members who, on hands and knees, linked themselves together to form a living platform. Climbing quickly to the top, he addressed the audience. "Welcome, all, to our performance," he said, his voice clear, deep, and fine. "We are happy to play for you. Today, as you can see by our costumes, is a special performance." A ripple of excitement fluttered through the audience. Bela drew out the moment, heightened the suspense. "Today we will perform *Ocean!*"

The Hyrgo loosed a roar of acclaim, chattering their approval. Bela allowed the outpouring to continue for a few moments and then cut it off just as it began to die away. He told them of the play's history, and briefly explained the various movements they would see. Yarden saw how expertly he manipulated the audience, working them into the proper mood for the performance. He ended by saying, "We do not wish to keep you from your midday meal, so please eat and enjoy the performance!"

With that the human stage broke and tumbled apart. Bela somersaulted once in the air and landed on his feet as the troupe scurried around him. In seconds the quadrangle was transformed into a blue-green sea where waves rolled over one another, rising, falling, rising, falling, breaking on the imaginary shore.

The players, arranged in staggered lines, each held the hem of the player in front, fluffing the garment in the air and letting it sink slowly down. Extra lengths of cloth had been sewn into each yos precisely for this purpose. As the billows filled and expired, the lines crouched and stood and stretched alternately, all the while murmuring in a low, throaty hum.

The blue and green of cloth and makeup became water, the voices water sounds. Yarden could hardly keep her mind on her part, so taken was she with the performance. She stole glances at the audience, seeing her own amazement mirrored in their eyes.

Presently the ocean's waves grew choppy, the water sound more discordant. Illusionary winds whipped the surface of the water, driving the waves onto the beach with increasing force. A storm was coming!

The players ducked their heads down and flailed their arms, snapping the cloth more frantically. The hum became a moan; rending sighs escaped as the waves towered and crashed, spilling over one another, pounding forward.

The crowd sat deathly still, totally absorbed in the clash of wind and sea.

Then, as the gale reached its crescendo, the sea waves gentled, the wind calmed. The storm passed.

Gasps of delight whispered through the audience. Yarden saw them transfixed, their eyes wide and staring. They were seeing the ocean, feeling it. The quadrangle itself had become a sea of faces, each one enthralled with the play unfolding. For the Hyrgo, the Chryse players *were* the ocean.

All day long Pizzle felt eyes watching him as he raked his way through the fields of muck. He would straighten and peer around quickly behind him, but would only see another Jamuna like himself, bent double, patiently turning over the drying crust. He would shrug, turn back to his work, and slog along a few rake lengths further before the feeling came on him again.

Finally, as the workday ended and the recyclers laid up their tools and began moving in from the fields, Pizzle saw two men standing on the rimwall of the field above. They were dressed like Jamuna Hagemen, but something about the way they stood—feet apart, arms held loosely at their sides—told him they had not been working the fields all day.

"They want you." Pizzle spun around to see Nendl coming

up beside him. He nodded toward the two men. "Go with them."

"Who are they?"

"They are friends. You won't be hurt."

"But—" Pizzle turned his face toward Nendl, trying to discover if there was cause for the alarm he felt. "I am afraid, Nendl."

"Go quickly. Don't wait. You must not be seen. They will take care of you."

"I want to stay with you," whined Pizzle.

Nendl took him by the arm and gripped it hard. "You must go with them. I've talked to them—it's all right."

"Then you come with me."

"I can't." Nendl darted a glance over his shoulder. As yet they had attracted no attention, but they could not stand talking together much longer. "You don't understand. I have to stay here. Go on!" He gave Pizzle a prod.

Pizzle took a few hesitant steps forward, then stopped and looked back. Nendl urged him on with a nod. "I will come later if I can. Now hurry!"

Other workers were walking along the rimwall toward the two men. Pizzle saw that he must make a decision. He lowered his head and moved off to meet them. When he reached the rimwall, he looked up to see that the men were now waiting for him at the entrance to the tunnel which led from the fields to the Hage warrens below. Jamuna Hagemen were passing by them into the tunnel; one of the men gave him a signal which meant he was to follow, and then stepped inside.

Pizzle followed, trying to catch the two men, but each time he looked up they were precisely as far away as before. They hurried through the Hage warrens, past dwelling blocks crowded with kraams, out onto open-air common areas, along boulevards lined with squat trees, across suspended walkways over terraced fields, and on. All he saw was new to him, and Pizzle realized there was no way back again, but also that the men had allowed him to draw nearer to them.

At last his mysterious guides disappeared into another tunnel which opened into the steep bank of a dwelling block overlooking a small lake fed by a splashing fountain in its center. Pizzle saw that the people at the lake's edge wore yoses he'd never seen before: gold striped with gold hoods. No one he saw wore the hood, however, unlike the Jamuna who wore them all the time except in Hage.

He stepped hesitantly into the darkened tunnel where the men had disappeared.

"Here, put this on. Quickly!" whispered someone directly in front of him. A bundle was thrust into his hands.

He stood for a moment, peering into the darkness. He opened his mouth to ask one of the many questions rising to his tongue, but felt hands on him, tugging at his clothes, before he could utter a syllable. There was a ripping of fabric, and his yos was stripped from him. "Put it on!" came the urgent whisper. Pizzle shook out the bundle and began feeling for the hem.

When he had pulled the yos over his head and tied the sash at his side, the guides took him, one at each elbow, and steered him back out onto the plaza where Pizzle saw that his new yos had gold vertical stripes like all the others he saw. They led him to the edge of the brickwork to where a wiry green lawn began its gentle slope down to the lake.

"Go on down there," said one of the guides.

"Wait at the water's edge. Someone will come for you," said the other.

With that, the two released him and stepped away. Pizzle turned back twice as he moved off toward the lakeshore. Each time he saw the two still standing where he'd left them, silently watching him.

He reached the shoreline and stood for a moment looking out across the lake to the fountain, gurgling and bouncing as it sent a thick column of water into the air. When he turned back, the two men had disappeared. Pizzle began strolling idly along the grassy shore, watching the others drifting, as he was, around the lake.

Short, round-topped trees, growing right at the water's edge, trailed vines into the water. Flowers with delicate white blooms floated up where the vines touched the surface. Pizzle stopped to examine the flowers, squatting down for a closer look. In among the stems and dangling water roots he saw the flash of a silver side and a swirl of fins. Also, reflected in the water's mirror, he saw two figures standing over him.

He stood and turned. One of the figures was a man, the other a woman. Both smiled at him and nodded. The woman stepped to his side and said, "I see you enjoy the lake." With the slightest tilt of her head, she turned him away from the water. "In that case we must come here again soon."

The man, still smiling, stepped behind Pizzle, and together the three moved up the slope once·more to the plaza. They walked easily along, passing before tiers of dwellings, each with a large round window and balcony facing the lake. Occupants in colorful Hage robes carried trays of food or sat at tables eating. Pizzle's stomach growled, and he remembered he hadn't eaten since midday.

"Where am I?" he asked.

"Tanais section," replied his companion. "Would you like to eat something? We thought a meal might be welcome soon."

"I am hungry," Pizzle admitted.

"It's just a little farther. There are some people who want to meet you, Pizol."

He looked at her suspiciously. "How do you know my name?"

She laughed easily. "Didn't you know you had friends looking out for you?"

"Nendl is my friend."

"Oh, he's our friend too. A Hageman does not betray his friends."

Pizzle contemplated her last remark—had it been made for his benefit? A reminder of . . . what? Loyalty? Was she instructing him?

They walked on in silence, moving around the lake and above it, their feet soundless on the spiral-patterned bricks. At the far side of the lake, they approached an immense, multi-towered block of dwellings—so tall it commanded a clear view of the entire section. Aerial walkways arched between the slender towers, joining the upper levels to one another.

Overhead, the dome was now nearly transparent. A blue-gray dusk, deepening with the approach of night, triggered the miniature yellow lights hidden in the branches of trees and strung along the serpentine byways, and soon Tanais Hage basked in the golden wash of myriads of tiny lights.

"Here we are," said the woman as they stopped before the central tower. She ushered him in through a narrow slit of an opening three levels tall. Pizzle slipped in and found himself in an enormous, triangular hall. The hall was nearly empty. Only a few Hagemen, dwarfed by the proportions of the room, moved silently across the polished surface of the floor toward one of the three spire-shaped openings.

"This one is ours—" She pointed across the hall to the opening on the left, and led them quickly across the expanse. Upon reaching the entrance, she paused and explained, "It's a lift. We will leave you here, Hageman Pizol."

The man behind him reached inside the doorway, adjusted something, and then motioned Pizzle into the lift. He stepped in and heard a whizzing sound as the lift climbed swiftly away. Bands of light ringed the transparent compartment, dropping past so fast it seemed that the lights moved instead of the lift. Pizzle pressed his hands flat against the smooth sides and held on. Presently the falling rings slowed, and the lift stopped without a tremor. The static fizz of the unidor cut out, and Pizzle stepped out of the lift and into a kraam many times the size of Nendl's.

Wherever he looked, flat white surfaces met his gaze— ceiling, floors, walls—all soft white and smooth, uncluttered with objects or decoration of any kind, the floors covered with gray and white weavings. Before him stood a man, dark and imperious in a long, emerald green Hage robe.

"We have been waiting for you, Hageman Pizol," said the man, coming forward to take him by the arm. "You are safe here. And very soon, you will remember who you are."

TWENTY THREE

Yawning, head pounding again, Treet sat hunched on a blue silk cushion, chin in hand, trying to keep his eyes focused. It had been a long day, filled with interminable questions and innumerable answers. Director Rohee had wanted to know everything about him and had questioned him endlessly. They had talked for several hours before the Supreme Director had gone, leaving him in the incredulous care of the inquisitors, who had also come heavily armed with questions.

All day long they had interrogated, and he had supplied answers—holding back only those aspects of his trip he thought best kept to himself: his time distortion theory, for one thing, and any direct references to Cynetics for another. Now he sat by himself, watching the three inquisitors discuss among themselves, trying to make up their minds about something. How best to proceed with the cross-examination, Treet thought. Whatever it was, he had lost interest long ago. They might have been planning to barbecue him and feed him to the blue kangaroos. Treet didn't care.

He hadn't done so much explaining since he had been caught crossing over from the New Frontier with a liter of Stolichnaya in his luggage. He just wanted to eat and go to sleep.

"Enough!" said Treet, standing up. He yawned and did a couple of toe touches by way of getting his circulation going again. "That's all. No more. I'm going to sleep."

The inquisitors looked at him. "We wish clarification on several points—" began the spokesman, a dry stick of a man named Creps.

"Come back next week. I'm through talking." Treet advanced toward them. "I'm hungry and tired, and you're becoming a pain."

"We will have food brought," offered Creps.

"You do that," said Treet, jabbing a finger at him. "And then clear out."

The three exchanged puzzled glances. "We do not understand," said Creps.

"Oh? Let me see if I can make it any clearer. Go away! Get out! Leave! Is that better?" Treet enjoyed the effect his words were having with the three stuffy inquisitors; expressions of horror bloomed on their officious faces. He continued, "You want to know something else? I'm tired of answering all your stupid questions. What about *my* questions? I'm not answering any more questions until I get some answers myself."

"We have been instructed to provide information," replied Creps. The other two nodded.

"Tell me this then: where are my friends? That'll do for starters."

After a quick consultation, one of the inquisitors turned and fled the room. Well, thought Treet, that got some results. I should have hollered sooner. Treet stood and glared at his two remaining guests until the third came back a few moments later.

"Food has been requested," Creps informed him. "Also, we have summoned the Supreme Director. He has asked to be informed of any unusual behavior."

"Fine," replied Treet. "Let's get the old boy back in here, and maybe we'll get somewhere." He plopped himself back on his cushion and sneezed as the dust swirled around his face. "And send someone up here to clean this dump!" he added.

A few minutes later, a guide—the one who had awakened him that morning—came in carrying a large tray, heavy with bowls of food: more raw vegetables, a thin, clear soup, and several small roast fowl. The guide placed the tray before Treet and backed away as Treet dove in. He seized one of the birds and tore off a leg.

Treet was licking his fingers and looking at the soup when Rohee entered the kraam. With a nod he dismissed the inquisitors, who looked relieved to escape. Treet smiled to himself; he hadn't realized it was that easy to intimidate these goons.

Rohee settled himself on a cushion and dipped his hand into a bowl of cherimoyas. He popped the fruit in his mouth and sucked the sweet juice, studying Treet, his eyes sharp and hard.

"Help yourself," said Treet, and went on eating.

"There will be no more questions," announced Rohee as he rolled another of the delicate fruits in his hand.

Treet swallowed. "Good." He took a tentative sip of the soup and added, "I thought you said you trusted me."

"Yes," replied Rohee thoughtfully. "But we are also curious."

"I'm curious, too. I want to know what happened to the people I came here with. You said you would tell me—I'm still waiting."

"They have not been harmed."

"So you say. But if they're all right, why can't I see them?"

The Supreme Director's wrinkles arranged an expression of extreme concern, but his eyes remained hard. "It is best that you be kept apart for the present. It is for your own well-being."

Treet's head snapped up. He swallowed. "What? Is that a threat?"

"It is a simple fact." Rohee gazed at him quietly. "I can explain."

"Go ahead." Treet wondered at the change in the old man. The first meeting had been stiff and formal, the second more friendly. And this—this was downright cozy. The Director was treating him like a confidant. Or, Treet reconsidered, a condemned man at his last meal.

Rohee tilted his head back and looked down his beak nose. "I am beset by enemies, Traveler," he began. "I am Supreme Director of the Threl, leader of all Empyrion. Naturally, my position attracts many who bow before my face, yet conspire for my power behind my back."

Treet wondered at this confession. Why was the old bird telling him this? "I understand. Are you telling me that my friends are in danger from your enemies?"

"Not precisely. If you have not guessed, Traveler, your arrival has put me in a very awkward position. My enemies would like nothing better than to get their hands on you and your friends. They believe that you could help them in their plots against me."

"I see. What do you think? We know nothing about any of this."

Rohee shrugged and reached for another cherimoya. "This is what they believe. I merely mention it because they are ruthless men whose schemes stop at nothing short of open opposition—which they dare not attempt." He lifted his shoulders again as if to say, I accept this; I live with it. "Therefore, I have instructed my allies to take each of your friends into Hage. They are hidden there, safe from my enemies. To move them now would endanger them needlessly."

Treet nodded. "I see." He wiped his mouth with the back of his hand and replaced the soup bowl. "Pardon me if I don't believe you for one microsecond."

"You do not know Empyrion," Rohee stated firmly. He returned Treet's gaze equably. "But when you have learned our ways, you will be reunited with your friends, Traveler. I, Supreme Director, have so ordered it."

Treet remained silent for a moment, considering. He had pushed the matter far enough for the moment; there was nothing to be gained by badgering Rohee about it. Best now to change the subject. "What's going to happen to me?"

Rohee smiled, his eyes becoming slits. "I have been thinking about what you said this morning—about your mission."

"Yes?"

"I have decided that you will fulfill your mission, Traveler."

"Is that so?" Treet eyed his benefactor suspiciously. There was a trade-off coming, he could feel it.

"It may be as you say—that it would prove beneficial to everyone. We will never know unless you try."

"I'll need some help," suggested Treet, pouncing on this unexpected opportunity. He wanted to see how much Rohee was willing to give.

"I will assign a guide to you. He will be instructed to help you in every way."

"Fair enough. But I want someone who knows his way around and can get me the information I need—not one of those three bozos—" He jerked his head toward the nonexistent inquisitors. "I want someone smart."

The Supreme Director stared and then lightened. He chuckled, "No, not one of those. They are Jamrog's security advisors—chosen to prepare a report to the Threl about you. Your arrival has naturally piqued the interest of our leaders."

"Why don't you let me meet them personally? I have nothing to hide."

"No. Not yet. In time, perhaps." Rohee shook his head, drawing his sparse eyebrows into a knot. "It is better for you to remain invisible for now."

"Enemies?"

"There are always enemies. You will be safer if no one knows who you are; you may pass more freely that way."

Treet accepted this. "Fine. Cynetics will be pleased. But soon I will need to see my friends again, of course."

"Yes. In time," said Rohee. He stood slowly, and Treet stood with him. "I open Empyrion to you, but no one may know what you are doing. Speak to no one else, do you understand? You will answer to me, Traveler."

Treet heard an unspoken threat in the leader's voice and felt the tension of balancing unknown factors, of coping with potentially lethal forces beyond reckoning. He then understood something of the risk involved in turning over the keys of the city to an alien. "You won't be sorry," he said, attempting reassurance.

Rohee only nodded, then rose stiffly and shuffled away. In a moment Treet was left alone again. He ate some more and lay back on the cushions, but soon discovered he was not the least bit tired anymore, so got up and walked around his new quarters, thinking, replaying all that had happened to him.

There were many questions left unanswered. But if he was very, very smart, he would find the answers. At least now he was being given the opportunity to dig them out for himself. Maybe that's what Rohee wants too, he thought. He wants me to find out for myself because . . . why?

That was something else to discover.

"He knows nothing," said Tvrdy in frank disgust, "and suspects less. In his present condition he is worthless."

Cejka nodded. "Patience. It will take a few days for the antidote to be absorbed into his tissues."

"Even then I'm not so sure we'll get anything. The damage is already done, I'm afraid."

"Where will you keep him?"

"Here with me. I have assigned guides to watch him so he doesn't wander."

"That could be very dangerous," the Rumon leader cautioned. "If he were seen, or if—"

Tvrdy brushed aside the warning. "No one will suspect he's here. I do not want him out of my sight."

155

"Have you notified Piipo and Kavan?"

"No, and they are not to know—not yet. Later, when he is ready to talk. For now, there is no need to tell them. There is nothing to tell."

"I agree." Cejka allowed himself a broad smile. "What a stoke of luck, seh? We've done it! Who could have dreamed it would be so easy?"

Tvrdy grinned, his lips curled in amusement. He placed a hand on Cejka's shoulder. "Jamrog will dig his heart out with his own hands when he learns what we intend." The grin faded suddenly. "But that is not for a long time yet. We must not become overconfident."

Still smiling, Cejka agreed. "Yes, yes, you're right. But it starts now—after all these years. So much patience, so much work . . . but worth the price, yes?"

"Did you ever doubt it?" Tvrdy smoothed the shimmering folds of his green Hage robe with his hands. "But we've yet to discuss taking the other spies."

"No," Cejka said. He pushed himself up from his chair and took up the orange Hage robe draped over a nearby table, pulling it over his head. "We've discussed enough for one night. I must get back to Rumon Hage before I am missed. Jamrog must not have cause to wonder about my movements. Besides, we must guard against overconfidence—yes? I think we should be satisfied with the one we have caught. We know where the others are; we can find ways to get them if that becomes necessary. Losing one will be enough of a shock to Jamrog." He smiled again. "I wonder what he'll do?"

"We'll find out. I wouldn't want to be in Hladik's yos when Jamrog explodes. That could be very messy." Tvrdy got up and moved to the lift with Cejka. "Do you want my guide?"

"I can find my way back. A guide might arouse suspicion. I'll be all right." He stepped into the lift and pulled the yos sash tight. "Send word when our friend is ready to talk."

"Of course. Good night, Cejka."

The unidor crackled on, and the lift dropped from sight. Tvrdy stood looking at the empty tube for a moment, chin in hand, thinking. Pradim came in silently and waited to be noticed by his master. "Nothing more tonight, Pradim," said Tvrdy when he stirred finally. "Just make sure our guest is comfortable before you go to sleep."

Pradim padded away quietly, his fingers waving in the air.

Tvrdy crossed the room and went out onto the balcony. Tanais Hage spread out before him, sparkling with the light of tiny yellow lights. The byways were empty and shadowbound; the intercrossed mazes of Empyrion wore night faces. The patter of the fountain echoed up from far below, and Tvrdy turned his eyes toward the dark outline of the lake. There, slipping among the trees winding along the shoreline path, a figure moved with quick stealth.

"Soon, Cejka," Tvrdy whispered to himself, "we will all walk in the daylight."

TWENTY
FOUR

Treet had been up for several hours and had taken his sweet time sampling the pleasures of his new sanitary stall. Warm water was a luxury, and the liquid soap he found in a crystal canister containing a pungent perfume with an astringent quality he found refreshing. He rubbed himself all over with thick, coarse-woven squares of fibrous grasscloth which, he assumed, served as both washcloth and towel.

I'd strangle a rhinoceros with my bare hands for a real bath, thought Treet. His skin cried out for a nutrient solution; he felt flaky and brittle all over and wondered how long it would be before his dry epidermis began peeling off in sheets. He sighed; at least it would be a passably clean hide.

He hummed as he laved the water over his face and neck, happy for the first time in a long time, having decided upon rising that he would play the Supreme Director's game—at least to all outward appearances. He would go along without a fuss and use his position to gather information, locate the others, and eventually reestablish contact with Cynetics.

There is no hurry, he told himself. The main thing is not to make anyone nervous or suspicious. I can wait; I've got time. My first task is to scope out the territory, get the lay of the land, and find out what these people are all about. What do I know about them really?

Not much. Only that they have changed. More to the point, *time* has changed. I'm seeing the colony at some point in its future, relative to Earth. Something happened in the colony's past to bring it to this state, and I have to find out what that something was.

The idea of a quest renewed in Treet a sense of adventure he thought he'd lost. Here he was, transplanted in a semi-advanced culture on an alien world—think of the possibilities! Who could tell what he might find, what secrets he might unlock?

The fire of adventure warmed Treet's blood. He was anxious to be off on discovery's road. He pulled his silver-striped kimono over his head and adjusted the sash, pulling the hem up to just above his knees, in the manner of the colonists. That was one thing he'd learned already.

He emerged from the stall ready to leap tall mountains and ravenous. He paused midway across the floor of his kraam, wondering how to summon breakfast. As he stood thinking about the problem, he heard a single chime and a moment later a young woman entered the kraam carrying a large oval tray.

"Breakfast!" said Treet. "Wonderful!"

The young woman looked at him curiously, ducked her head shyly, and proceeded to the nearest of Treet's tables where she set down the tray and began laying out the food. "I don't suppose there are any croissants on that tray—or coffee?" Treet muttered to himself.

"I do not understand, Traveler," replied the young woman in a clear, precise voice.

"So you *do* talk. Good." Treet sat down in a sleek chair of polished wood and began dipping into the various bowls. "Tell me then, when do I get this guide I'm supposed to have?"

The young woman regarded him closely. "I am to be your guide."

Treet sized her up: a slight but well-knit frame, shapeless under the flowing kimono; fine brown hair cut short over a high, spacious forehead; expressive hands with long, tapering fingers. Her quick dark eyes with a suggestion of epicanthic fold at the outer angle hinted at an oriental ancestry now far removed. With head erect atop a slender neck, she appeared intelligent and alert. "Great. Now then, you know your way around this dome of yours? You can get me into the places I want to go?"

"I have been instructed to help you in every way, Traveler."

"Okay." Treet nodded, chewing a feijoa. "First thing is cut out the traveler stuff. My name is Treet—Orion Treet. You can call me either. What do I call you? Friday?"

A puzzled expression played over the guide's young features. "I do not understand."

"What's your name?" Treet picked up a bowl of diced meat in a thick, white gravy and ladled some of it into his mouth with a paddlelike utensil from the tray.

She hesitated, as if deciding how to answer.

"My name is Calin," she said finally.

"Calin? Nothing else?"

"That is my name." She didn't sound any too convinced.

"Have you eaten this morning, Calin?"

The guide nodded, watching Treet carefully and still wearing the look of quiet wonder with which she'd entered the kraam.

"Well, drag up a chair and sit down here anyway. I don't like people hovering over me while I eat."

"You wish me to sit with you?" She acted as if she had never heard of sitting.

"Yes, I want you to sit with me. Look, unless I'm mistaken, we're going to be working very closely together for a while. I don't want anyone standing on ceremony around me. I have work to do, and I can't be tripping over formalities at every turn. See?"

Calin said nothing, but silently nodded her assent.

"Good," Treet continued. "Now why don't you tell me about yourself and we'll get acquainted."

Before the guide could speak, the chime sounded again and Treet looked up. "Company?"

Calin jumped up from the table as if her chair had suddenly become radioactive. "I have requested a shaver," she explained, running to the vestibule. She came back leading a humpbacked, bald-headed man in a white-sleeved kimono. The little barber carried a soft woven box and peered nervously at Treet, awe and fear mingled on his smooth-shaven face. "This one is a third-order Nilokerus. I requested the best."

"Good, Calin. You seem to have thought of everything. We're going to get along just dandy." He rubbed his prickly chin, turned his chair around and, tilting his head back, said to the barber, "You may begin."

With a tremble in his step, the Nilokerus shaver advanced, placed his box on the table, and went to work, rubbing sweet-smelling, clear lubricant on Treet's prickly face to prepare the beard. Treet closed his eyes and said, "The last guide I had was blind."

"Hage guides are blind."

"Why?"

"When they are assigned, their eyes are put out; otherwise the psi will not come to them. They are not magicians and have no other powers."

Such barbarism was not unheard of. Still, Treet winced. "But you're not blind," he pointed out. "How come?"

"I am a Saecaraz magician," she explained, pride creeping into her voice. "I was chosen by the Supreme Director because of my skill, and because I am a Reader. I have—"

"A magician did you say?" Treet opened his eyes and raised his head. The barber jumped back, razor in hand.

"Yes. Fourth-order."

"That's good, huh?" Treet put his head back down. "You'll have to explain that to me."

Calin shrugged. "There is nothing to explain. One serves one's function, and the priests reward one's achievement by advancing one through the orders. That's all."

"Well, we'll work on that a little more later. But I think I know what you're saying. Go on."

"There is nothing else to tell."

"Oh?" Treet cracked open an eye. "Are you single? Married? Do you live alone or with a whole bunch of other magicians? What does a magician do exactly? How big is this place anyway? How many people? Where does Empyrion gets its power? How do you grow your food? Why do you live under this dome? What's this business about Nilokerus and Saecaraz? What do you do for fun? How is the colony governed? Do you have laws? What's it like outside?" Treet paused for breath. "See? There's lots to tell."

"I am admonished," replied Calin, much taken aback with Treet's rapid-fire questioning.

"Don't worry about it. I just wanted to give you an idea of my interests. I'm interested in everything." Treet quit talking and allowed the barber to finish scraping his face clean of whiskers. When the barber took out his scissors, however, Treet waved him off, saying, "I'll skip the trim, if you don't mind. Next time." He rubbed his tingling face with pleasure. "Good job. Help yourself to a plantain or whatever those things are."

He turned to Calin, exitement bubbling through his veins. "I'm ready! Let's go!"

Calin smiled. She liked this unpredictable Traveler, and his enthusiasm swept over her like a rumor through the Hage. "Tell me where you wish to go. I will take you anywhere."

• • • • • •

They stood at the rimwall of the topmost terrace in Sae-caraz Hage—the highest point in all Empyrion. The dome directly over their heads—a scant hundred meters away, Treet estimated—was not perfectly bowl-shaped. It was more like the inside of an old-fashioned circus tent, complete with poles.

He could clearly see individual panes large enough to cover whole city blocks back in Houston; the cords that bound them, like the strands of an enormous spiderweb, were as big as the trunks of California redwoods. The gigantic support poles which poked up through the dome were as big as hypertrain tubes.

"Some view," remarked Treet after a long moment of silence. The effect was like standing on an alpine mountain summit overlooking deep valleys with their huddled villages below. Only here, the mountain was a squat pyramid of plates stacked atop one another in descending circumferences, and the valleys were plazas and greenspace, although at least one river of size wound its way along the lowest level rimwall to disappear around a terrace curve far below.

Treet was no accurate judge of distance, but guessed that on Earth, on a good day, he could see perhaps twenty-five or thirty kilometers. The other side of the dome appeared to be at least that far, maybe farther—he couldn't tell because there was no haze to cloud distance and offer perspective.

"We are near the center of Empyrion. This is Saecaraz Hage. Threl High Chambers and the Supreme Director's kraam are below us. Over there," Calin pointed across space to another terraced hillside in the distance, "is Nilokerus hage. And there," she swiveled forty-five degrees, "is Chryse. Tanais is next to it, adjoining Saecaraz."

To Treet these landmarks were fairly meaningless since he couldn't tell where one place left off and another began. Like suburbs of a metropolis, one place simply merged with another. "Just what is a Hage?" asked Treet. "Is it a place or a social designation? You see to imply both."

"I don't understand social dez-ik-nation."

"It's . . . ah, like a class or a family." From the frown on Calin's face Treet knew he had explained nothing. "It's who you are."

Calin bent her head in thought, her forehead wrinkled. "It is a place," she said finally, "when one goes there. It is a social dez-ik-nation when one comes from there." She smiled, proud of her definition.

Now it was Treet's turn to frown. "I see. You live there you mean. It's home."

"Home?" Calin shook her head. The word meant nothing to her. "We live in Hage, yes."

"Everyone lives in a different Hage?"

"Yes, the Saecaraz live here, the Nilokerus there," she pointed across the distance again, "the Chryse there, and the Tanais, and the others," she indicated with a sweep of her hand, "each in his own Hage." Her tone implied that this was a most obvious and elementary fact.

Treet began to see the arrangement. Whatever else it was, a Hage was clearly some sort of social marker which aided internal organization. A caste system, apparently. "I'm beginning to get it, I think." They turned away from the wall and walked back to the lift entrance. "Take me to a Hage; I want to see one close up."

Calin cocked her head to one side. "We are in Hage. We are in Saecaraz."

"No; I mean I want to go to a different one. Nylokeerus—is that how you say it?—let's go to that one."

The guide hesitated. "Perhaps Bolbe. It's closer."

"Fine," replied Treet. "Tell me about it on the way."

They reached the lift and began their descent to what Calin called Gladwater level. "The Bolbe are a small Hage, and have little stent, but at least they are above the Jamuna—although some of their magicians are equal to the best Chryse players." This fact was illustrated with the graceful flip of an upraised palm, which Treet read to mean that things tended to even out, at least for some members of a Hage.

Calin continued, "The Bolbe are weavers mostly, and tailors. I will take you to their Hageworks where you can see what they do."

The lift stopped, and they stepped out into a dark, cavernous gallery hollowed from the stone crust of the planet. Dim lights set in the walls cast pale illumination into an oblong room whose slab-cut ceiling echoed with the ping of splashing water. A pathway described by tiny yellow lights led down to a waterfront where people had gathered. There were, Treet guessed, a hundred or so colonists—the most he'd seen so far—and they appeared to be waiting for something.

"What's going on here?" Treet asked. His guide pursed her lips—an expression which meant he had asked an incomprehensible question. He rephrased it. "I mean, what are these people doing?"

"They are waiting for a boat," Calin said. "We will go with them to Bolbe Hage."

"By boat?"

"Unless you are afraid of boats." She regarded him with concern. "Many people do not like boats. I myself like them very much. I ride whenever I can."

"Boats are fine. Wonderful. I like boats, too—only I never expected to ride one here, that's all."

They had come to the water's edge to stand waiting with the others gathered there. Treet could see kimonos in several different colors: gold-striped, red-striped, turquoise-hooded with silver-banded sleeves, green-sleeved with yellow hems. Those wearing identical robes stood together—well away from the ones wearing different colors. His guess was correct: the robes were uniforms. "These are the colors of the Hage?" He indicated the various clustered groups.

"All Hagemen wear the yos so that they may be recognized," Calin explained simply.

"Black and silver—that's Saecaraz?" Treet plucked at his own uniform.

"The silver bands are Saecaraz," Calin replied, "and the gold Tanais." She nodded to a group wearing yoses with vertical gold stripes. "The green and yellow is Hyrgo; the red is Rumon." She named the various ones around them.

"Saecaraz, Hyrgo, Rumon," Treet repeated. "How many are there altogether? How many Hages?"

The magician looked at him oddly. "Eight," she replied as if this should be self-evident.

"Eight? Why not six, or ten, or twenty?"

Calin shook her head slowly. "There are eight," she began solemnly, and then looked away as the crowd around them surged forward. "Look, the boat is coming."

Treet could not see the boat. The cave was not well lit, and the people pressed close to the rail at the water's edge. He saw a dark shape glide up, and heard the hollow scrape as the hull touched the wharf. Someone called out something in a loud voice which he did not understand. A murmur went through the passengers on the dock. In a moment the crowd began to move forward.

When they reached the rail to board the boat, Treet saw

three men in red-striped yoses and short, blunt wands in their hands, standing at the head of a wide gangplank. Passengers passed before these men, who pressed the glowing point of the wand against the exposed flesh of each person's upper right arm.

"What's this?" asked Treet.

"To ride the boat costs two shares," said Calin. "They read poak as you board." She raised the sleeve of her yos and presented her arm. The boatman pressed the glowing point against her arm as she stepped onto the gangplank.

Treet followed her example, watching closely. He felt a pleasant tingle where the wand touched his arm. The bored boatman waved him on, and Treet climbed down into the boat. It was a squarish, boxy carrier—more barge than boat—made for transporting cargo and passengers short distances: flat decks—three of them, one atop the other over three quarters of the boat, with the small third deck over the rear quarter—surrounded by a woven rope rail. There were benches along the sides and in the center; all the rest was deck space—filled with passengers and, here and there, mounds of stacked bales and bundles.

"I always ride there," said Calin, pointing to the topmost deck. She pushed through the other passengers toward the midsection of the boat where a stairway led up to the upper decks.

Treet followed her up to the third deck, gripping the handrail as the boat swung away from the stone pier. In the darkness there was not much to see, but Treet felt a sensation of motion and glimpsed the yellow lights of the waterfront sliding backward. They were off.

They journeyed in gloom, but Treet saw that they had entered a channel. Rock walls pressed inward, and the boat picked up speed as the river ran more swiftly through the narrowed course. After what seemed an interminable length of time, Treet saw the mottled gray stone lighten as it closed on them, and all at once they were out of the cave.

"It's fantastic!" cried Treet, blinking in the bright daylight. "I've never seen anything like it!"

TWENTY
FIVE

If the view from above was impressive, the view from the river was spectacular. But, as Treet had noticed before, look more closely and you'd see that everything had a frayed and rundown appearance. The river—flat, broad, and blue-gray—crawled between undulating, step-sided mountains. Along the moss-covered lower rimwalls which formed the banks, short, knob-shaped trees trailed flowered vines into the water; fluffy, long-bladed grass of pale green fringed the water's edge.

The boat swept along with the water on its own unhurried way. Treet saw scores of people moving along the shoreline roads, some of them riding small, open-air vehicles, but most walking in tight little groups. The upper terraces were lined with curious, multiple-humped buildings, many four or more stories tall. Through the oblong windows he saw lights flash occasionally, which made him think of factories.

"What goes on up there?" he asked Calin.

She turned to where he looked. "One of the Saecaraz Hageworks," Calin explained. "That is where they repair the ems."

"Ems? What's an em?"

"Those—" She pointed to the movement along the terrace.

"Those little cars, you mean?"

"A kar is a veeckle, yes?" the young magician asked. Treet nodded, despite her mispronunciation of the word vehicle, so she continued. "As a Reader, I am allowed to examine certain old records. I have read of veekles such as kars."

"I see," said Treet. "Doesn't everyone read?"

Calin tilted her head to the side. "What would be the use? Only Readers read."

"Oh." Treet dropped the subject. He had decided that he would not offer the colonists observations about his world—even though he itched to point out the contrasts. In his travels, he had learned that such observations by foreigners were not only unwelcome, but most often had the effect of drying up the free flow of quality information—as if the host preferred not to toss his best pearls before the foreign swine. Who, after all, wants to risk himself, his country, or his customs to the ridicule of infidels?

A sponge I am; a sponge I will remain, thought Treet; and sponges do not make waves. He changed the subject. "Where does this river go?"

"It is called Kyan," explained Calin. She turned to view it, her eyes sweeping its curves. "It flows throughout Empyrion, through every Hage. There is a very old story about the river." She glanced at him tentatively.

"Go on, I'd like to hear it."

"The story says that long ago, before the cluster was closed, before there were Hages even, the old ones traveled on the water. An old one called Litol built a very big boat and took half the people with him to find a faraway place. While they were riding the water, the boat caught fire and sank, and Litol and all the rest were lost.

"Those left behind saw the red fire in the sky at night and knew that their friends would never return. They decided to make their own river, which they bent into a circle and filled with the tears from their eyes, for they wept over Litol and the lost. This is why the river flows as it does, so that whoever rides the water need never be afraid of getting lost since the river always comes back to its beginning."

Calin fell silent when she finished the story. To Treet's trained ear the story sounded familiar: just like scores of other folktales he'd heard. The story hid as much as it revealed, but it nevertheless countained elements of historic fact—grains of verity served up in a soup of mythic fancy.

"That's a nice story," remarked Treet.

Calin stirred, sighed. "It is a very old story. No one knows how old. There are others like it—I know them all."

"You must tell me more of them sometime. I like old stories." Yes, I do, thought Treet. Those old stories will help me piece together what happened here.

The river swept around the feet of the terraced mountains and now came to a place of sculptured hillsides which rolled gently down to the seamless rock wall of Kyan's banks. On a near hillside a dozen or so musicians, dressed in the turquoise and silver of Chryse, sat in a cluster playing for a small crowd of Saecaraz gathered below them. They were too far away to see or hear distinctly, but Treet caught a sense of the sound: light stringed instruments accompanied by dusky, low-voiced woodwinds.

Treet strained after the music, hearing it in wispy snatches. What he heard puzzled him, until he realized that it was the tonal equivalent of Calin's river story—pensive, possessed of a delicate melancholy. In fact, the music articulated the very atmosphere of the colony: brooding and old and tired, tottering to its fall.

Beyond the hills he glimpsed white towers, graceful spires linked with arches, rising above trees thin as tapers. The boat turned abruptly, taking the towers from view before he had a chance to ask about them. He turned and saw that Calin had moved to the other side of the deck. She held the rope rail and looked out toward the opposite bank. Treet joined her.

"You started to tell me about the Hages," said Treet. "I'd like to hear about them now. You said there are eight."

She nodded. "There are eight. The number corresponds to the Greater Requisites of the Sacred Directives. The Hages are Saecaraz, Chryse, Nilokerus, Rumon, Hyrgo, Tanais, Bolbe, and Jamuna. Each holds its place, and thus the eternal balance is maintained. This is also from the Directives."

"I see. And what are these Directives?"

Calin marveled at his ignorance. "You've never heard of the Sacred Directives? How do you live?"

Treet shrugged. "I manage. Perhaps I know them by another name."

"That could be," she allowed. "No one could live very long without them."

"Where did they come from?"

"Come from? The Directives have always been. Since the beginning. They were given—" She hesitated.

"Yes? Given how?" Treet pressed.

The magician's dark eyes darted right and left. She lowered her voice. "There are some things we don't speak of out of Hage."

"Oh? Why not?"

"I can't explain here," she whispered. "Later—I'll tell you later, when we're back in your kraam."

Here was a puzzle. What was there about these Sacred Directives that they could not be discussed in public? Presumably everyone knew about them—why the secrecy? Treet cast a glance to the others around them. No one seemed to be paying any attention to them. "All right, but don't forget. I want to know."

Presently the river widened and a boat traveling the opposite way passed by them. This boat was larger and sported three full decks, all of them crammed with passengers. It was brightly painted in carefree splashes of color—scarlet, yellow, and violet. Raucous music came across the water, along with the clatter of voices, laughter, and song. People mingled on the decks in colorful yoses, large jars in their hands, drinking, singing, laughing loudly.

"Some party," said Treet. The scene reminded him of a Mardi Gras celebration he'd witnessed once in Trinidad: flashy, forced, frenzied.

"It is a cruise," offered Calin.

"Oh, where are they going?"

"Going? They cruise—it is . . ." she paused, searching for a word Treet would understand. "A happy making," she said finally.

"They look happy all right." Treet watched the boisterous boatload pass. "What are they drinking?"

"Souile. Some call it shine. It is an intoxicant."

"So I see. Every last one of them is skunked!" As the party boat plied its way around the bend, several drunken passengers relieved themselves with obvious delight into the river from the aft decks. "They just ride around in circles on this boat and get waxed?"

"A very popular amusement. Once on board, the shine is free—also flash."

"Flash?"

"Pleasure seeds."

"I thought so. Free drinks and drugs! Welcome aboard! Some pleasure cruise."

"Look," said Calin, turning back toward the river bank, "we're coming into Bolbe Hage."

Treet followed her gaze and saw that on this side of the river, the hills had blossomed with color. Every meter of hillside was wrapped in fabric of the most dazzling color and design: shimmering reds and violets, swirls of emerald and chartreuse, glistening blues and deep vibrant browns, pearly whites. The hills were checkerboards with multicolored squares. Treet supposed that the display was a sort of advertisement for the Hage's handiwork.

A little further on, the hills gave way to a waterfront area—

a flat rectangular space ringed by banks of pale yellow mosque-shaped buildings. Two other boats were moored to posts beneath a long notch in the bank wall. Men in blue-hooded yoses were stacking bales on one of the boats, while men in green-and-yellow unloaded them from the other. The bales being unloaded were tumbled down an incline where they were picked up and trundled away on the bent backs of laborers. It was a scene typical of any waterfront on Earth—a thousand years ago.

The boat drifted closer to the wharf, nosing toward a post; ropes snaked out as the boat was snugged into its berth and the gangplank extended. As passengers streamed off, Treet and his magician guide joined the crush on the lower deck and eventually found themselves deposited on the wharf.

"This is where the Hyrgo bring the ipumn," Calin explained. "The Bolbe take it and begin making it into cloth."

"Ipumn is grown by the Hyrgo?" asked Treet. "They're the ones in the green and yellow yoses, right?"

"Yes, those are Hyrgo."

"And who are those in blue, over there—the ones with the medals around their necks?" He indicated a group of three Bolbe standing next to the growing mound of ipumn bales. One of the three held a flat clipboard object which he worked over with a glowing stylus. From a heavy chain swung a large blue-silver medallion which looked like the Greek letter pi with arms.

"Those are Bolbe priests," she said out of the side of her mouth. "They are recording the bring. All that comes and goes within the Hage, the priests record—as they record the dole." She steered him by the priests toward the nearest of the mosques.

"The dole? You mean handouts?"

"I don't understand han-douts," replied Calin. "The dole is given to all freely. It is the right of every Hageman to receive his tender."

"Food, clothing, shelter—that sort of thing?"

"Food and clothing, yes—these are given in the dole. The rest a Hageman must buy with his own shares, which are given by the priests at allotment."

Treet grasped the set-up. Very ingenious. Make certain nobody starved or went naked, meet the bare necessities, and then let them work for the rest, earn the currency with which they could buy the extras. A variation of the old-style socialism. "These shares," said Treet, "that's what the poak is all about?"

He touched his arm at the spot where he had been bruised. There was nothing to feel there now.

Calin nodded, smiling at him. "You learn quickly, Traveler Treet. The shares are given according to a Hageman's order and work record."

"The higher the order, the more shares you get. Slick. What's the highest order?"

"Six, I think, though I don't know if anyone has ever attained sixth order. I am fourth order—most Readers are."

"So you get more shares than a third-order magician, right?"

"Of course. But the allotment also depends on the stent of the Hage. Look there—" She pointed to several Bolbe before a low platform unwrapping the bales of stringy ocher ipumn. "They are perhaps third-order ipumn handlers. Those unloading the boats are first-order. These others," she gestured toward the Bolbe on the platform who were sifting the ipumn and sorting it into piles, "are ipumn graders—second- or third-order. They will receive more shares than the material handlers—as much as dyers, but less than weavers."

"I see," said Treet. "The only way to get more shares is to advance to a higher order or get a better job."

"Job is *function*, yes?"

"Yes. But how do you change functions? I mean, what keeps everyone from wanting to be a magician? If magicians get the most shares, I'd think everyone would want to be one."

"It is difficult to change functions, but it can be done. You must petition the priests. They decide."

"How do they decide?"

"I don't know. This is not for us to know. Although sometimes a Director will request a function change for a Hageman. Then the petition is always granted."

"The Directors run the show—isn't that always the way?"

"Please?"

"Never mind," said Treet. They wandered past the mosque-shaped buildings of the waterfront along a wide avenue bedecked with multicolored hangings and streamers and flags strung across the walkway on wires. At the end of the avenue, they entered a communal square where several work stations had been set up before flat-roofed sheds. Bolbe milled around the work stations, lugging bundles of ipumn. The air was filled with a fine ocher dust and the whine of high-speed machinery.

"This is where they begin breaking down the ipumn fibers. Over there," she gestured across the square, "they pull the fibers, there they separate them, and so on."

The air smelled of cinnamon—not unpleasant, but the dust was getting to Treet. He noticed that the workers wore no protective masks. "They breathe this stuff?"

Calin appeared unconcerned. She turned away, striking off along another path. They walked through Bolbe Hage following the ipumn through the various processes of becoming cloth. They saw spinners turning the raw fibers into hanks of glistening thread, fine as human hair; dryers with poles stirring long, loosely braided chains of ipumn in large pools of bubbling colored dye; dryers turning the braided chains on racks under lamps; weavers threading huge looms, and folding finished material onto square bolts. In all, Bolbe Hage fairly bustled with activity.

What impressed Treet most of all was the diligence and industry with which the Bolbe worked. Both men and women went about their tasks with quick precision; nowhere did he see any slackers or dawdlers. No one lingered over a job; no one sat with idle hands. "Everyone is so busy," he remarked to Calin when at last they headed back toward the boat. It was long past time to eat, and Treet was hungry. "It's remarkable. What keeps them at it?"

"The priests record transgressions against the Directives. Anyone who deviates from the Clear Way will be punished at allotment."

"His shares are cut, in other words?" Treet nodded to himself. Yes, very tidy. Keep them at it with incentives and threats. Reward the good workers, punish the bad. "The priests watch everyone all the time, I suppose? They know who's been naughty and nice."

Calin agreed solemnly. "The priests watch everyone."

They arrived at the waterfront in time to board for the return trip. As the boat pulled away, this time under the tug of a chattering engine, Treet turned for a last look at Bolbe Hage. "You know, we still didn't see where they make the really fine stuff." Treet gestured toward the glowing array of fabric spread on the hillside.

"That is Hage cloth, made in deep Hage. No one is allowed to go there."

"Never?"

172

Calin lifted a palm in that equivocal gesture which Treet understood to say, it all depends. She said, "The Bolbe guard deep Hage jealously. They allow no one from another Hage to enter. They don't want the secret of their craft revealed. It is the same with the Tanais and Rumon, but the Hyrgo and Jamuna allow anyone to come and go in deep Hage; they don't care. Of course, their craft has no art."

All the way back to Saecaraz and to his kraam Treet remained silent, digesting all he had seen and heard. Calin did not intrude on his reverie, and after seeing that food was brought for a late afternoon meal, she left saying, "I will come tomorrow the same as today, unless—"

Her listener glanced up distractedly. "Yes . . . come tomorrow, same time. Fine . . ."

Treet ate and lay back on his mount of cushions. Not bad for the first day, he thought. Innocent tourist—no surprises, no pointed questions, nothing to upset anyone. The Supreme Director will get a glowing report—he's probably getting it right now.

Treet knew that Rohee would be fully informed of his moods and movements, knew that he would be carefully monitored at all times. That was all right with him—let them watch until they got tired of watching. Then he'd make his move. Somewhere out there Pizzle, Crocker, and Talazac waited, and he meant to find them. One way or another he *would* find them.

The priest rubbed his long nose and gazed at Yarden doubtfully. Bela stood beside her, his hand around her waist. Coming to see the Hage priest had been his idea. He'd said that perhaps her memory would come back more quickly if she bought a benefice.

Together they'd walked through Chryse Hage, not to the temple, but to the Quarter—the place where the priests lived and held commerce with the populace. They waited in line for several hours as one by one the petitioners were admitted into a large mound-shaped structure built on a rise with steps leading up to a wide arched doorway.

"The priests will know what to do," he explained. "Very likely there is astral interference with your aura. If so, they will see it and recommend a suitable treatment."

Yarden thought about this, not understanding it completely. "Will I have to pay them?" she wondered, thinking that she did not have many shares in her poak.

"Of course."

"Is it . . . expensive?"

Bela had laughed. "Never more than you have. But don't worry. The priests understand. They will help if they can."

The room to which they were finally admitted was big and dark and sour smelling. Sweat, smoke, urine, and other unwholesome odors mingled together in a fetid perfume—as if whole generations of priests had lived and died in the room without ever cleaning or opening it to the light of day. The darkness and rank aroma were almost suffocating. Yarden gagged upon entering and would have turned back if Bela had not gripped her very tightly by the arm and urged her forward.

The priest, a bloated, rheumy fellow with drooping eyelids and a chin that rested on his swelling belly, sniffed loudly when they entered the room. He was sitting on a high-backed stool, his voluminous yos spread out around him so that he appeared to be floating in the air. A dirty medallion hung around his neck, shining dully in the light from two candletrees of smudgy candles.

"Step forward," he said tiredly. "Let me see you. What do you want?"

"Go on," Bela whispered as Yarden glanced at him. "Just tell him what you want."

"Well?" The priest cast a baleful eye at her, sniffed again, and sneezed into his hand.

"Tell him," Bela whispered. "Just say what I told you."

"If it please you, Hage Priest," she began in a tremulous voice, "I would like a benefice."

"A benefice," he had repeated flatly. "Of course. And what is the nature of this benefice?"

"My—my memory. I cannot remember things clearly. We—I thought a benefice . . ."

When the priest said nothing, Bela had stepped up, put his arm around Yarden, and explained, "She has been in reorientation, Hage Priest. Her memory is unfortunately—ah, displaced."

"Hmmph!" the priest snorted. He put a thumb in his nostril and blew. "Reorientation."

"Is there anything you can do?" Bela had inquired, thus plunging the priest into a period of deep contemplation during

174

which he stared at Yarden as if she were the carrier of a dread disease.

Finally the priest shifted his bulk and yawned. "How much do you have?"

"Not much," Yarden replied shakily.

"How much?"

"Ten shares."

"It's not enough," he said dryly. "You may go."

"Wait," interposed Bela. "Perhaps you can think of something. Hage priests supervise the allotment, do they not?"

"You know well that we do."

"Then perhaps at the next allotment you could arrange to give her extra shares. She could pay you then." In essence Bela was inviting the priest to name his fee and pay himself.

"It would be expensive," the priest observed. He shook his head slowly, already calculating how much he could get away with.

"Of course." Bela gave Yarden a little squeeze.

"Reorientation." The priest's porcine eyes narrowed. "As much as a hundred shares. Maybe more."

"Maybe two hundred?" inquired Bela.

"Yes. Two hundred."

"You'll do a benefice for two hundred?"

"Very well." He withdrew a short, ball-tipped wand from his clothing and struck a bell hanging from a stand next to him. Another priest came forward with a tripod on which a brazier full of burning coals smouldered. He placed the brazier in front of his fellow priest, then retreated, only to reappear a moment later with a tray. On the tray were bowls of powder in various colors.

"Prepare a healing benefice," said the Hage priest, stifling another yawn.

"Mind or body?" asked his assistant.

"Mind. Make it twice strong. She has been in reorientation and has lost her memory."

The second priest lay down the tray and picked up an empty bowl. He began dipping into the various powders with his fingers. "I will add a sarcotic too, to be sure." He tossed powder into the bowl and stirred it with his fingers before handing it to Yarden.

She looked into the bowl, and the assistant priest smiled, revealing brown teeth. He inclined his head and pantomimed

175

dumping the bowl into the brazier. Bela nodded in encouragement.

Yarden stepped up to the brazier and lifted the bowl, tipped it, and carefully emptied its contents onto the coals. There was a sputtering flash, and foul vaporous fumes arose from the coals. Resinous smoke rolled up into the darkness. Yarden stepped from the brazier, convulsed with coughing.

"*Benito, benitu, beniti,*" intoned the Hage Priest in a bored voice. He raised his hand in the air above Yarden's head. "In the name of Trabant, I cleanse the aura of all astral interference . . . and so forth. Let the Seraphic Spheres be content with the offering thus poured out. Restore—ah, what is your name, woman?"

"Yarden."

"Restore Yarden's memory to her in good time," continued the priest, "that she might serve her Hage and follow the Clear Way faithfully. Trabant Animus be praised."

They were dismissed then and left by a side door as the brazier was removed and the next petitioner ushered in quickly. On the way back to Bela's kraam, Yarden remained silent, reeling from the experience with the priest. She could not explain it, but felt dirty, as if she had wallowed in filth and now bore the stains on her face and hands. Waves of revulsion churned inside her. She gulped deep breaths and fought to keep from vomiting.

Bela watched her curiously, but said nothing until they were almost to the kraam. "Do you feel any different?" he asked.

Yarden shook her head, lips pressed tightly together.

"Oh well," said Bela sympathetically, "it often takes a little time. We may have to ask for another benefice if this one doesn't work."

"No!" Yarden turned horror-filled eyes on him. "No more."

Bela laughed. "All right. It doesn't matter. Let me know if you change your mind, though. I'd be glad to take you again."

Yarden turned away. *I never want to go back there,* she thought. Anger flared. *This was Bela's doing. He insisted I go. He knew that would take place. But no, Bela is my friend; he stood by me the whole time. It wasn't his fault, and nothing bad happened.*

Still, if nothing bad happened, then why do I feel so unclean?

TWENTY
SIX

The next day for Orion Treet, and the next, was much the same as the day before. In fact, for the next several days in a row he played the tourist, dutifully tagging along beside his guide, visiting each Hage in turn, viewing the life in each of Empyrion's spheres.

By day he was the sponge, soaking up all he could see and all he was told. By night he examined what he had absorbed. He paced the confines of his kraam, sifting facts and observations, trying to create, as with the tiny colored tiles of a mosaic, a single, sweeping picture of Empyrion.

The emerging portrait was that of a civilization in decline: old, decrepit, timeworn. The signs of advanced age were everywhere apparent—stone steps worn hollow by the tread of feet over the centuries; once-straight walls now sliding, tilting, wrapped in thick moss; towers whose shifting foundations bore the marks of decade upon decade of attempted repair; dwelling blocks in whose peeling facades one could trace the histories of whole generations of inhabitants, layer on layer; fetid catacombs where water-stained walls bore ancient graffiti. Empyrion wore a thick patina of time.

Treet sensed a primordial heaviness, the all-pervading lethargy of decay.

The untold years had witnessed the evolution of an extremely stratified society—not only distinct classes, each separate from the other, but classes within classes—and each stratum fiercely protective of its station and function while at the same time aggressively seeking to improve its position in relation to the others through a subtle ongoing competition, the rules of which Treet had not yet discovered, much less understand.

For the citizenry of Empyrion, the Hages were everything: home, family, country—all in one. A Hage was a political entity as well as a gear in a complex economic machine; it was both social matrix and utilitarian construct; it was a rigid caste system which created for its members a sense of place and purpose and belonging in return for work.

Each Hage was governed by a Director who, through his staff of Subdirectors, ruled his fief with despotic power, answering only to the Supreme Director, chief dictator among dictators. The power of the Director seeped downward through a bewildering hierarchy of priests and magicians. Hage priests supervised the allotment, paying out shares for work; they conducted the regular Astral Services and presided over the occasional feast day celebrations.

Calin had even taken him inside an Astral Temple. It was a big, black pyramid, empty but for rows of seats placed round a small stage. At a Service the priest read from the Sacred Directives—a body of writings that had come down from the earliest times—and exhorted their congregations to follow the Clear Way, a path of obedience leading to enlightenment.

The dome dwellers worshiped a god called Trabant Animus, Lord of the Astral Planes. It was Trabant who bestowed immortality on a soul and, if sufficient progress had been made during its lifetime, joined it with one of the many oversouls or spirits of the highly enlightened departed. Once joined to an oversoul, a soul journeyed through two realms or existences: Shikroth and Ekante. One, Shikroth, was called the House of Darkness; the other, Ekante, the House of Light. The journey through both was accomplished under the direction of sexless astral bodies known as Seraphic Spheres—entities of pure psychic energy.

The religion made no sense to Treet. Rather, it made about as much sense as any other religion he'd ever encountered. Treet had little use for religion, tending to see it merely as something to keep the dim, cold unknown from becoming too frightening. He wasn't easily frightened, so relegated religion to the dustbin of outmoded ideas.

Magicians, Treet learned, were just as mystical as priests in their own way, and just as bound up in an incomprehensible code of belief. Each Hage had at least six magicians assigned to it, and often many more. Their function was to maintain the electronic equipment and oversee the use of all machinery. They were technicians, but with a difference: in order to repair Empyrion's failing equipment, magicians had to steep themselves in technical knowledge—machine lore, Calin called it—which had been handed down from magician to magician for ages past remembering.

For this, some of them were schooled as Readers, as Calin had been, in order to scour old documents for references pertaining to the repair of machines. All were trained in psychic abilities, since most of the equipment was so old they often had to, as Calin put it, *merge* with a machine in order to repair it. The knowledge of how to manufacture the more complex machines had been lost in the second Purge. So magicians had their hands full just keeping up with simple maintenance and willing tired machines to go on functioning.

The rest of the tasks necessary for cohering a complex society fell to the workers. Everyone in the colony was assigned a job, and everyone worked. Children—and Treet saw very few children—were born into a Hage creche where, at the age of six months, they were assigned a function. Children were apprenticed in their crafts until the age of fourteen, when they were formally initiated into the Hage and took their places as adults beside the other workers.

Hage populations, therefore, were kept at fairly constant levels, adjusted as need arose. New workers replaced old. Treet had not learned yet what happened to those who were replaced. He presumed they stayed on in deep Hage, caring for children too young to work, since neither the very old nor the very young were visible in the places he'd visited.

This then was the emerging portrait of Empyrion. True, it bore little resemblance now to what its creators must have established. There was no trace of its original intent that he could see. Empyrion had evolved into a creature far different from any corporation colony Earth had ever seeded. The time shift, whatever its mechanisms, accounted for most of that, certainly. But there were other forces at work too, Treet knew.

He'd read of European miners in South America who, lost for years in the Brazilian jungle, had evolved a strange, cultic society with an entirely new language and culture. When they were discovered forty years later, none of the rescuers could understand a word they said, nor did the miners wish to return to civilization—they had their *own* civilization!

Something like that had happened to Empyrion. But what Treet saw around him had taken far longer than forty years to evolve. Just how much longer, he would have to discover. They must have a data bank, or some sort of official repository of information on the colony. And that, he thought, is the next place I want to go.

When Calin came for him the following morning, Treet hit her with his request. She did not react at first; she looked at him blankly, as if she had not heard. When Treet repeated himself, she became flustered. Her eyes slid away from his, and she twisted her features grotesquely.

"What's wrong?" asked Treet. "What did I say?"

"I—" She hesitated and started again. "We can't go there!" she managed to force out.

"What do you mean, we can't go there? Why not? And why are you whispering?"

"It is forbidden."

"Forbidden? The library is off-limits? I don't believe it." He laughed sharply. This seemed to agitate the magician even more.

"Don't talk so!" she rasped.

"I'll talk any way I please," sneered Treet. What had come over his guide this morning?

She reached out and plucked at his sleeve, inclining her head toward the door. Treet caught her meaning and nodded, and they both left the kraam without another word.

Once outside, Treet demanded, "All right, now suppose you explain what all that was about? Why the convulsions in there just now?"

Calin was pulling him along the corridor which led out to the Sweetair level terrace. "We could not talk in there," she said, glancing up at his face once and then turning her eyes forward once more. "Your kraam is . . . is—"

Treet supplied the word himself. "Wired? Is that what you're trying to say? Someone's listening in on me?"

Calin nodded solemnly. "They are listening."

"Who?"

"Invisibles." The word was a whisper.

"So what?" Treet shrugged. "I don't care if they listen. They can take pictures too, for all I care. I've got nothing to hide." Except my suspicions, he added to himself.

"It is not good to talk openly about such things," Calin said, returning somewhat to her normal demeanor.

"Not good for who—you or me?" Treet frowned and watched the dark-haired woman beside him. In the handful of days they'd spent together he had grown quite fond of her. She had loosened up around him to the extent that he felt he could ask almost any question that occurred to him. This little episode just now in his quarters served as a fresh reminder that he was not on a sightseer's holiday. These people were different from him in subtle yet fundamental ways; he would do well to remember that.

Treet stopped. Calin walked a couple of paces alone until she halted and faced him.

"Okay, spill it. What is the big secret around here?" he said. "I won't go another step until you tell me."

"I don't understand."

"You know what I'm talking about. You're all hiding something—what is it? What do you know that I don't know?"

Treet looked at her sharply. He hoped that his abrupt question would have the effect of shaking part of an answer out of her—if she knew anything. "Well? I'm waiting. Do we stand here all day?" Far down the corridor behind them came a group of Saecaraz Hagemen.

"I don't know what you mean," Calin pleaded. She glanced quickly at the approaching figures. "We must go." She turned, expecting Treet to follow. Instead he sat down.

Calin took a step and then turned back, her eyes growing wide with horror when she saw him squatting in the middle of the corridor. "Get up! You can't sit there like that!"

"Why not? I'm not hurting anything," Treet replied mildly. This was working better than he'd hoped.

"It is forbidden!" Calin stooped and tugged at his arm, trying to raise him. The Hagemen behind her came closer. They had stopped talking among themselves and were watching the scene before them. "Please, get up and let us hurry away from here."

"What happens if I don't?"

"The Threl will hear of it. The Supreme Director will punish me."

"Tell me what I want to know, and I'll get up."

The Hagemen were within earshot now, and were watching very carefully. Calin nodded, whispering desperately, "Yes, yes, I will tell you what I know."

"About the data repository, too?"

"Yes! Yes!"

The others were almost on top of them. Treet nodded and pushed himself up slowly, pressing his hands to his back. "I don't know what happened," he said loudly. "I must not have been looking where I was going. Nasty fall."

Calin had her hands on him, hauling him upright. She appeared properly concerned that he had not hurt himself. The Hagemen halted beside them, glancing at one another with puzzled expressions. "He is not hurt," she explained. They grunted and moved on, looking over their shoulders suspiciously.

"Easy, wasn't it?" said Treet. "Now, about those answers."

"We cannot talk here. But I know a place—the Riverwalk."

"Let's go."

The Riverwalk was a wide, ambling boulevard of square-cut stone which ran abreast of Kyan. Calin led Treet along the moss-grown rimwall which formed one bank for the river below. Hageman from various Hages—Saecaraz, Tanais, and Nilokerus mostly—moved along the tree-lined road, some in the small electric carts, ems, that looked like chariots without horses or visible wheels, and the rest on foot in isolated groups. Quite a few of the latter were pushing large hand-wagons of a type Treet had seen before in his travels: a sizable box slung over a U-shaped axle between two bicycle-type wheels with a third small swivel wheel in front. Each barrow was piled high with cargo, and those pushing strained to the task.

They had walked along in silence for some time. Treet could see that Calin was mulling the situation over in her head, trying to decide how and what to tell him. That was all right, but he didn't want to give her too much time; he'd get soft answers that way. "I think we've come far enough," he told her. "Let's talk."

"Many things are forbidden to us," she said simply. "We know this is for the best, so we do not question it. To question what does not concern you is unwise."

"Unhealthy, you mean?" He watched her closely; she walked with her head bent, eyes to the ground.

"Do not talk so loud," she warned, "and keep your mouth hidden. There may be lipreaders close by."

"Lipreaders—informants?"

Calin nodded. "The Invisibles use them."

"Okay, I'll be discreet. But tell me, why all the secrecy? What is everyone afraid of?"

"I have already told you," she said lightly. "It is for our good that certain things remain hidden. Only pain and death come from knowing."

"Ignorance is bliss, is that it? Keep the masses happy, give them bread and circuses, and trouble stays away from your door."

Calin peered at him strangely. Clearly, she did not comprehend sarcasm. "Your words bite, Traveler Treet. They veil your meaning."

"Never mind. So why can't we go to the library—or whatever you call it—where all the information about the colony's past is kept?"

She spoke into the folds of her yos, muffling her words. But her answer surprised him. "There are enemies among us who are trying to destroy our nation. They work in secret; so we use secrecy against them."

"I see. Who are they, and why do they want to destroy everything?"

"They are called the Fieri. I know very little about them, but I know that once, long ago, there was a great war in which the Fieri were overcome and cast out. They pledged eternal hatred toward us, and ever since have tried to destroy us. They have sown their evil among us and have won over some of the weaker of our people, twisting them with their hatred. That is why we must all be so careful. That is why we are watched and why we watch."

Treet knew enough about repressive regimes to understand that he'd just been fed the accepted party line. There seemed to be no reason to badger Calin about her explanation. Very likely she believed every word herself. He tried a different tack. "This war interests me. I would like to find out more about it."

"The Archives," she said softly. "The data bank you speak of."

His eyebrows went up. "Yes?"

"That is where you will find what you wish to know."

"I thought you said it was forbidden."

"It is. No one may go there—not magicians, not even Hage priests. No one but the Supreme Director himself."

"Or someone who had his permission perhaps?" Treet stopped in his tracks. "Take me to him now. I want to ask him."

Calin studied him for a moment, as if trying to read his thoughts from his face. "I will take you to him. But whatever answer he gives must be sufficient."

"Whatever he says goes. That's fine with me." They began walking the opposite direction, back toward Saecaraz deep Hage. "Do you think I have a chance?"

Calin smiled slightly. "I can't say. Perhaps. I know that he has given you special privileges for a purpose."

"What purpose I wonder?"

The magician shrugged. "He has not told me." Her tone became gravely serious. "It is said among us, however, that he who stands too near the Threl deserves his fate. You must be careful."

Treet gazed at the dark-haired magician. Her concern touched him; it was the first time she had given any hint of feeling for him. "I'll be careful," he told her. "Now, let's go see Rohee. I have a feeling he'll want me to see those Archives."

TWENTY
SEVEN

The Archives of Empyrion were like nothing Treet had ever imagined. The main room was a chamber half-a-kilometer on a side with a flat expanse of a roof a good fifty meters from the floor. In essence the enormous room was the colony's attic: a place where the flotsam and jetsam of an aging civilization was consigned to molder quietly into dust.

In entering the room, he and Calin had passed through a dark, steep downward passage protected first by sleepy Nilokerus guards and then by heavy metal doors at intervals of thirty meters, each with its own coded lock. The last door, twice a man's height and ten meters wide, had been sealed; it gave a whoosh of indrawn air when Treet, following Rohee's precise directions, pressed the code sequence into the pentagon of lighted tabs on the lock and twisted the opening mechanism. Dusky light filtered down from skylight wells overhead as they stepped down onto the floor of the chamber.

Treet had often fantasized about what it would be like to discover a lost Pompeii, or the forgotten tomb of an Egyptian Pharaoh in the Valley of the Kings. Upon setting foot in that silent room, his dream became reality. His heart palpitated; his throat tightened; his palms grew clammy and his knees spongy. Here was a vast treasure-trove of the unknown past, a mine of information about the colony's history. Its riches were his and his alone to discover.

Supreme Director Rohee had been cagey when approached about the Archives. He had not said no right away, neither had he agreed. Instead, with sly, hooded eyes, peering down his beak nose over steepled fingers, he listened to Treet's lengthy entreaty and then questioned Calin closely before making them wait six hours for his decision. The waiting had been maddening—all the time Treet suspecting he would be denied access to the Archives, and wanting it more by the minute. But his frustration melted at once when a Saecaraz Hage priest appeared at his kraam with the message that he was to come at once to Threl High Chambers. There Rohee had informed him that he and Calin would be allowed to examine the Archives in the company of the Hage priest who would keep watch so that the spirits of the place would not be disturbed.

The three of them had set off at once. It was still early evening and, since Treet intended to make his first visit a meaningful one, they had brought food and drink with them.

The Hage priest had not spoken a word since delivering his message. He remained a mute sentinel, hanging back as Treet tugged open the door, following warily, like a creature flushed from its natural surroundings. The priest's curious reluctance brought to Treet's mind a stock character in old 2-D movies: the cowering ethnic guide who is made to trespass on his forefathers' burial ground by gold-lusting fortune hunters.

"Jackpot!" Treet's voice rang hollow in the cavernous room as he stepped lightly down from the last of four steps which formed concentric ledges around the Archive's circumference. A fine gray film lay over everything—not dust, for the room was sealed. It looked like time itself, oxidized and deposited as silt to form a transparent shroud over Empyrion's past. Not a trace of a smudge anywhere, Treet duly noted; any intruders' footprints would be plainly visible on the floor. Therefore, he concluded that no one had entered the Archives in a very long time—years at least, perhaps centuries.

"I guess Rohee doesn't come down here much," said Treet, gazing around. The size of the room made his voice small. Directly before him lay a jumble of artifacts and machines and stacks and ranks of containers of various sizes and shapes, around and through which ran a maze of intertwined pathways. He fought down the impulse to dash forward along the first path at his feet and start prying into everything he saw. "We'll have to have a plan," he said, mostly to himself. "There's too much here to just run at it. We'd be here months before we even knew what we were looking at."

At that moment, the priest, above them on the steps where they'd left him, stretched out his arms and began chanting in a trembly sing-song. He held in each tight fist something that looked like a frayed black rope bound to the end of a stubby handle. As his voice rose and fell, echoing eerily back from the depths, he began flailing away with the ropes in loopy figure eights.

"What's got into him?" wondered Treet.

"He is clearing an astral zone for us to work in. There will be many spirits gathered here, clinging to the old things. He is reminding them that we, the living, are their masters. We should not have any trouble from them." Calin's dark eyes were wide with wonder as she spoke, her voice tinged with awe.

"Well, let's get started. There must be some sort of map for this place, or a floor plan or something. I would guess it might be near the entrance here. Let's look around for anything that might show us the layout."

Calin nodded, although she little understood all that Treet had said. Together they began searching the immediate area, stirring fine gray powder from everything they touched.

"Make a note: we'll need masks if we're going to be working in this stuff," said Treet after only a few moments. Clouds puffed up around his hands and feet; his clothes were already well decorated with powdery handprints. "We could use a vacuum cleaner, too. Hold on. What's this?"

Calin's head jerked around as she straightened up. "You have found something?" She came to where he stood bent over a pedestal set in the floor. It was covered with a cloth whose filth-encrusted folds had stiffened with age.

Slowly, so as not to dislodge an avalanche of "dust" onto whatever had been protected beneath, Treet lifted the covering. The pedestal was a free-standing data terminal, quite old—yet of a design Treet had recently seen on Earth.

A strange feeling of displacement stole over Treet. How odd, he thought, to find an object of the very latest modern design looking a thousand years old. Here was something that could not be more than five years in service at the more up-to-date corporate offices, yet bearing the marks of countless years of hard use. It was unsettling.

"Time travel," Treet whispered, letting the cloth drop at his feet. "I wonder if this thing still works." He regarded the terminal doubtfully. It was so *old*. And yet, silicon and platinum were hardly perishable substances. With a shrug he touched the sensor plate.

Nothing happened.

He tapped it and then punched it harder. Still nothing.

He turned to Calin. "You're a magician—do something."

The woman bent over the terminal and placed her hands against its sides. She closed her eyes, became motionless.

Treet stared at her in disbelief. His comment had been meant as a joke. But Calin apparently took him seriously, and acted on his suggestion. What could she be doing? he wondered. The colonists were afflicted with a weird regard for spirits and such, but did they believe they could communicate with machines too?

In a moment the dark-haired magician straightened and lifted her hands away from the terminal housing. She delicately placed a finger on the sensor plate and held it there. To Treet's amazement, the screen flickered to bright green life.

Magic?

"This one is very old. It needed coaxing," Calin explained.

"So I see." Treet scrutinized the young woman, seeing her in a strange new light. She appeared inexpressibly foreign to him just then: mystery wrapped. "No wonder they call you magicians," he said at last, then turned his attention to the terminal. "Let's see what we've got."

There were a half-dozen symbols embossed on the sensor plate and Treet recognized them as ordinary computer function designators. He brushed one with a fingertip, and a menu came up on the screen. "So far, so good. It's in the mother tongue at least."

At his shoulder, Calin squinted at the black letters. "This is the writing of the ancients," she said. "Very difficult to read."

"Oh, I don't know," remarked Treet, and rattled off a string of words from the menu.

Calin marveled at this achievement. "You know the writing of the old ones? But how?"

He decided on an evasive answer to save a lengthy explanation. "I learned it a long time ago." Treet scanned the menu and chose an entry called *General Reference,* made his selection, and watched as the screen cleared and another menu flashed up. He grinned at Calin. "Banzai! This is what we're looking for."

Among the entries on this second menu was a selection titled *Archival Orienting.* He chose it and watched as the screen drew a detailed floor plan of the enormous room, dividing it into multicolored sections. Lips pursed, chin in hand, Treet alternated his study of the screen with a survey of the room, fixing the layout in his mind.

Presently he looked up to find Calin sifting among a stack of sealed lightprint disks. "I found these over there," she said, inclining her head toward a formidable tower of barrel-shaped plastic containers whose base was littered with the disks. She held a handful out to him.

The magnetic ink on the yellowed plastic labels had faded almost beyond legibility, but Treet managed to decipher some of them. He read: *Maintenance: Fusion Core Ceramic Shields; Stress Factors in Spun Steel Suspension Systems; Integrated Circuitry and Biogenics; Crystal Patterning.*

"These are the instruction manuals," said Treet.

"Instruction manuals?"

"For the colony—all this." He waved his hand to embrace all of Empyrion. "Everything."

"Is this a *find?*" Calin asked.

"You pay attention, don't you? Yes, it's a find," Treet allowed. "But not exactly what I'm looking for." He turned back to the screen. "What we want is human documentation."

"Human doc—?"

"Records, files, disks, cartridges—but about people, not how to grow crystals," he said absently, studying the glowing screen before him.

There did not seem to be any particular place where documents were kept. What Treet hoped to find was a cache of diaries or logbooks of the colony's first years of operation. Surely such things existed. He had never heard of a colony that did not keep copious records on itself. Empyrion, being the first extra-system colony, would have monitored itself scrupulously and generated an ocean of data.

Treet heard a soft, grunting sound like an animal snoring, and looked back to the upper ledge where the Hage priest lay. He had spread his yos under him and now slept with his head on his arm. Strange bird, thought Treet. Doesn't he know what is here?

He punched up the menu again and spent the next hour trying its selections, but found nothing that promised immediate help. He sighed. This was going to be a long haul. Unless they stumbled over something accidentally, the information he sought would only be found through a methodical and painstaking search. The thought made him cringe—sectioning off a room this size with its jumble of articles . . . daunting, to say the least.

When Treet finally raised his head from the datascreen, he saw that the light had dwindled. Sinking into darkness, the shadows thickened in the room, fusing, deepening.

Where was the light switch for this place? he wondered. He

trotted back to the entrance, stepping over the body of the sleeping priest. He searched the area for a switchplate of any description, but found nothing. There must be lights somewhere, but where?

It was getting too dark to search, and without a clue to where the lights were, there was no hope of finding them in the dark. "Calin!" Treet called. "We'll have to come back tomorrow. It's getting too dark to see, and I can't find the lights. Calin?"

He listened. Nothing.

No sound came from the floor. She had been right there only moments before, standing next to him. Where could she have gone? He stared around him at a broken wall of dimming shapes, now pale and unreal in the twilight. In the silt of one of the many pathways through the mountains of discarded objects her footprints lay—but which one? It was now too dark to make out footprints anyway.

"Ca-a-l-l-i-n-n!" he called.

"Hageman, we want to talk to you."

Nendl, casting a quick glance over his shoulder, hesitated. Two Hagemen in Jamuna brown were coming up fast behind him. He hadn't known he was being followed. His kraam lay but a few meters ahead, so he put his head down and ran to it, slipped in, and snapped on the unidor. He lay panting against the wall.

They had seen where he went, he knew. But that could not be helped. At least he was safe in his kraam now, and it would be night soon; they would not wait for him all night. They would try to nab him in the morning on his way to the fields. But by then he would be safely hidden where they'd never find him.

He moved away from the wall and heard a heavy scraping sound, like someone boring through the stucco of his kraam. The wall began to vibrate. He put his hand out and withdrew it instantly—the surface was hot to the touch.

As he stood watching, the wall convulsed and a section collapsed inward, scattering dust and debris. The two men stood looking at him through the haze of dust. One of them had a flat, nozzle-shaped instrument in his hands; the other stepped

190

into the kraam through the jagged hole.

"Hageman, you forget your manners," he said. His eyes were hard, his voice soft and silky. "Your name is Nendl."

"No," the Jamuna recycler replied. He swallowed hard, his heart beating in his throat.

The man smiled thinly. "Perhaps that is not your private name, but Nendl is your Hagename."

"Who are you? What do you want?"

"Only to talk to you."

"Go away. Come see me tomorrow."

"We will go away when you tell us what we want to know."

Nendl glared at the man, but clamped his mouth shut.

"Tell us where your Hagemate is."

"I have not had a Hagemate in several years."

The man smiled patiently. "The one who has been living here with you—where is he? Answer quickly—we grow tired of your impertinence."

"I don't know who you mean."

"Liar!" the man roared. Smiling unexpectedly, he moved closer. "Try again. Where is he?"

"I don't know." Fear made Nendl's voice quiver.

The man spun on his heel. Nendl did not see the leg swing up and the foot snap out. The kick caught him on the point of the chin and drove his jaw backward, breaking off the lower front teeth and dislocating his jaw. Nendl fell backwards, blood spurting from his mouth. The man stood over him, smiling, then lifted his foot and ground it into the recycler's genitals. Nendl screamed.

"You should have shown us some courtesy, Hageman," said the man softly, watching his victim writhe on the floor. He turned away abruptly and jerked this thumb over his shoulder at Nendl. "Bring him," he said to his companion, and strode out.

TWENTY EIGHT

The message had been explicit; there was no mistake. Tvrdy had acted at once to arrange a meeting of the Cabal. Now he waited at the appointed place—a granary in Hyrgo deep Hage. He wore the green-sleeved yos of the Hyrgo and sat among bulging sacks of fresh-smelling grain. He waited patiently, knowing the others would join him soon, content to allow Piipo's personal bodyguard to keep watch over the meeting-place.

How long must we continue to practice our deceptions? he wondered. Not long, he guessed. One way or another there would be an end to their secret activity. The day was coming for open confrontation. He could feel the dread approach of that day in his bones. It would be a dark day. Yes, a dark, bloody day.

The quick flit of a shadowed figure hurrying along the aisle between the steep stacked bags of grain drew Tvrdy's attention away from his thoughts. He recognized the furtive step as that of Cejka's. He stood and welcomed his friend.

"No trouble tonight?" Tvrdy glanced past Cejka's shoulder—a reflex action born of years of exacting vigilance.

"I was not followed, nor was I seen. Don't worry."

"Did you see anyone else?"

"No one." Cejka studied him closely. "Should I have?"

"Piipo has several of his personals at watch. I thought it best to maintain extra security tonight."

"Your news is that important?"

A tight smile stretched the edges of Tvrdy's lips. "Do you think I would have pulled you from the arms of your Hagemate if it was not?"

"Listen!"

"That will be Piipo. He said he would come after us and seal the entrance. That way we will not fear discovery—at least while we are here."

There was a slight rustle of clothing close by, and Piipo

slipped into view from behind a small pyramid of grain sacks. He walked confidently toward them, his hood thrown back on his shoulders. "This is the best I could provide," he said, indicating their surroundings. "There was not much time." He regarded Tvrdy frankly.

"The information could no doubt have waited until tomorrow, but by then we might have lost an important opportunity to make contact with the intruder in Sirin's custody."

"Yes?" Piipo looked surprised.

"You were right to call us," said Cejka. "I wouldn't care to miss such an opportunity. How did you find out?"

Tvrdy settled back on his grain sack, and the others gathered close. "For several days I have been receiving reports of a stranger moving through the Hages in the company of a Saecaraz magician—a female called Calin. They have been careful not to go into deep Hage, but have moved freely enough among the populace. There does not seem to have been any attempt to disguise their visits."

"I have heard nothing of this," said Piipo.

"They came to Hyrgo two days ago," said Tvrdy dryly. "And to Rumon the day before that. It is not likely they would have been reported—the visits did not draw attention. They traveled on foot for the most part and were observed together at all times. There was nothing at all unusual about their visits."

"Then how do you know it *was* the intruder?" Piipo frowned, and Cejka glanced at him sharply. "I assure you I do not doubt your sources," Piipo hastily added. "But I don't see—"

"If Tvrdy says it was the intruder," Cejka cut him off decisively, "then stake your life on it."

Tvrdy raised his hands to quiet the two and continued. "Today, however, they stayed within Hage Saecaraz. In fact, they left the intruder's kraam three times only—yes, Sirin has given the intruder a kraam within the Supreme Director's chambers—and twice they went to see him in the audience room."

"A kraam for the spy?" wondered Piipo. "What does it mean?"

"And the third visit?" asked Cejka impatiently.

"To the Archives. They have not returned."

"The Archives!" Cejka gasped.

Piipo stared incredulously. "I don't understand. What does it mean?"

"It means," replied Cejka, recovering quickly, "that we may already be too late to learn much from the intruder. Either the psilobe has permanently altered his memory, or he has joined Rohee's reign."

"The Archives," Piipo muttered. "You put too much store by them. They cannot be that important."

"We have seen records—" began Cejka. Tvrdy warned him off with a stern glance. "You have no idea how important the Archives are. If we told you, you would not believe us."

"It is all old mother's prattle," Piipo scoffed.

"It doesn't matter," said Tvrdy. "All that matters now is whether we should risk trying to contact him. That is why I called you. I would not implicate you without your knowledge. If we tried and failed . . ."

Cejka nodded silently. Piipo looked from one to the other of his co-conspirators. Tvrdy's gaze was steady and patient. He had worked through the problem in his own mind, and wanted to allow the others a chance to reach the same conclusions for themselves.

"Well," Cejka said, breaking the silence which had grown heavy as the grain in the great vault of a room, "I see no other course but to try. We must be certain. And even if he has joined Rohee, we may discover a way to use him to help us gain entrance to the Archives."

"And you, Piipo?"

"I agree. In any case we have to know whether he has joined them or not. Yes, contact him as soon as possible."

"My thoughts exactly." Tvrdy beamed at them and began explaining his plan to make contact with the stranger. They discussed his plan from every angle and in the end agreed on how it should be carried out.

As they rose, stretched, and made to leave, Piipo asked, "Tell me—any news of our latest acquisition?"

Tvrdy shrugged. "Still too soon to tell. He was given a large dose—much larger than normal. They were taking no chances. But he is beginning to ask questions."

"That's a good sign," put in Cejka.

"Yes, there is some small hope. A partial recovery at least."

"What about the woman and the fourth intruder? Still no word?"

"The woman has been seen from a distance. Two attempts at contact have failed—the Chryse troupe she is with did not appear as scheduled. It could be that the troupe's leader has been instructed to keep her under close security." Tvrdy paused and added, "I wasn't going to tell you now—we've had enough bad news for one night . . ."

"Go on," urged Piipo, "we might as well hear it all. The night is too far gone for sleep anyway."

"The fourth intruder was taken to Starwatch level of Nilokerus several days ago. Condition uncertain, but he has been attended continuously by Ernina herself since his arrival."

"That's Jamrog's doing!" muttered Cejka.

"My source thinks not," replied Tvrdy. "There have been no official orders regarding his disposition upon recovery. I think Hladik is responsible and doesn't want anyone to know what has happened to the captive assigned to him."

"Conditioning?"

"That's my guess. I told you it was bad."

Piipo took a deep breath and squared his shoulders. "All the more reason to make contact with the remaining intruder as soon as possible. We are running out of alternatives." He smiled unexpectedly.

"Well? What is it, Piipo?" asked Cejka.

"Excuse me, I am still new to the ways of a cabal and I have difficulty believing in the need for such urgency. I am quickly learning, however, and I just had a thought. Why not take *all* the spies? We know where they are. It could be done. Isn't tomorrow a Holy Day?"

Tvrdy stared at Piipo, then broke into a wide grin. "Excellent! I like the way you think. I was afraid you were beginning to doubt your decision to join us."

"Never! It is the one thing I am pleased with in a very long time. I do not regret it. Once my word is given . . ."

Tvrdy clapped him on the shoulder. "It will soon get much worse, you know."

Piipo's smile broadened. "How else can it get better?"

The three sat down again and reformed the plan, each taking responsibility for securing one of the intruders. Another hour passed before they were satisfied and adjourned the Cabal. Piipo put his fist to his heart and then slipped away, dodging behind sacks of grain. Tvrdy and Cejka nodded silently, returned the salute, and then hurried off, leaving the way they had come.

• • • • •

Jamrog, forehead bulging menacingly, lips compressed into a tight line, twirled a bhuj between his quick hands. The spinning blade dashed light from its mirrored surface, flashing like the anger smouldering in the Director's eyes. Hladik sat to one side, frowning, dark brows pulled together into a ridge above his eyes, his jowls spreading over his collar.

Fertig, Nilokerus Subdirector, sweated into his yos and blurted out the rest of his news. ". . . but the usual procedures proved ineffectual. He lost consciousness when the second eye was burned out and died before we could administer revivants."

"What was he given before interrogation?" growled Hladik unhappily.

Fertig spread his hands in a show of innocence. "The usual pain enhancers. Nothing more. It was not known he had such a weak heart."

"Did you think to check his records?" Jamrog sneered.

"My men are better trained than that!" Hladik snapped. "Records are not kept on wastehandlers. Only the higher-order Jamuna have permanent files. This one was merely a recycler; the only record he possessed was his dole number. I looked into that myself."

Jamrog groaned and smashed the bhuj against the floor. A starburst pattern appeared in the cracked stone tile at his feet. "How is this possible?" he demanded. The Nilokerus at the ready behind Fertig stiffened.

"Calm down," Hladik soothed. With a wave he dismissed his aide, who, with the rest of the Nilokerus contingent, retreated gratefully without hesitation. "A third-order recycler's death—this Nendl, whoever he is—will not change anything. We'll get the spy back—where can he go? He has no friends; no one will help him. I would not be surprised if he were apprehended before the day was out."

"Are you really so stupid? Save your mindless chatter. I know better. We don't know how long Pizol has been missing. His absence was discovered this morning, but as far as we know he has not been seen for three days at least. Obviously he's been taken in somewhere. I suspect Tvrdy is behind this."

"What an accusation! Listen to yourself. Tvrdy is a Director, after all."

"A Director who will stop at nothing to worm his way into power over us. Don't be a fool. You know he is cunning. He's not a brainless lump like Dey or Bouc. Who can guess what he's thinking in that tight mind of his?" He glared at Hladik, defying him to contradict this.

"I know you and Tvrdy have your differences—"

"Differences? Hah! He'd kill me without a second's hesitation if I ever gave him the chance—and I would do the same. We are enemies, Haldik. Or are you talking this way because you are weakening?"

Hladik pulled a hurt face. So far his little exercise had accomplished his goal: averting Jamrog from further questioning him about their other prisoner—the one he had nearly killed through the conditioning. That had been his own idea, a little insurance. If Jamrog ever found out—better not to think it. That was inviting disaster. With any luck the spy would recover before Jamrog suspected anything was wrong. He made a mental note to pay the prisoner a personal visit.

Jamrog, still scowling, flung out his hand. "Stop playing the wounded innocent and tell me what we are to do now."

"As I said, Pizol will be found soon. In all probability he is still within Jamuna Hage. He will turn up. All dole kiosks have been alerted. It's only a matter of a few hours. Leave it with me."

"I wish I had your confidence, Hladik. All right, I will leave it with you."

Glad to change the subject, Hladik asked, "What have you learned about the Fieri spacecraft?"

"Very little. Their magic is of a different kind than ours. Completely different. Much of it is incomprehensible, although there are a few minor similarities, I am told."

"Is it genuine?"

"Yes, very much so. And that is the mystery of it. If the Fieri have regained flight, why did they send such a small force? It makes no sense."

"I begin to think we may have to interrogate the spy under Rohee's custody after all. I understand the Supreme Director has given him a kraam in the High Chambers. He's mad."

"Sirin is old but not insane. He has his reasons. We would do well to find out what they are before moving against the spy he has befriended." Jamrog fixed his eyes on a spot over Hladik's dark head. "I wonder—" He tapped the staff of the bhuj gently in his hand.

"Yes?"

"I wonder if we have not made a mistake in placing the intruders in Hage so quickly. You should have killed them."

Hladik's answer was direct. "The Supreme Director wished otherwise. We chose the best course open to us. If the Dhogs had found out about them, who knows what could have happened? This way we have kept them safely hidden from their own, and beyond the reach of Tvrdy's faction too."

"Ah, so now you admit that Tvrdy has a faction, do you?"

Hladik answered benignly, "Of course, was there ever any doubt?"

Jamrog's lips twitched in a thin, ruthless smile. "It seems to me he has shown less than a healthy interest in Threl unity of late. I think Tvrdy's kraam could bear additional watching."

"An excellent idea. I will see to it."

"Use Invisibles—this is no reflection on your security forces, but the fewer people who know about this the better. Agreed? I will see that Sirin sends his authorization at once."

Hladik nodded, pulling his chin thoughtfully. "If Tvrdy and his little enclave are up to something, we'll soon know it."

TWENTY
NINE

As Treet stood peering into the gathering gloom, wondering how and where to start searching for his lost guide, he saw what appeared to be a faint glimmer of light reflecting off the metallic surface of a large cylindrical object which rose up from behind the foremost rank of a series of stacked ventilator louver frames. He stared at the glow and it did not go away. So, tapping for the ledge's edge, he made his way toward the place, waving his hands in front of him like a blind man.

Ducking around a pile of motor housings, Treet lost sight of the light momentarily and spent a panicky few seconds trying to gain his bearings. When he found it again, the dull, yellow radiance was much closer than he had expected. He crept carefully around a pile of filthy hydroponic seeder tubes and stepped into a little circle of light cast by a yellow globe lamp on a stand. Beneath the lamp was what appeared to be an open, oval manhole in the floor.

Treet knelt down and hollered into the manhole. "Calin! Are you down there? Calin?"

He waited, received no answer, and cautiously placed his hand into the void while his mind constructed grisly pictures of Calin's broken body lying crumpled at the bottom far below. Dangling his arm just inside the hole, Treet found what he was looking for: the rungs of a metal ladder attached to the side of the hole just beneath the rim. He eased himself down into the hole, placing his feet gingerly on the unseen rungs.

If she had fallen in, wouldn't he have heard a scream or something? And who had turned on the globe? Maybe she hadn't fallen, he thought as he went down slowly, placing his feet securely on one rung after another. Perhaps she had climbed down—as he was doing—in order to check out what was hidden below. Then again, perhaps she was nowhere near the manhole in the first place.

He touched the floor and looked up to see the bright oval above him—a good five meters. He squatted on his haunches and touched the floor: dry, but not dusty. As far as he could tell, it was perfectly clean. There was no body huddled beneath the rungs, so he straightened and stretched out his arms. Fingertips brushing the walls on either side, he began to walk. The passage led down a fairly steady incline, and the walls were seamed at intervals, which made Treet think of pipe rather than a corridor. Perhaps this tube was part of a disused drainage system. If so, there was no real point in continuing the search—there was no telling where the pipeline led.

Just as Treet had made up his mind to turn around and go back, he came to a junction box. Two other large pipes converged to join into one enormous conduit, which showed a light a little further along. Treet entered the conduit and felt his way toward the light.

In a moment he stood blinking in the entrance to a large underground gallery lit with vapor tubes in long parallel lines above row upon row of metal shelving stacked with lightprint disks and holoreader cartridges. Amidst an untidy mound of disks sat Calin, her nose in a blue plastic-bound notebook.

"Comfortable?" Treet stepped into the room, gazing along the shelves and at the dark-haired magician engrossed with the book in her lap.

Calin smiled and looked up. "I have found a find," she said proudly, holding out the notebook to him.

Treet stooped to retrieve the book and closed its brittle cover to read the label: *Interpretive Chronicles—1270 to 1485*.

"Indeed you have, dear sorceress," said Treet softly. "You've found the granddaddy find."

"Banzai jackpot!" she shouted, beaming.

"Quadruple banzai jackpot!" He raised his eyes to look at the long rows of neatly arranged materials. It was all here—everything he needed, at his fingertips. "Do you have any idea what this means? It means that you have saved us both a carking fat lot of work, among other things."

He held the notebook in his hands and flipped it open at random. The pages were acid-free printout paper—thank the gods of small favors for that—written in a crisp hand, clear and readable in black ink. The margins were wide all around, allowing for the notes which had been added and initialed at a later date and in a different hand.

The dates caught Treet's attention. They were all wrong—unless, of course, the colony had simply begun its own reckoning. Even then, could they be right? He turned back to the title on the cover. 1485? Nearly fifteen hundred years?

He was convinced beyond the shadow of a doubt that the time displacement or compression or whatever involved probably several hundred years at least. But a millenium-and-a-half? Judging from the amount of material gathered on the long ranks of gray metal shelves, fifteen hundred years was just the beginning.

"Where did you get this notebook?" he asked, handing it back.

Calin pointed to a nearby shelf where a row of orange, blue, and green notebooks stood in an orderly row. "There are many more of these," she said.

"So I see." Treet stepped up to the shelf and scanned the dates on the spines of the notebooks. He called them out. "Foundation to 98, 110 to 543, 586 to 833, 860 to 1157 . . ." He ran his fingers along the row of notebooks as he moved to the end. "Incredible!" he cried as he came to the end. "It goes all the way to 2273!"

His head snapped around. "Calin, what year is this?" Why had he never asked her before?

The magician's face scrunched in thought. "It is the year 1481, I think. So say the priests."

That's why I never asked her before—they're dating from something other than the foundation of the colony. Think! There must be a key here somewhere. He scanned the orderly row of books. "If I go back 1,481 years—" He ran his finger along the spines of the notebooks, stopped, and frowned. "No, that's no good. I don't know how much time has elapsed since these books were placed here." His frown deepened.

At least he knew that the colony was 2,273 years old, and probably a whole lot older. The key to this mystery lay somewhere in these books, but finding it would take time.

Resisting the impulse to pull them all out at once, Treet went back to the beginning and gently tugged out the first notebook. The paper fluttered in his shaking hands as he read the first page. It was a personal note from the author, framed in the same steady, precise handwriting:

TO ALL WHO COME AFTER:
    These books are the work of one man's life. Treat them with respect. This record of Empyrion has been assembled from

many diverse sources, some of which were not completely reliable. It will be hard for anyone of a more enlightened age to understand the repression under which I have labored.

Where there are errors, know that they could not be avoided. I leave them for you to correct. But know, too, that what you hold in your hands is the truth—as far as can be told. I have told everything in the books.

Feodr Rumon
After Arrival 2273

Treet reread the short note and felt the uncanny sensation that the words had been written to him personally. He wondered how many others had read them. At least one other, judging from the margin notes he'd seen.

This was a find, all right. The one and only genuine original find of a lifetime. Trouble was, he was the only person in the whole wide universe who knew its significance. Not that certain others wouldn't be interested—Rohee for one, Chairman Neviss for another.

The Chairman's name triggered a chain reaction in his mind. Of course! It all fit. What a pinhead I've been, he thought. I should have guessed what was going on long ago. Of course Neviss knew what had happened—or had a Harvard-educated hunch—knew that the time distortion factor had royally screwed up the works. What was it that Neviss had said in their too-brief interview? Treet closed his eyes and remembered the words exactly: "The proposition I have in mind has to do with this colony. I want your help in solving a problem there."

So *this* was the "problem" Neviss had alluded to but never explained: a trifling matter of a few thousand lost years to be accounted for. Nothing to it. Send up a starving historian who'd sell his eldest daughter (if he had one) to the United Arab Emirates for a chance at the most significant historical discovery of the last several centuries and you could rest easy. Orion Tiberias Treet—bless his simple, hoodwinked heart—was on the job. He'd die kicking and screaming bloody murder before he'd let anyone deflect him from the trail once he got the scent.

And it had worked. Treet cursed the scheming Chairman and his smarmy assistant Varro and all of Cynetics' vast holdings and chattels. Yet, he admired the beauty of it. Despite himself, his historian's soul luxuriated in the golden glow of discovery. Although he had a good mind to call down the fates of economic failure upon Neviss and company, he also felt gratitude for being chosen to make the trip.

"That devious old scoundrel," murmured Treet, closing the notebook and placing it carefully back on the shelf, "trapped me with honey. He knew all along I wouldn't be able to help myself."

He turned to see Calin watching him closely. "Something is wrong?" she asked.

He grabbed her, gave her a big, sloppy kiss on the side of the mouth, and roared, "Nothing is right, my fine magician, but nothing is wrong." He released her and whirled back to the shelves. "Now then, let's see what other goodies are here, shall we?"

He scanned the ordered ranks of disks and cartridges, each and every one containing some piece to the Empyrion puzzle. Where to start, he wondered. At the beginning, like a good schoolboy? Or work back from the end, which might be quicker in some respects? Treet sighed. Why rush? He had nothing but time on his hands.

Starwatch level was nearly deserted as Hladik and his guide moved along the upper terraces and rimwalks. "Stay here and wait for me," he told the guide as he entered the physicians' cluster and walked among the beds there. Most were empty, but he wasted no time searching the others—he knew where to find the one he was looking for.

In a separate chamber two third-order physicians bent over the inert body in the suspension bed. As Hladik appeared, both straightened. "Good evening, Hage Leader," they said in unison, bowing at the waist. The physician nearest him added, "We were just about to—"

"Leave us. I wish to see the patient alone."

"Of course, Hage Leader." The physician took his instruments in his hands and nodded to his colleague; both backed from Director Hladik's presence.

Hladik approached the bed and peered down at the sleeping man. Although the slack features were pasty and deep blue circles swelled beneath the eyes, on the whole the patient's color had improved since the last time he'd seen him. Good, he was out of danger. "Kolari," Hladik whispered, using the postconditioning trigger name, "this is your Director. Do you hear me? Wake up."

The eyelids fluttered and opened, revealing dull, listless eyes beneath. "I am glad to see you are feeling better." He paused and glanced around. "Do you remember your theta key?"

The head bobbed once, then again. Excellent! The conditioning has succeeded, thought Hladik. "Good. I want to hear it. Repeat the theta key now."

Crocker spoke, his voice hollow, wasted. "The Fieri are our enemies. If they try to contact me, I go with them. I remain alert so that I may return and tell you where they hide. If anyone interferes . . ."

"Yes?"

"I kill them."

"Very good. Rest now. Close your eyes and sleep. You will forget that I was here. But you will remember your theta key."

THIRTY

Asquith Pizzle blinked his eyes and rolled out of bed. For the third night in a row he had been awakened by a feeling of suffocation. It started as a pressure in his chest which grew so great that his heart thumped wildly against his rib cage until his breathing stopped. In his sleep-sodden consciousness, it felt as though some dark malevolent being straddled him, pressing giant splayed thumbs against his windpipe, tighter and tighter, choking him until he awoke, panting and out of breath.

The feeling of immense oppression dwindled as Pizzle pulled on his yos, leaving only a quivery sensation through his midsection. Dressed, he sat on the edge of the bed, staring at the ceiling of the bare room, wondering for the nine billionth time in the last three days why he was here.

The man—Tvrdy, was his name—had helped him. He was sure of that. He could trust Tvrdy, even if he could not trust his own memory. And this was the mystery: where had he come from, why was he here, and where were the others who had come with him?

Each day he remembered more—as if the thick sheet of glacial ice which had frozen his memory melted a little more, uncovering a few more precious acres of once-hidden terrain.

He now remembered, imperfectly, faces of others whom he felt certain had come to this place with him. He remembered, too, that he had not always been in this room of Tvrdy's. He had been with someone else, had done something before coming here. But it was all fuzzy in his mind; he could have imagined it. Certainly most of what he remembered had an ethereal, dreamlike quality.

But Tvrdy had helped him there too, providing what he called a guide to lead him back along forgotten pathways to retrieve important facts and events. Under Pradim's gentle prodding, he had made considerable progress, though he still had a long way to go.

As Pizzle sat on his bed thinking, his hand strayed up to his face. Something was wrong there. What was it? The beard that had begun to straggle over his unshaven chin? No, his ears . . . or eyes . . . *glasses*. The word came to him from out of nowhere, spinning into his consciousness like a windblown leaf.

I wear glasses, he thought. Or once did. What happened to them? What has happened to me? An inky jet of melancholy gushed up inside him, filling him with phantom grief for all he had lost—or imagined he had lost, for he really did not know precisely what his former life had been like. But the feeling was strong, a tide that swelled and flowed over and through him, tugging him along. A big tear formed in the corner of each eye. He bent his head.

When Pradim came in a few moments later, Pizzle had not moved. The guide came quietly around the suspension bed to stand in front of him. "Pizol, our Hageman has returned. He wants you. Come with me now."

Pizzle raised his face, wiped his eyes with the heels of his hands, and got up. "Your misery?" asked Tvrdy's guide.

"Yes, but I'm all right. I remembered that I used to wear glasses. It seemed important."

"Glasses?" Pradim looked at him strangely. "Are you sure?"

"I'm sure."

They went through two rooms to the small inner chamber, Tvrdy's quiet room. The Tanais Director was waiting for them when they came in. "Thank you, Pradim. Go now and do as I instructed you. Bring me back word straightaway when everything is ready. Traudl is waiting for the signal. And tell Amuneet to stay close by in case I need anything. She can bring in breakfast as soon as it's ready. I'm hungry, and there will be no more sleep tonight."

Pradim vanished and Pizzle entered the room, sitting opposite Tvrdy on a low, cushioned chair. He had come to enjoy these interviews with Tvrdy; they helped ease his mind.

"I'm glad you are awake, Pizol. I would have had to disturb you otherwise." Tvrdy spoke gently and easily, but Pizzle saw fatigue in the down-turned lines of the Director's face and the slump of his shoulders.

"I couldn't sleep."

Neither could I." Tvrdy studied him a long moment, weighing him, gauging him for what would come next. Pizzle felt his interest quicken, and desperately hoped that he would measure up to whatever Tvrdy had to say so Tvrdy would tell him what was on his mind. Pizzle waited, feeling his nerves tighten with anticipation.

Finally Tvrdy spoke. "I have two things to tell you, Hageman Pizol." His voice was quiet, but his tone flat and hard, betraying an undercurrent of tension. "The first is this: there is trouble coming which I cannot prevent. You will be involved. You must get ready for it; I will help however I can, but it is up to you to equip yourself." He paused and when Pizzle did not say anything, nodded and continued. "The second thing I wanted to tell you is that I think it is time you knew about your friends."

"You know about the others?" Pizzle sat up. "I remember them—their faces. I *knew* I did not come alone."

"No, you did not. There were three others with you. We have found them, and so far they are safe—although they have been given psilobe too, and remember no more than you. They have been hidden within Hage, but we have seen them."

"Hidden? I—I don't understand. Why can't I see them?"

Tvrdy looked at him sadly, drew a hand over his face, and lay back against the cushions of his chair. "It is not easy to explain, but I will put it as simply as I can." He paused, his lips pouting in thought. At last he said, "There are some among us who thirst for power. Very soon they will force a confrontation which my friends and I cannot ignore."

"The trouble you spoke of just now?"

"That's right. If they win the struggle, there will be a Purge. In such event, the Threl Directorate would be overthrown, any who opposed them would be crushed, the Hages would be decimated. No one would be safe."

"And my friends are being held by these people?" Pizzle slumped in his chair. "You said you knew where they were."

"They have been seen, but not contacted. You are the only one we have been able to secure. And now that you have disappeared, the others will be much more difficult to reach. One is with the Chryse—a woman . . ."

"Long black hair, dark eyes. Slender with long limbs?"

Tvrdy smiled and nodded. "Good, you remember her. The other two are men—one, we recently discovered, is under care of the physicians."

"Is he all right? What happened to him?"

"We don't know. He was injured in some way, perhaps when you were brought in."

"And the other?"

"For some reason he was taken by the Supreme Director and has been given a kraam of his own in Threl High Chambers and freedom to move around. He is watched, of course, but we think Threl Leader is using him for some private purpose. We don't know what it is. It is possible he may have joined them."

"Light hair or dark?" Pizzle tried to think which of the two faces he remembered would have joined the opposition.

"He is a big man. Dark hair, heavy brows, and square head."

Pizzle nodded. Yes, that described one of the faces. "Treet!" The name spurted out and with it a dizzying string of associated images, as if another wedge had been removed in the logjam of memory, releasing its jumbled store. Pizzle sat stunned as the torrent of recollection tumbled through his mind.

"You remember something now," replied Tvrdy, gazing at Pizzle closely. He sensed what was happening behind the man's dazed eyes, and wondered if this was the time he had been waiting for—time to ask the question he most desperately wanted an answer to. He hesitated, then leaned forward, touched Pizzle on the arm with his hand, and asked, "Tell me, Hageman, are you a Fieri?"

Yarden followed the troupe along a low-lying rimwall through still-dark streets. Far above, the faceted planes of the dome pearled gray as new sunlight struck them. It was early morning, and they were on their way to what Bela had called an Astral Service.

"You'll see," he had said when she asked what it was. "Here, take this." He held out a pale, thin wafer. When she had hesitated, he added, "For your memory. I've explained that this will help you. You've taken them before, remember?"

She had taken the wafer and held it in her palm. Its center was discolored by a light purplish stain. She lifted it to her mouth.

"Bela, we should be going. The sanctuary will be filled before we get there, and we'll have to sit in the back," Dera had complained. She fixed Yarden with an icy stare and tugged Bela away.

"We're going now," he had said, sweeping Dera to him with his arm. "Come on, everyone! We will be late for the Service," he called as the troupe straggled together and led the way out of his crowded kraam.

Yarden had hurried after them. As much as she feared the Service, she did not want to be seen lagging behind. However, as soon as they reached the plaza outside the kraam block, she let herself fall to the rear of the party. As the troupe proceeded along walkways planted with ragged hedgerows, Yarden pulled her hand from the folds of her yos and, certain that no one was watching, dropped the wafer Bela had given her into the bushes. She then quickened her pace and overtook the last of the troupe.

At first Yarden had taken the wafers Bela gave her, believing that they were helping her remember. But the small white disks with the faint spot of purple in the center had the reverse effect—they increased the inertia of remembering and made her more forgetful, her memory more remote and ill-defined. This she noticed the third time she tasted the bland crust on her tongue.

Thereafter she had avoided taking them, successfully hiding the fact from Bela, whose insistence had made her suspicious. As a result, her memory improved dramatically. She now knew herself to be different from those around her, knew that she did not belong to the Chryse, knew that theirs was a world foreign to her. She also nursed an airy belief that she was separated from others of her own kind who could help her—a belief which, thanks to her intuitive distrust of Bela's drug-laced wafers, was hardening into a fair certainty.

Be patient, she told herself, it will come to you. Use your mind; fight the laziness. *Think!* Concentrate on the past. Try to remember. It will come back.

That was how she spent her every waking moment, fending off the lethargy which had been cast like a pall over her mental functions, peeling back that deadening numbness to free whatever lay trapped beneath. She was careful not to mention to anyone what she was doing, lest Bela find out. Careful, too, to keep up the dazed and perpetually confused demeanor which had first characterized her.

After palming the wafer for the second time—they were

given to her at two-day intervals—she knew that Bela was not her friend and that he meant to stop her from remembering. Why this should be, she couldn't say. However, since the encounter with the hideous Hage Priest she felt it as strongly as she felt the importance of restoring as much as she possibly could of her memory. And with each passing day the potency of the drug diminished, unlocking more of her memory.

Yarden kept her eyes open as she followed the Chryse band out of deep Hage toward the river she had been told ran through the center of Empyrion. In an hour or so they came to a wide, tree-lined plaza. Across the square, through the thin, gnarled, leaf-shy trees, the Kyan flowed dull behind its low-walled bank.

In the center of the plaza stood a great squatty black pyramid with ramps leading up from all sides. People streamed across the square, moved up the ramps, and disappeared inside the pyramid through pillared entrances. At the sight of the pyramid, the troupe surged forward and hastened across the white, stone-flagged square to the pyramid. Yarden unwillingly joined the crush of people forming at the foot of the incline and moved slowly up.

As the low arch closed over her head, Yarden experienced a sudden and overwhelming sensation of suffocation. She staggered, gasped, and clutched the sleeve of the Chryse nearest her, another young woman named Mina. The player took Yarden's arm and guided her into the sanctuary.

Inside the Astral Temple, the sensation of oppression swelled. It was as though a heavy object lay on her chest and constricted her breathing passages. Try as she might, she could not draw sufficient air into her lungs. She grew dizzy and her vision narrowed, becoming a pinched, black-bounded, unfocused field. Shapes swirled around her: indistinct and chaotic movement accompanied with bursts of raking sound. The voices around her were magnified into terrible shrieks, piercing her ears and penetrating her skull like hot knives.

Powerless to stop or turn or flee, Yarden was pushed deeper into the sanctuary by the press of bodies flowing into the pyramid temple. She reeled forward and was eventually pushed into a seat at the end of a long row. The influx surged past her; she became separated from her troupe in the moil of bodies.

Shaken, she sat down to await a thinning in the stream of worshipers, her only thought to get far away from the dreadful temple as soon as possible.

She watched and, when the human traffic abated, struggled to her feet, hands gripping the back of the seat. But as she stepped into the aisle, the light changed. She looked back toward the entrance where priests labored to slide enormous door panels into place, sealing the entrances. In moments the interior of the temple was plunged into stifling darkness.

Yarden collapsed back into her seat, a scream rising in her throat. Trapped! she thought, fighting to keep herself under control. *I am trapped!*

THIRTY ONE

Treet raised burning eyes and closed the book in his lap. His brain buzzed with information. He felt as if his skull had been opened up and the contents of a very large data bank dumped in and then stirred with a stick for good measure. How do I make sense of all this? he wondered, looking at the blue notebook in his hands. It—it's like nothing I've ever read.

Correction—it is exactly like something I've read: one of those ancient historical works penned by quasiliterate scribes in the dark ages.

However, knowing that it came to him from three thousand years in the future, in a manner of speaking, made the reading of it eerie and unsettling. Why unsettling? He looked again at the blue notebook, and the answer came to him: that manuscript, lettered so neatly by hand on computer printout paper . . . the subtle juxtaposition was strangely symbolic. Here was an artifact of a far-flung future, reeking of the long-gone past.

Or vice versa. Treet couldn't decide which. He still had trouble thinking of himself as having arrived in the colony three thousand years in its future, but that's the way the numbers added up. It made his mind flip-flop to think that he stood looking at a civilization that old when, strictly speaking, back on Earth none of the things described in the notebook had happened yet.

It was true. If he were strolling the Piazza D'fortuna in Fiorenze, Italy, right now and stopped to gawk up at the stars, chancing to glimpse that small spark of light called Epsilon Eridani, Empyrion's first colonists would still be poring over their initial environment probes of a virgin world. Yet, in this place and time those probes had happened so long ago they were not even remembered.

How is this possible? wondered Treet. Old Belthausen and

his *Interstellar Travel Theory* didn't know the half of it. Nothing he'd read in that book, with its incomprehensible charts, dizzy diagrams, and endless dry calculations, had prepared him for this.

He returned the blue notebook to its place in the center of the row of colored notebooks. It was the one Calin had pulled out at random; he had intended to begin at the beginning like a good and diligent scholar, but in flipping through the book he had become so absorbed in it he'd read it straight through. It had raised more questions than it answered, unfortunately. But at least he had glimpsed something of the scope his inquiry would have to take. And he knew a great deal about what had happened between the years 1270 and 1485—eventful years for the Empyrion colony.

During that time the enormous work of sealing Empyrion under the fabulous crystal domes had been completed, enclosing the eight separate cities of the Cluster. A deadly second Purge had shaken Empyrion to its core when the death of the first Supreme Director touched off a string of Directorate assassinations, ending in a citizen's revolt and the ultimate establishment of the Threl.

It was this last event, he had discovered, that the colony now dated from. The year 1485 added to the current year 1481 equalled 2,966—slightly less than three thousand years. Unbelievable, but true. He had arrived 2,966 years into Empyrion colony's future and stood looking down a long corridor of years at monumental and life-changing events.

Interspersed with these major events were smaller happenings, faithfully recorded by the patron saint of Rumon Hage: the yearly fluctuations in productivity, the rise and fall of birthrates and deathrates among the populace, the institution of assigned marriage, the abolition of assigned marriage, the slow succession of Directors, the dredging of Kyan, the advent of the poak, and much more. There was little doubt in Treet's mind that were he to read each and every volume, as he indeed intended, he would find them all equally exacting and painstakingly precise as the one he'd just finished.

Here in this orderly row of long-hidden notebooks were the answers to all his questions—including the primary one: what had gone wrong? He still didn't know the answer to that, nor to the other ten thousand that occurred to him, such as, who were the Fieri and why were they so hated in the first place? What had caused the first Purge? How had the colony been governed before the Directorate? Why had the Cluster been closed? And on and on. But the answers were here within his grasp—thanks to Feodr Rumon, who, nearly seven hundred years ago, had hidden his books in the unused sewer below the Archives.

Treet unfolded himself from his squatting position on the floor and stretched stiff muscles. How long had he been sitting there? Four hours? Eight? It seemed only minutes, but his back assured him it had been much longer. Next time he'd have to make sure to bring a chair—he looked around to see Calin sound asleep, stretched out on the floor behind him—and a bed wouldn't be a bad idea either.

"Rise and shine, Calin," said Treet, still pressing his knuckles into the small of his back, trying to loosen the kinks. "I've had enough for one night. It's time to go back." He stooped and shook her shoulder gently, lingering over the feel of her warmth through the silken smoothness of the yos.

She moved, and Treet withdrew his hand. She came fully awake and glanced around, remembered where they were, and relaxed again. "Yes, we're still down in the cellar, but it's time to go." Treet extended a hand to her and lifted her up. For a moment they stood close, then Calin lowered her eyes and stepped away.

"You wish to go back to your kraam now?" she asked.

"I'm exhausted. We'll sleep, get something to eat, and then come back here." He let his gaze travel the length of the room, sweeping the shelves and well-ordered rows. "There's a lot to do, and I want to get at it."

Calin nodded and then led them back into the pipeline. Treet walked beside her. "Tell me," he said, as they felt their way along in the darkness, "how did you know the secret room was down there?"

"I used my psi," she answered simply. "I knew it was there when I found it."

Treet thought about this. "Of course. But if you didn't know it was there until you found it, how did you know where to look for it?"

"My psi showed me."

"Your psi."

"You wanted to find records and disks, you said—about people. I asked my psi to show me. He led me to the place."

"*He* led you? Your psi is a *he*?" For a second it seemed like she was talking about some kind of psychic ability or magic. Now she implied that her psi was a person. "Explain him."

"Each magician receives energy from his psi—one of the higher entities who are part of the Universal Oversoul. The psi energy bodies give magicians their powers."

"Universal Oversoul? That sounds noo-noo na-na to me, Calin. I don't believe in any such thing."

Calin seemed not to mind his agnosticism. She continued, "I asked Nho—that's the name of my psi entity—where to find the records you sought. He led me."

"Yeah. Well, whatever." Obviously the trick worked, however it was accomplished. Who was he to argue with success?

They came to the junction box, took the left branch, followed the pipe to the metal ladder, and climbed it to the oval manhole above. The skylight wells cut into the ceiling of the Archives showed daylight once again. They'd spent the entire night in the hidden room. "Was this just open like this?" Treet indicated the oval hole in the floor.

"No, I uncovered it." Calin pointed to a massive cylinder.

In the faint daylight Treet saw a wide ring around the manhole. The circumference of the ring corresponded precisely to the circumference of the standing cylinder.

Calin touched the nearby lamp, and the globe went dark. She removed it and walked to the cylinder, placed her hands flat on its sides, closed her eyes, and grew very still—just as she had done with the computer terminal. A few seconds of silence ticked by, and Treet saw the huge metal vessel move. He stared as the cylinder trembled and raised from the floor the merest fraction of a centimeter and hovered toward the hole. The slender magician, palms still flat against the sides, not guiding so much as merely maintaining contact, did not appear under any stress at all. If the enormous object—it must easily have weighed several tons—caused her any strain, she did not show it. Her face remained as calm and expressionless as it had in sleep.

Treet gaped as the cylinder settled into exactly the same spot as before. "That's what I call impressive," he said softly.

Calin stepped from the cylinder and turned to face Treet. "Nho's energy is strong. It flows from the Universal Oversoul; I am merely a channel."

They threaded their way back to the entrance where the

Saecaraz Hage priest still slept. They climbed back up the wide steps to stand over the priest. Treet nudged him with a toe. "Should we just leave him here?"

"He must make a report to Rohee."

"How can he do that? He's been asleep the whole time." Treet kicked him gently and raised his voice. "Come on, Sleeping Beauty! On your feet—it's your turn to dance."

"Mff-ugh," the priest snorted. He climbed clumsily to his feet and shook out his yos; the creases were sharp and probably permanent. With a suspicious glare at Treet, he snatched up his black-handled ropes and retreated back through the Archives entrance.

Treet pressed his full weight against the door. It boomed shut, and he resealed the entrance before joining Calin, who was waiting a little way up the passage. The priest was nowhere in sight.

"He didn't waste any time, did he?" said Treet.

"Today is a Service day. All Hages celebrate the Service, and all priests officiate."

"A high Holy Day, is that it? Well, sorry I'll have to miss it. I've got more important things to do—like sleep." He yawned and they started off, back toward the first of many sets of metal doors fifty meters away.

Ernina sat over a bowl of spiced chayote broth, dipping a rusk to soften it. She pondered the night's reading: a book about genetic factors in blood and circulatory system diseases. As always, she was left awed and a little depressed by the ancients' skill and knowledge. Their words spoke to her across a chasm of years; they, long dead and forgotten, knew secrets she could hardly grasp—even when she read them for herself. Such knowledge, such power they had possessed.

Where had it all gone? Cynetics gives, and Cynetics takes away, she sighed. Even that name, once holy and spoken only with greatest reverence, had lost its significance. No one believed in Cynetics anymore. In fact, most of the lower-order Hagemen did not believe the ancients had ever existed. Even the priests had long ago stopped reciting the Credo in worship.

She sighed again, raised the soggy rusk to her mouth, and chewed thoughtfully. These last few days a pensive, almost wistful longing had filled her waking moments. She found herself returning again and again in her mind to thoughts of the elder times. This, she knew, was due to the presence of the Fieri in the room beyond her own.

His body of bones and flesh and blood was a living link between the here and now and those far-distant days, the First Days. His existence was proof of the Credo of Cynetics; and instead of bowing at his feet in all humility and honor, ignorant men like Hladik and Jamrog and all the rest did their best to extinguish memory of the old ones by hounding any who still revered them, reorienting believers or killing them outright.

It was madness—madness born of hate. Ernina had seen enough of it in her life to know that hate was the twisted child of fear. Why did they hate so? What did they fear that they had to destroy even the memory of a race long deceased?

But they were *not* all deceased. The Fieri in the next room attested to that. Somewhere, somehow they still existed. And this, no doubt, was what the small-minded men feared.

Ernina sipped the last of her broth and placed her bowl on its tray. She rose, went to her inner room, and closed the book she had been reading, then put it safely away.

Today perhaps her special patient would feel like talking. He was recovering rapidly. Soon he would be able to walk. And then what? He would go back to Hladik.

No; not if she could help it. The Dhogs knew and protected one another. The Dhogs, Hageless nonbeings, lived out a shadowy existence in the no-man's-land of the ruined Old Section, it was believed. She had never seen one, or known anyone who had. But if the rumors held any truth at all, they must have leaders and there must be a way to reach them.

In that moment Ernina made up her mind. She would risk all to contact the Dhogs. What does it matter if I am caught? she thought. What can they do to me they have not already done to many others? They can kill me but once. I will see this Fieri safely hidden among the Dhogs. At least they will know how to help him.

She heard a movement in the patient's quarters, and dashed back through her rooms. It was too early; he mustn't try to walk yet, even if he did feel stronger. He needed rest.

Ernina entered the room and froze. The bed was empty, her patient gone.

217

THIRTY
TWO

*I*n the darkness of the sanctuary Yarden huddled in her seat, knuckles pressed against teeth. She waited. The mass of bodies around her waited too, hushed and expectant. The air within the temple vibrated with the pulse of three thousand bodies, all straining for the moment of release and transcendence. All except Yarden who waited only for release from the stifling temple.

From the rear of the sanctuary a low, thrumming sound began, and a purple light shone down on the celebrants from above. Presently a line of priests carrying thick, smoking tapers appeared, moving slowly down the wide aisles from the four corners of the pyramid. They walked backward, chanting. M-M-M-Ah-Ah-O-O-O! M-M-M-Ah-Ah-O-O-O! The sound rose on the first syllable and fell on the second. M-M-M-Ah-Ah-O-O-O!

The congregation picked up the chant, and soon the entire temple hummed with the deep, resonant sound: M-M-M-Ah-Ah-O-O-O! M-M-M-Ah-Ah-O-O-O! M-M-M-Ah-Ah-O-O-O!

The chant grew in volume. M-M-M-Ah-Ah-O-O-O! M-M-M-Ah-Ah-O-O-O! Pulsing. Throbbing. M-M-M-Ah-Ah-O-O-O! M-M-M-Ah-Ah-O-O-O! The sound vibrated eardrums and diaphragm. It bored into the skull; the brain quivered with it. M-M-M-Ah-Ah-O-O-O! M-M-M-Ah-Ah-O-O-O! The blood pulsed with the rising sound. M-M-M-Ah-Ah-O-O-O! M-M-M-Ah-Ah-O-O-O!

The tempo quickened. M-M-Ah-O-O! M-M-Ah-O-O! The priests came closer. M-M-Ah-O-O! M-M-Ah-O-O! The candles stank of burning hair and fat. The priests moved backward down the aisles, holding their flickering lights high. M-M-Ah-O-O! M-M-Ah-O-O!

They reached the front of the sanctuary, came together, and placed their foul lights on stands, then raised their hands high above their heads. M-M-Ah-O-O! M-M-Ah-O-O! On each raised palm was the painted symbol of an eye, glowing faintly in the purplish light. M-M-Ah-O-O! M-M-Ah-O-O!

The entire temple rocked with the chant, now louder and more insistent. M-Ah-O! M-Ah-O! It rumbled from five thousand throats. Swelling. Booming. Rolling. M-Ah-O! M-Ah-O!

The sound was deafening. Yarden pressed her hands to her ears to keep it out, but the horrid noise beat through her palms and into her brain. She squeezed her eyes shut tight and held her head. M-Ah-O! M-Ah-O! M-Ah-O! M-Ah-O-O-M-M-M-M-M-m-m-m. . . .

The chant died away to a whisper.

The sanctuary shimmered in sparkling silence. Yarden looked at the faces of those around her. Bathed in the soft violet light, each was a mask of intense animal expectation—relaxed and ready, features slack, eyes alert, but vacant and inhuman. Yarden turned away from the sight of those blank faces and cringed back in her seat.

She forced her eyes back to the front of the sanctuary where a smaller pyramid, radiating a pinkish light from within, rose slowly up behind the row of priests. When the radiant pyramid came to a stop, suspended in the air above the priests, a seam opened in its side and it split into two halves, scattering rays of rosy light through the smoke-drenched air of the temple.

A faint, wispy music accompanied the opening of the pyramid—less music than the sound of air rushing over the mouthpiece of a flute, or wind sounding the open mouths of empty jars. From within the luminous pyramid came a voice, deep and sonorous. It spoke as from the depths of some dark recess, echoing through the sanctuary:

"Hear your god and remember!"

The celebrants responded in one resounding voice: "Trabant be praised!"

"I am Lord of the Astral Planes. The Shikroth and Ekante belong to me."

"Trabant be praised!"

"The Houses of Light and Darkness belong to me. The Seraphic Spheres hear my voice."

"Trabant be praised!"

Although the words meant nothing to her, as Yarden listened, the words entered her. The voice took control of her mind and pulled her consciousness along with it.

She saw a picture in her head: bright, transparent orbs of

219

light, swirling with color over luminous clouds. One of the spheres hovered in the center of the others, grew larger and larger until it blotted out all the others, and then shrank away, becoming the pupil of a gigantic eye. The eye in turn divided, becoming two eyes; below the eyes, lips formed a mouth. The mouth uttered the incomprehensible words of the voice from the pyramid.

"From Everlasting the Golim have sought me. The over-souls of the departed stand naked before me."

"Trabant be praised!"

"You who live and breathe are mine. Your hands are my hands, your feet my feet, your voices my voice. I am in you as you are in me."

"Trabant be praised!"

Yarden looked and could not keep herself from looking. The voice altered, took on a slightly higher pitch, became female. At the same instant the eyes and mouth became a female face attached to a female form. The body wore a glistening, filmy raiment and floated just above the iridescent clouds. The sky behind the figure convulsed with vibrant color, melding from red to blue to green to orange and back again almost simultaneously. The woman spread her lithe arms wide and said, "Come to me. Bring me the gift of your minds. Make your wills a fragrant sacrifice. Feed me with your desires. Put your flesh on the bones of my perfect way."

"Trabant be praised!"

"Your praises are the liquor of sweet communion. Your bodies are the mansions of my pleasure. Come to me that you may know me as I know you. Taste the life that death steals so quickly."

"Trabant be praised! Trabant be praised! Trabant be praised!" The voices of the celebrants rumbled in unison, escalating in volume as their features quickened. Many were standing now, reaching out their hands toward the floating pyramid. "Trabant be praised!"

Yarden felt herself rising toward the figure, her arms stretching out to the opened pyramid and its vibrating light, pangs of longing overwhelming her. In her mind the Trabant Woman looked at her with half-closed eyes, a sensual smile on her full lips.

"Come to me," she said breathlessly. "Consummate our love on the altar of pleasure and delight. Come to me."

The Trabant parted her lips with the tip of her tongue. Her head tilted back as her hands spread the shimmering garment and held it open, revealing full breasts, a firm, flat stomach, and shapely thighs. "Come to me." Trabant's voice was a whispered seduction. "Come . . . to . . . me!"

Yarden felt an ache in her loins, and her hips began moving rhythmically as around her the entire congregation swayed together. Her hands played over her body and then other hands joined hers. Yarden opened her eyes and saw that a man stood before her, stripped to the waist, his skin glistening in the rosy light of the pyramid.

She moaned. The man's hands were under her yos, roaming over her body, and she felt her flesh alive under his touch. She pressed herself against him, and he embraced her. Their mouths met hungrily and Yarden yielded to the kiss, clutching at her unknown lover.

The voice of the Trabant, now husky with passion, spoke inside her head. "I am your master. Feel me inside you. I will never let you go!"

An image of unspeakable horror flashed in Yarden's mind. She saw a vast host of corpses rising from a putrid swamp, writhing as decaying flesh fell from their long bones. The corpses mingled and began to caress one another, lipless teeth against shiny bone.

Bile churned up into Yarden's throat as a staggering wave of revulsion swept through her. The man before her, now naked in her arms, grasped her and pulled her to him. A dread as powerful and black as any she had ever known descended upon her, and she thrust the man away. He pulled at her, clawed her, his face contorted with lust.

"Give me your body!" demanded the Trabant. "Give me your soul!"

"Don't give in!" Yarden recognized the voice as her own, even though she did not know herself to have spoken. "I won't give in!" she said louder.

The Trabant became even more insistent. "Worship me and I will fill your life with pleasure. Come to me—let me satisfy all your longings."

Never! Yarden struck at the man before her with all her might. She caught him off balance as he pressed toward her, and he went down on his backside. Yarden whirled and pushed into the aisle, now swarming with the sprawling, convulsing bodies of men and women mingled in grotesque couplings. Stumbling over the conjoined pairs, she fought her way up the aisle to the doors where she crouched unseen and tried to push from her mind the awful ceremony being consummated around her.

Hold out, she told herself. They can't touch you as long as you don't give in to them. Hold out!

The last of the metal doors slammed shut behind them as Treet and Calin emerged from the debris-littered passageway that led to the Archives. Two Nilokerus sentries stood at their posts, looking bored and indifferent. Neither of the men gave them so much as a cursory glance, staring ahead, faces nearly covered by their crimson hoods. As Treet and his guide moved abreast of them, however, one of the guards stepped forward. He had a hand on Treet's arm before Treet knew what was happening.

"You will come with me, please," said the man, pulling Treet close. "Quickly! There is not much time."

Treet jerked back, but the man hung on. "What's going on? Let me go!"

Calin froze. "These are not Nilokerus!" she said.

The other guard stepped up, taking Calin by the shoulder. "No, we are not Nilokerus. Come with us, please. We only want to talk to you."

"We can talk here," said Treet, prying the first sentry's hand loose from his arm. "Start talking—and it better be good and interesting."

The first guard signaled the other one, who released his hold on Calin. He slipped the hood back from his face. "We have information for you about your friends."

Treet's head snapped up. "What about them? Talk!"

"We are instructed to tell you—but only if you come with us," answered the second sentry, still within clutching distance of Calin.

"No, you have it backwards. First you tell us, then we go . . . maybe." Treet put all the authority into his voice that he could muster.

"The change of guard is expected any moment. If they find us here—" began the first.

222

"Then quit wasting time and talk. So far you're not saying anything interesting."

A glance passed between the two false guards, and the first one made up his mind. "Your friends are being held by enemies. We know where they are."

"Where are they?"

"If you come with us, we will tell you."

"What enemies?"

"Your enemies."

"I don't have any enemies," replied Treet. But that wasn't exactly true. *Everyone* here was a potential enemy. "Calin, what's he talking about?"

Calin stared at the sentry. "You are . . . *Dhogs*." She said the word as if it were lethal.

Treet worked his mouth to speak. The first guard cut him off. "Listen!"

Footsteps echoed in the corridor beyond. "The Nilokerus are coming. You must come with us now. We can tell you no more."

Treet still hesitated. "No. Tell me where my friends are."

"We will take you to them."

"You said they were being held by enemies. How can you take me to them?"

"No time to explain," said the second guard hurriedly. He gestured to the corridor. "Come with us now!"

The footsteps sounded closer. Treet had to make up his mind. He was disinclined to go with the two men, but if it was true that they knew something about his friends—as apparently they did—if they could put him in touch with them—that was perhaps worth the gamble. "You will help me reach them?"

"Yes," replied the first sentry without hesitation.

Treet glanced at Calin; she had overcome her initial shock. Whoever they were, the Dhogs did not frighten her. "Okay, we'll go with you," said Treet at last.

Just then two figures appeared in the vestibule and advanced toward them. The false sentry nearest Calin put his hand under his yos and started to withdraw it. His companion telegraphed a quick warning with his eyes, and the man concealed the hand once more.

The new guards came ahead slowly.

"Go and wait for us at the end of the corridor," whispered the first sentry. "Now!"

Treet nodded to Calin and stepped forward. The two new guards looked at each other and then stopped them. "Is all in order here?" one of them asked.

"They have the Supreme Director's authorization, Hageman," replied the first false guard. "We have checked."

"Then be on your way," said the Nilokerus guard to Treet.

Treet and Calin continued on. As they reached the place where the vestibule joined the main corridor, they heard a voice utter a surprised exclamation. A sharp snap, like the crack of a whip, cut the air. A second snap sounded—an instantaneous echo of the first. Treet looked back in time to see one of the Nilokerus stagger and go down, his face smouldering. His companion, weapon in hand, was gazing in disbelief at a smoking hole in his stomach. The man toppled backward, his head cracking on the stone floor. The body rippled once and lay still.

The false guards came flying toward Treet. He stared at the two bodies and at the sooty smoke still rising from their wounds. One of the men grabbed him and spun him away. "Hurry!" he shouted and Treet was yanked along the blue-tiled corridor, his mind reeling with the horror of the violence he had just witnessed. He felt his stomach squirm and heave; he swallowed hard and allowed himself to be propelled from the scene.

THIRTY THREE

Yarden felt hands reach out to take her arms, felt herself being guided through the milling crush of bodies leaving the temple. Her eyes, soft and unfocused, stared dazedly ahead. She let herself be pulled along, unresisting, uncaring, her mind numb from the assault practiced upon it in the temple. She felt as if she had been raped.

It had taken every last grain of strength to resist the insidious presence of the Trabant. She had escaped—barely—but was exhausted, unable to fight anymore. She would return with Bela and the others to the Hage, or they would go somewhere and perform. It didn't matter. The Service—an orgy so hideous and unthinkable that her spirit recoiled from it as from the kiss of a corpse—was over and she had escaped. That's all she cared about.

They moved slowly down the long ramp, Yarden on wooden, unfeeling legs. Celebrants, sated and spent from their grotesque revelry, pressed in around her, but the hands still guided her. She turned to see who held her. "Bela?"

"Shhh, say nothing," instructed the woman beside her. She wore the turquoise and silver of the Chryse, but Yarden did not recognize her as belonging to their troupe.

They reached the foot of the ramp, and two guides pulled her quickly away, dodging among the retreating celebrants as they hurried across the white square to the shelter of a standing row of trees. Something in their movements—so quick and furtive and sure—assured Yarden that these were not members of her troupe. They were strangers, and they were leading her away from her Hagemen.

Let them take me where they will, she thought. It doesn't matter. Nothing matters anymore. I am lost.

They came to a place along the path out of sight from those following. They stopped. "Will you come with us?" asked the foremost guide, still clutching her arm.

"I don't know you," said Yarden, peering into their faces. What was that she saw there? Concern? These people cared about her. Why?

"No, you don't know us, but we are friends. We have been following you."

"You were. . . ," she hesitated, "in there?" She looked back. The temple was out of sight behind the sword-leafed trees.

"No; we saw you go in and waited for you to come out. There are people who want to see you. They are your friends, too. They asked us to bring you. It isn't far."

What would Bela say? she wondered. But at the thought she realized Bela did not care for her. When had she ever seen concern in *his* eyes? She remembered the wafer he had given her that morning. Had she taken it, she would have been incapable of resistance; she would have given in, become one of them.

"Will you go with us now?"

Yarden nodded. She had nothing to fear from these people. She could trust them far more than she could trust Bela. "Yes, I will go with you."

Then they were hurrying along secluded walkways, heading toward the winding river and away from Chryse deep Hage. Yarden kept pace willingly, though she had no idea where she was being taken. Whatever their destination, it would be safer then remaining with Bela and the others. Friends . . . safety—the words lifted the edges of the darkness that lay upon her soul. She felt her heart quicken with hope as she hurried on.

Through the labyrinth of Saecaraz deep Hage, up and up through the levels, out across terraces, past Hageworks and many-windowed kraam blocks, over connecting skywalks and through deserted market squares the fugitives ran toward snaking Kyan. Their flight was fast but measured, their progress sure. There was a purpose to the apparent aimlessness of their trail, which Treet decided was to confuse any pursuit.

When they reached the rimwalk at the river's edge, they paused at a clump of tall bushes with long, feathery yellow branches which arched up gracefully to twice a man's height. From a hiding place within the cluster of brown stalks, one of the guides tugged out a concealed bundle, opened it, and passed out black-and-gold yoses. He stripped off the Nilokerus garment and slipped on the new one.

"Tanais," said Calin. "I cannot wear this."

"Wear it," said the first guide flatly. "A Tanais boat will come by here in a few moments carrying only Tanais. It will pick up three *or* four Hagemen—you decide."

"Hold on! Are you threatening her?" Treet turned on the man, his head half in the yos. He pulled it down and glared defiantly. "I won't have it."

The man returned Treet's glare icily. The other guide spoke up. "He is merely saying what must be. It is a Tanais boat and will carry only Tanais. If she will not come—" His glance flicked to his comrade's hand beneath the yos.

"You'd kill her? Like you killed those other two back there?"

"We'd have no choice. She has seen—she knows!"

Treet saw how it was. Their escape route was set up to handle few variables and no surprises. "Well?" asked the guide. "The boat is coming."

"For crying out loud, Calin, get that thing on!" said Treet, snatching the yos from the man's hands and shoving it at the magician. When she hesitated, he took it and yanked it down over her head. She did not resist. "There. It just isn't worth getting killed over, okay?"

Calin gave him a dark look, but remained silent.

"All right, we're ready," said Treet. "What next?"

"This way," replied the second guide, shoving the Nilokerus yoses into the bushes.

They continued on along the rimwalk, with the gray river to the right, the long elegant steps of terraces to the left. Soon they came to a place where the rimwalk dipped down close to the water as the river crawled around a sharp bend. "Over here," said the first guide, scrambling over the stone breastwork.

Treet dropped over the edge and landed on his feet. The boat, a square-nosed barge of medium size riding low in the water, rounded the bend and came directly toward them. Four Tanais Hagemen stood idly on deck. But as the boat neared the shore, the four sprang forward and produced a short gangway which they pushed out over the nose. As soon as it was close enough, the first guide leaped onto the plank. Calin scurried aboard, the second guide close behind her. Treet followed, and no sooner did the boat touch the bank than the engines reversed, and it pulled away again. As the boat drew away from the shore, the four who had been standing idly on deck ran out onto the gangway and jumped to the bank, the last one barely clearing the water's edge.

A complete exchange, thought Treet. Very tidy. And all in less than ten seconds.

He looked around and noticed that this bend was fairly well hidden from the rest of the river. Also, a boat disappearing around the bend would be out of sight from the opposite shore until it emerged again on the other side. No doubt the place had been carefully chosen for that very reason. Every detail had been thought of—right down to the passenger exchange. These people were definitely not taking any chances.

Treet remembered the two dead bodies and grimly reminded himself that the stakes were very high. How many more people would die before this was over? Just what had he gotten himself into? He crossed his arms over his chest and watched the scenery slide by as the boat pulled itself back out into deep water and continued on around the bend.

They traveled against the current for a few kilometers, Treet guessed, before they entered a different Hage. He knew at once when they entered it by the change in architecture. He recognized the shapes of the buildings—tall, spire-shaped edifices with flying buttress arches—but couldn't remember its name.

"Calin," he said to the magician beside him. She had not said a word since setting foot on the boat. "Where are we?"

"Tanais Hage."

Was that resignation or despair making her voice so hollow? Treet turned and regarded her more closely. "What's wrong?"

"I am dead."

Her response startled him, and he laughed. "You're what? *Dead?* What are you talking about? There's not a scratch on you." The mirth went out of his voice when he saw the bleak futility in her dark eyes. "You're serious."

She did not answer, but stoically gazed out across the water.

"Calin, I know there's an awful lot I don't understand. But you're going to have to explain this to me. Are you afraid you can't go back?"

228

Tears misted over her voice. "I can never go back. When the Saecaraz discover what I have done, I will be erased. And the Tanais will not allow me to stay—I am a Saecaraz magician!"

She sounded so forlorn that Treet put his arm around her shoulders and held her to him. "Look, nobody is going to erase you." He realized how silly that sounded, but he was sincere. "I really don't think we have anything to worry about."

Actually, there was plenty to worry about, as Treet well knew. The deaths of the two Nilokerus and his own disappearance would not, in all likelihood, establish him further in the Supreme Director's good graces. Calin had a point: they *couldn't* go back.

Without his knowing it, he had booked them on a one-way flight. No return. Treet thought about this for a moment as he stood with his arms around the frightened magician. Then, as there was nothing he could do about any of it, he shrugged and held Calin out at arm's length. "I won't let anything happen to you, okay?" She pulled away and went to stand by the rail.

She was still standing there when the boat entered the Tanais marina. It was a semicircular jetty extending into a cove which had been carved out alongside the river. At least thirty other boats, large and small, were docked, and several more were at that moment entering the cove with them. Both the wide, curving dock and the waterfront area beyond were crowded with people milling about.

Treet saw the plan at once: pull in with three or four other boats—each, he noticed, with four passsengers visible on deck—and lose yourself in the crowd. Anyone following or watching would be pressed in the extreme to catch their trail. Obviously some careful thought and planning had gone into this operation. Yes, the stakes *were* high—maybe higher than he realized.

The boat slid into an empty berth alongside another craft of the same design. A third boat nosed in beside them on the other side, and twelve passengers disembarked at once to meld with the idle confusion on the dock. Single-file, they threaded their way through the ambling crowds on the waterfront. At the far side of the wharf they paused and allowed a group of four to move ahead of them and disappear down a shadowed walkway leading to deep Hage.

When the first group had gone, they moved on again, and after a few level changes, the entering and leaving of many

229

dwelling blocks, and a long wait in a dark tunnel while one of their guides went ahead to make sure the way was clear, they arrived at a generous plaza bordered on one side by a small lake with a fountain bubbling up in its center. Gently-sloped green lawns ringed the lake on every side, and around it grew lollipop trees which cast nets of white-flowered vine into the water.

Mirrored in the lake was an imposing structure made up of several independent sections clustered around a tall central tower and joined together at the upper levels with airborne walkways. The plaza and lakeside, like the dock and waterfront, swarmed with people wandering in groups of three or four. The guides struck off along a path that wound around the lake, eventually arriving at the plaza to lose themselves once more in the human maze.

Once across the square they wasted no time in entering the central tower, where they ran through an enormous hall over a highly polished floor to dive into a lift. The four crammed into the lift—clearly designed for one or two passengers—and up they went.

Treet lost count of the levels, but guessed that when the lift slowed, they were somewhere near the top. The barrier field withdrew, and Treet stepped out into a spare but spacious kraam. Standing in the center of the room were two figures, one of which he recognized.

"Well, well, Pizzle! Long time no see."

THIRTY
FOUR

"Treet? Orion Treet, is that you?" Pizzle bleated uncertainly.

At first Treet thought Pizzle had suffered brain damage, judging by the way he squirmed and squinted, but then realized the bookworm was not wearing Z. Z. Papoon's glasses. Treet stepped forward. "Yours truly, at your service. You okay?"

"I lost my glasses," said Pizzle, smiling broadly. "But it's not so bad. I'm getting used to it."

"So I see." Treet returned the smile and added a handshake and a slap on the back for good measure. He never in a trillion years would have dreamed he'd be so glad to see that homely, gnome-faced grin. He stood beaming and patting Pizzle's back as if he'd contracted a mild case of idiocy, and then noticed the man standing behind Pizzle. "Who's your friend?"

The man came forward, lips pursed, hands folded with fingers interlocked. He nodded to the two guides, who climbed back into the lift and vanished. "I am Tanais Director Tvrdy," announced the man. "We have been waiting for you."

Pizzle saw the look of cool appraisal Treet gave the Director and piped up, "You can trust him, Treet. He saved me. They were giving me psilobe—a kind of mind drug—and he got me off it. He wants to help us. Honest."

Treet glanced back at Calin, who still lingered near the lift. She looked like a small, defenseless animal that had been cornered by a much larger animal and now had given up, resigning itself to more powerful jaws. He decided to dismiss the polite formalities and get directly to the point. "They said you'd tell me about my friends. Here's Pizzle. Where are the other two?"

"The woman, Talazac, is on her way here now. I expect her to arrive within the hour. Crocker has been hurt and cannot yet travel. He has been removed to a place of safety. You can go to him if you like, but I would advise against it. You might be caught."

Treet appreciated the straight answer. He relaxed. "What's going to happen to us?"

Tvrdy appeared to consider the question carefully, looking at each one of them in turn. Finally he said, "I do not know. Much depends on your willingness to help us."

"Help you do what?"

"Help us save Empyrion," he said simply.

Jamrog and Hladik reclined together over a tiny round table in Jamrog's kraam, sipping the fiery souile from small round ceramic cups gripped between thumb and forefinger. Jamrog's Hagemate, a supple young woman in a filmy Hagerobe of radiant saffron, knelt between them with a ceramic jar over a warming flame, pouring more hot souile whenever their cups became empty.

Hladik let his eyes wander over the luxurious interior, coveting all he saw: vibrant Bolbe hangings and floorcoverings of intricate design, fine antique artifacts from Empyrion's Second Age, sleek furnishings of rare wood, exquisite Chryse metal carvings—two of them erotic pieces executed nearly lifesize. His envious gaze came to rest on the comely form of the young woman kneeling beside him. He smiled, his lips a straight line bending at the corners. "You live well, Jamrog. I commend you also on your good taste in companions."

Jamrog lifted a caressing hand to his Hagemate's flawless cheek. "If you find her to your liking, Hladik, take her," he said absently. The woman lowered her eyes.

"Be careful. I might accept your offer." Hladik made his tone light, but glanced greedily at the woman's curves beneath the transparent Hagerobe.

Jamrog let his hand fall away. His angular face hardened in a fierce smile. "I would be insulted if you refused, Hageman. Take her—I give her to you."

Hladik placed a hand on her folded knee, stroked it. "You are in a very generous mood today, Jamrog. Tell me, would this have anything to do with—" He halted. A peeping tone sounded from his clothing. He touched his shoulder and bent his head to one side. "Yes?"

"Fertig," came the answer. "Security protocol has been violated. I require instructions."

"Where?"

"Horizon level. Archives checkpoint."

"Do nothing. I am coming down." Hladik jumped up, swaying slightly as the souile rose to his head. "You will excuse me, Hageman."

"I am coming with you," said Jamrog.

"Until more details are known—"

Jamrog rose abruptly. "You waste time." He strode toward the door. Hladik cast one last glance back at the lovely woman still seated beside the low table, hands resting on her knees, then followed Jamrog out.

They rode Hladik's em through the secret connecting tube between Saecaraz and Nilokerus Hages. The tube had been installed in the early days of Saecaraz supremacy and was now forgotten, except by the few authorized to use it. Within minutes, thanks to the speed of Hladik's vehicle, the two Directors were standing in Hladik's private council chamber within the security section of Nilokerus Hage.

A very pale Subdirector stood before them. "The situation has worsened," he explained. "We have had two more reports."

"What is the damage?" asked Hladik. Jamrog stood to one side with arms crossed and head lowered, frowning.

Fertig gulped air and saw that he could not cushion the blow, so rushed ahead. "The Fieri woman has disappeared. Bela informs us that his troupe attended Service in Chryse Hage, and she was not with them when they came out."

"The fools! They should have been watching her more closely. I will have them all in for reorientation!"

Jamrog's eyes narrowed. "The other report?"

"Treet and the magician guide have not returned to the kraam. We have discovered that Rohee granted them permission to visit the Archives. They were admitted sixth watch yesterday and did not emerge until first watch this morning." He took a deep breath and continued. "There was a Saecaraz priest with them, but he has not been identified. Second-watch guards were found dead at their station."

"What of the first watch?"

"When they did not check in, a messenger was sent to the checkpoint. That was when the bodies were discovered. The first-watch guards have not been found."

"This is Tvrdy's doing!" howled Hladik. "I know it. He has stolen the spies right from under our noses."

"Aided by your incompetence," fumed Jamrog. Hladik puffed up in protest, but Jamrog's eyes flared in deadly warning. "Yes, it's *your* fault," he said icily. "I'm holding you responsible. You should have doubled the security on the others when the Jamuna spy disappeared."

"How could I have known that—"

"That is your trouble, Director. You have consistently underestimated Tvrdy's cunning and resources. He should have been dealt with."

"Under whose authority? Yours, Jamrog? Need I remind you that you are not Supreme Director yet? We cannot move openly against another Hage Leader."

"Rohee has issued his own death demand with this. He's mad—letting a Fieri into the Archives! I should never have left him alone with the spy."

"We can get them back," Hladik offered. "If we strike quickly, our Invisibles can recapture them."

"No, it has gone too far. The spies must be killed. They should have been killed upon capture. If they were to make contact with the Dhogs, it would strengthen the resistance. How could this happen now—when we are so close to ridding ourselves of them forever!"

"We've made mistakes," said Hladik, "but nothing is lost. We will kill the spies and put an end to this. We will also deal Tvrdy a blow from which he'll never recover. That should warn anyone else who might be thinking of joining him."

"All right, do it. Use Mors Ultima and strike at once. I will take care of Rohee personally. He will die quietly in his bed this evening. By tomorrow morning my power will be consolidated and," he paused, a rapacious leer spreading over his features, "by tomorrow evening the Threl will have a new leader and Empyrion a new Supreme Director."

Fertig stood mute with terror, wishing he had not heard this conversation. It would be his death, he knew, if their plan did not succeed, or even if it did. Already he could feel the cold flame of poison licking his limbs, seeping through his blood. I have heard too much, he thought. When this is over, they will not let me live.

Hladik turned on him. "Well, what are you waiting for? Assemble the Invisibles. I will meet with the squad leader Mrukk in the ready room in four minutes to plan operational strategy."

"By your command, Hage Leader." Fertig vanished gratefully, leaving the two to their schemes. He entered the security command post and placed the watch commanders on alert, then summoned the Mors Ultima squad of Invisibles. His tasks completed for the moment, he returned to his monitor station to await further orders.

I must find some protection, he thought desperately. There must be a way—there *must* be a way. He sat rigid in his chair, staring at the eternally revolving monitor screens. All at once he leapt to his feet. Yes! There was a way—perhaps the only way to save himself. But he'd have to act fast. He spun in his chair and tapped out a coded message on a blank disk with a light stylus.

He leaped to his feet and took the disk to dispatch. It would be dangerous sending the message from here; it could be traced. But there was no time to take it elsewhere, and the secure lines connecting the Directors' kraams were the quickest. Fertig handed the disk to the dispatcher and said, "Tanais Director. First priority. Destroy upon transmission."

THIRTY
FIVE

"**H**elp save Empyrion?" Treet cocked his head to one side thoughtfully. "And just how would we do that?"

Tvrdy's answer surprised him. "Do you know of the Fieri?"

"I am familiar with the word."

"For most of our people, the Fieri, if they are remembered at all, live only in children's stories of long ago. But there are those among us who believe they still exist."

"You, for example?"

"And certain others."

"This is interesting, but I really don't see a problem of survival here."

Tvrdy nodded and led them to cushions where they all sat down together. Calin did not join them, but stayed where she was—crouched next to the wall beneath a large, shapeless hanging. "Your coming has released an enormous amount of astral energy into our world. That energy must be dissipated or used."

"We've polarized their psychic plane," explained Pizzle. "We've upset the astral balance around here prodigiously."

Treet looked at him. "That's not all that's been upset apparently." He turned back to Tvrdy. "Exactly what are you trying to tell me?"

"Your presence among us is a catalyst for action. The energy you bring with you is strong—too strong to be resisted. It will be used; one way or another it will be used."

"Go on, what are you getting at?"

"For six hundred years the Saecaraz have ruled Empyrion—Subdirector succeeding Director."

"The line of succession runs through Hage Saecaraz. The Saecaraz Director always gets to be Supreme Director, is that it?"

"Precisely. Even though he is but a Subdirector, Jamrog sits with the Threl; his stent is equal to that of a Director. But when he becomes a Director—"

"Trouble with a capital T," put in Pizzle.

Tvrdy continued his recitation. "Sirin Rohee is old. Jamrog will not hesitate to remove him when he has outlived his usefulness. At present, the Threl is divided on what to do with you. Jamrog would use you as an excuse to seize power. My friends want to see Jamrog deposed and leadership of the Threl returned to the Directors."

"Ah, politics I understand," remarked Treet.

"Jamrog already suspects treason among certain members of the Threl. Should he come to power, there will be a Purge and Empyrion will be cast into chaos. Thousands—tens of thousands will die needlessly. Kyan will run red with the blood of our Hagemen, and we are powerless to prevent it."

"That sounds serious enough, but what's it got to do with this Fieri business?"

"They think *we* are Fieri!" Pizzle explained. "That seems to carry a lot of weight around here."

"I still don't see what everyone's so excited about," said Treet.

Tvrdy continued. "Fieri are stronger than we are, their numbers greater, their magic far more powerful."

Treet shook his head, "Fine, but we're not Fieri."

"I know that now. You are Travelers."

"How does that help you?"

"You could go the Fieri, explain what is happening here, and seek their aid. With the Fieri's help, we could overthrow Jamrog's regime."

Treet clucked his tongue. "Let me see if I've got this straight. You want us to contact the Fieri for you and see if they'll help you stop the opposition from tap-dancing on your heads. Right? Only relations have not been exactly cordial between you Dome Dwellers and the Outsiders for roughly two thousand years, give or take a few centuries. Just what makes you think they'll greet this proposal of yours with the proper degree of enthusiasm? Hmm?"

Tvrdy's eyes narrowed. "You have a quick mind, Orion Treet. You understand why we cannot go to the Fieri. That is why I ask you. You are Travelers. They will listen to you."

"Maybe. Then again, they might just assume we're spies and donate our bodies to the cause of Universal Misunderstanding. It seems to me others have done that around here."

Tvrdy said nothing. Pizzle, looking uncomfortable, tried to

smoothe things over. "It wasn't like that, Treet. They didn't know. It was a mistake."

"No mistake, Pizzy old boy."

"He's right," Tvrdy agreed. "It was no mistake. The things that were done to you were done intentionally. But I hope you believe that not everyone agrees with those tactics." He paused, features softening. "My friends and I have risked everything to save you. It would have been much easier to let Jamrog keep you."

"Oh, I'm not ungrateful," said Treet. "I just wanted *you* to know that *I know* what's going on around here."

Just then the lift arrived from below, and three more people tumbled into the Director's kraam. Treet only saw one of them. "Yarden!"

He jumped up and went to her, and would have taken her in his arms if not for the dazed expression on her face and the emptiness in her eyes. She looked directly at him without a flicker of recognition. "Yarden? Are you okay? Yarden, you're safe. It's Treet. Remember me? Orion Treet."

She stared around at her surroundings, and big tears formed in her eyes. She turned back to Treet and reached a quivering hand to his face. "I remember you," she whispered. The tears overflowed her lashes and streamed down her cheeks. She closed her eyes, swayed on her feet. "I remember . . . everything!"

Yarden collapsed into him, and he put his arms around her to hold her up. Long sobs shook her, and she buried her face against his chest and let go. Treet held her close, saying, "There now, you're safe. It's over. You're safe now."

After a while she stopped crying. At Tvrdy's suggestion Treet led her into the next room and made her comfortable on the suspension bed. She closed her eyes the moment her head touched the cushion; she was deeply asleep as Treet crept from the room.

"I think she'll be all right," he said as he rejoined the others.

"Sure," agreed Pizzle. He regarded Treet owlishly. "It's rough at first—takes some time to get yourself oriented. Once she's past it, she'll be fine."

Pradim, the Tanais Director's eyeless guide, entered the room. All turned to him and Treet saw from the man's pinched

238

expression that something terrible had happened, or was about to.

Tvrdy moved to him, and the two men spoke softly to one another head to head. Tvrdy turned away, and Pradim hurried from the room. The Director's features were calm, but his voice was tight. "An unprecedented development has taken place. I have received secret communication from the Nilokerus Subdirector informing me of an attack."

"The target?" Treet asked, already guessing the answer.

"Us. Invisibles are moving against us now. We have approximately six minutes to make our escape."

"Six minutes!" cried Pizzle. "That's not much time; we've got to get out of here!"

"Stay calm," advised Treet much more calmly than he actually felt. He went to the adjoining room where Yarden slept, took her shoulder, and jiggled it. "Sorry to wake you so soon, Yarden, but we're leaving."

Her eyes opened at once. "Oh, it wasn't a dream! You *are* here!" She sat up and looked at her clothes and the room and Treet sitting next to her.

"No dream. I wish it was," he said, standing. "We can talk about it later. Right now we have some disappearing to do."

They reentered the main chamber to find Pradim handing out yoses. "Put these on," instructed Tvrdy.

"This won't stop them," scoffed Pizzle.

"No," agreed Tvrdy as he slipped on the red and white of the Nilokerus, "but it may give us a split second. Sometimes that is enough. Ready? Follow me. I've had an escape route planned for years against this day."

"Somehow that doesn't surprise me," said Treet as they headed to the lift.

They squeezed in, and Tvrdy set the controls for a fast plummet. As the capsule raced down through the levels, Treet inquired, "By the way, how'd they know we were at your place? I thought this whole operation was ultra-ultra."

"Jamrog does not know. I am merely his most convenient first target. They hope to gain knowledge of your whereabouts through me. Naturally, finding you in my kraam would have made their task much simpler."

"No need to do that."

The lift slowed and bounced to a halt. Tvrdy cut off the

unidor, and Treet stepped out and into a man in the colors of the Tanais, holding an oblong instrument with a barbed prong at the end of it. Two more men with identical weapons were running toward them across the entrance hall.

"Wrong floor!" shouted Treet, flinging himself back into the lift. Tvrdy's finger was still on the controls, and the barrier field was back in place as the Invisible's weapon discharged. By then the capsule was already dropping once more.

He drew a shaky breath. "Split seconds, you were saying."

"How'd they get here so fast? It hasn't been six minutes," observed Pizzle.

"Obviously the advance force was already here."

"Some of your own men?"

"Invisibles disguised as Tanais."

"What now?"

"We will lose ourselves in deep Hage, make contact with my friends, and wait."

"And hope the Invisibles don't find us before help comes?"

"It should be safe enough," said Tvrdy. "It will take them many days to search us out."

"I have a better idea," said Treet. "Suppose we decide to opt for your Plan A. How long would it take to outfit us? When could we leave?"

THIRTY
SIX

Treet, Pizzle, and Tvrdy stood together at a datascreen set in the wall of a kraam located deep in the catacombed lower levels of Hage Tanais near the Isedon Zone, the ring of ruined Hageblocks that formed the boundary of Empyrion's Old Section. The kraam had been provisioned for just this sort of emergency. Every cubic inch of space was stacked with supplies. There was enough food, water, and weaponry to sustain a medium-sized insurrection indefinitely. Calin sat forlornly beneath a tower of transparent plastic water barrels. Yarden slept nearby, stretched out on a pallet of vantium shield sheeting.

The datascreen showed a map of a section of Empyrion. Tvrdy pointed to the lower left-hand corner and tapped the screen. "This is the Archive area," he said. "It is in Hage Saecaraz, as you know, so we will have to find a way to get you there."

"Can't we leave from somewhere closer?" asked Treet, peering at the map doubtfully. The route was so convoluted and confused he despaired of reaching the Archives without running into a party of Invisibles. "I don't see why we need to go to the Archives again anyway."

"You haven't been paying attention," said Pizzle. "Tvrdy already explained all that."

"Excuse me!" roared Treet. "I've got a few things on my mind at the moment. I missed it okay?"

Tvrdy gave both men a look of long-suffering exasperation and intoned, "You will need land vehicles if you are ever to reach the Fieri. If such are to be found anywhere in all Empyrion, they will be found in the Archives."

Treet nodded. Yes, that seemed reasonable enough. But he was still bothered by Tvrdy's lack of certainty. "You don't know whether there are land vehicles there or not, or if there are, whether they are still operable, do you?"

"You would be in a better position to answer that yourself. I have never been to the Archives. No one has."

"Well, you're right. And from what I saw, I'd say it would be a chancy enterprise. We couldn't count on finding anything useful."

Tvrdy shrugged. "We will go there in any case."

"Why not take us to our transport? We know that works." He saw Tvrdy shake his head slowly. "That is, it used to. What happened?"

"Jamrog will have disabled it. Saecaraz magicians have been studying it. Besides that, I have not been able to find out where it has been hidden." He glanced at Calin. "Ask her."

"Calin?" Treet turned imploringly toward the magician.

She rose and shuffled forward. "I do not know where the flight craft is."

"What about your psi spirit or whatever? Couldn't he tell you?"

The magician shrugged. "Nho is prevented from telling me. But I overheard talk in Hage. Your machine contained many wonders, they said, much strange magic."

"They took it apart?" whined Treet. "This is insane!"

"It's not that crazy," offered Pizzle. "You have to look at it from their point of view."

"Oh, do I? I'm tired of looking at everything from their point of view. I think it's time somebody looked at something from *my* point of view!"

Tvrdy continued equably, "Once inside the Archives, we can seal the entrance. There are doors here," he pointed to a further side of the bulge in the map, "which open to the outside beneath the landing platform. You will escape from there."

"What about Crocker? What happens to him?"

"He will stay here. Rumon Director Cejka is bringing him here tonight. You will see him before we leave."

Treet put a hand to his face and rubbed the stubble lengthening there. He looked at Pizzle. "Okay with you?" The jug-eared head bobbed readily. "I've got nothing better to offer. When Yarden wakes up, we'll put it to her. If she agrees, we go."

"Tonight will be eventful for all of us. Therefore, I suggest we all rest while we can." Tvrdy switched off the datascreen and sent them off to a light, skitterish sleep.

• • • • •

Treet awoke groggy and confused. An evil-tasting film filled his mouth, and his eyes felt as if cinders had been strewn beneath his eyelids. His sinuses were stuffed, and his head felt blocky. Great, he thought, I'm coming down with the plague—just when I'm leaving on vacation. Isn't that always the way?

He heard a rustle next to him and put out a hand. "Piz? You awake?"

A face, moonlike in the darkness of the kraam, rose over him. "I want to go with you," whispered a tentative voice.

"Calin, I don't know. I don't thi—"

"Please. You must take me with you. I will die here."

"Tvrdy won't let anything happen to you. I'll tell him. You can stay here with Crocker."

"No. Tanais owes me no protection. I will not ask for it."

Treet paused, thinking. He tried a different tack. "It'll be a hard trip. We don't even know where we're going exactly."

"I have been thinking you will need a guide."

She had a point. A guide would be helpful. "You can guide us? Outside the dome, I mean? You know your way around outside?"

"Nho can guide us. I will ask him."

It dawned on Treet then that the guides did not know any more about getting around Empyrion than anybody else. They were *psychic* guides. The thought of an astral entity leading them on a chase around a virtually unexplored alien planet made no sense at all, but at least it made no less sense than any of the rest. "Oh," he said. "I see. Well, I still don't know abou—"

"*Please!*" whispered Calin desperately.

"What's this about traveling?" A second female voice spoke up, and Treet felt Yarden slide in close to him. "Have I missed something?" Though he couldn't see her features distinctly, her voice sounded normal.

"You've been a little out of it," said Treet. "The long and short of it is we think it would be best to leave the colony for awhile. You have a vote."

"Go to the Fieri," she said softly.

Treet raised up on his elbows. "How do you know about the Fieri?"

"I am a sympath," she acknowledged simply. "I felt your thoughts."

Yarden a brain dipper? That explained something, thought Treet—that remote, mysterious quality he'd always noticed about her. Maybe that was it. "You read my mind," said Treet.

"That's what everybody believes," replied Yarden. "But receiving another's thoughts isn't like reading a newspaper. Ours is a highly developed sensitivity to certain individuals whose psychomotive scan patterns closely match our own."

"Like me, for instance."

"Like you."

"How long have you been able to tap my brain?"

"Since the first moment I saw you. But we do not *tap*, as you say. Brain dipper," she said harshly, "is a vulgar term. What I do is much more subtle, much more sensitive than that. Besides, we can only receive from a person who is willing to send. You must be open to sharing your thought before I can receive its impression."

"I see." Treet squirmed in the dark. The uncomfortable feeling he always had in her presence returned in force. Only now he knew why he felt weird around her. And knowing made it worse. "Well, about the Fieri—as I was telling Calin, it will be a difficult trip. We don't know what we might find out there. Crocker will be staying here. You could stay with him, as I've advised Calin to do."

"Which would be dangerous too," said Calin.

"Yes. Unfortunately we don't have a lot of wonderful choices just now. Circumstances have kind of degenerated around here."

"I'm going with you," Calin said, her voice a challenge.

"I'm going," Yarden declared firmly.

Treet said nothing for a moment, then decided it didn't matter what he thought about the situation. He couldn't very well dictate what anybody else should or should not do. Still, the implication was that he was somehow the leader of this little expedition. How had that happened? "Look, if you're both waiting for my blessing, forget it. What you do is up to you."

"Then we can go?" asked Yarden.

"No one is going to stop you."

Just then a light came up in the kraam, dim and hazy. Tvrdy entered softly and come to stand over them. "It is time."

"Crocker isn't here yet," said Treet, getting to his feet. "You said we'd get to see him before we left."

"Cejka must have been detained elsewhere and could not get word to us. We cannot wait any longer."

There was nothing to do but agree. "All right. Give us a second to pull ourselves together. Pizzle isn't awake yet."

"Yes he is," said Pizzle, climbing to his feet. "I am now."

They ate a few clumps of a sweet, gummy daikon bread and drank some water Tvrdy had brought for them. They washed themselves and stretched muscles that had tightened while they slept. As they moved toward the entrance to the kraam, Tvrdy handed each one a long, black outer cloak and a tubular pouch which was worn slung over one shoulder and across the chest. "Inside are emergency provisions," he explained.

Tvrdy unsealed the door and darted out into the passageway. The others followed like quick shadows and moved off down a long, twisting corridor, then followed it until it became a wide, disheveled gallery joined by several other disused corridors radiating out like the spokes of a wheel. At the entrance to one of them, blind Pradim stood waiting. He greeted the Director and without a word led them off at a near run.

Once they cleared the corridor, Pradim eased the pace somewhat, but kept them moving smartly. "There is transportation waiting," he explained. "But we must hurry."

After what seemed like hours of chasing through endless tunnels, corridors, galleries and passages, they at last came to a wide portal and stepped through it and out into the night. Three small ems were lined up at the entrance. Tvrdy jumped into the driver's seat of the first one, Pradim took the second one, and Treet the third. The others climbed in on the passenger side, one to each em, and they were off.

Treet had never driven one of the little cars before, but found it quite easy: press on the pedal and the electric vehicle spurted forward, ease up and it braked automatically. All he had to do was steer, which was simple enough. More difficult was following Tvrdy, since they drove without lights through winding terrace roads along the snaky Kyan. Once in Saecaraz, they abandoned the ems and struck off on foot again, avoiding well-used byways.

At first Treet feared discovery beyond every turn and around every corner. But then he guessed that their route had been cleared for them. At regular intervals along the way and at blind intersections, sightless Pradim slowed and searched along the path, sometimes stooping to trail his fingers along the walkway. He always found whatever it was he sought—a sign or mark of some sort that told him the way ahead was safe.

Treet's guess was confirmed when they reached the Saecaraz central lift where Pradim paused, hunched over, and pressed his fingers into a crack in the lower wall, then straightened and spoke to Tvrdy. "This mark is old—several hours. Something is wrong."

Treet was close enough to overhear, and said, "Meaning we don't know what's waiting for us on the lower level."

Tvrdy frowned, his face taut. "We cannot wait here. Anyone may come by at any moment. We have to go on."

"And the second we climb out of the lift—BLAMMO! You can talk about us in past tense."

"If we wait here any longer, discovery is certain."

Treet whirled to Calin. "Listen, we've got a little snag here. See if Nho could help us out. Is there anyone waiting for us down there?"

Calin appeared about to protest, but nodded once and grew very still. Her eyes glazed over slightly as she entered that other dimension where she and Nho rendezvoused. Just as quickly, she was out of it. She drew a breath and the spell snapped. The trance lasted only seconds.

"Well?" asked Treet, genuinely fascinated.

"Nho does not see death for us," she said.

"What does he see? Grievous bodily harm? Imprisonment? Torture?"

"I can't say more."

"It is enough," snapped Tvrdy with finality. "We go now."

Treet nodded, and they gathered themselves and dashed across the open chamber toward the nearest lift. Other corridors joined the chamber and as the lift came up, withdrawing its barrier field, footsteps sounded loud in one of the adjacent passages. "Hurry!" whispered Treet. "Someone's coming!"

The others were pushing into the lift when a guide clothed in Saecaraz colors came flying out of the passage. He stopped instantly, a look of horror washing over his eyeless face, made a desperate signal to Treet, and then fled back into the corridor.

Treet made to duck into the lift. There was a shout and the sound of a small explosion. Out of the corner of his eye, Treet saw an object flying toward him. He looked and saw the guide shoot out of the passage, skimming through the air. The man screamed and clutched his chest, flames and blood sprouting from a ghastly hole. The body fell hard, skidded into the center of the chamber, and lay sprawled in an inert heap. Smoke rose from the corpse's clothes, while blood pooled on the stones beneath it. Another shout. Closer. Treet dove into the waiting lift, the barrier field snapped on behind him, and the capsule dropped.

"What was it?" Tvrdy eyed him with concern as he climbed back to his feet.

Grim-faced, Treet answered, "I think your man just took a hole in the chest to save us."

Tvrdy nodded. No one else spoke. Finally Pradim broke the silence. "We'll get off three levels above Horizon and take another way to the Archives. They will know where we're going otherwise."

"They probably already guess," said Treet gloomily. The vision of the mangled body still filled his eyes.

"If we can make it to the doors, they cannot reach us without decoding the locks."

"Or blowing them off their hinges," Pizzle piped up.

"You *are* a cheery fellow, aren't you, Pizzle?"

"Just thinking out loud," he said.

"The doors are shielded," offered Pradim. "We will have some time once we are inside."

"*If* we can get inside," said Treet. "What if I can't remember the entry code?"

"Start remembering now," said Tvrdy as the capsule slowed and slid to an abrupt halt. "Or there is no point in going further."

THIRTY
SEVEN

The lift's barrier field snapped off with a pop. Since Treet was nearest the door, he stepped out first, tentatively, ready to dive back in. But the long, arched passageway was empty. At a distance of thirty or forty meters, the tunnel divided, the left-hand side bending away and down, and the right fork continuing straight until losing itself in darkness.

Pradim pushed past Treet and flew to the fork, motioning those behind to hurry, then ran into the downward-bending tunnel. Treet pushed everyone ahead of him and followed, allowing Tvrdy to bring up the rear. After many branchings and turns, Pradim stopped to listen. There were no sounds of the chase; no one was behind them.

They pressed on and in a few minutes came to a rectangular room with a round railing in the center. In the floor below the railing was a hatch. From the debris on the floor and the cobwebs hanging in filthy sheets from the pipes in the ceiling, it appeared that no one had entered the room for decades. Pradim opened the hatch and dropped through the hole. One by one the fugitives followed. A steel ladder joined the two levels, the lower one of which appeared to be a water conduit of some size, though dry and apparently unused.

Large grated drains opened in the sides and bottom of the conduit at regular intervals of twenty-five meters. Pradim counted them as they passed each one and stopped at the twelfth. He reached up and tugged on the grate, and surprisingly the heavy steel cover came off without effort. Pradim tossed it aside, and it bounced soundlessly. Plastic, thought Treet. He wondered how many other such doctored escape routes existed throughout Empyrion's endless tangle of byways.

Blind Pradim hoisted himself up into the oval opening and turned to lift down his hands to Calin and Yarden in turn; Pizzle came next and then Treet and Tvrdy. They crawled on hands and knees in near total darkness for an eternity. Treet's kneecaps and the heels of his hands grew tender and then sore and then painful before the conduit angled upward slightly and then entered a brightly-lit room containing a row of enormous valves—all peeling paint and rusting.

Directly above the valves was a circular opening with a steel ladder leading to a hatch like the one they had dropped through earlier. Pradim, wasting no time, grabbed the first rung, pulled himself up, and disappeared through the hatch. When Treet joined the others, he emerged to find himself in a closet just off a main corridor. Pradim was missing.

"Have you remembered the code?" asked Tvrdy in a tense whisper.

"I think so. We'll soon find out."

Pradim came soundlessly back and motioned for them to follow him. They entered a blue-tiled corridor, and Treet recognized at once that they were near the Archives guard station. In a moment they turned a corner. Two Nilokerus sat leaning against the wall, their legs out stiff in front of them, weapons clutched in their hands. Although their eyes looked straight ahead, they did not see the fugitives hurry past.

"Dead?" wondered Treet aloud.

"No. Sonic immobilizer," explained Tvrdy. "They will tell those after us that we did not pass this way. Still, we must hurry; they'll only be restrained a few seconds."

Treet turned his attention to the first set of doors, walked to the lock plate, and studied the pentagon of lighted tabs. "Here goes nothing." He raised his index finger.

"Wait!" Yarden pushed up beside him. "I can help you remember correctly."

"How?"

"Shh! Close your eyes and concentrate on the tabs."

Treet closed his eyes and tried to think of how he had pressed the code tabs before. All he remembered was walking through a succession of doors, dreaming of what might be locked away on the other side of the last one. He distinctly did not remember pressing the buttons. "Sorry," he said.

"Concentrate! You pressed them correctly once. Your mind remembers. Picture yourself pressing them in sequence. Feel the tabs."

Treet closed his eyes once more, but now all he was aware of was the nearness of Yarden Talazac and the warmth of her breath on his neck. "It's not go—" he began, then felt her cool fingertips on his closed eyelids.

"Picture it exactly as it happened," she said softly.

Treet saw himself approach the big doors, saw his hand reach out for the first tab, was aware of Calin beside him and the ridiculous priest behind, watching nervously—he had not noticed that before—and felt again the surge of excitement at what lay ahead. He saw the first tab as his finger moved toward it.

The sound of pounding feet echoed in the corridor behind them. "They're coming!" said Pizzle.

"Got it!" said Treet and pressed the first lighted tab. The light went out.

"Go on," said Yarden calmly. "You will remember."

Treet closed his eyes and again felt her fingertips on his eyes. "Okay!" He pressed a second tab and the light went off. "Two down, three more to go."

"Get on with it!" squeaked Pizzle. Their pursuers sounded closer.

Treet raised his finger, and the third tab blinked off.

"They're almost on us!" cried Pizzle.

"I'm doing the best I can!" replied Treet through gritted teeth.

"They're here!" shouted Pradim as a squad of Invisibles rushed into the guard station behind them. He pulled a cone-shaped device from the folds of his yos, moved to the doorway, and aimed.

A fizzling crack split the air, and the cone device exploded in a shower of sparks in the guide's hand. Pradim turned toward the others and raised an empty sleeve. Where his hand had been, only two nub ends of clean white bone remained. His face went grey, and he lurched forward. Calin grabbed him and pulled him away from the open doorway as a second shot sent chunks of the door frame ricocheting around them.

"We're going to be killed!" screamed Pizzle.

Treet stabbed at the fourth tab, and it went off. "I remembered!" he hollered as he smacked the last button. The locking mechanism clicked open. Treet and Tvrdy attacked the door and heaved it open a crack.

Firebolts streaked the air. Scorching metal and stinging hot debris pelted into them. Somehow they all shoved through the slim opening at once and threw themselves at the door to close it as sparks and cinders rained in upon them.

Treet remembered the next code easily—it was a simple

variation on the first. He stabbed the tabs, the lock clicked open, and they all pressed through and shouldered the door closed behind them.

"That was a little too close," said Pizzle, his body shaking as much as his voice.

Yarden and Calin stood with Pradim, wrapping improvised bandages on his raw stump. But there was little blood—the weapon had cauterized the wound. The guide's face had gone dead white, and his body trembled oddly; he seemed not to know where he was.

"The doors will slow them down," said Tvrdy. "Until they find the code."

"How long?"

"Who can say? Rohee is the only one who knows it— besides you."

"Would he give it to them?"

Pradim moaned. The pain was beginning to hit him. Calin sat him down and took his head in her hands. She spoke to him in low, whispered tones, and he slumped forward. "He will sleep for a time," she said.

Tvrdy nodded gravely and said, "I am certain Rohee knows nothing of what is taking place this night. He would not move against another Director like this. At least he would observe Directorate Conventions. But Jamrog might dare to use other means to gain entrance."

"Such as?"

"They could put a code-breaker on the lock," offered Pizzle. "With only five code digits it would take a good computer just a matter of minutes to click through all the permutations."

Treet turned on him. "Whose side are you on?"

"We ought to know all the possibilities," Pizzle replied, unrebuffed. "Don't you think?"

Tvrdy agreed. "Such devices exist."

"Then we have only a few minutes. We'd better get moving."

Tvrdy lifted Pradim onto his shoulders, and the fugitives fled through the succession of doors as quickly as possible and at last entered the Archives. Tvrdy stepped across the threshold and lay the unconscious guide down, covering him with his outer cloak. Then he turned to stand in quiet amazement, gazing at everything around him. "It is like looking into the past," he said in hushed tones.

"Sure," said Treet. "Take the tour later. Right now why don't we try to find these vehicles you say we can't live without, and we'll be going."

Tvrdy stepped lightly down the concentric ring of ledges onto the floor of the Archives, found a pathway, and disappeared into the welter of junk piled with haphazard care throughout the vast expanse.

"Okay, everybody," called Treet, "spread out and make a noise if you see anything that looks like it might put some distance between us and those goons out there."

"Look at all this stuff!" shouted Pizzle as he dove into it. "Just like the old Smithsonian!"

Yarden chose a pathway and moved off quickly. Calin knelt over Pradim, lay her hands on his head once more, and then joined Treet. "Nho helped us once," said Treet. "Would he do it again?" Calin nodded and grew still.

"This way," she replied, striking off toward the middle of the room.

Fifteen minutes, and two mystical consultations later, Calin stopped and pointed to a row of shroud-covered humps next to the great doors that opened beneath the landing platform. "Hey!" cried Treet. "Everybody! Over here!"

Pizzle stumbled up. Tvrdy and Yarden, who had also heard Treet's cry, arrived moments later. Pizzle went to the first hump and yanked off the shrouds, stirring a veritable fog of the fine, gray powder. When the fog subsided he was leaning against the hood of a strange machine, grinning. "Nice, don't you think?" He sounded like an antique car dealer showing off his latest acquisition.

"What is it?" Treet peered doubtfully at the elongated red-orange machine before him and at its two blue-and-black companions standing a little way off.

"Transportaion," said Pizzle grandly, adding, "I'm almost sure of it."

Tvrdy squatted to peer at the underside. "What do you think?" asked Treet.

"Excellent!" cried Tvrdy. "You have found them. I had forgotten about the blades."

"The blades?" Treet stared at the vehicle. On either side of a narrow, open-aired passenger compartment, two long, thin runners swept down from the pointed nose to flare like curved sabers along the full length of the vehicle. The contraption looked more like a skinny, old-fashioned sleigh with its runners flattened and turned on edge than anything else Treet could think of.

There were three humps in the floor of the passenger compartment which corresponded to three, ball-shaped flexible wheels, which were made of overlapping metallic bands. The ungainly craft balanced precariously on these wheels, tilting back and forth on the runner-blades.

"Yes, you will need these," Tvrdy was saying as he pointed to two other vehicles exactly like the first. All three showed signs of wear and tear—places where the paint was worn to the metal, scratches and dents, torn seat cushions. Obviously the machines had seen heavy use in their day—whenever that had been. "I had also forgotten the sand."

"Sand?"

Calin spoke up. "There is a legend about a great sand sea between Empyrion and Fierra."

"A desert. Of course. Just what we need."

Calin, eyes turned inward, began reciting:

"On blades that race the sea is cut,
And scattered by the skimmer's wake.
On and on, the dune sea rolls
White gold in endless waves."

She came out of her trance and explained, "Nho says it is from an old song."

"Great," Treet frumped. "Well, do we wait for those lovely lads out there to figure out a way to get in here, or do we make a graceful exit?"

In the skimmers they found an assortment of blue, red, and green singletons much like the ones they had been wearing when they arrived on Empyrion. Treet was the first to start stripping off his yos. Pizzle found one near his size and squirmed out of his yos too. "Come on, ladies. No time to be shy," remarked Treet, stuffing a leg into the garment. "Get some real clothes on." He flipped two of the smaller-sized jumpsuits to Calin and Yarden.

When they hesitated, he explained, "Look, I'm not much of an explorer, but I've been on a few excursions, and we don't know what kind of conditions we're likely to find out there. But whatever it is, we're better off dressed for the occasion. Okay?"

Yarden nodded and ducked behind a large louver panel. Calin shrugged and began pulling off her yos. Treet turned his back discreetly and met Tvrdy as he returned from making his check of the vehicles, carrying bubble helmets and atmosphere canisters under his arms.

"Aw, do we need those?" whined Pizzle.

"It is advisable." Tvrdy handed helmets around. "We would not think to move outside the dome without a breather pack."

"How long are these packs good for?" asked Treet. The helmets looked brand new and never used. Strange to think they were likely several thousand years old.

"Five hundred hours. I have put replacement canisters for each of you in the skimmer compartments."

"That gives us—" Treet began calculating.

"Twenty days per canister," said Pizzle.

"We ought to be able to find the lost tribes in forty days, eh?" It certainly seemed like a long enough time to be wandering around in the wilderness. He turned to Tvrdy. "What do we do when we come back? How do we get in touch with you?"

"Come back here to this entrance." Tvrdy indicated the massive fibersteel doors before them. "There is a code lock on the outside. Press it and I will come to meet you or send someone."

"Fine, but I don't know the code and neither do you."

"It doesn't matter. All locks are monitored in Tanais Hage. When someone attempts an inappropriate code, a warning signal is tripped. We will know you are here."

Treet looked at Tvrdy for a long time and then said, "You sure you wouldn't rather come with us? You might live longer."

Tvrdy smiled grimly. "I'll survive. Once he knows that you have escaped, Jamrog will not persist on this course. I will bring charges against him before the other Directors, and he will deny them, and that will be that—for a while."

"Whatever you say. We'll be back as soon as possible. I can't promise anything, but we'll do all we can to bring help."

"We will await your return, Hageman Treet. Tanais priests will offer benefices to the outland spirits for your safety." Tvrdy seemed about to say something else, but turned quickly away, donned a bubble helmet, and moved to a pedestal near the great curving door. He pulled off the cloth covering the pedestal and studied the mechanism.

"Everybody ready?" said Treet. Pizzle, Calin, and Yarden stood lined up behind him. All were wearing singletons and had their helmets under their arms with breather packs attached. "Okay, let's get 'em on."

Helmets in place, Treet gave Tvrdy a signal, and the Director punched a button on the console. Nothing happened. He tapped it again, but the door did not budge. Without a word, Calin went to the pedestal and placed her hands on it. A moment later the doors ground into motion on huge, complaining rollers, sliding apart slowly, ponderously.

Treet went to the nearest vehicle and climbed on, settling himself in the driver's seat. There was a joystick affair for steering and two pedals on the floor which could not be reached with his feet unless he stood. He puzzled over this arrangement for a moment before realizing that passengers were intended to straddle the central humps and ride the skimmers like camel jockeys. Portions of the long cushioned seat flipped up for backrests. With joystick in hand, the driver pressed the pedals with his knees—though what the pedals did, Treet had yet to discover.

Pizzle stood close and pointed to the panel under the stubby windscreen. "They're electric," he said. "With solid-fuel assist generators."

"I can read," Treet pointed out. "Get ready. You and Yarden take that one; Calin and I will take this one." He indicated the sleek blue-and-black skimmer nearby. "And you better let Yarden drive." Pizzle flapped his arms in protest, but Treet cut him short, saying, "You don't have your glasses, remember?" Pizzle snorted, but climbed on the vehicle behind Yarden.

Pale, watery light spilled in from the widening crack as the doors inched apart. Treet pressed the ignition plate, and the machine trembled to life beneath him with a sound like the whine of a ramjet turbine. Calin scrambled up behind Treet and pulled a strap across her hips, raising two handgrips into position near her arms. Treet nodded and gave a thumbs-up signal to Yarden, who acknowledged it with a wave.

The doors slid slowly open and as Treet eased back on the joystick, inching the skimmer forward, he glanced up just in time to see black shapes boiling in through the gap. He saw Tvrdy rush forward. Someone shouted.

Treet jerked the joystick back and the skimmer lurched forward, stuttered, and died.

The black shapes swarmed around them, cutting off their only escape. Treet cursed and hit the ignition plate. Nothing. A hand snaked out and grabbed him by the wrist before he could hit it again.

THIRTY EIGHT

Treet wrenched his arm away, but it was held fast. With his heart thumping triple time, he yelled for help, cutting his cry short in mid-yelp, for he witnessed a strange thing: Tvrdy running forward and embracing one of the attackers. Traitor! thought Treet. He has sold us out!

But no, they turned and came toward him together, Tvrdy slapping the side of his helmet. Treet found the radio switch on the neck and tapped it. A squawk of static burst in his ears, and out of the noise Tvrdy's voice emerged saying, "Cejka could not reach us. He and his men have been waiting for us outside."

Relief washed over Treet as the meaning of Tvrdy's words broke upon him.

"Crocker!" Pizzle leaped from his skimmer and ran to where Rumon Hagemen escorted a lanky figure through the door.

The pilot leaned heavily on those supporting him as he shuffled into the Archives. "Crocker, can you hear me?" asked Treet, throwing himself from the skimmer and rushing forward. "You okay?"

Crocker's voice sounded thin and wheezy in Treet's helmet. "I've been better." The Captain laughed, and the laugh lapsed into a dry cough. "I was afraid you were thinking of taking off without me."

"Wouldn't dream of it," replied Treet. "But are you sure? I mean—"

"You're *not* leaving me behind. I can make it." Treet heard desperation in the Captain's voice.

Treet glanced at Pizzle, who only stared noncommittally into space, and back to Crocker. "You're sure?"

Crocker nodded. "Please, I'll be fine."

"You may not thank me for this," said Treet. "But all right—if that's what you want, I won't stop you."

"It may be for the best." Tvrdy spoke up. "If Jamrog discovered he remained behind, his life would be in danger."

Cejka agreed. "It would be safer for everyone."

"You mean the chase will be off once we've disappeared." Treet nodded. "Okay, we'll take the other skimmer too. Calin, you're going to have to drive. Can you handle it?"

The magician nodded inside her helmet. "It won't be difficult."

"Good. Let's get going. As soon as we're out of here, we'll all feel a whole lot better." Cjeka's men helped Crocker to Calin's skimmer, made him comfortable, and strapped him in. Treet climbed up into the driver's seat once again and pressed the ignition plate, heard the muffled whine of the engine, felt the throb of mechanical life. When everyone was ready, he eased back the joystick and the skimmer scraped forward slowly, bumped over the outer doorseal, and pulled itself along under the superstructure of the landing platform—a dark forest of fibersteel pylons and beams.

The blade-runners carved through the bare earth beneath the platform, knifing a twin track in the dirt. Treet pulled the joystick back further and speed increased, stabilizing the tipsy craft somewhat. The wheels, flattened with the weight of the skimmer and its passengers, bit into the soil and churned them forward.

Now Treet cleared the edge of the platform and plunged into long grass, which dragged at the skimmer, swishing and hissing as the vehicle sliced through. He drove toward the rise of a low hill directly in front of him and glanced back to see how the others were navigating. "Everybody getting the hang of it?"

His question went unanswered. Just as he turned to look back, an explosion ripped the earth not five meters in front of him. "Look out!" screamed Pizzle, his voice sharp inside the helmet. Another explosion rocked the skimmer as a crater blossomed in the grass nearby. Chunks of smoking dirt rattled on the cowling of the skimmer as Treet hunched over the joystick, urging the machine faster.

"They're on the platform!" cried Treet, stealing a glance behind him as the vehicle plunged forward. Both Calin and Yarden had cleared the platform and were racing out over the grass. "Spread out! You're too close together."

Treet gained the top of the hill and slowed to look back. Calin had split off to one side, and Yarden had fallen behind somewhat. A brilliant flash leaped from the platform, and a sheet of flame engulfed the trailing skimmer.

"Yarden!" screamed Treet. His breath caught in his throat, and he threw the joystick forward.

"Keep moving!" cried Crocker. "Don't stop!"

Treet spun around and saw Yarden's skimmer come shooting out of a wall of boiling smoke and dust, the nose of her vehicle scorched black. "I—I'm okay . . . I think," she said into her helmet mike.

Three more fireballs exploded around them, but the skimmers reached the crest of the hill, plowed over the top, and were cut off from the direct line of fire of those on the platform. Treet leaned to the side, and the skimmer carved a graceful arc along the slope. "Hey, it's easy!" he said. "Like steering a sled—just lean into it."

The others followed his lead and they swept down the hillside, keeping themselves out of sight of the Invisibles on the platform. At the bottom of the hill, Treet turned to glide into a shallow valley between two hills. The valley flattened out after only two hundred meters, and once again they came into view from the platform. A volley of thundervolts strafed the ground, throwing charred landscape into steaming spires. The skimmers sped forward, sliding through the grass.

Desperate to get more speed out of the machine, Treet yanked the joystick all the way back. The action threw him momentarily off balance, raising his knees off the pedals. Instantly the skimmer streaked ahead—an arrow released from the bowstring—as the blades raised up.

Treet understood at once what had happened and informed the other drivers of his discovery. "On turf the blades drag; they're used only for steering. Raise up on the pedals and decrease the drag," he explained, and immediately the three were rocketing over the hills, rapidly outdistancing the hostile fire.

"Whee! This is fantastic!" chirped Pizzle. "Next best thing to flying."

Crocker spoke up. "If I remember the scan we took before landing, there was a minus eight dry land reading off to the southeast of the colony."

"Minus eight dry land. That would be a desert?"

"Think Sahara—that's minus eight."

"I caught a glimpse of it on one of our passes," said Pizzle. "I saw a river too."

Treet vaguely remembered seeing a river as the *Zehpyros*

streaked by, but so much had happened since they'd landed, that day and its events seemed impossibly remote.

Ahead, a rising slope flattened to a promontory. "Let's stop up ahead to reconnoiter," said Treet. "We'll get oriented, and then we can travel."

"Good idea," replied Pizzle. "But let's not delay too long. I wouldn't mind putting a few thousand kilometers between me and those Invisibles back there before lunch. They might decide to get serious about all this and come after us."

They stopped their machines on the little plateau and checked for damage. Other than a few more dents, and some fire-blistered paint on Yarden's skimmer, they all had come through unscathed. Treet craned his neck around and saw the magnificent silvery bubble cluster of Empyrion glittering like a jewel as the sun's first rays bathed it in early morning light. Far behind them, smoke spread and flattened on the breeze. There was no more shooting; the Invisibles had given up without a chase, or so it seemed.

Treet turned his eyes to the west. Pale green hills the color of turquoise stretched away to the horizon beneath a sky-bowl of pale, bird's egg blue. The country was wide and broad and astonishingly open. A rush of pure liberation whipped through him, and he realized just how cramped and confining the colony had been, how constricted and limiting.

"I was sure I'd never see the sky again," said Yarden softly. Treet turned, and she was beside him. He looked through the faceplate of her helmet and saw tears trickling down her cheeks.

"It's really something," said Treet. "I forgot what freedom was like. I don't think I'll forget again."

After consulting a very subdued Calin about direction, they started off, riding the green crests and valleys in search of the legendary lost Fieri.

Jamrog's eyes narrowed as he took in Hladik's information. When he finally spoke, his voice was ice and venom. "So Tvrdy had succeeded! Very well, let him believe he has won—it will make his fall the sweeter." He fell silent then, gazing into space while his fingers tapped restlessly on the side of the chair. Momentarily he came to himself again and regarded the Nilokerus leader sharply. "Well, tell me why I shouldn't have you thrown into your own reorientation cells."

Hladik had prepared for just this eventuality. He said simply, "Only that I may have delivered the Fieri into our hands."

"If this is a lie, Hageman, it is most ambitious. Tell me, how did you accomplish this remarkable feat?"

"One of the spies was placed in Nilokerus Hage . . ."

"Don't insult me, Hladik; I well remember. You said he had disappeared with the others."

"He did, but not before I had him conditioned."

Jamrog's smile was hard. "Your famous conditioning, yes. However, your subjects usually die, do they not?"

"Some do. This one survived. He is conditioned to return to me when he finds the Fieri."

"I see." Jamrog's expression became even more fierce. "Then let us hope for your sake that he finds them, Hageman. In the meantime we have Tvrdy and his cohorts to deal with. They must not be allowed to strengthen their position through this episode."

"I have some ideas about that, Director," offered Hladik hopefully. His face shone with a faint sheen of sweat. He knew how close he had been to invoking Jamrog's wrath against him. But now he could relax; the worst was over. "I suggest we discuss them over souile."

"Your tastes have become expensive, Hladik. I'm not sure I approve."

"It's no more than the Threl can afford, Hageman," he chuckled, keeping his eyes on Jamrog.

"Oh, in that case we'll drink to Rohee's health, shall we?"

"Yes—may it desert him in a most timely fashion!"

Jamrog laughed and took Hladik by the arm, and they went out together into Empyrion's twisted pathways.

THIRTY
NINE

"As I see it," said Treet, "our problems are only beginning."

The day had grown comfortably warm. Epsilon Eridani shone bright, a white disk directly overhead, smaller in the heavens than Earth's yellow Sol. Empyrion's sky fairly shimmered a fine, transparent blue—the color of flame. The company had stopped to rest and eat and, more importantly, plan their strategy for surviving in the alien wilderness.

Treet continued, "We have no food, no water—only the emergency rations in our packs, and at the rate they're going, those won't last long. In short, we're in it up to our furry eyebrows, friends."

Pizzle got up and wandered over to where the skimmers were parked.

"Am I boring you with this, Pizzle?" asked Treet, his voice crackling over the helmet speaker.

"No, I'm as concerned as you are. I just had an idea, that's all."

"We've got to rig up some kind of shelter," added Crocker. "We don't really know what the climate is like. It could freeze every night, or rain."

"We can at least make a fire at night," said Yarden. "Can't we?"

The group looked at one another glumly. No one wanted to add to the bad news by pointing out that they had no fire-making equipment and no fuel either. The treeless hills stretched out in every direction, an endless rolling sea of pale green, the color of turquoise or blue jade, without feature all the way to the horizon. Even if they managed somehow to make a fire, there was absolutely nothing to burn.

"Fire takes fuel, which we don't have. And speaking of fuel," said Treet, regretting his dismal inventory, "there's the matter of go-juice for the skimmers."

"They're electric," called Pizzle, bending over the side of the nearest skimmer.

"Gosh, thanks!" remarked Treet. "That helps ever so much. We already *know* they're electric, Whiz Kid. But their cells are recharged by generators which run on solid fuel."

"Yeah, and solar," replied Pizzle. "See?" He straightened and unfolded a winglike panel from the rear of the vehicle. "Solar cells. We can run on solar and, unless I'm mistaken, recharge the batteries at the same time. We'll save the fuel for emergencies."

Treet was impressed, but hardly felt in a congratulatory mood. "That helps a little," he admitted. "But it's going to take more than a few solar cells to pull us through. What else do you have there?"

"Give me a minute." Pizzle walked around to the other side of the skimmer and studied it, poking here and there around the machine, his putty face pursed in a scowl of concentration.

"Weapons," Crocker said. "We should have some weapons—even primitive clubs would be better than bare hands. There could well be carnivorous animal life around here."

"We haven't seen anything," said Yarden. "Wouldn't we have seen signs of any animals?"

"Not necessarily. They might be nocturnal." Crocker saw the face Treet made and continued, "Okay, maybe I'm wrong. My point is that we don't know this world at all and that until we get acquainted we better be on our toes."

"You're right, of course." Treet turned his attention to Calin, who had been strangely quiet all morning. "What about it, Calin? Any night-stalking meat-eaters we ought to be on the lookout for?"

Calin returned to awareness and looked blankly at Treet. "Animals?" She mouthed the word oddly. "I know of no animals. I have never been . . . outside . . . the dome . . ." Her voice trailed off, and she returned to her reverie.

"There's another thing I wasn't going to bring up—about the helmets," began Crocker.

"You might as well bring it up; we're on a roll. What about the helmets? We have enough air for forty days apiece."

"It isn't that. The thing is we can't take them off—which means we can't eat or drink."

Treet stared. It was true—there was no way to eat or drink without taking off the helmet. "We need some kind of airtight shelter. Fast!" He had a picture of them all slowly starving to death inside the oversized mushroom-shaped globes.

Pizzle's nasal yammer sounded in his ear. "I don't know if this will work or not," he said.

"If what will work?"

"This tent idea. Look here—" Pizzle came ambling back with a long, orange bag that bounced as he walked. He dumped it in front of them and set about emptying it. Slender fibersteel poles came sliding out, along with knitted nylon-type roping, thin and strong, and a flat packet of cloth that looked like crinkled orange silk.

Pizzled picked up the bright orange packet and shook it out, unfolding it into an ultrathin membrane with narrow pockets. They watched as he slid the poles into the pockets, stretching the material taut as the fibersteel bent into half circles. Within three minutes the tent was erected: a longish, ribbed tunnel affair with a mivex seal for a door. It looked like a culvert that had been flattened on the bottom and pinched down at one end. Clearly, occupancy was limited to no more than two people.

"*Voila!*" said Pizzle proudly, admiring his handiwork.

"Any more where that came from?"

"I should think so. There's a long, skinny compartment on the floor of the left-hand side of the skimmer. It was underneath the reserve air canisters. There should be one in each vehicle, and my guess is they're waterproof as well as airtight. You don't put a mivex seal on something unless you want to keep something in or out." Pizzle glanced around, lips wrapped around his imp grin. "You know this is just like *Escape from Nurakka*—I mean, they used airboats, but it's the same idea."

Crocker, pale and unsteady, leaned his hands on his knees and studied the tent. "We'd have to figure some way to bleed out the air inside and fill it again so we could breathe in there."

"We could use the spare canisters—valve off just enough to get a good mix," explained Pizzle. "We know that the air is not downright poisonous, so that shouldn't be any problem."

"Wouldn't we use up our oxygen faster?" wondered Yarden.

"Maybe. Not much though," replied Crocker. "We wouldn't be wearing our helmets inside the tent, so breathing time would even out somewhat. You'd lose a little every time you opened the seal, of course. Once inside the tent, we'd have to stay in."

Treet frowned inside his helmet. The whole enterprise seemed so half-baked in the clear light of day. "Then we eat only once a day," he grumped. "Fantastic."

"Twice," replied Crocker, straightening painfully. "When we put up the tents for the night and again just before we take them down in the morning. That won't be too bad."

"What about water? I can't go all day long without a drink."

"Maybe I could rig up some kind of straw gizmo and run it up through the neck seal of the helmet."

"We've got to *find* water first," Yarden pointed out.

"The river Pizzle mentioned is to the east. If we keep heading this direction, we'll hit it before long," said Crocker.

"What about the desert?" wondered Treet.

"Look," snapped the Captain, "one problem at a time. We'll solve 'em as they come, okay? You people are going to have to give up some of your ideas about creature comforts. This isn't a nature hike we're on. This is survival."

"Speaking of which," Pizzle chimed in, "I think we ought to be moving along. The further from that place back there," he jerked a thumb over his shoulder, "the better I'll feel. Since we can't eat or anything until we get the tents up, let's travel as far as we can."

The sun was aglow in the western sky, burnishing each hilltop a brassy green-gold and throwing each valley into deep blue shadow, when the company decided to stop for the night. Although the sun remained above the smooth horizon, away in the east faint flickers of starlight already glimmered. The sky seemed fragile and transparent, the sheerest of materials, lending the light an intense and vibrant quality—almost alive.

For the last two hours no one had broken radio silence. All were tired and preoccupied, steeling themselves for the rigors ahead. Treet had convinced himself that he would survive; one way or another he would make it. He would do all he could to help the others, but their survival, he reasoned, depended upon themselves. He was not responsible for getting them into this,

265

nor was he responsible for getting them out—that was a problem they all shared equally. In Treet's opinion they were *all* victims.

This was the way his thoughts were bending. So it was with a shock that he heard his own voice cracking in his eardrums: "I think we'd better find a place to make camp. Since we haven't done this before, we don't want to be fumbling around in the dark."

Why did I do that? he wondered. Why couldn't I let Crocker take command? If anyone should lead, *he* should.

Crocker ratified his suggestion. "You're right. We're losing the light. Let's stop at the next flat hilltop you see."

The next flat hilltop was two hilltops away. Treet slowed the skimmer as it crested the hill and parked it so the solar panel could pick up the last of the sun's rays. He slowly unfolded himself from the driver's position and stretched out the kinks. According to the odometer on the skimmer's control panel they had covered slightly over two hundred and eighty kilometers since their last stop, which worked out to around five hundred and sixty for the day. Not too bad for the first day.

Treet did a few quick toe touches and torso twists as the other climbed down from their vehicles. "I feel like one of those old-time cowboys," said Pizzle. "You know, like Roy Rogers. I believe I'm getting saddle sores."

"You look a little bowlegged," said Treet, flipping open the storage compartment of the skimmer and pulling out the long tent envelope. He carried the tent to a level spot and dumped it out. The others chose spots nearby and began setting up their tents.

"Let's keep them fairly close together," said Crocker, "so we can talk to each other."

"Who's going to be talking?" said Treet. "Once I crawl inside, I'm sound asleep."

"It's eat first and then sleep for me," said Yarden. "I'm starved."

Crocker warned, "We'd better make our food last. It might be a while before we find anything edible out here." When no one responded, he went on more insistently, "I mean it! No more than a few mouthfuls—eat just what you need to keep yourself going. And drink only a swallow."

"Aye, aye, Captain Bligh," grouched Treet. "We get the picture. Let's don't dwell on it."

"Look, Treet. Maybe you'd prefer leading this expedition yourself. It's not in my contract that I have to be Bwana, you know."

"I didn't mean that you—I mean, I—" stuttered Treet. "Oh, forget it. We're exhausted, and we're all stressed out. Let's just get the tents up and go to sleep."

The sun had nearly dropped below the fading hill line when they climbed into the tents: Treet and Calin into one—the magician would not go with anyone else—and Crocker and Pizzle in another, since Yarden did not express an interest in sharing quarters with either of them and the men were hesitant to suggest otherwise.

Treet backed into the half-hoop structure, pulling two spare air canisters in after him. He sealed the mivex entrance and then opened the connector valves of both flat canisters, allowed air to bleed off while he counted seconds, and then said into his mike, "I've had both valves wide open for ninety seconds. Now what?"

"Take your helmet off," said Pizzle.

"You take *your* helmet off!"

"It'll work, don't worry," Pizzle coaxed. "Trust me."

"I don't know why I'm the guinea pig, but here goes." He took a deep breath and placed his hands on either side of the helmet, gave a three-quarter twist, and lifted it off, holding it above his head for quick replacement. He let his breath out and paused, then sniffed experimentally. Okay, so far. He drew more air in and held it—nothing unusual. Calin sat cross-legged at the far end of the tent, watching him with wide eyes. Then he gulped a deep breath and announced, "It works! Hey, it works!"

He breathed deeply, in and out again a few times. Besides a faint metallic tang on the back of his tongue, the air seemed perfect. "It feels great to get out of that plastic bubble!" He heard a faint voice, like the voice of his conscience buzzing at him. He picked up his helmet again.

"You forget something?" It was Crocker.

"Are you all right?" inquired Yarden with some concern.

"Yeah, sorry. It works perfect. You can take your helmets off now." He waited a few seconds and then hollered, "Isn't that better?"

"Marvelous!" came Yarden's answer through the tent membrane.

"Sweet relief!" called Pizzle.

Treet took Calin's helmet off as she made no move to do it herself. She looked at him oddly and then curled up in a ball where she sat. He opened their emergency pouches and brought out some food for them—dry wafers with the texture and taste of dog biscuits. He gave a couple to Calin and crunched down two himself, then rinsed his mouth with a few sparing sips of water.

He placed one of the flat air canisters under his head for a pillow and stretched out. Calin remained curled at one end of the tent. Rather than try to move her, Treet lay diagonally across the floor so that he would not have to keep his knees flexed all night. "Nighty night," Treet called as he settled himself to sleep.

He heard some mumbling from Pizzle and Crocker's tent, but closed his eyes and was asleep at once.

FORTY

The dog biscuits tasted no better just before dawn the next morning, but by then he was hungry enough to eat rocks. At least the single sip of water he allowed himself was refreshing. Calin awoke at Treet's merest touch and rose without speaking. They donned their helmets and climbed out of the tent. Treet walked down one side of the hill, Calin the other as the sky turned pink low in the east. Treet stood looking at the dawn-dulled sky, noting a line of gray clouds with rosy feathered edges chugging westward far to the south. Otherwise, the heavens were uniformly void.

When he retraced his steps up the hill, he met Pizzle coming down. "Sleep okay?" he asked.

"Fair. Crocker muttered all night; I think he's still hurting."

"Crocker can hear you, you know." The voice was Crocker's, loud in their helmet speakers. "I'll be all right. Don't you worry about me. I won't slow anybody up."

"Sorry," Pizzle said quickly. "I wasn't implying anything."

Treet turned to see Crocker stumbling down the hill toward them. "Is it true, Crocker? Are you in pain?"

"No!" the Captain denied, a little too forcefully. "Just worry about yourselves."

"We could stay put for a day or two and let you get some rest . . ."

Crocker jabbed a finger at Treet's chest. "Nobody is doing any such thing on my account. We'd waste food and water which we might well need later on."

"I didn't mean anything," said Pizzle sullenly.

"Yes, we know you didn't mean anything," snapped Treet. "Forget it. Let's get the tents down and head out."

The sun's pearl-white disk was peeping above the eastern hill line by the time everyone was ready. The skimmer's whine, muffled by the helmet, climbed into the upper registers, and Treet eased back the joystick for another day's journey.

"Keep the sun to your back and spread out. We can't afford any accidents," he said as his skimmer slid out over the grass, gliding down the hill into the shadowed valley.

Treet again took the lead, Calin maintaining a steady speed a little ways back on his left hand, Yarden nearly even on the right. The three vehicles churned their way across the rippled landscape, passing from sunlight into shadow as the turquoise hills rose and fell in even waves.

The next two days were perfect copies of the first. They ate, slept, woke, and traveled the wide, hill-bound country, which showed no variation and gave no indication of ever changing at all. A more monotonous land Treet could not imagine.

This, Treet reminded himself, could be considered a blessing, for it meant that their travel was unimpeded by the more diverting variations of scenery and weather. If there was nothing much to look at, at least no obstacles hindered them.

About midday the fourth day out, they halted to stretch and take another directional reading—as much as possible. Treet sat on the ground, tucked his knees up to his chest, and rolled on his back, working the kinks out of his lower spine. While the others were walking and limbering up, he approached Calin, who was sitting by herself on the ground next to the skimmer.

Her eyes were focused on something far away in the distance when he came up. He squatted down beside her and tapped her helmet. When she failed to acknowledge his presence, he reached out and touched her radio switch. "Calin, I haven't heard a squeak out of you since yesterday. Are you feeling okay?"

Calin did not move when he addressed her, but remained immobile, arms encircling updrawn knees, vision fixed on the unvarying horizon.

"Did you hear me?" Treet leaned toward her. "Calin?"

"Can I help?" Yarden dropped down beside him on her knees.

"I don't know what's wrong with her. She hasn't said a word all day."

As Treet spoke, the magician's body began to shiver,

though the sun was warm and the breeze fair. "Calin? Listen to me. Calin?"

The tremors became more pronounced. She raised her head, and Treet saw in her eyes a vacant, mindless stare—the look of a wild creature shivering with fright. He placed a hand on her shoulder and felt her muscles rigid and cold beneath his touch. "She's stiff as stone!"

Her head began thrashing inside her helmet. Her mouth worked silently behind closed lips, and a keening moan sounded in the helmet speakers. Her eyelids fluttered as her eyeballs rolled up into their sockets. Blood trickled from her mouth. "Her tongue—she's chewing her tongue!" cried Treet. "We've got to do something!"

Yarden bent close, putting her arms around the trembling woman. "Calin, this is Yarden." She spoke softly, calmly. "I'm going to take your helmet off."

"You can't do that!" shouted Treet. "It could kill her!"

Yarden moved behind the magician and cradled her trembling body. "She'll die anyway—she's swallowed her tongue. She's choking!"

It was true. Calin's face was now tinted a ghastly shade of purple; her lips were blue.

Yarden put her hands on either side of the helmet and gave a sharp twist. She pulled it off and forced Calin's jaws open with one hand, reaching deftly in with her long fingers and flipping the magician's curled tongue forward.

Calin gulped air and instantly her eyes bulged out in terror. "Aaiiee!" She screamed a ragged, throat-tearing scream which, even through the sound-dampening properties of their helmets, sounded like a death rattle. Her hands clawed at the air.

"For God's sake, get her helmet back on!" boomed Crocker, running up.

Pizzle stood frozen a little way off, staring at the writhing woman on the ground before him. Yarden still knelt beside her, holding her head. Calin inhaled and screamed again, this time her voice faint and far away. "Aaiiee! It bur-r-n-n-s!"

Treet snatched up her helmet and thrust it forward.

"No!" said Yarden.

"You're killing her!" cried Treet. He moved to put the helmet over Calin's head, but Yarden shoved it aside.

"No, wait!"

"Talazac!" roared Crocker. "Get that helmet back on her right now. What do you think you're doing?"

Treet stooped with the helmet in his hands. Yarden resisted once more. "Please stop. It'll be all right. Just wait a moment."

"What's gotten into you?" said Treet. He hesitated, his hands thrust out with the helmet between them. "Do you want her to die?"

"Wait, she's right," said Pizzle. "Look."

Calin lay still now, her color improving and her breathing, though still ragged and shallow, developing a more regular rhythm. She whimpered and moaned, but her limbs had stopped trembling and her head no longer thrashed. "It *burns*," she rasped.

"Well, I never—" observed Crocker. "She seems to be coming out of it."

"Get her some water," ordered Yarden. Pizzle returned seconds later with one of the pouches. He held up the collapsible plastic canteen to Calin's lips and she swallowed, her features convulsing with pain. "Her throat's a little sore I imagine," said Yarden, putting her hands to her own helmet.

"Wait! You're not thinking of taking off *your* helmet." Treet stared incredulously at Yarden. "Have you lost your mind?"

"She needs me," replied Yarden simply. "I have to talk to her." She gave the helmet a quick twist and pulled it off. She paused, eyes closed, laying the helmet aside. Then she inhaled.

The pain twisted her features monstrously. She gulped air and shuddered, collapsing against the side of the skimmer. Her hands went to her throat, which she grasped as if she were trying to strangle herself. Tears streamed from her eyes. "Ahh! Ah-hh-hh . . ."

"Yarden! Put your helmet back on!" shouted Treet. He leaped forward, took up the headgear, and lowered it over Yarden's head. Her eyes flew open, and she knocked it away. "Help me, you two!" Treet shouted to Pizzle and Crocker, who stood motionless behind him. "Yarden, you're suffocating."

"She can't hear you anymore," said Crocker.

Treet raised the helmet once more, but Yarden reached out, gripped his arm, and dug her nails in. "She doesn't want it," said Pizzle. "She's over it."

Yarden's eyes opened slowly. She smiled weakly, painfully, then bent over the quivering magician and spoke to her. Treet saw her mouth move, but could not hear the words. Then Yarden straightened and turned to Treet, put her hands on his helmet, and nodded.

Treet shook his head furiously and grabbed her wrists. She smiled and mouthed the words, *Trust me*. He hesitated, then took a deep breath, and nodded. The helmet twisted and came off. Treet sat back on his heels, still holding his breath.

"Let it out slow and breathe in slow," said Yarden in a grating whisper. "It will sting like fury, but you'll be okay."

Sting wasn't the word for it. As Treet inhaled, it felt as if all his soft tissues had suddenly burst into flame—as if his nasal passages, throat, and windpipe had ignited. His lungs convulsed with the shock. Angry red flares erupted in his brain. It seemed as if he breathed pure fire.

The scream he loosed was far from pretty. It bubbled in his throat and tore up through his vocal cords in an explosive burst only to trail off into an agonized, choking wheeze. Tears blinded his eyes and he squirmed convulsively on the ground, thrashing from side to side.

"Don't fight it," Yarden soothed. He felt her hands on his chest. "Breathe in slowly. Stay on top and ride it out."

Treet fought the pain, pushing it down with an effort. He opened his eyes and saw Yarden bending over him, her eyes bright, coaxing him with encouragement. "You're almost through the worst," she said in a voice frayed and ragged.

He drew another shallow, shaky breath and felt his scorched tissues wilt. The pain seared through his lungs; it felt as though they had been turned inside out and singed with acid. He coughed and moaned.

His next breath was better, and the next better still. The pain subsided to a sharp tingle. He raised himself slowly, wiping the tears from the side of his neck. Calin sat looking at him, panting lightly as if she'd run a sprint to reach him. Yarden smiled. "Not so bad," she said hoarsely.

"Not if you're used to eating fire," replied Treet, his throat raw as frazzled wire.

Yarden motioned to Pizzle and Crocker to remove their helmets, but the two refused, backing away cautiously. Treet did not blame them in the least; in fact, he marveled at himself for acquiescing so readily to Yarden's request. Why had he done that?

"Let them keep them on if they want," rasped Treet. He

drew a tentative deep breath and though it still stung fiercely, the pain was not what it had been moments before. He could bear it. "Why did you do that, Yarden?"

She looked perplexed. "I don't know. I had a feeling about it—a strong feeling that we should do it. Calin had to have help in any case. I had to get to her."

"What do you mean we *should* do it? How could you know that?"

"I don't think I can explain it to you. It just seemed right, that's all. Besides, I couldn't bear the thought of being trapped in that thing for the rest of my life."

"Come on—the rest of your life?"

"I'm never going back to the colony." Yarden said this with utmost self-assurance, as if stating the most evident fact.

Before Treet could ask her about her declaration, Crocker tapped him on the shoulder. Treet glanced up into the faceplate and saw the Captain's mouth forming broad, muted words which he couldn't read. Treet shook his head. "You're going to have to spell it out! I can't hear you," he shouted.

"He says we should put our helmets back on. It's danger-ous without them," offered Yarden.

Treet straightened and slipped his helmet on briefly. "I really don't think it's dangerous," he said into the mike. "I think you should take yours off—both of you."

"Funny, you don't *look* crazy," quipped Pizzle.

"Suit yourselves. I don't care what you do. But I think Yarden is right—this way is better."

Pizzle and Crocker swiveled to look at one another. They shook their heads, and Pizzle spoke for both of them. "No way. We saw you jerking around on the ground."

"No pain, no gain," said Treet, removing the headpiece once more.

He turned to the women. "You gave us a scare, Calin. Do you feel any better now?"

The slender magician nodded slightly. "I was afraid."

"I'll say. But what were you afraid of?"

She looked at him blankly and made no answer.

"Well, I guess it doesn't matter. We can talk about it later. Right now we need for you to get in touch with Nho and ask him about direction."

Calin went still and her eyes lost their focus. Yarden looked at her and said, "You shouldn't make her do that."

"She does it. I don't make her," Treet replied. "You act as if all this is my fault somehow. Let me tell you—it's not my fault!"

Calin came to herself again. "Nho says we are going the right way."

"That's all? Would he care to elaborate?"

"There is nothing else to say now."

They each took a sip of water, Pizzle and Crocker looking on thirstily, then remounted the skimmers again to slide even further into the hill-rumpled waste.

FORTY
ONE

That night Yarden sat alone on the hillside just below the hoop-shaped tents. Pizzle and Crocker were sealed in their tent, and Calin, who had earlier decided to join Yarden, was asleep in hers while Treet walked the tightness out of his legs and shoulders, striding up and down the nearby hills, swinging his arms. His lungs still ached—as if he'd run a very fast ten thousand meters—but the sharp burning sensation was gone. He came upon Yarden and flopped down beside her. Neither spoke for a long time.

"It's amazing, isn't it," he said at last. "The quiet. It's so . . . profound."

The air was still and deathly silent. He had never heard such an absolute absence of sound in the outdoors: no piping birdcalls, no burring insects, no rustling leaves or ticking branches. Nothing.

This is what it's like to be deaf, thought Treet.

"Not deaf," said Yarden. "More like immune."

Treet thought about asking her what she meant, then thought that she already knew he was thinking about asking her and decided not to. Instead, he leaned back and gazed upward at the stars beginning to glow in the deepening twilight. Empyrion had no moon, so the stars shone especially bright in the darkening heavens. "Do you realize we're looking at constellations we have no names for?"

"Mmm," said Yarden, "stars should have names. We could make some up."

"It wouldn't be official."

"Why not! Ours would be as good as anybody else's."

"Okay, see that wobbly string of stars just above the horizon, with that bright one at the head? We'll call that one Ophidia—the snake."

"How about that one with the brightest star directly overhead? It looks like a bird—there's the head, and those stars

276

sweeping down on either side are the wings. A pretty bird—a nightingale, I think."

"Make that one Luscinia, then."

"Ophidia and Luscinia," said Yarden softly. "I like those. You're good with words."

"I'm a writer—or used to be."

"Used to be? What are you now?" she asked lightly. Treet could feel her eyes on him, but kept looking at the sky.

"I don't know what I am. Right now I seem to be an explorer."

"Yes, I see what you mean. None of us are exactly playing our usual roles." She lay back on an elbow. "I know I never will again."

"Fatalism?"

"No, I don't think so. More like realism. It's a feeling."

"Like the feeling you had about taking off our helmets?" Treet turned to look at her, noting her reaction.

"Something like that. Why did you do it? Pizzle and Crocker wouldn't, I knew that."

"I guess I'm easily influenced."

Yarden laughed, her voice still hoarse. "You are many things, Orion Treet. Easily influenced isn't one of them. I'm serious—why did you do it? Crocker is right; it could have been dangerous."

"Maybe I just wanted to be free of that blasted bubble."

"Your freedom is important to you."

"It is, now that you mention it. I guess that also explains why we're out here scooting across these God-forsaken hills." Treet pushed himself up on one elbow to face her. "I answered your question, but you still haven't answered mine."

"Which question was that?"

"The one I asked earlier: why you think you're not going back to the colony."

"You never asked me that," she said, giving his arm a push. It was the first truly spontaneous gesture Treet had ever seen her make.

"I thought about it—which is the same thing with you, isn't it?"

"I told you it doesn't work like that—I can't read minds. I just get thought impressions, that's all."

"You're evading the question."

She looked at him intently, eyes luminous in the dying

light, and said, "Empyrion is an evil place. I won't go back there."

Her answer surprised him. He replied, "I'll grant it could be better, but evil? It's not *that* bad." The look she gave him told him the subject was not open for debate, so he tried a different tack. "You were pretty shook up when they brought you to Tvrdy's kraam. What happened?" When she did not answer, he added, "You don't have to tell me if you don't want."

"It isn't that. I'm afraid you won't understand—I'm not sure I understand it all myself."

"I know that feeling, at least."

"Yes. Well, for me it was like this," she said, and began relating all that she remembered of her captivity among the Chryse. She told of the plays they'd performed and of the flash orgy and finally of the Astral Service. When she described the Service, Treet noted her voice growing smaller, fainter.

"If this hurts, we don't have to talk about it. Forget I said anything," offered Treet.

"I don't *want* to forget. I want to remember how close I came to giving in. I don't ever want to get that close again."

"Giving in?"

"To the evil of Empyrion." Her tone became intense, insistent. "I felt it in that Service, as I have never felt it in my life until that time—an overwhelming presence of inestimable hate, a force of pure, unremitting malevolence. Trabant, they call it— the name chills me! And this thing, this being is the essence of evil. It wanted me—*demanded* me. I resisted. If the Service had lasted any longer, I would not have been able to hold out."

"But you did hold out."

"Yes, and I never want to be tested like that again."

Treet looked at her a long time, considering her words. "You saved Calin's life this morning. I still can't figure out what happened with her."

"The same thing that happened to me."

"You lost me there."

"Fear."

"She said she was scared. I thought she meant scared of what we were doing."

"Put yourself in her situation. They have lived for untold generations under that dome of theirs. They never leave it for any reason—they view the outside world as an enemy. How would you feel if you lived your whole life believing that and were suddenly thrust out? The land is so big, so empty. It must have terrified her, and that terror worked on her mind until finally she just snapped."

"The same thing might have happened to you in the Service."

"Exactly."

They fell silent after that and just lay quietly in each other's company until Yarden got up and started toward her tent. Treet watched her go, called "Good night" after her, but received no reply. He glanced heavenward and saw that Ophidia had risen higher in the night sky, then got up and went to his tent and fell asleep pondering all Yarden had told him.

Early the next morning the company came in sight of the river. Yarden, with Calin riding behind her, was the first to spot it. She sped up and pulled the skimmer to a halt on the crest of a hill, allowing the others to catch up.

"Do you see it?" she asked.

"See what?" asked Treet. Pizzle and Crocker pulled up and sat staring from inside their helmets, looking at the others.

"The river. See? Down there beyond those hills. You can just see a little sliver of it shining through there." She pointed, and Treet followed her elegant finger to see a glittering spangle threading through the hills.

"Jackpot!" said Calin with a smile. She seemed wholly recovered from her ordeal of the day before—almost a completely different person. Yarden had apparently had a most beneficial effect on her.

"Yes, jackpot." Treet turned to Pizzle and Crocker, shouted at the top of his lungs, and pointed out the river. They looked and responded by nodding vigorously and giving him the A-OK sign. He squinted his eyes and estimated that the river lay at least four kilometers away. "We can be there in five minutes. Let's go. It'll be time for a rest stop when we get there."

They pushed off again and rode the hill swells to the river's edge. There they stopped and looked out over a broad expanse of flowing water, silver blue in the sunlight, its gentle, gurgling music a welcome relief from the skimmers' scream.

They dismounted and walked down to the water's edge. Treet squatted, stretched out his hands, and plunged them in.

The water was cool and clear, the bottom fine-grained sand. He cupped his hands and raised a mouthful to his lips, sipped cautiously, tasted, and then swallowd. The water had a slight astringent quality, but tasted as fresh and clean as its sparkling clarity promised.

"I say it's okay," said Treet over his shoulder to the others watching him. "See what you think." He dipped his hands and drank again and again and was immediately joined by Calin and Yarden. When he had drunk his fill, Treet rose, wiped his mouth on his sleeve, and beckoned to Pizzle and Crocker, who stood looking on like poor relations at a posh family picnic.

He pantomimed taking off a helmet and pointed at them. They stared doubtfully back at him, but made no move to remove the bubbles. Treet shrugged and turned back toward the water. The river stretched a good sixty meters across, flowing southward in unhurried ease, shimmering like quicksilver beneath a blue-white canopy. Although the channel appeared to deepen quite gradually, Treet estimated from its width that at midstream the water would be well beyond a skimmer's ability to navigate—even if the heavy machines had not already foundered in the soft river bottom.

Getting their transportation across would be a trick, no doubt about that. Just how it might be accomplished he could not imagine—until his gaze fell upon Calin, kneeling at the water's edge, drinking.

"We've got a problem, ladies," began Treet, settling beside them. "We have to find a way to get our vehicles across. I don't think they're made for underwater. Got any ideas?"

"A bridge?" began Yarden, then waved aside the idea at once. "Forget I said that." She looked at the desolate hills across the water. "That side is just as barren as this. We'll just have to look for a fording place."

"I guess so—unless Nho can help us out." He looked at Calin directly. "What about it?"

"Treet, no." Yarden put a restraining hand on his arm.

"Calin? Can your psi do anything?"

She considered this for a moment and then nodded. "It would be possible to carry them across perhaps. But I cannot— what is the word?"

"Swim?"

The magician nodded again quickly. "Yes. Swim."

"That is a problem," agreed Treet.

"You can't make her do it," said Yarden. "Do you have any idea what using psi power does to a person?"

"Not really," admitted Treet. "But we've come to a dead end, Yarden. I'm open to suggestions, but unless you know of a good ferry anywhere around, I don't know what else we're going to do."

"Couldn't we at least look for a place to ford? We might find one, which would make crossing a whole lot easier and simpler."

"True. Okay, we look. Here's what we'll do. You and Calin go south and I'll go north—say, for twenty kilometers."

"Thirty."

"All right, thirty. We'll meet back here and share what we've found. How's that?"

Both women agreed, so Treet pushed himself up and went to his skimmer, then donned a helmet briefly to speak to Pizzle and Crocker. "Look, you guys are going to have to get out of those hats. You're missing all the fun."

"What's going on?" asked Crocker.

"Well, we're trying to find a way to get across. Any ideas?"

Crocker glanced at the skimmers. "They're much too heavy to lift that's for sure. A ford, I'd say."

"That's what we decided. Yarden and I are going to split up and take a quick look both ways along the shore. You and Pizzle stay here with the other machine. We'll meet back here in an hour."

"Sounds good," said Pizzle.

"In the meantime, why don't you two work up your nerve and take off your helmets? As you can see, the air is fine. We're thriving. In fact, I think the oxygen content of the atmosphere is higher than Earth's. There's only a momentary discomfort, but that doesn't last."

"Momentary discomfort? Is that what you call rolling around on the ground screaming your heads off? No thanks," said Pizzle.

"Suit yourself. You're going to have to take them off sooner or later. Stay put. We'll be back soon."

Treet, Yarden, and Calin left, driving along the bank, following the slow curves of the river. It wound easily through the hills, and Treet noticed that the river valley was a narrow band on either side, which meant that the water course was relatively recent, geologically speaking. The river had not had time to cut away and flatten the hills along its sides.

Staying close to the bank, he steered the skimmer northward and noticed a ridge ahead which advertised a clear view of the waterway below. Treet left the bank and made for the ridgetop. The promontory did indeed offer a good survey of a fair stretch of river, and nowhere did he see any variation in its width which might indicate shallows. It rolled on placidly beneath the white sun and eventually disappeared beyond a ruffled row of hills away to the north. Though the skimmer's odometer read only fifteen kilometers, Treet decided to turn back, knowing that were he to proceed further he would find only more of the same.

Yarden and Calin were waiting for him when he returned. "There's a shallow place about twenty kilometers from here. It's real rocky and the river spreads out pretty wide, but it doesn't look like it gets more than knee deep," Yarden said, her face glowing with the excitement of discovery. "Did you see anything?"

"Nope. Let's go."

It was as Yarden had said. The river widened and flattened as it ran over a rocky shelf which it could not cut through as easily as the soft, earthy hills. As the others looked on, Treet waded out a few meters into water that came to just over his knees and announced that it appeared not to get much deeper. He sloshed his way back and stood before Calin.

"Well, shall we give it a try?"

Yarden spoke up. "There are a lot of rocks around; maybe we could—"

"What? Build a bridge? Yarden, for crying out loud, we'd be here for months. Be reasonable."

Calin stopped any further discussion. "I will do it." She pressed Yarden's hand, and Treet noted the gesture. An understanding of some sort, a sisterhood, had bloomed overnight between the two women—which was only natural, he supposed. They were, after all, the only females on this expedition, and they were entitled to their own company. But there was something besides the sisterly concern—a harmony between them. Perhaps the gifts they possessed drew them together in a unique way.

"I think it would be best for two of us to go with you. I could go on one side and Pizzle on the other—to steady you in case you slipped or something."

Calin nodded once. She had, Treet noticed, already begun retreating back into herself. Her dark, almond-shaped eyes dulled as her consciousness shifted to that other place where her power lay. She stared straight ahead for a moment, her body very still. Then she moved stiffly to the nearest skimmer, bent to place her hands lightly on its side just above the runner, and straightened. The vehicle floated into the air and hovered.

Pizzle and Crocker stood with mouths agape, and Treet chuckled to himself. He hadn't warned them about what they intended doing; the spectacle no doubt astounded them down to their toenails.

Treet stepped to Calin's side and gestured for Pizzle to do likewise. Pizzle only stared in uncomprehending amazement, so Yarden said, "I'll go with you." She put her hand on the magician's shoulder, and together they walked out into the water.

The river had worn the rock shelf smooth, but it was not slippery. Still, they carefully placed each step, moving slowly out into deeper water to midstream. Even at its deepest point, the water was clear enough to see the bottom, allowing Treet to steer them around the few holes he saw. Soon the water grew shallower again, and they were climbing back out on the other side.

Treet guided them to a flat place near the shore, and Calin put the skimmer down. She straightened, her eyes still dull, her face expressionless. "Do you want to rest or anything?" asked Treet. Calin shook her head, so he said, "Okay, only two more to go. Let's take it slow and easy; we're doing great."

The second crossing went as easily as the first, but when Calin released the machine, it slammed down heavily, bouncing on its suspension. Yarden's wrinkled brow showed concern; she threw a quick, imploring look to Treet which said, *Do something!*

"I think we should rest for a second, Calin," he said. "There's no hurry. We're almost finished."

But the magician turned and started back across the river once more. Yarden's worried expression accused Treet. "I tried to stop her," he said weakly.

The third crossing began like the first two, and proceeded

without incident until they reached midstream. Treet noticed trouble when the skimmer began to waver in the air. Calin stopped abruptly.

"Cal—" began Treet. The skimmer dipped dangerously toward the water.

"Shh! Don't disturb her," whispered Yarden harshly.

Calin became a portrait of exertion: eyes closed tight, sweat beading on forehead, features darkening with strain, knotted veins standing out on her neck. The skimmer bobbled, its bulk rocking wildly as if slipping through her grasp. One runner touched the water.

"Concentrate," cooed Treet. "You can do it. Go slow. Just a little farther; we're almost there."

They took one more step.

"Ahh!" Calin cried, falling back. The skimmer twisted in the air and plunged into the river with a tremendous splash.

FORTY
TWO

Water showered over them as the machine crashed down. The resulting wave knocked them backwards off their feet to flounder helplessly in the backwash. Treet, aware that Calin had fallen, blindly reached out for her, snagged her collar, and held on.

Though the current was not swift, it was strong and Treet was pulled downstream. He flailed his arms and kicked his legs as he fought for a foothold. Finally he managed to get his feet under him and stood, staggered as the water pressed against him, but stayed up. He felt hands on him and cried, "I'm okay! Help me get her out!"

Dashing water from his eyes, Treet saw Calin's limp form slung between Pizzle and Crocker as they sloshed toward the near bank. Yarden stood behind him, hair plastered to her skull and hanging in long sopping ropes. The fright in her expression was replaced with malice as Treet began to laugh.

"Just what's so funny, mister?" she sputtered belligerently, shoving dripping sable locks over her shoulder.

"You look like a wet cat," he laughed. "You okay?"

"As if you cared." She turned and stomped toward the shore.

Treet followed, watching her shapely form moving beneath the clinging wet singleton. Desire spread through him in an instant, shocking Treet with the force of its presence. Yes, he admitted, Yarden Talazac was a very desirable woman. Perhaps he'd wanted her since the beginning, or perhaps now she seemed more of a warm-blooded woman to him and less the cold, ethereal mystic.

He joined her on the shore and said, "I'm sorry I laughed. I just—"

"You just have no sense of compassion!" she snapped. Her light copper skin glowed with anger; a magenta blotch tinted the base of her throat.

"You're really mad." Treet's tone was quiet astonishment.

Yarden quivered—whether with rage or chill, Treet could not tell. Her voice, however, was stiletto sharp. "Of course I'm mad. You could have gotten us all killed with your stupid insistence. I tried to tell you, but you wouldn't listen."

"Wait a min—"

"You can't absolve your guilt in this one! It's your fault."

"My fault! How is it my fault?" Desire was dwindling rapidly as indignation piqued. "Just how do you figure that?"

"You made her use psi. I told you it was dangerous, but you insisted it was the only way. It is *never* the only way."

"Maybe not, but it was the best way."

"No, not even the best way."

"Suppose you tell me what would have been better?" Treet glared, and Yarden glared right back, the magenta blotch deepening and spreading up her throat.

"Oh sure, pretend ignorance. It won't work. You're not shifting blame, Orion Treet," she huffed. "Think about it." Yarden spun away, leaving him with a stinging reply on his tongue and no one to say it to. He watched her march over to where Pizzle and Crocker bent over Calin, trying to revive her by rubbing her hands. Except for the glassy helmets and breathing packs, it was a scene out of a Victorian melodrama where the ineffectual male drones cluster around a fainted female offering smelling salts and encouragement.

Treet snorted and splashed back into the river. The skimmer had landed on its side and was half in the water, one blade gleaming in the sun. Eddies in the current formed whirlpools around the machine, making little sucking noises along its underside. Treet tried to rock it back onto its runners, but even with the push of the current to help him, the vehicle was too heavy to budge. He gave up and joined the others on the bank.

Calin's eyes were open, and she blinked at those bending over her as she came to. She moved to get up, but Yarden said, "Rest a moment. You're safe now. Nothing happened."

She lay back again and her eyes went to Treet. "I—am sorry. I have disappointed you," she said.

"Disappointed me!" He knelt down beside her. "You haven't disappointed me. It was an accident. I'm just glad you weren't hurt, that's all."

Calin looked at him strangely, as if she were distrustful of anyone expressing concern for her. She glanced at the others around her and sat up, looking at the marooned skimmer. "I failed."

"That's all right," said Treet. "We'll find a way to get it out. Don't worry about it right now."

Treet donned a helmet from a nearby skimmer and put it on. "Is Calin okay?" asked Pizzle.

"She seems to be. We should try to get that skimmer out," Treet said into the mike.

"There's probably no hope. Water tends to ruin electric circuits something fierce." Pizzle shook his head dismally inside his helmet.

"We should try in any case," remarked Crocker. "It could be that the circuits and motor casings are sealed. We won't know until we fish it out."

"I suppose you don't want to take off your helmets for this little salvage operation. It would make things easier."

"How would it make things easier," inquired Pizzle, "to have us writhing and crying and coughing our lungs out?"

"It only lasts a second," said Treet.

"Later maybe," said Crocker. "Give us time to work into the idea."

"You've had enough time already." Treet clamped the helmet's neck seal down and felt it grab at the tabs on his singleton. The air inside the helmet smelled stale and unwholesome—like the air of a tomb—after breathing the stringent, light-drenched atmosphere of Empyrion. "I'm not going to argue with you about it. Let's get that skimmer out."

Together they waded into the stream and put their backs into rolling the skimmer onto its runners. They succeeded in getting it rocking and eventually managed to tip it right-side-up once more. Water washed over the sleek nose of the machine and flooded up through the floor to pool around the seats.

"Now what?"

Crocker peered at the craft dubiously. "You think your little magician could take another crack at it?"

"Maybe. But not for a while. She's pretty shaken up," said Treet. "After a good night's rest, who knows?"

"Sixteen hours in the water won't do this machine any good," Pizzle pointed out.

"You said the harm was already done. If that's true, sixteen hours won't matter one way or another."

"Right. So, what are you suggesting?"

"We stay here for the night, let Calin rest, and try it again in the morning if she's willing."

"What do we do while we're waiting?" wondered Crocker.

"I for one could use a bath. It's not a nutrient solution, but this water feels pretty good on this old skin. We don't know when we'll see water again; I'm suggesting that we make the most of it. Take a bath, do the wash, drink a few liters."

"We should also rig up some way to carry water. If we're heading into minus eight desert, we're going to need every drop we can take with us." Pizzle smiled, pleased with himself.

"Okay, Einstein, hop to it."

Treet explained the program to Yarden and Calin and then hiked downstream a few hundred meters and around a bend so he would be out of sight of the rest of the company. He stripped off his singleton and, after thrashing it furiously in the water for a minute or two, spread it out to dry on the bank. He slipped back into the water and lay down in the sun-warmed shallows, letting the water lap over him, feeling its tingle on his skin.

No, it wasn't a nutrient bath—that most blessed of modern conventions—but it was wet and took the parched, crackly quality out of his hide. He turned his face to the sun, enjoying the warmth on his flesh and the solitude. His thoughts turned immediately to Yarden.

What a tight bundle of contradictions she was. Last night she had shown him a side of herself that she rarely revealed. Probably only a handful of others in her entire life had ever seen the warm, caring, sensitive, romantic?—yes, romantic—woman he had seen. They had talked easily together, comfortable in one another's company. And she had seemed relaxed; that transparent barrier field she maintained between herself and everyone and everything else had faltered for a time, and she had shown herself an amiable companion.

Whatever he had seen last night, there was none of it left this morning, however. Her barrier field was back up; she behaved toward him as if the evening had never happened—as indeed, nothing of consequence *had* taken place between them.

Maybe I'm just moonstruck, thought Treet. Maybe I'm inventing something that was never there in the first place. I've been wrong about these things before—like that time in Lucerne with the Contessa Ghiardelli. Women, even under the best of circumstances, were impossible to read precisely. And this insane trek was far from the best setting for deciphering the mercurial movements of romance. If Yarden was behaving slightly schizoid toward him, who could blame her?

His head heavy with these thoughts, Treet closed his eyes and dozed, listening to the water sounds as the river swept by.

He awoke only moments later, seemingly, but the sun had slipped further down in the sky, and when he looked he discovered his singleton had dried on the bank. Treet got out of the water and stood on the bank with his arms outspread, letting the easy southerly breeze dry him before climbing back into his jumpsuit. His skin felt pliant and supple for the first time in a long time.

What was it Crocker had said about this planet? *By all accounts a paradise* . . . Paradise, thought Treet. Yes, there was a little of that here: balmy temperatures, soft warm breezes, and the like. But the landscape was peculiarly barren—too desolate, really, to be considered much of an Eden from any biological point of view. Where were the animals? The trees and larger plants? Where were the birds and insects? Even if nothing else could exist in this place, there should be insects.

Yet, there was only the grass—thin-bladed, wiry stuff that spread over the contours of the interminable hills like a shag carpet gone berserk, seamless and unvarying in its limitless turquoise expanse.

Some paradise. No palm trees; not even a parrot. Yet the atmosphere was congenial—once a person got used to it. The first few breaths of Empyrion "air" were undiluted agony—like breathing fire. Most likely the effect was due to the high concentration of oxygen in the atmosphere in combination with other gases which were either not present or were mixed in different proportions on Earth. Whatever caused it, the result was amazingly painful for those first few seconds.

Empyrion, thought Treet, realm of pure elemental fire, home of the gods . . . I wonder. Someone had shown a strange sense of humor in naming the place.

He sighed and rubbed droplets from the hair of his legs and chest, then pulled his singleton on. He would have preferred underwear, truth be told; wearing a jumpsuit without shorts felt slightly decadent. At least he was out of that foolish, flizzy yos, which was an improvement.

Treet strolled back to where he'd left the others and found only Pizzle, sitting on the ground with a helmet between his knees, working on it with some odd-shaped tool that looked like a cross between a hammer and a dinner fork. Treet tapped him on the helmet. Pizzle glanced up and mouthed a few words which Treet didn't catch.

"What are you doing?" asked Treet after he slipped on a helmet. "Where'd you get that tool thing? And where is everybody?"

"Curious thing, aren't you?" replied Pizzle. "Everybody else wandered away like you to take baths, I guess. I found this 'tool thing' in the skimmer kit. These neck seals are expandable, and I'm trying to see if I can't get them to seal all the way shut so we can carry water in the helmets."

"Good idea. Do you just come up with this stuff, or do you have to think all the time?"

"A little of both," replied Pizzle smugly. "Thinking wouldn't hurt any of the rest of you, you know."

"Let's just say none of us are in any immediate danger of overdosing on it. The way we act, you'd think we were on a tour of Versailles: 'Which way to the palace, my good man?'" He paused and watched Pizzle fiddling with the pliable neck seal, working it back and forth, open and closed. "They won't carry much water," Treet observed.

"About five or six liters, I figure. Maybe more. I intend taking out all the innards."

"Do you intend taking off *your* helmet too?" Treet jibed.

"I've been thinking about that. We really should have somebody inside a helmet so in case we come up against anything really unexpected, at least one of us could still function. I don't mind wearing it, so I volunteer."

"You don't mind wearing it!" Treet brayed. "Pizzy, my friend, you were the biggest baby of all when it came time to put them on. I distinctly remember you wimping about it. Crocker had to order you into it as I recall."

"I've gotten used to it," sniffed Pizzle.

"You'd get used to breathing this air too, if you'd give it a try."

"There could be wind-borne viruses or bacteria lethal to human beings. Something could eat away at our respiratory systems, and we'd never know it until we awaken one morning hacking up blood clots big as your fist."

"Yeah, and giant flesh-eating turtles could swoop down from the sky on leather wings with snapping jaws to gobble us up for hors d'oeuvres, too. In the meantime, I'll take my chances. Sometimes you just have to risk it or you're not really alive."

"You think what we're doing isn't risky enough?" Pizzle whined. "Life is plenty risky the way it is; I don't feel the slightest impulse toward increasing the stakes." He got to his feet and took up the helmet. "Now let's see if it works."

Treet watched his slope-shouldered companion waddle into the river, take the helmet, and carefully sink it into the water. He brought it out a few seconds later, made some kind of adjustment with his funny tool, and tipped it over. The water stayed in for the most part, although it dripped in a steady stream from the gathered seal.

"I think with a few more adjustments we'll be okay." He grinned at his own cleverness. "The main thing is it works."

"I still don't think it's enough water."

"Let's hear your idea, smart guy," huffed Pizzle.

"How about one of the tents? They're airtight, which means they're probably watertight, too, doesn't it? One of those would hold a lot of water."

"We'd take turns carrying it on our backs, I suppose. Do you have any idea how much a tent full of water would weigh?"

"No. Who cares? We could use one of the skimmers to haul it—have our own personal movable waterhole."

"Impossible," snorted Pizzle, striding toward the bank.

"Why—because I thought of it first?"

"No. The weight of a tank that size would—Hey!" Pizzle dropped the helmet and flung out his arms as he sank into the river. He disappeared with a plunk.

FORTY THREE

Treet sprang forward. "Pizzle!"

Pizzle's helmet broke the surface before Treet reached the water's edge. Pizzle's arms thrashed the water into a froth as he screamed into his helmet mike. "Help! It's got me! Something's got me!" He bucked and whirled as if fending off invisible sharks.

Treet waded in, looking for signs of whatever it was that had Pizzle in its grasp. Pizzle screamed and disappeared under the water once more.

"Pizzle, I'll get you out," shouted Treet, sloshing toward the spot where his friend had gone down. There were dark circles indicating holes in the river bottom all around the area and Treet stepped carefully around them. Just as he reached the place where he'd last seen Pizzle's helmet, the water erupted in a jet and Pizzle came flying up with a silver something attached to his chest. His hands clutched at it as he tried to tear it off.

Treet grabbed Pizzle by the arm and jerked him forward, his only thought being to get back on dry land. The thing in Pizzle's arms wriggled and flapped ferociously as Treet propelled them all to shore. Once there, he heaved Pizzle out and fell on the thing that had attacked him.

"Wait! No, wait!" hollered Pizzle, throwing up his hands. "Don't hurt it!"

"What!" Treet stopped.

"Wait," repeated Pizzle, throwing the thing off and rolling over. "Let's see what it is."

"I thought you were being killed."

"I was—at first. But I caught it," said Pizzle. "Look!"

Before them lay a long, floppy eel-like creature with a flat, shovel-shaped head which ended in a wide, fringed mouth. Two bulbous pink eyes on top of the head stared at them as the fish writhed on the bank. It was, for all practical purposes, transparent. Its small brain, veins, muscle tissue, and internal organs could be seen all too clearly beneath its smooth, silvery skin. Its shape was reminiscent of an overfed torpedo. Two sets of fingery protrusions flexed on either side of its loathsome head, and it emitted a greasy grunt—*reet, reet, reet*—as it jerked its finless body around in the grass.

"It's ugly!" said Treet. "Did it bite you?"

"I don't think so." Pizzle leaned forward on his hands and knees to study the creature more closely. "Just think—our first alien lifeform."

"And it had to be an eel." Treet grimaced. "Careful, don't get too close. It might take another nip at you."

"Look at that soft mouth—it can't have any serious teeth."

"Serious teeth or not, I wouldn't get too close. Maybe it squirts hydrochloric acid."

"This reminds me of *Six Trillion Tomorrows*, where these guys find this octopus thing in a crater on this asteroid flying around this binary star."

"What did they do?"

"Who?"

"The guys in the book with this octopus."

"They ate it."

"Ate it?" Treet looked at the pulpy thing quivering at his feet—it seemed to be expiring. "Are you actually suggesting we eat this . . . this ghastly little monster?"

"I wasn't, but it's not a bad idea. We're going to be running out of food soon. So far I haven't seen anything else around here that looks like proteins."

"Gack! I'd rather eat the tent poles."

"Relax. Let's skin it and cook it and see how it tastes. It might be a rare delicacy."

"And it might send us screaming into the night."

"I thought you were a gourmet."

"You don't get to be a gourmet by eating whatever slithers out from under just any old rock."

"How about snails?"

"Escargot? That's different."

Pizzle shrugged and picked up the fish by its pudgy tail. It gave a weak flip and hung still. It was about seventy centimeters long and weighed, by Pizzle's estimation, between four and six kilograms. "We could make a fire using some of the solid fuel from the skimmers."

"What's all the excitement?" Crocker's voice boomed in the helmet speakers. "I was taking a nap, so I turned off the radio. When I turned it back on, I heard the fight." Crocker, his singleton still damp from its washing, came striding up. He took one look at the eel-fish in Pizzle's hand and whistled into the mike. "Sweet Mother McCree! The catch of the day. Where did you get that . . . that repulsive reptile?"

"In a hole in the river," said Pizzle, and explained the events leading up to the capture of the specimen.

Crocker looked properly impressed, and Treet guessed he would be a good man to have along on a fishing trip. He took the eel from Pizzle, hefted it, and looked at it more closely. "It won't win any beauty prizes, but I wonder how it tastes?"

"You too?" hooted Treet. "I don't believe you guys."

Crocker shrugged. "You get hungry enough and you'll eat just about anything. I must confess, however, those survival wafers are starting to taste like billiard balls. I, for one, welcome a change." He held the eel up triumphantly. "Dinner!"

Pizzle had heaped a small mound of skimmer fuel in a circle of round rocks gathered from the river bank. He had disconnected two wires from the generator of the skimmer and held them poised over the powdery yellow fuel. It had taken him the rest of the afternoon to get the experiment set up, and it was now almost dark. The sun had set in a silvery haze nearly an hour ago, and night was sweeping in from the east.

"I'm almost ready. Everybody get back; I'm not sure what's going to happen here."

"Any day, Pizzle. It's getting past my bedtime."

"Whose fault is that, Treet? We could have been eating hours ago if you hadn't inflicted your dumb obsession on me." Pizzle's voice was hoarse and ragged.

"He *is* something of a monomaniac," cracked Crocker.

"Okay, okay—you win. Put your helmets back on if you want to. I thought you'd thank me for getting you out of those plastic prisons."

"Oh, no." Crocker wagged a finger at him. "You don't weasel out of it that easily. We've lived up to our part of the deal. Now it's your turn."

"Will you guys stop sniping at each other? Let's get on with it. We're starving!" Yarden sat sideways on the seat of a nearby skimmer, Calin next to her with chin on knees.

Shortly after Pizzle and Crocker had begun discussing how best to cook the prize catch, Treet struck a bargain with them: he would brave the first taste of alien eel if Pizzle and Crocker would take off their breather packs.

"What is it with you and these helmets?" Pizzle had demanded.

"He's one of those people who can't be happy unless everyone is exactly like him," said Crocker. "He can't stand it that we're different—it threatens his security to be disagreed with."

"Sure, that's it. I admit it. You're ever so right. So don't take them off—we'll communicate in sign language for the rest of this trip because I find it a pain to go hunting up a helmet every time I want a word with either of you. Your adolescent obstinacy is making it difficult for us to cohere as a single working unit."

"Lay it back at our feet," said Pizzle.

"He's right, you two," replied Yarden, who had returned shortly after the discussion started and had donned a helmet in order to get in on it. "We all need to work together. How can we when two of us are isolated from the others?"

In the end, with much protest and breast beating, Pizzle and Crocker gave in and the deal was struck. The next hour was spent coaxing them out of their bubbles and holding their hands while they underwent the trauma of taking their first breaths of Empyrion's astringent atmosphere.

Pizzle held his breath until, red-faced, eyes bulging, he had to inhale. His screams almost made Treet wish he hadn't made such a major production out of removing the breathers. Pizzle then rolled on the ground for an hour afterwards whimpering and cursing between clenched teeth.

For his part, Crocker faced the ordeal stoically, with an air of doomful regret—like a deposed monarch going to the gallows. He removed his own helmet, closed his eyes and inhaled deeply, clutched his throat, and doubled over while the tears streamed from his eyes. He moaned but did not cry out. When the worst was over, he perked up considerably.

It was a long time before either one of them would speak to Treet.

"Hit it!" croaked Pizzle now, and Crocker punched the ignition on the skimmer and engaged the generator. As the skimmer's powerplant revved, Pizzle brought the two bare ends of wire together over the pile of fuel.

A fizzly shower of sparks streaked out and the fuel erupted with a whoosh, sending up a ball of brilliant blue flame that knocked Pizzle on his rump and singed his eyebrows.

"You did it!" cried Yarden.

"Nice work," said Crocker.

"How long will this thing burn?" wondered Treet, watching the flames dubiously. Unlike a fire on Earth, the flames of Empyrion were pale blue, like the thin, almost transparent flames of burning alcohol.

"Long enough to cook dinner," squeaked Pizzle. "Here, you can do the honors." He handed Treet a makeshift spit—a tent pole on which chunks of the gutted eel had been speared.

"Here goes nothing." Treet grasped the tent pole at midpoint and lowered the eel to the flames. In moments the meat was sizzling merrily, and Treet's expectations took an unexpected upturn. Maybe it wouldn't be so bad after all.

He turned the spit continually, careful not to let any portion get too done. The others crept closer to the fire and commented on his cooking technique, wondering aloud what the fish would taste like. When at last Treet announced that it was done, they all leaned forward expectantly, their eyes shining in the light.

Treet raised the cooked eel to his nose and gave a studied sniff. "Slightly musky aroma," he announced.

"Get on with it," the others replied.

"Please, you asked my opinion, you're going to get your money's worth." He picked at a piece of flesh. It came off in a long, fibrous strand. "Composition stringy, but not objectionable."

"Taste it!" they cried.

"I'm getting to that." With a mild grimace Treet brought the strand to his mouth, took it in, chewed thoughtfully, then picked off another piece, chewed that, and swallowed, all the while his expression deadpan.

"Well?" asked Yarden. "What do those well-schooled tastebuds of yours have to say for themselves?"

Treet looked imperiously at the ring of faces around the fire. "Smoked olives," he said.

"Smoked olives! What kind of answer is that?" complained Pizzle.

"No," said Treet chewing again, "it isn't oily enough. More

like mountain oysters, only saltier. Or tongue marinated in a weak Marsala. Or maybe . . ."

"Treet!" Crocker interrupted the expert commentary. "Stop playing food analyst and tell us if it's edible."

"Okay. Since I'm not falling on the ground in a coma or retching uncontrollably, yes, it's edible, I think." He handed the wobbly skewer across to the pilot. "See what you think."

They solemnly passed the eel around, each taking a portion and putting it in their mouths. They chewed and swallowed and peered at one another timidly.

"Verdict?" Treet inquired.

"Sort of a cross between chicken and lobster, I'd say," offered Pizzle.

"Wrong," said Crocker. "It's veal, definitely veal."

"I don't know," said Yarden. "It has more a poultry flavor—like duck or goose."

They all turned to Calin, the only one who had not offered an opinion. She glanced around at the company and said, "I can't say what it tastes like; I've never eaten much meat. But I'd like some more."

The eel was divided up and distributed in roughly equal portions. They ate in silence, listening to the smack of lips, the flutter of the ghostly fire and, further off, the riffle of water around the drowned skimmer.

They really were an unlikely party of explorers, thought Treet: a bunged-up transport jockey, a wily executive mind-reader, an otherworldly magician frightened of all outdoors, a bookwormish Trend and Impact Analyst Boy Scout, and a knockabout history hack with delusions of grandeur. They were ill-equipped, ill-provisioned, and ill-guided, and right in the middle of an ill-fated mission.

So much for reality.

Treet licked his fingers and flicked the last curved rib bone into the fire. "Not bad, but it positively begs for garlic and herb salt. Now, if we don't die of some hideous toxic reaction in our sleep, we ought to be on our way tomorrow morning first light." He stood, brushing bones from his lap. "Good night."

FORTY FOUR

"Hold it! Not so fast," said Crocker with a voice that sounded like he'd swallowed live sparrows. "Sit down, Treet. I want to propose a change in our evening activities."

Treet sat. Crocker, having caught everyone's attention, went on to explain quickly. "I had an idea while we were all sitting here that this is a cozy little group. We've been through a lot together. And, Yarden, I admit you were right about the breather packs—it is better without them. Now then, since we can all talk to one another like human beings once again—"

Treet opened his mouth, but Pizzle cut him off before he could speak. "No wisecracks. Let's listen to what he has to say."

"Thanks," continued Crocker, "the same goes for you. Anyway, it occurred to me that all of us had different experiences while captive in the colony—we've each seen a slightly different view of things there. I thought it might be interesting to compare notes, you know, share impressions. Since I spent most of my time flat on my back in a floater, I'd especially like to know what went on with the rest of you." He looked across the fire. "Okay, Treet, you wanted to say something?"

"Only that I think it's a good idea. It would help pass the time."

"More than that, we may get a few clues to what we're up against here. Our survival could depend on it."

"I agree," remarked Pizzle. "And I think Treet should start."

"Me?" Treet raised his eyebrows.

"Sure. Apparently you were the only one free to roam around. The rest of us were drugged most of the time. So, with the exception of Calin here, you know the most about it."

"Maybe we should have Calin tell us all she knows," said Treet.

Yarden protested quickly. "No. She should speak last—after we're all through. Otherwise, what she said would color our own perceptions. She's lived in the colony all her life, and we would begin to see our own experiences through her eyes. I think we need to be as subjective as possible."

"Don't you mean *objective?*" asked Pizzle.

"*Subjective.* Look, we've all had different experiences, and we interpreted them in different ways. But it's the interpretation that matters—the gut-level feelings we got, the conclusions we arrived at, what the events meant to us."

"We certainly don't want our perceptions blunted by reality," scoffed Pizzle lightly.

"She has a good point," replied Treet. "Who can say what the reality of Empyrion is? It's too big, and we know too little of it and its past to speak with total objectivity. All we know for certain is what we experienced and what those experiences meant to us at the time. Let's get those out, share them around, and then we can begin to construct the big picture."

Yarden nodded at Treet over the campfire. Treet noticed that the fire made blue shadows in her hair and eyes. Her smile puzzled him. What did I do to earn that? he wondered.

"Agreed?" asked Crocker. "Okay, Treet, the floor is yours."

Treet held up his hands. "One more thing I'd like to suggest—that we postpone the start of our campfire stories until tomorrow night."

"Aww!" complained Pizzle.

"No, I mean it. I'd like each of us to spend tonight and tomorrow thinking about what happened and how we want to tell it. That could be important, I think."

"Fair enough," said Crocker. "Everybody agreed? Fine. Tomorrow night we begin."

The sun was already up when Treet emerged from his tent. He'd stayed awake a long time after retiring, thinking about how he wanted to tell his story the next night. He had finally fallen asleep undecided—there was so much to tell, he didn't know the best place to begin.

Pizzle and Crocker were already up and were standing by the shore, looking at the waterlogged skimmer out in the middle of the river. "Any hope?" asked Treet as he joined them.

Pizzle wagged his head dismally. "Not a chance in a zillion. I say it's ruined."

"We've got to find out one way or the other, which means we fish it out in any case."

"Maybe we could pull it out with one of the others."

"No rope or chain or cable or anything to tie 'em together. I already thought of that."

"Oh."

"The way I see it, Calin is our best bet."

"You saw what happened yesterday. I think Yarden would have something to say about her using her psi like that again."

"We need that vehicle," Crocker reminded them. "There's a desert out there somewhere and if we're going to get across it, we've got to have every available resource."

"So we ask her," said Treet.

"*You* ask her. Yes, you. She trusts you."

"Why do I get the feeling there's something distasteful about this?"

"Survival is distasteful to you?"

"That's not what I mean, and you know it."

"Just get her to do it. We'll all thank you later," said Pizzle.

When Calin and Yarden joined them a little later, Treet took Calin aside and explained the situation to her. He ended by asking, "Will you do it? Crocker's right; it could make the difference between life and death later on."

Calin's expression was one of pained reluctance. "I—I can't do it."

"What do you mean? You did it yesterday; we all saw you."

"I can't use my psi. Yarden told me that it's not good for me. It's dangerous. She made me promise never to use it again."

"She did what?"

"She told me many things I didn't know about it, and I promised her never to turn to it—to use it is weakness."

"Well, maybe just this one more time."

"Yarden said there will always be one more time, and then one more. I have to stop and never go back."

Treet stomped back to where Pizzle and Crocker waited. "It's no go. She won't do it."

"You're joking. Why not?" Crocker demanded.

"Yarden has given her some story about how using psi is dangerous and unhealthy. She made Calin promise never to use it again."

"Oh, great," sighed Pizzle. "Well, you can kiss one skimmer good-bye and maybe one or two of us as well."

"Stop being melodramatic." Treet frowned at Pizzle.

"Right. I forgot you volunteered to *walk* across the burning waste. We have one skimmer to carry the water, and we need the other two for passengers."

"You laughed at my idea for hauling water."

"I changed my mind."

"We're not getting anywhere this way," grumped Crocker.

"Have you tried driving it out?" The men turned to see Yarden watching them, arms crossed, chin thrust out, daring them to laugh at her. Calin stood quietly behind her.

"Well, no, we haven't," replied Crocker diplomatically. "There didn't seem to be much point."

"Why not?" Yarden came to stand with them as they stared out across the water to the skimmer—an island all its own in the slow-moving current.

"Why not? Uh, tell her why not, Pizzle," said Crocker.

Pizzle shot a venomous glance at Crocker. "It's my belief that the water has damaged the circuitry, or at least shorted it out. There's no point in trying to drive it out of there because it will never in a million years start while it's sitting in water."

"Do you know this for fact?" Yarden turned her eyes on him and bored into him. Treet enjoyed the show.

"Well, no. But, I—"

"Why not try it and see? It seems to me that any vehicle made to traverse the desert can probably take a little water."

"Yeah," echoed Treet, "why not try it and see?"

Pizzle rolled his eyes and harumphed, but Crocker said, "What have we got to lose? Give it a try."

Without a word Pizzle walked into the water and out to the skimmer, climbed onto the seat, and pressed the ignition. He nearly fell off when the machine started up at a touch.

"Pizzle, you're a genius!" hooted Treet. "Only trouble is, Yarden is a bigger genius."

She smiled acerbically and looked at the men with a smugly superior expression on her face. She and Calin walked upstream, leaving the men alone.

Pizzle drove the vehicle slowly out of the river, grinding the runners over the rocks. When it finally reached dry land, it gave a sputtering jolt and died. "Okay, so the motors and circuits are sealed. How was I supposed to know that? It would still be a good idea to let it dry out before running it again—just in case."

Treet raised his eyes to the sky. The sun was climbing

rapidly, spilling light over the hilltops and into the valleys. Another perfect day—like one more perfect pearl added to the string. "Shame to waste the day," he said. "What shall we do while we wait for that buggy to dry out?"

Crocker spun toward him. "I was just thinking the same thing. You know what? I think we should go fishing."

"Fishing!"

"I'm serious. That eel last night tasted pretty good, considering. And since none of us expired during the night from any unknown toxic effects, and since there are bound to be more where that one came from, I say we go after them."

Pizzle brightened, and Treet saw the computer chips that Pizzle used for a brain light up. "We could catch a million to take with us into the desert! I should have thought of that yesterday."

"How are we going to take a load of putrefying eels into the desert? They'll rot before we get two days from here."

Pizzle rolled his eyes in exasperation. "We *dry* them. On rocks. In the sun. It's easy. And we'll have food all across the desert. Water, too."

"This is just one big jamboree to you, isn't it, Pizzle?" sniped Treet.

"Starving appeals to you?" Crocker mocked. "Let's get started."

They discussed several techniques for catching the eels, including making rods and line from the tent poles and braided thread, and rigging up makeshift harpoons. Neither possibility, nor any of the others they considered and discarded just as quickly, suggested success. So they sat stymied until Treet said, "Actually Pizzle didn't catch that eel as much as that eel caught Pizzle."

"What do you mean? I caught it."

"If I remember correctly, you fell into the hole and it grabbed you. When you came rocketing out of the water, I saw that thing attatched to your chest. You were flapping your arms around trying to get rid of it."

"Oh, yeah?" Crocker turned an appraising eye on Pizzle.

"Hold it! What are you guys thinking? You can't be serious. I'm not—hey, wait a minute . . ."

"Food all the way across the desert, Pizzy," said Treet.

"You're crazy!"

"It's easy," said Crocker. "We used to do it all the time

when we were little kids—slip down along the river bank and find a hole and reach inside. A good grappler could catch some pretty big old catfish."

"You're *both* crazy!" Pizzle edged away. "I won't do it."

"It's the only way. Besides, it was your idea. You should get the glory."

"It's only right," agreed Treet. "We could tie something around you to hold on to so you wouldn't drown or anything; you have nothing to worry about. We'll be there right beside you."

Within ten minutes, Pizzle's protests notwithstanding, they were wading out into the river together, Treet and Crocker holding opposite ends of a piece of tent cording which had been secured around Pizzle's waist. "Look, there's nothing to worry about," offered Treet. "They don't have teeth. From what you said, they just sort of suck onto you and there you go. We'll pull you up if you get into trouble—so don't get yourself in a nervous tizzy."

"You'll be fine," assured Crocker. "In fact, after the second or third time, you'll start to enjoy yourself."

"If I live through this," muttered Pizzle darkly, "I'm going to get a good lawyer and sue both of you into debtor's prison. There must be laws against using a person for fish bait."

"You won't sue us," predicted Crocker, "you'll thank us."

They found the hole Pizzle had dropped into the day before, and several more near it, one of which was big enough to admit a man. With murder in his close-set eyes, Pizzle took a deep breath and dropped in. Treet and Crocker held the ends of the cord and counted, figuring they would give Pizzle twenty seconds to accomplish his task.

He was back in ten. The hole was empty. And so was the next. After several more attempts, they moved on a little further downstream and came to a place where more holes dotted the river bottom. Here their luck changed. The second hole Pizzle tried contained an eel about the size of the one he'd caught the day before. This one attached itself to his back and when they pulled Pizzle up, Treet grabbed it and flipped it onto the bank.

The rest of the holes in the area were empty. "We won't find any more eels here," said Treet after the fourth try. "These critters have territories. I think all the holes in a given area belong to one eel. If we want to catch another one we'll have to go further downstream."

"The water gets deeper," observed Crocker.

"We'll stick to the shore." Treet looked at the eel expiring on the bank. "This is going to take a lot longer than we thought. I think we ought to streamline this process. You two could catch them, and I'll gut them and get them drying out."

"Good idea. We'll get a regular little production line going." Crocker and Pizzle headed off downstream, and Treet—using a tool from the skimmer kit—made quick work of the eel and carried it back to camp. The two women were waiting when he got back. He gave them the eel, explained their plan, and repeated what Pizzle had told him about how to dry the meat on rocks in the sun. "We'll be back later on this afternoon," he told them.

By the time Treet reached the place where Pizzle and Crocker had been, he found another eel on the bank—this one half again as big as the other two they'd caught. The two "fishermen" were already working their way further downstream; he could see their torsos swaying above the water as they searched for holes in the riverbed.

The day stretched out into a rhythm of walking and working and waiting and walking again—a rhythm Treet found enjoyable. The eerie silence of the place was modified by the plap and gurgle of the river as it moved quietly along. With the sun on his back and the company of his thoughts, Treet went about his task happily, enjoying the solitude and serenity of the day.

By late afternoon they had worked far downstream. The sun dipped near the horizon, signaling the end of a good day's work. Treet lost count of the number of eels they had caught. He decided, however, that it was enough for one day and was gutting the last eel before hurrying ahead to call Crocker and Pizzle back when he heard the whine of a skimmer behind him.

Yarden, her dark hair streaming, piloted the skimmer expertly over the ruffled river bank toward him. He stood and waited for her. "Call it a day," she said. "Talazac taxi service has come to fetch you home."

"Thanks. Pizzle and Crocker are somewhere up ahead. Why don't you go get them and I'll finish up here. We can pick up our catch on the way back."

"You've caught enough to last three months. I counted twenty-eight, and I may have missed a few." She gave him a smile and a wave and glided away. Within minutes she was back with two tired fishermen in damp clothes. She had found them a little way downriver lying on the bank drying out before heading back. Treet squeezed onto the crowded vehicle and they worked their way homeward, stopping at intervals to pick up their catch.

They arrived back in camp as the sun faded behind the hills, washing the westward sky a pale eggshell white as the east darkened to indigo. Calin had a fire going and an eel on the spit as they climbed down and unloaded the toppling stack of flayed eels. Treet noticed that the tents had been moved and that beneath each one was a thick bed of bunched grass. "We've been busy all day, too," said Yarden proudly. "We made grass mattresses."

"My dear lady," said Crocker, "each and every one of my brittle, aching bones thanks you. If I weren't so hungry, I'd crawl in right now and go to sleep."

As they ate around the fire, Treet noticed that everyone's spirits were markedly improved. They all talked and joked and smiled at one another. Even Calin joined in shyly from time to time. Something important had happened to them that day; a milestone of some sort had been passed. Treet worked it over in his head and decided that the buoyant feeling was due to the fact that today was the first time they had worked together as a group toward a common goal of survival. Today they had become a team.

When all had eaten, they lay back as the blue flames flickered. "Well," said Treet, "I guess I'm the entertainment for this evening. Are you sure you all want to hear a story?"

305

FORTY
FIVE

Treet began like this:

"After the scuffle on the landing platform, I woke up by myself in a room—fuzzy-headed, naked, and sore. I put on the clothes I found in my cell and waited. I was brought food, which I ate, and I slept. Two or three days went by and I was taken to meet the Supreme Director of Empyrion, a cagey old cuss named Sirin Rohee.

"Three of his advisers showed up and asked me questions. I answered. We talked a little, and he sent me back. It was a day or two later, I think, when I remembered who I was, where I was, and who had come with me. The drug wore off, I guess—or maybe they didn't give me such a heavy dose. When Rohee sent for me again, we met alone. I told him I remembered, and told him *what* I remembered. For some reason—I still don't know why—he took pity on me and gave me quarters of my own. He provided Calin to be my guide and allowed me the run of the place, although I'm fairly certain I was watched constantly nevertheless.

"I toured each Hage of Empyrion—at least those areas open to inspection. There are places within Hage where outsiders are not allowed, and we of course stayed out.

"After about a week of this touring, I asked Rohee if I could see the Archives. He debated about it for the better part of a day and decided to allow me. I think he had some private plan in mind for me, or hoped I would discover something useful for him, or maybe he was just curious—I don't know.

"Calin and I, along with the obligatory priest, went to the Archives and looked around. The place was full of old machines, parts, and junk, and it was my impression at the time that the place had not been visited in many years, generations perhaps. Anyway, we didn't find what we were looking for—at least not at first. Then, as I was getting ready to leave, I noticed Calin had disappeared and went looking for her. I found her in a hidden room under the Archives—a room full of historical data on the colony which had been hidden and sealed about seven hundred years ago. That's an educated guess.

"On leaving the Archives, we were contacted—waylaid, actually—by some people who said they had information about my friends. These turned out to be Tvrdy's people, and they reunited us all. Things heated up, and we moved to the Archives to make good our escape. We fled the colony and have been making our way across some of the most desolate country I've ever seen.

"And," Treet summed up, "here we are."

Into the silence that followed Treet's account, Pizzle bleated, "That's it? That's what we've been waiting breathless all day to hear?"

Crocker made a move to join the protest, but Treet raised his hand for silence. "Not so fast. Those are just the bare facts. I wanted to construct the skeleton first; now I'll hang some observations on the bones."

He paused, gathered his thoughts, then said, "Empyrion is not the colony Cynetics established. Rather, it *was*, but is no longer. It has changed, evolved. As near as I can figure, we are seeing the colony nearly three thousand years after its foundation . . ."

"Three thousand years!" gasped Crocker. "Impossible."

"I knew it was old," said Pizzle, "but I never dreamed—"

"According to Belthausen's theories, it's possible," said Treet. "Someone who knows a whole lot more about these things than I do is going to have to figure it out, but . . . Well, let's just say we're dealing with a culture which has had a good long term of isolated development. Empyrion has evolved into an extremely stratified, regimented, organized, and highly repressive society.

"There are eight Hages, each with its own societal function. They're organized around necessities: food, that's Hyrgo; Bolbe, clothing; Saecaraz handles energy; Nilokerus takes care of security, health care, social services; Tanais is structural engineering, construction, housing, that sort of thing; Rumon is communication and what you might call production, traffic, and quality control—anything that has to do with movement of goods and services through the colony; Chryse is fine arts and entertainment; Jamuna is waste recycling."

"Don't I know it," remarked Pizzle.

"A Hage is more than a vocational guild, although it is that. It's also home, family, city, and state."

"It's a caste system," said Yarden.

"Yes," agreed Treet. "There are strong elements of caste in the mix. It isn't hard to guess how this caste system came about: survival. A colony arrives with all the basic components necessary for establishing a viable society. If something happened to cut the colony off from its source of supply, it would quickly organize itself into skill areas vital to survival.

"Whenever you have rigid occupational stratification—some jobs are essential, waste recycling for instance, though hardly the most prestigious or attractive, so these low-status tasks must be assigned—an enforced hierarchy soon develops. In order to preserve its place in the hierarchy, occupational protectionism takes over. If I am a genetics technician, which is near the top of Hyrgo Hage, and I want to stay secure in my position, I guard my professional knowledge and expertise jealously. Over time, it becomes nearly impossible for anyone not born into the caste to develop the knowledge and skills.

"Just as there is a hierarchy within Hages, there is a hierarchy of Hages within the colony as well, with intense competition for control of leadership. The top man of each Hage is the Director, who serves on a sort of Board of Directors called the Threl, with the Supreme Director acting as Chairman of the Board."

"They retained the old corporation structure," observed Pizzle.

"Yes, but how these people come to power, I don't know. They're not elected, that's for sure. I suspect the reins of power are handed down in much the same way as early trading companies or political parties handed down power: through hand-picked successors chosen by dint of their loyalty and adherence to the party line, then groomed for the job. Factors such as birth or qualification would have little to do with the choice. Once in power, it would be nearly impossible to get someone out of leadership since the whole structure of the system is designed to maintain the status quo.

"As time passes, the whole society slowly becomes ever more firmly entrenched in preserving the caste code that allowed its development. Any person or group threatening the code is seen as an enemy of the state. In the early years, malcontents would have jeopardized survival and would have been dealt with harshly. All energies had to be channeled into supporting the common good, and any deviation could have been disastrous.

"By the time survival became less of an issue, the system was firmly established and functioning autonomously. It became self-protecting. Physical survival was transmuted into ideological survival."

"I'm not sure I follow," Crocker broke in.

"Think of it like this: the system was set up to reach only one goal—the physical survival of the colony. It reached that goal. Then what?

"Apparently the leaders of Empyrion colony failed to appreciate their position, and instead of redirecting the colony on to higher, more universally fulfilling goals, they merely abstracted the old goal. Physical survival became political survival. Instead of threats from the outside, they became concerned about threats from the inside. The system equated opposition with danger, ideological purity with safety, loyalty with consensus agreement. In essence, the system emerged as an entity in its own right and claimed primacy over the interests of individual citizens. The leadership saw to it that the system continued serving itself, devoting as much energy to its own survival as it had previously devoted to the survival of its citizens."

"Those evil people," said Yarden softly.

"Evil? I don't know," replied Treet. "It was probably easier to go with the flow than dismantle the entire apparatus of colony government and redirect the energy of the citizenry to higher ideals."

"It could have been done. Societies have always done it," Yarden pointed out. "What monstrous selfishness."

"I suppose it could have been done, but remember they were cut off, isolated. The wormhole closed or shifted or whatever wormholes do. And anyway, the leadership had effectively silenced any opposition, so there was no real challenge to their authority or values."

"What about the Fieri?" asked Pizzle. "I thought they were the hated opposition."

"I was getting to that," said Treet. "The documents I've seen indicate that long ago—a few hundred years after foundation—something catastrophic happened. I have not read the specific documents to find out what it was, but it was a severe shock to the colony—maybe a natural disaster of some sort.

They came through the crisis, but in the following years there were disputes over how to reorganize and rehabilitate the colony.

"At one point, I believe, the colony actually split into three factions. There was a Purge, and the smaller faction was eliminated or consolidated. Sometime later one of the factions, the Fieri, left the colony or was forced out.

"You would have thought that would be the end of it, but their leaving signaled the beginning of about three hundred years of political upheaval. The power structure of the colony was gutted by the pullout of the Fieri; there were bloody coups and countercoups and eventually a revolt by the citizens, followed by a second Purge, which ended in the establishment of the Threl."

"When did all this happen?" asked Pizzle. He leaned forward, chin in hands, listening with rapt attention.

"About fifteen hundred years ago, by my reckoning. The Second Purge began what colony historians call the Third Age—a period characterized by continual, fanatical harassment of the Fieri."

"But why?" asked Yarden. "I thought the Fieri left. What reason could the colony have for persecuting them?"

"I don't know the details. My guess is that at first the Fieri were simply a covenient target—a scapegoat. The colony was in trouble. Among other things, it was rapidly losing its technology; things were beginning to run down and nobody knew how to fix them. The Threl chose to point to the Fieri as the source of all their ills. Persecuting them diverted attention away from the colony's real problems, which the Threl were no doubt struggling to contain.

"But even after that, when the Fieri were no longer a threat—if they really ever were—the Threl did not give up. Over the years the hatred, so useful before, became an obsession. Fantacisim grew up. They simply could not let it go. I think the Threl were jealous of the Fieri for having the courage to leave, to follow their own destiny. Since there was no other way to punish the Fieri, the Threl plotted to hound them into oblivion."

"And succeeded," said Yarden.

"That's what I thought, too—at first. But the Fieri still exist, though it's been a long time, a thousand years at least, since anyone in the colony has actually seen one. They thought *we* were Fieri, remember. And I doubt Tvrdy and his cohorts would have sent us out if they didn't believe we had a chance of finding them. They're desperate for help, so it wouldn't make sense to send us knowing there was no help to be found.

"That's it in a nutshell. I had planned, of course, to go back and study Empyrion history in detail, but—well, that's as far as I got. Things got too hot, and here we are." Treet finished and everyone sat silent for a long time, staring into the faint blue flames, watching the ghostly flicker, conjuring up visions of times long past in the Third Age of Empyrion. Without a word Yarden got up and went to her tent; Calin followed immediately.

Crocker yawned and rose. "You sure talk pretty, Treet," he said and shuffled off. Pizzle and Treet sat together for a time, staring into the dying fire, listening to the sizzle of the solid fuel as it burned away. When the last flame died, Pizzle crept away, leaving Treet alone with his thoughts and the star-dazzled night.

They stayed another day on the banks of the river to allow the eels caught the day before to continue drying in the sun. They swam a little and napped, resting up for the next leg of their journey. Pizzle fiddled with various ways of securing a water-filled tent to one of the skimmers and toward the end of the day came up with a solution that offered at least the barest possibility of success.

"There's no way to know if it will work until we try it," he said regarding his handiwork.

"Elegant it ain't," offered Treet, "but it ought to do the trick." He studied the limp tent encased in a latticework of cloth strips and cording and strung over the vehicle like a deflated balloon. Pizzle had removed the passenger's seat, creating a trough for the water bag to rest in. "You've done a fine job. By the way, where did you get the cloth?"

"I tore up a spare singleton. The thing is, we won't be able to fill it up as much as I'd hoped, which means we'll run out faster. We won't be able to travel as far. That worries me a little—we don't know how big this desert is."

"No way to know. We'll just have to do the best we can."

Pizzle nodded, but the frown that creased his brow did not go away. He fussed and mumbled for several more hours until Crocker came by and ordered him to go swimming and get his mind off the problem for a while.

By evening, everyone was rested and in good spirits, eager

to be traveling once more. They ate and discussed the rigors of the desert. Then, after a pause in the talk, Yarden said, "I want to tell my story."

She described her life with the Chryse in fine detail—their forays into various Hages to perform the plays and mimes, the flash orgies, rehearsing new plays, lolling around the marketplaces on allotment days, and other things she had experienced and observed.

"It sounds like you had it pretty good," remarked Pizzle. "How did you get your memory back?"

"I became suspicious of Bela, the troupe leader. At first he was kind to me, wanted to make love to me—tried on several occasions. When I cut him off, he changed toward me. He was still solicitous, but I saw an ugliness beneath his bonhomie, a duplicity that I distrusted. I came to feel he was using me in some way.

"In fact, he became quite brazen about giving me the mind drug. I think at first it must have been administered secretly in my food or drink, but later he offered it to me in the form of a little wafer and made me take it myself. I did the first time, but palmed the wafers and threw them away after that.

"I soon discovered that without the drug my memory started coming back. The drug blocked memory somehow, but if the doses were not kept up, the fog barrier thinned. It took some effort, but I was finally able to break through. It got easier after that.

"Unfortunately, I did not have time to regain my memory completely. On the last day I was taken to an Astral Service." Yarden's voice quavered, and her shoulders shivered with an imaginary chill. "It is still so vivid in my mind . . . the most horrible experience of my life." She paused, looked into the campfire.

Treet watched the light shifting over her handsome features. He'd heard the story before—she'd told him a few nights ago when they were alone on the hillside. As Yarden talked, Treet remembered that night, and wondered if they'd ever again be as close as they were those few moments. Strangely, he began to feel sorry for himself, and resentful of the fact that she was telling her story to the others just the way she'd told him.

Their time together that night had been an intimate moment, and now she was letting everyone else in on their shared secrets. It was like kissing and telling. He told himself it was silly to feel that way, but the argument lacked conviction and he succeeded only in stirring up a little guilt to go along with the self-pity. He retreated further into himself, reliving the intimacy of those moments.

"Don't be angry with me."

"Huh?" Treet raised his head. Yarden looked at him across the dying fire. The others were moving off toward the tents. He'd not heard the party break up. "I didn't— I'm not angry."

Yarden cocked her head to one side. "No, maybe not—not yet. I had to tell them, you know. We agreed."

"Sure."

"But I didn't want you to feel like I was betraying you."

"Why would I think that?"

"Not think, Orion. *Feel*. I sensed you were upset. Emotions have a logic of their own." She rose and came around the ring of stones to him, bent over him, touched his chin, and raised his face to hers. She kissed him lightly on the lips.

"What was that for?" asked Treet, his voice thick and unsteady. He was genuinely bewildered by the kiss, but trying valiantly to cover it.

"That's for us. It's something I won't share with anyone else."

She was gone then, leaving Treet to his befuddlement, still reeling from the kiss. When at last he took himself off to bed, he was no closer to an answer to the riddle of Yarden Talazac.

313

FORTY
SIX

The better part of the morning was spent filling the tent with water. After striking it for the last time, Pizzle arranged it loosely under the network of straps and they began hauling water from the river in their helmets. Pizzle oversaw the operation, keeping a tally of the number of helmetfuls that went into the tent. By his calculation one helmet full of water equaled one day's water supply for the group. When they had seventy-five helmetfuls he sealed the tent.

"But we can carry a lot more," said Treet. "The tent isn't even half full."

"That would be dangerous. Fill it any more, and we won't be able to steer the skimmer. Besides, the weight would snap the straps and the tent would roll off. This way it acts as ballast and lies relatively flat."

"He's right," said Crocker. "Let's leave well enough alone."

They snugged down the rigging, packing the dried eels under the straps all over the surface of the orange bag. "It looks like something out of *The Gypsy Pirates of R'Enno*," said Pizzle. "I hope it works."

"We'll soon find out." Crocker looked back at the river. "I suggest everybody take a good long drink of water. It could be the last fresh one we'll get until who knows when."

They drank their fill from the crystalline river and somewhat reluctantly mounted the skimmers. Treet and Crocker rode one, Yarden and Calin another. Pizzle, despite his myopia, piloted the skimmer with the water bag, claiming he was the only one who understood the physics of it. They started up and slid away. At the top of the first hill, Treet looked back over his shoulder to the river valley below. We forgot to name it, he thought. Then the hump of the hill took it from view as the skimmer began its glide over the downward slope.

The land changed almost immediately. Once away from the river, the grass grew shorter, more sparse. At a distance of forty kilometers, the hillscape flattened, and the hills became less rounded and further apart, separated by long, ramplike inclines.

By midday the carpet of pastel grass was worn thin and patchy. Treet noticed that the soil showing through the sparse covering was lighter, drier, sandier. When they stopped late in the afternoon to erect the two remaining tents for the night, the sandhills had become small bluffs whose soft soil was cut away by blowouts on the windward side. The blowouts showed white-blue in the fading daylight.

"The desert can't be much farther," remarked Crocker, scanning the barren countryside. "What a wasteland. It's so empty it scares me."

"What do you suppose could cause it?" wondered Treet aloud. He peered into the distance, noting how the violet shadows deepened and slid up from the lowlands to swallow the heights.

"Cause it? What do you mean, *cause* it? It's a natural landform. Lack of water is what causes it. Didn't you ever learn any physical geography?"

"I'm a purist." Treet shrugged. "It just seemed very *un*natural to me. Too empty. It's a total void. I've seen a few deserts, but nothing this completely—"

"Annihilated," put in Pizzle, finishing his thought. "Even deserts have life, but this place is antilife."

"You think this is something, wait till we reach minus eight," Crocker snorted. "That'll make this look like a rain forest!"

Crocker's prophecy came true two days later. The travelers climbed to the top of a long rise and stopped to stare upon a vista of white dunes. Like the endless swells of a milk-white sea, the humpbacked dunes swarmed to the horizon and beyond.

Speechless, the company viewed the spectacle in a silence broken only by the sound of their own breathing. The sun, behind them on its downward arc into the west, painted each dune a dazzling white.

After a while Treet turned his eyes back the way they had come. The barren hills showed light turquoise that smudged to powder blue in the distance. By comparison, the desolation they had passed through now appeared almost shockingly verdant, luxurious in its rampant fertility.

What a strange, wounded land, thought Treet, then wondered why the word *wounded* had come to him.

Minutes later, still without having spoken a word, the company began its descent to the desert floor. As the machines touched the sand, the blades sank deep. For an instant Treet feared they might founder. The sand buried the runners, making the craft grind ahead sluggishly. But Treet, remembering that the skimmers were designed specifically for desert travel, pulled back the joystick and leaned forward on the knee pedals, lowering the runner blades still further. The skimmer leaped ahead.

Amazed at the machine's response, Treet held the joystick back and allowed the skimmer to gather speed. Gradually the machine rose on its blades until it fairly sliced through the sand with all the effort of a skater flying over ice. Nothing they had experienced of the vehicles' capabilities had even hinted at the breathtaking velocity they could achieve.

Exhilaration flooded over him in an instantaneous gush—as if he had taken a plunge into a rushing cataract. His heart quickened; his blood raced as adrenalin pumped into his veins. He gulped for air and gripped the joystick tightly with both hands, then heard a long, high, wailing sound over the scream and whizz of the skimmer and realized Cocker was howling in pure delight as they dipped and glided over the undulating dunes. The still desert air snapped their clothing into sharp creases that rippled over their limbs.

Out of the corner of his eye he glimpsed a shape gaining on him. He glanced over to see Yarden leaning forward over the joystick, her knees pressed to the pedals, crouched like a jockey in the saddle of a thoroughbred racehorse, features compressed into an expression mingling ferocious intensity with rapture. Her long black hair gleamed in the sunlight as it streamed out horizontally behind her.

She streaked past, her skimmer's wake a high, white plume as the tiny scoop-shaped depressions of the metallic wheels jetted the fine dry sand into the air. Treet leaned forward to cut wind resistance, clenched the joystick, and urged his machine to chase, willing it to go faster. When he looked at the speedometer it read 400 kilometers per hour. He gulped, astounded by the speed.

He made a good race of it, cutting back and forth behind Yarden as they swerved along, threading the bases of the dunes, back and forth like a waterskier zipping in and out of a speedboat's wake. Gradually Yarden pulled away from him; he watched as the plume dwindled, eventually shrinking to a mere white puff which disappeared behind a dune far ahead. There was no catching her.

"I've never felt anything so absolutely, ecstatically thrilling in all my life!" shouted Yarden when they finally found her again. She had stopped to wait for the others. Her face flushed and ruddy from the excitement, eyes luminous with pleasure, she raised her hands to her windblown hair and smoothed it. "It's like a dream—like flying in a dream." She fairly hugged herself with ecstasy. "Isn't it wonderful?"

They all agreed it was indeed wonderful—Pizzle a little less enthusiastically than the others, feeling martyred by the necessity of having to drive the water bag at a snail's crawl while everyone else flew like eagles.

Treet was fascinated by Yarden's response. The flight of the skimmer seemed to have ignited an inner fire that burned from her eyes and made her whole body glow. He thought if he were to touch her skin it would sizzle. The sight was enchanting; he would have been embarrassed to stare so brazenly if not for the fact that Yarden was oblivious in her bliss.

"It reminds me of the first time I took a trainer up," said Crocker reverently. "Suborbital jumpjet—little more than a rocket engine with a seatbelt. I never wanted to come down."

With difficulty Treet tore his eyes away from Yarden, but not before she noticed his look and returned it with a smouldering glance of her own. He noticed Calin standing off to the side, watching them. She, too, radiated live heat, but her expression was impossible to read—composed of too many emotions, or of one that Treet had never encountered before. Her almond eyes sparked strange fire in their depths.

"Well, what say we make camp here for the night?" he asked.

"There's still a lot of daylight left," observed Pizzle.

"Oh, let's do go on," Yarden said a little breathlessly. "One more ride—I want just one more before we stop."

"This time *I* get to pilot," Crocker stated firmly.

"Fine," said Treet.

They rode for another hour or so. Epsilon Eridani bulged just above the horizon, a white incandescence that turned the sky and sand white gold.

Crocker was following Yarden's skimmer furrow in the

317

sand. Treet sat in the passenger's position behind Crocker, clutching the handgrips and hoping Yarden would have sense enough to stop soon, when he saw the blue mist. At first he thought it a cloud of insects—it had that swarmy, diaphanous quality—but it was much too big. It looked like the rain edge of a thunderstorm viewed from a distance as it sweeps across the landscape, though closer and not as dense or dark.

It hovered directly in front of them, an immense curtain several hundred meters in the air and perhaps ten or fifteen kilometers wide. It was hard to tell exactly because the curtain lost itself in the dunes at the edges and faded into the air high above. Before Crocker could pull up, they were through it, proving that the misty curtain was much closer than it appeared.

Treet felt a splash of coolness on his exposed skin, as if he had been sprayed with rubbing alcohol from an atomizer. Then they were through, the veil of mist behind them, shimmering pale silver in the sunset.

Moments later they rounded the foot of a low-humped dune and came upon Yarden and Calin. The women had dismounted and were waiting for them on the shadow side of the dune. Circling once, Crocker brought the skimmer in. A few minutes later they heard the whine of Pizzle's machine as it came sliding around the dune to park beside them.

"Anybody notice that fog?" asked Pizzle as he climbed down from his vehicle.

"Yes," said Yarden, "we noticed it. Rain do you think?"

"Not rain. At least not any kind of rain I ever saw," offered Crocker. "No clouds."

"It was wet like rain," put in Treet. "Like mist. Maybe Pizzle's right—maybe it was a fog of some kind."

"Fog in the desert?" Crocker scoffed lightly. "In bright daylight? That's a first."

Treet lifted his shoulders. True, there had been no change in temperature as they went through the curtain, which would argue against any kind of fog. Yet, he felt an unmistakable dampness as they flashed through. His forehead and the skin on the backs of his hands still tingled faintly. He rubbed his forehead, but it was now dry. Whatever had been there had likely evaporated.

The company went about setting up camp, pitching the two remaining tents on the flat sand between dunes. Night came on quickly, the stars intense in the desert dome. They made a small fire in a depression in the sand, then gathered around to talk quietly, their voices drifting in the silent air. They sipped water and ate some of the dried eel, which, to their surprise, tasted just as good dried as fresh, though chewy in the extreme.

After eating, Treet got up to stretch and walk before turning in. He climbed to the top of a dune, his boots sinking and sliding in the fine, loose sand. He did some torso twists, toe touches, deep knee bends, and side bends, then stood with his hands on his hips gazing up at the velvety sky.

Here in the desert the sky appeared darker, the stars brighter, their light sharper, more intense. He was still watching them when a voice behind him said, "Ophidia is well up already, I see."

Treet turned slowly. "Yarden, I didn't hear you come up."

"Am I disturbing you?" She came to stand beside him, and Treet felt a flutter in the air, as if an electric current vibrated the molecules between them.

"No, you're not disturbing me." He glanced skyward once more. "I was just thinking."

"Tell me."

"It was nothing."

"I'd like to hear it anyway."

"Well, I was thinking that this world, Empyrion, is far more different than it appears at first. It takes time to discover the differences; they're subtle."

"Hmmm," agreed Yarden, "I see what you mean. Some people are like that, too."

There was something in her tone he had not heard before. He turned to look at her face, but could not read her expression in the starlight. Is she talking about me, he wondered, or herself?

Before he could wonder further, she said, "You're very different than I first thought. There's a lot to you, but you don't make much of it. Most men, I've found, have an erroneously high opinion of themselves and don't mind sharing it at every opportunity. But not you. That's just one way you're different."

"There are others?"

"Oh, yes, Orion Treet. There are lots of others. I have not discovered them all yet. But give me time . . ."

She paused. Treet saw the liquid glint of her eyes as she gazed at him. He reached out and touched her arm, soft and pliant and warm. He pulled her to him.

"No," she whispered, tensing.

He put his lips to hers. She did not return the kiss, but pushed against him.

He held her in a tighter embrace. She struggled in his arms. "Stop!"

"It's all right—" he persisted.

"Let me go!"

She stiffened and pushed him away as he let go. Off balance, he fell backward onto the sand. She stood over him, her eyes flashing in the starlight. "You're no different!" she said harshly. He felt the bristling heat of her anger.

"Yarden, I—" he began, but she was already gone, confusion hanging in the air where she had been.

Treet picked himself up and slip-walked despondently down the dune to his tent.

FORTY SEVEN

Yarden's wild screech brought Treet out of a deep sleep. He was on his feet outside the tent, Crocker and Pizzle stumbling out behind him, before he knew what it was that had summoned him. The sky was light, but the sun was not yet up. A second later he heard a strange whimpering sound coming from the women's tent. He went to it and said, "It's Treet. What's wrong?"

Calin answered, "Don't come in here!"

The three men looked at each other uneasily. Crocker responded, "We won't come in, but you're going to have to tell us what's wrong."

"My—it's my . . . Ooohh!" Yarden moaned.

The men waited. Presently the tent flap opened and Calin stepped out, then stooped to help Yarden, who came out slowly, doubled over. She straighened, and Treet's heart dropped a beat. Pizzle sucked his breath in sharply.

"Good Lord, girl!" gasped Crocker.

Treet took a step closer.

"Don't touch me!" warned Yarden. "I might be contagious. Please, stay away."

"We need to see—how else can we help you?"

"I'll show you," she said, "but just don't touch me, whatever you do."

She raised her face and stretched forth her hands. Angry red blisters pimpled every square millimeter of skin, including eyelids and fingertips. The only places where the blisters were not in evidence were the crevices between fingers, the triangular expanse of skin under her chin, and the crescent folds behind her ears.

The blisters were raised bumps with translucent, fluid-filled caps, elongated rather than round, red at the base, but yellow at the top. They looked as if the slightest touch would burst them and disperse the fluid.

"What are your symptoms?" asked Pizzle. "Fever? Itch?"

"No fever." Yarden shook her head. "No itch. They don't hurt, although my skin tingles like crazy. I didn't feel anything or notice anything until I woke up like this. Oohh!" She raised her hands to her eyes. "What am I going to do?"

Treet could see that she was close to hysteria. He desperately tried to think of something comforting to say. "It isn't so bad," was the best he could come up with.

"Not so bad!" she wailed.

"That fog!" cried Pizzle. "Look, the blisters only cover the exposed places—wherever the mist touched. Everywhere else is normal—I mean, I assume it's normal?"

Yarden nodded. "Nothing so far. Only where the mist touched me."

"Then how come none of the rest of us have any blisters?" asked Treet.

Pizzle shrugged. "Different genetic makeup, different body chemistry—who knows? Maybe Yarden was allergic to whatever was in the mist and the rest of us aren't."

"I'm not allergic to anything," replied Yarden petulantly.

"That you know of," said Pizzle.

"It doesn't look like any kind of allergic reaction I ever heard of," observed Treet. "More like a disease."

"Thanks," muttered Yarden, chin quivering.

"Are you suggesting we quarantine her?" Crocker appraised her with narrowed eyes. "It might not be a bad idea."

"What good would it do?" objected Treet. "We all rode through the mist. It's just a matter of time until the rest of us come down with it."

"Oh, great!" Pizzle frumped. "Let's look on the bright side."

"Well, what do we do now?" wondered Crocker.

"Yarden, do you feel well enough to travel?" asked Treet. "One of us could drive for you."

Yarden nodded silently.

She's more shook up than she lets on, thought Treet. Why did this have to happen to her? All that flawless, porcelain skin now blotched and swollen and . . . ugly!

They struck camp and skimmed over a gray land into a hard pewter sunrise. The blades cut grooves in the fine sand as they rode the lift and fall of the round dunes like the swell of an ocean. They stopped once midmorning for a drink of water and a survival wafer. Yarden showed no change in her condition. She said she still felt okay, though worried.

When they stopped a few hours later to take a direction check, Pizzle's rubbery face showed distinct discoloration—clumps of spots on his cheeks and across the bridge of his nose. Crocker mentioned that his throat felt dry. Calin seemed okay, but said little. Treet noticed that his skin was tender where the mist had made contact. He knew it was just a matter of time.

Next morning three bloated and blistered faces peered at one another fearfully in the orange halflight of their tent. After a moment's examination of hands and a tentative exploration of facial features, Treet sighed. "It looks like we're in the game, gentlemen. What's our move?"

Crocker thought for a minute and said, "I say we keep going—as long as we can. We don't know the course of this . . . this condition, but if we could reach the Fieri we'd be better off."

"Keep going till we drop, eh?" cracked Pizzle.

"It's our best chance," snapped Crocker. "What do you suggest—that we just lay down and scoop the sand over our heads?"

"Stop it, you two. We've got to think about this. I agree with Crocker—we don't know anything about this malady, so we might as well keep going. Maybe it will go away in a day or two."

"Then again, maybe not."

"Yes, Pizzle. Maybe not. But laying around here won't get us anywhere. And as long as we don't *feel* sick, there's no reason to sit around wallowing in self-pity."

All day long the company monitored themselves for minute changes in their conditions. Calin, too, had fallen victim to the malady; but other than tingly, tender, blistered skin and dry throats, no one had anything new to report. By nightfall, however, Yarden had developed new blisters on her arms and chest. The condition, whatever it was, was spreading.

Then the itching started.

At first it was merely an upgraded version of the tingle they had become used to, but by morning the intensified tingle was a fire on the blistered hide, impossible to ignore or satisfy. Scratching didn't help—made it worse, in fact. The pustules burst at the slightest touch, oozing their syrupy contents onto the surface of the tortured epidermis, spreading the contagion.

"Don't scratch!" Treet shouted through clenched teeth. "You'll only make it worse." They were sitting in the shade of a dune near the tents, each with a helmetful of water within reach.

"Thank you, Doctor Feelgood," grumbled Pizzle. "Ooo! I'll go insane if this doesn't stop." He squirmed and writhed like a worm in hot ashes in an attempt to refrain from scratching his sores.

"I say we get on the skimmers and ride," offered Crocker. "It will help take our minds off the itch."

"Go kill yourself!"

No one else felt like traveling either; each nursed his agony in his own way. Yarden and Calin slept fitfully. Pizzle flailed and cursed, and at one point attempted to burrow into a dune headfirst. Crocker paced and moaned, clenching and unclenching his fists. Treet walked, swinging his arms and striding long strides, counting each step, willing himself not to scratch.

But scratching was inevitable. The blisters burst, and a yellowish purple crust formed on the pitted skin. The crust hardened and cracked, fluid oozed between the cracks, and the itching increased. They took off their clothes so the material would not stick to the skin and pull it off.

All night long Pizzle howled and thrashed. Treet and Crocker whimpered in their own misery and kept an eye on him so he didn't injure himself with his maniacal gyrations. The sound of weeping emanated from the women's tent—the soft, blubbery sobbing of utter despair.

By morning the blisters were so numerous over the rest of their bodies that no one got up. They all lay flat on their backs, sniveling, scratching until fingernails bloodied and pus ran red.

Treet slept—a nightmare-ridden, fevered torpor that gave no rest or relief. He dreamt of preying birds picking flesh from his bones, of steam springing from superheated rocks to scald him, of sitting up suddenly in bed and leaving his skin behind, stuck to blood-caked sheets.

When he woke he could not open his eyes, the crust was so thick. His throat felt shredded, as if he had been gargling hot razor blades. Breathing through his nostrils was difficult; the air wheezed in his lungs. In his groggy, partially coherent state he feared that the pustules were now forming in the soft mucous tissue of his breathing passages. He tired to speak, to cry out, but his voice would not come.

Then he noticed that the itching had stopped.

With quivering fingertips he explored his ravaged face. The crust was a lumpy shell, seamed over where, through some movement, he had cracked it and the fluid had bubbled out and dried. He could no longer feel the pressure of his fingers on his skin. Either the crust was thick enough to insulate feeling, or the delicate nerve endings were numbed . . . or destroyed.

From the nape of his neck to the balls of his feet, his whole body was now covered with the suppurating crust. Treet was literally encased in a cocoon several millimeters thick. Every movement cracked the cocoon and made the fluid run into the crevices. Underneath the crust the skin was dead, but at least that was better than the maddening itch.

The day passed—maybe two or three days, for time melted together to become a solid, ill-defined mass. Treet vaguely remembered rolling himself up with a tremendous effort, grappling with his empty helmet, and stumbling outside to get a drink, cracking his cocoon in a million places, making the foul yellowish fluid drip from him like poison rain. When he came to again, he was back in the tent as before; maybe it had been a dream after all.

He faded in and out of consciousness. Once he awoke to a bone-parching fever and imagined he was wrapped in foil and lying on red-hot coals. Another time the sound of his heart drumming double-time wakened him, and he was certain his heart had burst through his papery skin and was beating outside his body. He lay like a mummy. Inert. Unmoving. More dead than alive. Waiting for his vital functions to falter and stop. The sound of his heartbeat eventually dwindled away, and he knew he was dead.

Waking or sleeping, the terrible, fever-induced hallucinations continued. But as Treet sank further into unconsciousness, the nightmare images and sensations dwindled to dull discomfort. The fever raged, but Treet was beyond its reach.

Some time later the fever broke, and the weltering heat gave way to cool relief. He felt as if his withered body had been dipped in thick, cooling menthol balm. For the first time since the blisters appeared, he relaxed and slept peacefully.

The coolness persisted, and when Treet came to awareness once more he realized that the worst was over. This he knew instinctively. He listened for his heartbeat and heard a regular, strong thump-a-lump rhythm. He was hungry and achingly thirsty, but clearheaded and calm. The cobwebs and cloudiness had vanished from his brain, and along with them the gnawing fear. He still could not open his eyes, and breathing was difficult. He felt weaker than he ever had in his life, but he was, despite these modifications, himself again.

He must have slept again, without knowing it, for when he woke he could open his eyes—or at least open them inside the cocoon. Weird purplish light filtered through the crust, which seemed to have ballooned like an expanding foam. He felt a sudden urge to move, to break out of the cocoon.

Starting with his right hand, he wiggled the fingers and found that after a moment the interior of the casing loosened and he could move his fingers. With a little more effort he could twist his hand. Balling his fist, he succeeded in cracking the casing a little, then punched through it.

The cocoon came away in chunks after that—first the right arm and then the left. Then, hands pounding at the dense, pebbled surface, he cracked the area over his chest and peeled it away upward toward his throat and head until he was able to pull it from his face in one masklike section. With an Atlaslike shrug, his shoulders broke free and he sat up and looked around, blinking in the early morning light.

He was outside the tent on the sand next to one of the skimmers. The bottom half of his body was still trapped in a grotesque purple-black and marbled yellow casing that looked disturbingly like charred flesh—puffed up like a marshmallow held too close to the flame. The cocoon was at least three centimeters thick over his entire body. The shapes of his legs could barely be discerned as individual objects; they were joined from hip to knee. His feet were lumpy mounds.

Treet beat on the shell and broke it apart with his hands, freeing hips, thighs, and knees before kicking his feet out. He stood slowly, unsteadily and leaned against the skimmer.

It was then that he realized his skin was completely healed. Holding his hands before his eyes, he marveled that the skin was smooth and supple, slightly moist. His body hair curled in ringlets, holding tiny beads of moisture like pearls. There was not a trace of a blister or scab anywhere. The skin of his arms, legs, and torso was also uniformly without blemish. As far as he could see, there was not a mark on him. He had emerged whole and unspotted from the ordeal.

He snatched up a helmet from the seat of the skimmer and held its faceplate in front of his face to see himself in its smoky reflection. His bearded features appeared not only unharmed, but youthful. From what he could tell, there was not a line or wrinkle showing on his face.

As the awareness of this miracle broke over him, he was overwhelmed with giddiness—an intense, nonsensical desire to dance and sing, to prance and cavort and abandon himself to sweet, reckless joy.

He threw back his head and laughed, thinking, How wonderful to be alive! I am reborn!

FORTY EIGHT

Not a sound came from the tents. Treet didn't think the others were dead, but the possibility crossed his mind. The day was new, the sun not yet beyond the first quadrant. A partial breeze stirred the tent flap and lifted the hair on his rejuvenated skin, and Treet remembered he was naked.

He went to his tent and peered cautiously inside. Crocker's and Pizzle's grotesquely bloated shapes were stretched out like obscene vegetables, swollen and discolored, or like the ghastly larvae of some gross, monstrous insect. With more difficulty than he would have imagined, he dragged the unwieldy sarcophagi from the tent and into the open air. Then, after a moment's consideration, he did the same with the bodies of the two women.

Next, he fished his soiled jumpsuit from the heap outside the tent where they'd discarded them. It stank with a powerful, nose-shriveling stench and was so besmirched with urine, blood, and ooze that the cloth was stiff as cardboard. There would be no wearing that singleton again—best just to bury it, or better still, burn it. Burn them all.

He remembered Pizzle saying something about spare jumpsuits in the carry compartment of one of the skimmers. He tried the nearest one and, underneath some hastily folded yoses, came up with a new red singleton nearly his size. He climbed into it and then turned his attention to the bodies arranged before him. They looked like effigies sculpted in plastic foam and then baked in a fire pit, the scoring of the flames still evident on the tough shell.

Of the two women's shapeless forms, he thought he could tell which was Yarden and decided to free her first. He knelt down and lifted his fist to smack the shell, then hesitated—what if she was not ready? What if freeing her too soon would somehow interfere with the healing process? It was best, he decided, to wait until he detected some stirring from within. Then he could help and know it would be all right.

He had just settled himself to wait when he heard faint scratchings from one of the cocoons. He bent over the nearest one—Calin's, he thought. There was movement inside. With the palm of his hand he pounded firmly on the shell high up on the chest just below the base of the throat, cracked it, and then worked across and down the left arm.

In moments a soft, bronzed-skinned limb came forth, its hand scrabbling and grasping. Treet caught hold of the hand and squeezed it. "Calin, can you hear me? Don't worry. I'll have you out of there in a second."

He fell to the task with restrained fervor, smacking the hard carapace carefully so as not to injure the body trapped within. He heard a muffled yelp when he pressed too hard in removing the headpiece. But when he lifted it away, Yarden blinked and smiled faintly up at him.

"Don't look at me," were her first words. "I must be a horror."

Treet swallowed and whispered, "You are beautiful." He touched one flawless cheek with a finger and let it trail down along her throat. It was true—Yarden was even more beautiful than before, if that was possible. Her fine skin had lost none of its silkiness, and the tiny laugh lines at her eyes and the corners of her mouth had been erased. She appeared years younger.

She blushed under his gaze, a rosy tint spreading from throat to cheeks. He pulled away the cracked encrustment over her torso, allowing her to sit up. She shrugged her right arm free and brought it over to cover her breasts demurely. Now it was Treet's turn to blush. No stranger to female anatomy, he nevertheless turned away and handed her a yos to put on, keeping his eyes averted.

"How long have you been up and around?" she asked. "You can turn around again. It's incredible we're still alive."

"Not more than a minute or two." Treet bent to finish freeing her from her crumbling prison. She kicked her legs, the cocoon shattered, and she stood up.

She looked at her hands, legs, and arms with wonder. Treet followed her gaze, drinking in the glowing freshness of her body. She had never appeared more lovely, more desirable than at that moment. He felt a pressure in his chest, and his throat constricted. He couldn't speak.

"Ahhh!" yelped Yarden amiably. "Oh-h-h, it feels so *good* to move, to be alive!" She burst out laughing just as he had done, then shook out her hair, brushing away the clinging pieces of crust. Treet watched her with utter fascination.

No woman has ever had this effect on me, he thought. It's like I've never seen a woman before. I feel like an awkward kid.

"What's wrong?" asked Yarden, her eyebrows arching gracefully. "You're looking at me funny."

"I—I am?" Treet blustered. He turned away. "I feel a little funny."

"Come on, let's get the others out of those horrible body casts!"

Together they worked at pulling Pizzle, Crocker, and Calin from their loathsome cocoons and finding the newly-released captives something to put on. When all were presentable, they stood around gazing at one another, beaming foolishly, grateful and happy to have survived, and full of the wonder of the transformation each had undergone. Even Pizzle's looks had improved; he appeared less jug-eared, his features less haphazard than before. His straggle of beard had thickened out, and the little bald spot on the top of his head grew new hair.

"There's no explaining it," said Treet. "We can't even begin to know what happened to us. Even if we could explain it, I'm not sure I would believe it anyway—it still seems far too incredible. By all rights we should be moldering corpses. Instead, we're all standing around fresh as baby's breath, looking fifty years younger."

"An exotic virus or bacterial infection—" put in Pizzle.

"I don't care," said Crocker. "I'm just glad we survived. Did any of you others have dreams?"

"Did I!" Yarden said. "They were terrible. I've never had such bad dreams."

"I know—maybe an enzyme of some kind," continued Pizzle, shuffling away deep in thought.

"How long do you figure we were out?" wondered Crocker.

"Your guess is as good as mine," Treet answered. "I have no idea. The last thing I remember is getting up to get a drink. That was maybe two days ago. At first I thought it was a dream, but I woke up out here on the sand, so maybe not."

"You got a drink?" Something in Pizzle's tone made them stop and turn toward him. He was staring at the skimmer with the water supply.

"Yeah, I think so. Why? What's wrong?" Treet exchanged a quick glance with Crocker.

"Then this is *your* fault . . ." Pizzle turned to the others, his face grim, the light dying in his eyes.

"What's my fault?" Treet moved toward him, then froze. The waterbag was limp, deflated. "No!"

Pizzle spoke softly, but his words boomed in their brains. "It's all over now. We've had it. We're out of water."

"We can't be!" shouted Crocker, dashing forward. He stopped in his tracks when he saw the tent, now flaccid, its mooring straps hanging loosely, the whole thing collapsed. The inner flap that had sealed in the water gaped, having been carelessly ripped open and not closed properly. The seal had dropped below the waterline, allowing the water to leak away. The sand beneath the skimmer was a shade darker, still damp from the water it had absorbed.

Long seconds passed before anyone spoke. Treet stared in disbelief at the empty tent, his face ashen. Pizzle and Crocker turned on him as one. "You did this!" they accused. "Because of you we're all going to die!"

"I—I'm sorry . . . I didn't know . . ." Treet mumbled, stunned.

"It's all your fault," said Pizzle darkly. "This whole expedition is your fault—it was your idea in the first place. We're going to die out here because of you. We can't last even three days without water."

Treet bristled at this. "What choice did we have? You tell me that."

"We could have stayed in the colony. We could have hidden somewhere and been safe," snapped Pizzle.

"That's crazy!" Treet turned imploring eyes on Crocker. "Tell him it's crazy, Crocker. We had no choice."

Crocker scowled darkly. "What's crazy is being out in the middle of this wasteland without water. He's right, it's your fault."

"Stop it, you two!" Yarden charged into the middle of them. "It is *not* his fault. How dare you blame him? He was out of his head with fever—as we all were. He didn't know what he was doing. Besides, we don't really know what happened at all. It could have been any one of us. Maybe *you* didn't close the seal properly, Pizzle!" She thrust a finger in his face.

"Me!" Pizzle flapped his arms in exasperation. "He's the one that got us into this mess. Why are you defending him?"

"No one got us into this predicament. We all went willingly. Only Treet had the courage to follow his instincts. Let's forget about laying blame and figure out a way to survive."

Pizzle crossed his arms and stalked away.

Crocker fumed for a while, but eventually came to his senses. "We just got a little panicked, that's all. It's a bad shock." He looked at Treet with raised eyebrows. "No hard feelings?"

Treet nodded, accepting the apology. "Pizzle's right though," he said glumly. "We won't last three days without water. What are we going to do?"

FORTY
NINE

"**M**aybe Nho can help us," suggested Crocker. He glanced around quickly. "Hey, by the way where is Calin?"

"She was here just a second ago," said Treet. "Check the tent."

They searched the tent and the immediate vicinity. Treet turned up some footprints leading away from camp. He found Calin sitting hunched up in the sand at the foot of a dune, head down, her arms drawn around her knees. He sat down beside her.

"We've been looking for you, Calin," he said gently.

She made no answer.

"If it's the water you're worried about—"

"It's not the water," she said, her voice trembling.

He waited, but she did not continue. "What then?"

"It's Nho . . . I can't—he's . . ." She raised a round, tear-stained face, lips quivering. "He's gone!"

Treet sat looking at her for a moment, then put his arm around her shoulders. "Hold on now," he soothed. "What do you mean he's gone? Where could he go?"

Calin shook her head in dismay. "I don't know, but it happens sometimes. I've heard of it before. The psi gets angry and leaves, and the powers vanish. There is no way to get it back. I've been trying to contact him, but . . ." Her voice quivered, and the tears started again. "I'm not a magician anymore!"

Treet pulled her close, feeling a little foolish. How do you comfort someone whose psychic entity has disappeared into astral never-never land? "There, there," he said. "Maybe he will come back. Maybe you just need a little time to recharge your batteries, you know? You've been pretty sick. Maybe that has something to do with it."

They sat for a long time clinging together. Treet surprised

himself with a sudden outpouring of tenderness for the stricken magician. She was weak, vulnerable; she needed him. He rather liked the feeling, like the yielding nearness of her.

"I think we better go back now," he said finally. "I'll tell them about Nho if you want me to. Crocker won't like it, but there's nothing anyone can do. We'll just have to wait and see."

Only Yarden was cheered by Calin's loss. She took her shoulders and looked her in the eye. "Don't you know what this means? You're free!"

"Yeah," griped Pizzle, "and we're history. We have no compass anymore. No water. No nothing. We're sunk."

"Squelch the doom forecasts," said Crocker. "I've been assessing our situation. We didn't lose all the water. While you've been belly-aching Yarden and I measured out what's left. We've got about twenty liters, by our best estimate, besides what's in our emergency flasks."

"So we postpone the inevitable four or five days. Whoopee."

"Pizzle, you're a crybaby, you know that? You're a spoiled brat of a crybaby," Treet said. "Here we all are, trying to pull together for survival, and all you can think of to do is carp and whine because things aren't absolutely peachy."

"I beg your pardon! The prospect of immediate death makes me a little testy," Pizzle japed.

Crocker ignored him. "I figure if we push ourselves as hard as we dare, we ought to be able to make ten thousand kilometers in four days. That should take us out of this desert—it *can't* be much bigger than that."

"Want to bet?" muttered Pizzle.

"Can we go that fast?" wondered Treet.

"I don't see why not. Didn't you tell me we topped out at four hundred kilometers per hour?" Crocker patted the side of the skimmer he leaned against. "That's flying."

"But that was a race. We couldn't drive like that all day."

"Only short bursts. I figure all we have to do is maintain an average of two hundred and fifty per hour over ten hours travel time per day. We could do that, I think."

"We'd have to double our average," pointed out Yarden. "Before we got sick, we were doing a hundred and twenty-five. I kept track."

"Impossible," said Pizzle, but he stood and came over to join the discussion. "I mean, we'd have to push it to the limit.

And even if we were somehow able to keep from going around in big circles, we still don't know precisely where we're heading."

"We keep the sun at our backs in the morning and aim for it in the afternoon," remarked Crocker. "Just like we've been doing."

"Too bad we can't travel at night and use the stars," Pizzle mused, "like in *Dune*."

"That's another one of your adolescent fantasy stories, I take it?" said Treet archly.

"Only one of the most famous classics of all time."

"Never heard of it."

The company struck camp and proceeded on their way, pushing the skimmers as fast as safety would allow, and changing drivers regularly. The pace wore down muscle tone and reflexes fast. But they soon developed a rhythm of driving and resting, and the kilometers fell away beneath the gleaming, sand-sharpened blades of the skimmers.

At the end of the first day they had covered nearly two thousand kilometers. "We're five hundred short for the day," said Crocker, "but we had a late start. We'll do better tomorrow."

They did do better the next day, covering almost three thousand kilometers of dune-strewn desert. They climbed down from the skimmers in the early twilight gritty, bone-weary, parched, and triumphant. In their sleep that night they relived every dip and swell of the sand-filled wilderness as they slid once more over the endless white void in their dreams.

On the third day disaster struck.

Pizzle was far out ahead of the group—they took turns leading one another so those behind could relax somewhat since it was easier to follow than to forge the trail. Treet was second, watching the high white plume of Pizzle's skimmer weaving its way over the desert landscape when without warning the plume disappeared in a great puff of sand and dust.

Treet gunned his vehicle to the spot and skidded to a stop beside the smoking wreckage of Pizzle's skimmer. Crocker bounded from the passenger's seat and dashed through the clouds of hanging dust to where Pizzle lay spread-eagle on the sand fifty meters away. Treet approached as Crocker rolled Pizzle over.

"Is he dead?" asked Treet. Pizzle's head wobbled loosely on his shoulders. One side of his face was turning a bright red from an ugly scrape, and the heels of both hands were raw and bleeding. It looked as if he'd slid across the desert floor on his hands and face.

"I don't think so," replied Crocker, placing two fingers beneath Pizzle's jaw at the carotid artery. "I've got a good pulse here. He's just out. I don't see anything broken."

Treet straightened and turned back to the ruined skimmer. The smoke was clearing, revealing a twisted pile of metal half-buried in the face of a dune. "Oh, something's broken all right."

Yarden and Calin came skidding in and ran to them. "Is he—" began Yarden, glancing fearfully at the limp body cradled in Crocker's arms.

Holding up his hands, Treet said, "We don't know yet, but we think he's okay. He's scraped up pretty bad—that's all we can tell right now."

Pizzle gave a long, low moan that sounded like a snore. "If I didn't know better, I'd swear he was sleeping," said Treet.

Crocker peered at him doubtfully. "He's coming around." He patted Pizzle's cheek gently. "Pizzle, can you hear me? It's Crocker—hear?"

Pizzle's eyes fluttered open. "O-o-h-h . . ." A hand went to his head. "What happened?"

"You had a wreck," said Treet. "Where does it hurt?"

"All over . . . O-o-h-h. I don't . . . remember . . . a thing," he said, rolling his head from side to side. "I think my neck is broken."

"I doubt it," said Crocker. "But it probably should be. Can you get up?"

"Just let me sit here a minute." Pizzle closed his eyes again. "I must have blacked out."

"Like a light," said Crocker. "Tell us what happened."

"I don't know. I mean—I was driving along, I looked down at the instrument panel to check my speed, and the next thing I know I'm waking up here." He rolled his head again. "Oh, baby! Is my skimmer all right?"

"Total loss," said Treet. "You were lucky." He studied Pizzle closely. His eyes narrowed. "In fact, more than lucky, I think.

336

The only people who walk away from accidents like this in one piece are drunks."

"What are you saying? Pizzle certainly wasn't drunk," Yarden remarked.

"No, he wasn't drunk. He was *asleep*."

An expression of recognition spread across Crocker's face. "Is that true? You fell asleep?"

Pizzle blanched. "How do I know? Everything's kind of blurry. Maybe I did get a little dizzy just before—"

"Just before you fell off?" said Treet with disgust. He stomped off to examine the smashed skimmer. The machine looked like someone had tried to fold it in the middle. It's sides were crumpled and bowed; its blades stuck out in artistic angles.

"Pizzle, you grouthead!" exploded Crocker. He stood up quickly, dropping Pizzle onto the sand. "Look what you've done!"

A sickly grin warped Pizzle's face. He pushed himself back up on his elbows. "Sorry, guys. I don't know what to say. I didn't mean to. I guess I got mesmerized or something. Rapture of the road, you know? It's never happened before."

"Well, we don't have to worry about it happening again. You'll have to ride with Yarden. You take the prize, Pizzle, you know that?"

"Ease up on him," said Yarden. "He could have been killed."

"Maybe that's not such a bad idea," said Treet, joining them once again. The tone of his voice made the others glance at him. "We've lost the rest of the water. The tent was punctured in the crash. It's all gone."

Pizzle groaned. Crocker swore under his breath.

"We've still got the emergency flasks," Yarden pointed out.

"Well, this is an emergency."

"We're never going to make it," moaned Pizzle.

"Not if we sit around here much longer," said Treet.

"He's right. I suggest we get moving again pronto. We can't get out of this desert fast enough to suit me," Crocker said.

They left, but not before Pizzle had stripped everything of possible use from the damaged vehicle. That took some time, but Pizzle convinced the others that it would likely pay off in the long run. When at last they got underway again, the sun was starting its slide down toward the western horizon and a stiff breeze had picked up, sending sand devils twirling across the flats.

A ridge of cloud appeared away to the south, and the breeze turned into a steady wind. Treet noted the clouds and pointed them out to Crocker. When he looked again, he was amazed to see that the ridge had swelled to a hard, brassy brown bank that was moving toward them fast. He held up his hand and slowed to a stop.

"I think we're in for a storm," he said, indicating the clouds. The wind whistled over the tops of nearby dunes as sand snakes hissed up the smooth dune faces. The sun had become a pale platinum disk in a sky of brittle glass.

"Maybe we can outrun it," said Crocker.

"We can try," agreed Treet.

They pushed the skimmers as fast as they would go, but at the end of another hour the wind had become cold and strong, flinging the sand into their faces, stinging exposed flesh; it became apparent they would not be able to outrun the storm. Crocker cupped his hand and shouted, "Let's find the biggest dune around here and pitch our tents in the windshadow."

Visibility had dropped to a scant few meters by the time they found a place to stop. Copper clouds opaqued the sky and all but obscured the sun, which burned with a ghostly pallor, like a candle shining through burlap. They managed to get one tent up and anchored between the two skimmers when the gale hit.

The wind roared with the sound of a rocket thruster throttled flat out. Overlaying this was a harsh, shushing rasp that was the wind-driven sand in flight. The company huddled together in the crowded tent and listened to the storm. Its howl absorbed all conversation, so they lay back in the dim orange half-light and watched the fabric of the tent stretch and flutter, hoping against hope that their fragile shelter would last the night.

Some time later Treet awoke. The wind had died away to a murmuring whisper. He slipped quietly out of the tent, shoving sand away from the flap with a swimming motion of his hands. He stood and looked around. It was early evening. The sun was down, but the sky still held a leaden glow. Stars burned coolly overhead and the newly-rearranged dunes stood like bleached shadows, silent and immobile, their crests touched with silver.

Treet surveyed their position. One of the skimmers was completely buried in the sand, the other only half-buried. The curved roof of the tent jutted beween them. He climbed to the top of the nearest dune and scanned the horizon, letting his eyes sweep the undulating desert beneath the twilight sky. He had completed a ninety degree arc when he saw the obelisk.

FIFTY

"It's no use," sighed Pizzle. "I've done everything I can think of to do. I don't think it's going to start."

He sat in a ring of scattered skimmer pieces—cowling, chain, sprocket gears, screen mesh, wire, sealed bearings—his face and hands smeared with grease, peering doubtfully into the complicated innards of a dead sand skimmer.

Crocker sat on his heels next to Pizzle, scratching his head and frowning. "I'm sure I don't know what else to do." He drew a soiled sleeve across his brow, jerked his thumb over his shoulder to the skimmer gliding up, and said, "You want to give 'em the bad news or should I?"

"What bad news?" asked Treet as he, Yarden, and Calin, who had become little more than a ghost since her psi deserted her, climbed down from the last working sand skimmer. They had driven to the obelisk Treet had spotted the night before to check it out.

Crocker squinted up into the sunlight at Treet. "We're down to one vehicle. We can't get this other one to start."

"That's bad," said Treet. "But at least we still have one."

"Yeah," said Pizzle darkly. "Keep your fingers crossed and hope it holds out."

"What did you find?" Crocker unfolded himself and stood, squinting in the direction of the obelisk—a narrow white slash in the pale blue sky.

"It's some kind of signal tower—that's my best guess. It's huge—I'd estimate close to two hundred meters tall. The base is one hundred meters in circumference—Yarden paced it off—five sides, twenty meters to a side. There are some funny markings on the base, like numbers or letters, only they're not. The rest of it is completely smooth—some kind of plastic sheeting that covers it to about halfway up, then bare metal beams and struts like a radio antenna all the way to the top."

"Anything on top?" asked Crocker.

Yarden answered, "Some kind of dish—like a satellite dish."

"Could be a microwave reflector," mused Pizzle. "Those have to be pretty tall like that. Any way to climb it?"

"There is a ladder of sorts that begins about five meters off the ground on the south side. But the thing is almost straight up and down. I wouldn't want to go climbing around on it."

Crocker nodded thoughtfully. "Well, let's get packed up here and take a look. The day is getting away from us as it is. We'd better make some good use out of it, or we've wasted a day's ration of water."

The skimmer fairly groaned under the weight of its passengers. All five managed somehow to crowd aboard—along with the tents and the gear Pizzle insisted on bringing in case of a breakdown. They drove to the tower, a short ride of about six kilometers. Crocker parked the skimmer in the shadow of the soaring object and then walked around it.

"Sure is a big old thing," he said. "I think one of us should try to climb it. Maybe we'd see something from way up there that could help us out."

"You mean like an oasis or something? Forget it," said Pizzle. "You're dreaming."

"Or like a river, or green hills, or anything that shows us the way out of this desert," said Crocker.

"Or like a city," put in Yarden. Everyone looked at her. "Is that so farfetched? We're looking at a signal tower of some kind. Whoever built it must have built something else, too. Maybe we could spot it from up there."

"Sure, why not?" asked Treet.

"Then you're going up?" said Crocker.

"Not me. You go up—*you're* the pilot."

"Don't look at me," said Pizzle quickly. "I'm barely functioning without my glasses the way it is. I'd never see anything from up there."

"You were functioning well enough to wreck a skimmer," Treet needled. "Now all of a sudden you're blind."

"I'll go up," offered Yarden. "I'm not afraid of heights."

"Neither am I," remarked Treet. "It's the fall I can't stand."

"You won't fall," said Pizzle. "You'll be extra careful."

"It *was* your idea," added Yarden.

"It was Crocker's idea!"

"No, I mean this morning—when we first saw it. You said

341

someone should go up and check out the view." Yarden nodded, chewing her lip as she raised her eyes to where the shallow, round dish gleamed from the top. "It probably isn't all that high. I don't mind going."

"I'll go," muttered Treet.

"You don't have to." Yarden smiled at him, then said, "You'll be all right, just hang on tight."

So Treet found himself standing on Crocker's shoulders, reaching for the vertical ladder. "I can't reach it! It's about a finger too far," he called.

"Lean against the base—we'll boost you up."

He leaned full length against the base while the rest of them grabbed his feet and pushed him up higher. There was a single rail next to the indented rungs. Treet caught the bottom of the tubular railing where it joined the plastic sheeting and hauled himself up. The rest was relatively easy—as long as he kept his eyes on the rung just ahead.

He climbed, one hand on the rail, one hand on the rung at eye level, stopping every other rung or so to sweep sand from the indentation. When he finally reached the place where the sheeting stopped and bare metal began, he crooked his arm around the rail and looked out.

A sun-washed whiteness met his gaze on every side, shimmering in heat waves off the sand, melting into light blue in the distance. There was no green, no river, no city, no oasis— nothing but sand dunes and still more sand dunes, looking like the humped backs of white whales from high above.

Treet called down his observation, and Crocker's voice came drifting up to him. "Go higher! Higher!"

Treet gritted his teeth and edged onto the metal superstructure. He could, he quickly found, climb the inside beams at the intersections of joints. This took him higher in a zigzag pattern and gave him good footing and something to hold on to with both hands. In a few minutes he was half again as high as he was when he'd given his first report, but still only halfway up the tower. Far below, the others were mere dark spots on the ground with round white centers which were their upturned faces.

A slight breeze rippled his singleton and stirred his hair. The landscape was a wrinkled ocean whose waves were frozen white ice. Nothing could be seen south, west, north or east— except the same monotonous monochromatic dunescape. As

Treet moved to begin climbing down again, he caught something out of the corner of his eye. He stopped and looked.

Nothing. The heat shimmers were playing tricks on his eyes, he decided. He turned to lower his foot back onto the next joint and he saw it again—off to the southeast, the faintest vertical slashmark on the horizon. He looked again and saw nothing, but tried looking slightly to the left of it and saw it again—the lone spire of another tower barely nudging above the dune line. It disappeared into his blindspot whenever he tried to look directly at it, but became visible when he looked away.

Treet marked its direction and began climbing down. It was a long, slow, muscle-knotting climb, but he finally reached the bottom of the ladder and slid down the base to drop onto the sand.

"Well?" asked Crocker. "What did you see?"

Treet raised a fist of white sand and let it sift through his fingers. "A lot more of this same white stuff, friends."

"I was afraid so," grouched Pizzle.

"*And* . . ." Treet paused, drawing them out.

"Yes? Do we have to guess?" asked Crocker.

"Another tower like this one, I think. Away to the southeast. The same general direction we've been heading all along."

"How far?" asked Yarden.

Treet shrugged. "I can't say. Pretty far. It's hard to tell."

They all looked at each other. "Is everyone thinking what I'm thinking?" asked Crocker.

"We are," replied Yarden, "if you're thinking of following these towers to wherever they go."

"Trouble is," replied Pizzle, "that wherever they go is probably a million kilometers from here. They may not lead anywhere at all. We don't even know if they're still operational, or if whoever built them is still around."

"Do we have any better options?" asked Treet. "We've got four days of water left, and that's at half rations. After that . . . well, we start dehydrating . . . seriously."

"Stop," said Yarden. "All I can think about now is how thirsty I am."

"So let's quit standing around here and get moving. The quicker we find the way out of this place, the better off we'll be."

"You're starting to repeat yourself, Crocker," said Treet.

They climbed back onto the overburdened skimmer and

started off in the direction Treet had indicated. Thirty minutes later—traveling at a top speed of one hundred and ninety-five kilometers per hour—they reached the second tower, an exact duplicate of the first.

"I suppose you want me to climb this one too," said Treet, craning his neck to look upwards. Why did they have to be so blooming *tall?* he wondered.

"If you wouldn't mind—just to be sure," said Crocker.

The view from the second tower was precisely the view from the first in every respect—including the illusive suggestion of a third tower on the southeastern horizon.

"It's there," said Treet as he dropped back exhausted to the ground. "If we keep going this direction, we'll hit it."

A little over a half-hour later they reached the next tower.

"I'm not going up again. I'm not selfish; let someone else have the thrill."

"Not necessary," said Crocker. "We're moving at a forty-five degree angle to the arc of the sun. I imagine we'll find another tower if we keep on going."

Two towers later, they stopped for a drink of water. Fortunately the weather of Empyrion, even in mid-desert, remained uniformly friendly—twenty-five degrees centigrade during the day, dipping at night no more than eight degrees—with a light breeze, when there was a wind at all, so that the travelers did not sweat overmuch, or in fact have to worry about excessive heat at all.

They decided to push on as far as they could go under sun power, and, by carefully increasing the skimmer's speed, were able to pass a dozen more of the strange towers before the sunlight grew too weak to power the vehicle. The sun was low in the sky, throwing the shadow of one of the towers out ahead of them when they stopped.

"As good a place as any," replied Crocker. They erected the two remaining tents and then sat around glumly munching survival wafers and dried eel flesh. They allowed themselves one more sip of water before turning in for the night.

Treet rested for a while, but could not sleep, so slipped out of the tent and, despite the need for conserving energy and body fluids, went for a walk. Walking helped him think, and thinking was what he needed most at the moment.

He thought about their chances of survival—nothing much

to think about there. Then he thought about the towers: incredibly tall and finger-thin, spaced at precise intervals across the desert. What were they for? Who used them? They looked quite old. Perhaps they had been built long ago, their makers dead a hundred generations, their purpose now forgotten. Perhaps, as Pizzle suggested, the towers led nowhere.

The stars came out and splashed themselves over the sky. Treet found a place to sit at the bottom of a nearby dune and lay back to watch the sky. The sand, warmer than the air now that the sun had set, felt good against his back as he gazed up into the alien heavens.

How many times have I seen this sky, he asked himself, and not really seen it? Empyrion's sky was a magnificent creation, like Earth's, but unlike it at the same time. The planet's purer atmosphere made the stars appear much brighter, closer, more readily accessible. But they, like Sol, were just as faraway as ever. But which one was Sol? Which of all those shining flecks of light held his own azure bauble in its gravitational field?

"I thought I'd find you out here."

Treet heard Yarden shuffle up. "You mind?" she asked, when he did not respond.

"Uh, no, help yourself," he murmured, raising his head and then lying back. Here she is, he thought, as much a puzzle as ever. Why can't I get on the same wavelength with her? Maybe it's her sympathetic ways.

"I couldn't sleep either," she said, nestling into the sand beside him. "I thought I'd keep you company." She did not look at him, but followed his gaze skyward. "What are you looking at?"

"Nothing . . . everything. I don't know. Stars. They're all the same, but all different. You never get tired of looking at them. I wonder why?"

"Maybe it's because we know deep down that somehow they represent mankind's future and past and everything in between."

"Huh?"

Yarden smiled in the dark—Treet could tell she was smiling because her voice softened, became warmer. "I mean that when you look at a star you're seeing light from thousands of years ago—that's the past."

"Right."

"And the stars themselves represent the future—going there, visiting them, discovering things, spreading the human race through the galaxy—that sort of thing."

"And everything in between?"

"Well, that's what they represent right now—something to light the night, to give us something to steer by, to look at and wonder at, to plot a life's course by."

"Yarden, I do believe you're a romantic."

"Hopelessly," she sighed. "You are too. I can tell."

"Me?" Treet scoffed. "Never. I've seen too much."

"What's that got to do with it?"

"I mean I don't harbor any illusions about life. It turns out like it turns out. There's nothing anyone can do to change that. Certainly going all starry-eyed over things won't help."

"You don't believe that really."

"Believe what? That getting sappy about life will make it turn out better than it's going to anyway? A man would be a fool to believe it." He paused, and when Yarden did not say anything, he added, "How did we get on that subject anyway?"

"You started it. But the stars *are* nice—like that big one over there. I don't know when I've ever seen one brighter."

"Which one?" he asked.

"There." She lifted her hand and pointed to an intensely glowing star near the horizon to the northwest. "See? So big and bright. Blue-white."

"It's a beauty," allowed Treet. "And as a matter of fact, we haven't seen it before."

"That's strange."

"Not really—we've probably crossed some meridian or equator or something and its visible now. But it is bright."

"Maybe it's Sol."

"Maybe . . . but I don't think so." Treet's voice sounded as if it were strained through a sieve. Yarden looked at him, but could only see the outline of his head dark against the light sand. "Yarden . . ."

"Yes—" She shared at him in the darkness, trying to see his expression. "What is it?"

He sat up bolt upright. "Yarden, it's moving!"

"What is?"

"That star is moving! It's coming this way!"

FIFTY
ONE

"I don't see any movement." Yarden fixed her eyes on the bright star. "Are you sure?"

"Wait! Hold still, take a deep breath, and look . . ." Treet poised perfectly still for a few seconds. "See? It's getting bigger. That is definitely no star. But whatever it is, it's coming this way."

They watched for a few moments more, and then Treet went to rouse the others. Crocker cupped his hands around his eyes to shut out all extraneous light, watched motionless, and then announced, "You're absolutely right. It's a craft of some sort, and it's headed for us. Judging by the angle of flight, I'd say it was low altitude and only moderate speed."

"Helicopter?" wondered Treet aloud.

"Like a helicopter, yes."

"It's following the line of the towers," observed Pizzle. "Look where it's coming from. Bing, bing, bing—right down the line."

"Pizzle, I do think you're right," said Treet. "Now why would they do that, whoever they are?"

"They're navigational towers," explained Crocker, indicating the dark mass rising up into the night beside them. "The pilot homes in on the towers to stay on course."

"That's a stupid way to fly," said Treet.

"Primitive," agreed Crocker, "but effective."

Yarden broke in, "You don't suppose they are looking for us?" Her stress on the word *they* made the others stop and look at her in the starlight. There was no doubt who *they* were.

"Chasing us? You mean . . ." began Treet. "No, why would they?"

Crocker shrugged. "We'll find out soon enough. ETA is less than twenty minutes by my guess. Maybe we should be ready to make a run for it in any case."

Working feverishly in the dark they struck camp, keeping one eye on the ever-growing light in the sky. They took down the tents and loaded the skimmer, then gathered at the base of the tower to sit and wait. The disk of blue-white light increased by slow degrees until it outshone every other star, and still grew brighter and larger.

Then they heard the engines, softly at first, a mere burring rumble on the night air, like distant thunder. Gradually the rumble grew into a great booming throb that pulsed in heavy waves as it echoed among the dunes. By then they could make out a great dark shape above the light—a huge, black spherical mass that blotted out the stars around it. The bright light emanated from the bottom of the craft, shining down at an oblique angle, playing across the desert as it came. They could see the light striking the crests of dunes, flaring white and sliding down the slope to disappear from view, only to flare again on the crest of the next.

"I think we should get out of the way of that light," cried Crocker. He had to shout above the monstrous thrum of the oncoming engines to make himself heard.

They ran from the tower to lay in the sand atop a small dune near where the skimmer was parked. There they waited. Three heartbeats . . . four—then the mysterious craft was upon them, blacking out a fair portion of the night sky as it glided by, engines roaring, pushing the flying machine past them at a stately pace.

The light swept over the exact spot where their tent had been, flashed over the tower, and continued on. A tremendous black sphere filled the sky above them, below which dangled another, smaller shape that looked like an elongated teardrop. A row of green lights appeared near the front end of the horizontal teardrop, and a dull red glow lit up the rear.

In a matter of seconds it was gone, churning off into the night, the sound of its mighty engines dwindling rapidly, its black smoothness melting into the night once more, the light fading, leaving only the faint suggestion of a red glow behind. Then that, too, was no more.

A feeling of sadness descended over the group with the passing of the craft. No one spoke for a long time.

Finally Crocker broke silence. "What in blue blazes was that?" he asked. Awe, and the stillness of the night after the boom of the craft's engines, made his voice sound thin. "I've never seen anything like it."

"It was an airship," said Pizzle.

"We know that," snapped Crocker, "but—"

"No, he means like a blimp," Yarden offered. "Right?"

"Right. Airship—as in lighter-than. Did you see the size of that thing? Oooeee! Incredible. It must be making a good hundred k's per hour, which for all that mass is doing all right."

"Who were they?" asked Yarden, expressing the obvious question in everyone's mind.

"Calin?" asked Treet, turning to the silent young woman. "I think you can tell us. They weren't Hagemen looking for us, were they?" he said.

Calin shook her head. Her voice came soft in the darkness, touched with wonder. "No, they were not looking for us. They were . . . Fieri."

"Just what I figured," replied Treet. "They didn't even know we were here. We just happened to stumble onto the Fieri air route."

"Amazing, your powers of deduction," quipped Pizzle. "I was about to say the same thing."

"At any rate, that settles the problem of our next move," put in Crocker. "We keep following the towers right to Fieriland."

"And hope the water holds out," said Treet.

They followed the Fieri towers for three days, passing them at regular intervals every thirty minutes. The overloaded skimmer gave out toward the end of the third day. Tempers frazzled by thirst and the monotony of desert travel snapped when the skimmer lurched, chugged, and shook to a bone-rattling halt.

"That tears it all to hell," said Pizzle, throwing a three-way wrench at the broken vehicle. He'd been tinkering with it for over three hours, and the sand was littered with skimmer pieces. "It's probably some routine maintenance thing that we don't know about. But it's kaput! We're done for."

"Lay down, Pizzy, I'll scoop sand over your head."

"Drop dead!"

"Isn't that what you're suggesting?" Treet said snidely.

"We're not finished yet," said Crocker. "Not even close."

"Oh?" Pizzle turned on him. "I'm overjoyed to hear it. I thought people usually died of thirst when they ran out of water in the desert."

"We're not out of water yet," said Yarden.

"You're right," said Pizzle. "I forgot. We've got a whole half day's ration of water. We could all take baths and wash our hair we've got so much. Whatever shall we do with it all?"

"Cool off, Pizzle," said Treet. "I don't want to hear any more of your spoiled-brat theatrics."

"If I had a stillsuit and crysknife your water would be mine," Pizzle muttered.

"What did he say?" asked Crocker, watching him strangely.

"He thinks he's someone called Paul Dune or something—a character from one of his books. Thirst is warping his brain," said Treet. "Let's leave him here."

Treet picked up his sling, slipped it over one shoulder, and started off. Yarden and Calin fell in behind him. Crocker watched them go, picked up the two slings at his feet, and held one out to Pizzle. "The machine's finished. Even if you knew how to fix it, there's nothing to fix it with. Come on or I *will* leave you here."

He turned and trudged off. Pizzle glanced at the skimmer, hefted the sling onto his back, and shuffled after the others, head down, in his slope-shouldered gait.

Night found them halfway between one tower and the next. But they walked on, having decided to travel by night and therefore minimize evaporation of moisture from their bodies. The hours passed slowly as they dragged themselves over the desert, becoming more aware of the burning in their throats with each and every step.

No one said much. They mostly kept their heads down and conserved as much energy as possible, wasting neither words nor motion. An hour before dawn, the sky showing like oxidized aluminum in the east, they halted, erected the tents, and went to sleep.

Treet awoke from a dreamless sleep feeling like he'd taken a big bite out of a sand dune. He coughed and would have spat, but was afraid to waste the spit, so swallowed instead, which did nothing for the gritty dryness in his mouth. He took up his water flask, jiggled it to test how much remained—only the barest hint of a slosh at the bottom of the flask—and decided to forego the drink he'd promised himself upon waking.

Then he remembered what had awakened him: the sound of an airship's engines.

He rolled to his feet and stumbled from the tent, almost

tipping forward onto his face as he straightened. He was a little light-headed from lack of water and thought perhaps he was hearing things—the aural hallucinations of a dying man. But he was just being melodramatic; he was nowhere near far enough gone to start having hallucinations, aural or otherwise.

He turned his eyes to the sky. It was early afternoon by the sun. A Fieri tower loomed over the dunes to the southeast about four kilometers away. The airship's engines thrummed lightly from out of the northwest, though without its single large headlight it could not as yet be seen. Treet stood squinting into the sky, straining for a glimpse of the craft as the sound grew steadily louder.

"Wake up!" he hollered. "An airship is coming! An airship! Quick, wake up! We've got to try to flag it down!" he hollered, dashing from one tent to the next to rouse the others. By the time they tumbled out upon the sand, the shape of the Fieri airship could be vaguely discerned—a rust-red disk in a cerulean sky.

"This is it," said Crocker hoarsely. "We've got to make them see us. It's our only chance."

"If we only had a signal flare—" griped Pizzle.

"Take down the tents. We'll wave those," commanded Crocker.

Pizzle dived into the tent, fished out his sling, and dumped it out in the sand. He grabbed up a small canister and some other objects and started fiddling with them.

"Now what are you doing?" asked Treet in exasperation. "We could use your help."

"Shut up and leave me alone!" snapped Pizzle. "I've got an idea."

The Fieri's craft loomed closer. Now they could see its bulk casting a rippling shadow over the dunes.

"There!" said Pizzle shortly. "I hope it works." He held up his handiwork for all to see. Attached to the canister were several wires and a broken piece of a solar cell.

"What is it?" asked Treet.

"A smoke bomb. This is from the skimmer I wrecked—it's filled with solid fuel, and the cell ought to heat up the wires and blow the fuse inside. It might be enough of a spark to touch off the fuel. I figure it should smoke two or three minutes."

"Pizzle, you're a wonder," said Treet. "Want us to do anything?"

351

"Yeah. Stay out of my way."

"You better get it going right now. That airship will be here any minute."

Pizzle climbed a dune and hunched himself over the canister, holding the solar cell by the edges, tilting it toward the sun. In a few moments a hissing sound came from inside the canister. "It's getting hot in there."

"Look!" cried Yarden. "The airship is almost here!"

Treet glanced skyward and noted the looming shape of the Fieri airship. "It that thing going to work?" he hollered.

"Shh!" warned Crocker. "Give it a chance."

The hissing grew louder. "Go baby, go-o-o," coaxed Pizzle. "Do it, do it, do it. Make your papa proud."

"It's not going to work," said Treet.

Yarden looked at him with worried eyes. Calin stood silently, watching with a stricken expression. Crocker pounded his fists against his thighs, his face intense, looking like a gambler whose winnings were riding on a heavy-odds underdog.

"Will you shut up!" cried Pizzle. "It'll work—just give it a second."

"The ship is almost here!" said Yarden. "Ooo, come on, come on . . ."

The canister hissed loudly and gave a muffled pop. Yellow smoke erupted from the top of the canister along with sparks and a sharp sizzling sound. "There!" said Pizzle triumphantly. "I told you it would work."

But the words were no sooner out of his mouth than the sizzling stopped. The sparks fizzled and died; the smoke evaporated. "No!" cried Pizzle, diving for the canister.

"So much for the miracles of modern science," said Treet, already dashing away. "Get those tents!"

"I can get this going again, I know it." Pizzle jiggled the wires and tapped the canister. He held the solar cell to the sun.

"Forget that!" barked Crocker. "Find something shiny to flash. The rest of us will signal with the tent fabric and hope to God they see us!"

The airship was almost directly overhead by the time they started waving the orange tents from the top of the tallest nearby dune. Treet could make out individual windows in the bulbous, teardrop-shaped cupola suspended below the gigantic gas-filled sphere of the airship. But if anyone aboard was watching, he couldn't see a face. The thundering engines reverberated across the desert, bouncing sand from the dunes below, vibrating diaphragm and eardrum alike with their deep, sonorous sound.

As the giant airship's shadow slid over them—a rusty moon eclipsing the sun—Treet shouted, "We're too much underneath it! They'll never see us!"

He snatched the tent from Crocker's hands and fled into the sunlight again, sliding, slipping, rolling down the side of the dune. He ran hard, trying to keep up with the craft, waving the tent fabric over his head, yelling, falling, sprawling, getting up, and running again.

The airship floated on without so much as a tip of a trailing stabilizer to them. In a little while the Fieri craft became a mere blip in the sky, leaving only the purr of the engines behind.

Treet lay panting in the sand, watching the airship disappear once again. He felt stunned and sick and foolish. To think they would die out here now after all they had been through. That airship had been their last real hope, and it had just vanished over the bleak horizon. The cursed white desert—nothing but bleached dunes beneath a waxy blue sky—would soon cradle their bones in its vast desolation.

The unfairness of it! Treet wanted to cry, but it would be a waste of precious tears and would do no good. He rose slowly and ambled back to where the others sat waiting, their expressions mirror-images of his own dejection.

"Well, we're awake now," Crocker was saying. "We might as well get moving."

"Why?" grumped Pizzle. "What difference does it make whether we die here or fifty kilometers from here? It's all the same to me."

For once Crocker did not snap back at him; he didn't even bother to reply, just turned sad eyes toward him and shrugged. The resignation in that heavy lift of the pilot's shoulders cut at Treet's heart like a razor. Never had he witnessed such an elegant statement of despair. He looked away, a lump the size of a melon swelling in his throat.

Yarden jumped to her feet; her dark eyes narrowed in quick anger. "I defy you to give up on us!" she shouted. Treet swiveled around to see her face livid with rage, fists clenched and shaking. "It is a sacrilege!"

Crocker looked properly chastised, but Pizzle glared back defiantly. "Bitch!" he spat.

Yarden's slap sounded like the retort of a gun. The white

imprint of her hand on Pizzle's cheek was already turning deep red before Pizzle knew what happened. A rich interplay of emotions—shock, bewilderment, outrage, innocence, guilt—pinwheeled over his homely features. He settled on an expression of unalloyed astonishment. "You hit me," he observed softly.

Yarden's eyes flared, but she answered coolly, "I'm not sorry. You deserved it. Get on your feet, and let's get moving."

Calin rose and came to stand beside her, saying nothing, but showing quiet courage in the gesture. Treet, still on his feet, took a half-step closer. The three of them waited, looking down at the two men.

"Looks like we're bound for a little more sightseeing, Pizzy old boy," said Crocker. He got up slowly, patting dust from his clothes.

Pizzle climbed to his feet, now contrite and apologetic. "Okay, okay," he said. "Why's everybody always taking these things so seriously?"

Yarden's lips remained pressed firmly into a straight line. But the hard light in her eyes softened, and satisfaction radiated from them. She spun on her heel and stalked down the face of the dune, starting off once more across the desert.

FIFTY
TWO

Yarden's steely determination carried them three more days. On the fourth no one got up. They lay in the tents, too weak to move, too demoralized to care, merely waiting for the end, hoping it would not be too painful.

Treet drifted in and out of consciousness. The last two days had been cruel torture. Simple thirst had ceased, only to be replaced by a most compelling agony: his tongue swelling in his mouth, every tissue giving up its stored water, internal organs shutting down for lack of moisture. He and the others had nevertheless stumbled on doggedly, dimly aware of where they were and what they were doing.

Nothing mattered. Beyond care, beyond regret, beyond every other human response, now only the slow, inexorable approach of death held any interest for him. To be alive and know you were dying and know too there was nothing you could do about it, thought Treet in one of his lucid moments, was surely the worst trick of a whole universe full of lousy tricks.

By the fevered whispers and the soft sighing moans emanating from those around him, Treet knew that he was still in the land of the living. But as the day progressed, the hours dragging by in leaden succession, each one too long and too laden with the thick, foul presence of death, the moans and whispers gradually ceased.

The bright orange light inside the room was fading when Treet roused himself from a trancelike stupor in which he imaged the deep pulsing thunder of airship engines as the great spheres passed, one after another, oblivious overhead. He rolled weakly, painfully onto his side and listened. He heard a droning buzz and could not place the sound. He listened for a moment, and the sound resolved itself into voices—Yarden was talking to someone in the hallway outside. They were talking about him.

"He is dying," she said. "We're all dying, don't you see. It's okay though—really it is." She was obviously trying to convince herself as well as her companion that death was an acceptable outcome of their ordeal. "Actually, I could have predicted it from the beginning. Failure is nothing to be ashamed of. It happens. Anyway, we all have to die sometime."

There was more that Treet could not get. Such stupid talk, thought Treet. Odd coming from Yarden. She was the one who had used every ounce of her own stubborn will to urge them all on when nothing else would have kept them going. Now here she was telling whoever she was talking to, most matter-of-factly, that it was perfectly proper to lay down and die. That wasn't like Yarden at all.

Tears came to Treet's eyes, hardly more than a mist wetting his hot, dry eyes. I've lost her, he thought. I should have told her I loved her. Not that it would have made any difference—but no, it always made a difference. I should have told her. Now she would die without knowing . . . but it didn't matter. He would die without saying it, so they were even.

"You know what burns me," Yarden was saying to her listener. Her voice came from just outside the curtained door. "I could have sworn that Orion Treet and I were friends—more than friends, if you know what I mean. I mean, I did everything I could to let him know how I felt. A girl can only do so much though. It was up to him to meet me halfway, but he never did."

"I can't understand it," the stranger's voice replied. "It was obvious to everyone else how you felt about him. But look at it this way—you're probably better off the way you are."

"Dead?" Yarden asked in mild surprise.

"No, I mean better off without him. He wasn't much after all. You could have done much better. You were young, you had lots of other opportunities."

"Had," huffed Yarden softly.

"Yes, had. Well, like you say, it can't be helped. You certainly did all you could. No one could have done more, I must say."

Treet groaned. Why were they talking like that? It was life and death they were talking about, not the price of eggs in Egypt. This was *his* life, *his* death—he wanted it treated with a little respect.

"Stop it . . ." he murmured.

But the voices went on talking in that odd, insane way. He could no longer distinguish the words, but he heard their buzz and at one point recognized Calin's voice among them—a man's voice, too, but not Crocker's or Pizzle's—his father's voice. They were all talking about him, about his miserable life and even more miserable death—he knew it and resented it. "Stop!" he said again, his voice rasping in a dry throat, the mere rush of wind over desert sand. "Stop, damn it!"

Treet pushed himself up on his elbows and inched toward the tent flap. His muscles, stiff and unyielding, trembled and resisted the feeble effort, which was, he knew, his final mortal act. They can't talk about me like that, he thought. I'm dying. It isn't right . . .

He flopped forward and reached the door, pushed his head through the curtain. Though it nearly exhausted his ebbing strength, he stretched his arms forth and hauled himself halfway through the opening, where he stopped. The air was cool on his skin, the light dim. Either it was getting dark or his eyesight was going, probably the latter. He didn't care. The voices stopped as he emerged from his room, he noted with grim satisfaction.

Good, he thought, I've given them something to think about. They didn't know I could hear them; now they'll think twice before writing anyone off quiet so casually. But there was something else he wanted to do—one final thing. It was why he'd crawled out into the hallway. What was it? His head was no longer clear; the thoughts wouldn't come.

Fog-wrapped images played before him. He saw once again the face of his father, looking at him in frank disgust over a priceless M'yung Dynasty perfume jar smashed into smithereens. He was seven years old and had not meant to break the ancient thing; it slipped while he was looking at it. "You'll never learn, will you?" said his father. "You're hopeless."

It would have been better if his father had hit him, walloped him a good one for his clumsiness. That he could have accepted. But the once-and-for-all pronouncement was too severe and unremitting. There was no appeal.

"I'm sorry," breathed Treet. "S-sorry . . ."

The drone of the voices returned again, more insistent. He'd given them something to think about. Treet smiled, feeling his lips crack as the skin stretched. He tasted blood on his tongue. The taste brought him around somewhat—at least to the point of remembering why he had crawled from his death-bed. He had a message.

"Yar-den . . . I . . . love you."

Again the voices buzzed over his head. Dark spots swam in the air above him. Flies, he thought. Not voices . . . flies. They were only flies all along.

Pizzle heard the sound of his heart beating in his brain. It thumped with a droning monotony on and on and on. Beating, beating. Growing louder and ever louder. The sound reminded him of the Fieri airship's engines beating in his dreams—the airship that had passed over them, thus condemning them to death. The sound made him angry. His anger propelled him up through unconsciousness, fighting through layers of heaviness like a swimmer ascending from cold, obscure depths.

With an effort he pushed himself up on his elbows; Crocker lay beside him. Treet lay half in, half out of the tent. Both were still, barely breathing, the light inside the tent making their faces livid and grotesque.

He licked his lips with a thick, dry tongue. The sound of the thrumming engines persisted. Now it came from outside. The sound became a hateful thing—a mocking, ugly thing. He would silence it.

With a groan he lurched over Treet's body and out into bright sunlight, where he lay on his back with his arm flung over his face. But the sound, the sound of the airship engines, grew louder. He roused himself to look up.

The hot white sun dazzled his eyes. When his eyes could take the light, he saw an empty, uncaring sky, the blazing disk of the sun the only feature. As he watched, the sun went into eclipse. How strange, he thought, to witness a solar eclipse. I'm dying and I see an eclipse.

Since when do eclipses make noise? he wondered. Wait . . . wait . . . this is not right . . . Muddled thoughts surged around in his head. What is it? What is it about this that is not right?

Pizzle was on his feet now, swaying, peering through his shielding hands at the sun. An airship! It had to be. He had one more chance. One more chance to show the others, one more chance to survive.

He staggered to the tent and thrust his arm in, dragged out the sling, and opened it. Out tumbled the smoke canister he'd made. He picked it up and knelt over it. His eyesight wavered, but he forced himself to concentrate on jamming the wires down inside the container. He held the fragment of solar cell toward the sun and felt the wires grow warm in his hand.

Last time it had failed and he had let everyone down. It would not fail this time; he would not be the butt again.

"Go-o-o," he cooed, his voice a breeze through dry grass. "Ple-ease, go-o-o."

A fizzing sound came from the canister. "Go-o-o!" He willed the canister to ignite.

Smoke started pouring from the top of the cylinder. But it wasn't enough. The hole in the top was too small and only a thin, wispy trail of gray smoke emerged.

"No!" he cried, jerking the wires out. Pizzle grabbed the top of the canister, but the cone-shaped top was hot and the metal seared his hands. He yelped and dropped it in the sand.

He scooped it up again and scratched at the top, heedless of the hot metal or the pain. His fingernails tore, but the lid refused to budge. "Arghh!" he roared, scrabbling with his bloody fingers on the burning canister.

His hands were blistered now. The airship was closer, almost directly above him. He held the smoke bomb in the crook of one arm and braced it there, screaming in pain. "Ahh-hh!" He placed all four fingers on the ragged edge of the lid, gritted his teeth, and pulled. "Off! O-off-ff!" he cried in agony.

The stubborn lid finally loosened and spun off. Oxygen flooded in to touch the solid fuel inside, and the canister erupted like a small, mobile volcano.

F-f-f-whoosh!

Smoke and fire spurted out in a huge fireball that rolled up into the sky. Pizzle fell back, reeling, dazed, his face burned and blackened, his hair smoking.

The orange-and-black fireball rolled heavenward—up and up—higher and higher, passing right in front of the airship.

Pizzle rubbed the ashes of his eyelashes out of his eyes and looked up. The airship's shadow passed over him, and he saw it glide by. He fell back, exhausted by his futile last attempt.

It was then that he noticed the absence of sound.

He had gone deaf?

He shouted and heard his voice croak. No—not deaf! The

engines had stopped! He squirmed and rolled over on his stomach, raising his head weakly. The airship, totally silent now, was heeling majestically around. It was coming back!

Pizzle lay facedown in the sand and cried.

FIFTY THREE

"What do you think that is?" asked one of the Fieri pilots idly. He leaned over his instruments, gazing down at the immense white sheet of desert beneath them.

"Where?" his copilot responded.

"There—just off beamline to the south. I thought I saw something—a glint of color. It's gone now."

"You'd better tell Bohm."

"I don't know. It was probably nothing. You look too long and you start seeing things down there."

"I know what you mean. Still," the young man peered down at the dunescape as it rippled beneath the airship, "let's take it down a bit closer and see. Bohm's instructions are explicit."

"Do you really think they saw something?"

"Oh, they saw something. But they should have turned back to check it out."

"Would you? Look at it down there. As many times as I've flown this route I've never seen anyth—" He stopped in midsentence to watch a bright red-orange and black ball of flame billow up right in front of the craft. "Now that was something! I'm turning back. Get Bohm—I think we've found what he's looking for."

The Fieri airship hung like an enormous rusty moon above the two forlorn tents of the spent travelers. The rescue party had wasted not a second, deploying the survival cylinder the moment the airship hovered to a stop over the tents. Fieri physicians hit the sand running and quickly reached the dying wayfarer whose signal had alerted them. In the next fevered seconds, electrolyte fluids were administered and the condition of the patient was carefully noted. He was placed in the cylinder and whisked back to the airship, while the rescuers turned their attention to the women in the first tent.

The Fieri spoke softly to themselves, wondering how the fugitives could have come so far in the desert, remarking on their unusual, old-fashioned clothing, coaxing their patients to live just a little longer so they could be cared for properly aboard the airship.

They had been startled when one of the refugees, lying half out of the second tent, partially revived before they had a chance to minister to him.

"Get him out of the sun!" said Bohm, director of the rescue operation. "Quickly! Get him a stabilizer!"

"He's saying something," said Jaire, a young female physician. "Flies? I don't understand it."

"He's delirious. Here—you two," Bohm directed two aides, "help Jaire get him wrapped up. He will go after these two."

"There is one more inside this tent," said one of the aides.

"Bring him out. I'm almost finished here. Take these two to the cylinder. Gently, now." He touched a triangular tag dangling from an epaulet. "There are five. Three alive so far. Two are on their way up now. I want them started on fluid replacement and stabilization."

The Fieri leader hurried to the next tent, glancing at Treet as he passed. He peered into the face of the fugitive and whispered, "Infinite Father, guide our hands and minds; help us save them."

When all had been brought aboard, the airship, its engines booming echoes into the dune valleys, moved slowly off, gaining altitude as speed increased, leaving behind two orange tents and a scattering of footprints in the sand.

Considering what one had to go through to get there, death was not so bad. At least it was peaceful and the body no longer ached. There was even a muzzy sort of awareness—call it a phantom persistence of being that allowed inconsequential thought—little more than *I am ... I am ... I am ...* over and over and over.

Most surprisingly, death was not black. It was red. Rather,

it was vermilion with clear blue highlights. And it was anything but the everlasting silence Treet had always believed it would be. Death was a clattering din, truth be told. There was a droning hum that drummed like an irregular heartbeat, an aggravating click like that of many steel balls smacking together simultaneously, and the sound of static electricity snap-crackling as from an oversized Leyden jar.

Were these the sounds of his own dissolution? He did not know. If not for the noise, he could have gotten used to it. But the incessant racket kept him from the quiescence of his insubstantial thoughts.

Treet opened one eye a crack. Surely that wouldn't hurt anything—being dead and all, one was allowed certain license, and as yet no one had read him any rules regarding the conduct of a corpse. He supposed that on opening his eye he would see that oft-described sight of his own empty husk of a body splayed where his soul had left it, staring blankly up into everafter, a poor advertisement for the tenacity and resilience of the human species.

Instead he saw a woman with long henna-colored hair tied back to grace a slender neck, bent as she peered into the screen of a machine, not much bigger than a common calculator, which was emitting all those annoying clicks. Treet liked what he saw, so he opened the other eye—fearing that so flagrant an action might cause an immediate forfeiture of his corpse status, but being unable to help himself anyway.

The woman sat perched atop a tall stool. She was dressed in a smock of sea-foam green with a loose, open jacket edged in blue. The jacket had deep pockets and a blue belt tied at the side, accenting the slimness of her waist. Her long legs were sheathed in soft white boots that laced to just below her pretty brown knees. Sunlight from an oval window flared her hair, making a halo of red gold around her head. A wisp of cloud trailed by the window, giving the impression of flight.

This must be an anteroom of the afterlife, thought Treet, complete with angel and cloud city.

Directly over him a cone-shaped instrument hummed and crackled with static electricity as a ruby light glowed from within it. He lay on a flat, padded table, his head held in position by a contoured pillow something like a sandbag. A white, gauzy cloth covered his loins or he would have been completely naked. Yet he was not cold. In fact, his skin glowed with the rosy hue of a sun-worshiping health freak, rather than the insipid pallor of the recently deceased.

The rest of the room, from what Treet could see without moving his head, was kept in shadow. But the shadows were uncluttered, and apparently he and the angel were alone. He worked his mouth and found that it moved quite easily, although it took a few moments for his voice to emerge. And when it did, he did not recognize the raspy wheeze as his own.

"Are you real?" he asked. The gummy film on his tongue tasted as if something nasty had crawled in his mouth and died.

The angelic being turned from the clicking screen and fastened concern-filled eyes on him. Her eyes were the exact color of her hair—ruddy brown with flecks of gold. Delicate arched brows drew together, and her lips pressed firmly in a frown of competent care. She reached a long-fingered hand toward him and placed it on his chest. Her hand was warm on his skin.

"Am I . . . dead?"

The frown turned into a light-scattering smile. "No," the angel laughed, her voice soft and full and throaty. "You are not dead, nor will you be for a very long time." Her speech was understandable, though colored with a light dialectal lilt which made it seem decidedly otherworldly.

"Oh," Treet whispered.

The angel touched his face with the back of her hand. "You sound disappointed."

Treet only stared upward into the lovely, flawless face, noting the sweep of her dark lashes and the silky smoothness of her cheek. He wondered what it would be like to look upon such perfection for an eternity. "No," he croaked finally, "not disappointed."

Just then a door opened somewhere in the room behind them. Treet felt a rush of cooler air that entered with the new arrival. "So, Jaire, our Wanderer is awake, eh?" said a sharp, trumpet tenor. "Has he said anything?"

The woman, Jaire, glanced up and smiled as a man with a cap of white frizzled hair came to stand beside her. Though he appeared well-aged, his muscles were firm, his skin supple. Vitality burst from his quick blue eyes like z-rays from uonium. Apparently there was no way to contain it—the life in the man simply overwhelmed its slight but sturdy container.

"Yes, Bohm, we have been talking about life." She winked at Treet. "He has decided to remain on this side of the Transformation."

"Was there ever any doubt?" said Bohm. He placed a ready hand on Treet's cheek, glanced at the cone-shaped instrument, gazed into Treet's eyes for a moment, and then declared, "The life force is stronger—no question about it." He looked at Treet and said, "Your Creator has seen fit to grace the world with your presence a little longer. Ours is the benefit."

Treet swallowed, then gagged. His tongue felt twice its size and sticky. A green cylinder appeared in Jaire's hands, and a curved straw was placed at Treet's lips. "Drink slowly," she instructed.

A cool, slick liquid slid down his throat, which felt like baked cardboard. "Thanks," he whispered, and drew in another lengthy sip. "What about the others?"

"Your friends are resting comfortably," said Bohm as Jaire pulled a thin sky-blue coverlet over Treet. "They are still asleep at the moment, but should awaken before we reach Fierra. Please, don't worry about them. Think no negative thoughts. Your trial is over. All will be well."

A little pinging sound came from another room. "Ah!" said Bohm, turning away. "Another has awakened to join us. I will look in and return when I can. Rest well, Wanderer." He patted Treet's shoulder as he went by. The door whished open, and he was gone.

"Bohm is a busy fellow," observed Treet, noticing the light in Jaire's clear eyes as she watched him. "We're on our way to Fierra, which means you must be Fieri."

"Yes," she replied, pleased, and a little surprised, Treet thought. "You know our ancestral name. Now you must tell me yours."

"My name is Orion Treet."

"Two names? Which do I call you—Orion or Treet?"

"Either."

"Then I will choose Orion. It has a mysterious sound." Her eyes sparkled merrily. "What does it mean?"

"What does it mean? Oh, it's the name of a great hunter whose image is remembered in the stars."

"A good name for you then," she said. She gazed at him with open admiration, making Treet feel like a rank impostor for presuming to use his own name. She reached down, pulled the coverlet up beneath his chin, and tucked it around his shoulders. "Bohm has said that you should rest. I will leave you now."

"No, don't. I wa—"

"I will be close by should you need anything. Rest now. Anyone who has come across the Blighted Lands needs all the rest he can get. Think no negative thought."

Jaire left quietly, and the lights dimmed as the door whished once again, leaving Treet in the soft light from the oval window. He closed his eyes. Yes, it felt good to rest. He would doze for just a moment before getting up.

FIFTY FOUR

The moment must have been a long one, for when he awoke again, the sky through the little oval window showed steel-blue dusk. He felt better than when he woke up the first time, so raised his head slowly from the table. The movement made him slightly woozy, but it passed almost immediately and Treet swung his legs over the edge of the table and stood up, draping the coverlet over one shoulder like a toga.

He tiptoed to the window and looked out. From his vantage point he surmised that he was in a Fieri airship, flying eastward at an altitude of about a thousand meters. It confirmed what he already knew to be true—that they had been rescued from the desert at the point of death by the Fieri and were now en route to the Fieri settlement.

Below, he could see a slice of landscape—not oyster white and dry as bone, but dark green and lush, and not the washed-out green of the hill country either—fertile looking, with gently mounded hills and shallow valleys filled with small round-topped trees. The silver blue threadwork of a river wriggled beneath the airship as it pushed its way through the lowlands. The rest was cloudless sky, sinking into twilight.

Treet heard the door slide open behind him and tightened his hold on the folds of his improvised toga. He turned to meet Jaire, standing in the doorway. "You are up, Orion. Good. Bohm thought you would be." She held out her arms, and he saw that she carried clothing. "I brought these for you to wear." She stepped closer, placing the bundle on the table. "When you are dressed, come out. I want to show you something."

"Thank you." Treet nodded. "I will."

He stared at the place she had stood long after she had gone. There was a woman worth getting to know on more intimate terms, he thought. I should be so lucky.

He shrugged off the toga and sorted through the pile of clothing she'd brought for him. There was a pair of loose-fitting underwear which he donned at once, and a pair of trousers of a softspun, loosely woven material, sandy colored, with a voluminous, three-quarter sleeved shirt to match. He put on the trousers, the pantlegs of which stopped well short of his calves, and then tried the shirt, discovering that it had no buttons. The next item from the pile was a wide, plum-colored sash. He took the shirttails and overlapped them around his waist—noticing that he'd lost every ounce of the life-support system he'd carried with him for the last thirty years—stuck the tails into his trousers and tied the whole works with the sash.

Next he perched on the edge of the table and drew on high boots, dove-gray in color, and made of a canvassy material. He pulled the corded laces tight and wrapped them around the top of the boots, stuffing the few centimeters of pantleg into the boot tops before tying the laces just below the knees. He stood, bounced on his heels a few times to get the feel of his boots, and decided he was ready to join the human race again.

He approached the door and put out a hand, only to have the thing slide open of its own accord. He stepped through to meet Jaire, waiting for him with her back turned, leaning a graceful hip against a rail. She tossed him a glance over her shoulder as he moved to the rail and saw that they were on a circular balcony overlooking a large, circular room. At intervals, short flights of stairs joined the balcony from below, where three male Fieri—each dressed similarly to Treet, except for the fact that they wore their shirttails out—engaged in various tasks related to flying the airship.

"Come with me," Jaire said, moving off along the rail. "How do you feel?"

"Much better," Treet said, taken aback by the grating rasp of his voice. "Though I sure don't sound like it."

"Bohm says that will pass." She put a hand to his elbow and led him around the circular railing to a bank of windows which curved both above and below the balcony, following the contour of the bulb-shaped nose of the craft.

"This is my favorite way to see Fierra," explained Jaire, "at dusk, just as the light of the city begins." They stopped at the first window. "See?" She indicated the view with a sweep of her hand. "Isn't it beautiful?"

Beautiful was not a strong enough word for it. Enchanting, was closer. Below them, unfolding as the airship descended slowly toward it, was a vast, gleaming city, winking like crystal in its own light. Treet's first impressions was of an entire plain sprung up with sparkling faerie castles, or of a glowing cathedral stretching endlessly for kilometers in every direction. It was a city of light—like nothing he'd ever seen, except perhaps in a dream.

He'd had the idea—from something he'd read in Feodr Rumon's *Interpretive Chronicles*, most likely—that the settlement of the Fieri was a simple encampment of mud huts or skin tents, more a wide place in the wilderness than an actual walls-and-pavement city. But this . . . this vision of splendor was simply beyond all expectation or imagining.

The airship swung closer, and Treet saw tall, freestanding towers with spires like needles, their points glowing like fiber-optic threads. He saw the sweeping arches of numerous bridges spanning a river that flowed through the city to merge with an enormous, shining lake—shining because fully half the city appeared to be built right out over the water. The mirrored surface glittered with golden light from wings and causeways stretching between luminous mansions. The jetties connecting these float-ing palaces were so numerous that they formed a glittering webwork—nets of light flung out over the royal-blue deep.

There were pavilions and courts and halls, groves and gar-dens and bright arcades joining plazas and parks. Meandering, tree-lined avenues wound through expansive residential districts whose dwellings radiated soft rosy light from high round domes.

Treet's eyes blinked in a prolonged visual gasp as his mind sought words to describe what he saw. Then they were descend-ing to a great square marked by rows of blazing pylons. Flood-lights played over the spherical shapes of airships anchored in a hollow square formation.

Treet became aware of the voices of the airship's pilots as they communicated with the ground crew. Their forward prog-ress halted, and the ship slid down vertically to its berth. The pylons rose up; the airship hovered, then kissed the ground . . . once . . . twice . . . coming to rest like thistledown upon a new-shaven lawn.

"What do you think of Fierra?" asked Jaire, regarding him with bright, amused eyes.

"I do believe I've died and gone to heaven," replied Treet in an awed whisper. "It's totally . . . unbelievable!"

His answer pleased her, he could tell. He was properly impressed and didn't mind letting her know. She smiled, took his elbow, and guided him away from the window toward the nearest ramp of stairs.

Bohm met them at the railing, beaming with keen intensity. "You look well, considering your test," he said. "I would easily mistake you for one of us—a Mentor, perhaps. Still, I hope you won't mind being noticed."

"Will I be noticed then?" asked Treet, catching an undercurrent of meaning in the old man's words.

"Most certainly you will be noticed. I have communicated with the Mentors. They are most anxious to greet you personally." He paused, waiting for Treet's reaction. When it was not forthcoming, he hurried on. "But all that can wait until you are feeling up to it. You and your companions are to be our guests, Orion Treet. I ask only that you recuperate and enjoy Fierra."

"I am in your debt." He turned toward Jaire and said, "I think I would recuperate much faster if I had someone to show me your impressive city."

"My father has already requested the honor," she said, linking her arm in his. "I will take you to my parents' pavilion on the lake—that is, if you wish."

"I wish." Treet smiled, then remembered his neglected companions. "Unless, of course, my friends and I would be too—"

"I have made separate arrangements for your friends," interrupted Bohm. "You are not to worry about them. They will be well cared for."

"Yes, I'm certain of it," agreed Treet. "It's just that I haven't seen them since we were rescued. I ought to check on them at least. Where are they?"

"Come with me," said Bohm, already leading the way. "If it will help ease your mind, I think you should see them."

One by one, Bohm led Treet into small rooms along the circular balcony. Each room had a padded table like the one Treet had awakened on, and the same conical hood above, making the same crackly static sound over the inert body of one of his companions. All were peacefully asleep—Pizzle was even snoring—and all appeared none the worse for being dragged bodily back from the very threshold of death's dark and silent gate.

The sight of Yarden comatose on the table sent a pang of guilt through his midsection.

"I hate to leave them," said Treet as he crept from her side.

"Maybe I should wait until they wake up and we can talk about this."

"If you prefer," said Bohm. "But that really isn't necessary. Besides, it could be several hours before they respond." He gave Treet a fatherly pat on the arm. "Please, allow me to take care of them for you. Go with Jaire, and do not concern yourself about their welfare."

Treet hesitated, but there was no reason to doubt Bohm's word. "All right, I'll leave them with you for the night."

"I will send word to you tomorrow about when you can all be together." Bohm ushered them down the stairs through the airship's command station, through an open hatchway, and down a short ramp to the landing field. The gigantic spheres of Fieri airships, looking like colossal mushrooms, each one tethered to a pylon, met his gaze as he set foot on the grassy field. "Good night, Wanderer. May you find in Fierra all that you are looking for."

"Good night. And thank you . . . thank you for saving my life," said Treet as Jaire took him into the softly glowing night.

FIFTY
FIVE

"**I** think I'm going to like it here," said Treet. He and Jaire were riding along the wide boulevards of Fierra in a low, driverless two-seater which had met them at the airfield. Jaire had pressed a code into an alfanumeric pad and off they went, cruising silently through the city, guided by the vehicle's internal navigator.

Everywhere Treet looked he saw handsome people, some in silent cars like the one he and Jaire were riding in, but most afoot, going in and out of the glowing, dreamlike buildings, or thronging the generous walkways. Treet did not know which impressed him most—the Fieri or their architecture.

The people were on the whole tall and statuesque, with well-proportioned limbs and torsos, graceful in movement and aspect, their features fairly formed and expressive. In general appearance, they resembled the ancient Etruscan sculpture Treet had become enraptured with as a student—gods come to life. The women possessed a willowy femine allure that complemented the unadorned masculine vigor of the men. A more elegant race would be hard to find anywhere.

The architecture, on the other hand, was equally attractive in its own way. Whether clustered together in metropolitan communion, or standing alone on a favored acre, the buildings were individual works of art—given to upsweeping lines and simple, flowing curves, subtle tapers and clean edges. Apparently the Fieri were fascinated with spires, for nearly every structure possessed at least one, and usually more than one of the blade-thin towers. The effect was of an entire city straining heavenward, poised for imminent flight to the stars.

Most arresting, however, was the fact that the buildings themselves glowed. They were not transparently luminous, like some type of exotic glasswork, for the buildings appeared solid enough; but those same solid surfaces gave off soft, steady light.

Most of the Fieri habitations radiated a subdued rose-colored glow, but others shone topaz, pearl, and marbled blue and green, richer than the rarest peacock opal.

"What makes the buildings glow like that?" asked Treet, waving his hand toward a block of lambent residences. "Some kind of stone?"

"You're very astute," replied Jaire. "We use sunstone from the Light Mountains in the north. Nearly everything in Fierra is made of sunstone."

"It certainly creates an effect."

The car whisked them along through the city toward the lake—now crawling slowly through heavier traffic, now speeding over seamless causeways, the sponge-vinyl tires whispering on the pavement, the wind cool on their faces as it swirled around the low windscreen. The sky overhead faintly gleamed with relument luster—a ghostly aurora of reflected glory—making the night seem alive.

Treet took it all in—as much as he was able—in silence, too dazzled to speak, letting the panorama unfold around him as he moved through it until he was almost drunk with wonder. The alien beauty of the place made his head swim, and he sopped it up greedily. Soon, though, he felt his eyelids growing heavy as sleep snuck up to overtake him. He struggled to stay awake, but the long days in the desert had eroded his strength, and he had reached the end of his endurance for the day. Finally he let his head flop loosely on his chest and sank into sense-numbing slumber.

He was still asleep when they reached their destination: a spacious pavilion built on stilts over the lake, connected to the shore by a wide, curving jetty which served neighboring pavilions as well. The car crept to a halt in front of Jaire's parents' pavilion, and they were greeted by a slender young man who looked enough like Jaire to be her twin. Treet roused himself just enough to help them bundle him from the car and into the house.

He walked mechanically through a brightly lit interior, the details of which were fogged with sleep, and allowed himself to be stretched out on a soft pallet in a dark room, one side of which was completely open to the lake. There he was left alone, and he soon drifted to his dreams once more.

• • • • • •

373

The sun had turned the lake to burnished platinum by the time Treet awoke. He stirred and sat up suddenly when he remembered where he was. He looked around at a large square room devoid of furniture except for the bed and a stand on which were hung several outfits of clothes like the one he wore. The walls were buff-colored with broad borders of cinnamon, textured with an indented pebble grain. Two facing walls bore a curious printed design: a triangle with wings outspread, glowing from its center, sending out rays that become tongues of fire. The same design was printed over the curtained door.

A fresh breeze ruffled the loosely woven curtains at the open end of the room and flicked up small waves to lap against the pilings. Out on the silver-white water the curved scarlet sails of a sleek windrunner leaned into the breeze as the boat slashed through the water.

Without thinking about it, Treet found himself leaning his elbows on a balustrade on the walkway outside his room, staring out over the lake. The shoreline stretched in a long scimitar sweep into the distance; he could not see the opposite shore from where he stood, but reasoned that the body of water before him was more inland sea than lake. The air smelled fresh and clean, and Treet detected the citrus scent of orange blossoms.

His stomach growled, and he realized he had eaten nothing for quite some time—nothing that he could remember anyway. So he moved off along the balsutrade in search of some nourishment. At intervals above him were balconies with canopies affixed to crossed poles. No one appeared on any of the balconies as he passed by.

Treet reached the far side of the great house and turned the corner, continued on along a blank, sun-baked wall, turned again to pass through a breezeway between two freestanding wings of the house. A walkway joined the upper stories. He walked twenty paces and entered a huge courtyard, covered by a bright yellow canopy.

There Treet stopped. The pavilion was built around the courtyard, and it was easy to see that it was indeed the centerpiece. Rooms opened directly onto it from every quarter, both on the house's upper and lower levels. Every square meter of the courtyard was filled with plants of the most outlandish varieties. The yard was a veritable jungle of exotic vegetation: all in shades of deep blue-green, with waxy leaves and spiraling, fleshy-podded tendrils and wild iridescent flowers.

The canopy overhead formed a lemon-tinted sky and was made of the same open-weave cloth as the floor-length curtains in his room, allowing the sun's rays to fall through the loose pattern of the weave. It rippled like a parachute in the breeze off the lake, causing hot, bright spots of sunlight to flitter like phosphorescent butterflies over the plants and shrubs and painted floor tiles of the courtyard.

Treet gazed at the lush profusion around him and took a step forward, nearly treading on the tail of a creature which at first glance appeared to be the largest black leopard in captivity. The animal turned its massive head toward him, winked huge green eyes, and lazily withdrew paws the size of dinner plates. It yawned at him, showing a furrowed pink tongue and a double row of shining white triangular teeth like shark's teeth, then slid down to lay on its lightly spotted stomach, stretching muscled legs out into the greenery, effectively blocking the pathway beyond.

Taking a long, slow step backward, Treet attempted to remove himself from the animal's presence. He backed two paces and bumped against something that felt like a fur-covered fireplug. Looking down, he discovered another creature identical to the one directly in front of him. This second one raised a paw and took a swat at him, missing by only millimeters. Before he could dodge away, the next swipe hit his thigh and spun him around and down. The great leopard thing grinned at him and put its head forward, licking velvet lips.

"Hsoo!" Jaire shouted from the upper gallery. Treet glanced up to see her staring down, hands on hips. "What do you think you're doing? Let him up at once. He's a guest!" She dashed for a stairway.

The giant panther cocked its head and came closer to nuzzle his prize, sniffing Treet indiscreetly. "Hey!" cried Treet involuntarily. The next thing he knew he was being licked in two directions at once—one beast slurping left to right, the other right to left. "Hey-y-y!"

"Jomo! Hsoo! Stop this instant! He's a guest. Leave him alone and let him up." Jaire arrived in a flurry of exasperation, grabbed the foremost of the two creatures, and dug her hands into its thick black pelt, pulling with all her might. The animal allowed itself to be diverted and moved off sedately. "You, too, Hsoo. Go take a swim or something. You're not to bother Orion again."

Treet watched the two animals lumber off, their hides bunching and smoothing over rippling muscles. "I'm glad they weren't hungry," he remarked.

"They're such nuisances sometimes, but don't worry. They eat only fish, so they're not really dangerous."

"Except to fish."

Jaire laughed, filling the air with a shimmery ring. "I don't think they'll likely mistake you for a fish. Wevicats are highly intelligent. *Too* smart I often think. Jomo and Hsoo know what effect their appearance has on strangers. They were playing a joke on you."

"I'll remember to laugh next time," said Treet, trying to think of another question just to keep his beautiful companion talking. I could listen to that lilt forever, he thought. Jaire led him along the green pathway through the courtyard to a wide entrance on the ground floor. "Are there any more creatures lurking around I ought to steer clear of?"

"Only old Bli, but he's a rakke."

"A what?"

"Rakke—a water bird. He's ill-tempered, but likes to stay close to his perch in the sun, so you probably won't run into him." She looked at Treet closely. "I know I'm not supposed to ask, but don't they have animals in Dome?"

"Dome? You mean the colony—Empyrion?"

"This is Empyrion." She waved a graceful hand to indicate the whole world. "What do you call the Dread City?"

Treet stared at her and scratched his head. "Are we talking about the same place? The colony? Bubbletown?"

Jaire nodded uncertainly. "Y-yes . . . I think so."

"Is that where you think I came from?"

"Where else?"

I could tell you, but I don't think you'd believe me, thought Treet. Instead he replied, "Who said you weren't supposed to ask me about it?"

"My father," she replied. "In fact, he's waiting to see you. I was on my way to find you." They entered the pavilion and moved across a spacious, polished floor to a smaller receiving room.

"Ah, at last I meet my guest. Welcome to my home, Orion

Treet." The voice was *basso profundo,* a rumble of rich and operatic sound. Treet glanced up to see a very large man dressed much as he was with the addition of a long sleeveless coat over his shirt. The pattern worked into the sea-green cloth was light gold—intricate interwoven arabesques that glittered dully. His tall boots were dark brown, matching his dense, curly beard. There was a thick band of lustrous gold metal around his neck.

The man crossed the room in three strides, moving quickly for a person of such size. He held out both hands to Treet as he came close. Treet did not know what to do, but reached out and took the hands—and had his own wrung severely. "I am Talus, Mentor of Fierra. My daughter you have met already; this is my son, Preben."

Treet blinked and saw that a younger man accompanied Talus. The younger man was an exact duplicate of Jaire, only done up in male flesh, with unmistakably male features and attributes.

"My brother," Jaire said, "you met last night, though I don't think you would remember."

Treet gripped Preben's hands too, and said the first thing that came into his head. "Yes, I've met you both before—by various names: Zeus and Apollo, Poseidon and Ares, Odin and Thor . . ." He realized what he was saying and broke off. "Forgive me for rambling on. I—ah, did not mean any disrespect."

Talus nodded gravely, studying him. Measuring me for a straitjacket, thought Treet. But then his host smiled and laughed, the sound a merry earthquake. "Your words are strange, but there is no offense in them. I think the Mentors will enjoy you."

"Were they friends of yours?" asked Preben.

"Zeus and Apollo? Yes, in a way," replied Treet, feeling more at ease. "They were friends of my youth."

"How are you feeling?" asked Talus. "My daughter tells me that you were very near death when they rescued you. No one to my knowledge has ever traveled across the Blighted Lands and lived."

"I guess we were lucky." Treet shrugged. "We didn't have much choice."

"Luck? Ha!" Talus said sharply. "The Protector Aspect was full on you, or you would not have survived." He softened, apparently remembering the welcome he'd just extended. "But we will discuss all that later. I imagine you are hungry, so let's not waste time better served eating."

Jaire chimed in, "I've already prepared the food. Mother will be waiting for us."

"I will serve," said Preben. He ushered them through the wide entrance, through a great hall to a smaller room at one end. Inside, at a huge table covered with a cream-colored cloth edged in silver, a slightly older, more mature Jaire was arranging an overflowing bower of plants in a basket with deft, quick motions of her hands. "Mother," announced Preben, "our guest has joined us."

The woman looked up, a smile lighting her eyes. "Welcome! I see you have met my family. Now I too have the pleasure of meeting you. I am Dania."

Treet suddenly felt quite formal. "Yours is a most gracious home," he said stiffly. "I hope my presence is not an intrusion."

She smiled again, looked at her husband, and then back at Treet, saying, "Such intrusions are all too rare here at Liamoge." She absently tucked a wayward flower back in place and straightened. "Sit here in the honor seat," she patted the back of a graceful chair, "that I may serve you myself."

It was an awkward moment for Treet, being seated by a woman while the others stood looking on. Dania then took up an oval platter and, as Preben offered each in turn, began filling it with food from the various vessels on the broad table. She placed it before him and reached for her own platter. Treet waited until all were seated, using the time to study his plate.

There was sliced meat—pink like ham or rare roast beef—pale yellow cheese, a salad of chopped pulpy fruit, miniature loaves of dark bread, chunks of fish marinated with vegetable pieces in a pungent sauce, steaming lumps like orange speckled potatoes, something that looked like pasta in the shape of a horn (stuffed with cheese, bread, and spiced meat and covered with red gravy), and four tiny cakes glazed with green frosting. It all looked delicious to Treet; he sucked his teeth to keep himself from drooling.

When all had been seated, Treet picked up his fork—a two-pronged utensil with a carved stone handle. He was about to spear a slice of meat when Talus raised both hands and, with eyes fixed on a point on the ceiling, said, "Receive our thanks, faithful Provider. Your blessings spill over us like the rains in Rialea, and we praise Your many hallowed names." Lowering his eyes once again, he smiled and said, "Eat! Enjoy! The blessing of the Provider is given."

They all dug in. Treet ate with abandon, giving himself to the task with an enthusiasm that would have been considered rude in polite company, if not for the fact that his hosts matched him nearly stroke for stroke. Forks flashed, and teeth chewed, and food dwindled on the platters. No one spoke until Talus, midway through his second helping, said, "Life is good always, but best at table. Don't you agree?"

"Mosht shertainly," Treet mumbled around a mouthful of bread. The food was excellent—apart from the fact that even leek gruel and dried crusts would have tasted like *haute cuisine* after weeks of dried eel. Despite his long deprivation, Treet's taste buds registered a meal that would have thrown the staff of any five-star restaurant into contortions of envy.

Talus rose, grasped a large pitcher, and proceeded around the table, filling tall white-gold goblets with a light green liquid. When he finished, he replaced the pitcher and, still standing, lifted his goblet into the air. "To new friends!" he cried, beaming at Treet from behind his bushy beard. "There is nothing so fine as a new friend, for in time they become the most precious of all the Comforter's gifts—old friends!"

He put his goblet to his lips and drank deeply. All at the table followed his example. The liquid was tart and refreshing, like lemon water, but leaving a piquant hint on the back of the palate, like anise. Treet let the beverage roll over his tongue and kept his nose in his cup after everyone else had come up for air.

Preben stood and said, "To new friends! May they stay long, and leave only to cheer us with their quick return."

They all drank to Preben's toast and then turned to Treet. He stood, and in order to give himself more time to think of an appropriate toast for the occasion, picked up the pitcher and proceeded to fill the goblets of the others himself. Talus protested gracefully, but smiled with satisfaction as Treet worked around the table. He refilled his own goblet last and lifted it high. "To new friends," he said, looking at each one in turn. "May hearts beat fondly, life flow richly, and time pass slowly when they are together."

They finished the meal with a sweet cordial that tasted of spiced cherries. Jaire and Preben dismissed themselves, confessing pressing errands, and Talus and Dania led Treet to a grouping of cushioned chairs in a nearby corner of the courtyard. They sat down together, and Treet waited patiently while his hosts gazed at him for some moments in silence.

Is this where they give me the bad news? he wondered. Sorry, big fella, we're going to use your brain for fish food. He had been waiting for the other shoe to drop ever since he had awakened aboard the airship. Surely, no one was as kind, thoughtful, charitable as these Fieri—especially to strangers. There had to be a catch somewhere. They wanted something from him, or they intended using him in some way. But what could they want? How could they use him?

Talus fingered his beard and slumped in his chair, looking like a king settling back on his throne for a season of thought. At last he spoke, his voice a low rumble in his deep chest. "I imagine there is much that you have to tell us," he said.

Here it comes, thought Treet; this is it. He tried to gaze unconcernedly back.

"Here I must ask your indulgence."

Yep, thought Treet, they're up to something. "What indulgence is that?" he asked innocently.

"Only this: that you save your story for the College of Mentors. We would all very much like to hear it, and it is our opinion that repeating it too often will distort it."

That was nothing like what Treet had been expecting. He said, "If that's what you want, Talus. However, I want you to know that I wish to keep nothing from you. Whatever I can tell you, I will tell you freely."

"Could you come with me this evening?"

"This evening?"

Dania remarked, "If you knew, Orion Treet, how much this request chafed Talus, you would understand his eagerness. The Mentors are curious boys, despite all their dignity. If it had been up to them, they would have had you before them the moment you stepped from the balon. But the Preceptor thought differently, so you were brought here that you might refresh yourself first." She paused and glanced at her husband, then back at Treet. "You are not to meet with them until you feel ready, and that you must decide for yourself."

This is weird, thought Treet. Are they trying to smother me with kindness? Is this some sort of test? What are they after?

"Dania is right to remind me of the Preceptor's wishes. I merely thought . . . if you are feeling well enough . . . that you might—"

"Talus, leave our guest alone. You are as bad as Jomo and Hsoo in your own way."

Treet smiled emptily, looking from one to the other of them. He made the best answer he could. "I have no wish to leave your gracious home so soon. But I would be happy to repay the kindness you've shown me in any way I can. If answering your questions will help, so be it."

He tried to be sincere—he certainly was not misrepresenting his true feelings. He was grateful to be alive and happy to help those who had helped him. But he felt awkward at the same time, as if he were betraying someone by being too cooperative or aiding and abetting a suspected enemy. Why should I feel that way? he wondered.

The answer came back: perhaps I just don't understand true generosity of spirit when I see it. I'm not used to it; it makes me nervous, and things that make me nervous make me wary.

"There is one other thing," Treet added. "I'd like to see my friends as soon as possible."

"They are being cared for," said Dania. "I chose the receiving homes myself. Their welfare must not concern you."

"Their welfare, no—I know they're in good hands. It's just that they may worry about *me*. They might wonder where I am, or think I've deserted them or something, you see."

"Think no negative thought in this regard," said Talus. "All is well, I assure you."

"Still, I'd like to see them," said Treet. Talus and Dania glanced guiltily at one another. "Is there some reason I can't?"

"The Preceptor has asked that you be kept apart from one another. We are obeying these instructions," Talus admitted.

"Oh." His frown must have given away his negative thoughts.

"Please, trust us in this," said Dania quickly. "Our Preceptor is a very wise and revered leader. Your welfare is our only concern. You'll see."

"You mean I can't see anyone until after my interview with the . . . College of Mentors, is it? Anyway, I can't see them until then?"

"It would be best." Talus nodded gravely.

"What if I refused?" Treet didn't like saying that; it seemed like a dirty trick. But he had to know.

"That would be unfortunate . . ."

Ah ha! thought Treet. At last we come to it. The velvet dagger in the neck. "I thought so," replied Treet. "I should have kn—"

Before he could finish, Talus continued, ". . . because it would disappoint the Preceptor. She knows what you have gone through, and she has suggested this rule for your welfare."

"What do you mean exactly?"

"She understands what life must be like in Dome. She is anxious that none of you feel threatened by the others." To Treet's puzzled look, he said, "She wants each of you to be able to speak freely and openly with us. To ensure that, she has asked that you be kept apart until each has had opportunity to speak."

Understanding dawned slowly on Treet. "You mean that if one of us had some hold over the others, he wouldn't have a chance to reassert his power or make threats or whatever. I see. Yes, very smart." Smart from several points of view. They wouldn't be able to compare stories either, if by some chance they meant mischief—spies on an espionage mission, for instance.

"It is for the best," offered Dania. "I hope you see the justice of it."

"I guess I do," replied Treet. "Very well. Let's do it tonight then. We'll get it over with, and that way I can see my friends that much sooner."

Talus leaped to his feet so fast it made Treet jump up too. "Good! Good! I will notify the Clerk of the College at once, and he will arrange it." He bounded off, leaving Treet a little dazed, wondering what he had acquiesced to.

Oh well, not to worry—think no negative thought, he reminded himself. I'll find out soon enough.

Treet spent the rest of the day in the agreeable company of Jaire, who looked after him like a combination nurse-and-private-tour-guide. She led him from room to room in the great house, showing him the various *objets d'art* and items of interest in each. Treet's respect and admiration multiplied as the day went on. It was clear that the Fieri were possessed of immense artistic talent and took that talent and their art seriously. For every room contained at least one object—a carving or painting or metal etching—which would have been a museum centerpiece anywhere on Earth.

The house itself was a work of art: large, spacious, conceived on a grand scale, yet not overbearing or gauche for its size. The furniture—what there was of it, for the Fieri apparently liked their interiors Spartan—and other appointments were simply designed in the same clean, uncluttered style. Each piece of furniture or work of art became an integral part of the room. And each room appeared exquisite in conception and execution individually, and at the same time part of a greater whole.

About the time they completed the tour, Treet heard Talus' voice booming from the lower level. "Jaire! Bring our guest to the entrance. The evee will be here soon."

"We have to go now," said Jaire apologetically, looking at him candidly with her deep brown eyes. "I hope you were not bored by my discourse."

"Most enjoyable. I would not have missed a moment of it. I only wish I didn't have to leave so soon."

"My father is anxious for you to make your appearance. For many years he has been urging the Mentors to establish contact with Dome," she said as they made their way to the main entrance of the pavilion. "He thinks it would be highly beneficial."

"I see," said Treet thoughtfully. "I don't see how I can help, but I'll try. Tell me about these Mentors."

Jaire shrugged. "What can I tell you? They are men and women who serve Fierra."

"What do you think they want to hear from me?"

Jaire did not have time to answer, for they had descended to the entrance. Talus came forward, snatched Treet by the arm, and all but dragged him outside where one of the Fieri's small driverless vehicles was at that moment rolling to a stop—this one slightly larger than the one that had brought Treet to Liamoge.

Preben stepped forward and opened the single door on the side of the sleek car, helped Treet and Talus climb in, and then entered himself, folding down a jumpseat in front. With a nod from his father, the young man entered the destination code into the keypad on the dash, and the car slid quietly away.

The sun was lowering and would soon dip beneath the western rim, leaving the sky whitewashed blue and radiant, but fading quickly. The evee swept along the causeway over smooth, chrome-colored water, past numerous pavilions—some larger, some smaller than Talus' home, but all the same lackluster gray. The sunstone gave no hint of its coming transformation.

Closer to the heart of the city, traffic thickened. Other driveless vehicles sped along beside them. Treet noticed that the evee adjusted its speed according to the traffic patterns around it. Most of the vehicles appeared to be heading toward the same destination: a great seven-sided obelisk surrounded by a half-circle of smaller obelisks and set on an expanse of rising land amidst a carefully tended grove of miniature trees.

The evee swung into a long circular drive at the foot of the rise below the edifice, and they disembarked, joining the throng moving up the hill. With the lowering sun directly behind the obelisk, scattering the last of the sun's rays, the slim spike seemed to become a spacecraft lifting from its launching pad on a burst of white fire. Men and women were disappearing behind the standing ring of smaller stone obelisks, and coming closer Treet saw that a steep hollow had been dug in front of the main structure, forming an open-air amphitheater. Fieri were streaming down into the amphitheater, taking seats along the stair-step sides.

Treet and his companions approached the standing stones, passed between them, and descended into the amphitheater. Only then did Treet remember that he was the featured speaker for the evening. The realization gave him a sudden case of stage fright. His palms grew clammy, and his stomach fluttered; his feet stumbled as he moved down the narrow aisle. He felt instantly awkward and forgetful, afraid to open his mouth—whatever might come out was beyond his control.

Talus apparently sensed his discomfort, for he put a large hand on Treet's shoulder, leaned close, and whispered, his voice small thunder, "Be at ease. All you see here are your friends. They wish you well."

"I wish there weren't so many."

"Ordinarily there would not be this large a gathering. But you and your friends have stimulated our interest, so we are meeting in the amphidrome tonight. I'll stay with you every moment."

They made their way down to the floor of the amphidrome and found seats on the first row. Preben excused himself and disappeared as two men came hustling up, one white-haired, the other dark-haired but with a beard graying in the center and at the edges. Both wore faded blue cloaks over their clothes. The white-haired one Treet recognized as Bohm, whom he had met at the airship. Bohm spoke first, greeting Treet and Talus, and presenting the stranger to Treet. "Orion Treet, allow me to introduce you to Mathiax, Clerk of the College of Mentors."

The man's bright eyes glittered with excitement as he extended both hands, palms upward in the manner of the Fieri. Treet took the hands and squeezed them, saying, "I am pleased to meet you, Mathiax."

The Clerk nodded and glanced at Bohm, his expression stating emphatically, Oh, this is really something. He even speaks our language! Treet felt like a lab specimen on display, a feeling that escalated with each passing second. But when Mathiax replied, it was in the warm, intimate tone of one trusted confidant to another. "You must forgive us our ebullience at your expense. We sometimes forget ourselves in our haste to embrace new awarenesses."

These people are so polite, considered Treet, so formal, so different than I expected. It's hard to believe they share the same common ancestry as those who live in Dome.

"I am only too happy to—ah, serve in any way I can."

Mathiax nodded happily and said, "We will begin in just a few minutes. I want to be certain all are here, so if you will excuse me . . . Talus, you will act as Prime Mentor this evening. I will give you the signal when it is time to begin."

With that he and Bohm left, hurrying off together. Treet heard the Clerk say to Bohm, "Yes, I see what you mean . . ." as they passed from earshot.

"Please be seated," said Talus, lowering himself to a seat. He patted the one next to him with his hand. "Relax. There is nothing to be concerned about. You will do well."

Treet sat down absently, scanning the rapidly filling amphidrome in the process. "How does this work?" he heard his voice asking.

"This?" Talus waved a hand to the rows of spectators. "A conclave is a general session of all Mentors and certain invited guests who have an interest in the subject area under investigation."

"Am I under investigation then?"

Talus wagged his head earnestly. "No, no. We only want to hear what you can tell us."

"What can I tell you?"

"What you know." Talus seemed about to elaborate further when Preben arrived with a blue cloak for his father. The big man put it on and was about to sit down once more when the clear pealing tone of a bell rang in the air, a pure and beautiful note as if rung from a crystal bowl. "Ah, that is the signal." He smiled and rubbed his heavy hands together. "At last we can begin."

Talus stepped out onto the floor of the amphidrome and held up his hands. The audience grew silent instantly, as if the sound had been switched off a holovision. He raised his resounding voice in a brief invocation to someone or something called the Seeker Aspect. Treet did not catch all the words—he was too busy wondering what he would say to all these people who had turned out to see him. Had he known he would draw such a crowd, he might have prepared a speech, or maybe sold tickets.

Then Talus was saying his name and waving him forward. Two high-backed stools were produced by aides in green cloaks. As Treet climbed into the nearest one, his aide pressed a diamond-shaped tag onto the front of his shirt. In the center of the tag a glittering bit of glass or crystal winked in the early twilight. The obelisk rising behind them held a golden luster as if the sun were striking its surface, though the sun had set behind it. The sunstone was beginning its night's work of converting Fierra into a city of light.

Talus nodded at Treet encouragingly. Treet turned his eyes to all the faces peering down at him from the rising gallery, fierce in their intensity, expectant. What could he say to them? What had they come to hear?

"Go on," whispered Talus. "Don't think about it, just say what the Teacher puts into your mind to say."

Okay, thought Treet. Here goes nothing. He swallowed hard and opened a mouth gone suddenly dry. "I am—" he croaked, and heard the echo of his amplified voice ripple through the amphidrome. The Mentors waited, leaning forward in their seats. He took a deep breath and plunged in headfirst.

"My name is Orion Treet, and I come to you from a world beyond your star . . ."

FIFTY
SEVEN

When Treet finished speaking, it was very late. The sky over the amphidrome glimmered with its ghostly aurora, through which the stars winked like jewels from behind a shimmering veil. The assembled Mentors sat in awed silence, gazing upon this mysterious stranger who had materialized in their midst. Treet expected questions to come thick and fast, but the crystal bell tolled once more and the entire gathering rose and began climbing the steps, filing quietly from the amphidrome to disappear into the night.

Treet breathed a long sigh of relief for having survived his ordeal. He'd told them, as simply as he knew how, nearly everything—which was more than he'd planned on telling, certainly. But once he'd gotten started he hadn't known where or how to stop, so he dumped it all out—everything from the arrival of their transport to their rescue by the airship.

Talus rose from his stool on Treet's right hand and came to him. "Do you think they'll vote for me?" asked Treet.

"I do not understand," said Talus, shaking his head slowly. "Much of what you said I do not understand."

"Never mind. What about the parts you do understand?"

"Those I find most disturbing."

"You don't believe me?"

"No, I believe you. No one could speak as you do if it were not true. And that is what troubles me."

"I think my friends will tell similar stories," pointed out Treet.

"Again, I believe you. Understanding—that is another matter entirely."

Just then the busy Clerk came running up. He shoved a folded card toward Talus. "This has just come from the Preceptor."

Talus took the card, unfolded it, glanced at it, and handed it to Treet. "Your presence is requested. At once."

Was it something I said? wondered Treet

They whisked along the near-deserted streets of Fierra. Over delicate arches and through brightly lit tunnels, past open markets and blocks of dwellings, along thoroughfares lined with glowing pylons they went—Talus and Treet accompanied by Preben and Mathiax. Treet could tell by the long sideways glances he was receiving from the others that they were dying to ask him some of the millions of questions that were bubbling up inside their brains like lava from a hot volcano. Mercifully, they let him sit quietly and watch the enchanted city slide past.

"There is the Preceptor's palace," said Mathiax, pointing to a many-tiered pagoda rising from a clump of trees ahead. The evee slowed as it turned into a narrow lane, and the Preceptor's palace swung full into view, glowing, thought Treet, with a rosy luster like those floodlit castles that were so popular with the postcard crowd. The drive ended a few meters inside the grounds, and the vehicle stopped. The passengers got out and made their way across a wide, dark lawn, spongy underfoot with thick vegetation.

Two Fieri, one male and one female, met them at the open entrance to the palace. Both were dressed in a high-necked jacket with deep sleeves and a large triangular patch of bright silver over the heart. On the patch was a symbol Treet could not make out. It looked like a ring of circles, each one blending into the next, yet somehow separate from the others. The image appeared to be spinning so that each time he tried to look directly at it, the symbol blurred and shifted.

The male attendant held out his hand, and Talus placed the folded card on his palm. "Thank you for attending our request," said the woman. She smiled warmly. "You will find our Preceptor awaiting you in the audience room. I will be glad to show you the way."

"No need," said Mathiax. "I know how to find it."

"As you wish," she said and waved them through.

The Clerk led them up three levels on a sweeping spiral staircase to an enormous room that took up nearly the entire third level. "This is the reception hall," explained Talus as they trooped across the threshold. The interior of the hall was lit by several large columns of sunstone, which cast a soft, rose-tinted light all around.

Treet thought, upon entering the reception hall, that the room was empty, but then saw a tall, slender figure standing before heavy, floor-to-ceiling curtains worked in designs of green and gold. The Preceptor wore a short copper-colored robe over silver knee-length trousers. The robe was cinched at the waist by a silver belt; silver boots met the trousers at the knee. Yellow sunstone chips glimmered in a wide silver band around a graceful throat.

The Preceptor waited for them to come close, her long, fine hands clasped in front of her, gazing intently at them as they crossed the polished expanse of floor, their footsteps tapping the stone. She smiled as they came to stand in front of her, extending her hands to Treet, and then to the others in turn, saying, "I realize you must be tired. You do your leader a kindness by coming at this late hour. I won't keep you long."

She stepped lightly to the curtain and pulled it back. The audience room was a small chamber concealed behind the draperies. They filed into the room, and the Preceptor entered, waving them to long, low divans arranged in the center of the room. She seated herself across from Treet and gazed at him with intense violet eyes that probed his directly. He realized that if he remained very long in this woman's presence, he would have no secrets left. Those eyes—hard and bright as amythests, set in a face of intriguing angles above a straight, aquiline nose and a strong, almost masculine jaw—would pierce like lasers anything that did not yield instantly to them.

"I listened to your story," she began. "I was much amazed by all you said."

"You heard me?" It was a dumb question, but it was out before Treet could stop it.

She pointed to the badge still stuck to the front of his shirt. "My crystal is tuned to receive sympathetic vibrations. I heard every word." She studied him for a moment, as if making up her mind about him. Then she said, "No one has ever come across the Daraq. The few who risk the journey die in the attempt. We find them, but always too late."

"Others have come before us?"

"Not many. And not for a very long time. But the Protector

390

went with you, and the Sustainer watched over you until we could send a balon to rescue you. Therefore, we can assume that the Infinite Father has a purpose in sending you here."

Treet sat still. He had nothing to say on that score. The Preceptor continued, "We must find out what that purpose is so that we may fulfill it. Would that be agreeable to you?"

"Yes, of course," said Treet. "What do you want me to do?"

"Stay with us, learn our ways. My kinsmen Mathiax and Talus will guide you, and all of Fierra will be open to you. Then, when the All-Wise reveals His purpose, teach us."

"That's it? That's all you want me to do?"

The Preceptor nodded slightly. "Yes. What more is required than that we fulfill our spiritual purpose?"

"Can I see my friends?"

"If you wish. Your love for your friends is commendable. But it would be better if you wait until each of your friends has spoken before the Mentors. However, this is a request I make, not a precept. You are free to do as you will."

"Talus explained your request to me. I accept it, although I'd like to point out that I hold nothing over any of the others."

"But they might hold power over you."

Treet considered this, and rejected it. "No, there's nothing like that at all. I'd know about it, wouldn't I?"

"Perhaps not. Power comes in many subtle forms, some most difficult to recognize."

Treet saw that he was getting nowhere, and decided to abide by the Preceptor's request. "I don't mind waiting. May I send a message to them?"

She shook her head imperceptibly. "They already know that each of the others has been saved and that all are being cared for. I know it is difficult, but have patience—you will all be together again soon."

It occurred to Treet that he'd heard a similar promise recently; Supreme Director Rohee had mouthed words to the same effect, and look what happened. He had been lying. Was the Preceptor also lying? Before Treet could wonder further, she rose, signaling an end to the audience. Mathiax, Talus, and Preben, none of whom had said a word throughout the interview, stood and extended their hands. The Preceptor clasped hands and spoke a few intimate words with each one before they were ushered from the private chamber, back across the empty reception hall, and down the spiral staircase and out into the dwindling night.

It will be dawn in a few hours, Treet thought. And in a few hours I resume my career as a sponge.

He should have been ecstatic at the prospect of probing into the secrets of the Fieri—delving into exotic cultures was his life, after all—but there was something missing. Something had a name, and the name was Yarden.

He walked out onto the darkened lawn, heavy with bitter disappointment. He puzzled over the feeling and realized that subconsciously he had been hoping up to the very moment of their dismissal by the Preceptor that he would see Yarden. He would turn a corner and she would be there, or he would enter a room to find her waiting. The whole time he had been with the Preceptor, he had been hoping Yarden would step unexpectedly from behind the curtain.

Without knowing it, he had been waiting to see her. Now he knew that he would not—at least not for several more days. The thought depressed him.

By the time they reached the waiting evee, Treet was in such a black mood that he sat sullen and silent all the way back to Liamoge, staring blankly at the bright wonders of Fierra. They had, for the moment, ceased to hold any charm for him.

FIFTY
EIGHT

"The thing you keep forgetting," said Mathiax, looking directly at Treet, his fingers combing through his graying beard, "is that each and every Fieri is aware of the Infinite Presence at all times. We are permeated with this awareness—it informs all we do."

Treet thought about this. Yes, in the last several weeks he'd certainly seen evidence of this awareness Mathiax was talking about. "I understand your religion is very important to you, but are you telling me that it even influences your technology?"

"Why not? Why should that be so hard to accept?" Mathiax leaned forward and tapped Treet on the arm. "Let's walk a bit further—it's good for the brain."

They were sitting on an empty stretch of beach by the silver lake. They had been walking most of the day, stopping to rest and discuss, moving on when they reached an impasse in communication or came to a subject which required additional thought in order to translate it into terms Treet could properly understand. Mathiax was a quick and able teacher, and it had been his idea to take Treet out away from the city to walk along the lakeside for part of each day's session. "Less distraction," he'd said. This gave Treet time to assimilate what he'd seen and heard before returning to Talus' pavilion.

In three weeks' time Treet had learned much about the Fieri. Most of it had to do with their simple religion. Apparently everything the Fieri did or thought was in some way rooted in this intense spiritual awareness Mathiax had been describing. The Fieri religion was not difficult; its central tenet could be summed up quite simply: A Supreme Being existed who insisted on concerning Himself with the affairs of men in order to draw them into friendship with Him.

That was the basic idea, plainly stated. The Fieri believed that this Being was a pure spirit who expressed Himself in many different personality modes or Aspects. They recognized any number of the Aspects—Sustainer, Protector, Teacher, Seeker, Creator, Comforter, Gatherer, and so on. But all were merely individual expressions of the One, the Infinite Father, as they called Him.

Treet got the idea that they were a little reluctant to pin the Deity down to one name or expression. They preferred a much more flexible and elastic approach. But although they spoke of Him in many different ways, depending on what they wanted to say about Him, it was always understood that to invoke one Aspect implied all the rest. The Infinite Father was One, after all, indivisible and ultimate in every sense.

This was the Fieri doctrine—not complicated or obtuse, but ripe with enormous implications. For once a person accepted the idea that the Infinite Father of the entire universe actually desired commerce with individual men, literally no sphere of mortal endeavor was untouched. Each and every thought and action had to be examined in light of an expressed partnership with an infinite and eternal patron.

These were not utterly new ideas, Treet knew. There were several Earth religions that espoused the same general themes. The difference here, as far as Treet could tell, was that the Fieri's beliefs had created a vital, thriving society of nearly eight million souls in love with truth and beauty and kindness to one another. Nowhere else he'd ever heard of had that happened on so great a scale.

In Treet's experience, personally and scholastically, theocracies produced miserable societies: stubborn, resistant, suspicious, intolerant, highly inequitable, and so hidebound they could not function in the face of change or conflict.

The Fieri had apparently avoided all that and stood at a pinnacle of social experience unique in human existence. They had discovered Utopia, had been smart enough to recognize a good thing when they saw it, and had worked at making the vision reality. For this they had earned Treet's respect and admiration. Orion Treet also recognized a good thing when he saw it.

The one item that puzzled him in all this, however, was how such a society could have developed at all, considering how they had originated. The Fieri were part of the same population of the colony ship that had landed on Empyrion in the beginning.

According to the colony's official historian, Feodr Rumon, a group of dangerous malcontents had been cast out, or had left of their own accord, but under protest. Exactly what had taken place wasn't clear; Rumon's *Chronicles* were slightly schizophrenic on this point. Still, the proto-Fieri had been forced from the safety of the colony and condemned to wander the wild wastes of Empyrion.

But the homeless nomads had somehow transformed themselves into a culture that in almost every respect surpassed the highest achievements of any Earth had ever seen. At least, in three weeks of scrutiny, Treet had not discovered any flaw. Theirs was a perfect society: no poverty, no disease, no crime, no homeless, no idle lonely old.

Now he and Mentor Mathiax walked along the coarse, pebbled beach of the inland sea the Fieri called Prindahl. The wide water shone flat and metallic beneath the white sun, a quicksilver sea over which the knife-hulls of boats with sails of crimson and ultramarine raced, trailing diamonds in their rippling wakes. Closer in, the sky held the gliding bodies of long-winged birds, rakkes, diving and soaring, feathering the gentle wind to rise high and then plummet to shoals of sparkling yellow fish.

A little distance away, graceful Fieri children frolicked at the water's edge with their wevicats, dark and feral beside the angelic youngsters. Together the huge, lithe animals and their diminutive masters abandoned themselves to play, tromping the shallow water into foam, lost in laughter and the joy of the moment. The children's voices rang clear like notes struck from silver bells.

Treet watched the boats and the birds, creatures of the wind, so fast and free. He listened to the sound of the children playing. A pang of envy shot up in his bones, an ache for something he'd scarcely been aware of lacking: peace. Not merely the absence of tension or conflict, but the complete unity of body, mind and spirit, the total harmony of life in all its parts. That is what the boats and birds and children symbolized: creatures at rest within themselves and in harmony with their environment. Not fighting it, but accepting it, shaping it and being shaped by it to live in it and beyond it.

That, Treet decided, was exactly what the Fieri were about as well: transcending the conditions of their existence by the force of a unity of spirit so strong it re-created all it touched. They had discovered the secret of this harmony, and he envied them.

For most of his 153 years, Treet had thought it was freedom he was after. He realized now that it was harmony. Without inner harmony, no amount of external freedom would ever make one free. One would always be a slave to selfishness, to pettiness, to passion, or to any of a jillion other afflictions of the soul.

This spiritual harmony had finally to rest on something absolute—this was what Mathiax had been trying to tell him for the past weeks. The Fieri peace was not the absence of something negative, but the presence of something positive—a solid force knitting the center together, and around which everything else moved: a starmass whose gravitational field held all lesser bodies in their orbits, described their movements, kept them spinning in their flight.

For the Fieri, that solid force at the center of everything was the Infinite Father.

"Tell me something," said Treet, breaking the long silence that had wrapped them as they walked. "What do you remember of Dome? Why did the Fieri leave?"

Mathiax pursed his lips and scowled. He took a long time to answer, but at last said, "No writing has come down to us from the Wandering. But in earlier times, the old rememberers said that a great change swept through Dome—a change that left it forever twisted. Those in power no longer respected life; they respected expediency. Any who argued for life over expediency fell under suspicion, were persecuted and eventually driven out. For Dome to exist, it was said, all had to yield to the greater good. The Fieri—only our name and these few memories come down to us from those times—said that what could not be good for one individual, could never be good for the whole. If one person suffered, all suffered. The rulers of Dome could not accept this. Persecution began—terrible suffering for all who stood with us. Rather than retaliate in kind or endure the injustice of persecution, our forefathers left their homes."

"And then?" Treet weighed this version of the story with the one he'd read in the colony's official records.

"We wandered. Empyrion was a vast, rich world designed by the Creator for sustaining life. The land welcomed us, and our people roved the world and learned its secrets. Later, much later, we built great cities on fertile plains and raised a strong people under peaceful skies . . ." Mathiax drifted off. The

Clerk's gray eyes gazed far out across the lake, remembering things he'd never seen.

"What happened?" Treet asked softly.

"The Burning . . ." Mathiax made a choked sound deep in his throat, and Treet turned toward him. Tears streamed down the man's face.

Afraid to speak lest he intrude on the Mentor's sorrow, Treet looked out across the lake to where the boats were but smears of color in the distance.

After a moment, the Mentor came to himself again and wiped his eyes. "These are things which cannot be remembered without sorrow," he explained.

"I understand," replied Treet. "If you'd rather not talk about it—"

"No, no. You will hear it. But perhaps I'm not the one to tell it." Mathiax turned, and they began walking back to the waiting evee. The lesson was over for the day, and Treet had more than enough to think about.

On the way back to Liamoge, Treet felt again the sense of urgency he had begun experiencing at odd times in the last several days: a straining forward, a quickening of the blood, a momentary catch in the heart's rhythm, a skipped beat in the anticipation of an unknown event speeding toward him. He wondered, not for the first time, if the feeling was in some way connected with the *purpose* the Preceptor had spoken of. A purpose he did not recognize yet, but felt drawing inexorably nearer with every passing hour.

Treet did not wonder about his purpose; he figured he'd know it when he found it. Or rather, when *it* found him—the sense of being pursued was that strong. The urgency puzzled him, however. While content to let whatever was pursuing him catch him, he also felt that time was in some sense running out—for him, for the Fieri, for a person or persons unknown. And if he did not act soon it would be too late—although what *act* or *too late* meant Treet could not guess.

All this provided Treet with the overall impression of being impelled toward a far-off destiny, a fate already chosen for him from the first—although he believed in neither fate nor destiny.

Still, he sensed that events beyond his control were aligning themselves around him like lines of magnetic force, and he was powerless to prevent it.

And now, as he and Mathiax sped along the seamless causeway over sparkling Prindahl toward Talus' pavilion, Treet allowed the surge of confused emotion to play over him, savoring the heightened awareness emerging from the muddled wash.

Yes, something was about to happen; it waited only for him to set it in motion. I am the catalyst, he thought. It's up to me. But will I know what to do when the time comes?

FIFTY
NINE

When they reached Liamoge, there was a large, multi-passenger evee waiting outside the entrance of the pavilion. Treet walked briskly through the entryway and into the main hall where Talus and Dania stood talking to several guests. One of the guests turned as he entered, and Treet found himself looking into the face that had begun to haunt his dreams.

"Yarden!" He stared, afraid to move lest the vision vanish.

She approached him slowly, almost shyly, he thought, until he saw that she was studying him closely. "You've changed," she said. "But I don't know how."

"You haven't," replied Treet. The others had stopped talking and now looked on. He told Talus, "Excuse us for a moment. We—"

Dania answered, "You have much to say to one another. Walk in the courtyard; no one will disturb you."

They walked through the hall and into the deep green confusion of the courtyard. He had so much he wanted to tell her—he'd been saving things up for months, it seemed—and now that she was here, he could not think how to begin. His mind went blank. After a few steps they slowed, turned, and gazed at one another.

"How have you been?" he asked. No, that's not what he wanted to say at all. Just say it!

"Well," Yarden answered, looking away. "And you?"

"Fine . . ." This was getting them nowhere. He glanced down at his hands and noticed that they were quivering. "Look at my hands—they're shaking."

Yarden placed her hands over his. "They're cold too." She stepped closer to him, raised her eyes. "I've missed you, Orion," she whispered. "I've missed you very much."

Then, without his knowing how exactly, his arms were filled with her warmth. "Yarden . . . I began to think I'd never see you again. The last time we were together . . . I was afraid—"

"Shhh," she soothed. "Not now. Just hold me."

Treet stood with his arms wrapped tightly around her, cradling her softness. They stood for a long time without moving, without speaking, letting their embrace find its own eloquence. At last Yarden pushed back to look at him. She raised a finger to trace his chin. "Funny, I'd forgotten about your beard," she said.

"I'd forgotten how beautiful you are." Her long dark hair was smoothed back from her face to fall in a loose cascade behind her shoulders. Her eyes, jet beneath sweeping brows, hinted at depths unexplored. She put her cheek against the hollow of his throat, and he smelled the freshness of her hair. "I never want to let you go."

"I could tell when you were thinking about me," she said almost absently.

"I wondered if you would know. What did you get?"

"I'm not going to tell you. But it let me know that I was right about you."

"I thought you considered me an ogre."

"Crusty, conceited, and too independent for your own good, but not an ogre."

"Coming from you, ma'am, that's a compliment." Still holding her, he led her to a grouping of chairs in a far corner of the courtyard. They sat together in one of the larger chairs. "I thought I had so much I wanted to say to you, but I seem to have forgotten everything. It hardly matters though."

"But I want to hear it. I want to hear about every minute of these last weeks."

"All right," agreed Treet. He pulled her close and began relating all that he'd experienced since stepping off the airship that first night. When he was through, Yarden straightened and turned toward him, drawing up her legs and crossing them.

"Now it's my turn," she said. Her story was nearly identical to Treet's. By the time she came to, the airship that had rescued them had landed. Still very drowsy, she was taken to the home of a young Fieri woman named Ianni.

"I was half-asleep for the first two days," said Yarden. "But Ianni understood and did not press me too hard, although she was very excited to learn all about where I'd come from, how I'd gotten here—everything I could tell her." She paused in her recitation and said, "Oh, Orion, aren't these the most wonderful people you've ever encountered? They are so loving. Fierra is simply incredible . . ."

He agreed that he'd never seen anything close to it, and she continued, "Ianni took me everywhere. She is an excellent teacher, very sensitive. She introduced me to everything Fieri. We were up every morning at dawn and went to bed late every night." Yarden told him of their long days of discussion and travel around the city, about visiting the Preceptor and sailing out across the lake one night under the stars. She ended by saying, "I've seen the most amazing things, eaten the most delicious food, been exposed to wisdom and kindness I never dreamed existed!"

"So have I," murmured Treet, pulling her close once again. "But that's not all. I learned that . . . I love you."

He would have said it again, but her lips were on his, her arms around his neck. He drank in the heavy, honeyed sweetness of her kiss. He returned it with all the desire that was in him, demanding more and more of her, of himself, until they broke apart, breathless, clinging to each other.

"Yarden—"

Just then a shout came from the other side of the courtyard. "Hey! Where is everybody?"

"Pizzle!" Treet felt as if someone had dumped ice water on him.

A moment later the scraggy, jug-eared head poked through a tangle of foliage directly in front of them. "There you are! Hey, don't get up—I'll join you." He slid a chair up and plopped in. "Boy, isn't this some place they got here? I never would have imagined it could be like this—not after seeing the inside of Dome. You guys look great! Just great! I was starting to wonder whether we'd ever get back together. Not that I worried about it—there is just so much to do here, you know. Unbelievable!"

He sat there beaming at them and shaking his head. "It's good to see you, too, Pizzle," said Treet. He'd forgotten what a bother the egghead could be, but was quickly remembering.

"I understand we have you to thank for saving our lives," said Yarden. "You flagged down the airship that rescued us."

"Yes, we owe you a lot," added Treet. "How are your hands? Mathiax said you were burned pretty bad."

Pizzle held up his hands and wiggled his fingers. "Never better. These Fieri are genius doctors—I don't have a single scar

401

to show for my heroism. But to tell the truth, I thought we'd had it out there in the desert. I figured I'd jigged my last jig. I know I was more dead than alive when they picked us up, 'cause I don't remember much about it. Seems like it happened a hundred years ago."

"I know what you mean," agreed Yarden. "So much has happened in such a short time it all seems like a bad dream—like it happened to somebody else. I'm just thankful we all made it."

"Speaking of which," said Treet, "have you seen Crocker or Calin yet?"

"Crocker's due here any minute. That's what Talus said. I don't know about Calin." Pizzle grinned, putting all his teeth into it. "I'll tell you what—isn't this some place though?"

"I've never seen anything to compare," agreed Treet.

"If you're here and Crocker's coming," Yarden said, disentangling herself from Treet's embrace, "it must mean that you've spoken before the College of Mentors."

"Correct. Very attentive audience, I must say. I take it you two have done your bit?"

"I spoke yesterday," said Yarden. "I talked myself hoarse, and they would have sat there all night long. When I finished though, not a word—they just got up and went away. Strange."

"They did the same with me," said Pizzle. "I guess it's their way."

"I think they plan some sort of free-for-all later. Right now they only want the facts as we see them."

"You don't think they believe us?" asked Yarden.

"Oh, they believe us," replied Treet. "But we've really upset them more than they let on. They don't know what to do with us—that is, with the information we bring with us." Treet paused and pursed his lips thoughtfully. "I've observed a few lapses in the Fieri code of impeccable conduct. If you're interested, I'll tell you what I think they mean."

"I'm all ears," said Pizzle happily. He was living every SF fan's keenest aspiration: high adventure on a distant planet.

"Well, here goes. One: our reception here was odd, to say the least. We're packed off to private residences, rather than greeted by their representatives of law and order. Why? For all they know we could be killer commandos come to take apart their city stone by stone. It's as if they want us to think our coming was no great shake at all—yet, our appearances before the College of Mentors indicates a considerable degree of healthy concern."

Yarden opened her mouth to speak, but thought better of it and nodded for Treet to continue.

"Okay? Two: Talus imposes a gag order on his own family in order to keep me from talking to them. He's a Mentor—which I'm sure you've figured out is pretty high up in the Fieri chain of command—and he set great store by my speaking before the assembly just as soon as possible—my second night here, in fact. Yet, he's asked me no questions and has not really spoken to me since that night—except to say hello and good-bye and have some more salad.

"Three: After my little speech, Mathiax, not Talus or Jaire, becomes my official tutor. We spend the next weeks wandering around this incredible city of theirs while he fills my head with stories. But every time I begin to make a comment or observation about what I see, or compare it to Dome, he cuts me off—doesn't want to hear it. It's like he wants me to soak it up, but not let anything run out."

"Same for me," offered Pizzle.

"Four: when I speak to the Preceptor, she doesn't ask me a single question about where I come from or what I'm doing here. Instead, she tells me to discover my spiritual purpose. What's that mean? And what's that got to do with any of the rest of this?"

"The point?" asked Yarden.

"The point is, I know the curiosity must be killing them, but for some reason they're going to great lengths to cover up the fact, or at least not to let it influence them in their treatment of us. Hence, they are rolling out the red carpet for us, but in a very casual, almost secretive way."

"So?" wondered Pizzle, chin in hands.

"It's obvious, I think. They are uncertain—not to say suspicious—of us. On the one hand they treat us like we're just folks, long-lost cousins come to visit—"

"On the other hand, they don't want to risk offending us in case we turn out to be emissaries from on high." Yarden finished his thought for him.

"Exactly."

"So they bend over sideways trying to make us feel at home," said Pizzle, "getting us to understand what they're all about, showing us how great everything is here so that when we decide to do whatever we've come here to do, our actions will be tempered with the knowledge of what we've seen."

"Something like that," agreed Treet.

Yarden frowned. "They're highly intelligent, highly compassionate people. What would you expect them to do?"

"I don't know, but it strikes me as slightly screwy. The reception we got at Dome made more sense."

"Cynic," said Yarden. "Looking for the cloud behind the silver lining."

"I might add that they are desperate to convince us of their sincerity, and the integrity of what they have here."

"I'm convinced," said Pizzle. "They have nothing to fear from me. I only hope they let me stay."

"Sure." Treet nodded thoughtfully. "That would be great, only . . ."

"Only what?" asked Yarden, regarding him with a sidelong glance.

"Only it may not be that simple."

SIXTY

"**W**ell, well, Crocker, you look your handsome, dashing self," said Treet. "I see Fieri food agrees with you." The three had rejoined Talus and his party in the reception hall, now nearly filled with people—most of whom were watching their visitors with keen, if scantil disguised, interest. They found Crocker standing with a group of Fieri talking about airships. The group broke apart discreetly as they approached.

At the sound of Treet's voice, Crocker looked up, smiled broadly, and reached out to take their hands, then hesitated and withdrew awkwardly. The light died in his eyes. "After all those weeks in the desert together, I didn't think I'd be so glad to see your scruffy faces again. It's good to see you. What's it been? Six months?"

"Seems like it," said Pizzle. "They give you the grand tour?"

"I've examined every bit of real estate from lakeshore to kumquat grove, and I'm here to tell you I've never seen anything like this place in all my worldly days. What they have here—it's a monument to genius, that's what it is." Crocker's words were warm and even enthusiastic, but his tone lacked conviction—as if he were reading a written speech he'd grown tired of reciting.

"I agree," replied Yarden. She reached out and pressed Crocker's hand, scrutinizing him closely. "Still, I'm glad we're all together at last."

"Not quite all," said Treet. "Calin isn't here . . . Ah, Pizzle, you and Crocker hold forth. Yarden and I will go and see what we can find out about Calin." He pulled Yarden away with him and they wound through knots of convivial Fieri, who stopped talking and watched them as they passed by.

"You're not worried about Calin," said Yarden when they reached a far corner of the room. "You're worried about Crocker."

"Did you see that? He slammed the door shut so fast, I'm surprised he didn't pinch his fingers when he yanked the welcome mat out from under our feet."

She confirmed his observation with a sharp nod. "I saw. It was definitely not the Crocker I know."

"You told me I'd changed—"

"Yes, but not like that. Something's happened to him."

"Sometimes severe trauma warps a person. They feel guilty for surviving, or that they have to mend their ways somehow."

"I don't think that's what's ailing Crocker. After all, he didn't survive at the expense of any of us. We all made it together."

"Maybe he knows something we don't know."

"Could be, but what?"

"Do you get anything from him?"

Yarden scrunched up her face in concentration. After a moment she said, "No, nothing. But then, Crocker and I have never been on the same wavelength. I've never received good impressions from him about anything. He's opaque to me." She looked at Treet seriously. "What did you mean when you said it may not be that simple?"

Treet ran a hand up and down her arm and gripped her hand. "I'll tell you later. Right now let's check on Calin and then get back to Pizzle and Crocker. I have a sudden funny feeling we're about to have a rude awakening."

Talus greeted Treet and Yarden with gusto, clapping them both in fierce bear hugs. It occurred to Treet that the big man's smile looked pasted on. When Treet described his concern for the missing member of their party, Talus replied, "I understand. But you need not fear for her welfare. She is well . . ."

"But?"

Talus filled his bellows of a chest with a deep breath. "Your companion has shown no response to our continued efforts at reaching her."

"What do you mean, no response?" asked Yarden.

Talus' eyes became grave. "She remains listless and will not speak. Although we have tried to engage her interest in activities and conversation, she does not reply or acknowledge our advances in any way."

"She's okay physically?" Treet fixed Talus with a direct stare. "She eating and sleeping and all that?"

"Oh, yes, although she eats very little. Still, we can find nothing wrong with her." Talus spread his hands in an expression of genuine helplessness. "She will not speak to anyone."

"Talus, there's something I should tell you about her." Treet paused, looked at Yarden, who gave him silent encouragement, and then plunged ahead. "Calin is not one of us—that is, she's not a Traveler. She's from Dome."

Talus pulled on his curly, ram's fleece of a beard and puffed out his cheeks. "I see," he said finally. "Yes . . . that might explain her behavior. But," he looked up decisively, "it would not have altered her care. We would have done nothing differently."

"I appreciate that, Talus," said Treet. "But it might be best now if we could see her. If she knows we're still here with her, she might snap out of it. For all we know, she thinks she's landed in the enemy camp and you're all waiting for a chance to kill her."

Talus wagged his head back and forth with a heavy frown. "No one could believe such a thing of us."

"She's from *Dome*."

"She's also lost and very, very frightened, Talus," pointed out Yarden. "You have to remember that neither she nor anyone she's ever known has ever ventured outside Dome and lived. We had a similar experience with her out there—the landscape overwhelmed her and she went into convulsions. If we could see her—"

"Don't say no, Talus," put in Treet. "I know what your Preceptor has advised, but she did say it was only a recommendation. We're free to choose our own way in this, right?" Talus nodded slowly. "Well, I'm choosing for Calin since she can't choose for herself. I say she'd feel better if she could see us, be with us."

"If she would speak—"

"She won't. Anyway, what do you need her for? You've already heard from the rest of us. That should give you enough of whatever you're looking for."

"But she's from Dome! She could tell—"

"Look, let us go to her, or bring her here. Maybe when she gets over it, she can talk to you." Treet could see his argument was succeeding. He pressed it home. "Think it over. You'll never get anything from her any other way."

Talus admitted defeat. "It is as you say. Yes, I'll have her brought here, and we'll hope that she responds to your care. The love of friends is a powerful remedy. I'll do as you suggest."

"Thanks, Talus. You won't regret it," Treet assured him. Talus moved off to fulfill the request, and Treet turned to Yarden. "That's done. Now we should rejoin the others and figure out what to do next."

"About whatever it is that you think is going to happen here tonight?"

"Right. I don't know what form it's going to take, but I suspect a major confrontation."

Yarden scowled at him. "You make it sound like they're going to throw us to the lions."

Treet gazed around the throng, noting the humming undercurrent of tension in the voices and the sharp tang of anticipation in the air. "Could be, Yarden," he muttered. "Maybe they are."

SIXTY
ONE

Treet could tell when the Preceptor arrived—excitement rippled through the room, voices grew hushed and then resumed their chatter but at lower decibels. The assembled Fieri, most of them Mentors, Treet suspected, formed a phalanx around them, hemming the travelers into a corner of the reception hall. "This is it," said Treet, looking around. "The moment we've all been waiting for."

"I'm still skeptical," said Pizzle. "They don't . . . hey, they're all looking at us!"

"Don't say I didn't warn you, okay?" Treet turned to face the Fieri, who, as Pizzle had said, were indeed regarding them intently. A path opened in the wall of people as the Preceptor drew near.

She came to stand before them, dressed in shimmering black with a close-fitting cap of silver that hugged the crown of her head. The cap was trimmed with yellow chips of glowing sunstone so that she fairly radiated a golden halo. Her amethyst eyes gave no hint of her intent, but the set of her jaw spoke of determination, and there was gravity in her step.

Talus, Bohm, and Mathiax closed ranks behind her. Each of the men shared their leader's seriousness. All talk in the hall fell away as the Preceptor came close and stopped before the travelers. She inclined her head toward them in a dignified greeting.

"You honor us with your presence, Preceptor," Treet told her. His companions remained silent.

The Fieri leader smiled gravely and answered, "You speak so lightly of honor, I wonder if you know what it means."

Treet was taken aback by this reply, but recovered and said, "I meant no disrespect, Preceptor. I am cert—"

She waved aside the apology. "Please, I spoke out of frustration. Take no offense. I only meant that the Infinite Father alone is worthy of honor." She paused, folded her hands in front

409

of her, and said, "My friend Mathiax has informed me that you inquired about our past, about the Wandering and the Burning. He did not answer you because I asked him to allow me to tell you in my own way." She raised her hands to indicate that here in this place, before all these people, was the way she had chosen.

"I understand," offered Treet. His stomach tightened, and his pulse quickened. Yarden pressed nearer to him; her hand closed over his and squeezed.

The Fieri formed a silent wall of faces. Their anticipation charged the atmosphere in the hall until it fairly crackled. Did they know what was about to come?

The Preceptor closed her eyes, her hands frozen in the gesture she'd begun. A sound came from her throat: a long sighing moan, aching with sadness and melancholy.

"Hear the story of the Fieri," she began abruptly, eyes still closed, head tilted back slightly. "The Infinite Father awakened His people in the midst of folly and led us out from the dark cities to roam fair Empyrion and make a new home where light could rule. So we wandered."

"We wandered," replied the Fieri in unison. Treet realized that the story was a litany all Fieri knew by heart.

"In the West we found the fields of living crystal, and in the East the mountains of light where our fathers dug the first sunstone; in the North we saw the Blue Forest, alive with her creatures, magnificent and old; in the South we found gentle hills and clear running water, and the Marsh Sea with its floating islands where the talking fish birth their young. And we wandered."

"We wandered."

"When we had learned the secrets of our world, the time of wandering came to an end. We harnessed the living crystal for power, and quarried the shining sunstone. Our fathers built great cities of light and lived under the sun in harmony with all things. We remembered our brothers in the dark cities and sent emissaries to them, bringing our most precious gifts to share. They welcomed us, and greedily learned all we could teach them, then turned against us, using the knowledge we had given them to make weapons. They covered their cities with crystal and became Dome."

"The cities of darkness became Dome," the chorus replied.

"They turned jealous eyes upon us. In darkness they cursed

our light and dreamed our destruction. The fever of hate inflamed them, and they went mad in their delirium. Then, when the evil in them grew too great . . ." The Preceptor's voice cracked with emotion. All in the room held their breath. "Then came the Burning."

"The Burning," answered the chorus in a hushed whisper. The effect was chilling. Treet stood spellbound.

"The Burning," the Preceptor sobbed. "Fire fell from the clear sky without warning, raining down on the cities of light, destroying them in clouds of smoke that blotted out the sun, consuming even the stones. No one survived. Young and old alike perished in that terrible day. It was over in a moment, but the black smoke rolled up to heaven for many days to become a shroud to cover the sky. On that day, our bright homeland became the Blighted Lands, a desert where no living thing could ever survive."

Tears escaped from under the Preceptor's closed eyelids. She let them fall and in a little while resumed. "But the Fieri survived. A very few, it's true. Some of our people were working the crystal mines in the West when the Burning took place. Others were away in the mountain quarries to the North. These few survived to wander once more.

"A dark epoch followed. Sickness became our constant companion: our men grew old too quickly and died suddenly; those of our women who were not barren gave birth to dead babies or produced monsters from their diseased wombs; our flesh withered while still young; little children lost teeth and hair, they vomited blood. Our proud ancestors became a nation afflicted with sores and running wounds.

"All that we knew passed away; all that we loved died. The treasures of our great civilization fell into dust. We lost the knowledge we had worked so hard to discover—we lost everything to the dark time.

"Yet, we survived."

"We survived," came the murmur from the chorus.

"We lived, for the Infinite Father heard our people and took pity on them. As they wandered the land, sick and sore, the Seeker found them, the Gatherer brought them together, and the Sustainer led them here, to the shores of Prindahl, where we were given a new beginning."

"Glory to the Infinite Father!" said the Fieri behind her.

"He bound our wounds and healed our sickness. He gave

411

us the light of hope to guard us, and taught us a deeper love than any we knew. The Infinite Father raised us from the ashes of death, and He claimed us for His own."

"Praise to the Infinite Father!"

The Preceptor opened her eyes and regarded the visitors with unutterable sadness and compassion. Treet was overwhelmed with a rush of jumbled emotions—outrage at the crime that had been visited on these noble people, grief for their loss, wonder at the meaning of the Preceptor's words, and astonishment at their incredible will to survive. For what she had described was a nuclear holocaust.

Out of jealousy and spite, the inhuman monsters of Dome had leveled the bright cities of the plain with atomic weapons. They had turned once-fertile soil into a wasteland scorched white and sterilized by radiation.

As one who had passed through that man-made desert, Treet felt the cruel injustice of it like a hot brand in his heart. It was some time before he could speak. "Such horror . . . I never guessed . . . ," he murmured.

"The worst that could ever happen to any living thing happened to us," said the Preceptor. "But the Infinite Father in His love sustained us."

"Sustained you? He let it happen in the first place!" snapped Treet without thinking. Every eye in the place turned on him.

"How so?" the Preceptor asked softly. They might have been the only two people in the room.

"He could have saved you, but He didn't. He let it happen," mumbled Treet, dreadfully sorry he'd said anything at all. He felt Yarden tugging at his sleeve.

"We did not know the Infinite Presence then."

"But He existed, didn't He?"

"Yes, and He revealed Himself to us through our pain. He taught us with our tears."

"It seems a hard lesson," remarked Treet finally. "Too hard." Yarden tugged again.

"No, you do not understand. Our pain was His pain first. If we grieved, how much more did the Comforter grieve. He became our sorrow; the death of our loved ones was no less death to Him, the Light of All Life. He took our sorrow to Himself and transformed it into love and gave it back. That is His glory."

412

Treet caught only the barest hint of what the Preceptor was saying, but he let it go. "You've stayed away from Dome ever since?"

"The Protector gave us Daraq, the desert, as a shield. Dome will not cross the Blighted Lands. Now they live turned in among themselves. Their disease will not be healed. It festers within them; it devours them and will in time destroy them. We leave them to their madness."

Treet stared at all those around him and knew in that instant why he had come here to this place. Words bubbled up from inside him and fought their way to his tongue. He felt like shouting, like hiding, like running from the hall screaming, like weeping and singing all at once. He began to tremble and felt Yarden's hand on his arm.

He clamped his mouth shut, determined not to make a bigger fool of himself than he already had. But his mouth would not stay shut. Hot pincers gripped his tongue, and the words came of their own accord. "The horror is starting again!" His voice grated in the hushed room.

The assembled Fieri looked at him strangely. The Preceptor nodded and said, "Speak freely. Tell us what has been given you."

Treet drew a quivering hand across his damp forehead and said, "You know that I—that is we," he included those with him, "escaped from Dome. But while I was there I saw the signs—the madness you spoke of just now—it's all beginning again. Already the leaders of Dome are searching for you, fearing you without reason. It's only a matter of time before they overcome their fear and come for you."

His words sent shockwaves of surprise coursing through the assembly. "Treet!" came Yarden's urgent whisper. "What are you doing?"

The Preceptor merely nodded once more, pressed her palms together, and brought her fingertips to her lips. Treet waited. Needles pricked along his scalp from nape to crown.

She leveled her eyes on him. "What will you do, Traveler?"

The question was not what Treet expected. "Do?" He looked to Talus and Mathiax for help. They merely peered back at him with narrowed eyes waiting for his reply. "I'm sorry—I don't know what you mean."

"Your purpose has been revealed to you," the Preceptor explained. "Now you must decide what to do."

413

"Why me?" Treet sputtered, looking around helplessly. "I mean, this affects every one of us. We all—"

"*You* must decide," said the Preceptor firmly.

"I'm going back." The words were out of his mouth before he could think, but once said he realized he'd been waiting to say them since the moment he'd set foot in Fierra, perhaps even before. "The signs are there—I've seen them before. We've got to stop Dome or they'll destroy everything. Come with me."

The Preceptor regarded him silently and then said, "We have seen what war can do; we carry in our hearts its terrible wounds—wounds which can never heal." She shook her head. "No, Traveler, we will not go with you. We will not fight Dome."

"But they wi—"

"The Fieri have vowed eternal peace. We will never lift a hand against another living being."

"They will annihilate you," Treet said wonderingly.

"So be it." The Preceptor's eyes glittered in the light. "It is better for us to join the Comforter in the pavilions of the Infinite Father than to increase the hate and horror of war by participating in it. We have vowed peace; let us live by our vow."

Treet could not believe what he was hearing. He looked to Mathiax and Talus for help, but they merely looked back emptily, their faces drawn in melancholy. "You will die by your vow," he said, shaking his head.

The Preceptor turned and moved away. The ranks of Fieri broke and the hall began to empty. Treet watched them go and then turned to his companions. Each regarded him with expressions of incredulity and contempt mixed in equal portions.

Crocker said, "You put both feet smack in the brown pie this time. Coo-ee!" He strode off.

Pizzle shrugged. "What can you expect from a guy who's never read *Far Andromeda?*" He shuffled away, following Crocker out into the courtyard.

"I'm going to my room," Yarden said icily.

"What did I say?" whined Treet. "Yarden, listen!" He hollered at her retreating figure, but she did not turn back. In a moment he was all alone. No one has any use for a doomsayer, he thought; and that's just what I am.

SIXTY
TWO

"**Y**ou're insane, Orion Treet! Is this some kind of kinky death wish? Is that what it is?" Yarden seethed. Anger flared her dark eyes with flecks of fire and honed her words to piercing points like needles of ice. Treet had never seen such fury in a woman and stood back in awe, as from a flame-sprouting geyser.

"Yarden, be reas—"

"Be reasonable yourself! If you weren't so infatuated with that gigantic ego of yours, you'd see how crazy it is!"

Treet flapped his tongue in response, but his reply was lost amidst Yarden's fresh tirade.

"It's a fool's errand. You'll get yourself killed for nothing. You have some kind of misguided messiah complex, and you think you'll change Dome. But you won't. They're *evil*, Orion. Through and through evil—rotten with it. I won't stand here and listen to you delude yourself."

"It's not that bad, Yarden. Honestly, do you think I'd—"

"Think you'd walk into that nest of vipers unawares? Yes, I do. You don't know them for what they are. You did not see them like I did. Please, listen to me. Stop this stupid, stupid plan of yours now. You don't have to do it. No one will care whether you go or not. No one will think less of you for not going. Give it up."

"I can't give it up! Can't you see that?" He'd tried the calm-down-cool-off-let's-talk-about-it approach, and it had proven about as effective as a pup tent in a hurricane. Yarden's reaction mystified him. She had blown up instantly, without warning. He hadn't seen it coming. "Someone has to do something about Dome or the holocaust will begin again."

"You have no proof of that."

"I know what I've seen. I know the pattern from history— I've seen it time and time again. The machinery of war is already in place. We've got to stop them before they get full control of it."

"How do you intend to stop them?"

She had him there. He had no idea. "I don't know, but I'll find a way. Come with me."

"No! I won't be a party to your suicide. I love you. I won't watch you kill yourself."

"I'm not saying it isn't dangerous. I know it is. I'll be careful. But dangerous or not, it's got to be done. Don't you see that?"

"No, I don't. The Fieri have lived for two thousand years avoiding Dome. Why should that change now all of a sudden?"

"It's the age-old pattern, the cycle of hate. Dome despises the Fieri, and over time that hate builds up until they can't contain it anymore and it explodes. Last time they incinerated the Fieri cities—changed a million kilometers of fertile farmland into a sterile desert waste; they blasted three generations of civilized human beings into sizzling atoms in less than two seconds. They'll do it again unless they are stopped."

Yarden stared at him. Her lips were compressed into a thin, straight line. Her face was clenched like a fist, teeth tight, jaw flexed. "I can't believe you'd do this to us," she said finally.

"To us? You think I want this?"

"Yes. In some strange way no one will ever understand, you do want this or you wouldn't insist on going."

"Yarden, I don't *want* to go. I'm no hero. But someone has to go, and there's no one else. You heard the Preceptor. None of the Fieri will go. Fine. I'm not bound by any sacred oath. Besides, I promised I would go back."

"You what?"

"I told Tvrdy I'd return. They're desperate for help, and they're waiting for me to bring it. I told them I'd come back with help, and I meant it. That's why we left, remember?"

"I don't believe this," Yarden huffed. "After all you've seen here, you can still think about returning?"

"They're waiting for me—us—to come back with the help they need."

"They're using you, Treet! Open your eyes. Suppose you helped them overthrow Jamrog—what makes you think Tvrdy would be any different, any better than the fiend he replaced? They scream about injustice and brutality. Yet, when the new regime comes to power they show themselves worse villains than the villains they replaced: more brutal, more unjust, more

416

repressive. It's the politics of terrorism—you end up replacing one terrorist with an ever bigger terrorist!

"Wake up, Treet; they're using you. You owe them nothing. You're not bound by anything—except your own inflated ego!"

"You don't know—"

"Give it up," Yarden pleaded. "Please, give it up. You don't have to go. You don't owe them anything. What goes on in Dome doesn't concern us any longer. We're free. Forever free. The life we've always dreamed of—that all mankind has always dreamed of—is here. And it's ours for the asking. Please, Orion, stay with me. We'll be happy."

"I want nothing more. You have to believe that, Yarden. But what happens inside Dome *does* concern us. Can't you see that? Dome will strike again; they can't stop themselves, so they have to be stopped and there's no one else to do it. I have to try. I don't want to, but I'm going." He moved toward her, raising his hands to touch her. She stiffened and turned away.

"I'm leaving," she said.

"No, wait. Don't go, Yarden. Let's talk about this."

"You've made up your mind. There's nothing more to talk about."

He watched her rigid form move through the doorway and disappear in the darkened corridor beyond. He knew that everyone in Talus' pavilion had probably heard them fighting, but he didn't particularly care anymore. He sank into a chair and shook his head wearily. Of all people, he expected Yarden, if not to support his decision, at least to understand it. Instead, she had reacted in the worst way possible.

Was she right? Was he being a stubborn, egomaniacal ass? Had he misread the signs entirely?

He thought about this, remembering the haunted expressions he'd seen on the faces of Dome's inhabitants: that vacant, sunken-eyed hopelessless that in the strange alchemy of repression was transmuting the simple desires of an abused people into a volatile ether awaiting the proper spark to ignite it. The spark would be a leader who, to slake his unquenchable greed and power lust, would turn the force of firestorm toward the innocent Fieri. The Fieri would become the hated enemy whose destruction would be presented as the panacea for all Dome's ills.

Treet knew that torturous trail for what it was. He'd seen the bloody cycle repeat itself too often in history not to recognize it now. The mystery was, why did no one else recognize it?

He would have gladly agreed with Yarden if there had been even the smallest particle of doubt in his mind, if there was any other logical explanation for what he had seen and heard. But he knew in the marrow of his bones he was right, and his scholarly integrity was too keenly developed over too many years to allow him to back away from his assessment just because it was inconvenient or threatening.

He was right. Dome would attack again, probably very soon. Something had to be done. It was all well and good to appeal to two millennia of peace and invoke a sacred oath of nonviolence. But the rabid, power-mad rulers of Dome would not think twice about violating peace or sacred oaths when they could conceive of neither.

As soon as Dome whipped themselves into enough of a killing frenzy, they would strike. They would venture out from under their enormous crystal shell with death in their hands; they would seek out the Fieri and annihilate them. They would do this, Treet knew, because, as it had happened time and time again on Earth, the mere presence of the Fieri challenged their warped existence the same way a single ray of light jeopardizes whole realms of darkness. Dome could never be reconciled to the Fieri—the differences between them were too great.

The problem was classic: how do you appease an enemy who will not be appeased by anything less than your death?

If the Fieri could accept annihilation out of religious conviction—as the Preceptor had pointed out, they knew the horror of war better than anyone else and had vowed that they would never increase that horror by participating in it—so be it. Treet had taken no such vow.

Besides, there was a chance that Dome could be diverted from its present course if he acted soon enough. And he wouldn't be alone: Tvrdy and Cejka and their followers already struggled to dismantle the war machine, or at least halt it. Perhaps with help they could succeed—perhaps not. But in any case there was absolutely nothing to lose. If they failed, there would be no life for the Fieri anyway.

One day soon Dome would again fill the skies with fire, and there would be no escape. To think otherwise was utter delusion. Besides, what kind of life would it be to awaken every morning wondering if this was the day the world would end? What kind of happiness could exist as long as the specter of inevitable destruction loomed larger every moment? What kind of feast is it where hooded death sits at the head of the table?

He had to go. There was no other way.

"I think you're nuts, too," said Pizzle when Treet saw him in the courtyard the next morning. "If you think you're going to talk me into going back with you, then you're more than nuts—you're psychotic."

"I knew I could count on you, Pizzle. True blue."

"So sorry! I've just never been much of a martyr. Aversion to suicide is one cultural trait I approve of. It's very practical."

"I wouldn't expect you to be anything but practical. That's you all the way—good old pragmatic Pizzy." The sarcasm in his voice finally got to Pizzle.

"Look, if you want to toddle off on some lunatic crusade, go right ahead. Who's stopping you? Anyway, you should thank me: a coward like me would only slow you down. You could save the world a lot quicker without me hanging on your back."

"You're right about that. But, loath as I am to admit it, Pizzle, you've got a cool head on your shoulders when you choose to use it. You'd be a help."

"Right. And this head is staying fixed on these shoulders. Thanks, but no thanks."

Treet got up and looked down at Pizzle with dismay. "You don't have to make up your mind right now. Think it over, I'll be back."

"Suit yourself." Pizzle shrugged and looked myopically up at him. "But I'm not leaving Fierra. Ever. Jaire is taking me sailing today. You know what? I've never been sailing in my life. I've never been alone with a beautiful woman either, as a matter of fact. And this is just the beginning. I intend to start doing a lot of things I've never done before. I'd be a fool to leave this, and so would you."

"Don't you think there's the slightest chance you could be overdramatizing all this?" Crocker sat across from Treet, leaning toward him, resting his forearms on his knees. The courtyard was cool and quiet in the midmorning sun. The yellow canopy made them both look slightly jaundiced.

Treet shook his head slowly. "No. I wish I could make myself believe I was wrong, but I've seen too much, I know too much. Pretending it doesn't exist won't make it go away."

"I agree," said Crocker. "If you feel that way, I think you should go."

"You do?" Treet looked at the pilot closely, studying him for any trace of the odd aloofness he'd displayed since the travelers had been reunited. Crocker seemed himself, but Treet remained wary. "Why do you say that?"

"Well, if you can have an opinion, why can't I agree with it?"

"I mean, why do you think I should go? No one else does."

"No big secret there, Treet. I just think a man has to do what he thinks is right no matter what."

"Code of the wild west, eh? A man's gotta do what a man's gotta do."

"Go ahead, make fun of the only person who believes in this crazy scheme of yours."

"You say you believe and you still call it crazy. Thanks a lot."

"I'm willing to go along with you."

That stopped Treet cold. "You what?"

"I'll go with you—back to Dome. What's the matter? Isn't that what you want?"

"Sure, but—"

"But what? Isn't that what this little conversation was leading up to—asking me to go with you?"

"Yeah," Treet admitted, feeling unsettled, but not certain why. "I *was* going to ask you to go with me."

"So I saved you the trouble. This way, if anything goes wrong you won't have to feel responsible. You didn't recruit me—I volunteered."

"You really want to go, huh?" Crocker's reaction was so different from what he'd received from Yarden and Pizzle, Treet was suspicious.

"It's not a question of *wanting* to go. But let's just say your little speech last night convinced me. Something has to be done, or we might just as well lie down in a deep hole and pull the sod over our heads. I'm not ready for that yet. If there's a chance we can prevent it, we've got to try. That's how I see it."

"Crocker, you're a wonder," said Treet. "I figured you'd laugh in my face like Pizzle did."

"Pizzle's a spineless, self-seeking coward! He's not worth spit," replied Crocker with a vehemence that surprised Treet. Crocker and Pizzle had been the best of friends throughout their desert ordeal. It wasn't like Crocker to denounce him so strenuously.

Treet got to his feet, and Crocker slumped back in his chair, staring up at him. Treet said, "Thanks for the vote of confidence. I'm going to look in on Calin. We'll start making plans for the return trip in the next day or two."

"Fine." Crocker nodded slowly. He looked gray and exhausted, as if wilting before Treet's eyes. "I'll be here."

Treet left the courtyard quietly and made his way to Calin's second-floor room, knocked once, and went in.

SIXTY THREE

The room was dark, the woven draperies drawn, letting in little light from the open balcony beyond. The muted plashing of water mumbled like liquid voices, and the lake breeze soughing through the drapes made the room breathe as if alive. Calin lay on a low platform-bed on her side with her knees drawn up to her chest. She did not move when Treet came in, and at first he thought her asleep. As he came to stand over the bed, he saw that her eyes were open, staring into the dimness of her room.

"Calin," he ventured. No response. "It's me, Treet. I came to see how you're doing. Mind if I sit down?"

He sat on the edge of the bed, stretching his legs in front of him and leaning on his elbow. "You know," he said, trying to keep the anxiety out of his voice, "you've got our hosts climbing the walls. They can't figure out what's wrong with you. If there's anything you want to tell me, I'd like to listen."

Treet waited, heard the faint ruffle of her shallow breath. "I know you can hear me, Calin. And I was hoping you'd talk to me. If anyone has a right to hear from you, I guess it's me. After all we've been through together, if you can't trust me, you really are out of luck."

He grimaced at that last part, but Calin gave no indication that she'd heard him at all. He blustered ahead. "I was hoping you would at least talk to me . . . I, uh—I've got something to tell you."

The Dome magician might have been in some kind of cataleptic trance for all the interest she showed in his news. Treet had heard of people who could simply will themselves to die, and wondered whether Calin had the knack.

"Anyway," he told her matter-of-factly, "Crocker and I have decided to go back to Dome. There's unfinished business back there, and it's important we go as soon as possible. I don't know how we're going to get there yet, but . . ." He paused, then added impulsively, "I was wondering if you wanted to go back with us?"

Treet surprised himself with the question. When he entered the room he had no idea of asking her, and even as his lips formed the words he did not seriously consider that she would be able to respond to it.

But to Treet's amazement, Calin rolled over and looked at him. She blinked her eyes, and Treet saw her presence drifting back as if from far, far away. Her hand made a motion in the air, and Treet followed the gesture and saw a low table at the foot of the bed. A carafe of water and a cup sat on a tray. He poured water and lifted her head while she drank.

When she had sipped some water, Calin said in a creaky whisper, "Please . . . take me with you. I want to go back . . . back home."

He stared at her for a moment, considering what he'd done. "Well, uh—I . . ."

"Please." She clutched at his sleeve pathetically. "I will die here."

What she said was likely true. One way or another she would die here. So, on impulse, he agreed. "Good. I want you to go with us. I need you, Calin—you're my guide, remember?"

The mention of her old function brought a sad, lost smile to the young woman's lips. "Your guide," she said. "I will be your guide again."

"Yes, but before we go anywhere you're going to have to pull yourself together. Okay?" He went to the draperies and yanked them open. Bright sunlight streamed in. "First, let's get some fresh air in here." The breeze floated in, balmy and inviting. "There, that's better." He came back to the bed. "Let's see if we can get you on your feet."

She pushed herself up slowly from the bed. Treet put an arm around her and lifted her effortlessly. She was nearly as weightless as a shadow. This shocked him more than seeing her in her cataleptic state. "We've got to get some food into your stomach. You're withering away to nothing, and it's a long trek back to Dome."

Calin moved easily enough once she got going, and Treet knew that she had snapped out of whatever self-induced spell she'd been under. The simple mention of going home had done it. Though he could in no way imagine such an attachment, for

423

Calin the twisted, teeming warrens of Dome were home, and she missed it.

In the smaller dining hall they found food laid out. Treet broke the magician's fast with good bread and soft fruit, then offered her some cold, sliced meat which she gobbled down. Treet ate too, chewing thoughtfully, watching Calin and pondering about all that had happened in the last twelve hours or so:

He had somehow volunteered for a kamikaze mission behind enemy lines, alienated the one person in the entire universe who loved him, antagonized a very useful comrade, become nursemaid to a hothouse flower that couldn't live in the real world . . . not to mention loosing the fear of war among the most amiable, peace-loving people that ever lived.

And all this without meaning to, which, for a man who never put on his underwear in the morning without a strong conviction, was highly uncharacteristic of him to say the least. What could I have accomplished if I'd set my mind to it, he wondered.

He heard the low vibration of Talus' voice somewhere close by and got up, saying, "Stay here and finish eating. I'm going to talk to Talus. I'll be right back."

Talus was standing with two other Mentors: Bohm and Mathiax. The three formed some sort of triumvirate of Fierran leadership which Treet hadn't figured out yet. They looked up as Treet came toward them. Talus stroked his beard, and the others crossed their arms over their chests and studied him coolly.

"I guess I stirred things up here last night," he said. "I'm sorry if I embarrassed you."

"If you are right about what you said," replied Talus slowly, "you need have no concern for my feelings."

Mathiax said, "As a matter of fact, we have been talking about how to aid you."

"I thought the Preceptor made it quite clear that I could expect no help from the Fieri." Treet glanced quickly at the three grim faces.

"That is so," answered Talus. "We have no wish to violate a precept, but Mathiax here has suggested that perhaps a greater precept claims authority in this special case."

"What might that be?"

Mathiax answered, "The most fundamental precept of our

people requires that we extend ourselves to the aid of another whenever and wherever and in whatever way required."

"You have no obligation to me," said Treet.

"Oh, but we do," said Bohm. "We do because we choose to, and will always choose to. To refuse aid when aid could be offered would be a greater error than breaking the vow. Our precepts make us Fieri, not our vows. Even so, we need abandon neither."

"What Bohm is saying," explained Mathiax, "is that there might be a way of helping you, while at the same time observing our vow of peace."

Treet frowned. "I'd be grateful for whatever you could do, but," he shrugged, "going back is something I've chosen. You don't have to feel obligated."

Talus and Mathiax shook their heads sadly. "You still don't understand," said Mathiax. "Never mind. It doesn't matter. We have decided to offer you transportation. One of our balon routes lies just north of Dome. Ordinarily our navigators avoid flying within sight of Dome, but if one of them happened to let his balon wander a few hundred kilometers to the south, no harm would be done."

"I see. Yes, and if I happened to be on that balon, it might even touch down momentarily. No harm in that certainly."

The three Mentors shared sly smiles between themselves and nodded. "Thanks," said Treet. "You've helped me more than you know."

Talus put a large hand on his shoulder. "It was a difficult decision. But the truth was in you last night, and that we cannot ignore. May the Protector go with you."

"I have a feeling I'm going to give your multifaceted Deity a workout before this is over," said Treet lightly. "I'm going to need all the help I can get."

SIXTY
FOUR

*E*vents spun past Treet with dizzying rapidity. Plans were laid and provisions secured for the return to Dome. Despite their vow of nonaggression, the Fieri willingly involved themselves in all phases of Treet's preparations. Bohm provided detailed maps of the balon route and the area where the travelers would be dropped off: along the river about twenty kilometers to the north of Dome.

"It's very simple," explained Bohm, stabbing a finger at the map. "The route lies between Dome and the Blue Forest. You will land here—where the river ends its slow curve around Dome's plateau. Then you can either move southwest away from the river, or follow it to here and turn in westward. It's roughly the same distance either way."

"You're sure it'll be all right? What if Dome sees the balon? I don't want to endanger your crew."

"They have been informed of the risks, and they all want to help. But to tell you the truth, we've never had any indication that Dome has ever seen one of our balons. At least not in the last five hundred years—as long as the airships have been flying."

"Is that so? How did you travel before that?" wondered Treet, suddenly interested.

Bohm smiled and laughed. "Oh, I thought you knew. You used them yourself, I understand."

"The sand skimmers?" Why did that seem so odd?

"Of course. In the very early days we traveled overland to the crystal mines. But that is tedious—despite the speed of skimmer blades."

Treet nodded. "Then the skimmers we found in Dome belonged to you, to Fieri I mean. They were yours."

Bohm looked surprised. "Yes! Certainly they were. Who else would have made them?"

What a lump I've been, thought Treet. A cheese-headed

lump! Dome had no use for sand skimmers. Why would they develop vehicles to traverse a desert they never entered? That brought up an obvious next question: "How did the skimmers get there, Bohm?"

The old man frowned and said, "They were captured—must have been. Though I can't recall ever hearing about anything like that."

"It's at least five hundred years ago, as you said, maybe longer."

"Yes." Bohm nodded thoughtfully. "Still, if you are interested, there would be a record of any such event in the Annals. As Clerk, Mathiax would be able to find it. Shall I have him look?"

"No, it's not important. I can guess what happened. It was an interesting fact, that's all."

Mathiax had a slightly different interpretation of that fact when Bohm told him about it later. The Clerk had joined them at Bohm's house near the airfield, and Treet confirmed the story by describing the skimmers in detail from shining blade tip to trailing solar panel. Mathiax listened, eyes half closed, nodding and grunting agreement.

"It is strange how the Provider works, is it not?" he said when Treet and Bohm had finished. "I had not stopped to consider it before, but now that you bring it up, I see the hand of the Infinite in this."

"Oh?" Treet didn't see it himself, but as a scholar he respected the Fieri's beliefs about their Deity.

"Yes, it's obvious. Don't you see?"

Treet gazed blankly back at his friend and said, "Frankly, no. But I'm not used to looking for such things."

"You should get used to it, Orion Treet. The Infinite Presence has chosen you for a task. When He chooses someone, He makes it possible for His agent to carry out the task for which he was chosen. You see?"

"You mean to tell me," replied Treet skeptically, "that five hundred years ago your Infinite Father arranged to have sand skimmers captured just so I'd have transportation when I needed it?"

Mathiax considered this for a moment and then agreed. "It amounts to that, yes."

"But what happened to those who were riding the skimmers at the time? They would have been imprisoned—killed, more likely. I'd call that a heavy price to pay just so I could have a ready getaway."

"We do not presume to fathom the ways of the Provider. It could be that those who were captured had their own tasks to complete. But we recognize that the Creator works in all times and places, turning even the very worst of circumstances to His purpose."

"It is so," agreed Bohm. "All praise!"

Two days later, they were ready to leave. Treet awoke on the morning of their departure heartsick. He had not seen Yarden since the night of their argument. He had looked for her, expecting to find her at Talus', and was told that she had returned to Ianni's house. He sent messages to her which she ignored. When, on the night before the balon was to leave, he had Jaire take him to Ianni's, they found the place empty. Yarden was not there.

Treet was forced to conclude that she was avoiding him, refusing to see him or speak to him. He considered delaying the trip another day or two on the off-chance that he might find a way to see her and talk to her again, but what was the use? She doesn't want to see me, he told himself. If I stayed another month she'd find excuses not to speak to me. It's over for us. I blew it. I might as well go now; there's no reason to stay.

And there was at least one very good reason to leave as scheduled: fear. Treet was afraid that if he didn't go now, he'd lose his nerve. The thought of actually returning to Dome and finding a way to do what he had to do there had become almost overwhelming. He couldn't think of it all at once, only in small chunks—hiking to the colony, making contact with Tvrdy, losing himself in the colony underground . . . the rest became fuzzy. But vagueness at this point he considered a blessing.

As the hour of departure neared, Treet grew more anxious. He wanted just to be gone, or at least moving. He couldn't stand the waiting any more. Each moment brought something that reminded him it was not a holiday vacation he was undertaking. He looked upon every Fierran vista as the last. See that? he told himself. You'll never see it again. He did not add that if his quest failed *no one* would ever see it again, but knew it just the same.

Crocker's mood could not be guessed. Treet checked with

him several times prior to departure, and each time Crocker appeared preoccupied and busy with his own preparations, though what those might be, Treet could not guess and Crocker didn't say. Treet left the pilot to himself, thinking, There'll be plenty of time for catching up later.

Now Treet stood next to a gleaming pylon on the edge of the airfield, the rising sun stretching his shadow across the expanse of close-cropped green lawn where the enormous red sphere of the balon, the Fieri airship that would take them to Dome, glowed against the pale blue sky. The oversized beachball shapes of balons tethered to the ground formed a bulbous, multicolored mushroom hedge around the field. Beneath the yoke-shaped gondola, the ground crew moved with unhurried efficiency. The wide loading ramp was down, but Treet didn't feel like climbing aboard just yet. He waited.

In a little while he heard Talus' resonant tones rolling across the field and turned to see Crocker and Talus striding toward him. Crocker had his kit slung over his shoulder and a grim, determined look in his eye. "Morning, Treet," he said, glancing toward the balon. "Good weather for flying."

Talus clapped Treet on the back and said, "This day has come too soon."

"You're right, Talus. I feel like I'm turning my back on the treasure of a lifetime. I'm going to miss you all very much."

"You won't change your mind and stay with us?" the Mentor asked earnestly. Crocker's head swiveled sharply to note Treet's reply.

"Thanks, Talus, but no." Treet shook his head wistfully. "I can't stay."

The big man regarded Treet with utmost compassion. "Follow the light that is in you, Traveler Treet. The Protector will watch over you, the Sustainer will keep you, the Comforter will give you rest. Go in peace and in peace return."

Treet didn't know what to say. No one had ever given him a benediction like that before. "Uh—ah, thanks, Talus. That's really nice."

Crocker made a sound in his throat, turned, and walked toward the balon. Talus watched him for a moment and, lowering his voice, said, "I wonder about that one. He is too much involved with himself."

"Crocker? He's okay—just a little nervous maybe. This isn't a joyride we're going on, you know." Treet spoke lightly, but his heart felt the implied foreboding of Talus' words. "What about Calin? I thought she was coming with you."

"Jaire will bring her." He gave Treet a knowing look.

"Maybe I should go—"

"It will be all right. We have a little time yet, and Mathiax has something for you."

As if on cue, an evee approached and came to a halt on the grass a few meters away. Mathiax climbed out and joined them. "I see all is ready . . ." He hesitated, then added, "I wish we could do more."

"You're doing enough," Treet reassured him. "You said yourself this is my task. I'll be all right."

"You may depend on it," the Clerk said solemnly.

An awkward silence grew between them, so Treet spoke up. "Talus said you had something for me."

"Oh, yes!" He pulled a folded card from his purple vest and handed it to Treet. "The Preceptor asked me to give you this. You are to read it after departure—alone."

Treet tucked the card into the pocket of his brown Fieri jacket. "Thanks. I will." Silence overtook them again. "I—uh, guess this is good-bye." The two men extended their hands to him in the Fieri manner, and Treet gripped them tightly. "Good-bye," he said, his throat tightening inexplicably.

"The Infinite Presence goes with you," said Mathiax. "Trust in Him to lead you."

"I'll try." Reluctant to take his eyes from their faces, Treet stepped backward from them and collided with someone standing a few paces away. "Sorry!" He turned, his hand frozen in midair. "Yarden, I—"

She was dressed in a white sleeveless jacket with white trousers and boots. Her black hair hung loose, gleaming with blue highlights, feathered by the breeze. His heart lurched in his chest. She said nothing but drew him aside with her. When Treet looked back, Talus and Mathiax were climbing into the evee to leave. They continued walking.

Halfway to the balon she stopped and faced Treet. "I haven't come to say good-bye, if that's what you're thinking."

"Why have you come, Yarden?" He ached to take her in his arms and hold her, to bridge the distance yawning between them.

"I came to give you one more chance to call off this asinine scheme of yours. Stay here, Orion. Stay with me. I . . ." Her cool,

430

matter-of-fact manner faltered. The next words were spoken from her heart. "I need you. Don't go . . . please." She searched his face for a sign that he would amend his plans, but found only resolution. "That's it then. You won't change your mind."

Treet looked away. "I . . . Yarden, I can't."

"Then I won't either!" she snapped. "When you leave, it's good-bye."

"I'll come back."

"I won't live like that. No, it's forever. I never want to see you again." She stepped away from him, and he felt as if he had been jettisoned into deep space without a suit.

"Yarden, don't go! Please!"

She turned away slowly and began to walk across the field, spine straight, shoulders squared.

"I love you, Yarden!" Treet called. Her step halted, and her shoulders slumped; her head dropped momentarily. Treet saw a hand rise to her face, but she did not turn back. In a moment she continued on as before, but more quickly.

Treet stumbled toward the waiting balon. When he reached the ramp, Yarden was a small white figure against the green of the field. He watched until she passed behind a pylon and disappeared, then blindly pulled himself up the ramp and into the airship.

reet spent most of the flight cloistered in his quarters aboard the balon, emerging only occasionally to check with the navigator on their progress. The first time he went down to the bridge, they were high over deep folds of thickly forested mountains whose creases sparkled with freshets and silver cascades. Only a few hours later they reached the outer fringes of Daraq, the great desert shield.

Leaning with his elbows on the rail at the curving observation window, he gazed down on the glistening humps of white sand, watching the tiny round shadow of the balon dip and glide as it rippled over the wrinkled dunescape. Calin crept catlike up beside him and stood with eyes fixed on the spreading whiteness far below. Treet wondered if she knew how the desert had been made by her own people long ago. No, the Fieri would not have told her; they would have spared her that.

Still, something in the way Calin stared at the endless waste sliding away beneath them told Treet that she grasped part of the truth. "It is so dead," she whispered after a long while. "So dead and sad. I feel a sorrow I did not feel before."

"We were busy before," offered Treet, "just trying to stay alive."

Calin did not say anything, but Treet knew she did not accept his explanation.

He left her at the rail and returned to his quarters, threw himself down on his flight couch, and pulled the folded card from his pocket for the sixtieth time, opened it, and read the fair, handwritten script.

Traveler Treet, you stand at the center of events beyond your knowing. I ask the Infinite Presence in your behalf, not for strength, but to give you wisdom, that you may know what to do when the time comes for you to act. You suppose your arrival upon our world to have been chance; yet, though the designs of the Creator are most complex, every thread is woven in its place with His full intent. As you have said, you come from a world beyond our sun—a world we remember only as the shadow of a dream of long ago. Your presence reminds us that we cannot forget the lessons of the past. We *are* our past. I ask you to remember this. And also to remember for us who we were, for this we are beyond remembering. Know that you are the perfect agent for the task before you. Mathiax has told you, but still you doubt. Put your unbelief aside, and do not be afraid. You are well chosen.

The Preceptor

The trip lasted four days, and most of that time Treet spent thinking about what the Preceptor was trying to tell him in her enigmatic way. There was encouragement, yes, but something else less easily defined. At heart, her message seemed to be hinting that the key to succeeding in his task lay in understanding Empyrion. This understanding, she seemed to be suggesting, was to be found in his knowledge of his own world. Perhaps that's what she meant by making reference to his world beyond their sun. As for the part about remembering, he didn't get that at all.

And what did she mean, "we *are* our past"?

Maybe she simply meant that the Fieri were shaped by their past. Isn't everybody? Yes, but the Fieri were products of a past they could not remember. Their memory had been effectively wiped out in the holocaust.

But he, Treet, could remember. He knew, probably better than anyone else alive on Empyrion at the moment, the origins and history of their race. The Preceptor was asking him to remember for them the things they could not remember themselves—their past.

Was this so important? Ultimately, what did it matter? They could not change the past. Even if they all remembered perfectly the events which had led their ancestors out from Dome, or before that their colonizing journey from their original home, Earth, what could they do about it but accept it?

Adopting his familiar role as historian, Treet settled himself for some serious thought on the problem and finally came to the conclusion that for the Fieri, being shaped by a past beyond memory meant that they could never be certain about their future. As odd as that might seem on the surface, there was ample precedent in history for such a notion. Many ancient

Earth cultures believed that the past actively influenced the present and future. Nothing extraordinary there.

But what if one was cut off entirely from the past? That, perhaps, would mean a fairly one-dimensional future, a flat future, devoid of the richness and texture of the informing past. Also, the mutiplied chance that the past, in some way, because it was unknown, could repeat itself and they would be powerless to stop it.

The more he thought about it, the more unhappy Treet became with this line of reasoning. It did not account for much that he had seen in his too-brief stay there. There was something else that it did not account for: the curious reception given the travelers.

This had bothered him from the first.

If the Fieri were really as ignorant of the past as he supposed, why didn't they pump him for information day and night? They had in Treet a mobile data bank packed full of just the sort of fascinating tidbits they—according to his theory—ought to want to know: details of their home planet, their colonist patriarchs, what the colony must have been like in the early days, what caused the tragic split with Dome.

Inexplicably, the Fieri (and Dome, too, for that matter) appeared manifestly uninterested in any details of that sort. This perplexed Treet utterly—until he tried to put himself in their place. How would he react if a strange humanoid showed up on his doorstep one morning saying, "Hi there, I'm from another world and time, and I was just passing through the universe and thought I'd drop in. By the way, I can solve the riddles of the ages. Want to know the origins of life on your planet, huh? Go ahead, ask me anything."

All things considered, the Fieri reacted quite intelligently. Back home on Earth the supposed visitor would have been enrolled in the nearest noodle nursery before you could say DNA. Everyone he'd met on Empyrion so far seemed to consider him just an ordinary tourist and this, Treet decided, was what bothered him the most. Treet and his companions were from Earth! Yet the inhabitants of Empyrion seemed universally unimpressed.

Perhaps, he concluded, they simply had no way of comprehending it any more than he would have of comprehending the time traveler who appeared on his doorstep. Yet, the canny

Preceptor had put her long, well-manicured finger on it—Treet's veracity was of crucial importance to the survival of Empyrion. If indeed he was who he said he was, then somehow, some way it was up to Treet to do what only he could do.

But what?

Orion Treet, now on his way to confront his peculiar destiny, had absolutely no idea.

Late in the afternoon of the fourth day, the balon began its descent. Treet joined an excited Crocker at the railing and watched the airship gently lower itself from an opal sky. Below them, stretching northward to the broad, unvarying horizon, lay a heavy carpet of forest so dense and deep and dark it looked blue.

Emerging from the leading edge of the Blue Forest was the shining course Pizzle had dubbed Ugly Eel River. Along that river to the south, Treet knew, lay the glittering, multipeaked monstrosity of Dome, sparkling beneath the white sun of Empyrion like a diamond mountain. Treet glanced at Crocker and saw that the pilot stared into the southern distance as if hypnotized.

"I don't see it, do you?" said Treet.

Crocker pulled himself back and replied, "No . . . still too far away. It's down there though."

"You don't have to go. Calin and I can find it. You can stay on board—"

"No!" Crocker's face distorted in genuine anguish. Treet noted the reaction with alarm.

"Hey, it's okay—either way. I only wanted you to know that I'm not forcing anyone to do anything they don't want to do."

"You don't get rid of me that easy." Crocker forced a smile that looked like a death rictus. Treet felt a chill creep up into the pit of his stomach from the soles of his feet.

"I don't want to get rid of you, Crocker," he replied.

They watched the landscape drift closer, gaining definition with their descent. The river widened as they approached and eventually slipped beneath them and out of view. The pale turquoise hills that formed their landing field were as uniformly desolate as he remembered them, the turf just as wiry and

435

tough. The balon dropped vertically the last thousand meters and bounced like a bubble on a forlorn hilltop. The wide hatchway opened, and the ramp descended to the ground.

The travelers watched the balon float away silently, rising straight up in the air. Then, when sufficient altitude had been reached, the engines cut in, pushing the spherical craft onto its northwestern course. There had been no fanfare for the travelers' leaving. They had said good-bye to the Fieri and climbed down the ramp, followed by a small, three-wheeled cargo carrier. The carrier was self-guided, programmed to follow the trailing member of their party at a distance of four meters.

Treet glanced at the map in his hands and oriented himself to the river, which he could see as a dark line curving away to his left a kilometer or so distant. "It's straight ahead, friends. We can walk a couple of hours and make camp for the night. With any luck, I figure we'll reach Dome sometime tomorrow afternoon."

"Suits me," said Crocker, staring off into the distance. Without another word he started walking.

Treet watched him, then said to Calin, "I'm a little worried about him. He's not himself."

The magician's eyes flicked from Treet to Crocker and back again. "I sense fear . . . and—I don't know . . ." She bent her head. "I'm sorry."

"Don't be. It's not your fault. I'm a little scared myself. How about you?"

Calin nodded and hugged herself. Standing there among the featureless hills, small, vulnerable, it was the gesture of a lost child. Treet gathered her into his arms. "It's going to be all right. Believe me. Nothing's going to happen to us."

They held each other for a moment, and Treet remembered how she had put her childish trust in him at the beginning of their odyssey. Now here they were again, about to reenter a strange, forbidding world. Her world. He would need her there just as much as she needed him outside it. Treet pulled her close and then, quite without premeditation, put his lips to hers.

The kiss was brief, but it lingered in his mind for a long time after. He took her hand and they followed Crocker, who had disappeared momentarily into a fold in the hill line. At their movement, the robo-carrier whirred. Its lenses swiveled in its sensor panel, fixing the proper distance and when four meters stretched between them, its wheels rolled forward and it came tagging along behind.

Crocker unrolled his sleeping pallet as soon as he'd finished eating. They had hunched together over the small pellet-fuel fire they'd made to warm their food. The Fieri had provided them with all they could think of to ease the rigors of the hike. Even though it was only twenty kilometers, they were outfitted for a journey across the entire continent. Treet wished they had been so provisioned on their first trip.

Their meal had been simple, filling, and eaten in almost total silence. Calin nestled close to Treet, and they sat together across from Crocker, who ate with his head down, dipping his hand mechanically into his bowl. It seemed to Treet that the pilot was avoiding eye contact with him, but he put it down as fatigue and jitters about what lay ahead of them. The times Treet attempted conversation evoked no response. Crocker sat with his long frame bent over the bowl balanced on his knees, staring alternately into the fire and then into the darkening sky.

By the time they finished eating, night covered them with its blanket of stars. Treet and Calin followed Crocker's example and fished their pallets from the robo-carrier and unrolled them next to the fire. The pallets were made of a soft foam bottom layer bonded to double layers of a heat-reflective blanket material. Weary travelers would slip between these blankets and sleep comfortably all night.

But Treet did not sleep well. He lay for a long time listening to the enormous silence of the hill country, watching the impossibly bright stars glaring down at him from a firmament that shone like the inside of a burnished iron bowl.

He could not stop thinking about what lay ahead, could not help but think that he was hopelessly unequal to the task and foolish for even considering that what he might do could make any difference. He had no plan, no weapons, no help that he could count on. Visions of futility shimmered in the flames beside him as he lay on his arm, gazing into the fire.

The fire had burned itself out when he awoke again. The night was bright with stars, and he sat up. Calin kneeled over him; her touch had awakened him—that and an odd sound: someone moaning pitifully.

"What?" he asked. "Crocker?"

The pilot groaned again, this time a deep, guttural sound like that of a wild animal—a wolf perhaps, readying itself to attack. Treet pulled his feet from the pallet's envelope and went to Crocker, put his hand on his shoulder, and jostled him gently. "Crocker, wake up. You're having a bad dream. Crocker?"

The man growled again, savagely, and came up, muscles tense and rigid, teeth flashing in the cold starlight. "No!" he shouted. "No! Ahh!" His eyes bulged. Sweat glistened on his forehead.

"Take it easy, Crocker," said Treet. "You're having a nightmare. It's over now. You're here with us. You're safe."

In a moment Crocker relaxed, the tension leaving his muscles all at once. "I—don't know what came over me," he said, shaking his head and rubbing his neck. "It was like a—I don't know—like I was frozen inside a block of ice, or fire, or something. I couldn't break out. I was dying."

"It was only a dream. You're okay now. Take a deep breath."

He lay back down and was asleep seconds later. Treet was not so lucky. He lay awake waiting for Crocker to dream again, but heard only the heavy, rhythmic breathing of deep sleep. After a while he felt a light touch on his arm and glanced up to see Calin's face above his. "No, I'm not asleep," he said softly.

The magician came around and bent close to him. Treet lifted the blanket and let her slide in beside him. He wrapped his arms around her and held her body close. The comfort in that simple act sent waves of pleasure washing through his soul. Entwined together, they slept until morning.

Crocker sat watching them when Treet awoke. The sun was barely touching a pearl-gray eastern sky, and a light wind stirred the longer blades of grass on the hilltops. Treet came fully awake the second he saw Crocker's face—half of it was smeared down, as if someone had run a torch over the left side of a wax mannikin's face. His eyes were lusterless, dead. His mouth pulled down on one side and up on the other in a ridiculous, ghoulish grimace.

"Crocker!" Treet cried. Calin started from sleep and looked up, cowering.

Treet disentangled himself from his bedroll and got to his feet. The pilot looked at him dully and then began to laugh. It was a ghastly sound—hollow, disembodied, half mocking, half pitying. He stopped abruptly, like a recording switched off.

"What's wrong with you? What's so funny?" asked Treet, shaken. Calin cringed.

"Wrong? Nothing's wrong." His voice was soft. Too soft. "I was just thinking . . . what a shame to waste it . . . eh?"

"Waste what? What are you talking about?" Treet took a step closer. Crocker threw up a hand to stop him.

"Your girlfriends—I don't see what they see in you."

Jealousy? Was that it? Crocker had never shown anything like that before. "Look," Treet said, "you had us worried last night. You had a nightmare—remember?"

Crocker rose, yawned, stretched his arms out wide. Treet noticed the tremendous reach of those long arms. "I slept like a baby." His lips twitched into a wolfish grin. "So did you, it looks like."

"She was scared," said Treet, then wondered why he was explaining. "So was I. You really had us going."

"Speaking of going . . ." Crocker stooped, rolled up his pallet, and stuffed it into the carrier. "Let's get it over with."

He watched while Treet and Calin put away their bedrolls, then turned and headed off. When he had passed from earshot, Treet whispered to Calin, "We've got to keep an eye on him. Something's wrong."

She nodded, but said nothing, and they started off once more.

By midmorning they had reached the halfway point, Treet estimated. They sat down on a hilltop to eat some dried fruit. "We ought to be able to see it soon," he said.

Crocker nodded, chewed silently, and swallowed.

"We should probably talk about how we're going to get inside."

"Plenty of time later," said Crocker.

"Okay. Sure. Later."

When they moved on, Crocker fell behind them, shuffling

along flat-footedly now, where before he'd swung his long legs in an efficient, ground-eating stride. Calin hung close to Treet's left hand, glancing back at regular intervals. Treet refrained from looking back, but once, when he could stand it no longer, he peered over his shoulder to see Crocker's mouth working silently, as if he were debating with himself. Crocker stopped when he saw that Treet was looking.

They stopped a few hours later for their first good look at Dome. The sun was high overhead, blazing in the crystal facets of its enormous webwork with white brilliance. From this distance, it would have been easy to mistake the structure for a glass mountain whose peaks and tors glittered as the sun's rays played over its polished surface. From a closer vantage point, individual sections of dome clusters would be seen, giving Dome the appearance of a mound of soap bubbles dropped on an endless flat lawn.

"There it is," said Crocker through his teeth. He turned to Treet, but looked through him.

Treet glanced away. "We can be there in a couple of hours. We'll have plenty of time before sundown to find a way inside . . . *if* Tvrdy is still watching, that is."

They started down the hill to the last valley before the long, gradual climb to Dome's low plateau. Crocker fell behind again, and Treet halted when he reached the bottom of the hill to wait for the pilot to catch up. Crocker waved him on. Treet, with Calin stuck like a second shadow to his side, continued on, growing increasingly worried. Something was terribly wrong with Crocker, he knew. What? Nerves? Treet was nervous himself; it wasn't that. It was something deeper, more sinister.

After walking for an hour or so, now beginning the trek up the slope to the plateau, Treet looked around to see Crocker, his back turned, standing over the carrier. "Anything the matter?" he hollered back.

"Yeah, this robot is jammed up. It can't make the climb. We'll have to leave some of the gear."

"Stay here," Treet told Calin under his breath.

Calin, staring down at Crocker, nodded. As Treet turned away, he felt her hand on his sleeve. "Be careful," she whispered.

"What's the problem?" he asked as he joined Crocker. The man was sweating through his clothes.

"I don't know. I heard it laboring, and I looked back and it was stuck."

"We've had tougher climbs than this. It always made them before."

The pilot shrugged. "Maybe its gears are shot."

"Let's take some of the stuff out and see if that helps." Treet bent over the carrier and started undoing the straps that held down the webbing. "Are you going to stand there or are you going to help?"

Crocker stood rock still.

Treet stooped, pulling articles from the three-wheeled robot. "Well?" He looked back just in time to see Crocker's arm swinging down in a murderous stroke, sunlight gleaming on the object in his hand. Calin screamed.

Treet ducked, but the blow caught him on the top of his right shoulder, missing his head, but smashing the median nerve into the clavicle. His arm fell to his side, paralyzed. Blinding pain flared from the shoulder a microsecond later.

Treet collapsed and rolled on his back to avoid the next strike. He started screaming. "Crocker! What are you doing! It's me, Treet! Treet! Crocker! Stop! Sto-o-p-p!"

The metal bar blurred in the air. Treet squirmed on the ground, dodging away as best he could, as the improvised weapon dug a little furrow in the dirt bare centimeters from his left temple.

Treet heard another shout and saw Calin flying to his aid, arms flailing. She attacked her heavier adversary with her claws, raking red welts into the side of his face and neck. The pilot threw her off, but she was at him again, scratching like a she-cat. A slashing backhand blow sent her spinning into a heap.

The diversion had allowed Treet to get to his feet, however. He lunged toward Crocker, his useless arm dangling. He thought to knock the mad pilot off-balance and somehow wrest the bar away from him.

Crocker, with the quickness of the insane, roared and jumped to the side, wielding the short length of metal in a deadly arc. The swing grazed Treet on the lower jaw, tearing a ragged gash along the jawline. Blood spilled down the side of his throat. "Crocker," he said, gulping for breath, "in the name of God, give it up."

The pilot lunged again, a strangled, inhuman sound bubbling from his throat, his eyes flecked with blood. With dreadful clarity, Treet's pain-dazzled brain registered that Crocker meant to kill him. His only hope now was flight; he could try to outrun his assailant and escape, or at least put some distance between them until Crocker came to his senses.

He turned to flee, shouting, "Run, Calin! Run for it!" The magician had circled around Crocker and now stood only a meter or two to Treet's right. She did not move. Her eyes were half-closed and her face rigid in concentration. "Calin!"

Treet flung out his good hand, snagged Calin by the arm, spun her around, and shoved her forward all in the same motion. He felt a sharp jab in his upper back, and then the force of the thrust wheeled him sideways. He tripped over himself and fell headlong to the ground.

He landed on his right side. His dead right arm failed to break his fall, and he hit hard. The air rushed from his lungs in a terrific gasp. Black circles with blue-white edges dimmed his eyesight. He heard himself yelling for Calin to run for it.

Standing over him now, Crocker, with a mighty snarl of rage, brought the metal bar down with both hands from high over his head. Too late to dodge, Treet threw his left hand up to divert the blow, expecting to see his forearm splinter as the heavy bar slashed down upon it. The second stroke would crush his skull like an eggshell.

Instead, he saw the metal bar fall with lethal accuracy only to glance aside at the last second. One instant it was a deadly blur descending toward him, the next it was sliding away. He was untouched.

Crocker appeared dazed. The weapon dangled in his hand. Treet threw himself at it, grabbed. With only one hand, Treet could not hope to hang on. The weapon slid by centimeters from his fingers as Crocker's superior strength overcame his single-handed grasp. The pilot kicked out; Treet's knee buckled and he toppled.

The pilot staggered back, clenching the bar in his upraised hands. Howling, he swung the bar down. Treet's eyes closed reflexively. Again the bar bounced harmlessly aside before impact.

Crocker roared in pain—like a berserk rogue elephant stung by the dart of a keeper. He whirled away.

"Calin!" Treet struggled to his knees. The magician stood with one hand upraised, her eyes closed, sight turned inward. Treet recognized the posture as her trance state. "Calin, look out!"

Crocker's furious lunge drove the end of the metal bar into

Calin's neck. They both fell together, Crocker sprawling head-long over his victim. The metal bar rolled on the ground. Treet scooped it up with his left hand and swung blindly at Crocker's huddled form.

The bar, awkward in his hand, slipped as he struck out, catching the pilot on the hip. Treet glanced down and saw his hand dripping red; the bar was slick with Calin's blood.

Crocker gathered his long frame to spring. Treet braced himself, raising the bar. The pilot rushed forward with a howl, his face twisted almost beyond recognition: eyes bugging out, mouth gaping, jaws slack, tongue lolling. The bar thumped inef-fectually on Crocker's chest and bounced out of Treet's grasp as he stumbled backward.

He lay facedown, panting, knowing that even as he thought it, the metal bar was closing on his skull. He waited. Rather than the sound of metal singing through the air to splat-ter his gray matter over the turf, he heard an odd grunting noise and the faint whir of a machine. Treet glanced up to see the demented pilot limping away, the little robo-carrier rolling after him.

Crocker's body jerked spasmodically, arms loose, legs stumping woodenly, shoulders rolling. He looked like a puppet whose strings were fouled. As he lurched along, a loathsome gagging sound came from his throat. With a shudder, Treet realized the pilot was weeping.

On hands and knees he crawled to Calin's side and gath-ered her up. The wound was deep. The bar had been plunged into the soft flesh of her throat and ripped upward, leaving a ragged hole. Blood streamed from the hideous wound; her jack-et was drenched in crimson and sticky to the touch.

"Calin," Treet huffed, his stomach turning itself inside out. "You're going to be all right. He . . . he's gone."

She opened her eyes slowly, and from her unfocused stare Treet knew that she could not see him. "Hold . . . me," she whispered airily. Her larynx had been crushed, or torn apart. "S-s-o . . . da-ark . . ."

Treet drew her close, cradling her head against his chest. "You'll feel better in a moment," he told her, hating the lie. "Just rest."

Calin's lips parted in the gesture of a smile. "Nho," she wheezed. "Nho . . . came . . . back."

"That's good," he soothed. "Now rest."

She swallowed, pain convulsing her features. When she opened her eyes again, Treet saw the effort it had cost her. Still, she struggled to speak.

"What is it?" He put his ear to her lips.

"Ahh . . . I am . . . magician again . . ." She sighed, so lightly that Treet thought she had fallen asleep. When he looked he saw the empty, upward gaze, her dark eyes clouding with death.

SIXTY
SEVEN

Treet closed her eyes and kissed Calin's forehead, smoothing her tangled hair from her face. He sat for a long time, cradling the body, rocking back and forth, oblivious to the tears streaming down his face, murmuring, incoherent in his grief.

Slowly the warmth seeped from the body; Calin's limbs grew cold, and at last Treet let her go. He laid her gently down, pulling his jacket around her to hide the thickening stain on her clothes. "I'm . . . Calin, I'm sorry. . ." he told her, lifting his face to the sky. "So sorry . . . I should have known . . . seen . . . protected you. I'm sorry. Forgive me, Calin."

Time passed—how much time he did not know. But his shadow stretched long when he finally raised his head and looked around at the vacant hills, thinking, I can't leave her here like this. I have to bury her.

Where? He had no tool to dig a grave—only his bare hands, and the turf was too thick, too dense. He turned his eyes toward Dome. Then, carefully gathering the body into his arms, Treet stood and began to walk.

Night was far gone by the time Treet reached Dome. All the muscles in his back and legs had long ago twisted into throbbing knots, but he had walked on, ignoring the pain, his senses numb, heeding only the stubborn will to put one foot in front of the other and move on.

The sun had set in a ghostly yellow fireball, tinting the Western sky briefly before night extinguished the golden glow and plunged the lonely hills into darkness. Dome loomed larger with every aching step, the conical peaks and bulging humps holding the sky's last light long after the sun had sunk beyond the hills. Now its hulking mass brooded in the dark, except where starlight glinted cold from the planes of the crystal shell.

At the foot of Dome's foremost cluster, where the fibersteel and crystal sank into the earth, Treet lay Calin's body down. The grass grew long around Dome, and the earth was soft. Treet pulled, and the stiff grass came up by the roots, dragging large, heavy clods with it. He cleared an oblong swath and dug his fingers into the soil, smelling the deep, rich scent.

The stars bled dim light over him. With nightfall a haze had crept into the upper atmosphere, casting a pall over heaven's face. With his fingers he gouged out a shallow depression, scooping the earth away in clumps. His fingernails tore and bled, but he toiled on until he had carved a rough grave beneath Dome's roots.

He slid Calin's body into the grave, knelt over it, and, placing a hand against her cold cheek one last time, said goodbye. He started crying again as he heaped dirt over the body, watching her pale, smooth flesh disappear under the dark earth. When he had finished, he replaced the grass atop the mound and stood, brushing the dirt from his hands and knees.

He turned to go, but felt that there ought to be some sort of ceremony; some words, at least, should be said. He stared at the rude mound, but could think of nothing suitable to say—until it occurred to him to recite the benediction Talus had given him.

Raising his face to the dim stars, he imagined the magician's spirit hovering nearby. He said: "Follow the light that is in you, Calin. May the Protector watch over you, the Sustainer keep you, the Comforter give you rest. Go in peace." After a moment he added, "Infinite Father, receive this one into your care."

He turned away and began walking around Dome's vast perimeter.

Dawn found him standing at the edge of the canopy formed by the superstructure supporting the landing field. He entered, moving among the heavy fibersteel pylons as through a dark forest of smooth, branchless trees. As he came near the place where the doors opened into Dome's Archives, he halted. The air held the retchingly sweet odor of decay, and as the light grew stronger he saw a grisly sight: two semidecomposed corpses lying where they'd fallen a few meters from the door.

The events of that hectic day flooded back as Treet remembered their harried departure from Dome and the ensuing firefight. The moldering corpses offered a stark reminder, as had Calin's death, of the seriousness of his task.

Treet swallowed hard and moved toward the doors. He searched for and found the code lock with which he was to signal Tvrdy, but the mechanism had been blasted. Nothing remained but a scorched spot where the fibersteel had bubbled. There was no way to signal Tvrdy—if Tvrdy still lived and waited for his return, which he had begun to doubt. How would he get in?

He stepped to the great doors and saw that his entrance was provided: a third corpse lay pinched between the doors. The wretch had fallen on the grooved track, and the closing doors had crushed him. But not completely. The body had jammed the track as the doors ground shut, leaving a crack half-a-body wide.

Treet grimaced as he stepped over the corpse and wedged himself into the crevice. Darkness and panic swooped over him. His mind filled with doubt. What if Jamrog's men were waiting for him inside? What if Tvrdy had lied? What if he and his men had all been captured and executed?

He fought down the fear, and in a moment the darkness cleared and he saw himself standing poised on an imaginary line. He gritted his teeth and took one last look at the narrow band of blue sky and green hills glimpsed from under the landing platform.

"Now it begins," he told himself. Then, squeezing through the narrow way, he disappeared inside.

BOOK TWO

The Siege of Dome

The Siege of Dome

PROLOGUE

*I*n the year 98 A.A. Colony suffered a killing contagion that severely decimated the population. This was the time of the Red Death, and many whom Cynetics had raised up were alive then. These were the Original Ancestors, of whom little is now known, except that they were wise in the ways of Expertise and Machine Lore.

The disease spread despite heroic efforts of the Medico Expertise to contain it. Quarantine measures proved ineffective, and it soon became apparent to the Ancestors that most of Colony would succumb to the Red Death—so termed because of the blood welts that formed on the skin of the victims at the slightest pressure.

I have seen old records which indicate that the Red Death struck with frightening suddeness, producing chills, vomiting, loss of muscular control, slurred speech, lethargy. The eyeballs of the afflicted were said to become red from burst blood vessels in the eyes. Mucus ran freely from nose and mouth, making breathing difficult, and later impossible as the lungs filled with fluid. Victims of the Red Death drowned in their own mucus, choking, gagging, whimpering in agony as each touch brought a new and painful blood welt to swell the skin. Where these welts burst, a vile, suppurating crust formed. But at this stage, the victim was normally comatose and beyond care. Death followed within thirty-six to forty-eight hours of the disease's onset.

In those terrible days one Ancestor in three was taken by the Red Death. The Ancestors knew that for Colony to survive, healthy breeding stock from each Expertise had to be preserved. Those selected for survival were sent out from Colony to live apart in the Hill Country. Others, fearing the disease, attempted to escape by exiling themselves to the wilderness also; but lacking tools and provisions, many of these died from hunger.

In time, the exiles who had managed to live by eating fish and small mammals returned to find less than a fourth of Colony left alive. The surviving population numbered four thousand. Not one of the Original Ancestors survived.

The Ancestors attempted to replace every Expertise, organizing survivors to form the HSCs—Human Survival Cells. Each HSC was dedicated to preserving its own Machine Lore, and in this way each Expertise was preserved—all except one called Biogenics, which many survivors believed had created the Red Death.

It has been said that from this time Cynetics turned its face away from its people, abandoning its children because they fell away from the worship of true spirits. The Cult of Cynetics grew up among the survivors who believed renewed contact with the Divine Spirit would aid them.

The Four Thousand became the Progenitors of old, who reformed Colony after their own desires, vowing that nothing like the Red Death would ever happen again. Thus began the First Age of Empyrion.

Feodr Rumon
Interpretive Chronicles, Volume 1
After Arrival 2230

O rion Tiberias Treet lifted his face from the page swimming before his eyes, sat up, and glared around, red-eyed, at the untidy stack of blue plastic notebooks he had been reading nonstop for the last few days. He rubbed his whiskered jaw and stood creakily, began swinging his arms, pacing and stretching to get his blood circulating.

Five days—maybe more, he couldn't tell for sure—in the subterranean Archives of Dome, reading Feodr Rumon's *Interpretive Chronicles,* had given him an ache in his head to match the one in his stomach. He had not eaten since returning to Dome, even though, upon entering the Archives, he had found the provisions he and Calin had left behind on their first visit—a time that now seemed impossibly remote.

The food had long since spoiled, but the water in the sealed jar was good; so he drank sparingly from it and settled down to discover all he could of Empyrion's lost past. He knew he might never have another chance to read the notebooks, and knew, too, that once he left the safety of the Archives, he might never return. Several days of hunger were worth the price.

Upon leaving the Archives he would be a hunted man; so Treet was in no hurry to leave his work. He would have to leave soon, though. Already hunger was making him light-headed and weak. If he waited too long, he might not have strength or wit enough to successfully elude capture and provide some help to Tvrdy and his allies.

Of course, not knowing what had happened since his escape from Dome, he was at a distinct disadvantage in the strategy department. He assumed the worst. That way he would not be unduly disappointed.

He wondered what he would find when he decided to leave his hidden enclave, wondered whether there had been a Purge, and whether Tvrdy and Cejka had survived or been brought down. Assuming that they had survived, he wondered how to make contact with them, or with anyone else in a position to help him.

These matters he pushed from his mind whenever they intruded, and he forced his attention back to his reading. Old Rumon's *Chronicles* offered a wealth of information to be mined. He had only to pick up one of the ancient notebooks to be transported to some long-forgotten age of Empyrion's past. A past which Treet sincerely hoped would offer a clue as to how he might begin averting the catastrophe he had so clearly seen looming over the future of the planet.

This once-strong hope had turned into a wormy anxiety. For now, having returned, he was far less certain that he'd read the signs of disaster aright. *I was so sure of myself before,* he argued. *Nothing has changed—so why do I doubt myself?*

Doubt was a mild word for it. Whenever he thought about what he had committed himself to, snakes began writhing in his bowels.

Treet had lived his life trusting his instincts, never looking back. Life was too short, he often told himself, to spend even a second in regret. Now, it appeared that his ever-trustworthy instincts had betrayed him and backward glancing would become a way of life.

On the strength of his gut feeling he had left the Fieri and their magnificent civilization to return to Dome on the narrowest of chances that he might somehow forestall the doom that only he seemed to see.

On the strength of his gut feeling he had sacrificed his own best chance for future happiness by alienating the only woman he'd ever really loved, the only woman who, quite possibly, had ever loved him.

On the strength of his gut feeling he had set in motion a series of events which had caused the messy death of a beautiful friend. He missed Calin—would have ached for the loss of her had not grief numbed him. Still, the thought of her death and the sting of his own guilt for the part he played in it were never far away. And the gruesome battle between him and the demented Crocker, which had claimed the gentle magician's life, was replayed nightly in his dreams in brutal, bloody detail.

All this—the torment of those memories, of second-guessing himself, dark bouts of self-accusation—he struggled to hold aside long enough to learn as much as possible about Empyrion Colony's past in the short time he had to give to the task. And, despite his growing uncertainty about his mission, he still felt this to be crucially important.

So, ignoring all else as he ignored the vacuum in his stomach gnawing at his concentration, he returned to the nest he'd made for himself on the floor and opened the notebook he'd been reading for the last few hours. The binding, brittle with age and cracked in a dozen places, bore the handwritten tag *Volume 19*, signifying he was one-quarter of the way through Empyrion's Third Age, as classified by Rumon.

He took out his bookmark—a folded sheet of paper bearing the notes he had scratched with an old polymer stylus found in a nearby bin—and read what he'd written:

Colony Foundation	=	1 AA
Red Death	=	98 AA
Plebiscite Rejected	=	309 AA
Colony Splits	=	311 AA
Second Split	=	543 AA
First Purge	=	586 AA
Directorate Installed	=	638 AA
Flight of the Fieri	=	833 AA
Fieri Settlement Est.	=	1157 AA
Cluster Closed	=	1270 AA
Fieri Scattered	=	1318 AA
Directorate Overthrown	=	1473 AA
Second Purge	=	1474 AA
Threl Established	=	1485 AA

It was the record of civilization born to turmoil, much the same as any civilization. But what made Empyrion's record so sad—and this was the part that really got to Treet—was that the colony had advantages never possessed by any other civilization he'd ever encountered: they had started out with all the tools for creating Utopia right from the very beginning; they had all of history to teach them how to organize and govern themselves. They might have chosen to recreate Eden.

Instead, they chose Hell.

Treet's list of major historical events was the record of a society descending inexorably into tyranny. From the rejection of the first citizens' plebiscite to the establishment of the Threl, Dome had consistently chosen the downward course, evading at every turn the opportunity to rise; choosing—not once only, but time and time again—the collective will over individual rights, manipulation over liberty, expedience over benevolence, repression over freedom.

Through years of upheaval, through painful splits and bloody purges, the leaders of Dome relentlessly pursued the downward track. It was all right there in the notebooks—the damning evidence of a society throwing away human rights and freedoms with both hands, shedding all the higher and ennobling qualities that enlightened governments had fought so hard for since the dawn of time.

Yes, Treet thought gloomily, it was all there, faithfully recorded in the notebooks.

He still had nine fat notebooks to go, but was beginning to doubt whether he could finish before hunger made it impossible. Already the hand-lettered printout pages swam before his eyes, and his concentration was so fragile he was forced to read a single paragraph several times to get anything out of it. But at least he had discovered that catastrophe had taken place in Empyrion's past to shape its future—a future he was living now: the Red Death.

Based on Rumon's scant reference, Treet strongly suspected a genetic experiment gone haywire. Perhaps they had been attempting to adapt an indigenous lifeform or create a new bacteria strain for some purpose past remembering. However it was, once the contagion was loosed upon the colony, nothing could stop it. The disease had killed, by Treet's calculation, close to twelve thousand people, three-quarters of Empyrion's total population; by comparison, not even the plagues of the Old Middle Ages were so devastating.

When the Red Death had finally run its course, Empyrion was changed forever.

Treet found his place in the book and began reading. In just a few minutes he was exhausted, but struggled to keep at it for a few hours more. In the end, he had no choice but to admit defeat and lay the notebook down carefully. He had to have something to eat. Now. But before he could eat, he'd have to find a way past the guard station outside the Archives and then a place to hide until Tvrdy could be contacted.

He took out the map he had found on his first day back in the Archives. There was no telling how old the map was, or how accurate. Though it only showed two lower levels, one of which was mislabeled Archives Level, he supposed it could be trusted to point the way to the Old Section where he hoped to find refuge.

Treet stood and steadied himself as spots like tiny black fireflies swarmed before his eyes. He left the hidden room, taking a last look behind him as he entered the dry pipeline and made his way back to the Archives floor. As he walked along, one arm outstretched, touching the side of the pipe, he thought again about how he might elude the guards. Surprise would be on his side, he figured, for whatever that was worth. And he supposed that he might find some sturdy hunk of something to use as a weapon. Beyond that, he had no notion of how he might proceed.

He retraced his steps to the junction box and continued along the second pipe until he reached the metal ladder leading to the Archive floor, placed his foot on the first rung, and hauled himself up. It was then that he heard the clang and groan and felt the tremor of a heavy machine rumbling across the floor above.

Tanais Director Tvrdy crept along the darkened tunnel, pausing every few meters to listen again. He heard only the tick of his own footsteps echoing off the endless tile. He hunched his coat over his shoulders and wished for the millionth time that Pradim had not been killed. He would have trouble finding another guide—*if* he were ever to find one—who could be trusted so completely in so many delicate areas. Over the years, Pradim had become less a tool than a confidant and friend, and not incidentally a strategist of impressive powers.

If he missed the blind guide, the Cabal would miss him more. Reeling from the defeat Jamrog had forced upon them—for that's what Sirin Rohee's sudden and as yet unexplained death was: a crippling, paralyzing defeat—Tvrdy fought now just to maintain his position within the Threl. One way or another, Jamrog meant to have his head.

And one way or another, Tvrdy meant to keep it. If staying alive meant abandoning his Directorship, so be it. Only a fool like Hladik would insist on clinging to his dwindling power to the death. If Tvrdy allowed Jamrog to kill him in his bed, the Cabal was finished. And if the Cabal, small though it was and ill-equipped, passed from Empyrion, all resistance to Jamrog's rule would effectively vanish.

That was why he was making this journey now, alone, in the stark, predawn hours of a bleak and hopeless day, to make contact with Giloon Bogney, legendary leader of the faceless nonbeings, the Dhogs.

A message had been sent through the Rumon messenger network—Tvrdy didn't know how Cejka managed, but was thankful for such a clever and resourceful ally—and, what was most miraculous, an answer in the form of detailed directions had been received. Giloon agreed to a meeting in the Isedon Zone, that empty ring of ruined Hageblocks that formed the no-man's-land between the Hages and the Old Section. The condition was that Tvrdy come alone and bring some proof that he was in fact a Threl Director.

Tvrdy hated the thought of meeting the repulsive nonbeing alone in unfamiliar territory, but he was desperate. He would see Giloon, find out what his help would cost, and, with luck, estimate what that aid would be worth. The fact that Giloon had replied at all was a good sign; the crude map he'd sent was a better one. The Dhog wanted something, or he would not have responded at all.

Tvrdy came to a place where the tunnel ended, opening onto a deserted plaza lined with the charred stumps of once graceful feng trees. He consulted the Dhog's drawing and confirmed what he already guessed, that this was the entrance to Isedon, center of one of the original cluster of long ago; the only one still remaining. The dwelling-blocks on either side of the square—those still somewhat intact, at any rate—were smaller than in Hage, and were built in the ancient style: straight lines and flat surfaces. Tvrdy much admired the style and had copied it in his own kraam. The decrepit structures were dark and empty now. At least he supposed they were empty. The feeling of invisible eyes observing him intensified as he moved hesitantly to stand in the center of the plaza, overgrown with wireweeds and squatty lofo bushes that had insinuated themselves into crevices between the broken paving stones.

Tvrdy stopped when he reached the center and drew a shaky breath to calm himself. The air smelled foul and old, rank with decay. He shivered involuntarily; the place was a pest hole. He looked furtively around, imagining all sorts of crawling vermin creeping in the rubble of the tumbled buildings, and pulled his coat more tightly around him. The stiffness in his left arm reminded him of why he had come.

He and Cejka had had Cynetics' own luck that day when the Invisibles found them in the Archives. In the confusion of the Travelers' escape, he and Cejka had—he still didn't know precisely how—convinced the savage Mrukk, Commander of the Mors Ultima Invisibles and Jamrog's personal lackey, that killing two Directors outright and without proof of treason would be a mistake that would be paid in blood.

Mrukk, his face rigid with hot frustration at seeing his quarry racing away on Fieri skimmers, had made the decision to try to stop them, leaving Tvrdy and Cejka behind as he turned his attention to the fleeing spies. Cejka's men had attacked the small security force as soon as the shooting started on the landing platform.

Cejka lost several good men that day—Tvrdy himself had been wounded—but the Directors had escaped.

Then followed one demoralizing setback after another as all their careful plans failed or were neutralized by some evasive tactic of Jamrog's. The Saecaraz Subdirector seemed always to be one step ahead of them as the rebel Cabal scrambled for leverage to force events their way. So far, success had proven as elusive as a Hage priest's blessing, and as costly. They had lost many followers, and their network of agents and informants lay in ashes.

Tvrdy was startled out of his morose inventory by the appearance of a short, thick-limbed figure scuttling toward him over the slanting stones of the deserted plaza. The man wore a long cloak that dragged at his heels and held a short bhuj in his right hand; the wide, flat blade glimmered dully in the murky light as its owner scrambled forward on stump legs.

The Dhog leader came to stand before Tvrdy, his face begrimed, the hair of his beard virulent, matted, and greasy. A vicious purple scar divided his low forehead like a jagged lightning bolt, parting his hair and plunging diagonally down to the left cheek, warping the left eye so that it looked upward askance, as if Giloon were continually watching the sky-shell of Dome for a sign.

"So, Tanais!" he said, his round face splitting like an overripe fruit. Ocher teeth shone through the mat of hair, and his pudgy nose wrinkled in wry good humor. His voice was coarse gravel grating on glass, a sound to inspire abhorrence. An odor like that of rotting meat came off the Dhog's filth-encrusted clothes—actually, rags patched with rags—offending the nostrils as much as their appearance assaulted the eyes. On his chest he wore the medallion of a Jamuna Hage priest: a double-ended arrow bent into a circle.

Tvrdy took this in with a grimace of disgust, almost gagging, but forcing a sickly smile of greeting. Why had he come? There was no point. The odious creature could do nothing for him. His heart shrank in despair, but he reached into an inner fold of his yos and brought out a packet which he offered.

The Dhog spat and looked at the packet. "Giloon don't needs it. Giloon be knowing you, Tanais, withouts it."

Tvrdy replaced the packet, actually relieved not to have the Dhog paw through his personal documents. "Thank you for agreeing to meet me. You took a chance, giving me directions."

Giloon tilted his face up and laughed. The sun had risen, but the weak light filtering in through the stained crystal panels overhead remained dusky. Very likely Old Section residents knew only two variations: twilight and deep night; their days were spent in the dim half-light of eternal gloom.

Giloon's laugh died. "What Tanais wants of Giloon Bogney?"

"Is that who you are?"

The Dhog raised the bhuj and laid the flat of the blade against his cheek and rubbed. "Who else? Anyway, as Giloon a nonbeing it matters no big much, seh?"

"I want your help," Tvrdy said simply. He had been prepared to use elaborate persuasion and rhetoric to state his case, but decided to cut the interview as short as possible so that he could get away. There was no point in drawing out the hopeless affair.

"Help!" Giloon spat, dribbling spittle over his chin. "Help he wants!" He spun the bhuj in his hands and leaned on the haft, looking at Tvrdy with wild amusement on his dirty face.

He's insane, thought Tvrdy. I never should have come. "Help, yes."

"And what you be giving in return? You slicing Giloon's throat, seh?" He drew the blade tip of the bhuj across his neck.

Tvrdy took a deep breath and said, "If you help us remove Jamrog from power, we will grant the Old Section stent—you will become a Hage."

"And Giloon being a Director?"

Tvrdy grimaced, swallowed his revulsion, and said, "Yes, you would become a Director."

The Dhog squirmed—whether with delight or torment Tvrdy couldn't tell—raised his face once more, and laughed deep in his warty throat. "Giloon liking a man who lies big and fearless! You eating the night soil with both hands, Tanais, but Giloon liking you. That is why he not killing you now. Directors must be talking, seh? We talking."

• • • • •

461

The two women walked along the shore of the glimmering quicksilver sea, Prindahl. Chattering rakkes strafed the shallows for the quick yellow fish, scattering diamonds among the waves with every plunge. It was still early morning, but the day was warm and fair; a seaward breeze flipped the wavetops and swept the hair from their foreheads as the two ambled along, steeped in the comfort of each other's company.

Presently Ianni stopped, finding a place to spread her fishing net. Already barefoot, she lightly doffed the saffron knee-length trousers she wore beneath the belted tunic and waded out into the water.

Yarden Talazac watched for a moment and then sat down on a large flat rock nearby and let Prindahl's cool waters lap over her feet. Face turned toward the small white disk of Empyrion's sun, she let the rays warm her skin and allowed her mind to drift as she listened to the shimmering beauty of Ianni's song.

Ianni, like most Fieri, had the gift of song in her soul. She could spin a melody as easily as she cast the light net in her hands while wading the crystalline shoals. Ianni's songs were webs of fragile, sparkling beauty: fine and delicate and intricate, possessed of a poignance that made Yarden yearn for places she'd never been, for things she'd never seen and did not know.

Fierra itself, the shining city of the Fieri, came very close to fulfilling Yarden's nameless longing. It was all she could have dreamed of and more: a spacious, gracious city filled with gentle, loving people; an entire civilization whose highest aim was the pursuit of truth and the nurture of beauty in all its varied forms.

In Fierra there was no want, no trouble, no pain, no violence of any kind. In fact, none of the noxious weeds that had poisoned other societies had taken root in Fierra. It was a charmed, enchanted place. Charmed and enchanted by the Presence, the all-infusing Spirit of the Infinite Father, whom the Fieri worshipped in nearly every word and deed. Here in Fierra, among these inspired people, it was easy to believe in their God, easy to feel His relentless, questing spirit drawing the faith of all men and women to Himself.

Yarden wanted to believe. In the last weeks she had felt the prickly, fidgety squirm that signaled an inner awakening. This stirring in her soul she knew to be, in part, a deepening desire of hers to actually become a Fieri. In believing in the Fieri's God, she would be like them in a most fundamental way. There was more to it than that, but the rest remained inarticulate and unformed. Her heart had its reasons that her head could never know. She was content to let the matter rest there for the moment, to let belief come to her in its own time and in its own way—if it would.

As for the rest—a whole realm of thought and feeling she was ignoring, holding back, and denying, most of it having to do with the disturbing person of Orion Treet—she simply refused to entertain even the smallest fragment of a thought or emotion. She had shut him out of her life the moment she turned her back on him at the airfield and had maintained her stoic decision ever since.

Ianni's song stopped and Yarden shifted her thoughts, focusing her sympathic awareness on her friend. The two women had grown so close in their months together that it was easy for Yarden to receive Ianni's thought impressions—they came through clear and strong. In fact, Ianni had developed a habit of mindspeaking whenever she thought Yarden might be listening to her.

Bohm returns this morning. The balon will arrive soon. We could go to the field if you wished.

Yarden opened her eyes and looked at Ianni, who was still standing with her net in her hands, gazing into the water. No, she thought, and wondered if Ianni would receive her answer. I don't want to speak to Bohm about . . . the trip.

You cannot forget him, Yarden. He will need our prayers.

I mean to forget him, thought Yarden. That's exactly what I intend doing—as quickly as possible. He made his choice, and I have made mine. I will have nothing more to do with him.

She closed her eyes once more and lay back on the rock, feeling its sun-soaked warmth seep into her. She *would* forget him.

THREE

Asquith Pizzle let the rudder line go slack in his hand as the sleek sailboat turned itself into the wind, scarlet sail flapping. He gazed at the Fieri woman sitting across from him, now regarding him with a quizzical expression.

"I feel like letting it drift for a while," he explained.

"Are you hungry?" asked Jaire, reaching for the bundle riding in the sling between them, her henna hair flaring red-gold in the bright sunlight.

"Starved."

"You're always starved." She laughed lightly. "What an odd word."

"I'm still a growing boy." It was true—spending every waking moment with Jaire made him feel like a youngster whose fondest birthday wish had come true. "I could look at you forever," he said, speaking his thoughts aloud. Never in his life had a woman as beautiful as Jaire allowed him within fifty meters; most hung out "Forget it, Buster!" signs the second they saw him coming. Jaire was different. And despite the fact that she was, technically, an alien—or maybe because of it—he was ankles over elbows in love with her.

Jaire favored him with one of the dazzling smiles she gave so effortlessly, bent her head, the lights off the water filling her eyes, and with deft fingers tugged open the bundle in her lap, bringing out the sweet fruitbread she had prepared. "I am going to the hospital tonight," she said, passing him a thick slice, over which was spread a soft nut-flavored cheese.

"Is someone sick?" He took a bite and savored it.

"No . . ." Jaire shook her head. "It is my—what is your word for it?"

"Shift. Your work time is called a shift." He had been teaching her Earth English, as she had been teaching him Fieri.

"It is my shift." Jaire worked at the Fieri's single central medical facility—a hospital devoted mostly to the care of expectant mothers and the delivery of babies. There was little disease among the Fieri; so being a physician meant obstetrics and pediatrics almost exclusively.

Also, since disease had long been in decline, the medical profession among the Fieri ranked about the same as the position of computer operator back on Earth, as far as Pizzle could tell. Not that the Fieri worked all that hard at any particular occupation. Theirs was a culture wholly given to job-sharing. No one, apparently, held down a single career. Each of those tasks necessary to the maintenance and functioning of society was divided among any number of people.

And since there was no such thing as wages—they simply had no concept of money—it didn't really matter who did what. People tended to do what they liked to do, receiving training in several different occupations and then pursuing them most casually. This had the effect of removing such societal ills as avarice, ambition, and stress from the work environment. The Fieri ascribed no status to what a person did; they were more concerned with the quality of the life being led.

"How long?" Fieri work schedules bewildered Pizzle; he didn't see how they kept all their various tasks and commitments straight.

"Ten days."

"Every night?"

She laughed, "Yes, every night. You will have to ask Preben to take you to the concerts instead of me."

"But I don't want to go with Preben—I want to go with you. I'll miss you."

Jaire passed him another slice of fruitbread and looked at him in that mysterious, enigmatic way Pizzle regarded as her Mona Lisa look—a look she had begun giving him a great deal in the last few days. It hinted at both humor and high seriousness, combined with several other elements he couldn't decipher. Something completely female, and therefore foreign to him. He had no idea what it meant.

Pizzle continued, changing the subject. "I've decided what I want to do with my life here. I want to learn all I can about your people—every single thing."

"That will not take long." Jaire lifted the sweet bread to her mouth and chewed thoughtfully. "There is not much to learn."

"I disagree! There's everything to learn." He held up the half-eaten slice of bread. "For example, I don't have the slightest idea how or where you grow your food, or where you go to get

465

it, or how you divide it up. Or how you get along without money, or anything like that. Where I come from, *everything's* money! Without money you can't live."

"You have told me about money before. Forgive me, but I still don't understand it."

"Never mind. But you see what I mean? There's a whole world to learn." He waved his bread in an arc that took in the whole of the Empyrion horizon, glittering with the sun off the distant pavilions.

"And what will you do when you learn everything?"

"I don't know. Write it down, maybe. It doesn't matter. I want to know all about you." Pizzle tucked the last morsel of bread into his mouth, lay back, and closed his eyes, letting his mind drift in the glory of the day. He felt positively reborn. Nothing else mattered but that he was here and that he would always stay here, just like this, now and forever. He felt his shriveled soul expand, shaking out folds and wrinkles he'd thought were permanently impressed.

He breathed a long sigh of profound contentment and let the gentle waves rock him to sleep as Jaire composed a nursery song she would sing to her infant charges later that night. Yes, thought Pizzle dreamily, this was the life. Heaven itself could not be sweeter. A man would be a fool to leave—for *any* reason.

• • • • • •

Treet hung on the metal ladder in an agony of indecision. Should he go back and wait until whatever was happening up there in the Archives was over, or should he risk discovery to find out what was going on? This debate raged for several minutes, and would have gone on longer, but his fingers grew tired. Rather than drop back down, it was easier to go up—which he did with utmost caution, inching up the ladder, watching the hole overhead for any sign of discovery, ready to let go and fall the instant he saw anything suspicious.

He saw no reason for retreat, however, though the clangor and rumble grew perceptibly louder the higher up the ladder he went. At last, clinging to the top rung, he pushed his head up just above floor level to see that nothing had been touched near his secluded hole. The sounds he had heard came from a point midway between him and the inner doors of the enormous circular room. A quick check confirmed what he already guessed—that the outer doors were now sealed tight once more. Whoever was running the machine stood between Treet and his only exit.

Wasting no time, Treet pulled himself the rest of the way out of the manhole and darted to a nearby stack of electrostatic filter frames, crouched, and peered cautiously around. He saw no one nearby, so began threading his way through the mazework of discarded machines and obsolete junk, creeping with all the stealth he could muster.

The din grew as the incessant clang began to include other sounds as well: the screech of rending metal, the groan and pop of fibersteel breaking, the crash and clatter of objects being thrown and smashed against one another. Treet worked his way toward the activity, pausing frequently to look over his shoulder. If he were caught now, it would be over before it began. Fortunately, the noise of the wreckage covered any inadvertent sounds he made, allowing him to get closer than he might have otherwise.

What he saw when, crouching behind a plastic water tank, he peeped out across a cleared expanse of Archive floor was a huge orange machine lumbering across the floor and stirring up the fine gray powder into a thick haze. The thing was little more than an engine on treads, with a flat metal plate hung on the front for banging a pathway through the accumulated jumble. A half-dozen Saecaraz stood watching the mayhem as the improvised bulldozer rammed the circle larger, punching the perimeter outward from the center. The heavy metal plate smacking against the treads created the deafening clang that he'd first heard.

The Saecaraz seemed intent on what they were doing—creating more room, Treet guessed, though why they should care about that now puzzled him. After all, the Archives had been ignored and unvisited for generations. Perhaps it had something to do with the events which had taken place here recently. Treet did not especially want to see those events replayed; so he ducked down and looked across to the doors. He saw that one was open and, wonder of wonders, was unguarded.

He backed away quietly and, keeping a safe distance from the Saecaraz, moved around the cleared circle to the doors. He had reached the halfway point when the machine stopped. The wash of noise evaporated into silence. Treet froze. He could hear the voices of the Saecaraz. Apparently they had finished their work and were leaving. They were coming toward him!

Treet continued on, hurrying to stay ahead of them, but taking pains to remain silent and unseen. The voices were closer behind him when he reached a place where two pathways crossed among the towers of cast-off equipment. He hesitated. One path appeared to lead directly to the door, while the other bent around and wound back into the welter. With the Saecaraz closing on him from behind, he chose to make a stab for the door rather than muddle through the maze.

He dashed for the door, thinking that if only he could reach it before the others reached the ring of steps he would have a chance of slipping through unseen. The Saecaraz were coming perpendicular to him now, making for the same path he had chosen. From the sound of their voices, Treet guessed that some were approaching from behind him, and others were just ahead, having chosen different paths to the single exit.

Treet put his head down and ran for it, but had not gone more than three paces when one of the Saecaraz stepped onto the path ahead of him, his back to Treet. Treet skidded to a stop.

The man turned toward the door and moved off. Treet remained unnoticed, but knew now that he had to get off the path. He glanced around and saw a stack of vent covers and stepped onto it. The stack shifted under his weight, and Treet was pitched backward into the path, while the vent covers cascaded around him in a clattering avalanche. The insidious gray film that lay thick over everything in the Archives powdered up in dusty clouds. Heart beating wildly in his throat, he looked up to see that the Saecaraz ahead of him had not turned around. Was the man deaf?

Furiously scrambling for his feet and scattering more of the infernal vents, Treet picked himself up. The startled shout from behind him caught him with his rear end poised in the air in the act of standing up. He glanced behind him—two Saecaraz Hagemen stood together, both wearing expressions of amazement. The foremost of the two shouted again, this time for the help of his comrades. The Saecaraz ahead of Treet turned around and started running toward him.

Treet stood for an instant, poised for flight but with nowhere to go. Then, without thinking what he would do, he threw himself forward, crashing through the stack of vent covers and into a glassy wall of electrical insulators. He tore down the wall, and stumbled through the breach—heaving ceramic insulators big as a man's head behind him as he went—and fell into a tightly packed corridor on the other side, the sounds of the chase close behind.

He flew down the corridor, formed by banks of heat deflector shields, and ran headlong into a dead end. Panting, Treet halted and turned to meet his pursuers.

FOUR

Horatio Crocker plowed through the heavy underbrush, searching for the trail he hoped he would find somewhere just ahead. The robot carrier tagged faithfully along behind, riding its treads over the foliage Crocker tramped down.

For six days Crocker had stalked the lonely hills. Dazed, senses numb, whimpering pitifully to himself, he pursued a meandering path that roughly paralleled the river. On the seventh day he had come to the edge of the Blue Forest—a tractless expanse terminating the desolate hill country like an enormous curtain of deep blue-green vegetation.

He had no thought but to lose himself in the darkness of that many-shadowed land—and even this was not a conscious desire. He simply moved because he could not stop moving. At first there had been some urgency in his flight, but as time and again he glanced fearfully over his shoulder and saw nothing to cause him alarm, he gradually relaxed and pushed a less hurried, though still wary, pace.

He did not know why he ran, or where. All consciousness—that part of himself that knew himself, spoke to and governed himself—had been obliterated. He had a ghostly recollection of a shattering event back there in the hills: of blood and death, and an agony like a firebrand cleaving his skull and burning into his soft brain tissue. His mind had become an inflamed and tortured thing, and he bellowed out his pain to the empty sky.

As day gave way to day, Crocker retreated deeper and deeper into the core of his being in an effort to escape the drumming pain. He moved with the same cunning and stealth as a wild animal, and with as much self-regard. He ate when he was hungry and slept when he grew tired. He drank from the river, never far away, though he had water in three canteens in the carrier. He considered the robot a companion, accepting it as being alive in the same way that he was alive. In the space of a few days, he came to derive comfort from the machine's presence. It followed him—moving when he moved, stopping when he stopped, purring idly while it waited—giving Crocker a sense of kinship.

When, on the sixth day, he had stood atop a high promontory and saw the hillscape descending in rippled steps to meet the forest, he knew that he would go there and seek solace beneath the dense dark mass of its interwoven canopy. No one would find him in there; nothing would hurt him anymore.

Without so much as a backward glance, he had pushed his way into the thicket fringe that rimmed the forest, protecting it like a daunting barrier reef around a vast, serene, imperturbable lagoon.

Now he labored, pulling himself through brush grown so lush and tangled that it was a solid wall. Above the wall he could see the tops of nearer trees; he watched these to mark his progress, lifting his head now and again as he thrust arms and legs and torso into whatever openings he could force through the growth. His clothes snagged and tore. His hands bled. But he did not heed the little pain, for it was drowned inside the greater, all-pervasive pain that he had become used to.

As he pushed past a broad-leafed shrub, thick-bodied and twice as tall as a man, he stuck his hand into a hole in the dense covering of leaves. An instant later the bush erupted in a flurry of flashing wings and screams. He threw his hands before his face as the shrieking birds took flight, and then, with instinctual quickness, reached into the feathery melee and closed his fist on the warm body of a bird as its head appeared in the hole, its wings half-unfolded for flight.

In the same motion, he brought the creature to his lips, put its head in his mouth, and bit down hard, feeling the crunch of delicate bone and hot blood spurting over his tongue. He drank the thick, bittersweetness and then spit the head out, tossing the carcass away. He smiled and wiped his mouth. "Meat," he muttered to himself.

• • • • • •

"How Giloon knowing Tanais be doing as he says when big noise finished?" The Dhog leader put his loathsome face close to Tvrdy and smiled maliciously. "Tanais Supreme Director be forgetting his Dhogs, seh?"

Tvrdy stared at Giloon, trying not to show his disgust. They were sitting in one of the dwellings across the plaza from where they had met. The kraam had been hastily appointed for the meeting: two filthy cushions had been put down on the grimy floor and a much abused table between them. Beside the low table stood an improvised brazier made of cast-off pieces of fibersteel riveted and bound together with wire. Foul-smelling chips—dried dung, Tvrdy suspected—burned in the brazier, giving off a thick, noxious smoke. There were two skewers with chunks of ratty-looking meat and a few sorry vegetables sputtering on the odorous coals.

Giloon reached over and turned the skewers expertly, casting a sidelong glance at Tvrdy and grunting with satisfaction. Tvrdy wanted to be away from this stinking place, but his opinion of his squat companion was changing. Giloon Bogney might well be crazy—probably was—but his madness bore a wide streak of stubborn self-interest that, under the proper circumstances, Tvrdy recognized as extremely useful. So, the Director sat in the ruined hovel, permitting himself to be alternately offended and insulted by the Dhog's presence and broad insinuations.

"You don't know me," replied Tvrdy, "if you think I would turn my back on any who gave aid when I asked. Saecaraz and Nilokerus may forget any service when it suits them—"

"But they be remembering any crime!"

"Yes, that's true. But the Tanais are not like that. We live by our word."

"When you getting fat on it."

"Watch your tongue! We make sure the terms are right before we make a deal. We never have to go back on our word—unless, of course, the other party attempts treachery."

Giloon chuckled, an ugly sound, full of malicious glee. "Giloon being a Director then, because Dhogs doing what Giloon says." He snatched up a skewer and thrust it at Tvrdy, who took the unwholesome thing and looked for a place to throw it. "Dhogs helping you, Tanais. Giloon giving his word, seh?" He tore off a scrap of meat, raised it in salute, and flipped it into his mouth.

Tvrdy followed his host's example and swallowed the meat without chewing. "I will send men to you—Rumon and Tanais, perhaps Hyrgo too. They will train those among you who are fit enough to fight."

"Dhogs not needing your training."

"We will face Invisibles armed with thermal weapons. You *will* be trained."

Giloon begrudged him the point with a grunt. Tvrdy continued, "You will give these men any aid, supplies, or information they require. Hold nothing back. If we fail, Old Section will not become a Hage and you will not become a Director."

"What we having, you having." Giloon spat on the table.

"My men will bring supplies with them which they will share with you—as they see fit. You must keep your people organized. There is to be no trouble between us. This is of the highest importance."

"You think Dhogs needing your aid, your training, your supplies? You throw us out of Hage, our names being erased; you taking away our life and thinking to starve us. If you be finding us in Hage, you kill us. Ah, but Dhogs live! We go down into the pits, we taking what you throwing away, use it. We living a long time this way, and we being still alive to roll your bones, Tanais."

Tvrdy put the skewer down on the table and leaned forward, his face hard, his tone steel. "Listen to me! You call yourself a leader—act like one. If you do not control your people, you will be of no use to us. If we do not have help, we will fail. And then how long do you think you will be allowed to live?"

Before Giloon could answer, Tvrdy went on, "When Jamrog is finished with us, he will turn on you. Rohee tolerated the Dhogs because you were useful to him: those who displeased him, he made nonbeings and sent to you. He used you as a threat to enforce his will. Jamrog is not like Rohee. Jamrog lives only to destroy. He will see the Old Section razed and the Dhogs slaughtered. I know him; that is his plan. Your head is full of night soil if you think to survive the Purge."

Giloon had sunk into a sulky silence. He fixed Tvrdy with a murderous glare and said nothing.

"You don't like what I've said, but you know the truth when you hear it, seh?" Tvrdy sat back, folded his arms across his chest, and returned Giloon's stare boldly.

The silence spread between them, but Tvrdy let his words sink in. Giloon frowned and fingered the bhuj's blade in his lap. When at last he spoke, his voice was a hissing whisper. "Giloon maybe kill you, Tanais."

"You'd kill your only friend for speaking the truth? Then you have much to learn before you ever become a Director."

Giloon sniffed, picked up the bhuj, and slammed the blade into the table. "Giloon being a leader greater as you. I control my people."

Tvrdy rose. "See that you do—your life and the lives of all your people depend on your cooperation."

"There being no noisy guts between us, Tanais." Giloon climbed to his feet and led Tvrdy out of the kraam and back across the square. Tvrdy saw the ghostly shapes of Dhogs watching from behind piles of rubble. As he moved away, the nonbeings came out of hiding to watch him leave, so that when he turned to give some last words to Giloon he saw a whole throng, gray as the shadows they inhabited, gathered at the far end of the plaza, watching silently.

"My men will begin arriving tomorrow. They will come one by one, or in twos. Receive them and make them welcome. We will soon have rumor messengers so that we can talk, but it is best if we do not see each other again until the plans are set. Do you understand?"

Giloon nodded, eyes squinted up at the Director. Tvrdy guessed some sign of official recognition of the Dhog leader before his people would go a long way toward smoothing future relations between them; so he took off his cloak and placed it on Giloon's shoulders. "There," he said, "now my men will know that I recognize you as a Director."

The Dhog's face squirmed into a great grin. He raised the bhuj and touched Tvrdy on either side of the throat with it, then turned abruptly and, hitching the cloak around himself, swaggered off across the ruined plaza to join his people.

Tvrdy watched him go, then turned and fled the Old Section as fast as decorum allowed.

FIVE

Treet gulped air and watched the Saecaraz come toward him. There were four of them. The two others had presumably gone for help. They slowed as they came nearer, and Treet sized them up: two were taller, heavier-looking, their bodies bulky beneath their black-and-silver yoses; the other two were slighter of build and not as tall, but looked more fit. Clearly, he would have trouble taking on all four, but it looked like he would have no choice.

So, figuring his best advantage lay in initiating the fight, he lowered his head and charged into them, bellowing as he ran. He plunged his shoulder into the first Saecaraz and sent him sprawling into the deflectors, spun off the block, and caught the second man as he attempted to dodge away. Treet gave him an elbow shot in the small of the back and shoved with all his might. There was a crash and a groan behind him as Treet dove for the onrushing feet of the third, who gave a yelp of surprise as his legs were cut from under him. The man landed on his face and skidded into his crumpled partner.

Treet came up running. The fourth Saecaraz stopped in midstride when he saw Treet gathering himself for another charge. For an instant the two stood looking at one another; then Treet yelled and lunged forward. The Saecaraz backpedaled and spun, tangled his legs and went down. Treet dashed for him, placed one foot square on his breastbone, and ran right over him and back into the main pathway, reaching the door seconds later.

He paused only long enough to pull the door shut and seal it, then ran for the first of a succession of doors leading to the guard station and the lower levels of Hage Nilokerus beyond. Once beyond the second set of doors, with those doors sealed behind him, he paused to listen and heard someone coming toward him from the opposite way.

The two Saecaraz who had gone for help were returning with the Nilokerus from the guard station. He could hear their feet pounding down the corridor—one, maybe two doors beyond. There was only one thing to do. Turning to the door he'd just sealed, he tapped the entry code into the lock and opened it again, then dashed the fifty meters to the next door, went through it, and pressed himself flat against the opposite wall and waited.

A moment later the Saecaraz appeared, followed by three Nilokerus with weapons drawn. They slipped through the huge doors and raced toward the next one ahead. Treet waited, holding his breath and praying none of them would glance back and see him standing there playing chameleon. None did; all five, hurrying to get to the Archives, pounded straight ahead.

Treet inched his way to the door and slipped through. He waited until the corridor was empty and then sealed the door he'd just exited. Then, listening carefully, he made his way to the next set of doors, which he also sealed behind him. No one seemed to be following him. They would not know he had evaded them until they conferred with the others inside the Archives; that would give him a minute or two before they came racing back after him. The doors would stop them only momentarily as they reentered the code at the lock, but every second counted.

He was thinking about how best to lose himself in Hage as he burst through the last set of doors—which is why he failed to see the Nilokerus guard waiting for him on the other side.

· · · · · ·

Nilokerus Director Hladik was reclining in his suspension bed, stroking the soft flank of his hagemate as she fed him cherimoyas from a silver bowl, when a chime sounded in the next room. A moment later his guide came silently into the sleep chamber.

"I told you I was not to be disturbed," Hladik said.

"Forgive my intrusion, Hage Leader," said the guide tentatively, his fingers sifting the air, eye sockets staring emptily into space. "It is from Supreme Director Jamrog."

Hladik sighed and lifted his deeply creased face. "Since Jamrog has become Supreme Director, I have not had one moment to myself. Well, what is it, Bremot?"

"The messenger did not say. You are to go to Threl High Chambers at once. Jamrog is waiting for you there."

Eyeing his bedmate hungrily, he said, "I must go, Moira, but wait for me and I will return soon." She yawned as he kissed her neck, then pulled a sheet over her body and went to sleep.

Hladik pulled off his hagerobe, donned a yos, and strode into the next room where Bremot stood waiting. "I hope Jamrog is brief this morning. I wish to return as soon as possible."

The blind guide led his master through Nilokerus Hage to a lift. They rode the tube down to Greengrass level and entered a guarded corridor where an em stood waiting. At the sight of their Director, the two Nilokerus snapped to attention. Hladik frowned, but passed by without a word, too much in a hurry and too preoccupied to offer the obligatory reprimand.

Under Bremot's precise control, the em sped along the empty corridor as it bent around and down, dipping below Kyan and coming up on the other side in Saecaraz Hage. The corridor had been constructed well before Sirin Rohee's time, and had served many Nilokerus Directors, providing a well-used shortcut to Threl High Chambers.

At one time Hladik had dreamed of becoming Supreme Director. But he feared Jamrog, and in that he showed wisdom. Jamrog's ambition was fiercer than his own; he knew Jamrog would ruthlessly remove any rivals to his claim. So, in those early years of Rohee's reign when the Directors were still vying for position and favor in his regime, Hladik had tipped his hand—a risk, certainly, but a very small risk—and let it be known that he considered himself successor material. Jamrog, still assembling his power base then, had been in no position to challenge him since Jamrog himself was a Subdirector and, technically, wielded an authority inferior to Hladik's.

This had forced Jamrog into the position of having to win Hladik over through gifts and favors. And Hladik allowed himself to be won, selling his ambition for the Supreme Director's kraam, but at a very fine price. He had never regretted his choice—except now, when Jamrog interrupted his intimate affairs for trifles.

Eventually Bremot brought the em to a stop and led them to another lift. They rode to the upper levels of Threl High Chambers. "Wait here," said Hladik as he stepped from the compartment. "This will not take long." Bremot nodded and remained in the lift.

"I suppose you don't know anything about this," Jamrog cried as he entered the Threl meeting room. No one else was in attendance, save Opinski, Jamrog's guide, standing quietly in a far corner of the room.

Hladik glanced at the flimsy yellow communique fluttering in Jamrog's hand and said, "Of course not, Supreme Director—seeing as how you have not yet shown it to me."

"Read!" Jamrog threw the sheet in Hladik's face.

Hladik took the transcript and read it. "Yes, I see."

"That's all you have to say? *I see?*" Jamrog fumed.

"I see, yes. I see no reason for you to be upset by this—" He snapped the sheet with a finger. "—this routine report."

"Your own guards caught someone in the Archives, and you call it routine."

"A Dhog, Supreme Director. What else?"

"A Dhog in the Archives. On the day before Rohee's funeral?"

"Coincidence. What else could it be?"

Hladik shrugged, outwardly trying to remain unconcerned. Inwardly he seethed. Why had those idiots allowed the Saecaraz to be contacted first? The communication should have been sent directly to him if Nilokerus guards were involved. Or perhaps Jamrog had intercepted it? "What do you suggest, Supreme Director? I fail to see—"

"You fail to see a great many things these days, Hageman," Jamrog barked, then dismissed Hladik's hurt expression with an impatient flick of his hand. "All right, I may be oversensitive just now, but it's only because I am concerned that nothing interfere with Rohee's funeral. Everything must take place precisely as I have planned. The people must witness a glorious spectacle. There must be no distraction."

"What could go wrong?"

Jamrog dropped into the Supreme Director's thronelike chair and passed a hand over his eyes. "I have not slept for two days, Hladik. I'm tired."

Hladik approached and sat down next to him. He waved Jamrog's guide away. Opinski withdrew discreetly. "Now, suppose you tell me what's really troubling you, Jamrog. I know there is some other reason you sent for me."

Jamrog stared upward and then closed his eyes. "I'm so tired."

"Rest then. Rest now so that you can enjoy your triumph tomorrow all the more."

"How can I rest when Tvrdy plots against me? He is out there even now, scheming with that Cabal of his to steal the bhuj from me—and I have not even been installed yet."

"That is but a tiresome formality—it gives the priests something to do. No one, not even the ridiculous Tvrdy, doubts that you are Supreme Director now. Besides, you have worn Tvrdy down. His power is gone; the Cabal you speak of is smashed. There is nothing left. He has no choice but to accept defeat gracefully if he would save his skin."

"You do not know Tvrdy at all if you believe I have won so easily. He will resist me to his last breath."

"Forget him. He's nothing."

"What if he is behind this incident in the Archives?"

"Well, what if he is? He will have discovered nothing. His agent was caught before he could make a report. There is nothing to worry about. If you wish, I will have the man brought to the tank and questioned and—" He hesitated.

"Yes? I'm listening. Go on."

"I was about to suggest having him conditioned after questioning and returned to his master. That way, if he is one of Tvrdy's men, we will have eyes and ears inside Tvrdy's network."

Jamrog's eyes narrowed with cunning. "Sometimes I underestimate your resourcefulness, Hladik. Yes, have the man conditioned and then allow him to escape."

Hladik forced a laugh. "Think of it! We will have an agent inside Tvrdy's network."

"Not an agent, Hladik," Jamrog said, his eyes narrowing to slits. "I want a weapon."

479

"It will be all right, Asquith, you'll see. You wanted to go to the concert and since I cannot go with you, I asked my friend to take you." Jaire was pulling a reluctant Pizzle along the upper gallery of Liamoge to the receiving hall. "She'll be here any moment."

"It won't be the same," complained Pizzle in his nasal whine. "I'd rather not go if I can't be with you."

"You'd miss a good concert—they're doing the *Naravell* tonight. You said you wanted to learn all about our ways, and I promised to introduce you to people who could teach you. My friend is much more knowledgeable about music than I am, and she'd be disappointed if she couldn't meet you."

"She would?" Pizzle asked suspiciously, not at all certain he wanted to meet anyone who wanted to meet him. That, in his experience, always betokened disaster at the hands of someone even less socially acceptable than he was.

They came to the wide, curving stairway and descended. "She's here!" said Jaire, giving Pizzle's arm a squeeze. They were only halfway down the stairs, and Pizzle didn't see anyone in the hall. Jaire propelled him down the stairs and out the doors to the curving drive outside. A sleek blue two-passenger evee was just pulling up to the entrance.

Pizzle saw only the single occupant sitting in the center of the passenger seat and purposefully turned his head away so that he didn't see her clearly. He heard the evee door open and, eyes on the ground now, saw two buff-booted feet come to stand in front of him. Jaire embraced her friend and they exchanged greetings, which Pizzle ignored.

Jaire said, "Asquith, I want you to meet my friend Starla."

Pizzle sighed and looked up. He'd heard of people claiming they'd been shot by Cupid's arrow. For him, it was as if he'd been impaled on the pudgy little love cherub's spear. He stared, transfixed by the vision before him: a young woman clothed all in white with buff-colored accents, her fine, platinum hair swept back by the light evening breeze, looking at him with pleasure and excitement mingled in her large, dark, oak-brown eyes. She was half-a-head shorter than he was and wore a silver bracelet on each wrist; her arms, bare in a sleeveless jacket, were tanned and smooth, as was her elegant, graceful neck.

An impartial observer might have said that her eyes were too big and perhaps too wide set, her chin too small and her nose a little thin. Certainly, her lower lip protruded when she was not smiling. But in Pizzle's eyes, she was, if possible, even more beautiful than Jaire—his fantasies made flesh.

"Starla," he said, repeating her name. And again, "Starla."

"I'm pleased to meet you—" She hesitated.

"Pizzy," he said, and embarrassed himself when he realized he'd just given her the least favorite of his many objectionable diminutives. "Just call me . . . Pizzy. Everyone does."

Starla laughed lightly. Pizzle reconciled himself to the name in that instant; it was worth all the years of misery and embarrassment if that name could evoke such a sound from one so lovely. "I'm pleased to meet you, Pizzy. Jaire told me you liked music . . ." She paused again because Pizzle was staring at her. Glancing at Jaire, who nodded toward the vehicle, she said, "Mmm, shall we go?"

Jaire took Pizzle by the arm and pushed him forward, saying, "Yes, you'd better hurry or you'll miss the best seats. I'm sure you'll both have a wonderful time." She took Starla's hand, placed it in Pizzle's, and bundled them both into the evee. Starla leaned forward and pressed their destination into the console; the car rolled silently away. Pizzle did not look back to see Jaire smiling in smug satisfaction.

• • • • • •

Stepping into the forest was like stepping into a cathedral. Enormous trees with smooth trunks stood like huge pillars, holding up a dense, blue-green layer of leaves, a vaulted roof a hundred meters above the forest floor. In fact, there were, Crocker noticed at once, two forests: the older, taller forest formed a towering leaf roof over a younger forest of slender trees and squat, fleshy shrubs all sewn together with innumerable vines and creepers. Around the massive smooth columns of

481

the supporting trees, braided pathways wound and converged and split, only to join and rejoin again.

The light filtering down from the leaf ceiling was bronze-green and soft, melting into the humid, water-drenched air. Vaporous wisps snaked along the forest byways, curling upward like tendrils of a growing plant to evaporate on unseen currents. And everywhere beneath the forest roof there was the rich, heady smell of damp, fecund soil and vegetation run riot—odors as palpable as the chitterings, clicks, and chirrups of the host of insects hidden in the foliage.

Higher in the leaf canopy, the shrill, chattering calls of birds and jarring whoops of mammalian tree dwellers—along with all sorts of murmurings, cooings, blarings, gruntings, yawpings, toatings, and gugglings—let Crocker know that the forest brimmed with unseen life, even as the heavy air reverberated with its raucous music.

The Blue Forest was a world unto itself, and Crocker felt secure here. As he walked further into its majestic fastness, the oppression of the open spaces fell away. He took the thick closeness of the forest and wrapped it around himself like a robe. He would be safe here among the creatures of the forest; he would become like them, and like them he would survive.

He struck along a path wide enough for the robot to follow and began moving deeper into the interior, the last glimpses of blue sky and green hills disappearing as the forest closed behind him. He walked along silently, moving with caution and stealth, adapting himself to the ways of the forest.

Like an animal, Crocker wandered the soft pathways, pausing now and again to sift the air for scent and sound of water. It had been exhausting work burrowing through the brushline to the forest, and he was thirsty. Eventually he came to a place where a small brook lapped around the gigantic roots of one of the forest pillars. He knelt down, cupped his hands, and drank.

The water was warm and had a distinctly earthy taste. He sipped and swallowed and spat the rest out. To get clean water he'd have to find a deeper source. Without thinking about it he moved off along the little brook, following it as it made its way over and around the roots of the giant trees and through stands of rushes with large lacy fan-shaped leaves. The brook took him deeper into the forest, deeper into the living green solitude.

At one point he pushed through a bristle-bladed hedge and found himself in a walled clearing. He looked up and saw the walls of the hedge rising above him for many meters. The clearing was carpeted with thick, bluish moss made up of tiny coiled filaments like wire springs. The sunlight striking through a thin place in the leaf canopy fell to the forest floor like heavy gold. In the center of the clearing lay a pool of deep blue-black water, filled from a spring which welled up from the center of the pool, splashing and sending ripples to the pool's outer rim.

The forest's discordant music, muted by the hedge walls, sounded far away. In the clearing, only the gentle plipping of the spring as it ruffled the water could be heard. Crocker stared at the water for a long moment and then began mechanically stripping off his clothes.

He lowered himself into the pool, feeling its chill refresh and revive him. He sank down into the ooze of the cool mud bottom and let the water close over his head, then kicked off and swam the length of the pool underwater, coming up for air when his head touched the far bank. It felt good to swim, to feel tight muscles relax as the knots loosened.

After a few minutes of swimming, Crocker felt wholly restored. He climbed out on the spongy bank and lay down in a patch of sunlight to dry off. The sun filtering down from the upper boughs warmed his skin, and he closed his eyes and went to sleep, his mind blank, unthinking, undreaming. He was part of the forest now—as much as any of her natural creatures. And, in his own way, just as wild.

SEVEN

Yarden watched as the dancers whirled and spun on the grassy field before her, their shimmering clothing reflecting the sun's last rays. Three men and three women, each tracing a complex interaction of movements with each of the others, danced for an audience of a hundred or more rapt spectators. Several musicians sitting around the ring of observers accompanied the dance on their instruments: long, hollow tubes, curved into polished semicircles. The flutelike instruments emitted low, rich, mellow tones, and though the musicians were scattered throughout the crowd, their music formed a single, seamless stage upon which the dancers performed.

Never had Yarden seen such exquisite movement, so lithe and free and—there was no other word for it—holy. The music and the dance were one and the same expression, so beautifully did they complement one another: sound giving impulse to movement, dance giving visual emphasis to the music, and each doing what the other could not do, thereby creating a total experience greater than the sum of the parts.

Yarden stood entranced. She'd seen dancers perform before, of course—some of the best in the world—but never with such abandon—almost as if they were creating their intricate movements spontaneously, yet in complete harmony with the others, for each dancer moved as an individual and as a member of a larger body at the same time. She knew they must have performed together for years to be able to create such intricate and harmonious movement.

This appreciation made the dance all the more wondrous to Yarden. She knew the cost of such perfection and loved the dancers for their extravagance. She watched with total concentration, savoring every fleeting, endless moment as the dancers spun and leapt and turned, coming together, forming patterns, breaking apart to create new patterns, until all the field and music and spectators coalesced into a single, creative awareness, joined by the movements of the dance.

When the dance finally ended—the dancers breathless and

exhausted, the music trailing off in whispers—the audience all exhaled as one, and Yarden realized that she, like all the others, had been holding her breath. She sighed, closed her eyes, and savored the moment, knowing that she had experienced true beauty and had been touched by it in a most intimate way.

She felt a nudge and opened her eyes. Ianni smiled at her and indicated the crowd, typical of Fieri gatherings, moving away silently. Yarden saw that the dancers, having gathered themselves together, were smiling at each other and talking together in low tones, their faces flushed with satisfaction and exhilaration. It seemed somehow wrong to Yarden that this performance should go unrewarded by the audience; there should be some recognition paid the dancers—applause, at least.

"I'll be right with you," she told Ianni. Turning to the dancers, she approached hesitantly. One of the women in the ensemble glanced up as Yarden came near. She smiled and held out her hands in the Fieri greeting, but Yarden stepped close and put her arms around the woman. They embraced and Yarden said, "Thank you for sharing your dance with me."

The woman pressed Yarden's hands and said, "It is our joy to dance. If you find pleasure in it, praise the Giver. He gives the dance."

"Your dance is praise itself," replied Yarden. "I will never forget what I've seen here today. Thank you." She then rejoined Ianni, who was waiting for her a little way off.

"Why did no one acknowledge the dancers?" asked Yarden as they walked back across the meadow toward the Arts Center, a palatial edifice made of rust-colored sunstone, with numerous wings and pavilions radiating from a common hub. "Or praise them for their artistry?"

"Praise belongs only to the Infinite," Ianni explained gently, as she had explained so often to Yarden since becoming her mentor. "Would you have us praise the vessel for its contents?"

"I don't know. It just seems that one ought to show some appreciation for the dancers, for their art, for the joy they bring in the dance."

"The joy of the dance was theirs."

"They shared it with us, then."

"And we paid them the highest tribute—we honored the beauty of the moment, and respected the serenity of the performance."

485

Yarden thought about this. "By leaving like that? Without a word, without a sound—just leaving? That was your tribute?"

Ianni, a tall, dark-haired woman, slender with long graceful limbs, folded her hands in front of her and stopped walking, turned to Yarden, and said, "We shared the moment together, and we took it to ourselves. We have hidden it in our hearts to treasure it always. What more can one do who has not created? It was not our place to judge, only to accept."

They walked again, feeling the warmth of the day and the pure rays of the sun on their faces. After a time Yarden nodded, saying, "I think I understand what you are saying: the artist practices her art for herself alone, but she performs as an expression of praise to the Infinite Father for the gift of her art—a gift she shares with her audience."

"Or with no audience at all."

"Yes, I see. The audience does not matter."

"Not to the performance, no. But if the audience is moved to praise the Infinite too, so much the better. Let praise increase! Of course, an artist is pleased when the audience is pleased. That is only natural. But, since she performs her art for herself and for the pleasure of the Infinite, the audience's response or lack of it is of no concern."

"The only concern is how well she has performed."

"Yes, whether she has used her gift to her best abilities. If she has, what does it matter whether she had an audience or not, or what the audience thought about the performance?"

Yarden understood, though she still thought anyone who could create such beauty as she had just witnessed ought to have more for their trouble than mute enjoyment, no matter how appreciative the crowd.

They continued on in silence until they reached the nearest of the outflung wings of the Arts Center. "Do you wish to return to the paintings?" asked Ianni. They had been viewing Fieri commemorative artwork in the gallery before their stroll of the grounds and their encounter with the dancers. Yarden looked up at the imposing entrance to the gallery and hesitated. "Or we could come back another time."

"You wouldn't mind?"

"Not at all." Ianni smiled. "One can only absorb so much."

"And I've absorbed all I can. Now I need time to think

about what I've seen." She took Ianni's hand and squeezed it. "Wasn't it beautiful though? I never imagined anything could be so perfect, so right, so expressive."

Ianni eyed her thoughtfully. "Perhaps you have an artist's heart, Yarden. Would you like to learn?"

Yarden shook her head sadly. "I could never dance like that."

"How do you know? Have you ever tried?"

"No, but—" Yarden's eyes grew wide with the possibility. "Do you think I should try?"

"Only if it appeals to you."

"Oh, it does. You have no idea how much!"

* * * * * *

The place where they brought Treet was an underground complex carved into Empyrion's bedrock, a cave with square-cut walls and passageways—the Cavern-level bastion of the Nilokerus. It was here that Hladik maintained the infamous reorientation cells: row upon row of stone cubicles, barely big enough for a person to stand upright or stretch out full length. Each cell had independent heat and light controls so that one cell could be floodlit and heated to a swelter, while the one next to it was plunged into total darkness and bone-chilling cold, depending on the whim of the reorientation engineer.

Treet was dragged roughly from the Archives vestibule, through an endless succession of corridors and galleries until he was handed over to the keepers of Cavern level. He had kept his mouth shut and answered none of his captors' questions, since it was clear from the beginning that they had already decided what to do with him and anything he said would make no difference.

From the conversation of the guards, he gathered they thought him a runaway—someone who had left his Hage to lose himself in Dome's underground mazeworks, hoping perhaps to make contact with the Dhogs. They presumed he had sneaked into the Archives when they themselves had entered. It did not occur to them that he had been in the Archives all along. Neither did it occur to them that he might be a Fieri spy.

For that he was grateful. At least they considered him no

487

more important than the typical runaway, which meant that he might be released sooner or later if he kept up his part of the charade.

"Your name?" asked the bored Nilokerus officer, glancing up from a green screen. He sat behind a large console and gazed at his prisoner with weary, watery eyes. The air in the caves was warm enough, but humid, and the stone was chill, making the atmosphere clammy and hard on the sinuses. "What is your name?"

Treet thought fast and said the first thing that popped into his head, "Stone." He tried to make his tone properly contrite, still hoping he could yet convince them it was some sort of mistake.

"What were you doing in the Archives?" the officer asked, punching keys into the terminal before him.

"I—ah . . ." Treet tried to come up with a plausible explanation. "I saw the doors open and I went in. I didn't know it was—what did you call it?—the Archives."

The intake officer looked up. "Were there no guards to stop you?"

"I suppose they didn't see me."

The guard gave a snort of contempt—whether for Treet's answer, or for the slackness of the guards on duty, Treet couldn't tell. "Hage?"

Treet said nothing. He was desperately thinking.

"Your Hage? Answer quickly."

"Bolbe." Treet blurted the name, and then gritted his teeth, hoping that he'd chosen a good cover.

The officer punched a few more keys. "No Stohn in Bolbe," he announced. "What is your Hagename?"

Mind whirling frantically, Treet searched his memory for a name that might serve him now—a name he had heard in passing that could be documented. "Bela," he said finally, with what he hoped was the right amount of resignation. Wasn't Bela the name Yarden had told him was the name of her Chryse keeper?

The officer shifted in his seat, tugging on his red-and-white yos as he punched in the name. "Yes," he murmured at length. "Here it is. Bela. You are a second-order ipumn grader."

Treet nodded and lowered his eyes.

"You will be returned to your Hage, Bolbe—"

Treet started to breathe a sigh of relief. His dodge had worked. Evidently, Bela was a common enough name.

The Nilokerus officer continued, "—after reorientation."

"No!" shouted Treet. The Nilokerus loafing in another corner of the room looked up sharply. "Please, I've never done anything like this before. I'll go back gladly. I'm sorry."

The officer gazed at Treet, hesitated. Would he let Treet go? With a shrug he said, "Standard directive punishment. No exceptions." He motioned to a nearby guard. "Take him to J-5V. Begin reorientation at once."

"No!" Treet screamed again. "Please! No!"

Two guards grabbed his arms and pulled him away; he was marched down one of the branching corridors and shoved into a cell. He heard the fizzling crackle of the barrier field as it snapped on, and he was left alone in the darkness of his cell.

EIGHT

Crocker came instantly awake, fully alert. His sleep had been deep and long, but a part of his awareness remained sharp, even in sleep, so that he awoke when he heard the faint rustling in the dry vegetation on the side of the pool opposite where he slept. He did not move, but merely opened his eyes to see a fat, furry creature the size of a small but well-fed pig ambling out of the brush.

The sounds of the forest were hushed now as the denizens of the day settled to their nests; the forest's nocturnal population had not yet begun to stir. Night came quickly to the world beneath the leaf-roof of the forest, and Crocker gazed out across the evening-dimmed circle of his bower at the intruder, his pilot's eyes keen in the failing light. He watched the animal pause in its slow shamble to the water, raise up on short hind legs to sniff the air, and peer into the murk with tiny round eyes. The thing had stubby legs that curved under its bulk and a long, fleshy tail that it carried straight up in the air. Its face was long and pointed, like a rat's elongated snout, but its eyes faced forward and its ears were the velvet exclamation points of a rabbit.

The animal appeared happy with its survey of the glade and continued down to the water's edge. Crocker eased himself up on palms and toes and made his way around the pool, maintaining careful silence on the cushiony moss. He came up behind the creature as it poked its long muzzle into the water and slurped noisily. Crocker eyed his prey for a moment—the creature was totally oblivious to any danger—and then, gathering himself for the spring, pounced on the animal, his hands quickly finding its short neck.

A terrified squawk bubbled from the creature's throat as it wriggled furiously. Crocker picked the animal up and shook it, squeezing the soft neck until the feeble fight went out of its body. The animal gave a convulsive quiver and died with a gasp.

He was standing by the water's edge, examining his catch,

when out of the brush behind him came a ball of bundled fury, charging right for him. He spun around, flinging the dead animal aside, just as his feet were swept from under him. He went down on his hip and squirmed to his knees as the burly ball of lightning attacked, long ears flattened to its back, sharp incisors bared.

Crocker saw enough in that second before the animal sprang to know that he was being challenged by the mother of the creature he had just killed—it was an exact replica of the first animal, but easily twice its size. He put his hands up and rolled backward as the animal leaped for him, catching it under the chin and pulling it over the top of him, his legs lifting its body up and over with the aid of its own momentum. The animal raked at him with its short, clawed feet and snapped at him with its long jaws as it went over, and then it was sailing through the air to land with a heavy thump on its back a few meters away.

The animal grunted and came up snapping, gathering itself for a second charge. Crocker did not wait, but leaped headlong at the animal. It twisted away, but Crocker landed on its back and his fingers found its neck and dug in. The creature yelped— a confused, mewing sound—and tried to roll over. But Crocker, adrenalin pounding through him, clamped his knees against its fat sides and kept his place on its back. The fleshy tail lashed his back ineffectually and the animal stumbled, grunting and squirming, digging its short claws into the moss and flinging patches skyward.

Sitting atop the thrashing beast, Crocker was overcome by a sudden rush of pure ecstasy and, with his hands buried in the creature's neck, choking the life from its body, he threw back his head and laughed. The sound rang in the glade, shivering the leafy hedge round about—a strange, strangled sound of tormented delight.

He laughed until his sides ached and then, as the unearthly echo died away, looked down to see that the animal beneath him struggled no more. Gradually he released his hold and got up. The creature lay still, unmoving. He looked at it for a long time and then knelt down beside it and put his hands on its body.

The fur was luxurious, thick and fine; the flesh beneath well-muscled, but soft. He stood abruptly and walked around the pool to the place where he'd entered, then stepped back through the hedgewall. There, patiently waiting for him on the other side, stood the robo-carrier. Since it could not force its way through the thick hedge, it had simply stopped on the trail to wait for its human controller to return.

Crocker retrieved the camp pack from its rack and then went back into the glade, opened the pack, and dumped out its contents. There was a utility knife among the articles in the pack, small and of no use as a real weapon, but Crocker took it up and went to the larger of the two animals he had killed.

Within a few minutes he had the rear haunch of the animal skinned and had cut away a large section of its liver; his hands were steeped in gore to the elbows. He sat back on his heels to look at his handiwork, the smell of blood heavy in the air. He raised the piece of liver to his mouth and licked it, tasting the thick sweetness, then hungrily devoured the still-warm portion. When he had finished this delicacy, he wiped his mouth with a blood-streaked arm and, taking up the knife again, began hacking at the meaty loin of the hapless creature.

When he had freed a good-sized piece of the haunch from the rest of the carcass, he sat back and, nostrils flaring with delight, began tearing off still-warm strands of meat and devouring them, smacking his lips and grunting his pleasure at this fine feast.

· · · · · ·

The concert had been over for hours, but Pizzle still sat with Starla in the soft night, gazing at the sky and talking in the empty amphidrome. The *Naravell,* a moving retelling of the long years of the Wandering and a monumental piece of music by any standard, went by Pizzle as if it had been a jingle for foot powder. He could concentrate on nothing but the entrancing creature beside him.

Starla had shown herself to be charming, fascinating, captivating, engaging, bewitching—all this, and she had not spoken more than a half-dozen complete sentences throughout the course of the evening. Mostly, she had listened raptly as Pizzle discoursed on whatever subject happened to pop into his head—everything from *Arabian Nights* to Zen. Her presence, like a heady wine imbibed too quickly, had not only loosened his tongue, but made everything he said seem to him wise and wonderful and sparkling with wit.

He spoke like one drunk on the sound of his own voice, but it wasn't his words that fascinated him—it was that *she* was there listening to him. He would talk just to have her listen, just so he could watch her listen—for he'd never experienced anything so marvelous in all his drab life. For indeed, his whole life did seem lackluster and inconsequential up to the moment of meeting Starla.

Pizzle paused for breath—his voice was going hoarse—and Starla laid a hand on his forearm and said, "Let's walk for a while."

They'd been sitting for hours, but Pizzle hadn't noticed. To him, the evening had been but a moment as it sped by. "Sure, sounds good," he said, getting to his feet. He looked around and saw that the amphidrome was dark and empty. "Cleared out fast, huh?"

Starla led him up the aisle and out of the amphidrome and along the broad boulevard planted with feathertrees—slender trees whose long, supple branches grew delicate blossoms like goose down. They walked along for a while in silence. Pizzle, having interrupted his monologue, could not now think of a single word to say. He was absolutely tongue-tied.

"Smell the air," sighed Starla. The feathertree blossoms sweetened the warm night air with their light fragrance.

"Mmm, nice," said Pizzle. He looked at his ravishing companion. If Starla by daylight was a vision, Starla by starlight was a dream. Her platinum hair shone like silver, and her eyes were liquid pools of darkness fringed by long, sweeping lashes. "You're nice, too," he said, and blanched. Without premeditation he'd just given her his first compliment. What a night!

"I must go soon," she said. They walked on a little further in silence. "We could go to another concert sometime . . . if you like—"

"Oh, I would," agreed Pizzle heartily. "Tomorrow night. Okay?"

Starla laughed. "I don't know if there is a concert tomorrow night."

"Then we'll go sailing. Anything. Please? Say yes. I'll come pick you up. Where do you live?"

"Very well," Starla agreed. "We will meet again tomorrow evening."

"What about tomorrow morning? As a matter of fact, I'm free all day tomorrow."

"But I work tomorrow."

"Where? What do you do? Tell me about it. I want to know about everything you do. I want to know all about you."

"Most often I serve the Clerk at the College of Mentors. There are twenty-four of us, and we help Mathiax administrate the Mentors' resolutions." She stopped and smiled at Pizzle. "But the day after tomorrow I am free."

"You are? Good! Let's spend the whole day together. Okay? Say yes."

"Yes." Starla laughed, a warm, throaty sound, full of good humor. "I'd like that very much." She paused, glanced down at her feet and then up into Pizzle's eyes. Growing serious, she said, "I know you are a Traveler, and that you come from another world. Jaire has told me much about you. I must seem very plain to you after all you've seen." Pizzle opened his mouth to tell her just how wrong she was, but she silenced him with a gesture and went on. "Forgive my presumption, but it's hard for me to think of you as someone so different. I think we are more alike than different. And though I don't know you very well, I like you very much, Asquith Pizzle. I would like to be your friend while you are here."

He looked at her, standing against the heaven-scented background of the feathertrees, and swallowed a lump in his throat the size of a melon. "No one has ever said anything like that to me," he said. "I'm going to stay here forever."

NINE

Cejka, Director of Rumon Hage, took up his ceremonial bhuj, turned the flat blade so that its polished surface faced the correct quadrant, thrust out his chin, and squared his shoulders. Though his days as a member of the Threl elite might well be numbered, he would appear among his own people as their worthy leader: imperious, unafraid, powerful. Opposites, to be sure, of how he really felt. Covol, his Subdirector, arranged the hood of his black-and-red striped yos, nodded once, and stepped away. Cejka began walking slowly, a phalanx of Hage officers and functionaries behind him, leading his delegation through Rumon to the docks where they would board one of the official funeral boats that would take them to Saecaraz, where Sirin Rohee's funeral was to be held.

As they moved through Hage, he thought again about his message from Tvrdy. Though the Cabal had suffered crushing defeats of late, it was no small tribute to his own skill and cunning that his network of rumor messengers was still virtually intact. For this he was thankful.

The meeting with the Dhog, Giloon Bogney, had been, in Tvrdy's estimation, a success. They had gained the nonbeing's promises of support—though at a very high price, it seemed to Cejka. Hage stent for the Old Section? Such a thing was inconceivable even bare weeks ago. No doubt Tvrdy had only done what he'd been forced to do.

Ah, Tvrdy, my friend, thought Cejka gloomily. What is to become of us? Jamrog will not let us live, I think. Already I feel his hands on my throat. I hope you know what you are doing. An alliance with Dhogs! Unthinkable!

Be that as it may, Cejka now had to select the men who would go to the Old Section to begin training the Dhogs in the ways of covert combat. That, too, rubbed Cejka the wrong way—teaching Rumon secrets to nonbeings. But Tvrdy had insisted. There could be no holding back now. Jamrog had gained the Supreme Directorship, and the only way to survive a Purge was with an army at your back—even if it had to be an army of Dhogs. It was to Tvrdy's credit, Cejka reminded himself, that he'd not only considered turning to the Dhogs; the ever-resourceful Tanais leader had actually joined forces with them. This was something Jamrog could never have foreseen.

The Rumon entourage, purposefully a large one so Jamrog would have no cause to accuse Cejka of being unsympathetic, passed slowly through the streets and byways of the Hage, followed by other Rumon Hagemen making their own way to Saecaraz to see the funeral spectacle. A delegation of Rumon priests, chanting loudly and raising a din with their cymbals and horns, took up a position in front of the official party and led the way to the dockyard.

The entire waterfront area was crammed with boats and people waiting to jam into boats. There was an air of festivity and high spirits among the populace. After all, it was a special day—no work in the Hages and free food for all in attendance at the funeral. It promised to be a tremendous spectacle, and no one wanted to be left out; all who could were making their way to Saecaraz.

"There is the funeral boat," said Covol, pointing out the red-draped decks and gangway of the large tridecker. Cejka led his entourage to the gangway and boarded the boat, which was to pull away from the dock as soon as the last official squeezed aboard.

Cejka made his way to the topmost deck and took his place at the forward end, his guide on one hand and his Subdirector on the other. There arose a commotion from below, and when he asked what was taking place Cejka was told, "Some Hagemen have attempted to board, but they are not of the official party. There will be a slight delay while they are put off."

"Oh, let them come along," replied Cejka impatiently. "If there is room, let them all aboard. It will only make our number appear larger, which cannot hurt. No delays! We must arrive at the scheduled time."

The Hagemen were allowed aboard, the gangway was pulled in, and the boat drew slowly away from the wharf, backing carefully through the small, congested harborage of Rumon, the scene ringing with voices of pilots and passengers as all made for the river beyond.

Kyan's gray and turgid waters were choked with watercraft of every size and description. Anyone in charge of a vessel of any size was ferrying Hagemen to the funeral. There were tiny two-seat paddleboats, large triple-deckers, Hage pleasure barges, and a host of the solid, double-decked cargo boats, all crowded with people making their way to Saecaraz for the big day—and every last one flying a red funeral banner.

The festival atmosphere was inescapable. A Supreme Director's funeral was a rare event in the first place, and Jamrog had appropriated huge sums to be spent in making Rohee's funeral the most lavish of any in living memory. Cejka distrusted this, though Jamrog's motive escaped him.

"I would have thought Jamrog content with a private cremation," Cejka whispered to Covol as he scanned the enormous flotilla stretching out both ways along the river. "Why, a man could walk across Kyan without getting his feet wet! Look at them out there. We'll be lucky if half the population of Empyrion isn't drowned today."

"Perhaps Jamrog seeks to gain more than the approval of the populace with this tactic," replied Covol, a small man powerfully built and possessing a quick mind. He would one day make a good Director.

"Say what you think, Covol," directed Cejka. "There are none among us in Jamrog's keep." It was true. Cejka had rigorously maintained the purity of his own ranks for years; he knew there were no traitors in his top echelon.

"By making much of Rohee's death, he will gain favor with those whose loyalty is easily won."

"Of course."

"But he will also create the illusion of being greater than Sirin Rohee himself. Only a divine can pay homage to another divine, so the priests say."

"I see," said Cejka thoughtfully. "He will be seen not only as Rohee's successor, but as greater and more powerful than Rohee ever was—and all because he makes a greater show of Rohee's death than Rohee himself would have. Yes, I see."

"For the price of a day's food and drink, the populace will see him as Cynetics incarnate."

Cejka sighed heavily. "I am afraid you are right. And we—we support the illusion by seeing to it that our whole Hage turns out to glorify dead Rohee—a man who was barely worth his night soil all his life long."

"It is strange."

"More than strange, Covol. We will see a frightening thing today. We will see a man make himself a god. There will be no stopping him now."

"Yet, he must be stopped," said Covol, wanting to believe that it was possible. "We will find a way."

Cejka looked at him sadly and then turned his eyes back to the river, saying, "Kyan will run red with the blood of our Hagemen before Jamrog will be stopped. Enjoy the funeral today, Covol. It is our own."

• • • • • •

"An artist must be pure of heart," said Gerdes, "for true art is the expression of the artist's innermost being. To create beauty, one must *be* beautiful"—she pressed her hands to her bosom—"in here, in your heart of hearts."

Yarden listened intently. They were meeting in Gerdes' home which was, like most Fieri homes, an exercise in studied simplicity: spacious and comfortable, open to the sun and air. The room in which they sat facing one another across a low table of polished wood opened onto a meticulously tended garden. Fine paintings hung on the walls, delicate, expressive, gentle shadings of light and color, giving the room warmth for all its airiness.

Ianni, as promised, had brought Yarden to meet Gerdes, and once the conversation had begun, excused herself so the two could talk alone. Gerdes did most of the talking, and Yarden thrilled to be in the older woman's presence, because Gerdes, teacher of dance, was unlike anyone Yarden had ever met, and certainly unlike anyone she would have imagined as a dancer: thickset and short-limbed, with short, grizzled, gray hair and a ruddy face, small rosebud lips that turned down at the edges in a frown of motherly disapproval, frank hazel eyes that fairly sparkled with enthusiasm and intelligence. Her manner was gruff, but her tone patient and caring.

But it was not her appearance or her manner that Yarden found so fascinating—it was the extraordinary things she said. Yarden had never heard such words, such ideas. Gerdes talked about art, about creating beauty, and the way she spoke was beautiful too. Yarden glimpsed possibilities of expression she had never known existed; whole worlds of wonder opened up to her as the woman spoke. She saw herself poised for a plunge into a shimmering sea of promise. How she would emerge, she could not say, but she would be changed and the change would be wonderful.

"I understand," said Yarden softly.

Gerdes looked at her closely. "Do you? Do you really understand? It is not easy to be pure. It is hard work. The hardest. The discipline required of an artist is enormous. Many people—most, it seems—simply do not have such discipline, such single-mindedness of purpose and patience. It takes years to develop a craft; years of painstaking, difficult work. The discipline is beyond all but the most dedicated."

"What about talent?" asked Yarden. "Doesn't that count for something?"

"Oh yes, talent is good. Talent is commendable, for it makes the discipline easier to endure, and the dedication comes more naturally. But talent alone isn't the answer. Talent is raw; it is a beast, wild and untamed. Talent must be mastered; it must be trained so that it can be used with wisdom and purpose. It must be pruned like a tree so it will bear only the best fruit." Gerdes paused to shake her head slowly as she paced before Yarden. "No, talent without discipline is only an empty promise—the glitter of an unworked crystal. It is nothing of itself."

Gerdes returned to her chair opposite Yarden. She sat down and leaned back, placing her hands on the arms of the chair. The older woman studied Yarden for a moment, searching her eyes. Yarden gazed back hopefully, confidently, knowing herself to be in the presence of a wise and powerful teacher. "Tell me, daughter," Gerdes said at last, "why have you come to me?"

Now that they had finally come to the reason for Yarden's visit, Yarden found her voice had dried up. She forced the words out: "I want to dance. That is, I want to learn to be a dancer."

Gerdes peered at her and nodded absently. "Stand, please. Walk for me." She made a back-and-forth motion in the air with her hand.

Yarden stood and walked slowly, passing before Gerdes once, twice, and then again, conscious of the woman's sharp appraisal. "Yes," said Gerdes, "that's enough. You may sit."

Yarden returned to her seat. "Will you teach me?"

Gerdes nodded slowly, keeping her eyes on Yarden's face. "I'll teach you—but not to dance."

Yarden's smile disappeared instantly. "I don't understand. Why not, may I ask?"

Gerdes leaned forward, reaching out a hand to touch Yarden's knee. "You move well. There is grace and ease in your step. No doubt you have great natural abilities—talent, yes. But, daughter, you are too *old*."

This pronouncement shocked Yarden. She'd never been told she was too old for anything in her life. Why, she had at least a hundred and fifty good, productive years left, probably many more than that. How could she be too old? "Are you sure?" asked Yarden.

"I know what you are thinking," replied Gerdes. "Ianni has told me that your lifespan is not like ours. You will live long, many times longer than will I. In this you are like the Ancients of our own people. This is what you are thinking, yes?"

Yarden nodded silently.

"Of course. But the dancers that you saw yesterday, that filled you with such longing to dance, have been working at their craft since they were small children. Their bodies have been adapted to the dance, formed by it; their minds think in terms of movement and rhythm. Everything they think and do is dance."

"You don't think I could learn?" asked Yarden, disappointment making her petulant.

Gerdes simply shook her head. "No," she said, and then quickly explained. "Oh, you could learn the steps, the movement. You could dance, probably very well, I imagine. But never well enough to suit yourself, or the Fieri standards of excellence either, for that matter. If you danced, you would always be reminded just how inferior your craft remained. You would see children dance with greater skill and proficiency than you would ever achieve, and you would envy them.

"In time, your envy would turn bitter—you would hate yourself for not being better than you can ever be. This hate would destroy your craft and art. It would destroy your heart, your soul. In the end it would destroy *you*. Rather than being a blessing, dance would become a curse."

Yarden was amazed by what she heard. Never had anyone

spoken like this to her. "But—you said you would teach me," she replied, shaking her head in confusion.

Gerdes patted her knee and then leaned back once more, smiling. "Yes, I'll teach you. But not to dance. I'll teach you to paint."

"To paint?" The idea had never occurred to her.

Gerdes laughed. "You would be surprised to learn how close the two are to one another. There is much movement and rhythm in painting—it is dance of another kind, and more. I will teach you to paint, if you are willing."

Yarden blinked back, bewildered. "I don't know what to say."

"No one can decide for you. But I will tell you this: you have the heart of an artist; you are sensitive, you feel things very deeply in your soul. You long to create beauty and to share it. These things are good and necessary.

"What is more, painting is an art that requires a special kind of intelligence. I sense in you that intelligence—wise, intuitive, loving. This is important. If you lacked it, there would be no way to learn it, and neither I nor anyone else could give it to you." Gerdes gazed levelly at Yarden. "But think about it. When you have decided, come to me. I will be here."

Their meeting at an end, Yarden stood slowly and took Gerdes' hand. "Thank you for talking to me. I'll need some time to think about all you've said."

"There is no hurry, daughter. Come back when you have chosen."

Yarden nodded and thanked her host again, then left, stepping out into the sunlit day. She walked along the wide, tree-lined boulevard back to Ianni's house. Ianni lived some distance away, and the walk gave Yarden a chance to think about all she and Gerdes had discussed. By the time she reached home, she had made up her mind. Please, she thought, let me be an artist.

"Did you enjoy your talk?" asked Ianni as Yarden entered, glancing up from her work of cutting vegetables for a meal.

"It was—" she began, and then changed the subject. "Ianni, you *knew* that I could never be a dancer, didn't you? That's why you took me to Gerdes. You knew what she would tell me."

Ianni ducked her head to hide a smile and began putting

the sliced vegetables in bowls. "I suspected, yes. But you were so full of the wonder of the dance, I could not spoil it for you. What you felt was good and true, and I did not want to discourage you in any way. I knew Gerdes would know how to tell you. Hers is a wise spirit." She raised her head slightly. "You're not angry with me?"

"No, not angry. You were right. I am glad to have met Gerdes. And—" She hesitated, finding the title a little presumptuous, but then plunged in anyway. "I'm going to be an artist. A painter. More than anything, that's what I want to do."

TEN

Treet stared into the utter blackness of his cold rock cell. Huddled in a corner, he sat with his knees drawn up against his chest and waited for the reorientation to begin, knowing that it would be, could not be anything other than, disagreeable in the extreme.

He'd read about prisoners in one of Earth's senseless wars being forced to undergo what they called *brainwashing*—a cruel form of mental abuse designed to destroy a person's will, among other things. Some prisoners of war, though, came through the experience with their faculties intact. These men were mentally tough to begin with, but they also used a few basic survival tactics to counteract the brainwashing. They recognized that the pointless cruelty practiced upon them had no rational basis other than to wear down their mental defenses; all the meaningless tasks and contradictory orders and physical harassment and verbal abuse was an attempt to weaken the inner man and break the mind.

Just recognizing this went a long way toward defusing its effectiveness. Once a prisoner knew what he was up against, he could take steps to counteract it. The survivors, forced to give up control of the major aspects of their lives, learned to regain control in other, subtler ways, thereby retaining a degree of independence and a sense of personal freedom. Maintaining this control, however limited, was the key: a determined man with even a tiny amount of personal autonomy could not be broken. He might be killed, but not broken. And almost to a person, the survivors Treet had read about had vowed they would die before giving in.

The general idea of survival was to beat the enemy at their own game, to control them while they were controlling you. When taken for interrogation and ordered to sit down, the prisoner went to the chair and moved it slightly so that he sat, at least symbolically, where he chose; when captors came to his cell, he invited them in and directed them to places on his mat, subtly showing that he controlled the terms of the visit; when dragged from his cell at dawn and ordered to dig his own grave, the survivor determined where to dig, thereby exerting control in the choosing of his own plot; and when at noon he was ordered to refill the grave, he planted a seed or a clump of grass so that his work would have symbolic value, rather than, as intended, remain just another meaningless exercise meant to unhinge him.

Treet steeled himself with these thoughts and planned strategies to meet whatever barrages they threw at him. His overall plan was to make an outward show of resistance early on in the game and then give the appearance of having succumbed to the reorientation so that when he was released he would still have his head in one piece. He didn't know if he could pull it off, but it was his only chance—as long as they didn't use drugs. Against drugs—like the amnesiant they'd used on him the first time—there was little he could do.

He sat in his cell for hours—perhaps much longer, he couldn't tell—waiting for something to happen. When something finally did happen, it surprised him with its mildness: lights hidden in the rock ceiling came on, shining dimly, and with them a sound like that of an ocean washing over a pebbled shore. Nothing more.

Not too bad, thought Treet. I can handle this. He closed his eyes and went to sleep.

Some time later he was awakened by a pinging sound, like a small hammer tapping a scrap of steel plate at regular intervals. This pinging sound had been added to the ocean sound, and he noticed, too, that the lights were brighter. Clearly, they meant to hammer at him with sound and light for a while—in the manner of cooking a live frog: toss the frog into a pot of cold water and then gradually bring up the heat until the pot boils; the frog will never know what's happening until it's too late to hop away.

"This frog is wise to their tricks," Treet told himself, and unzipped the front of his singleton and began worrying an inner pocket, which he eventually succeeded in tearing off. He took the pocket and tore it in half, rolled up the halves, and stuck one in each ear. His improvised earplugs worked quite well and he curled up and went to sleep once more. Better to sleep now while he could, and conserve his strength. There was no telling what might come later.

When Treet awoke, the sound had stopped and the lights

were dim again. On the floor of the cell before the unidor lay a tray with a bowl and a jar. The bowl contained boiled beans—tough little legumes that tasted like leatherbound cardboard pellets; the jar contained water, tepid but fresh. He drank the water and tossed down a handful of beans before remembering that the food and water could well be drugged. He sniffed the bowl and tasted another bean, but could detect nothing out of the ordinary. He replaced the bowl. Hungry though he was, he did not want to risk drugging himself so early in the game.

The sound came on once more, louder this time. The ocean rolled, and the hammer pinged more insistently. Treet could see how that sound could get on a person's nerves after a while. He replaced his earplugs and closed his eyes, grateful for the escape of sleep.

A sharp, stinging pain on the side of his head brought Treet out of his slumber. His eyes flew open to see a Nilokerus guard standing over him with a stiff rod. "Get up," said the guard. Treet moved to get up, quickly removing his homemade earplugs and stuffing them in his pocket. The guard didn't appear to notice; he turned on his heel and walked out. Treet followed him, not knowing whether to feel apprehensive or hopeful. Were they releasing him, or getting down to business at last?

The guard led him through the cell block back to the central admitting area where he had come in. A different guard sat at the console, and this one looked particularly put out about something. Without preamble, he told Treet what was upsetting him. "I'm missing the funeral because of you," he growled.

"There's been a mistake," offered Treet—as if he'd gladly clear up the misunderstanding so the guard could toddle off to the funeral. "I think it can be worked out."

"Oh, it has been worked out," said the administrator, reaching out to tap a few keys into the console. "You are to be made an example of." He glanced at the Nilokerus standing behind Treet, slapping the rod against his hand. "Take him to the conditioning tank."

"No, wait! You're making a mistake. Let me go. I won't cause you any trouble. Please!"

The guard prodded him with the end of the rod, pushing him away from the console. The administrator glared at him and said, "Director Hladik has ordered this himself. Perhaps you'd care to discuss it with him?" He laughed as if he'd made the

505

perfect joke, and Treet was steered down another of the rock-cut corridors radiating from the central room like the arms of an octopus.

The conditioning tank was an enormous transparent six-sided aquarium filled with green fluid. It looked like a jumbo nutrient bath; however, Treet strongly doubted its designers had any such benevolent purpose in mind. Several harnesses of webbing and electrical wire dangled from a gridwork suspended above the tank. There was no one in the tank at present, and only one other person in the hexagonal room—a rather stout toad of a man with a mashed-in, wrinkled face. Hair stuck out of his red-striped yos at the neckline, and his hands looked as if he wore fur gloves. He grunted when Treet and his guard entered the room.

"Here's one for you, Skank," said the guard with the rod, shoving Treet forward. "Take good care of him. Hladik wants him undamaged."

The one called Skank grunted again and shuffled over to Treet, appraising him with his eyes as if he were being asked to bid on a piece of spoiled merchandise. "Undamaged," snorted Skank, prodding Treet with hairy fingers. Treet was aware of a sour smell, like stale sweat or urine or both, and something else. Saltwater? He looked at the giant aquarium; there appeared to be algae growing in the water—which explained its charming green color, no doubt.

Treet stood passively and allowed himself to be poked. Skank turned him around and pounded him on the back, looked into his mouth, and felt him under the armpits. The guard watched this inspection idly and then turned to leave. "Where do you think you're going?" hollered Skank. "Get back here and help me put him in the soak."

The guard huffed and rolled his eyes, but did not speak. Very likely, he knew any protest would be lost on Skank, who was now grumbling and shuffling off to a small pedestal where he flicked a few switches. There came a grinding sound, and the metal grid began descending from the ceiling. "Take off your clothes," said Skank, returning with a large brown ball of waxy substance in his hands.

Treet undressed slowly, saying, "You're all making a big mistake."

"Save your breath," grunted Skank, grabbing the nearest harness as it came down. "You're headed for the tank."

The guard lifted Treet's arms and held them out at shoulder level while Skank fastened a band around Treet's chest and passed two straps between his legs. Next, webbing was wrapped around his torso and snugged down. His hands were bound loosely to his side; he could move his arms in shallow arcs, but could not touch his face or any other part of his body. The electrical wires, each with a flat electrode on the end, were attached to his skin at various points: over his heart, on his throat below his right jaw, on each temple and cheek, at the base of his spine, on his abdomen.

Treet submitted to this strange indignity, trying to appear far more calm and unconcerned than he felt. His stomach fluttered, but that might just have been emptiness; and his palms sweated, but it was quite humid in the room. He knew his act of aplomb was unconvincing when, as Skank's back was turned, the guard leaned close and whispered, "Don't fight it. Just relax. It will go easier for you if you don't resist."

Skank turned back, and Treet saw that he had fashioned a sort of mask out of the waxy ball. The mask had a mouth plug into which Skank inserted another electrode, and two protruding mounds where Treet's ears would be. The keeper of the tank glanced at Treet's face and made some small adjustments on the wax mask in his hands. Lifting the mask, he pressed it onto Treet's face with both hands. "Trabant take you! Open your mouth!"

Treet opened his mouth, and the wax plug slid in like a tongue. The mask was pressed tight to his face, sealing ears and eyes and mouth. A panicky moment came when the mask closed off his nostrils and he couldn't breathe. "Hold your breath," said the guard; Treet heard his voice muted by the wax plugs in his ears. "It won't last."

At almost the same instant, Treet felt himself lifted off the floor in his harness, dangling like a doll on a rope. Still holding his breath, he began to worry about what was to happen next. Surely they didn't mean to drown him—what purpose would that serve? Yet, there had been no provision made for getting air to him underwater.

These thoughts ricocheted around in his brain as he felt his toes touch the water. He drew back in shock, but forced himself to relax and, as he dropped lower, swirled the water, making swimming motions with his feet. The water closed over him . . . now to his thighs . . . and now his hips . . . his waist . . . chest . . . neck . . .

The water was neither warm nor cold, but exactly skin temperature. Within moments of entering the tank, he could no longer feel whether he was wet or dry. In fact, he couldn't feel anything at all. He moved his hands, but could not even tell he moved them. The liquid was like water, but heavier, bulkier, more elastic. It did not register on his skin at all.

Sensory deprivation, Treet knew, used such heavier-than-water fluids to cut off sensation to the brain. He also knew such techniques were highly effective, that if left very long in isolation the subject could expect aural and visual hallucinations, as well as a host of mental experiences bordering on the psychotic. Insanity was an almost guaranteed side effect for anyone left too long in a deprivation chamber. At least with brainwashing he knew what to expect and had a survival plan. If anyone had ever found a way to beat a SD tank, Treet had yet to hear about it.

A more immediate concern, however, was the fact that he could not breathe. He knew he could hold his breath for six minutes. Six minutes was a good long time . . . but it was not forever.

ELEVEN

Threl Square in Saecaraz was draped in red: red banners hung from wires across the square, red streamers hung from every tree, red bunting wrapped the imposing columns of the Threl Chambers entrance. Everywhere one looked was red, the color of death and mourning. Tvrdy slipped through the standing crowds already thronging the square and moved toward the section designated for Tanais dignitaries. His Subdirector would already be there, along with as many other Tanais of stent that could be crammed into the numbered space.

Moving among the populace of Empyrion, he gauged the mood as one of restrained festivity—subdued now because of the nature of the ceremony about to be enacted. But later all restraint would give way to revelry, dead leader or no. Tvrdy knew that Jamrog had foreseen this—knew what effect this sort of celebration would produce. The masses were too easily won by simple pomp, and once won, too easily led.

It was the great irony of leadership, he thought, that in order to be a good leader, one had to give everything to a people unworthy of the sacrifice. He sighed; perhaps it was always so.

He pressed his way through the quickly coagulating crowds, and eventually arrived at the designated section to squeeze in among his Hagemen. Subdirector Danelka snapped to attention and handed the bhuj to his superior, whispering, "I was beginning to think you would miss the ceremony."

"So did I. But today of all days I suspect Jamrog's surveillance to be lax. There would never be a better chance of reaching them." To Danelka's unspoken question, Tvrdy said, "Yes, it went well. We are allies as of this morning."

Danelka grimaced and replied, "I know I should be pleased, Director, but . . ."

"Don't worry. I do not expect anyone to relish our arrangement, although it might be helpful if we learned to mask our true feelings for the Dhogs. Revulsion and resentment cannot help our cause. Besides, I think we will come to value them greatly."

Danelka shook his head doubtfully, but said nothing more.

"Did anyone suspect I was missing?" Tvrdy pulled his hood closer and turned the bhuj in his hands to display the Tanais face.

"I don't see how," answered his Subdirector. "I carried the bhuj and remained hooded the whole trip. The boatmen paid no attention to our boarding, and the Saecaraz who met us at the square's entrance merely inquired about the number, but did not count us themselves."

Tvrdy grinned suddenly. "Jamrog's laxity will be his undoing yet. He does not have the stamina to rule as he should. He is sloppy, Danelka. Sloppy and lazy."

"And dangerous," added Danelka.

Just then a blattering of horns sounded. When the blast died away, and with it the commotion of the vast crowd, a single large drum could be heard emanating from within the Threl Chambers. The booming drumbeat grew louder, and a Saecaraz Hage priest appeared between the pillars at the entrance, an enormous drum preceding him. The drum was affixed to long poles which were carried by four underpriests.

Behind the drum-beating priest came a whole regiment of Hage priests, each with a silver horn shaped like a crescent. As soon as these reached the steps below the pillars, they raised the horns to their lips and blew the long, low ringing note that had commenced the ceremony. Saecaraz Hagemen followed the priests: Jamrog came first, walking alone, wearing a red mourning cloak over his black-and-silver yos; he was followed by row on row of assorted Hage functionaries.

In the midst of the ranks of Saecaraz came Rohee's bier, borne up on the shoulders of his Hagemen. The red-shrouded coffin seemed to float above the heads of the crowd, making its slow, circuitous way around the square, pausing before each official Hage delegation to allow the Hage Leaders to pay their official respects—which they did by tossing black and silver paper streamers, symbolically representing Sirin Rohee's long life, over the pale, ashen gray body.

When the bier stopped before Tanais, Tvrdy flung his streamer over the body too, surreptitiously tearing a short length off one end—privately stating his suspicion that Rohee's life was cut short. No one else saw the gesture, and the severed length of streamer fell to the stone flagging unobserved.

The procession moved on, and when the last Hage had paid its respects, the priests began the funeral chant, calling on Great Trabant to ease Rohee's passage through the Two Houses, Ekante and Shikroth, and to send sympathetic Seraphic Spheres to guide him. They asked the Oversouls to remember Rohee's long life and account his deeds with greatness. On and on the chanting went while the bier circled again and again. Finally, after nearly two hours, the chanting stopped and the casket was placed in the center of the square.

"What's this?" Tvrdy nudged Danelka. A ramp was being pushed through the crowd to the bier; at the end of the ramp was a red-draped platform. The ramp stopped with the platform directly above the bier. Jamrog appeared at one end of the ramp and moved slowly up to take his place on the platform. The assembly, restless after the long ranting of the priests, fell silent once more as, stone-faced and regal, Jamrog ascended.

"I heard nothing about anything like this," whispered Danelka. "Most unusual."

Jamrog raised his hands for silence, although the throng was already hushed and every eye was on him. He stared out at the great crowd, assuring himself of their utmost attention. He drew the moment out, opened his mouth to speak, but did not, then slowly lowered his hands to indicate poor dead Rohee beneath him. He raised his face, and a cry of grief came from him: "Rohee-e-e!"

A thrill tingled through the vast audience. What was the new Supreme Director doing? Why was the body not being consigned to the flames?

"Ro-hee-e-e-e!" came the cry again. Silence followed as Jamrog looked about dolefully. A full minute elapsed as the Director gazed with sorrowful eyes across the sea of faces. When the tension reached its peak, he said in a loud voice, "Our leader is fallen! He is dead! Dead!" The word was a shout, followed by a softer echo. "Dead."

Jamrog drew a deep breath and began to speak more softly, so the crowds had to strain forward to hear him. "Our beloved leader of so many years has fallen to the sleep of death, and will never rise again. Farewell, Sirin Rohee. Your people salute you and mourn your passing." Gazing intently at the body, Jamrog raised a hand in farewell. The gesture was simple and touching.

"I almost believe he means it," whispered Danelka.

"Shh!" replied Tvrdy. "I want to hear what the liar says."

Jamrog continued: "Look, my people, look long on the body of your dead leader. Remember him always. Remember him in noble death. Remember him . . ." He spread his hands wide over the body. "Look and remember."

"Remember how he raped the Hages!" said Danelka under his breath. Tvrdy gave him a threatening glance, as Jamrog went on to recite a long catalog of Rohee's benevolent achievements, most of which, it seemed to Tvrdy, centered on the old cut-throat not maiming an opponent worse than he might have, and not crushing the people with any more impossible regulations than they could absolutely bear.

"Sirin Rohee was a man born to greatness, and that greatness will not be diminished in death," Jamrog went on. "I will not allow his body to be consumed by flames or corruption. Even though he is dead, I will see to it that he remains with us: his body will be embalmed in crystal and laid in Threl Chambers, where a special mausoleum will be prepared. Then, you, his beloved people, will come to look upon him and honor his memory. He will be with us always!"

Jamrog had so drawn his listeners along, carefully building the drama and emotion of his words, that no sooner had his last words been uttered than the amassed mourners loosed a tremendous, bone-shaking cheer. The great shout echoed through the empty streets of Empyrion, ascending to the dome's crystalline shell far above.

The crowd surged forward and seized the platform on which Jamrog stood, tearing it away from the ramp. The severed platform—with Jamrog standing placidly in the center of it, hands outstretched—was lifted high and borne through the square to ringing shouts of acclaim.

As Tanais Hagemen of lower stent streamed past him to join the melee, Tvrdy turned away from the spectacle. Danelka caught up with him as he stomped from the square. "So that's his trick," muttered Tvrdy. "I should have guessed. He has given them a show they will never forget. Already he is greater than Rohee ever was—and far more deadly."

Subdirector Danelka asked, "What do you want me to do?"

"Stay with the delegation. I'm going back to my kraam.

512

Come to me later and tell me what has happened." He looked at Danelka wearily. "I'm tired . . . tired." With that he slipped away through the clamorous crowd and disappeared.

· · · · · ·

Talus and Mathiax strolled the path through the long grove of fan trees behind the Clerk of the College of Mentors' shoreside home. The air of Fierra was soft and warm, as always, and lightly scented with the fan tree's aromatic resin. An edge of gray cloud worked the upper atmosphere, drawing a light overcast across the great shining face of Prindahl from the North, giving the midday sun the appearance of white gold.

"It's going to rain," observed Mathiax to himself.

"Too early," Talus grunted absently, and the two walked on.

At length they stopped and faced one another. "We have been negligent," said Mathiax. "There is no denying it. We should not have let him go without first making some provision for communication."

"What could we do? The Preceptor's ban—"

Mathiax dismissed the thought with a quick shake of his head. "I'm not suggesting we should have gone with him—only that we should have found some way to allow him to reach us in need."

Talus frowned and rubbed his curly beard with the back of a broad hand. "The woman—Yarden—she told us she was a sympath. She could reach him."

"She won't." At Talus' sharp glance, Mathiax answered, "I already tried. I asked Ianni to bring the subject up when Bohm returned."

"And?"

"Ianni tried, but she refused to discuss it. It appears the two quarreled, and now she will have nothing to do with him."

"Something between lovers?"

Mathiax nodded. "Ianni says Yarden warned him not to return to Dome, and since he insisted on going she severed their relationship."

"I wish I had known that. Still, she may change her mind."

"Yarden is a strong person. Hers is a most formidable will and not easily influenced. We could grow old waiting for her to change her mind in this matter."

"I don't know what else to tell you, Mathiax. We did all we could do for him without violating the Preceptor's ban. As it is, we came very close."

"We believed he was right," pointed out Mathiax sternly.

"Of course. But even so, we must follow the Infinite Father's leading. War is an abhorrence to him. The Fieri will never lift a hand against—"

With an impatient wave of his hand Mathiax turned and began walking again. "You are right to remind me of our most holy precept. But I am uneasy, Talus. I tell you the truth: I cannot rest, thinking about Orion Treet. I think of him and feel a deep foreboding. It is a rare sensation with me, and one I do not like."

"What can we do? It is out of our hands, Mathiax. He is in the Sustainer's care now."

Mathiax nodded solemnly. "Yes. Yes, of course. But my foreboding may also be of divine origin, Talus."

Just then a large, glistening drop of water fell on the path between them, splattering heavily and sending up a little puff of dust. Talus looked up and saw that the cloud cover had thickened as lower-lying rainclouds had formed beneath the high leading edge. Another drop landed close to the first, and the sound of still other drops could be heard as they fell among the leaves of grass and trees close by.

Talus looked at the dark damp spots on the ground and then back at his friend: "I do not dismiss what you say, Mathiax." He indicated the heavy drops falling all around them now. "After all, you were right about the rain."

TWELVE

The rain fell in slanting sheets upon the roof of the Blue Forest, striking the natural thatch of closely interwoven leaves to trickle slowly down to the smaller trees and plants of the forest floor far below. Crocker heard the rain as a subdued roar overhead, and felt the heavy, moisture-laden air cool as the water seeped down from above, drip by drip. The forest—so loud with its exuberance of life only moments before the rain—now lay still, deserted as its creatures sought shelter from the damp.

Crocker, naked except for a broad waistband torn from his tattered jumpsuit and wrapped around his middle to form a pouch in which to carry the utility knife and a few other small articles he required, huddled under a low, spreading tree whose broad, waxy leaves shed the drops that were now coming more quickly as the forest canopy became saturated. He looked placidly around him, alert but unconcerned. His senses were becoming attuned to the forest's living awareness, that invisible web of consciousness formed by the combined mental activity of all forest dwellers.

He could now detect subtle pulses of communication humming through the webwork, but could not as yet dicipher them. Still, knowing that all around him the forest continually spoke to itself gave him a secure feeling. He belonged here and in time would learn to speak the language of the web, and then would become one with all the other creatures.

The rain percolated down to the forest floor, soaking into the thick, dark soil. Trails became trickling runnels, bubbling over root and vine, carrying water away to hidden pools and larger streams. The smell of rain-damp earth and foliage filled the air as vaporous wisps rose like ghostly snakes to writhe and disappear on unseen currents. Crocker had settled back in his little shelter and was listening to the tick and dribble of the rain when suddenly an earsplitting scream shivered the air.

The shattering cry sounded like the fighting scream of an enraged cat—only the cat that had made this sound must have been the size of an elephant. This fearful cry was followed by an answering call—a booming bellow, like that of a buffalo four stories tall—a sound that actually shook the earth where Crocker sat.

The next thing the human heard was the sharp crack of splintering trees and the groan of bushes uprooted as the two mighty beasts closed on one another. There were tremendous thrashings and crashings, and he could hear branches being stripped from trees. The ground shook under the pummeling of the animals' huge feet.

Cringing back deeper into the shadows of his rain shelter, Crocker listened, his heart pounding wildly. He was helpless should one of those prodigious creatures come for him—or even if, in turning to flee the scene of battle, it should run over him. And from the nearness of the sounds, he guessed the clash to be taking place just beyond the curtain of vine hanging from the lower branches of the pillarlike trees directly in front of him.

It was over in seconds, and the last cries echoing through the forest shook the rain from the leaves of Crocker's bush. Straining into the silence that followed the brutal encounter, Crocker listened and at last heard ponderous footsteps moving away slowly, bulling through the underbrush. This he imagined was the buffalo creature. Of the cat, he could not detect a sound.

Very likely, the buffalo-thing had killed the cat-creature and now lumbered off to lick its wounds, which were certain to be grievous. The cat-creature surely lay dead or dying, its lifeblood pouring out through its mangled body.

After a time, the rain ceased, though the drip, drip, drip of the leaves would continue for a long time as water filtered down from above. Only when Crocker was certain he could hear nothing at all of either of the animals did he creep from hiding. Crouching, he crawled out, senses keen and wary, muscles tense, ready to flee. He pushed silently through the undergrowth, passing between the twin columns of two forest giants, ducking beneath the shroud of vines. He expected to find the blood-soaked battlefield before him, but instead saw only more underbrush and more trees. A trail led through the tangle, so Crocker took it and began walking—warily, lest he meet up with a wounded creature out of its mind with pain.

He walked far longer than he estimated he would have to

before he came to the scene of the titanic battle. It was a clearing in the forest where a stream flattened and formed a shallow pool hemmed in by trees and thick brush. He stood and looked long and hard, scouring every inch of the clearing for movement, before stepping into it.

There was no dead cat-creature in the clearing, and no wounded buffalo-thing gasping out its last breath, either. But all around were signs of the monumental conflict: branches stripped from trees three meters off the ground, bushes squashed and flattened out of shape or uprooted altogether, smaller trees toppled and larger trees broken like twigs, the earth ripped into open furrows, mud from the pool bottom splattered over everything, depressions sunk ankle-deep in the forest floor.

The creatures that wreaked the destruction, he saw, must be the very lords of the Blue Forest. He stood alone looking at the gaping holes in the earth, the roots dangling in the air, the broken tree limbs strewn over the battlefield, and felt his bowels squirm inside him. There were creatures abroad in this world that dwarfed anything he could imagine. This realization made him feel small and vulnerable.

A weapon! He mouthed the word to himself and understood its meaning. He would find a suitable weapon, and then he would be safe. Other creatures would fear, but he would not.

He turned at once and began walking back to his hidden pool. Tomorrow he would begin searching for his weapon. And then . . . and then he would hunt down one of the great creatures and prove himself a forest lord.

· · · · · ·

It had been three minutes, Treet estimated, since he had entered the tank. He still dangled from the harness, but could no longer feel it. In fact, he could not feel anything: all sensory stimulation had ceased. He could will his arms and legs and hands to move, but whether they moved as directed, he couldn't tell. It felt as if he no longer had a body at all, that he was a mind adrift, cut off from all physical attributes—except hunger, which still gnawed at him, more insistently now than ever.

Approaching four minutes, Treet began to worry. Surely

517

they would pull him up soon. What good would it do to drown him? And if that's what they intended, why go to all the trouble to truss him up like a turkey? Nothing made sense. But, rational or not, he would have to breathe soon. His lungs were beginning to ache.

Come on, pull me up! thought Treet desperately. Pull me up!

He fought down the impulse to swim for the surface. Thrashing around in the water would use up air too fast, and he could not be certain of swimming in the right direction—he might just as easily swim to the bottom of the tank as the top. It was best just to remain calm and wait. *Wait.*

Treet put his mind to work, concentrating on his keeper, holding the man's squat image on his mental screen, willing him to punch the button that would bring the harness up.

Push the button! Treet screamed mentally, putting every atom of his will behind it. Push the button—NOW!

The ache had become a burning, searing flame. His lungs felt as if they would burst.

Ordinarily he would expel some of the air, and this would allow him to stay submerged a little longer. But with the wax mask plastered on his face, and the wax plug between his teeth, he could not exhale. The pressure in his lungs increased.

He reached out with his mind and attempted to touch the mind of his keeper. Push the button! he screamed with his brain. Push it, damn you!

His lungs at the point of rupture, Treet knew that his captors had no intention of bringing him up. They intended letting him die. With this thought came a desperate plan: blow the mask off! Perhaps the force of his breath could tear the wax mask from his face; then he could see the surface and swim for it.

With this thought came the decision to do it—the two were simultaneous. He had nothing to lose.

The exhausted air burst from his mouth with as much force as he could put behind it. The result astonished him: the stream of air bubbles passed right through the mask! It was as if it wasn't there at all. His ears remained stoppered and the plug remained in his mouth, so the mask was still in place.

Panic seized him and wrung him. I can't breathe! I'll suffocate!

He thrashed his head from side to side in an effort to dislodge the mask, but could not tell if he were actually thrashing at all, or only imagining his thrashings. His lungs convulsed in agony.

Air! I must have air!

The vacuum in his lungs became too great. He could not hold back any longer. He had to inhale, even though the mask stayed on. His mind presented him with a picture of himself trying to suck air through a plastic bag, suffocating, the plastic molded to his features, cutting off his life.

A split second later moist air was streaming into his lungs.

Treet had been so busy fighting it that when the involuntary impulse to draw air took over, he did not even notice. The quick inrush of air shocked and confused him—maybe it was water. Maybe this was what it was like to drown.

But no. He drew oxygen deep into his lungs and expelled it experimentally. The air seemed thicker, heavier than ordinary air, and damp—as if he were breathing through a wet sponge—but not at all like water. No, he was not drowning—at least he didn't think so. Somehow, he was breathing, and for that he was thankful.

He took a few slow, calming breaths. Obviously, the mask was some sort of oxygen-permeable membrane that allowed an air breather to breathe underwater. It held, still tightly plastered to his face, but from what he could feel of the plug in his mouth, the wax substance had changed consistency: it was soft and glutinous, molding to his features like dough.

Slowly Treet relaxed, his speeding heartbeat calmed, muscles unknotted and slackened. Whatever else happened to him in the tank, at least he wouldn't drown. That was a small comfort.

He drew oxygen through the membrane and tried to think about how he would survive the ordeal before him. His own mind was his greatest enemy in this struggle. Without the stimulation of data from his sense organs, his brain would begin to manufacture its own data in the form of hallucinations. He would begin to hear sounds and see images; he'd feel and smell things that were not there.

And as much as he would tell himself the hallucinations weren't real, there would come a time when he wouldn't be able to tell illusions from reality. Then the terror would start. He would experience the horror of his own nightmares, and he would not be able to stop them. His brain, like a runaway computer caught in an endless program loop, would run on and on and on. Cut off from his physical sensations, his brain would, like a prisoner too long deprived of sunlight and food, begin devouring itself in the darkness.

In the end he'd be nothing but a mindless shell of a man, demented, blithering. Unless . . . unless Hladik had other ideas. He had not considered that before, but considered it now. Of course, they had a purpose for him. He would be no use to them insane; therefore, his conditioning would likely stop short of that.

The question was, could he hold out?

Grimly, as Treet assessed his predicament, the thought came to him that, one way or another, he would find out.

THIRTEEN

Pizzle watched the rain sweep in undulating curtains across the flat, beaten-iron face of Prindahl. The fresh sea scent filled his nostrils, and he sighed contentedly, thinking about Starla and their long, dreamy evening. Never had he met a more engaging woman: warm, responsive, caring, a joy to behold and to be with.

The wind off the lake stirred the curtains of his room, and he turned away from the vista of rain-swept water to go in search of Jaire. He found her, auburn hair upswept and tied in a gold ribbon, lighting candles in the smaller dining room; the long table was already set.

"Can I help?" he asked.

"Thank you, Asquith. Yes, if you like. Over there you'll find goblets. Fill them from the pitcher, please."

He went to a tray on the sideboard and took up the crystal pitcher, carefully pouring the contents into the goblets on the round tray and wondering how to pose the question he was itching to ask.

"Did you enjoy the concert last night?" Jaire asked, favoring him with a bright smile.

Pizzle, trying not to reveal too much about his current emotional state, steadied his hand and replied in a matter-of-fact tone, "It was all right. Nice."

Jaire blew out the long wick with which she was lighting the tapers. "I'm glad you liked it. Did you find Starla an amiable companion?"

At the mention of her name, Pizzle gulped; a muscle in his eyelid twitched. He cleared his throat. "Oh, fine, I guess."

"She was *nice,* too?"

"Yeah, she's a nice lady, I—" He forgot what he was going to say next.

Jaire stood looking at him. If he hadn't been so flustered, he would have noticed the amused expression on her face and the knowing sparkle in her gold-flecked eyes. "I'll be sure to tell her that," replied Jaire, laughing.

Pizzle colored; his ears became crimson flags. "Does it—ah, show so much as all that?" he asked.

Jaire came to him and took his hand. She led him into the next room and to a cushioned chair where they sat down together. "You were out all night—it was nearly dawn when you came back."

"You waited up for me?"

"No, I was at the hospital, remember? I returned home only moments before you. I heard you come in."

"Uhh, hmmm. I see." Pizzle's features scrunched into a frown. "Did I violate some kind of a social taboo?"

Jaire blinked back at him. "A what?"

"You know, etiquette. Good manners, ethics, propriety—that sort of thing."

"Not that I am aware of. Did you?"

He almost leapt from his seat. "I—we, that is, didn't do anything improper, if that's what you mean."

"It *was* very late."

Pizzle nodded morosely. "Look, Jaire, I'm new here. I don't know what's proper and what isn't for courting a Fieri." He realized what he had just said and blanched.

"Courting?" Jaire tilted her head and peered at him, humor twitching at the corners of her lips. "That is a word I have never heard."

"It means . . . well, when two people, a man and a woman, like each other, see . . . well, they court. I mean the man courts the woman—he sees her."

"Sees her?"

"You know, they spend time together . . ."

"Ah, yes. I see what you mean."

"Well, what do you call it?"

"We call it pairing."

"Oh."

Pizzle looked so confused that Jaire laughed and put a hand on his arm. "Is that what you were doing?"

"I don't know. It wasn't like that—I mean, I didn't plan to stay out all night. It just happened."

"You do find Starla attractive?" It was more a statement of obvious fact than a question.

He nodded. "More attractive than anyone I've ever met. I

only—" He stopped, swallowing hard, and went on. "I only hope she likes me, too."

"Maybe you can ask her tonight."

"Ask her?" Pizzle glanced up sharply, his expression equal parts hope and terror. "Tonight?"

"Talus and Dania are away this evening, and Preben is dining with friends. I thought you might enjoy meeting some others. I've asked some of my friends to join us, Starla among them."

Now Pizzle did jump up. "I've got to get ready. What time is she coming?"

"They will begin arriving within the hour. You have time to—"

"Barely." He cut her off as he dashed away. She watched him fly back to his room on the upper story of the great house, smiled, and went back to her preparations.

• • • • • •

The Dhogs had gathered to celebrate the passing of Supreme Director Sirin Rohee. From throughout the Old Section they had come, each of the sixteen families represented in force. Giloon Bogney sat on a three-legged stool with his bhuj in his hand, the very picture of the revered tribal chief accepting the homage of his people. In fact, the gifts were donations of food and beverage that each family brought with them to provision the celebration.

Giloon smiled and nodded, rising now and then to embrace an especially worthy family head, exchanging jokes about the Surpreme Director's demise while the mound of foodstuffs and libation grew. From the look of the pile, there would be a fine feast tonight, and enough brew to produce a pleasant brain-numbing buzz for one and all.

Some of the Dhogs brought with them livestock—bakis (a variety of plump scavenger fowl) and prudos (the porcine equivalent of an ambulatory fertilizer factory). Dhog livestock had been bred for the ability to turn almost any organic substance into nourishment. The beasts, like their human masters, could survive on dry husks and chaff, and thrive on a meal of rinds and scraps. Both the bakis and the more substantial prudos would be butchered and roasted on spits around the bonfire to be lit at dusk.

As soon as they had heard that Rohee was dead, the Dhogs had begun collecting combustibles and had a large heap of flammable material amassed in the center of the dilapidated New America Square in the heart of the derelict section of Dome.

The Old Section had been, a little over three thousand years before, the site of the original Cynetics colony ship's landing. It was over New America Square that the first temporary dome had been erected on sterilized ground, and there the first Earthmen touched alien soil. But that was long, long ago—so long ago the current inhabitants could not even imagine that their crumbling ruin of a home had not always existed.

The Old Section had had a succession of names: Empyrion Base, Colony Administration, Plague Central, Fieri Ghetto, Dome Project Headquarters. As each name implied, the uses for the sprawling section, with its structures in ranks radiating from the central square, had been varied. Now it might have been called, simply, Sanctuary, for that was its current function—providing a home for Dome's nonbeings, the unfortunates who had, through one transgression or another, forfeited both Hage and stent, whose poak had been erased and their names expunged from the Hage priest's official rolls.

A Hageman who suddenly found himself without Hage or poak had only two choices: suicide or the Old Section. Most chose to join the Dhogs, accepting an existence—it could scarcely be called a life—of continual want amidst almost unimaginable squalor. To be a Dhog, the lowest of the low, was to be a nonentity, neither alive nor dead, but somewhere between the two, waiting for either to happen.

It was impossible to reach the Old Section from the Hages unless one knew the secret entrances and exits maintained by the Dhogs. Since no one did know—not even guides whose psi entities stubbornly refused to cooperate where the Old Section was concerned—new nonbeings were forced to wait until the Dhogs made one of their infrequent visits to the Hage refuse pits. The wretch who managed to convince the Dhogs to take him in was assigned to one of the sixteen families which were responsible for caring for their own members. The families worked to raise livestock and make any articles the family needed for survival.

Raw materials were scavenged from the Hage refuse pits—always a chancy enterprise since any Dhog caught in Hage was subject to the harshest abuse: torture always, and often death. So hated were they among the Hages that Dhogs risked life and limb simply by setting foot in Hage; hence they tended to move about only at night, and then only in twos and threes.

Though the refuse pits were their primary targets on their scavenging forays, anything not nailed down or too big to carry off was fair game for a Dhog: tools, vessels of various types, unattended cargo—these were the most highly sought rewards for a night's work. The Dhogs were careful never to take too much, or make their theft blatant, for they feared retaliation—against which they would be virtually defenseless. Even more, they feared making the Hages wary and overcautious, preferring a little carelessness on the part of their providers. If a tool that had been forgotten and left out disappeared, that was one thing. But if an entire tool bin were ransacked, that would force tighter security and stricter policing of all Hage goods, and that was one additional hardship the Dhogs definitely did not care to precipitate.

Therefore, their thefts were always judicious and cunning. Though it hurt terribly sometimes, they would leave a great haul untouched—a stack of ipumn bales left overnight on the wharf, or Hyrgo grain sacks waiting outside the granary—making off with just a single item so suspicion would not fall to them.

Giloon Bogney ruled his people with a genius composed equally of shrewdness and common sense, keeping order and dispensing rough justice, holding the reins of power with a firm, if filthy hand. Cleanliness was not a Dhog attribute. Water was to drink, not to wash in. The water teams had a hard enough time keeping up with their families' needs without worrying about providing wash water. People washed only when the opportunity presented itself, which was seldom.

When the last of the family heads had been formally greeted by their leader, Giloon signaled for the foodstuffs to be taken away and readied on tables provided for the purpose. Moments later, the squawks and squalls of the prudos and bakis rose above the festive commotion. A cry went up from the throng, numbering close to fifteen thousand by Giloon's estimation, for

525

nearly every Dhog who could walk, hobble, or crawl had come: "The fire! The fire! Light the fire!"

Giloon cast an eye toward the dome far above; the last light of day glimmered weakly on the sectioned panes. He shrugged and called for the fire team to bring a brand. A runner was dispatched at once and returned moments later, threading his way through the crowds, firebrand lifted high.

The flaming torch was presented to Giloon, who, with exaggerated pomp and ceremony, took it and moved to the center of the square and the large mound of combustibles there. The Dhogs parted and formed an immense ring around the pile, their dark eyes and grimy faces keen in the torchlight.

Giloon raised the torch in his pudgy hand and said in a loud, ironic voice: "The Big Man be dead!"

"Better him than us!" shouted someone from the crowd, and everyone laughed.

"And it's being no too soon!" Giloon continued. "We knowing he liking the Afterworld—he sending so many of our people there always."

"He maybe gets a Dhog welcome," added the voice from the crowd.

"And maybe gets a Dhog Oversoul to lead him," shouted another wag. More laughter came as Giloon lowered the torch to the pile. The bundled rags used for kindling leapt to the flame, and the bonfire blazed. Freshly butchered carcasses were brought forth on spits by the dozen and set all around the perimeter of the blaze as closely as possible. Soon the aroma of roasting meat mingled with the varied scent of the burning rubbish.

Games and music began—both rude and uncouth to a more civilized observer, but spirited nonetheless. Tall, standing torches were lit throughout the square, and lines began forming at the beverage and food tables. Every face wore a carefree expression, for tonight of all nights there would be plenty to eat and drink for everyone, young and old alike.

Giloon, with his personal entourage, strolled the square, talking to his people, sharing their merriment, and receiving mock condolences as well as genuine toasts to his own health and longevity. As a leader, Giloon was appreciated and honored by the Dhogs, who admired his legendary shrewdness.

His feats of stealth and guile were remembered and told as

exemplars to the young. Like the time he had diverted a whole shipment of rice from Hyrgo Hage to the refuse pits simply by switching destination tags. The rice was sitting on the Hyrgo docks awaiting transportation to Saecaraz. He had scoured the Saecaraz refuse pits for the tags and then affixed them to the grain sacks. It had taken all night, but he had only to collect the sacks from Saecaraz the next night. The reward for that one exploit was over a thousand kils of rice, and everlasting glory.

When he finished making his rounds, the Dhog leader retired to a platform that had been set up overlooking the square. There, in the company of his closest friends, he entertained the heads of the Dhog families and watched over the festivities. It was a wild revelry: raucous, gluttonous, riotous.

The celebration lasted far into the night with dancing, singing, eating, and drinking until not a single Dhog was left standing. Children and older adults huddled in impromptu heaps; young people paired off and crept away for more intimate sleeping arrangements. The bonfire dwindled and died as dawn tinted the smudgy carapace of Dome overhead. Sirin Rohee was dead, and the Dhogs had celebrated. It would be the last celebration for many of them.

FOURTEEN

"It was grotesque," said Cejka, grimacing in distaste. "I have never seen anything so . . . so *bestial* in all my life. Not even at Trabantonna! Whole Hages swarming in drunken madness! Seven Jamuna were killed when Chryse torch dancers accidently set a draped pylon afire and the crowd surged away; three were trampled and four crushed against a rimwall. And theirs won't be the only bodies found tomorrow, I fear. Rohee's funeral is a death orgy! You were wise to leave when you did, Tvrdy. I am still shaking from it." The Rumon Director held out his hand to show how it trembled.

"At least it's over," replied Tvrdy, pouring out two glasses of souile and handing one to his friend. "A drink will calm you."

"But it's *not* over, as you well know." Cejka took up his glass, saluted Tvrdy, and took a sip. He sat back with a sigh. "This is quality souile, Director," he observed. "In memory of Sirin Rohee?"

Tvrdy gave Cejka a dark look. "Sorry, a bad joke," Cejka admitted, taking another sip.

"We drink not to Rohee's memory, but to our own," said Tvrdy. "And because I mean to deplete my stock. Once the Purge has begun, all will be confiscated, no doubt. I, for one, would rather see it poured into the cesspit than allow even one bottle to fall into Jamrog's hands."

Cejka looked stricken. "Don't talk so! Even if you are joking—and I think you are not—it produces bad ether. We must not even think of a Purge."

"You said it yourself just now: it's not over yet. In fact, today was only a beginning. The funeral was a signal to any keen enough to see it. Jamrog means to eliminate all opposition to his total authority."

"As he did away with Rohee? He can't do it. The Threl will not allow it. If he moves against even one of us, the rest will—"

"Will what?" Tvrdy snapped. "Stand by and watch him do it? Yes. Don't lie to me, Cejka, and most of all don't lie to yourself. Even if we all opposed him—which would never happen—he'd disband the Threl. If we sought to overthrow him, he'd have us executed as traitors. Jamrog will make himself answerable to no one."

Cejka stared into his drink. "Your words are harsh, but true. You speak my fears and I do not like it, but I know you are right."

"We are dead men, Cejka. We have no hope." Tvrdy's tone caused Cejka to look up sharply. He'd never heard the Tanais Director so depressed.

"No hope? This is souile talking, not my old friend."

"It is reality! Jamrog was more powerful from the start than we ever suspected. He hid it well. We put too much trust in Rohee's ability to guard his own selfish interests, and not enough in Jamrog's ability to use those interests for his own ends."

"You overestimate him and underestimate yourself," pointed out Cejka.

"He *murdered* Rohee, by Trabant! And no one has breathed a word against him. Wake up, Cejka. We have lost."

Cejka rose stiffly, drawing himself up full height. "I will not stay here and listen to you rave, Tvrdy. You are no coward. Why do you talk so?" Tvrdy made a weak gesture, but Cejka continued. "We have been through too much together for me to believe you mean what you say. Go to sleep, Tvrdy. It has been a long day. Tomorrow will look different to you."

"Yes," replied Tvrdy morosely, "tomorrow will look different. It will look worse!" He shook his head sadly. "Sit down, Cejka. At least let us enjoy this fine souile like good friends. It may be the last time we drink together."

"I think I should go," said Cejka quietly. "You need rest. You are exhausted. You must sleep."

"We'll have plenty of time to sleep, Cejka—once we've joined Rohee."

Cejka turned away and strode toward the lift tube on the opposite side of the room. "Good night, Tvrdy. I will talk to you again when you are sensible." With that, he left.

Tvrdy poured the last of the souile into his glass and drank deeply, then got up and walked to his balcony to watch a pink dawn tint the planes of Dome's crystal shell. He tilted his head back and drained the glass, held it for a moment, and then hurled it from the balcony. "That's one treasure you won't get, Supreme Director Jamrog," he said and went to find his bed.

• • • • • •

Yarden was up at first light, excited to begin her new life as an artist. Since her talk with Gerdes, it was all she could think about. She imagined all the wonderful paintings and drawings she would create—whole rooms full of beauty. She would dedicate herself heart and soul to art, and would pursue it with everything in her. She would learn all Gerdes could teach her and study the great Fieri masters; she would develop the talent she had been given and, in time, become a master herself.

Yarden dressed in a sand-colored chinti, which was what the Fieri called the suit of blouse and loose, knee-length trousers they all wore. She pulled on soft boots a shade or two darker and crept quietly down the stairs to the kitchen on the first level of the small house. There she set about making breakfast.

When Ianni joined her a little while later, the sun was up and bright in the trees in the garden just off the open kitchen. Fieri architecture revered open spaces, so that their homes always had at least one entire wall exposed to the outdoors—usually overlooking some restful scene: a garden, the lakeshore, a park. Ianni's kitchen was arranged so she and her guests could eat in the garden when the weather permitted. Given Empyrion's paradisiacal climate, this was nearly every day of the year.

"Good morning," said Yarden cheerfully as Ianni entered the room. "I thought we'd have fruit this morning. I've already set our places outside."

Ianni gave her a look of approval and said, "Now I know you feel at home here. This is the first day you have fixed breakfast."

"Have I been an inconsiderate guest? Believe me, Ianni, I didn't mean to be. Really, I never thought—"

The Fieri woman shushed her. "I didn't say that for you to chide yourself. I am happy to serve you. But when you start serving me, you are no longer a guest. You are family."

Yarden smiled at the compliment. "Thank you, Ianni. You have done so much for me, I'll never be able to repay you."

"It is not to be repaid. What I did for you, I did for the Infinite."

"I understand," said Yarden. "But I still want to express my gratitude for all you've shown me and taught me. And most of all, for introducing me to Gerdes."

"Were you not even a little disappointed when she said you would never be a dancer?" asked Ianni as Yarden handed her a plate of fruit. They walked out into the garden to the table and chairs surrounded by shrubs flowing with cascades of scarlet flowers. Little fuzzy insects, like tiny balls of lint, toiled in the blossoms, spreading fragrant pollen from flower to flower.

"Disappointed? Maybe I was, but only for an instant. Gerdes told me the truth and I accepted it," Yarden explained as they began to eat. "She also gave me hope that I could become an artist of a different kind. And since she had told me the truth about my dancing, I could trust her about painting."

Ianni nodded, chewing thoughtfully. "You are anxious to begin, I know, but I wonder if you might consider delaying your study for a time?"

"Delay it? Why?"

"It's just an idea," Ianni said as she speared another piece of sweet, succulent ameang, a pulpy tree-grown fruit with tender white flesh. "I thought perhaps you might like to come with us to the Bay of Talking Fish."

Yarden laughed at the name. "Talking fish? Are you serious?"

"The name comes from before the Burning, so I suppose it does sound strange to you."

"Strange yes, but more fanciful—whimsical, I should say. I'm fascinated; tell me about it."

Ianni put down her fork and began telling Yarden about the wonderful creatures of the bay. "In the Far North country, in the region of the Light Mountains, there is a great ocean inlet that forms a bay—a body of water much bigger than Prindahl."

"The fish live there?" asked Yarden, her eyes dancing, picturing this magical place.

"No, the fish live far out in the deep ocean. But once every seven years they return to birth their young in the gentle waters of the bay." Ianni paused, remembering with a look of quiet rapture on her face. Presently she came to herself and continued, "It's a long trip; we travel by river through the mountains, and it takes several weeks."

"It must be quite an experience—the way you speak of it."

"The Preceptor could tell you better than I—I don't have the words. But yes, it's utterly exalting. We go, as many as can make the jouney, and arrive at the bay a few days before the fish arrive. We wait for them. Then they come. You can see their tail fins riding high in the water as they enter the bay. They know we will be waiting for them, and they begin to leap and play." Ianni's eyes lit up as she told about the fish. "It's the most beautiful sight: thousands of blue fins shining in the silver water as they come. The leaders bring the school right into the shallows, and we wade out to greet them."

"Do they actually talk?" Yarden had some idea that the noise the fish made sounded like talking. Ianni's answer surprised her.

"Not the way you mean. They talk yes, but not with words—it's more the way you do, when you choose to. We talk to them in our minds and hearts."

"Really!" Yarden looked at her host in wonder. "The fish communicate sympathically?"

"It's very similar, I believe. Mathiax could tell you more about it."

"Unbelievable!" The more she heard, the more fanciful Ianni's story seemed. "But, you—that is, the Fieri don't use mind-speech ordinarily. You have not developed it among yourselves."

"True," admitted Ianni, "but with the fish, it's different. We can speak to them, and they speak to us. Oh, it's wonderful, Yarden! I want you to come with us."

"I will! I want to very much—if it's as you say, I wouldn't want to miss it. When do you leave?"

"Very soon. Preparations are already being made."

Yarden's sympathic awareness caught Ianni's sense of awe and excitement; she definitely wanted to go, yet felt slightly disappointed in delaying her study. "But what will I tell Gerdes? I had planned to begin studying today."

"Gerdes will understand, I'm sure. She'll urge you to go. You can begin your studies when you return."

FIFTEEN

In the darkness of the blackest night he'd ever known, Treet felt the cold, wet kisses of snowflakes alighting and melting on his skin. The wind howled miserably, sending the flakes swirling over him. He felt their fleeting stings as they found him, spinning out of the vast, hollow emptiness to caress him and vanish.

Then the darkness began to pulse, convulsing in rhythmic shudders as cataclysmic tremors pounded through the black emptiness. Gradually the darkness changed, fading to deep red, as if a terrible sunrise trembled on some lost horizon. And the snow changed, too, becoming tiny biting insects—midges that swarmed and stung the skin where they touched. In an instant, Treet's hide was covered with minute swelling bumps. He cried out—not so much in pain, as in torment. The insects continued to swarm, and he was powerless to stop them.

The deep red grew brighter and the ponderous convulsions more regular and pronounced. Pounding, pounding, pounding, each pulse reverberated in his brain. Treet's insides quivered with every tremor as the vacuum grew brighter still, turning blood crimson. The insects changed in turn. They were insects no longer, but oblong cells floating in slow motion all around him, surging and subsiding with every booming thump of the drumming pulse.

Treet knew then where he was. Somehow he had become trapped inside his own heart!

The resounding tremor was his heart beating with laborious regularity; the tiny cells swimming around him were his own blood cells and platelets, surging with the tide of his blood through the chambers of his heart. And he was caught there with no idea of how to get out. He would drown in his own blood.

Instantly, as if reacting to this morbid thought, the heartbeat quickened, lurching rapidly and wildly. The blood fluids tugged erratically at him, pulling him first this way and then another. The cells and platelets assailed him, driven on by the wash of blood through his heart. Now he could see the walls of his heart constricting. The organ was shrinking with every beat!

Treet watched in horror as the fleshy walls of muscle closed around him. He opened his mouth wide and screamed.

The heart squeezed down, harder and harder, clamping him in a death grip. His heart beat faster now, grasping him tighter and tighter. He would be crushed to death by his own body. The insanity of it made his brain squirm. He screamed again for it to stop.

The heart stopped beating.

The blood, surging violently around him an instant before, stopped. The thunderous thumping stopped. Everything ceased.

My heart has stopped, he thought; I'm saved! The implication of this struck Treet even as relief overtook him: that means I'm dead!

The irrationality of this paradoxical event shocked Treet. Whoever heard of anyone dying in order to live? Preposterous! I can't be dead, he thought. And yet, if I'm not dead why can't I see? Or hear? Or breathe?

No, there is nothing wrong with me. I'm just sleeping. I'm all right. I will survive. I'll make it. I won't let a little nightmare unhinge me.

The terror, so real only moments before, quickly faded, and a sense of expanding euphoria took its place. Treet drifted in the warmth of the feeling until he realized that it was remarkably similar to another sensation: hunger. This roused him. He had not eaten in some time, except for the handful of beans and the sip of water he'd had in his cell, and who knew how long ago that had been?

Fully awake now, floating in the thick soup of the conditioning tank, Treet decided to again try an experiment he'd been conducting from the moment he'd been lowered into the tank: an experiment in sympathic awareness. Something Yarden had once told him had come back to him—probably in light of his futile attempt at swaying the tank operator to push the button on the console that would bring him up.

"Are you a sympath?" she had asked him aboard the *Zephyros*. "Some people are natural adepts and do not know it, Mr. Treet. You could be one of them."

The idea that he might be a sympath had unsettled him for a while after that, though he could not at the time think why.

He'd chalked it up to an ambiguous fear of disorder—a man of clear-eyed logic and cold rationality worshiped order and sense. The sympathic awareness and its sense-defying tendencies frightened him. Treet had always figured that a man needed a firm anchor in reality to survive all the insanity the modern world threw at him.

And so he did. But all of Treet's logic and rationality had not saved him. Here on Empyrion, these things were of little consequence or value, apparently. Therefore, lacking any better weapons, Treet had decided to fight back with the only tool he had—his own mind.

He had intermittently been sending Yarden messages of his demise. Without knowing precisely how the sympathic awareness worked, he had no real hope that he would be able to receive actual messages from Yarden, but he thought he might be able to nudge her consciousness somehow or otherwise make himself known to her. Once alerted, she would be able to receive his "thought impressions"—to use her term. Then it was up to Yarden.

He could not believe that she would be so cold to his plight that she would ignore him. She would come with help . . . wouldn't she?

The thought of Yarden coming to him made his heart ache with emptiness. He wished he'd been able to persuade her to return with him. Return to what? he wondered. To this? To capture and mental torture at the hands of their enemies?

No, it was better this way. At least she was free. Even if he had to pay the ultimate price for his foolishness, at least she would be spared joining him. She would never know what became of him.

Hard on this thought came the sobering realization, not for the first time, that if he failed, he would not be the only victim. Unless he found a way to alter the course of events, the relentless flow would carry the Fieri to death and destruction once more. Nuclear holocaust would be repeated as Dome in its unfathomable hatred and stupidity turned against the loving Fieri again—for the second time in fifteen hundred years. If that happened, as he was sure it would, none of his friends would live through it.

More and more, it appeared he would be the first casualty of the hostility. No, sadly, not the first—merely the latest in a long, long crowded line stretching back nearly three millennia.

The futility of his situation stung him. His helplessness mocked him bitterly. So much depended on him, and there was absolutely nothing he could do. Nothing but wait, hold out as long as he could, and hope.

. . . . . .

Far from the cells of Cavern level, Jamrog strolled the secluded pathways of Rohee's private pleasure ground high above Threl Chambers. Mrukk walked beside his master, hands clasped behind him, dressed in the light gray yos the Invisibles wore when in Hage. When prowling through Dome, the Invisibles took the colors of whichever Hage they happened to be passing through, blending in with the Hagemen at will. An easy trick, but always effective.

"What did you observe, Commander?" asked Jamrog placidly. The day before had been the triumph he'd hoped for and more. He'd slept well, after an evening spent entertaining two female companions, and risen early, eager to begin his rule by removing the first obstacles to his total authority.

Mrukk, a brooding hulk of a man, gave a quick sideways flick of his keen eyes—more out of habit than suspicion—and answered in a low voice. "The Directors were all in attendance, as you no doubt have been informed by your Hage priests. The Hages were well represented, and no overt signs of disapproval have been observed or reported."

Jamrog turned to him. "You don't sound convinced of that. Why?"

"There is an unsubstantiated report that Tvrdy was seen leaving Threl Square alone just after your speech."

"Hmmm." Jamrog's eyes narrowed. "Who saw him?"

"One of the Hage priests recognized him and reported it to Nilokerus security. By the time the report reached us, it could not be confirmed. However, his presence was noted when the Tanais returned to Hage, so perhaps the priest was mistaken."

Jamrog nodded slowly. "It doesn't matter. I do not care to trap the Tanais so easily; I have better plans for him. When I am finished with Tvrdy, his own Hagemen will deny they ever knew

536

him." Jamrog chuckled easily. He was well on his way to becoming invincible, and after so many years biding his time, waiting in Rohee's shadow, it was a very heady feeling.

Mrukk said nothing; his cold gray eyes stared ahead impassively. The fearsome commander of the Mors Ultima knew Jamrog well and knew how quickly the man's mood could change. But he knew also that he was more than a match for his master. His ruthlessness and cold brutality had been rewarded time and again as he advanced through the ranks to become leader of the elite force of the Invisibles. There was nothing he would not do for his master, true, but his loyalty had its price. He wondered sometimes how much Jamrog was willing to pay.

They walked a little further together, Jamrog frowned in concentration, clenching and unclenching his fists absently, his soft-shod feet whispering on the paving stones. "Commander," he said after a time, "I want you to see to it that the Invisibles are rewarded for their service yesterday."

"Of course, Supreme Director. Did you have a sum in mind, or should I use my own discretion?"

"Five hundred shares."

"Five hundred is very generous, Director," Mrukk said slyly. "Perhaps a lesser amount would serve as well. Some of the men may not know what to do with so much, seh?"

"Five hundred," said Jamrog decisively, glancing up quickly. "And make certain they know it is a reward for service. Instruct them that they can expect such rewards from now on—for good service, of course. Poor service will be punished in like manner."

"I understand, Supreme Director. It will be done immediately."

"Good," replied Jamrog. "You may return to your duties. Oh, there is one more detail. Do you remember the discussion we had some time ago about Hladik's usefulness?"

Mrukk's eyes narrowed; a thin smile twitched the corners of his cruel lips. "Of course."

"I have reason to doubt the Nilokerus Director's sincerity of late."

"Would you like me to have him watched by one of my men?"

"I think it best. It would not do to begin my rule with anything less than the total confidence and loyalty of all my

537

Directors." Jamrog dismissed the commander with a gesture and walked on by himself, musing on his various schemes, letting his feet wander where they would among the trimmed hedgeways and flowered paths.

This very pleasure ground was where Rohee had met his death in the form of a cordial, laced with a special poison which Jamrog had concocted.

Sirin Rohee in his last years, weary of ruling and of the spoils of his handsomely exploited position, had taken to spending long hours in his private pleasure grounds—a garden park planted with miniature trees and fragrant flowering shrubbery of every type produced by Hyrgo Hage. It was his habit to spend the afternoon hours walking off his meal amidst the greenery of his park, often with a nubile Hagemate (of either sex; it made no difference at all to Rohee).

He also enjoyed a cordial made from sweetened cherimoyas and distilled souile, which he sipped as he took his daily tour of his gardens—changed continually by Hyrgo growers so that the Supreme Director would not become bored with his favorite pastime. It had been a simple matter to drop the poison into the old man's drink. Jamrog had merely arrived to discuss a bit of business and slipped the powder into the bottle. He'd had his talk and then left.

Later that night, the news of Rohee's unfortunate demise had reached the ambitious Jamrog. The poison, slow acting, though excruciating in its irreversible final stages, had taken effect, and the Supreme Director had died screaming in his bed in the middle of the night, frightening his Hagemate out of her wits. Jamrog had been summoned at once, but it was by then too late. Sirin Rohee was dead. The girl swore no one had been near the old man all day and that he had eaten nothing that she herself had not eaten.

It was not especially important to Jamrog that he remain above suspicion in Rohee's death, merely convenient. The Hage priests would cooperate more readily if they did not have cause to accuse him of muddying the ethereal realms with the negative energy produced by murder. He needed the Hage priests for a special program he planned to institute soon, and their cooperation would be most helpful.

Therefore, when he had examined the problem from all possible angles and had decided that he had no further use for

Rohee, he poisoned his old master and established himself in his place. Exactly as he'd planned from the beginning.

Jamrog gave a great sigh of contentment. It was good, and the best was yet to come.

SIXTEEN

Pizzle lay in bed, having just passed one of the most baffling nights in his relatively brief but confusing life. In utter chagrin he reviewed the events of the previous evening one by one, examining each moment as it unfolded in his brain, trying to perceive where he'd gone wrong.

Jaire's guests had arrived and he'd been introduced. To his dismay, Starla had not been among them. A few of the guests had expressed interest in Pizzle's impressions of Fierra, and others wanted to hear about his journey. Surprisingly, no one seemed interested in hearing about Dome, or about Earth either. At least these topics were avoided in open discussion. The reason, Pizzle guessed, was because Dome, and Earth also for all he knew, held negative associations for the Fieri.

It wasn't that they forbade hearing about such things, or made it a rule to avoid them, but more that they did not wish to entertain anything of a negative nature for any length of time. This was why the facts of their arrival on Empyrion and their sojourn in Dome had been described only once—at an appropriate time before the assembled Mentors. Nothing more was said after that. There was no inquisition, no endless sessions of debriefing, no covert poking and prodding into the visitor's intentions or motives in coming.

This was the real corker for Pizzle. He'd expected a completely different response. On Earth, alien space travelers would have been instantly quarantined and subjected to endless inquiry and study. It was like Treet had said: "Our reception at Dome made more sense."

The Fieri were not fainthearted, Pizzle thought. And they didn't appear prudish in their approach to life. They just weren't interested in hearing about Dome. As it had been expressed to him by Mathiax one day, "What good can come of contemplating darkness?"

For the Fieri, darkness was a force always active, always encroaching on the light, and therefore always to be resisted in whatever form it took at the moment. Not ordinarily given to strong conviction himself, Pizzle nevertheless found himself admiring the Fieri devotion. But the way he felt now, it was hard *not* to admire everything about the race that had produced his beloved. If for no other reason, Pizzle would have adored the Fieri *en masse* for the one noble achievement of rearing a daughter so fair.

While he related the facts of his desert journey and consequent rescue by a Fieri airship—aided, of course, by his own ingenious signal device and his heroic actions, which he never failed to mention—he watched the room's entrance for Starla's appearance. She did not appear. Nor did she arrive during his monologue about his impressions of their amazing city.

Jaire had called them to the table, and the gathering drifted leisurely to the dining room. Pizzle, frankly disappointed, had decided to make the best of it by seating himself between two charming Fieri women. He had just settled in his chair and turned to the dinner companion on his left and . . . there, in the arched doorway, stood Starla, talking to a young man who was holding her tightly by the hand.

Pizzle's heart lurched; he felt as if he were a gourd that had just had its insides scooped out. He turned his eyes away quickly and sat down before she saw him looking at her, then clamped his mouth shut so hard his jaws ached. His eyesight blurred and he sat through the entire meal without looking to his left, where *she* sat toward the end of the table. He could hear her voice, now and again, talking in intimate tones with her escort. His ears burned, and his mind seethed.

Jaire served the meal—smiling, gracious, oblivious to his pain. He longed for the torture to be over so he could flee to the solace of his room and take up once more his foreordained solitary existence. Starla had obviously deceived him, leading him on with no intention of following through. Probably she thought the whole thing a great joke at his expense, a game to satisfy her idle curiosity. Sure, that's all he meant to her: an oddity from another planet, a freak, a conversation piece, something to tell her grandchildren about: My date with a Space Geek.

Pizzle sank lower in his chair as his heart sank lower into melancholy. He cursed his blind foolishness and wallowed in wave after wave of self-pity that rolled over him. By the meal's third course, he was so deep in his despair that he became frantic and began talking loudly and volubly to those around him. His two dinner companions exchanged looks of bewilderment. What had gotten into this foreigner? Silent as a stone through the first half of the meal, he was now boisterous to the point of hysterics.

Pizzle did not see the looks exchanged around the table. He did not see the stricken expression on Starla's face as he proceeded to make a monumental ass of himself, capping his performance by spilling his glass into the lap of the guest next to him. Jaire attempted intervention, trying her best to calm him, but to no avail.

Finally Pizzle, fearing some greater humiliation, excused himself and walked out into the canopied courtyard. The sunshield was drawn back, and the stars looked down in icy disapproval of his behavior at the table. Pizzle sighed morosely and shuffled over to a seat, slumped down, and closed his eyes in misery.

Some time later, an hour perhaps, he became aware of a perfumed presence. He opened his eyes and, with his slightly fuzzy vision, saw a dream drifting toward him. Starla came to stand before him, a look of hurt and disappointment on her lovely face. Pizzle needed no explanation to know what she was feeling, for her expression fairly well mirrored his own. But *why* she should feel this way he couldn't figure.

"May I sit down?" she asked.

"It's a free country," sniffed Pizzle. She gave him a questioning glance. "It's an expression—it means go ahead, nobody's going to stop you."

"You wish someone would stop me from sitting with you?"

"No, I didn't mean that. I meant—look, just do what you want, okay?"

Starla sat down in a woven chair across from him, crisp in her blue chinti. She looked at him with her large, dark eyes, liquid in the starlight. "I thought you'd be glad to see me," she said softly. "I thought we were friends."

"Yeah, I thought so, too," grumped Pizzle. "And I *was* glad to see you—until I saw you were with someone else."

"I brought Vanon to meet you."

"Great. I love meeting a girl's boyfriends."

"I do not understand you, Pizzy. Explain yourself please."

She was asking for it, was she? Very well, he'd give her both

542

barrels. "I'll explain myself. I was hoping to see you tonight—I waited and waited for you to show up, and when you finally do it's on the arm of some bozo you say you want to introduce me to. Why? You want my blessing or what? I'm sure you'll both be very happy together. How's that? Now why don't you run back inside before he comes out here looking for you. One thing I don't need is to see you leave with him."

A shocked expression replaced the hurt look on Starla's face. "What's the matter?" asked Pizzle. "Didn't anybody ever talk like that to you before?"

Mute, Starla shook her head.

"Too bad," snarled Pizzle. "People talk like that to me all the time. You get used to it."

"I came looking for you—" she began.

"So you could rub it in? Don't bother."

"I wanted . . . to be with you." Her voice quavered as she stood to leave.

Now Pizzle felt like a prize jerk. Why couldn't he just leave well enough alone? Why did he always have to push a thing too far? Because I'm a pin-headed stupido, he thought, kicking himself. "Look, you're not going to cry or anything, are you?" he said weakly.

Starla shook her head again and looked away momentarily. Pizzle thought he saw the glint of a tear on her lashes. "You're angry with me," Starla observed. "But I don't know why."

"I'm not angry with you. I mean, I *was,* but not now. Sit back down a minute."

Starla sat stiffly, folding her hands in her lap, glanced up at him, and said, "Vanon is my brother. He's my only family."

Pizzle groaned and slid down in his chair. "Somebody shoot me."

"If my bringing him here to meet you was wrong, I am sorry. I did not wish to hurt you."

It was, Pizzle reflected, probably genetically impossible for a Fieri to willfully hurt another human being. What a blundering, self-centered, gravel-headed dizzard I've been! What a toad! "I—It's just—I can't—" He stumbled over the words. "I'm sorry, Starla, I thought . . . I don't know what I thought."

"You thought I didn't want to be with you tonight?"

"Yeah, that's what I thought all right," Pizzle admitted. "I've got mashed potatoes for brains sometimes. I'm sorry. I should have trusted you." He swallowed hard. "You'll forgive me?"

"I forgive you, Asquith," she said.

He leaned closer to her and caught her scent in the warm night air. "Back on Earth there's a custom," he said softly, his heart pounding, "that when lovers quarrel and make up, they kiss."

She gazed steadily back at him and replied, "We have the same custom."

The next thing Pizzle knew, Starla was in his arms and he was kissing her, his heart bumping so loudly in his chest he thought he was having a heart attack, but didn't mind in the least.

"I love you, Starla," he said when he came up for air, astonishing himself with his declaration. He'd scarcely admitted it to himself. What am I doing? he wondered. Why can't I control myself?

Starla drew away from him, looked at him calmly, and said, "I love you, too, Asquith. I have from the first night when you told me all about *The Hobbit*."

"You did?" Pizzle stared. This is terrible! What am I going to do now? She's in love with me! I've really done it this time. "You really did?"

She nodded and reached for his hand, took it, and held it. Pizzle entered the seventh dimension—a place where time stood still and flashed by at incredible speed simultaneously. His head swam, and his feet perspired. His throat tightened, and his eyes spun in his head.

"I . . . Starla, I've hardly ever—that is, never—loved anyone before." His tongue grew thick and unwieldy in his mouth. "Not really."

She looked at him strangely. "Was there never a woman for you?"

"Oh, sure, lots of women—but none of them would ever have anything to do with me. I am, I guess you might say, just not what every woman looks for first in a man. Let's face it, I'm no holovision star."

Starla puzzled over his words. "I still do not understand many of the things you say. But I see into your heart, and I know you are a gentle spirit."

Pizzle could only stare. No one had ever said anything like

that to him before, and he didn't know how to respond. He simply sat holding her hand very tightly. A few minutes passed this way before either one spoke. Finally Pizzle broke the silence by saying, "Well, what do we do now—get married?"

The words were out of his mouth before he knew what he was saying. To her credit Starla did not leap up and run screaming into the night. She sat beside him, gazing at him intently, the starlight shimmering in her hair. She acted as if what he had said had some basis in logical possibility, as if she were actually considering it.

"I must introduce you to my brother first. Among Fieri, marriage is not entered lightly," was all she said.

"Oh, right. But maybe I shouldn't—I mean, what I said just now . . . well, that was . . . Sure, let's go meet your brother." Pizzle stood abruptly, before any more ludicrous words could cross his lips, and together they went back inside to rejoin Jaire's dinner party.

The rest of the evening went pinwheeling by in a blur. Pizzle, reeling from the implications of his hasty suggestion, wandered dazed through the introduction to Vanon, Starla's brother. At some point the party was over. The guests departed, Starla disappeared, and he found himself standing before the open end of his room, staring unseeing out upon Prindahl's calm, starlit face.

Eventually he found his bed and lay down in it, not to sleep, but to toss restlessly as his mind wrestled with the idea of marriage . . . MARRIAGE!

Now, as he lay contemplating his probable fate, Pizzle had regained most of his wits and composure. As dawn's pearly light streamed into his room, he remembered more clearly what had transpired last night in the courtyard. Starla had not said they *would* get married, only that marriage was not entered into lightly.

Feeling like a prisoner granted a surprise reprieve, Pizzle rose, ready to face the day. With any luck at all Starla would not even recall their conversation.

SEVENTEEN

The tree Crocker found was perfect: about six centimeters in diameter and arrow straight. Although merely a sapling, its trunk was tall and strong, its wood dense. Using his small utility knife, he trimmed off the few inconsequential upper branches and then proceeded to cut off the trunk near the roots, patiently shaving away the wood layer by layer in a tapering cone shape. It took him many long hours, but when he finished, he had a sturdy javelin as tall as he was.

He spent the next hours sharpening his weapon, whittling the cone into an elongated pyramid shape—four lethal triangles for strength. Once finished he began practicing with it, studying its balance and attitude of flight. It took much shaving of the shaft to get it properly balanced, but as he worked and practiced he discovered he could throw his spear nearly thirty meters with accuracy.

He had not heard or seen any traces of the behemoth lords since the titanic struggle overheard several days ago. The thought that such creatures existed and moved through the forest both frightened and thrilled Crocker. Whenever he happened to recall the terrible clash a twitch in his gut, a physical memory of fear, reminded him of the exquisite thrill he'd experienced in those dreadful moments when he believed the creatures would discover him.

Crocker spent the next several days ranging the forest for small game, traipsing only as far as he could go and still return to his secluded bower by nightfall. He still slept by the little pool and swam there. He had eaten on the carcass of the plump animal he'd killed until the meat had begun to rot. But that had been days ago, and no more animals had visited his pool to drink. He was hungry again, and anxious to try his weapon in earnest.

The Blue Forest abounded in wildlife of all kinds—most of it, unfortunately, inhabiting the upper regions of the leaf canopy, well above the reach of his spear. Birds and small mammalian creatures watched him pass along the forest pathways far below.

But there were larger, less wary animals to be found as well. He saw their spoor and occasionally caught a glimpse of a sleek hide gliding into the brush just ahead.

As hunger became more acute, his stealth improved in direct proportion. By the third day, he crept through the verdant byways as silently as the creatures he stalked. Although much of his human awareness was gone, Crocker still possessed a superior animal cunning. And if he neither knew nor remembered anything of his former life, at least certain latent portions of his mentality were responding vigorously to the stimulus of life in the forest. In place of memory, for example, he was developing an extraordinary patience and perseverance, allowing him to sit unmoving in a single spot or slog along a promising path for hours on end without complaint or exhaustion.

Of these things he was ignorant, however, for not a speck of consciousness remained. His life was governed by the most basic of forces: day and night, hunger and thirst.

He wandered the Blue Forest unaware of who he was or where he had come from, simply reacting to his needs of the moment, thinking no further ahead than the next meal. The robo-carrier did not accompany him on these forays, for the soft whirr of its motors and the shush of its treads as it passed through the brush made too much noise. Crocker had carved a tunnel for it to enter his secluded bower: once there, he switched the machine off.

Crouching atop a moss-covered rock overhang from which he could survey the trail below, he sat with his javelin resting loosely in his hands, waiting for an animal to pass beneath him. Several hours had gone by, and he was just about to give up his vigil and move on when he heard a rustling of dry leaves. He had placed a fallen vine across the path a little way up the trail. Something was coming!

Instantly alert, Crocker's grasp on the spear tightened. His muscles tensed. He leaned forward, rising on the balls of his feet. The rustling persisted. Not one animal only, but many.

Just then the first creature appeared on the trail below. It was smaller than he'd hoped, with stringy red-brown hair over a barrel-shaped body supported by four spindly legs that looked too delicate to support it. Its narrow head sported a longish, semiflexible snout which waved in all directions, searching the becalmed air of the forest for scent traces. Crocker, keen to kill, would have let fly with his spear, but some recently awakened instinct stayed in his hand. *Wait!* this newfound voice cautioned. *Larger prey is coming. Wait.*

He paused, and shortly the first animal moved on, snuffling at the ground with its floppy proboscis. Immediately behind it came another, slightly larger version of the same animal. Crocker raised the spear once more.

No, came the voice again. *Be patient. This is not the one. You will know it when you see it.*

Crocker obeyed the instruction, lowering the weapon slightly, biding his time. Two more creatures scuttled by on the trail below—neither one acceptable. He waited and was about to give chase when he heard again the rustling of the vine. This time the animal that passed beneath his gaze was slower and much more stout—its belly nearly dragged the path as it walked along, snout writhing, sampling the leaves of all the plants it passed.

Now! cried the voice in his head. *Strike now and you will eat well tonight!*

Crocker's reaction was instantaneous. He felt a tension in his arm as he drew back the spear and sighted down its length. Teeth clenched, he heaved the shaft forward with a rolling motion of his shoulder.

The spear flashed through the air. A frightened squeal shattered the stillness. The animal dodged. It tried to run, but its body would not move—the beast was pierced through its thick neck and pinioned to the earth.

It struggled feebly and then expired. Crocker scrambled down from his rock and raced to his kill. He let out a whoop as he stood shivering with excitement over his handiwork. The spear flew true, it's sharp point easily penetrating hide and muscle. His aim had been good, and the animal died quickly.

Good. You have brought down a leaf-eater. Their flesh is tender and warms the stomach.

He bent to retrieve his weapon and noticed a shadow moving toward him along the trail to his left. He whipped the spear around as an enormous black feline sauntered up, its midnight fur glistening in the patchy light, large golden eyes watching him keenly.

Crocker's hands stiffened on his spear. *Do not move,* his

inner voice cautioned. *Your spear is useless against a wevicat. Do nothing.*

On huge silent paws the beast padded forward, the nostrils of its great muzzle twitching. It gave the man a look of intense curiosity and then yawned mightily, revealing a grooved pink tongue and very sharp, very white triangular teeth lining wide jaws in a double row.

The man gave ground, backing away slowly, keeping the spear ready should the enormous feline charge. The cat blinked unconcernedly at him, yawned again, and nuzzled the fallen beast.

Crocker stood motionless and watched the cat rip into the carcass of the leaf-eater. He rebelled at losing his kill, and though he feared the wevicat, he would not be robbed of the meal he'd worked so hard for. The wevicat glanced up from its work, snorted in his direction as if to dismiss him, and went back to delicately peeling the hide from the haunches of the dead animal.

Rage leapt up in the man as he watched the wevicat nonchalantly stealing his food. Hands shaking, he tightened his grip on the spear and raised it above his head, bringing it down square on the wevicat's big head. Thwack!

The huge black beast spun, ears flattened to its skull, snarling. Crocker stood erect, challenging, the spear leveled at the spitting cat. *His claws scream for your blood, foolish one.* The voice was a terse whisper in his brain. *Your life is his.*

Crocker thrust the spear forward into the big cat's face. Quick as a blink the wevicat lifted a paw and swiped the spear aside, but Crocker, still shaking with rage and fear, brought the spear back. The cat's muscles rippled beneath its glistening coat, its golden eyes narrowed to vicious slits.

For a long tense moment the two glared at each other, neither backing down. *The smell of fear fills his nostrils,* said the disembodied voice inside the man's brain. *Flee and you will surely die.* The prospect of the hairless beast challenging him for the prey seemed to perplex the cat. It relaxed and sat back, gazing at the man warily. Here was something new—a creature of obvious weakness that did not run when threatened. The wevicat shook its great black head.

Crocker lowered the spear and tapped its tip on the side of

the dead animal's neck where the wevicat had begun to feed. The cat looked from the prey to the man, seemed to consider for a moment, then placed a paw on the side of the dead animal. *He says there is enough meat,* whispered the voice. *The wevicat respects you now. You will not sleep hungry this night.*

The cat returned to the kill and began stripping great chunks of meat from the carcass and devouring them whole. Crocker hunkered down to wait and watched the choicest pieces disappear into the wevicat's gaping maw. In time, however, the cat stood, licked its muzzle, yawned, and sauntered off a few paces. It lazily dropped onto its side, stretched out, and went to sleep.

Crocker crept forward and looked at what the cat had left for him: the stringy meat along the ribs and backbone and a portion of the forequarters between the front legs. Crocker took his small knife from his rag pouch and began cutting the meat into strips, chewing the still-warm meat slowly. From time to time, he glanced over at the wevicat to see if it might wake up. But the animal's sides rose and fell rhythmically in deep sleep, so Crocker went on with his meal.

He gorged himself on the sweet flesh, and soon the forest sounds buzzed in his ears and his head felt heavy. Tucking a last morsel into his mouth, Crocker pushed himself away from the decimated carcass, stumbled along the trail, and curled up under a bristle bush.

EIGHTEEN

"An excellent idea!" replied Gerdes when Yarden told her she'd like to postpone the beginning of her studies so she could go on the trip to see the talking fish. "I will go, too. It has been too long since I last saw them. I'll invite some of my other students, and we can work along the way."

Yarden was quick to second the idea. "It's the perfect solution, Gerdes. Still, I can't wait to begin."

"We won't wait," said Gerdes, smiling. "We will begin as planned. Are you ready?"

"Begin now? Certainly. I'm ready." Yarden glanced quickly around the bare room in which Gerdes conducted her instruction. "But I don't see any paint or brushes or surfaces."

Gerdes smiled. "Nor will you for a very long time. Painting does not begin with the paint, but with the *painter!* We must first explore Yarden and find out who she is and what kind of artist she may become. We will begin with movement."

"Dance movement?"

"You remember what I said, good." Gerdes nodded approvingly. "Yes, I told you painting and dance had much in common. To paint well, you must move well and understand movement and rhythm. You will learn it by learning to move rhythmically." Gerdes moved to a near wall where a crystal was mounted on a panel with a row of colored tabs beneath it.

These triangular crystals, Yarden had learned, were employed by the Fieri in various tasks of communication. Evidently the crystals could both transmit and receive vibrations which could be used to carry signals. Exactly how this was accomplished, Yarden did not understand, but she had seen the devices often enough. Mentors like Talus and Mathiax were rarely without one affixed to their clothing.

Gerdes touched a colored tab, and the room filled with music: soft, lilting music, gentle and evocative. "Close your eyes, daughter. Listen for a moment. Concentrate. Let the music seep into you; let it fill you up until you cannot hold it any longer."

Yarden did as instructed, closing her eyes as she stood in

the center of the room. Gerdes' voice became softer, remote. Yarden listened to the music, letting it touch every part of her. She felt it in her fingers and arms and legs first.

"Drink it in as if you were very dry and the sound was cool water for your thirst. Feel it in every muscle, every fiber of your body." Gerdes went on talking, slowly, softly, speaking in time with the music.

Yarden allowed the music to fill up all the places within her that she could think of—shoulders, neck, stomach, chest, hips, thighs . . . everywhere.

"When you cannot contain it any longer, let the music overflow in movement. Make your body a vessel for the music to flow through, and become yourself that motion. Let it carry you as you carry it."

Yarden hesitated, uncertain how to interpret Gerdes' last instruction.

"Don't think about it, don't try to make too much sense of it. Just do what you feel. Hear the music, let it fill you and overflow in motion. Move with it."

Feeling awkward and uncertain, Yarden began to move— tentatively, jerkily. She lifted an arm, dropped it. Stepped forward, stopped. She glanced at Gerdes. "Keep your eyes closed. I know it feels clumsy. That's because you're thinking too much. Don't think about it, just do it. Let your body interpret the music, not your brain."

So, feeling very awkward and not a little self-conscious, Yarden began to move, slowly, haltingly at first. Arms outspread, legs taking hesitant steps, she turned in a tight circle.

"That's right," said Gerdes. "Feel the music. Translate the sound into motion. Good . . . good." With this encouragement, Yarden began to take bigger steps and move her arms in circles around her body, approximating the circles the melody made as it circled through the song.

"Relax," soothed Gerdes, "There are no steps to this dance except those you make yourself; so there is nothing to be afraid of. Fear makes you stiff. The music is fluid; you must become fluid, too."

It was true—Yarden was afraid of looking foolish before her teacher, afraid of making an awkward movement. She slowed her turning steps and concentrated on relaxing her body. Gerdes noticed the difference at once.

"That's better," she said. "Let go of your fear. See? The tension is leaving your shoulders. Now, let your backbone bend—it is not made of wood, it will become supple if you allow it. The music will show you."

Yarden stopped. "I can't. It's too—"

"Shh. Don't speak. Don't think. Begin again." Gerdes came close and put her hands on Yarden's shoulders lightly. "You're trying too hard. Don't fight what is already within you. Your body knows what to do, but your mind intrudes. Relax. Let your body do what it knows. Begin again."

Yarden closed her eyes once more and began to move, forcing herself not to think about anything. Instead, she willed her consciousness into the music, emptied herself into it, let it cover her and pull her along in its smooth, gently unfolding rhythms. She was surprised to find that her body was already responding. Slowly, but with increasing confidence, she moved, not arms and legs only, but torso and shoulders and hips and neck.

It felt good to move with such freedom. Burrowing deeper into the music, she allowed the music to dictate the motion. For once she had succeeded in silencing that sharply self-critical voice that judged and reported her every action. That was the trick—to divorce the judging self from the feeling self, to remove the bothersome self-awareness altogether so it could not intrude on the pure emotional response, allowing the body to move freely.

"Yes, yes," said Gerdes with obvious satisfaction. "Much better. You're feeling the music now. Go deeper into it; let it fill all the empty places. Take it in, and transform it into motion."

Eyes closed, Yarden moved to the music, her motions growing ever more sure. Gerdes brought her along with softly uttered encouragement until she could feel the music deep inside her as it coiled and spun and flowed like rippling water from the well of her soul. She became the music, entering into it completely, merging with it, taking it in and letting it out again as pure, free-form motion.

She did not notice when the song changed and the tempo became faster, but merely felt the rhythm undulate more quickly, demanding more of her willingness to give herself to it. Gerdes' words intoned in her ears, but she did not hear them as much as she felt their presence. In fact, she was aware of nothing but the transmutation of music into motion that was taking place in her body.

When the music finally stopped, dwindling away like a whisper on the wind, Yarden felt her limbs slow and sag and knew the dance was over. She stood motionless for a moment and savored the warmth the exercise had generated. Exhaustion and exultation mingled, producing in her a pleasure close to ecstasy.

She opened her eyes to see Gerdes holding out a cloth to her and watching her with a quizzical expression. Yarden rubbed the soft cloth over her sweating face and neck, not ready yet to break the spell of the moment. Finally she could bear Gerdes' silence no longer; she had to know what her teacher thought of her exercise. "Did I do well?" she asked, somewhat timidly.

Gerdes gazed at her pupil intently. "That is a question you must answer for yourself, daughter. What does your body tell you?"

Yarden shook her head and felt sweat-damp curls slap against the back of her neck. "I scarcely know. I feel . . . almost dizzy with delight. It's the most wonderful feeling." At that, her words tumbled out in a rush. "Gerdes, I became the song—I was inside the music. I felt it throughout my body, inside me as I was inside it. I've never experienced anything so strange and wonderful."

The older woman gave her an appraising look and led her to a grouping of soft-cushioned chairs. They sat, and Yarden leaned back and felt the delicious looseness of a body totally relaxed. Gerdes said nothing, but continued to watch her student with the same thoughtful, questioning expression on her face.

Yarden sensed sympathically that there was something more than curiosity in her instructor's mind. She sensed something else. Fear? No, not fear, but close. Awe. This puzzled Yarden. She would have pursued the matter using her sympathic abilities—Gerdes would likely be compatible—but refrained. She did not want to know anything her teacher did not choose to say to her directly. Still, she could not help sensing the force of Gerdes' mental and emotional reaction.

The two sat for a long time until Gerdes finally arrived at what she wanted to say. Looking at Yarden directly, she placed her hands together and began, saying, "We are all given gifts freely from the hand of the All-Gracious Giver, who gives to all as He will. In my years I have seen many whose gifts shine bright as sunstone within them—and many of lesser endowment whose best efforts are nevertheless worthy enough to adorn the Preceptor's palace.

"Though I've seen gifts great and small in the most unlikely places, I've never seen any like yours. You, my daughter, are the bearer of a rare and special gift."

"Are you certain?" asked Yarden. The Fieri woman's words filled her with a mixture of apprehension and delight.

"Perhaps I was wrong about you becoming a dancer," intoned Gerdes, speaking mostly to herself. "I believe you have the ability and could be trained. But dance, I think, would use only part of the gift. There is something deeper there—I could see it when you forgot yourself and entered into the music. I could see it, but I don't know what it is."

"I felt it, too," replied Yarden. "I've felt it before, but never as strongly as I felt it today. I can't describe how it was, but I seem to have stepped outside myself. I was not conscious of what I was doing—each movement flowed through me, dictated from some other, greater source." She smiled suddenly. "Oh, Gerdes, it felt so good, so free and pure."

Gerdes nodded thoughtfully. "Yes, that is the body responding to the inner gift. The body knows how to move—it's made for movement after all. We have no need to teach it what it already knows."

"Liberating the body to do what it knows how to do—is that it?"

"Yes," agreed Gerdes. "You learn quickly."

Yarden jumped up. "I want to do it again. Please? Right now. I don't want to forget the feeling. I want to remember exactly how I did it."

"Very well," said Gerdes, rising slowly and making her way to the panel on the wall. "Ready yourself."

In a moment the music drifted into the room and Yarden, poised, ready to receive it, heard the first wispy notes and began to sway, guiding herself into the music and away from the critical awareness of her movements. It was easier this time, now that she knew what she was attempting. In no time at all she had entered into that state where her mind soared up through the dreamy, many-toned layers of sound, leaving her body free to respond in its own way.

The session left Yarden exhausted, but flushed with triumph and eager for her next lesson. "Thank you, Gerdes," she said, a little reluctant to leave. "I intend to practice every moment until I return. To think I had this—this wonderful gift inside me all this time and never knew it. I'll never be able to thank you enough for showing it to me."

"Your joy is thanks enough," Gerdes replied. "But you must not think that it will always be so easy. We have much hard work ahead of us, and yes, some pain as well. Tears are as much a part of creation as joy."

"I know that, Gerdes."

The older woman shook her head gently. "No, you don't. But it's all right. We will take it as it comes. Good-bye now."

Yarden said good-bye and walked home, luxuriating in the deep, warm, languorous feeling of physical exhaustion and the knowledge that her special gift had only begun to be explored. There were much finer things awaiting her, she knew; she thrilled to think what they might be.

NINETEEN

It seemed to Treet that he floated in space wrapped in cloud-soft vapors that curled around him, enveloping him and bearing him through endless corridors of darkness. He had floated this way from time immemorial, eternally traveling, yet never really going anywhere at all.

This celestial voyage was perpetually interrupted by vivid hallucinations: the one where he became trapped inside his own heart was a favorite torment, but there were others equally grotesque and frightening. One of them concerned being swallowed by a great transparent eel and enduring a living death inside its hideous stomach. Another saw him entombed inside a coffin-sized slab of crystal, frozen forever, unable to move or cry out, while all around him people moved and lived and breathed, oblivious to his torture.

In his lucid moments, Treet still knew himself to be suspended by wires in a tank of buoyant liquid, undergoing the process of conditioning. He knew this and told himself over and over in what had become for him a litany: *I will survive. . . I will survive . . . I will survive . . . I will . . . survive . . .*

But the periods of lucidity were shrinking, and the boundaries between consciousness and the nightmare region grew ever more amorphous. And his litany of resolve sounded more like naive optimism, cheap and mocking in his own ears.

Still, he would not give in to the creeping despair he could feel gathering around him, and instead continued to fight for his clarity of mind. Yet, to give himself over to the insanity of his weird visions would be far easier than constantly maintaining such a scrupulously tight rein on his mental processes. What did it matter whether he thought he was inside a giant eel? What did it matter what he thought about anything? He was never going to leave the tank with his head intact. In many ways it would be easier on him to simply give in, accept whatever insanity presented itself, and be done with it. Then at least he'd be released. The longer he held out, the longer he'd remain in the conditioning tank and the longer the torture would continue. Better to give in and regain freedom as quickly as possible.

A lesser man would have given in, as untold hundreds of Hladik's victims had. Here, however, Treet's innate stubbornness and frugality came to his aid. As a man who had lived the better part of a century with little more than the price of the next meal in his pocket at any one time, he simply could not allow himself to give up anything that had taken so much precious effort to accumulate in the first place. His mental acuity was a hard-won possession, arrived at only after years of painful and painstaking effort. It was, Treet had learned during the course of his life, no small achievement to be completely sane.

Mental clarity required such tremendous expenditures of discipline, vigilance, and perseverance that Treet was awed to think he had succeeded where so many, many others had utterly failed. He did not fault those who had failed. Theirs was a fate he had come too close to sharing for him to find any wide margin of comfort in his success.

But little by little, despite Treet's heroic efforts, the machinery of the conditioning tank worked on its victim. He found his sane moments fewer and more tenuous and the hallucinations fiercer, more frequent, relentless. He felt his grip on reality eroding bit by bit; the plunge could not be far off.

Nevertheless, striving to hold off the inevitable a little longer, Treet undertook yet another of his experiments in sympathic communication. Thus far these efforts had produced nothing of benefit, save giving him something to do. As he had done many times before, he began by sending his thoughts like hands outstretched, feeling, like radar waves spreading out, searching.

Only this time, instead of his mental radar streaming out into the endless void, something came back. Like the echoed ping of sonar bouncing back from a solid object, Treet sensed something moving at the farthest edge of his awareness. Something massive. He felt like one of those oceanic divers who, in the cold, dark depths of an arctic sea, feels the turbulence of the giant humpback's flukes as the creature glides silently, invisibly past.

The contact shocked Treet so much, his fragile concentration shattered. What was that? Another hallucination? Had he begun hallucinating that he was lucid and receiving impulses from his mental experiments? Or had it really happened?

Cautiously, Treet flung out his mental net once again. He caught nothing, so forced himself to concentrate, to stretch the strands to the utmost. The effort was taxing; the hair-fine filaments of consciousness trembled with exhaustion. He was about to collapse the tenuous net when he felt the mysterious shudder again, and stronger this time.

There was no mistake. He was not imagining it. It was there.

A presence, an intelligence that was not his own, hovered nearby, watching him, regarding him with keen interest, dwarfing him like the whale dwarfs the deep sea diver. Yet, he had nothing to fear from the leviathan his net had snagged. This he sensed intuitively even as his net shrank reflexively from the contact. Whatever he had attracted with his feeble efforts meant him no harm. That much came through instantaneously.

Treet attempted another probe, but could not sustain the effort and withdrew to puzzle over his surprising discovery. There was something out there—he had imagined his mental universe as space, infinite and empty . . . until now. Now, there was a presence lurking out there on the rim of his imagined universe. Something or someone.

Could it be Yarden? Treet wondered. He dismissed the possibility at once. Yarden, he reasoned, would feel familiar to him somehow. Her presence would be colored by her personality, and he would know her. This thing, this entity was no one he knew. Perhaps it wasn't even human. Perhaps it was something entirely indigenous to Empyrion, an alien intelligence drawn by his puny experiments. Of course, it could easily have nothing at all to do with Empyrion—a being of pure mental energy inhabiting a separate plane of existence, perhaps.

The possibilities were endless. He simply did not have enough information to know what he was dealing with, and until he did it was useless to speculate. So Treet put the matter aside for the time being and determined to rest up for another attempt at contact later. He wanted his next effort to be his best. He did not know if he'd have another chance.

• • • • • •

The Nilokerus glanced up quickly from his work as his superior came in. He stiffened and made a hasty salute. "Forgive me, Director, you were not announced."

"Does order and efficiency exist only when I am announced?" The scowl on Hladik's face made it clear that no answer would be sufficient and none was wanted. The Hageman kept his mouth wisely shut. "Where's Fertig? I want him."

The Nilokerus glanced around the stone-cut room quickly, as if the Subdirector might be found crouching in one of the corners. "He has not been seen, Director."

"Find him. I want to see the new prisoner. Where is he?"

"Skank—"

Hladik turned abruptly and started for the conditioning chamber. "Find Fertig and send him to me. I want to see him immediately," he called over his shoulder as he marched into the narrow corridor of cells leading to the room where the conditioning tanks were kept. It had been a sour day for the Nilokerus Director, a day for distractions and irritations. He had the uneasy feeling that things were imperceptibly going wrong, that his authority was crumbling under his feet and he could not see it. He'd soon put it right, however.

He'd crack a few skulls to demonstrate his displeasure, and soon his organization would be back to normal. It was all this business of Rohee's death and Jamrog's funereal spectacle that had made everything lax. A demonstration was needed. Fertig would make a good example. Where was the man? He'd been noticeably scarce since—well, since the Fieri escape. That long ago?

Hladik snorted. Fertig would have some explaining to do. Perhaps it was time to designate a new Subdirector. Yes, that might do. Fertig's demise would serve as a handsome warning to any Nilokerus tempted to slough their duties or allow zeal to flag.

He arrived at the conditioning chamber and entered. The room was dimly lit, the only illumination coming from the tank itself, which had two bodies suspended in it. Strange thought Hladik, I was aware of only one prisoner. Where had the other come from? What is going on here?

He spun on his heel. "Skank!" he shouted in his best outraged Director's tone. "Present yourself! Skank!"

His summons was rewarded by a shuffling sound from the adjoining room as the lumpy bulk of Skank came lumbering into view. The man gave Hladik a look of frank disapproval, which the Director ignored as he did the stench of the place. "Where have you been?" Skank opened his mouth to answer, but Hladik threw a hand toward the tank. "Why are there two prisoners in the tank? I come to see one and find two. Under whose order was this done?"

Skank peered at his leader with open contempt, spat on the floor, and said, "Two, did you say?"

"Yes, two! Are you blind as well as stupid? Look!" Hladik whirled around and gestured at the tank and at the single figure floating there. Stunned, he sputtered in protest. "Th-there were two just now. I saw them clearly with my own eyes. Two men in the tank. I saw them."

Skank spat and shrugged. "There's but one now."

The Director clenched his fists and would have struck the insolent Skank, but remembered what he'd come to do. "Yes, there is but one now. I want a report."

"The prisoner is as you see."

"His mental status?"

"Heavy alpha and beta activity. This one has stamina, Director. He resists with force."

"Then increase the stimulus. I want him broken."

Skank rolled a foul eye at his master. "My orders were to keep him undamaged."

"I give the orders, Skank. Do as you are told, or I will find someone who will." Hladik stepped close to the tank and peered at the captive suspended motionless inside. Was there something familiar about this one? Hard to tell—they all looked alike after a while.

He turned away. "Send word as soon as he is ready to receive the theta key." He fixed Skank with an ominous stare and marched from the stinking chamber, pausing to steal a final glance at the tank. Strange, he thought, I distinctly saw two.

TWENTY

Fertig stole a last look around his kraam. Had he forgotten anything? No, he had checked and checked again. He had all he could take with him in the bundle beneath his yos. It was time to go. Now. Before he was missed, before Hladik sent Invisibles to find him.

The day the Fieri had escaped, Fertig had chosen his course. To save his life he had only one hope: making his way to the Old Section to join the Dhogs—if they would have him. To help persuade the Dhogs that he was a valuable asset, Fertig had spent the last weeks searching for information of likely use to the nonbeings. Now, armed with an assortment of facts—enough, he hoped, to buy himself a place among them—Fertig was ready to depart.

Hladik had not mentioned the Fieri debacle since that day, but Fertig knew the Hage Leader had not forgotten. The Subdirector had time and time again seen Hladik pull out from his formidable memory long lists of past transgressions to indict a victim. Fertig knew Hladik had not forgotten his presence in the room the day he and Jamrog had ordered the Mors Ultima to strike another Director. And he knew it was only a matter of time before his role in the escape of the Fieri was discovered and his death warrant issued.

He had considered joining Tvrdy, but contacting the Tanais Director was too risky. Jamrog now had Invisibles seeded throughout Hage Tanais, and Tvrdy was under closest observation. Fertig strongly doubted he could reach Tvrdy without being recognized and reported the moment he set foot on Tanais soil. Besides, time was running out for Tvrdy too. Jamrog was closing for the kill. Thus, the only path left Fertig led to the Old Section.

Desperate as he was, Fertig found no comfort in the prospect of joining the Dhogs. If even a fraction of the tales were true, life among them was certain to be raw misery. But Fertig feared death more than discomfort—and death was certain if he stayed. Already Jamrog's instability was manifest for anyone with eyes to see it. Empyrion was spinning into a chaos of blood and destruction. Who would be left alive when the smoke cleared?

The Nilokerus Subdirector walked to the unidor, put his hand on the switchplate, and stared at the open portal as if it were the gate into the netherworld, which in a way it was. He shifted the bundle beneath his yos, took a deep breath, and departed.

· · · · · ·

The first word back from the men he'd sent to Giloon Bogney put Tvrdy in a better frame of mind than he'd been in for many days. The message had come during the night: contact successful . . . Dhogs well organized . . . cooperation complete . . . ready for supplies . . . send second contingent . . . more weapons needed . . .

Tvrdy read the decoded message once more, wadded the flimsy sheet into a tight ball, swallowed it, and smiled. The men he'd sent to the Old Section had made it. Giloon had lived up to his word. Here was a glimmer of hope at last: a most remote chance, but a chance nonetheless, that Jamrog could be stopped. He was not fooling himself; there was a staggering amount of work to be done before Jamrog could even be challenged, let alone unseated, but now at least there was a place to stand. That's all Tvrdy needed.

"Is anything wrong, Director?" Danelka, Tvrdy's industrious Subdirector, watched his leader casually.

"No, nothing." Tvrdy glanced up quickly. How long had the man been standing there? He cringed from the thought; it was unworthy. That's what came of suspecting everyone. Danelka was one of Tvrdy's five most trusted Hagemen, a man of unquestioned loyalty. "I want you to call them now. It is time."

"Of course. Is that all?"

"For the moment."

The man left to carry out his errand, and Tvrdy dropped into a chair. He had put off the decision long enough. It had to be today, while he could still control the circumstances of his decision. He would go on his own terms, and not on Jamrog's. Danelka would become Director, and one of the four underdirectors must be chosen to take Danelka's place as Subdirector. Over the years Tvrdy had groomed his men carefully; he knew each one and knew there was not a traitor among them. But now one must be raised over the others to a position of utmost sensitivity. The future of Empyrion might well depend on the choice. Which one would it be?

Within minutes, the first of the candidates had arrived. When all were assembled, he joined them, meeting their eager glances with keen appraisal. "You will have guessed, I think, why you are here," Tvrdy began.

Some of the men nodded; all stood mute and tense. The chance of a lifetime had come. To be advanced to the position of Subdirector meant high Hage stent—almost the highest. The tension was almost more than they could bear. "I won't waste words," the Director was saying. Had he already chosen then?

"I am leaving. Danelka will become acting Director. Which one of you will serve him?" The underdirectors looked levelly ahead. No one answered.

"You see how it is," Tvrdy gently intoned. He stood slowly. "This is one decision I will not make. It might be well for Danelka to choose, but as the one chosen will come under Jamrog's intense scrutiny . . ." He looked at them and spread his hands. "*You* will decide who it is to be." The underdirectors appeared shocked, so Tvrdy repeated himself. "You will choose among yourselves which it is to be. That way, you will all be satisfied with the choice."

The foremost of the candidates, a young man named Egrem, spoke up. "How will we choose, Director?"

"That is up to you. Decide however you like, but I must have an answer today. Any other questions?"

The underdirectors made no reply. Several glanced sideways at their companions as Tvrdy turned and left the room, saying, "I will be waiting in my kraam. Bring me your answer."

The Tanais Director was resting on his suspension bed when the signal sounded from the terminal across the room. He got up and stabbed a lighted tab, allowing the lift to come up from below. He went to greet the new Subdirector and was surprised to find all four tumbling out of the small lift.

"Well?" he asked when they had assembled themselves.

Illim stepped forward. "But if it pleases you, Director, I wish to make an explanation."

"Yes?"

"We have a condition among us, Director."

"Which means you require my assent."

"Yes."

"What is the condition?"

"We have agreed that the one chosen must forfeit—" The assistant halted, unable to make himself say the rest.

But Tvrdy had already surmised the agreement. "Will forfeit any claim to a possible future Directorship should Danelka and I be killed—is that it?"

Illim nodded.

Tvrdy smiled to himself. Yes, it was an admirable solution. That way the one chosen would not diminish the others' chances. They could still serve with hope in their hearts, and the chosen one would not have to fear their ambition. It was a solution worthy of the Tanais. Tvrdy made a show of turning the idea over in his mind before answering.

At last he said, "Am I to understand that the one chosen to serve the Hage is the one with the least ambition among you?"

The underdirectors looked abashed at the suggestion. Egrem said, "Send us all away if you think that, Director."

Tvrdy smiled and allowed his underlings to see his pleasure. "No, it is well done. I was right in trusting you. It was a hard decision. No one knows that better than I." He paused, then snapped back to business once more. "All right, I agree to the condition. Illim, present yourself." Illim stepped forward solemnly. "Illim will become Subdirector, but will forfeit his chance at a Director's kraam in the future. It is done."

"I will serve the Hage well, Hage Leader."

"I do not doubt it, Illim," said Tvrdy. "As for the rest of you, I have given Danelka orders to increase your poak by eighty shares each. Your loyalty is to be rewarded." The underdirectors could not conceal their happiness at this news. Eighty shares! They'd be almost as rich as magicians.

Tvrdy brought them quickly back to reality. "You will earn your increase, Hagemen. The lines of force are drawn. Already Jamrog plots against the Threl. I believe he will attempt to have each Director removed. If he cannot do it outright by assassination—as he did with Sirin Rohee—he will work among those closest to the Director. Make no mistake—he will try to turn you to his side."

The underdirectors darted defiance from their glances, but Tvrdy continued. "He will promise you wealth and power in exchange for treachery. He will make it easy for you to accept, impossible for you to refuse. But you must be strong. Do not believe his lies, and do not give in to him.

"Our only hope of survival is to remain steadfast. Report any contacts to Danelka at once. We must be strong or Jamrog will not be stopped.

"For your own protection," Tvrdy continued, "you will not know where I have gone, or when. Only Danelka has been briefed. He is to be the only contact between the Hage and myself from now on. He will pass only the information I instruct him to share with you. This also is for your protection."

The underdirectors had never heard their leader speak this way; certainly he had never addressed them so candidly. They were flattered, gratified by his confidence in them, and left pledging their strength and loyalty to Tvrdy, to the Hage, and to one another.

TWENTY
ONE

Hladik pushed away his hagemate's hand, but the tickling sensation that had roused him from sleep did not stop. "Enough," he muttered thickly. "No more tonight. Go to sleep."

Still the tickling continued. He opened his eyes. It was dark in the sleep chamber, but he sensed someone else in the room. "Who is it?" he said softly. "Who's there? Bremot?"

He put his hand out and touched the lamp next to the suspension bed. The globe came on, glowing softly. Hladik's eyes went wide with horror as he saw the bloody pool thickening beneath his hagemate's body. Her eyes stared emptily upward, a thin red line sliced across her lovely white throat.

There was a movement at the foot of the bed, and a figure emerged from the shadow. "Mrukk!" Hladik moved to get up. "What have you done?"

The assassin moved close, the blade glittering darkly in his hand. "You will approve, Director. I am removing a traitor from our midst."

"What do you mean?" He threw a frightened glance at his bed partner. "She—"

"Not her, Director . . . you!" Mrukk's eyes glinted as they narrowed to evil slits.

Hladik struggled to get up. Only then did he notice the dark stain spreading across his own bedclothes. The tickle that had awakened him had suddenly become a fiery burn. With a strangled cry he threw back the thin sheet and stared in disbelief at the deep cleft running from pubic bone to sternum. "Jam—rog-g . . ." he gasped, the name gurgling in his throat.

The Nilokerus Director clutched at his stomach, and lurched to his feet; he staggered two steps before his strength gave out, and collapsed at his assassin's feet. Mrukk's lips drew back in a sneer as he stooped to wipe his blade in his victim's hair; he had expected more courage from his former superior. Hladik moaned weakly as his limbs convulsed in death spasms.

"Jamrog, yes. Your benefactor, Director. I'll tell him you

thought to thank him for his last gift." Mrukk gave the body a shove with his toe. The mass of flesh jiggled and lay still. Replacing the knife in its sheath beneath his black yos, Mrukk stepped over the body of Hladik's guide and stole from the kraam, silent as the dead he left behind.

. . . . . .

The last few days had been a happy blur to Pizzle—his daylight hours filled with pleasant, if exhausting, labor as he worked side-by-side with the Fieri readying the ships that would make the long trip to the Bay of Talking Fish. By night he and Starla met to be together and share the details of their day. Neither mentioned marriage again, much to Pizzle's relief. Apparently Starla had forgotten that the word ever passed between them—which was exactly what he had hoped would happen.

There was so much to be done before they could set out on the journey. Pizzle had been intrigued by the notion of talking fish, and volunteered immediately when Jaire's brother, Preben, had told him about it. "Come with us," Preben invited. "It is an experience never forgotten."

"Gee, I'd like to," replied Pizzle. "Could I? You'd really let me?"

"Certainly," laughed Preben. Pizzle's eagerness was so childlike. "Anyone may go who cares to. Many hundreds will make the journey. And as I am to command one of the ships, you can travel with me."

"Great!" shouted Pizzle. "This is fantastic! Wait till Starla hears about this . . . How soon do we leave? Can I do anything? Do they really talk?"

"We will leave within a month, before the beginning of the next solar period."

Pizzle counted the days on his fingers. Based on what he was learning about Fieri timekeeping it worked out to—"That's less than three weeks away."

"The Preceptor will choose the appropriate day. We must be ready to leave at her signal. And since you ask, you *can* help me. I want our ship to be among the first. The Preceptor may choose ours to carry her, which would be a great honor."

So Pizzle had thrown himself into the preparations, helping

Preben's crew gather and stow supplies, scrape and repaint the ship top to bottom, check lifesaving gear, and freshen every one of the several dozen sleeping compartments below the wide, flat deck. The days sped by, each full of activity and anticipation.

One evening Pizzle went to meet Starla at their prearranged rendezvous—a secluded hill overlooking a cove on the shore of Prindahl. The sun still lit the twilight sky, though the first stars had emerged to take their places in the cloud-spattered heavens. He arrived early and waited, stretched out on the grassy turf, breathing the night air fresh off the great, dark water soughing gently on the shore below.

This is paradise, thought Pizzle idly. He had never been more happy, more satisfied, more at peace with himself. He wanted nothing else but for life to go on and on and on just the way it was. If only it could last forever. The Fieri actually believed that it would go on forever, that the Infinite Father had made them for eternity.

It was a notion Pizzle had always found quaint and somewhat ridiculous before. Now he saw it as profound wisdom. This kind of life, this heaven, made sense. For the first time in his life, he had begun to suspect that one lifetime may not be enough.

Then, quite without warning, a swift and poignant sadness rushed over him and he began to weep. Big, salty tears rolled from his eyes.

It would end. His life would end. He would die one day and it would be over, finished, no more. He would leave Starla behind and descend into dissolution and dust. And that would be that. Death at this tender moment seemed bitterly cruel and perverse, an outrage. To take away all this . . . this happiness, to be cut off so suddenly, so completely and finally was, Pizzle now considered, a monstrous and tragic injustice.

He lay on his back, staring blindly at the sky as the tears slid quietly down his cheeks. Starla found him that way. He heard her approach and sat up quickly, blotting his eyes with the heels of his hands. "What's wrong, my love?" she asked, settling down beside him.

He felt her cool hands on his face and produced a bleary-eyed smile for her benefit. "Nothing," he said. "I—uh, just got a little wrapped up in something I was thinking."

"Sad thoughts?"

"Not particularly." He tried to laugh. "No, not sad." He drew a long shaky breath and fell silent as he turned and gazed out on the water.

"What was it? Tell me, Asquith. I want to know." Starla's hand found his and clasped it warmly.

The nearness of her, the love and warmth that flowed from her to him, he found, in his present frame of mind, unbearable. The tears began again. He bent his head and let them fall.

"Darling . . ." Starla gathered him in her arms. "What is it?"

It was a long time before Pizzle could speak. At last he sat up and wiped his face on his sleeve. "I'm sorry," he said, "I'm not handling this very well. It's just that you're the most beautiful woman I've ever known. I don't deserve to be with—I don't deserve you."

"Shhh, don't talk so—" she began.

"It's true. I'm nothing—less than nothing. If you had known me on Earth, you wouldn't've given me the time of day. Please. Don't say anything," he said and looked away quickly again. "But by some miracle I'm here. I accept that. It's a dream. I know I don't deserve any of this, but here I am and I love it. I love you, I love Fierra, I love my life.

"I know this probably sounds dopey to you, but for the first time in my life I love my life."

He was silent for a moment, then sniffed and continued. "This—" He waved a hand to take in all Empyrion. "All this just overwhelmed me is all. I know it can't last, but . . . you don't know how much I wish it *could* last."

"It *will* last," said Starla softly. "It will last forever."

"I wish I could believe that."

"Believe it, Asquith. It's true."

"Yeah."

"Why do you doubt?"

Pizzle lifted his shoulders heavily. "You don't know how much I'd like to believe." He sighed heavily. "If I thought it could be true . . ."

"What you felt tonight was the voice of the Searcher calling you to Him, as He calls each of us. The Gatherer is reaching out for you, Asquith. Go to Him. Accept Him."

"I wish I could," Pizzle said sincerely. "There's just so much I have to sort out first."

"I understand," Starla said and snuggled closer. They talked of the approaching journey and the preparations to be made. Then they grew silent and simply drank in one another's company. At last they rose and made their way back down to their waiting evees, kissed good-night, and parted. The melancholy which lay heavily on Pizzle's heart stayed with him through the night. He went to his room at Liamoge and sat staring out at the deep, star-flecked water for a long time before slipping off into a light, restless sleep.

"**H**ladik's ashes and those of his hagemate will be entombed in the Hall of Directors in Nilokerus Hage," Jamrog said stiffly. His expression was bland and unreadable; his eyes shifted continually around the ring of Directors. The Threl took the news of Hladik's death in shocked silence. There was not a man among them who believed Jamrog's story of the incident. But the Supreme Director pushed the charade further, saying, "Subdirector Fertig will be apprehended. Even now the Invisibles are closing on his trail. He will face justice, Hage Leaders. This abominable deed will not go long unpunished, I can assure you."

Threl High Chambers were silent; each Director had understood Jamrog's implicit message: do not interfere with my plans or you will suffer the same fate as Hladik.

Into this tense silence came the tapping of a bhuj on the floor. "You wish to offer condolences, Rumon?" asked Jamrog sweetly.

"Condolences, yes," said Cejka. "But I would also ask the other members of the Threl to note our leader's remarkable fortitude in the face of this unimaginable tragedy. Hladik was, I believe, your closest friend and ally, was he not?"

There was nothing but innocence in Cejka's tone. Still, Jamrog watched him suspiciously, his eyes flicking between Tvrdy and Cejka. "It is true, I am deeply grieved by Director Hladik's unfortunate death," said Jamrog. "He was my friend and the·ally of us all. To be sure, we will all feel the loss."

"Most unfortunate," agreed Chryse Director Dey. "I am saddened and outraged."

"As are we all," put in Bouc, offering a doleful smile of sympathy.

"Murder," said Tvrdy sternly, "is always a cause for outrage."

There were murmurs of assent all around. "May I suggest that Subdirector Fertig stand before the Threl and answer for his crimes?" added Cejka. "I, for one, would hear his confession from his own lips."

The others tapped their bhujes on the floor in agreement.

"Thank you, Directors, for your concern and sympathy," said Jamrog tersely. "I will give the order that Fertig is not to be harmed. He will be made to stand before this body and give his confession." He stood abruptly and slammed his bhuj down. "This emergency assembly is dismissed. I am in mourning."

With that Jamrog fled the chambers, his face set in a fierce scowl. When he had gone, the others left quietly, avoiding one another's eyes. Tvrdy passed a secret signal to Cejka as they filed from the room. They met a little while later in one of the disused corridors of the Threl meeting place.

"That was a dangerous game you were playing," said Tvrdy once their guides were positioned to afford them privacy. "Why did you do it?"

"The monster!" Cejka blurted. "I could not sit there and hear him speak his lies any longer. I wanted the others to know I did not fear him."

"You would risk all our work for a show of bravado? Everyone knows what happened last night."

"Bouc and Dey—they make my stomach turn. Did you see them? Even after what happened to Hladik, they still try to worm their way into Jamrog's confidence." Cejka made a face of gross distaste.

"Forget them; they have chosen their destruction. I have news."

"Bogney?"

Tvrdy nodded. "He has lived up to his word."

"Amazing."

"We are to send more men and supplies as soon as possible. When can you be ready?"

Cejka smiled. "I am ready now. They will leave tonight."

"Good. I am ready, too. The sooner we join them, the better." Tvrdy looked at the Tanais bhuj in his hand. "The day has come when it is too dangerous to hold one of these." He let the ceremonial weapon clatter to the floor where it lay among broken bits of tile.

"You think there will be a Purge?"

"Cejka, open your eyes. The Purge has begun!"

• • • • • •

The machinery ground into operation, and the wires suspending Treet in the conditioning tank tightened. Skank watched as the body was slowly lifted, adjusting the levers to swing it over the tank's rim and drop it to the floor where it lay limp in a puddle of reeking fluid.

"Unstrap him," said the Nilokerus officer, pointing at the unmoving body. "Get him out of here."

"Unstrap him yourself," replied Skank, spitting on the floor. "I received no such order."

"Hladik is dead. Killed in his sleep last night by Subdirector Fertig. Now I am responsible for Cavern level, and I will not answer for this."

"And I received no order for his release!"

"Shut up! Don't you understand? There is no Threl authorization. This was another of Hladik's secrets. Who knows what the Director intended? There will be a new Hage Leader selected soon. What if the new Director finds out I kept one of Hladik's experiments? How am I to explain? What if the Threl finds out? I would be held responsible, and I will not sacrifice myself for Hladik's memory."

"Ahh," said Skank, winking slyly, "what if they find out you released him?"

"With Hladik's death he disappears. That's all I know."

Skank spat. "Take him then. I never saw him." He turned and lumbered away.

The Nilokerus stood looking at the huddled mass of inert flesh before him, then stooped and began tugging at the straps and wires, freeing Hladik's last captive.

• • • • • •

Treet felt nothing. No sensation of movement signaled his release. Cut off from all external stimulation, his senses had long ago ceased to function, his muscles to respond. In his mind he floated, drifting on endless waves or through endless corridors of empty space.

The fearful hallucinations had diminished along with his own dwindling consciousness. Until the last, he had kept up his effort to contact the alien intelligence he had attracted with his mental experiments. Each time he tried, the contact was stronger than the last. Although no thoughts were exchanged directly, Treet had the distinct impression that the entity allowed itself to be brought nearer, revealed more of itself to him. Treet had begun to suspect that in some way the mysterious presence had initiated the contact in the first place.

Treet's concentration waned as his mental energies depleted themselves. He lapsed into unconsciousness for longer periods, emerging only with great effort. The last time he regained awareness, the presence had been there with him, waiting for him. Treet had wanted very much to reach out to the entity—he sensed it was somehow very close to him—but it was all he could do to keep from sliding back into oblivion.

So he had merely held himself out to it, allowing the entity to behold him in whatever way it could. Here I am, Treet thought. I'm yours. To Treet's amazement, the presence had entered his mental space—simply merging with his awareness, but without violating him in any way. The effect was intensely comforting to Treet, who could not have prevented such an invasion in any case.

The exhilaration Treet felt when the entity entered his consciousness was electric. It inundated him, swallowed him, overwhelmed him like a tidal wave washing over a pebble on a storm-tossed beach. Even so, he sensed that the entity was holding back so that he would not receive the full force of the contact.

Treet accepted this and derived comfort from it, though he did not try to understand. There was something there with him, close to him, comforting him—that's all he understood. That, and that this entity was many times more immense than he could imagine.

These had been among Orion Treet's last conscious thoughts. Soon after the contact he had slipped into unconsciousness—though not before he had received a very strong sensation of calmness and assurance from the alien intelligence, a sensation designed to tell him that there was nothing to fear—a strange concept to communicate since there were certainly any number of things to fear, and with more than ample reason.

Treet accepted this offered assurance in the same way that he accepted the fact of the alien entity's existence—simply and without question. He did not have the strength for questions.

Treet had succumbed then, and the clouds he had labored to hold off descended, covered him, and bore him away.

TWENTY
THREE

Some time later, Treet became aware of a pressure on his chest and, of all places, his left cheek. He put up with the annoyance as long as he could and then squirmed. The shock of his hand smacking against a solid surface sent spasms rippling through his long-neglected muscles. The seizure left him exhausted, but simply aware that his environment had been altered; it now had hard surfaces.

This discovery roused Treet slightly. Light streamed into his brain, and he realized his eyes were open. He could see! The hideous wax mask was gone, and he could see. The pressure in his lungs reminded him that he could also breathe. He took a breath and immediately choked. Green liquid came gushing out of his nose and mouth. He vomited the vile stuff, aspirated it, and choked again.

When his lungs and stomach were finally empty, he drew a ragged breath and felt the cool air sear like a firebrand into the tissues. The pain brought him around. He perceived himself to be lying on the floor of one of the cells, more dead than alive. But alive nonetheless.

For that he was thankful, though he still wondered a little ungratefully what his next torture would be. Not eager to find out, Treet closed his eyes again and devoted himself to the luxury of sleep—a luxury soon interrupted by the arrival of a Nilokerus guard with a harsh voice that boomed in his sensory-deprived brain like the report of a cannon.

Throwing his hands over his ears, Treet writhed on the floor, then felt hands on him, lifting him, jerking him roughly upright.

"Get these on," the guard said, shoving a bundle at him. Treet's eyes fluttered in his head, and his skull vibrated with the noise of the guard's proximity. The room bucked and swayed. "Make it quick if you want to get out of here."

Treet could make no sense of the words. The man's mouth moved, his voice grated inside Treet's brain, but the words were gibberish.

The guard stared at Treet and then turned around and

stomped out. Treet staggered back, collapsed against the wall of his cell, and slid to the floor, still clutching the package that had been thrust into his hands.

Moments later the guard came back with another dressed in the red and white of the Nilokerus. "We'll have to dress him. He doesn't know where he is," the first explained.

"Can he walk?" asked his companion doubtfully.

"No, we'll have to drag him."

"Why can't we just leave him here?"

"Uri wants him gone right away. You heard about Hladik?" The other said nothing, but frowned and nodded.

"That's why we've got to get rid of him."

"What'll we do with him?"

"I've got an idea. You'll see."

They pulled the yos over Treet's head and stuffed his legs into the trousers. "I'll get an em—it will be quicker that way," said the first guard. "Wait here."

The Nilokerus looked at Treet distastefully, as if he were a hunk of meat that had spoiled. Treet closed his eyes again and tried to marshal his meager resources. If only they would leave me alone, he thought, and recognized that it was a coherent thought. The brain cells were starting to warm up again.

A few minutes later the other guard was back, and Treet was pulled up and slung between them and dragged out into the corridor where he tried to swim to the waiting em, swinging his arms and legs in random order. The Nilokerus barked at him to be still and dumped him in the back of the vehicle.

Treet's next impression was of speeding through a snaking pipeline: rising, twisting, turning, falling, looping around and around and around endlessly until at last they came to a halt. Treet was hauled from the back of the em and dragged across an empty expanse. His head happened to flop back, and he saw stars gleaming through the transparent panes of Dome's crystal roof far above.

He was propelled up a short flight of steps by the guards, who were by now cursing their duty, and at last flung down before an arched doorway. He heard his captors exchange a few mumbled words and then the sound of their footsteps retreating back down the steps and across the empty square. He was left alone, whimpering, limbs quivering, bewildered brain buzzing with sensory overload.

That was how two third-order Nilokerus physicians found him a few hours later.

• • • • • •

The big cat had followed Crocker for several days, padding along on huge, silent paws, a dark, fluid wave in motion. At first this unnerved the man, but he soon grew accustomed to glancing back over his shoulder and seeing the enormous feline creature a few meters behind him on the trail.

After their shared meal, Crocker had slept and then crept away, leaving the wevicat stretched out beside the carcass. When he happened to stop along the trail an hour or so later, he realized he was being followed. It was near sundown, the dense green of the forest was deepening to indigo all around, and the trails were becoming shadowed canyons. The cat was difficult to see, but Crocker knew it was there. His voice told him, *The cat's still back there. Go slowly. It has eaten, so it is not hunting. The creature is just curious.*

Crocker obeyed the voice and went on slowly, pausing now and then to look back, sensing the cat by the prickled hair of his scalp. When he reached his hedge-protected pool, he hesitated. Should he go in? Or find somewhere else to spend the night? A high tree?

Go in, his voice told him. *The wevicat will not follow you.*

The man obeyed and passed through the hedge. He dropped the meat scraps he carried and went down to the pool's edge to drink and wash himself, then returned to where the robot stood, placed his spear in the carrier, and lay down on the spongy turf to sleep.

The next morning, when Crocker left his bower the animal was waiting for him, tail curled around forefeet, great golden eyes gleaming with ferocious curiosity. They stood looking at one another for a long time, Crocker frozen with indecision over the presence of the beast, until his voice rescued him by saying, *The creature means to follow you. Show it that you accept it. It will not harm you.*

Crocker put down his spear and stepped forward. The cat yawned, came to the man, and pressed itself against him, knocking him to the ground. The huge furrowed tongue came out and licked the whole side of Crocker's head in one wet flick. The friendship was sealed. From then on, the wevicat had followed the man more or less continually—sometimes disappearing into the bush for a few hours on errands of its own, but always bounding into view again just when the man thought the beast had finally lost interest and had gone off to seek a new diversion.

The next night the wevicat joined Crocker in his lair, and the following morning they hunted together. They caught another of the slow bush cattle, and though the cat still claimed the kill, it left a slightly better portion for its human companion.

They ate and slept and took their time returning to their shared lair. The day had been sticky and hot, and now, as he neared the hedgewall, the man thought of the pool beyond and remembered how good a swim would feel on his sweaty skin.

Slipping through the hedge, Crocker stowed his spear in the carrier, stripped off the loinpouch, walked to the water's edge, paused to gaze into the cool depths, and dove in. The wevicat heard the splash and jumped to the edge of the pool where it crouched, ready to spring.

Crocker's head broke the surface. He gulped air and let himself slide under the water again. He came up splashing a moment later, shaking himself with pure, animal pleasure. The wevicat took one look at the man's head bobbing in the water and, with a lightning snap of its tail, leaped. The cat's body flashed through the air in a graceful arc and plunged in feet first almost on top of the man.

The next thing Crocker knew he was being hauled bodily out of the pool, his entire right shoulder and much of his right side wedged firmly in the wevicat's mouth. The cat dropped him on the springy turf and stood dripping over him, looking gaunt and skeletal in its sopping coat.

Crocker's round-eyed fright gave way to laughter when—after he'd checked himself to make sure he was not bleeding from several score puncture wounds—he realized the wevicat had not attacked him. Rather, it had rescued him. *It thought you were drowning,* explained the voice. He shuddered involuntarily, thinking about all those razor-tipped teeth piercing his soft flesh. But the animal had been extremely gentle, cradling him as it would one of its own cubs.

He climbed to his feet and looped his arms around the big

cat's neck and pushed against it with all his might. The beast stepped backwards, and they both tumbled into the pool where Crocker began whooping and splashing, kicking up the water and flinging handfuls into the wevicat's face.

The cat growled lightly and slapped out at the man with huge paws, pouncing and rolling, knocking him down or trying to catch him as he dove. Once Crocker climbed on the creature's back, and the wevicat spun in circles trying to dislodge him. Crocker noticed, however, that the animal was careful to keep its ebony claws sheathed.

After their watery rollick, the two dragged themselves from the pool and flopped down on the bank. The air was a thick blanket, causing skin and fur to dry slowly. They lay side by side and listened to the night sounds creep into the evening stillness as the twilight chorus limbered its voice. Some of the sounds Crocker could identify: the eerie, echoing howls belonged to fat flightless birds high in the upper levels of the forest; the gnawing chatters and barks were those of fuzzy tree rats; the gurgling squeaks and coos were tiny, wide-eyed lemurlike primates. The rest of the pips, croaks, hoots, gabbles, snorts, and startling yelps belonged to a large assortment of unseen mammalian throats of various sizes.

Crocker listened to the sounds as he had each night, and for the first time felt totally secure among them. Peace seemed to flow directly from the imperturbable presence of the great cat beside him. A bond had formed between them; they had hunted together, shared meat, and played together. An emptiness he had not even known existed had been filled in the man. He put out his hand and felt the sleek warmth of the beast beside him and stroked it gently; the cat loosed a deep, resonant purr that droned sleepy contentment. Night closed its fist around them, and they slept.

ourteen ships lay at anchor on the glass-smooth sea. Prindahl's mirrored face reflected the long, low hulls of blue and white and green. The sun's first rays stained the early morning sky watery blue. The day was but a promise; yet scores of Fieri already lined the shore, and more streamed down to the water's edge with the approach of dawn.

Yarden was among the first. Having found it impossible to sleep, she and Ianni had come to the shore to await the Preceptor's arrival. They joined those who had held vigil, marking the occasion with laughter and song through the night. The eve of leave-taking was a festive time, a time of keen anticipation and fond remembrance.

Flickering campfires dotted the shoreline, illuminating the ring of excited faces around each one. In between songs and stories, baskets of food were shared to keep up the reveler's strength.

The jovial mood reminded Yarden of Christmases she had known as a youngster, when the house had filled with relatives and friends, and the children had been allowed to stay awake late into the night to welcome the joyous day with gifts and games. This observation made Yarden pensive; it had been a long time since she had thought about her Earth life, a life that was now, quite literally, light-years away.

It was still early when the Preceptor appeared; clothed in her sky-blue travel garb and attended by three Mentors, she greeted her people as she passed slowly among them, accepting their best wishes for the journey. Yarden watched as the regal figure made her way to the foremost of the tethered boats, expecting a ceremony of some sort—a speech perhaps, or a christening. At very least, a prayer offered up for safe passage.

Instead, the Preceptor and her party merely boarded the vessel and took their places on deck. This was a signal to all the others who were waiting to go aboard. Instantly the crowd surged forward, and each of the fourteen ships rocked as their wide decks filled with passengers.

Yarden was swept forward with all the others and found herself standing in shallow water gazing up at a mast pointing skyward, its furled red sails bright against the new sky. Ianni, who had been right beside her only moments before, was nowhere in sight. Fieri clamored around her and called to their friends finding places on deck. She was trapped among a happy host and for a moment feared she would miss boarding altogether.

"Ianni!" she called. "Ianni, where are you?"

A voice sounded above her. "Yarden, what are you doing down there? Are you coming with us?"

She turned and looked up to see Pizzle's elfin grin beaming down at her over the rail. Next to him stood a young woman who smiled prettily. "You're Yarden?" she asked. "One of the Travelers?"

Yarden nodded and said, "I'm looking for my friend, Ianni. We were to board together, but I seem to have taken a wrong turn somewhere."

"Here, hold on," said Pizzle. "I'll get you aboard."

"What about Ianni—" began Yarden, but Pizzle had disappeared already. She sighed and ducked back into the crowd in an attempt to force her way to the gangplank, lost her footing, and fell backward with a splash. She was hauled onto her feet by nearby Fieri, who took her predicament in such good humor that it was difficult for Yarden not to laugh too.

"Now what are you doing?" Pizzle found her squeezing water from her clothes and hair. "Come on." He led her through the throng and pushed her up the gangplank. "What did you say your friend's name was?"

"Ianni," said Yarden. "I'm not sure if this is the boat we're supposed to be on or not . . ."

"Not to worry—I'm sort of second-in-command here, unofficially. I'll find you a place." He dashed back through the press around the gangplank and pulled Yarden along in his wake. People were eager yet considerate despite the excitement, and let them pass.

"We were supposed to meet Gerdes, my teacher, here," Yarden explained as they stepped off the gangplank and onto the deck. "I'll never find them now."

"Your teacher?"

"I'm studying painting. That is, I'm going to start."

"Going to be an artist, huh? Real nice," remarked Pizzle. "Let's talk about it later. I'm helping Preben—he's got command of this boat, and we're second in line. We've got to make ready to cast off."

"Wait! What about Ianni and Gerdes?"

Pizzle darted into the milling throng on deck and called back, "Later—we'll find them later."

Yarden sighed and looked around helplessly, hoping to spot one or the other of her friends. She fluffed her wet clothes and wished she could start the day over.

"Yarden?"

She turned and saw the woman who had been standing next to Pizzle at the rail. "I'm Starla," the stranger said. "Please don't be concerned for your friends. You'll find them."

"But how? I don't see them anywhere. They'll be looking for me."

"They'll find you." The young woman smiled again, and Yarden felt some of the tension leave her.

"I suppose you're right," Yarden admitted, relaxing just a little.

"It's a very long journey. We'll stop often along the way. If they are not on this boat, you'll find them on one of the others."

"Yes, of course." Yarden smiled at her own silliness. "I wasn't thinking. I can join them later." She noticed the young woman studying her intently and grew suddenly self-conscious.

"Forgive my forwardness," said Starla simply. "But you are very beautiful and I—"

Yarden guessed what the young Fieri woman was trying to say. She had encountered it elsewhere. "You are curious about what a female Traveler would look like?"

"Yes. And there is another reason . . ." Starla hesitated and then, when she saw that Yarden really wanted to know, said, "Asquith has said he finds me beautiful—"

"As you are," Yarden assured her.

"And he has described you as a very beautiful woman. I merely wanted to see . . ." She hesitated, glancing up at Yarden from under her long lashes.

"To see his definition? And I must look a sight—standing here dripping all over the deck." To Starla's puzzled look she added, "Never mind, I understand."

"I hope I have not offended you."

Yarden smiled warmly. "How could I be offended? It seems Pizzle has a good eye. We should both feel complimented."

"You are very kind. I can find you some dry clothes."

Just then Pizzle returned. "Hey, you've met. Great! Yarden, I've got it fixed for you. We're a little jammed up—all the ships are full to capacity. But you can share with Starla until you get back in touch with your friends. Okay?"

"Fine. Starla has explained already."

"Come on, let's get a place at the rail. Look—" He cast an eye to the top of the mast where a thin red banner fluttered in the rising breeze. "We're about to cast off. You won't want to miss this."

"What is it?" Yarden followed them to the rail and found a place next to Pizzle.

"It's the send-off. Preben told me about it."

The barge ahead of them had unfurled its great triangular sail of royal blue. It fluttered lightly and then puffed. The boat began to draw slowly away from the shore, turning out into deeper water.

A rippling of fabric sounded above them; Yarden turned to see a crimson sail shaking itself out and filling with the breeze. Then they were gliding away, taking a position behind and a little to one side of the first boat. The third vessel came on in its turn and all the rest, one by one, until all were under sail.

They passed along the shoreline and came to a place where rounded hills tumbled gently to deep water. The boats came close to the steep banks, and Yarden saw that the hills were lined with people. Fieri in small groups scattered over the hills from the heights right down to the water's edge, stood watching them quietly. The passengers aboard the barges fell silent. Yarden felt her pulse quicken with expectation.

Then, as if on signal, the multitude gathered on the hillsides began swaying slowly and singing, lifting their arms and waving. Some had bright squares of cloth which they held aloft in the breeze as they moved. Their song was a simple, rising, falling, melodic chant, sung slowly, over and over, as the hillside host swayed, some with linked arms and others with outspread arms, and all facing the rising sun and the ships moving slowly away.

The Fieri song sounded clear over the still water:

With peace we send
  you on your way;
In peace your journey wend.
Protector lend
  fair wind this day,
And joy to your journey's end.

The words were simple, but together with the plaintive melody—sung over and over in the style of a round, one hillside starting the tune and the next picking it up and beginning again when the first reached the end of the stanza, repeated again and again, from hillside to hillside—altogether it created a beautifully evocative and moving ceremony: the colorful ships plying slowly along green-cloaked hills asway with Fieri, faces bright in the rising sun, singing their loved ones away with a gentle blessing.

Yarden listened, enchanted by the simple beauty of it, drinking in every nuance of the experience. When she looked along the rail, she saw more than a few eyes shining with tears and noticed her own misting over as well. "It kind of gets to you," Pizzle sniffed.

The boats slid away from the hills; and although many of the singers followed along the shore, they were soon outdistanced and the song faded on the morning wind. "Wonderful," sighed Yarden; she felt as if she were coming out of a dream. "I wouldn't have missed this for the world."

"These people grow on you," said Pizzle. Yarden noted the way he stared at Starla when he spoke. "There's no doubt about it. This is going to be some trip."

• • • • •

Morning came to the Starwatch level of Nilokerus Hage, although Treet, in his sense-numbed stupor, did not comprehend the gray lightening of the great crystal panes above him. He did understand that the floor he lay upon was cold and hard and that his body ached in as many places as it was possible for a human body to hurt.

He had lain here all his life, it seemed. He could not

remember a time when his body had not ached and he had not huddled on the cold stone of a strange doorway. This being the case, he saw little sense in moving. And anyway, moving might make the pain worse.

He drowsed and woke and drowsed again. He dreamed that some Nilokerus guards came and trundled him off to their distant torture chambers, glad for another chance at tormenting him. In his dream he heard the crackle of electricity as they tuned their instruments of torture. Faces drifted in and out of his dream—one face in particular: round and lightly wrinkled, with concern in lively green eyes. A woman's face. How odd.

Treet puzzled over this endlessly. It was to him the riddle of the universe. Why a woman's face? Who was she? Where had she come from? What did she want? Why had she joined his torturers?

There were voices, too. *Rest . . . rest,"* they said. *You are safe . . . safe . . . nothing can happen . . . happen . . . to you . . . safe . . . sleep . . . sleep . . .*

There was comfort in these voices, reverberating as they did inside his head. Treet grasped the comfort and hugged it to him. Such solace was difficult to find in this world and must not be shunned. Cast it roughly aside and it might never return.

Treet hung for the longest time lightly suspended between the conscious world and the unconscious, sometimes more in one than the other, but never totally in either. Thoughts came infrequently into his mental never-never land, and those that did were flimsy, awkward things, insubstantial as phantom butterflies.

He thought about a dark-haired woman with a face made of rain; a great, troubling hole in the ground filled with broken glass; a thundering, yellow sky that burned and burned forever; a man who wore a turtle's shell on his back and hid from the sun. These and other whimsical images floated through his lazy awareness.

Far back in the further recess of his mind throbbed a sense of urgency: a charge had been given him; he had a duty to perform. Time was slipping away. The sense was anesthetized, the urgency dulled. But it was there, a clockwork, muffled and slowed though still ticking . . . ticking . . . ticking.

TWENTY
FIVE

"Tell me, Mrukk, what did Hladik say when he died?" Jamrog reclined lazily in his chair, features slack, eyes half-lidded from the effects of the flash he'd been sampling all day. His hagerobe was carelessly draped over his lean frame. A young woman heated souile in an enameled jar over a small brazier.

The chief of the Mors Ultima studied the Supreme Director carefully, wondering, not for the first time, what kind of man his master was. Certainly he showed little of the restraint or discipline that had helped propel him into the Supreme Director's kraam; he had given in to his vices so quickly. That showed weakness. Mrukk detested weakness in any form.

"He invoked your name, Hage Leader," replied Mrukk.

"How considerate," smirked Jamrog. "To think of me at the moment of his demise." He giggled obscenely at his joke, his head lolling from side to side as his body shook. "I did not know I inspired such devotion."

Mrukk stood stiffly, eyes narrowed as his cold heart calculated: a quick blade thrust between the ribs—what would be the outcome of such an action?

"Here, Mrukk," said Jamrog, offering a souile cup from the lacquered tray held by his nubile companion. "A drink to Hladik's memory. Our loss is Trabant's gain, seh?"

Mrukk took the cup, held it between two fingers, and lifted it to his lips as Jamrog did. The warm liquor touched the tip of his tongue and no more. He replaced the cup on the tray. Jamrog lifted himself to his feet, swayed, and gathered his robe around him. "Come, Mrukk, walk with me."

They turned, moved out from under the multicolored canopy, and strolled into the Supreme Director's garden. "I have another task for you, Commander," said Jamrog when they were out of eavesdropping range. "One of the Directors challenged me before the Threl yesterday—as much as insinuated that I had no right to take Hladik's life." He paused, but Mrukk said nothing, so he continued. "I cannot countenance such flagrant impertinence. If left unchecked, it soon renders the office of Supreme Director impotent. I will not be made impotent, Mrukk, do you understand me?"

"I understand. Which traitor challenged you?"

"Rumon." Jamrog said the word as if tasting his revenge in the sound of it. "I think a lesson similar to Hladik's would be instructive. See to it, Mrukk."

"As you will, Supreme Director." The fierce Mrukk stopped and faced his master. "Is that all?"

"Yes, for the time being. However, I expect you will be very busy in the days to come. To tell you the truth, I suspect a plot against me by members of the Threl. You will inform me when the Invisibles have gathered the proper evidence. No doubt your men welcome the opportunity to prove their loyalty and express gratitude to their Hage Leader for his recent generosity."

Mrukk said nothing, merely inclining his head in mute assent. He turned and stalked away. Jamrog watched him go and then called his Hagemate to him, pulled her close, and kissed her violently. "More souile!" he shouted, pushing her away. "I must celebrate. More souile!"

• • • • • •

Giloon Bogney strode through the ruined Hageblock. His cloak—the cloak Tvrdy had given him—was thrown across his shoulders to sweep along behind him like a wing. His nasty face was matched with an equally nasty frown. The diminutive ruler liked the appearance of enhanced power which the strangers gave him before his people. But dealing with the loathsome interlopers was beginning to wear on his goodwill. The Old Section positively reeked with their presence.

It was one thing to tolerate them, but quite another to have to suffer their incessant badgering. Tvrdy's men were at best a continual pain in the lower belly. The Dhog was beginning to wonder why he had agreed to the arrangement in the first place.

"Why Giloon not knowing more Tanais and Rumon coming?" he demanded, bursting through the doorless arch of the ground-floor room he had given the Tanais as a command post.

The leader of the Tanais contingent, an exact man named

Kopetch, was as unbending and precise as the levels and plumb lines he'd handled most of his life. His engineer's love for accuracy had made him a formidable disciplinarian: implacable and unforgiving. Tvrdy had assigned him the unenviable task of creating some kind of order within the Old Section, readying the place for its coming transformation into an armed camp—the first step necessary to begin forming the Dhog rabble into something resembling a fighting unit.

If he was unbending and unforgiving, he was also fair. And not easily shaken or roused. He moved with an inexorable and patient logic in all matters of heart and mind. Glancing up unconcernedly as the Dhog leader flew into the room, he said, in words measured and sure, "If you care to explain what you are talking about, I will be happy to listen to you. If you go on gibbering, I will ignore you. There are important arrangements to be made this morning—I assume it *is* morning."

Bogney ground his teeth and fumed, his face livid through the grime. "Things happening and Giloon not told."

"As you are speaking of them now, I assume you must have been told about them. Therefore, your anger is irrational."

The Dhog leader stomped toward the Tanais engineer menacingly, who turned to regard the threat with a calm, equable expression. "Dhogs not needing you, Tanais. You go away!"

"And how would that help the Dhogs become a Hage?"

"Grrr-rrr!" Bogney ground his teeth at the man. "Trabant take you!"

"To answer your initial question, you were not informed because there was no time for advance warning. Rather than waste precious time sending messages back and forth—messages which could have been intercepted by Invisibles—the Tanais and Rumon came directly upon receiving our all-clear." Kopetch paused and, out of concern for his mission, offered, "If this disturbs you in some way, accept my apologies."

"Giloon say who coming to Old Section."

"They came on Tvrdy's order. Would you countermand his order?"

"Giloon Bogney not under Tanais hand."

"We are *both* under Director Tvrdy's authority—as are the Rumon—until the Purge is over."

The Dhog glared at his erect and unperturbed adversary. He was not used to being talked to this way. It stung and rankled. Bogney was still searching his vocabulary for a suitable expletive when the Tanais said, "Our leader has sent you a special gift. I was about to have it brought to you. As you are here, perhaps you'd like to have it now."

"A gift for Giloon?" His eyes swept the room crammed with supplies and weaponry.

Tvrdy was right, thought Kopetch. The Dhogs *were* like children still in creche. "He thought this might be of use to you." The Tanais reached into a fold in his yos and brought out a slim, tubular object with a flat handle.

Bogney reached out and took the metallic thing, pleased with its dull, blue-black color and its cool weight in his hand. He hefted it and then took it by the handle, which just fitted the palm of his hand. He waved it around, pointing, aiming. "This weapon?"

"A projectile thrower. Very old, but still lethal."

"Tanais sending this to Giloon?" The Dhog smiled happily, eyes glittering at the sight of his new prize. No one else he knew of had ever possessed such a thing.

"He thought you might have need for it one day soon and wanted you to have it."

"Giloon accepting Tanais gift, but Director talks to Director, not to underman."

"That might be sooner than you think," replied Kopetch, moving back to his work. "The Tanais bring word that the Purge has begun. The Directors may not remain in Hage much longer. Also, Hyrgo may be joining us soon."

"Hyrgo!" Giloon was about to protest the further invasion of his realm by yet another disagreeable horde.

Kopetch headed him off by suggesting, "Of course, with your permission, they will want to begin setting up hydroponics and food processing centers."

"Food," said Giloon, rubbing his filthy beard.

"We must become self-sufficient as soon as possible."

"Dhogs making Old Section good place for growers. Giloon seeing to that."

"You are steps ahead of me," replied Kopetch, picking up a map from the stack of papers on the table. "If I might suggest this area here . . ." He pointed to a place on the map. "Donner Heights I think it's called."

Bogney squinted and studied the map, fingering it with his

greasy fingers. "This place ruined," he announced at length, shoving the map back. "Old map."

"Yes, so I assumed. But since we have so little time, and the Hyrgo will need a place to begin food production . . ."

Bogney thumped his chest. "Giloon seeing to it. No making noisy guts on that."

"I knew you would see the potential," said Kopetch dryly. "Was there anything else, Director?"

At the engineer's use of the title, the Dhog leader felt a shiver of delight quiver through him. He smiled importantly, eyes round and gleaming. "Much to do. You be wasting good light talking." With that he swept from the room, leaving only a lingering odor in the air to suggest that he had been there.

Kopetch returned to his work of reordering the Old Section. When his Hage Leader arrived, he wanted everything to be ready. Now, having placated the loathsome Dhog for the time being, it appeared he would have a good chance of getting something accomplished.

Still, he had to wonder whether there was no other way— to join the Dhogs of all things! Who would have imagined it? All they needed now was time. The best plans took time. Patience and time—they would need plenty of both.

TWENTY
SIX

*T*he day slid by easily as the ship carved the smooth water, tugged along by the steady breeze. They lost sight of land a little past midmorning; silver water shimmered on every side, broken only occasionally by shoals of leaping fish, whose bright fins burst through the surface, scattering light in shining fragments. The sky remained clean and cloudless and remote in its blue solitude.

To Yarden it was a magical day. The send-off, as Pizzle called it, provided by the Fieri had cast its spell over her heart, and she felt enchanted still. She strolled the decks wrapped in the gentle glow of a soft inner radiance that made everything she saw seem new-made and charmed. She felt as if this day, this very instant, her life was beginning, that all that had passed before was merely a prelude to this moment.

The other ships—twelve of them stretching out in a staggered line behind, the last one almost too distant to see clearly—plied Prindahl's deeper waters with solemn majesty, sails puffing proudly, painted hulls glistening, graceful outriggers slicing the low waves. Yarden thrilled to the sight; the procession reminded her of something out of the *Arabian Nights* or the *Tales of Sinbad*, and she found herself time and again, on one of her rounds of the deck, simply standing, staring out at the long string of boats sliding over the platinum sea.

Pizzle found her standing at the aft rail, her hair streaming in the breeze, eyes glazed in wonder. "I've been looking for you," he said.

"Umm," was all she said.

"Haven't seen much of you—I thought we might talk."

With an effort she turned her eyes away. "What about?" she asked dreamily.

"If you're busy, I can come back."

"Busy?"

"You want to be alone?"

She shook her head and took a deep breath. "The air is so

fresh!" She gazed back out at the colorful sails of the trailing barges. "So beautiful."

"I'll come back."

"How have you been, Pizzle?" she asked absently. "I haven't seen much of you lately."

"Is that so?"

She turned to him again with a questioning glance. "What did you say?"

"Nothing. It's just that you seem a little preoccupied right now. I guess you're thinking about Treet, huh?"

"Who?" She appeared genuinely puzzled.

"Orion Treet? A friend of ours—yours. Tall guy with lots of hair everywhere, likable, if a little poached topside. Remember him?"

"Treet . . ." A look of sharp vexation crossed her features. "I don't want to remember—to talk about him, I mean."

"Huh? I thought you two were real close." Pizzle wagged his head in amazement at female fickleness. "What happened? Lover's tiff?"

"I don't want to talk about it."

Pizzle was quiet for a moment, and Yarden thought he had gotten the message. "I guess he was probably too bullheaded for his own good," he said after a while. "Imagine, him going back there—back to Dome, I mean. I can't figure it. I didn't think he'd really do it."

"How dare you inflict him on me!" Yarden snapped. "I told you I don't want to talk about him. You're ruining everything. Just leave me alone."

"Hey, I'm sorry. I didn't know you two had scrapped it up. I was just wondering, okay?"

"Go away. Just . . . go away." Yarden turned abruptly, setting her jaw.

"Right, I'll see you later," said Pizzle, shuffling off.

Curse that Pizzle, she thought. Everything was beautiful until he'd mentioned Treet. I don't want to remember. I *won't* remember him. She pushed herself forcefully away from the rail—as if she were shoving away his memory. She continued her stroll once more around the deck, determined to regain the magical mood that had, like dew in the desert sun, evaporated at the drop of Treet's name.

• • • • • •

"I told you that he was not to be left alone—not even for a moment," said Ernina, raising an accusing finger at the slacker. "Where were you? Answer me."

"I just stepped out for—"

"I don't care. I don't want excuses, I want obedience. Someone is to be with him at all times. Understand?"

The first-order physician nodded ruefully.

"All right." The flinty old healer softened somewhat. "I know you are tired; I will send someone to relieve you soon." She studied her newest patient as she placed the fingers of her right hand against his throat. "I don't want anything to happen to him," she muttered.

"Is he someone important?" asked the young man.

Ernina delivered her answer with a look of reprimand in her quick, green eyes. "*Everyone* who needs our help is important."

"More important, I mean?"

The old woman evaded the question. "He has a mental disorder which requires constant attention. Should he awake, I wish to be notified at once." She turned on the young physician again. "When was the last time you read his aura?"

"Green, stabilized," he answered at once, "some shrinkage in the red, passing to yellow. His blue is still well below range."

Ernina nodded. "Any black showing?"

"Transient flares—nothing stable." He paused and looked thoughtfully at the man in the suspended bed. "He speaks aloud."

"It's to be expected."

"He speaks of his mishon. What is a mishon?"

Ernina shrugged. "Perhaps he will tell us when he is again in his right mind. Anything else?"

"Just muttering—nothing coherent."

She nodded and said, "I'll send your relief at once." Ernina left the room. This patient had a good chance to recover if his will to live was strong enough. Time would tell. She had done all she could for the moment.

How he had come to appear at her door, she didn't know. But she recognized Hladik's handiwork readily enough. The tortured man was a Fieri—that she also knew the moment she had seen him lying there shivering. Now that he was here, she was determined to protect him at all costs.

The news of Hladik's assassination had shaken the Hage. Not that she cared for the licentious Director, but his death augured ill for the future. Jamrog was, if possible, a worse tyrant than Sirin Rohee. And if, as the rumor messengers suggested, Hladik's death was the beginning of a Purge, her choice was clear.

Her patient could not be moved now—maybe not for a long while. But as soon as he was able . . .

In the meantime, there was so much to be done, so much to get ready before that eventuality.

She smiled grimly to herself; she had been given another chance to save the life of a Fieri. I lost the first one, she thought. One that I pledged to protect. I will *not* lose this one.

· · · · · ·

Cejka climbed the steps of the communications tower which rose like a spearhead from the center of Rumon Hage. He paused to look out over his domain, peaceful in the hazy midday light. Clumps of trees in a long sinuous line marked the banks of Kyan; low, blue-tinted Hageblocks, scattered among green quadrangles, stepped up from the river's edge.

Rumon was not large, but its people were fiercely loyal—a fact Cejka had always appreciated and never abused. Within Rumon's neat borders, Hagemen came and went without fear and spoke their minds freely, for Rumon priests were not given to greed and petty malice as were most others. Cejka saw to that, keeping the bloated priesthood in check just as he kept his rumor messengers quick and subtle.

Under Cejka's leadership rumor messengers had become the main, often the only, source of reliable information for the common Hageman. Consequently, there was not a single Hageblock in all of Empyrion where a Rumon rumor messenger was not welcome. The swiftness of the network contributed to the messengers' high stent among the people of the various Hages, who for the most part considered rumor messengers on a level with magicians, so quickly did they appear and vanish.

The Rumon Director was now grateful for the speed and efficiency of his beloved network. He had known within seconds the precise moment that Mrukk had set foot in Rumon. Even though the Mors Ultima commander had appeared in disguise as a Rumon Hageman, he was instantly recognized and reported, his movements since then carefully observed.

There could only be one reason for the assassin's sudden appearance, and Cejka knew what it was: Jamrog had ordered his death, no doubt in retaliation for his remarks in the Threl session the day before. Now Cejka had two choices and a decision to be made quickly.

Reluctantly he turned his eyes away from the deceptively calm landscape before him. Death waited out there. He hurried inside the tower and rode the lift to the top, where he had established the heart of the rumor network. Subdirector Covol was waiting for him when he entered.

"Where is he?" Cejka came into the large, machine-crammed room. As always it was humming with activity, but today there was an edge to the excitement. Hagemen glanced up briefly as the Director walked by and then returned to their tasks, many of them staring into glowing screens or speaking softly into microphones; others, their heads encased in remote viewer helmets, sat motionless, their fingers twitching on the lighted panels before them. And everywhere magicians scurried, tending the machinery, keeping it going.

"Still on Riverwalk level," answered Covol. "He appears to be working his way toward Hage center, slowly; he is in no hurry."

"Has he attempted to contact any of the known Invisibles within Hage?"

"We have detected no contact. None of the Invisibles are near him at present." Covol regarded his chief. "What is your decision? Should we try to apprehend him?"

Cejka clasped his hands and bowed his head. When he raised his face again he said, "No."

"He is alone. We can take him."

"It would be too difficult and the loss of life too great. If we fail, we will have shown Jamrog the strength of our network."

"We can take him," insisted Covol. To Cejka's quick dismissal he said, "At least let us kill him. We can have him surrounded by weapons carriers within two minutes."

Cejka considered this. It was tempting. Yes, they could have Rumon snipers within range in minutes, and at least one enemy would be eliminated. But it wouldn't stop Jamrog. Losing his prime assassin would drive the Supreme Director into a killing frenzy; he would order a massive strike on the Hage, and thousands would die.

"No," he said.

Covol heard the finality in his leader's voice and despaired. "Do you propose to do nothing to protect yourself?"

"Where I am going, Covol, I will be well protected." The Subdirector stared. "What's wrong? We have planned for this day. The time has come, sooner than expected perhaps, but it has not caught us unaware. Are you ready to assume the Directorship?"

"You'll still be Director," pointed out Covol.

Cejka nodded. "Yes, yes, but since I will not be here to take care of them, our Hagemen will look to you for leadership. Jamrog may even have you formally installed." He silenced a quick protest. "You know what to do. We have agreed on the plan, and we will follow it."

"Yes, Director." Covol squared his shoulders.

"Good. I will leave with the Hyrgo tonight. Now, alert Tvrdy; he must be informed of my plans at once." Cejka took a last look around the busy command center he had worked so hard to create. It was possible that he'd never see the place again.

He pushed the thought from him. The Purge was just beginning; many decisive battles remained to be fought, and Cejka meant to see Jamrog's head on a bhuj in Threl High Chambers before it was over. That, he considered as he disappeared into his private rooms, was a prospect worth further contemplation.

Near sundown on the fifth day the Fieri sailboats reached the northernmost shores of Prindahl. The sails were furled as the first ships slid into a sand-rimmed cove and anchored in the clear, shallow water. The passengers disembarked to make camp on dry land for the night. The cove had been used by the Fieri as a stopping-place for generations; there were open-air pavilions and fresh-water wells scattered among the cool groves of flat-leafed shade trees lining the cove just above the sand line.

No one seemed to mind that they had to wade ashore, and the festive atmosphere was quickly rekindled among the convivial travelers. Yarden sloshed through the warm, knee-deep water, and would have given in to a swim—as many of the Fieri were doing—if not for the fact that she wanted to find Ianni and Gerdes as soon as possible. She looked among the laughing, splashing bathers from the first boat for her friends, but didn't see them.

On the beach, she wandered along the fine, white sand, stopping at each boat to search among the passengers in the water and coming ashore. The fifth ship, spring green sails with a bright yellow hull, was just gliding in when Yarden arrived. She waited as the anchor dropped with a splash and the gangplank was thrust out into the water. The first passengers off were youngsters who dove off the gangplank and into the turquoise shallows like seals too long pent-up for comfort. Amidst their happy squeals, the other passengers filed off. Among the first was Ianni.

"Over here!" Yarden cried, waving an arm above her head.

Ianni glanced up, smiled, and waved. "So you found a berth after all," she said as she joined Yarden on the beach. "I knew you would, or else I would have come back to look for you. I'm sorry, I guess I should have warned you about the boarding."

"It doesn't matter. I've enjoyed every minute of the trip so far, and I'll enjoy the rest even more now that we're together. Where is Gerdes?" Yarden asked, searching the oncoming throng for her teacher.

"She'll be along. I saw her earlier this afternoon," replied Ianni. "I know she's eager to get her pupils together. You're not the only one to get separated from her."

They began walking along the sand, listening to the laughter ringing in the still air. "As much as I love sailing," said Yarden, "it's good to feel solid ground beneath my feet." She fell silent then and was quiet so long that Ianni turned her head to study Yarden from the corner of her eye.

"Something is troubling you," observed Ianni. She stopped and drew Yarden down beside her, stretching out her long legs as she reclined.

Yarden's first impulse was to deny her friend's assertion. But it was true. Off and on the last few days she had been moody. "I'm . . . I don't know—I feel restless, unsettled."

Ianni said nothing, but merely waited for Yarden to continue. The sun touched the flat, metallic surface of the lake and spread white fire across the far horizon and long shadows on the beach. Yarden sat with her legs drawn up, arms folded on her knees, eyes closed in searching thought. Finally she lowered her head onto her arms. "It's Treet," she said.

"Go on."

Yarden sighed heavily. "I thought I could forget him. I nearly did—at least I thought so. Until that stupid Pizzle . . ."

"It wasn't Pizzle," Ianni said softly.

Yarden lifted her head. "No, I suppose not. Not really."

She fell silent again, watching the sun slide into the water. The remaining boats had slid into the cove, and their passengers now strolled the beach or swam, their voices clear as light in the air. There were tears in her eyes when she turned to Ianni. "I didn't want this to happen. I wanted to be free of him. I wanted to start a new life. It isn't fair. Why should he have this hold on me?"

"Are you certain it's Treet?"

Yarden nodded. "Who else?"

"The Seeker has His ways."

Pondering this, Yarden said, "I have been faithful to my call. I have sought the Infinite's leading. I have asked to be shown how to grow in belief and understanding. I have—"

"You have cut Treet from your life," Ianni pointed out gently. "And closed that part of your life to the Teacher."

"But I don't see how that matters."

"The Infinite requires an open heart, Yarden, and an open life. All of life is to be shared with Him. You ask Him to help you grow, yet set limits to that growth."

"But Treet—I want to give him up to follow the faith."

"I know. But perhaps the Infinite requires something different from you."

Yarden didn't like this. "You're saying I'm stuck with Treet? No matter what I happen to think or feel about it?"

Ianni laughed. "No, I didn't mean it like that. I only meant that there is obviously something to be accomplished between you. The Seeker has been prodding you to see this. Your rejection of Treet is unhealthy; it has made you unhappy, restless."

"What am I supposed to do? He's God knows where, doing God knows what, and I'm here. Just what am I supposed to do?"

"I can't answer that, Yarden. Nor, I think, could the Preceptor. This you must discover for yourself."

Yarden frowned unhappily. "I'll think about it."

"Yes, think about it. But don't think too long."

• • • • • •

The sumptuous Supreme Director's kraam had been stripped of its fine furniture and art objects and transformed into a palatial banqueting hall—complete with a bubbling fountain and pool with live fish near the entrance. Miniature trees had been placed around the perimeter of the room, and a circle of tables erected in the center. Behind screens and in secluded clusters conveniently hidden by hanging plants were soft couches and mounds of cushions for the assignations of his guests. Braziers on tall tripods lit the room with yellow flames that burned day and night, flickering before glistening Bolbe hangings of the very best quality.

The Supreme Director was entertaining with increasing frequency; he was busy cultivating a coterie of sycophants, stooges who would do his bidding without qualm or question and never dream of challenging his authority.

Jamrog entered the kraam, surrounded by his Mors Ultima bodyguard. Since Cejka and Tvrdy vanished, the Supreme Director had taken to moving about in public in the company of handpicked Invisibles. Subdirector Osmas, his Saecaraz successor, and a thin, sunken-eyed Nilokerus—one of Hladik's underdirectors, elevated to the Directorship following Fertig's disappearance—stood waiting with several Chryse and Bolbe artisans.

"Splendid!" Jamrog clapped his hands when he saw them. "You have something for me?"

The toady Osmas squirmed forward, rubbing his hands. "I have reviewed the work myself, Supreme Director. I think you will like the results."

Jamrog, eyes gleaming in anticipation, observed the dour Nilokerus. The man, though young, had sunken cheeks and a deathly pallor, suggesting a wasting disease. "What about you, Diltz? What do you think?"

The voice that answered was forceful enough, but had something of the tenor of the tomb. "You will be pleased, Supreme Director."

Jamrog made stirring motions with his hands. "Let's see it then, by all means." Osmas ushered the artisans forward. With some trepidation they produced a huge length of cloth and unrolled it on the floor, stretching it between them. As the folds were carefully shaken out, there appeared a gigantic image of the Supreme Director with ceremonial bhuj in uplifted hand painted on cloth of Saecaraz silver with black edging.

Jamrog studied the likeness carefully, striding right into the center of the cloth to stare down at his own portrait. The artists glanced at one another fearfully. But slowly the mercurial leader smiled and looked up. "I am pleased," he announced. "Well pleased. You have rendered my likeness admirably, and for that you will receive a thousand shares each."

"A thousand shares!" gasped one of the Bolbe. He clamped a hand over his mouth and, abashed, shrank back behind the others.

"What, not enough?" mocked Jamrog, turning on the man. "Two thousand then—but you'll have to earn it, greedy Bolbe."

The artisans were stunned; they'd never heard of such sums. However, one enterprising Chryse found his voice and asked, "How may we further serve you, Supreme Director?"

"I want a thousand just like this," Jamrog said, tapping the long-handled bhuj on the portrait beneath his feet.

"A thousand!" sputtered the Chryse in disbelief.

"Two thousand for one thousand," smiled Jamrog sweetly. "I want them ready for the Trabantonna."

Seeing the artisans quail at the request, Osmas stepped forward. "The Feast of the Departed is nearly upon us, Supreme Director," he interceded. "Or did we misunderstand?"

"No, you understand completely. I will have my image displayed on every Hageblock in every Hage and at every feast site. This will remind all Empyrion of their leader's thoughtfulness for them." He looked around him for any to gainsay the plan.

"Of course, Threl Leader," replied the Chryse spokesman. "It can be done."

"You see, Osmas? No misunderstanding." To Diltz he said, "The Nilokerus will see that the banners are hung to best effect in each Hage. When I make my appearances at the Trabantonna feasts, I want to see my image well represented."

The Nilokerus Director assented silently. "Excellent!" Jamrog said, tapping the image with the bhuj again. "Correct me if I am wrong, Directors, but I think this sort of thing helps our Hagemen tremendously. It focuses their attention, you see, makes them continually aware of me as I am of them."

"Oh, undoubtedly, Hage Leader," gushed Osmas.

"All the more reason to proceed with haste," offered Jamrog helpfully. "We have our Hagemen to think of in this matter."

The artisans dismissed themselves and were whisked away by several of the ever-attentive Invisibles. "Now then," snapped Jamrog when the others had gone, "what of the fugitives?"

"Latest reports are not encouraging, Supreme Director," explained the Saecaraz Subdirector. "There has been no sign of them."

Jamrog whirled on Diltz. "What about your security forces?"

"As I have explained, Supreme Director, we do not have checkpoints at all Hage borders—"

"Establish them at once," Jamrog ordered. "I want those traitors found."

Osmas attempted to soothe his leader. "Certainly you can have no serious thoughts for them now. They mean nothing."

"Tvrdy is a cunning enemy, and Cejka is no fool. Together they are twice the threat. The longer they are free, the more impudent they will become. All opposition to my leadership must be silenced. Traitors like Tvrdy and his puppet Cejka encourage other weak-willed malcontents to harbor treason in their hearts." He stepped close to Diltz and thrust a finger in his face. The man did not flinch. "The Nilokerus will begin a Hage by Hage search for the two enemies. Any help will be generously rewarded—five thousand shares if we find them. Publicize it."

"As you wish," Osmas replied. Diltz merely offered his silent acquiescence.

The Supreme Director sighed with satisfaction. "Ah, I'm hungry. Have my guests arrived?"

"They are waiting in the anteroom, Hage Leader."

"Let them come in. Bring me a hagerobe, and send the food at once." He dismissed Osmas to carry out his orders, and stood with his legs wide apart, gazing at his enormous image on the cloth beneath his feet. "It *is* a good likeness," he said. "Think—it will hang in every place of prominence. My reign, Diltz, my reign is the beginning of a glorious age, the like of which Empyrion has never seen!"

"Undoubtedly," intoned Diltz in his sepulchral voice, a spidery smile twitching his lips.

Jamrog put his arm around the man's bony shoulders, threw back his head, and laughed.

TWENTY
EIGHT

He would live. There was no doubt in his mind about that. Neither was there any doubt that he was changed. Subtly perhaps, but definitely changed. Treet knew this, knew it in his heart and bones. He was simply not the same anymore.

At first he thought the conditioning had done its abominable work. But the more he thought about it—and he had a lot of time to do absolutely nothing but think—the more he was inclined to discount the idea. The way he had been yanked from the tank and dumped on the physicians' doorstep suggested that the process had been aborted. Secondly, the conditioning, he reasoned, was designed to remove, replace, or at least alter one's personal awareness, not heighten it.

This last fact was what strengthened his conviction that he had miraculously escaped before the procedure was completed, for Treet's awareness had clearly, decisively, unmistakably been boosted. He felt himself tingling with the sense that he *knew* something—some radical insight had been granted him, or some hidden inner secret of the universe had been revealed to him.

True, he didn't know what his secret revelation was—hadn't a clue—but the inner thrill of *knowing* was as unshakable as it was irrational. Treet delighted in a keenness of perception that had no object. And though he could hardly lift head from pillow, he felt strong and invincible, as if he could part oceans with a word.

The physical sensations did not stop there. His scalp prickled and his face, especially around the eyes and forehead, felt as if it were radioactive, as if he had stood too close to an atomic blast.

This was, however, not an entirely disagreeable feeling; nothing like a sunburn, for instance. He thought it could be an aftereffect of the wax mask he had worn in the tank, but the skin surface itself was not at all sensitive to the touch. The warmth seemed to emanate from inside, radiating heat outward. He imagined that his face might glow in the dark.

Combined with this burning-face phenomenon, there was a lightness in the pit of his stomach—like hunger only softer, more diffuse. He felt buoyant, as if his body were made of a less dense material: air perhaps, or light.

Absurdly, it seemed to Treet that he was floating inside himself. When he closed his eyes, he could feel himself drifting upward, or rising rapidly on invisible currents, streaming toward an unknown destination.

Taken together, these sensations might have alarmed him, or at least frightened him a little. Treet, however, experienced not a second's apprehension over any of his bizarre symptoms. This lack of concern was due to a continuing awareness of the alien presence he had contacted while in Hladik's torture tank.

The entity remained near him, unintrusive but present. As close as thought—as if a part of Treet's consciousness had been permeated by this other, but in such a way that increased rather than diminished his personal awareness—which accounted for his heightened sensitivity, no doubt. If consciousness were pictured as a great miasmic sphere inside which self-awareness dwelt, then a portion of Treet's sphere had been gently interfused with the alien entity's sphere. As a result, he was more himself rather than less.

Curiously, Treet found this pervasion a benign and wholesome affair, completing in him areas of previously unrealized deficiency, as if hidden gaps had been cemented, or wounds healed. He felt centered: a runaway planet that had been captured, stabilized, and pulled into useful orbit around a life-giving sun.

This was how he knew he would live, and how he knew he had changed.

The change, Treet knew in all his being—for the knowledge continually coursed through him like blood through his arteries—was toward life and away from death. There was a certainty, an inevitability to his life now that had been absent before. What is more, he knew that his life would be forever changed. No one, he reasoned, could undergo such an infusion of (there was no other word for it) goodness and remain indifferent or unchanged.

● ● ● ● ● ●

The wevicat padded silently through the forest, stopping occasionally to sniff at a new scent as it crossed the trail. Crocker followed, loping easily along behind, content to have the cat lead the way back to the lair. They had been hunting again that afternoon and had caught nothing but three of the plump, flightless birds. They had surprised the hapless creatures on the ground, making their slow way to new trees and better feeding. A flurry of feathers, squawks, and a quick wevicat nip on their short necks, and supper was assured. Now, late in the afternoon, the ground mist already starting to curl around root and bole, they were returning with their catch.

Cook the birds over a fire, the voice in Crocker's head had suggested. *You could make a fire. The meat would taste good that way.*

Crocker was puzzling over the word *fire* when he saw the wevicat freeze. The man stopped and stood rock-still, eyes and ears instantly alert. The great cat's nostrils twitched; the tip of his tail quivered.

A scent on the air, his voice cautioned.

Crocker detected nothing save the ordinary earth smells of the deep forest, but knew the cat's senses were infinitely more keen than his own. Something stopped the animal in its tracks. Game? An enemy?

The wevicat jerked its head around and looked at its human companion, then sprang forward, bounding headlong down the trail. Crocker leaped ahead too, and came flying into a clearing a few meters away—just in time to see the enormous cat clawing its way up a stout tree that emerged from a pile of moss-bedecked rock at the far end of the clearing.

Gripping his spear in one hand, the man began following the cat's example, but much more slowly and with greater care, standing on a rock to reach the first branch a good two meters off the ground. He had cleared the second branch and was reaching for the third when he heard bushes rustling and branches snapping—together with a horrendous snuffling sound like that of a rooting hog amplified fifty times—on the trail behind him. He froze as the beast making the sound lumbered into the clearing.

The first glimpse of the creature almost knocked Crocker from his precarious perch. The thing was perfectly enormous—

big enough to make the awesome wevicat appear insignificant.

Crocker recognized instantly that here was one of the lords of the forest he had heard that rainy day when he had hid quivering under a bush, fearing for his life, feeling the very ground tremble beneath their unseen combat, hoping against hope that he would not be discovered by the titanic warriors.

The beast lumbering into the clearing below had a smooth, almost hairless hide, thick and blubbery, bulging around its sturdy limbs and around its neck and the hump of his massive shoulders. It walked on four legs—the first two a good deal shorter than the thick-muscled rear limbs—and held a horn-plated, knob-ended fleshy tail out almost perpendicular to the ground as it moved. Its head, balanced by the knobby tail at the other end, lolled this way and that, showing the tiny glints of black eyes squeezed nearly shut by the puffy flesh surrounding them. The head was round with the tag ends of ears sticking out oddly atop the expansive hillock of a cranium.

The animal moved slowly, slogging forward in an absurd rolling gait—an earthquake in motion. The behemoth was a mottled two-tone: a dusty reddish color above, gray-brown below. Much of its pitted hide was slick with greasy effluence. There were scars criss-crossing its back, pink and new, attesting to its contentious nature. It paused as it came directly into the center of the clearing, filling the closed space with its bulk.

Crocker shrank back. It was almost close enough to touch.

The creature snuffled the ground and, to the man's horror, reared back on its tremendous hind legs and raised its head, eyeing the tree hungrily. The monstrous face was split in half by two hanging lip flaps beneath wavering nostrils like convulsing tunnels. The gross flaps spread as the jaws opened to reveal flat-crowned, green-stained teeth and a prodigious, questing tongue. The stench of rotting meat and vegetation filled the air.

The man's heart thumped wildly in his chest. Above him, the cat tensed. The grotesque head wobbled closer, nudging leaves, then drawing a whole branch into its sinkhole of a mouth with the prehensile tongue to be crushed to pulp by the grinding teeth. The tree shook as the branch snapped off. The wevicat teetered, claws digging for a better hold.

The next bite nearly yanked the man out of the tree. The beast seized the very branch Crocker was hanging on to with his free hand, causing him to drop the spear and scrabble for a new handhold. The spear fell, slid into the animal's terrific maw, lodged sideways.

The monster worked its mouth up and down in an effort to dislodge the irritant, but succeeded only in wedging the spear further. Crocker struggled for a better handhold, slipped and plunged, catching himself at the last instant to scramble higher into the tree.

The behemoth just below heard the commotion caused by the man's fall and stopped. The head came up slowly until its eye was staring right into Crocker's terrified face.

TWENTY NINE

The beast let out a snort that nearly blew Crocker out of the tree. Then, as the man fought to regain his foothold, the great elastic tongue thrust out and wrapped itself around his thigh, yanking him closer to the cavernous mouth.

Tightening his grip on the branch, he felt his arm and shoulder muscles stretch as his leg was wrenched and pulled closer to the behemoth's grinding stumps of teeth. One hand gave way. Crocker screamed.

The monstrous tongue pulled him closer. The lip flaps parted to receive him. Crocker shrieked as, with a jerk of the beast's head, his hand was torn from the branch and he swung into the creature's mouth.

The teeth ground together, and Crocker felt himself crushed between them. The air rushed from his body. But something prevented the teeth from closing on him completely. He looked and saw his spear sticking into the side of the animal's fleshy jaw.

Twisting his body sideways, he squirmed to the spear. The teeth came down again. He cried out as the tremendous pressure ground into his bones. His hands closed on the spear, and he held on.

The teeth parted again. Crocker thrust the spear up, jamming the weapon further into the soft tissue. The behemoth grunted. The spear bent, splintered, snapped in two.

Crocker felt himself sliding into the tremendous gullet. The huge teeth came down over him.

Just then he heard a sound that jellied the marrow in his bones: the blood-thinning battle cry of an enraged cat. The wevicat leaped from its perch in the upper branches straight for the behemoth's face, claws extended like curved steel scimitars. One swipe of its massive paw and the behemoth lost an eye.

The startled beast roared with fright, and Crocker felt himself momentarily free. The animal's mouth opened and he was expelled, falling to the ground, where he landed on the rocks beneath the tree.

Bruised, bleeding, slimy with the beast's saliva, the man scrambled for safety among the rocks as the fight commenced above him, the cat spitting, raking its lethal claws at will over its enemy's head as the monster lurched ineffectually here and there, trying to dislodge the angry wevicat, bellowing with a sound that shook the very stones in the ground.

The huge cat dug in and held on. The behemoth shook its head ponderously and flailed with its knob-ended tail, tearing great gaping rents in the earth and flinging clumps of soil skyward with its feet. In desperation the behemoth drove straight toward the tree where the man was hiding.

Crocker flung himself to the side as the tree groaned, leaning toward him. The cat leaped lightly onto the monster's back, sinking its fearsome teeth into the bulging shoulder hump.

The behemoth bawled as the pain fought to its brain. The clublike tail smashed limbs from the tree as the beast whirled in torment. It lowered its head and lurched toward the tree.

There was a popping sound deep in the earth as roots snapped. The tree tilted and fell, black roots showering dirt into the air. The wevicat sprang with compact grace from the behemoth's back. Landing on its feet, it spun and reared, ears flat against its skull, paws spread wide. The behemoth lowered its huge ugly head, and, with a roar that rattled Crocker's teeth, whirled, whipping its thick tail through the air with surprising speed.

The wevicat was faster, leaping straight up into the air. The horn-plated tail struck the earth, carving a deep slash in the turf. The cat came down snarling and slashing the behemoth's blubbery hide, laying open the skin in ragged pink gashes. Blood bubbled from the horrendous wounds. The cat was covered with it.

Twice more the behemoth's tail plowed the ground, to no avail. The agile cat moved like caged lightning, always just out of range of the deadly tail. Crocker hunkered behind the fallen tree, shivering with shock and fright, breath coming in shallow gasps, pulse pounding in his ears.

Then, just as the behemoth's tail recoiled for another strike, the beast turned and staggered away, leaving the field to the victorious wevicat. As the crashing, thrashing sounds of the behemoth's retreat died away, Crocker crept from his hiding place and went to the cat. Its fur was spiked and sticky with blood, but it was unharmed.

The man put his hand on the cat's back; the cat snarled, jumped up, and spun toward him, then recognized him and sat down. *The cat has saved your life,* Crocker's internal voice told him.

"Saved my life," Crocker repeated aloud, his voice small in the clearing where the sounds of ferocious battle still hung in the air. He went to the animal and put his arms around its neck, hugging the creature as it calmly began licking its fur. Then, dusk swallowing the forest clearing, both man and cat rose and padded silently back to their lair.

● ● ● ● ● ●

"Well, let's have it," said Tvrdy. "I can see by your expression that it isn't good."

"Not good at all," said Cejka. "Covol says Jamrog is offering five thousand shares for information leading to our capture."

Tvrdy nodded, frowning.

"Five thousand," Piipo snorted. "The fool."

"There's more. The Nilokerus are setting up checkpoints in every Hage—all entry and exit points, as well as internal junctions. They are to be manned day and night."

"This is sooner than I expected. I did not think Jamrog would act to control Hage movement so quickly. What do they check?"

"Poak—for now. Covol belives they will soon issue identity cards and travel writs."

"Messy," said Tvrdy unhappily. "This could cut our supply lines completely."

"Director, if I may—" began Kopetch. He had been silent during the briefing.

"Yes, speak freely."

With a nod of deference to his superiors, he said, "I believe this unfortunate circumstance could work in our favor. Once these cards and writs are issued we can obtain them, alter them, or duplicate them. We can then travel at will without fear of discovery—with the proper precautions, of course. They will come to rely on the documents and not on their own eyes and ears. As long as we hold the documents, we will not be suspected."

"An ingenious suggestion worthy of a master strategist!" Tvrdy smiled with approval. It was the first time he'd smiled in many days. His escape from the Hage had been much sooner than he'd planned, and although it had been accomplished without incident, he was still anxious over the way he'd left his organization. And despite Cejka's repeated assurances and messages from Danelka that the escape had caused no unforeseen repercussions, the Tanais leader remained uneasy, feeling that some detail had been overlooked.

Now he relaxed a little. Men like Kopetch—and his organization was built on such—could be counted on. Somehow, they would find a way to meet each new challenge as it presented itself. "Pradim could not have done better himself," Tvrdy said.

"Excellent!" Cejka beamed. "We can issue our own cards and writs. If we could get a poak imprinter, we could even create identities for the Dhogs. Why, there's no limit to what we could do. Think of it! Think of the confusion we could cause."

"Tell Covol to obtain the documents as soon as possible—and any machinery necessary to duplicate or alter them." Tvrdy paused, his expression soured momentarily. "There is one other thing. Bogney insists that he be allowed to attend the briefing sessions. I think we must agree, although I see nothing but trouble from it."

"I don't like it any more than you, Tvrdy," Piipo said, "but we must begin treating the Dhogs as equals. Soon we will be asking them to die for us."

"I might suggest maintaining our nightly briefings in secret," put in Kopetch. "Bogney and one or two of his men could attend a morning session."

"Two briefings." Cejka chuckled. "Tvrdy, I think we have found Pradim's successor."

"Is there anything else tonight? No? All right. I will inform Bogney of our decision to have him join the briefing sessions. We will set the first for tomorrow morning before drills, but will meet together as usual tomorrow night—no, make that one hour later from now on."

With that Tvrdy dismissed the meeting, and they all filed

out of the fire-gutted building which had been hastily designated as a meeting place, occupying as it did a central location within the Blazedon district of the Old Section, overlooking a flat, rectangular desolation formerly known as Moscow Square.

Tvrdy returned to his rooms in the Tanais Hageblock and entered to find Giloon Bogney waiting for him. "Is courtesy not observed in a man's absence?" he asked, confronting the Dhog leader directly.

Bogney waved the objection aside with an impatient flick of the bhuj. "Giloon not liking Director talking big plans and him not hearing." He glared acidly at the Tanais Director, defying him to push the point.

Instead Tvrdy replied, "I understand. That is why I have decided to ask you to join us. The briefings are becoming too important not to have the leader of the Dhogs present. Will you join us?"

Bogney stroked his greasy mat of a beard, satisfaction gleaming in his bright little eyes. "So? Giloon joining Directors, seh?"

"I think it best."

"Giloon be joining. Night meetings?"

"No. Tomorrow morning at first light. Bring one or two of your men with you, but you must warn them: the matters discussed are to remain secret. If we discover any leaks—"

"Be saving your threats, Tanais. Dhogs knowing how to keep secrets."

"I'm sure you do." Tvrdy looked at the disgusting creature before him. "Was there anything else?"

"Giloon talking it tomorrow." Bogney screwed up his face into a grotesque smile. "Giloon being Director soon."

"You think it will be easy, do you?"

"We fight. We win."

"There will be fighting, yes—but not for a good long time, I hope. We're not ready yet. We don't have the supplies necessary to sustain a prolonged battle against Jamrog's Invisibles, much less win one. But the time will come."

"Giloon being there tomorrow." He gathered his cloak—the cloak Tvrdy had given him—around his sloping shoulders and waddled from the room.

Tvrdy restrained the impulse to slam the door after him, but the relic would probably have shattered into glassy fragments. He looked around the room, but nothing had been touched. He went to a ramshackle table that had been put in one corner, scanned the orderly rows of reports he had collected since his arrival in the Old Section, and, picking up a nearby reader, retired to his bed, popped the cartridge into the reader, and began to scan the contents.

With any luck at all, and no further interruptions, he'd finish before morning, and have an hour or two for a nap.

THIRTY

Treet swayed as the floor tilted up under his feet. He pitched forward, toward the bed, but the physician's hands held him up. "You're doing well," coaxed the young man. "Don't stop now."

"I—uh . . ." Treet puffed. "I—need to . . . lie down . . ."

"Just a little more and you can rest. You need to move your legs."

"Ohhhhhh!" Treet groaned. "Let me die in peace!"

"Die is just what you will not do." Treet glanced up as Ernina swept in with a tray in her hands. She had a habit of showing up when least expected.

"Just a little sickroom humor," offered Treet. "Nothing against my wonderful nursemaid here." He grimaced at the first-order physician and painfully kept moving. He completed one more circuit around the bed and then collapsed gratefully upon it. The suspension bed bounced in the air with his weight, righted itself, and hung steady. "Ahhh, that's better."

"That *is* better," replied Ernina. "Better in every way. You'll be able to move about on your own soon." She handed Treet a cup of steaming liquid and told him to sip it, then signaled to the physician, indicating that she wished to be left with the patient. When they were alone she said, "I think you are well enough now to talk."

Treet gazed calmly at the woman whom he had come to think of as his savior, and guessed what was coming. And although he had thought about it a great deal since regaining consciousness, he still did not know precisely what he would say to her.

He'd learned from his nursemaids, as he called them, that he'd been left on the healing center's doorstep, which meant, he guessed, that he was still somewhere in Nilokerus Hage. He had also found out that Hladik had been assassinated, and suspected his release had something to do with that. As for the rest, he didn't know how much anyone knew about him. At any rate, it was too late to invent anything now. He'd have to play it by ear. He waited for her to begin.

She did not waste any words. "I know who you are." This was accompanied by one of her most direct, probing gazes.

"You do?" gulped Treet, dashing down some of the hot herb mixture.

"You need not fear me. I have pledged my life to help you."

"You have?" This was not at all what Treet had expected.

Ernina glanced cautiously around, as if checking that the room was still empty. "I know that you are a Fieri." She sat back, satisfaction glowing in her brilliant green eyes.

Treet sipped the medicinal tea through pursed lips. "How long have you known?"

"From the first."

"I see."

"No one else suspects. To my staff you are simply another patient—one of Hladik's victims. We have seen many of those. Only I know the truth, and I have kept your secret."

"Why?" asked Treet. He needed to know how far he could trust her.

"It is difficult to explain, but I will try. Some time ago I was summoned to Cavern level to resuscitate a dying prisoner—another victim of Hladik's conditioning, I thought. And so he was, but when I examined him closely, I discovered the secret: he was a Fieri." Ernina said the ancient word, and her eyes shone with the wonder of it.

Treet nodded; it had to be Crocker she was talking about. So that's what had happened to him. "I know all about conditioning," replied Treet.

"The priests say that the Fieri don't exist anymore—maybe never did. But there are old, old stories, and many Hagemen still believe. The nonbeings are said to know how to find them. They—"

"Nonbeings?"

"The Shadow People, the Dhogs. They are Hage outcasts whose poak has been erased and stent forfeited. They live in the Old Section, it is believed, though no one ever sees them. They exist, but do not exist."

"Why are they called Dhogs?"

Ernina lifted her shoulders in an eloquent shrug. "No one knows."

Treet was silent for a moment—something the woman had

said . . . what was it? "Go on with what you were saying—about the other Fieri."

"I vowed to save him and, eventually, to help him escape. But Hladik came for him—took him from his bed before he was completely healed." She added sadly, "I never learned what became of him."

Better you don't know, thought Treet.

"But I will *not* let those murderers succeed a second time." She smacked a tight fist into her palm. "I have made plans. Hladik is dead. They say Subdirector Fertig is responsible, but I smell Jamrog's handiwork in it. And that isn't all: rumor messengers have been saying that a Purge is beginning. Two Threl Leaders have disappeared."

Treet groaned. "Not Tvrdy and Cejka?"

The physician nodded gravely. "Tanais and Rumon, yes. You know them?"

"I—ah . . ." He paused to rephrase what he'd been about to say. "Yes, I was helping them—we were trying to prevent the Purge. But then Hladik caught me."

"He won't catch you again, nor will anyone else. I will see to that." She stood and took his cup, then placed an experienced hand against his throat. Treet felt comfort in the gesture. "Rest now. We will talk again soon and make plans. You are safe here for now. Rest and grow strong."

"All right, I'm all yours," he said. He was tired of talking anyway, and she had given him more than enough to think about for a while. Treet settled back and closed his eyes.

● ● ● ● ● ●

In the room adjoining Treet's, the young physician replaced the broken tile near the floor and crept from behind the multicolored Bolbe hanging. His breath was shallow and his feet unsteady as he moved off. A Fieri! his mind shrieked. The patient was a *Fieri!*

No one, not even the Nilokerus who contacted him and persuaded him to become a lipreader, could have guessed he would discover anything this important. His Nilokerus instructor would be pleased. But should he tell?

Yes, that is what his training had been for. And think of the shares he would earn. But who would pay the most for this information? The priests? The Hage Leader? The Supreme Director himself?

• • • • • •

The boats lay motionless, the water making little licking sounds as it lapped between the hulls. Laughter echoed from the rafters of the pavilions scattered around the bay as stories were remembered and recounted. Firelight glittered through the clustered groves, and music sighed on the soft night air.

The white sand beneath his feet shone blue in the starlight as Pizzle wandered the beach, lost in the enchantment of the night. Starla walked beside him, humming now and then as snatches of tune caught her fancy. The Empyrion sky was alive with stars, and their winking faces were mirrored in the calm deep of the lake, and in Starla's eyes.

"Tomorrow we start upriver," said Pizzle absently.

"Taleraan," replied Starla just as absently.

"What?"

"The river's name—"

"Right. Preben told me." They walked on in silence a while longer. "Too bad Jaire couldn't come along."

"She chose to remain at the hospital with the children."

"I know." He put an arm around Starla's shoulders and drew her to him. "I'm glad you're here, though. I wouldn't have wanted to experience this without you."

"I have spoken to my brother," she said.

"That's nice," said Pizzle absently. "What did he say?"

"He said he trusted me to make a wise decision."

"I'm sure you will."

"I've decided to ask the Preceptor."

"Good."

"She will know how to advise us."

"Advise us?" Pizzle replayed their conversation back in his mind. "Starla, what are we talking about exactly? What did you ask your brother?"

"About our marriage."

Pizzle stopped and held her out at arm's length. "You what? Marriage?"

"Out of respect for her parents, a woman seeks their wisdom regarding her marriage. But my parents are with the Infinite Father. Therefore, I asked my brother. Vanon likes you. He still talks about the story you told him—what was it?"

"The Rune Readers of Ptolemy X," sighed Pizzle. "It was one of Z. Z. Papoon's best efforts." He wondered what ol' Z. Z. would have said to the notion that the plot of one of his novels would endear a woman's family to the idea of marriage to an alien on a world eleven light-years from his home in Mussle Head, Massachusetts.

"Yes, that was it," continued Starla. "He allowed me to make my own decision. I think, though, it would be wise to ask the Preceptor to advise us."

"In case there's a regulation against someone marrying an alien, huh?"

"The Preceptor would know."

Pizzle reflected on this for a moment. "Are you saying you *want* to marry me?"

"You spoke of marriage. You haven't forgotten?"

"I haven't forgotten. But I thought you had." Now what was he going to do? He looked at her standing before him in the starlight, watching him expectantly. She was beautiful, desirable, a joy to be with and behold—what was he waiting for? Still, there was something holding him back, and he knew what it was. How could he tell her? Well, see, Starla, it's nothing really major, it's just that I'm from another planet and all.

"What's wrong, Asquith?" she asked softly.

"N-nothing . . . well, it's just that . . . we're different."

"I know that. I love you, Asquith. I believe you love me, too."

Pizzle looked at her and melted. "Oh, I do, Starla, believe me I do." He drew her close and held her for a long time.

• • • • • •

Yarden sat alone, her back against a tree, watching the firelight shift the shadows of those gathered around the campfire, enjoying its warmth and light. She heard the songs and stories, heard the laughter, but felt herself slipping further and further away from those convivial sounds into a barren and lonely place.

And it was all because of Treet.

One way or another, Treet was behind her unhappiness. Therefore, one way or another, he was responsible.

Yarden had never been one to show any dependence upon men. Why all of a sudden she should be mumbling and fretting over someone she didn't even particularly like, confused and upset her more than she cared to admit.

Sure, there had been a time when she thought she was in love with Treet. But likely as not, that had merely been a physical infatuation: two people surviving a harrowing experience, glad to be alive and eager to show it—that sort of thing. Had she, in her heart of hearts, ever had any genuine feelings for Orion Treet? At all?

Well, maybe. But whatever she felt—if anything—had flown right out the door the day Treet decided to go traipsing back to Dome on his lunatic crusade.

She still believed that she had been right to cut off their relationship right then and there. To sever it cleanly, once and for all. That was the best way. The only way. She wouldn't live with the anxiety of not knowing where he was, what he was doing, whether he was in trouble or hurt, alive or not—any of a jillion things a lover could find to worry about.

But we *aren't* lovers, Yarden insisted to herself. Not now. Not ever.

No.

She would *not* change her mind. In spite of everything Ianni might say, she had chosen her course and Treet had chosen his. There was nothing she could do about him anyway. He was back in *Dome*—the very word filled her with sick dread. There was no way she would go back there, and nothing could make her. Yarden had felt the evil of Dome, felt it most powerfully. She knew it for what it was. And because she knew, she would not go back lest the same power seize and overtake her as it very nearly had the first time.

If no one else could understand that, too bad. No one— not Ianni, not the Preceptor, not the Infinite Father himself— was going to make her change her mind.

Saecaraz Subdirector Osmas stared at the two Nilokerus before him. Two Saecaraz underdirectors, their faces pursed into identical scowls of authority usurped, stood behind. "What do you mean coming here like this?" he demanded. "Application must be made—"

"A matter of utmost urgency, Hage Leader," replied the more intrepid of the two. The other, a young man, hung back with an expression mingling awe and fright on his beardless face.

"It must be if you expect me to disturb the Supreme Director at this most inconvenient hour," Osmas growled. "What is it?"

"That, I think, we must wait to tell the Supreme Director."

"Wait you will—he sees no one at this hour."

The Nilokerus looked at one another. The brave one said, "Tell him that it—" He hesitated, choosing his words carefully. "That it concerns an escaped Fieri."

Osmas eyed the two suspiciously. "What are you saying? Explain yourself!"

The Nilokerus only shook his head slowly.

"I can have your poak erased." The Subdirector's voice was taut, but the threat brought no response from the Nilokerus. "You insist on meeting with the Supreme Director? All right, I warned you. Wait over there." Osmas pointed to a long bench against one wall of the anteroom, turned, and disappeared into the convoluted corridor leading to the cluster of kraams and chambers making up the Hage administration center beneath Threl High Chambers.

The Subdirector returned a few minutes later, bothered and anxious. "Come with me," he said and led them back into the cluster, where they entered a lift and rode up several levels to the Threl Chambers. Osmas said nothing, but his dark glances let the two Nilokerus know that he was not at all pleased with this development. Without ceremony he ushered them into the cylindrical meeting room and brought them to stand before a disheveled-looking man flopped in the Supreme Director's chair who frowned drowsily at them and demanded, "What's this about an escaped Fieri?"

Osmas nodded to the foremost Nilokerus, who stepped forward cautiously.

"Well? You have dragged me from my well-deserved sleep to hear this lie—" He yawned. "Let's hear it."

"I am a Nilokerus trainer, security section—" the man began.

"Yes, yes, we know all that. What about this Fieri?"

The Nilokerus turned to his young companion and said, "Tell him what you told me."

The young man crept forward timidly, although the Supreme Director appeared more sleepy than fierce. "There is a patient in Hage who claims to be a Fieri—I've seen him myself . . ."

Jamrog glanced at his Subdirector. "You brought me here for this?"

Osmas sputtered. The first Nilokerus spoke. "He's nervous, Supreme Director. I can speak for him."

"Then do so!"

"He is a lipreader—a first-order physician on Starwatch level." The young man nodded to authenticate the detail. "Yesterday he discovered that one of the patients in their care was a Fieri spy—escaped, apparently—who had come seeking help from the physicians."

"Escaped?"

"Apparently."

"How? Escaped from where?" These questions were directed to the physician.

The young Nilokerus plucked up his courage and said, "We found him one morning—many days ago now. He was wearing a Nilokerus yos, but was unconscious, unable to move. Believing him to be one of Hlad—" A terrified expression blossomed upon the young man's face as he realized what he was about to say.

"One of Hladik's prisoners?" Jamrog supplied the words equably.

"We took him in," the physician continued, "and stabilized him. He improved. Yesterday Ernina came to talk to him. She was the one who discovered he was a Fieri. She told him she knew—he didn't deny it. She told him she has vowed to protect him."

"Protect him from what?"

The young man glanced at his companion, who winced. "I don't know," he answered hesitantly.

The Supreme Director's eyes narrowed. He clasped his hands and leaned forward. "A Fieri among Nilokerus physicians," he said thoughtfully. Yes, it came back to him now. The fugitive caught in the Archives—thinking him one of Tvrdy's agents, Hladik had wanted to condition him. A Fieri?

According to Mrukk the Fieri had all escaped—aided, of course, by Tvrdy. Jamrog remembered the debacle well. It was Rohee's handling of the Fieri fiasco that had convinced Jamrog the time had come for him to seize power. If I had been in control then, considered Jamrog, the matter would have been handled differently. Huh! It would be just like Hladik to bungle the conditioning. Luckily this lipreader had some sense. Perhaps now he would have another chance to discover the truth about these Fieri agitators.

His head snapped up. "I would see this Fieri, Osmas. Send for Mrukk."

The Subdirector hurried away to summon the chief of the Invisibles. Jamrog sat nodding in his chair. "I suppose you think you deserve a reward?"

"It has been said that the new Supreme Director is most generous," replied the Nilokerus instructor uncertainly.

Jamrog sneered, his lips drawing back from his teeth. "Most generous." He staggered from his chair, clutching his wrinkled hagerobe. "Go now. Wait below, and I will have Osmas bring your reward." The Supreme Director lurched off, leaving the two Nilokerus gaping.

They found their way back to the lift, dropped down to the main level, and returned to the bench they had occupied before, there to wait in squirming anticipation.

At the sight of the Subdirector both men leapt to their feet. How much would it be? A thousand shares? Two thousand?

Osmas came toward the waiting men, Mrukk treading softly beside him. "I have brought your reward," he announced when they had drawn close to the waiting Nilokerus.

The instructor flashed a quick, greedy smile at his pupil. "Our thanks, Subdirector."

"Three thousand apiece." Osmas produced a poak imprinter from his yos and raised its glowing point. "The Supreme Director wishes to demonstrate his unquestionable generosity to those who aid Empyrion. Tell your Hagemen."

He held the stylus up and took the first Nilokerus by the arm.

"Allow me," said Mrukk, suddenly stepping close.

No one noticed the naked blade as his hand flicked out and up.

Blood cascaded down the Nilokerus' yos, and a look of astonishment appeared on his face. His mouth worked, and his hands fluttered to his neck, trying to rejoin the rent in his throat as he toppled to the floor.

The young lipreader cried out and turned to flee. He dashed a few steps and stopped, arms twisting backward, hands grasping, clawing at a spot between his shoulderblades where Mrukk's knife had suddenly appeared, buried to the hilt in his flesh.

Osmas stared at the carnage, horrified. "What have you done?"

The chief of the Invisibles stooped to retrieve his weapon, and wiped it casually on the clothing of his victim. "I have saved the Saecaraz treasury six thousand shares."

"When Jamrog finds out about this—"

Mrukk laughed. "You think he doesn't know?"

"But the reward . . ."

"Keep it for yourself. A bonus."

"I couldn't."

"Then give it to someone who knows what to do with it." Mrukk laughed again and pushed up the sleeve of his yos. Grimly, Osmas set the imprinter and pressed it to Mrukk's muscled arm. "Now then," said Mrukk, stepping over the body of the Nilokerus at his feet, "let's go find this Fieri."

• • • • • •

Just a little east of the tranquil bay, pastel green hills slanted up from the northern shore of Prindahl, to march away into

624

the shimmering blue distance. The hillsides were covered by small round trees with leaves so dark they appeared blue in the morning light, making the hillsides look dotted with minature balons ready to take flight on the first breeze. Through these hills wound the deep waters of Taleraan, upon whose broad back the Fieri boats would embark this day.

The glass-smooth lake reflected a high, cloudless sky of chromium blue and a sun rising white into a new day. The ships floated in the crystalline water, painted hulls gleaming, rigging glinting like silver tracery in the sunlight. Atop the tall masts several rakkes had taken residence, holding their wings out to warm in the new sun.

On shore, the travelers awoke to breakfasts of fresh fruit, tea, and flat loaves of sweet bread. They talked excitedly while they ate, some of the younger Fieri slipping off to swim one last time before boarding. In all, it was a leisurely start to the day. Although everyone expressed eagerness to depart, no one appeared in any hurry to leave—a fact Pizzle found slightly maddening. Even if no one else cared to start, he was ready—had been ready for hours before sunrise. In fact, he had not actually slept the night before: he'd been too excited.

After saying good-night to Starla (a process that took well over an hour), he had wandered the beach aimlessly, his head filled with thoughts of love and marriage and family. Then he'd scooped a shallow depression in the warm sand and laid out under the stars contemplating the harmony of the universe.

Now he was anxious to be off, but first he had to locate the Preceptor and request an audience. He lingered near the first ship, the one in which she traveled, hoping to be in the right place at the right time when she appeared. He was not disappointed.

Pizzle was standing at the water's edge, looking hungrily at the happy breakfasters in a nearby pavilion when he turned and found the Preceptor standing on the deck of the boat behind him, watching him.

"Good morning, Preceptor," he called. "Have you had breakfast?"

"Good morning, Traveler Pizzle," came her reply. "I have just come from my devotions and have not eaten yet. Will you join me? I would like to speak to you."

"Sure, whatever you say." He waded out to the gangplank

to meet the Fieri leader. She had changed her white chinti for one of amber yellow, and her hair was braided and tied in a sheer yellow scarf. She came gracefully down the gangplank and entered the water. Pizzle met her and offered a hand which she accepted regally, allowing herself to be escorted to the beach.

A place was made for them at the table inside the pavilion and food served at once. Most of the Fieri were finished eating and vanished discreetly. "Actually," Pizzle said after the Preceptor had asked a blessing over the food and they began to eat, "I wanted to speak to you, too. I would like to have an audience."

"Oh, yes?" The Preceptor looked at him curiously, her amethyst eyes bright with interest.

Pizzle nodded, picked up a small, red plumlike fruit, and bit into it. Juice ran down his arm. "Yesh," he said with his mouth full. He swallowed and then added, "If it's not too much trouble. It's for myself and Starla."

"I see." The Preceptor continued to gaze at him—for such a long time that Pizzle became uncomfortable.

"Is there something wrong?" he asked.

The question was met with a smile. "Please, think no negative thought. I was asking the Teacher for leading."

"Oh." Pizzle picked up another plum fruit and ate it thoughtfully.

"I am happy to give you an audience," the Preceptor said. "Would this evening suit you?"

"That would be perfect." Pizzle grinned happily.

"You are much changed since you came to us," the Preceptor observed.

"Was that what you wanted to talk to me about?"

"Yes, and to ask you if you are happy here."

Pizzle grew solemn. "I've never been happier in my whole entire life. I never knew anyone as happy as I am—I didn't even know it was possible to be this happy," he declared. "Really."

"Have you discovered your purpose among us, Asquith?"

"My purpose?"

"Everyone has a purpose given them by the Infinite Father. In order to find true happiness, it is necessary to fulfill your purpose."

Pizzle thought about this for a moment and had to admit that he didn't know what his purpose was.

"There is time to discover it, Asquith," said the Preceptor

gently, humor shining in her eyes. "But it does not do to put off the search too long."

Pizzle nodded. "I'll do my best."

The Preceptor rose. "I'll be waiting for you." She smiled lightly. "Until this evening, then."

"This evening," confirmed Pizzle. He got up slowly, and the Preceptor moved off to greet her people, many of whom had gathered to wait for her. He watched her move among them, giving and receiving blessings, and sharing with them the joy of the day.

Presently he came to himself. Hey! I've got to find Starla and tell her! He grabbed a loaf of the sweet bread and trotted off down the beach.

THIRTY
TWO

The Invisibles appeared so suddenly, there was no time for Ernina to put her plan into action. No time for anything except quick thinking and a desperate hope.

One moment she had been bending over Treet. The next, Mrukk and three of his Mors Ultima were standing in the doorway. She stepped around the bed to meet them. "It took you long enough to get here," she said angrily. "What kept you?"

Mrukk's eyes flicked from the man in the bed to the flinty old physician. She did not wait for a reply. "Didn't my Hageman tell you it was urgent?"

The Mors Ultima chief regarded her suspiciously. "No."

"What *did* he tell you?" Ernina demanded, hands on hips.

"Out of the way, woman." Mrukk made move to push past her. She put her hands on his chest and held him back.

"I sent him to tell the Supreme Director. I found the Fieri. The reward is mine. What did he tell you?"

"You sent him?" Mrukk glared at the immovable woman, and signaled to his men to go ahead with the abduction. They went to the bed and pulled Treet from it. He awoke startled, saw the shimmering black yoses, and hollered. He was dragged from the bed kicking and screaming.

Ernina did not risk so much as a backward glance. "Well? Answer me."

"The Nilokerus and the Hageman with him said he was a lipreader. They said you had vowed to protect the Fieri—" Mrukk glared at her fiercely.

"Protect the Fieri! Trabant take him!" she shouted, her face livid.

"Ernina!" Treet yelled as he was jerked through the doorway. "What are you doing? For God's sake, help me!"

"Don't you see what they have done? They have cheated me out of my reward. I intend to see the Supreme Director about this. The Fieri was mine! The reward is mine!" she screamed shrilly. "It's mine!"

Mrukk backed away a step. "I know nothing about the reward."

"Liar!" Ernina advanced toward him.

Treet's cries echoed in the corridor beyond—confused, enraged, helpless.

"The reward is mine. I'm going to the Supreme Director."

"Do it. I have what I came for. I don't care what you do." With that, Mrukk spun on his heel and disappeared.

Ernina fell back on the bed, stunned. So it had been Uissal. She had guessed the moment the Invisibles appeared, mentally cursing herself for being so blind. It was all there for her to see: the young physician's absence that day, his habit of lurking nearby whenever she spoke privately with a patient, his perpetually guilty expression . . .

She jumped to her feet. There was no time now for that. She had to move at once. She swept through the medical cluster to her own chambers, gathered up a large bundle from her table, and stood a moment looking at her beloved ancient books, running her hand along their disintegrating spines. Then she swung the bundle over her shoulder and departed.

• • • • • •

Tvrdy watched the drills from the wrecked tower of twisted metal that had once served as the outer stairway to a Hageblock long ago reduced to rubble. In the dirt-covered field below, ranks of Dhogs labored to become soldiers: moving here and there in ragged packs, running, diving, lunging, shouting, flailing arms and legs at imaginary enemies under the tutelage of Tanais and Rumon instructors.

The resulting display was so miserable that Tvrdy's frown had passed directly from anger to despair. The Dhogs were a hopeless rabble—dirty, ill-clothed, and ignorant. Even under tight Tanais discipline, they could not be organized; confusion reigned on the drill field. After he'd seen enough, Tvrdy descended from the tower and called one of his lieutenants from the field for a consultation.

"What is going on out there?"

The Tanais, sweating, his face dark with frustration, answered readily. "The Dhogs cannot be taught. They are too stupid for even simple exercises."

"Do they accept your leadership?"

"It isn't that. These nonbeings, Hage leader, they think with their stomachs only. They say they are hungry."

"Are they?"

The man shrugged. "They're always hungry. We all are."

Tvrdy folded his arms across his chest, lowered his head for a moment in thought. "All right, continue as best you can. But tell them that tomorrow, and from now on, before drills they will be given a meal. Also at night. See that they understand."

The Tanais instructor nodded to his superior. "As you say, Hage Leader." He didn't ask where the food was going to come from, although he wondered.

Tvrdy turned and walked from the drill field. How could men think when their bellies were empty? How could they work without food?

The Tanais Director walked briskly across the field to the Hageblock opposite, where Piipo had set up the Hyrgo headquarters in order to be near the Directors' command posts, although the growing fields were being established on the Old Section's outer ring much further away.

"Ahh, Tvrdy!" The Hyrgo leader looked up as Tvrdy entered the ramshackle room. He stood with several Hagemen who were holding transparent sacks of soil for his inspection. "I did not expect to see you again so soon this morning." To his men he said, "Begin revitalization. I'll join you in the fields."

They trooped out and Piipo came over to Tvrdy, dusting his hands. "The soil is dreadful—still, not so bad as I expected. We'll be able to work with it."

Tvrdy noticed a keenness in the Hyrgo's glance and tone. He said, "I believe you are enjoying this, Piipo."

"It's true. I can't explain it, but I find this all very stimulating." He noticed the gravity in Tvrdy's tone and asked, "What is it, Hageman?"

"How close are we to feeding ourselves?"

The question took Piipo aback. "You're serious?"

"Always."

"Tvrdy, we have not even planted. It will be months. The soil . . . the water . . . four or five months at least. I told you at the first briefing."

"Yes, I know. How long can we sustain ourselves on the supplies we brought with us?"

"At the present consumption level—until the first crops come in. This I also explained during the briefing. Why are you asking me these things?"

"I want to begin feeding the Dhogs."

"Feeding nonbeings?" Piipo's expression showed pure astonishment.

"They have no food. They are so hungry they cannot complete even simple maneuvers. We have to build them up if we are ever to make fighters of them. It's that simple."

"Starvation is also simple. We feed the Dhogs and our supplies vanish overnight. We can starve right along with the rest—what will that accomplish?"

"I don't propose to starve, Piipo."

"Then you must propose to bring in more supplies, because I can't make the seeds sprout any faster."

"What word from your Hage?"

"Subdirector Gorov is to be installed as Director pending an investigation of my disappearance. He says the Hage is in full production. The Purge has not touched the Hyrgo yet."

"This is good." Tvrdy tugged on his lower lip thoughtfully.

"What are you thinking?"

"I think we must bring in more supplies."

"Of course, but how can we do that? Jamrog's checkpoints—"

"Not through the supply route," said Tvrdy. "We must visit your granaries, Piipo."

"Raid the granaries!"

"It's the only way. We don't have the equipment yet to issue the travel writs and identification. But with Gorov's help, we should be able to get in and out unnoticed."

"It's dangerous."

"Of course."

Piipo was silent for a long time. Finally he said, "I don't like it, but it could be done. Unfortunately, Hage Nilokerus abuts. If anything went wrong, it would not take them long to get to us."

"Us? You'll stay here, Piipo. We need your expertise."

"No, I must go with you. Who knows the Hage better than its Director?"

"We'll take one of your underdirectors."

"No. I'm going."

Tvrdy saw it was no use arguing with the Hrygo, so he

said, "Meet me at the briefing kraam in an hour. We will all sit down and plan the raid. Then Cejka will arrange to get instructions to Gorov at once."

"When will the raid take place?"

"Tonight."

THIRTY
THREE

*T*he pale green hills drifted slowly by the ships which stretched out in a long, snaking train along Taleraan's undulating curves. The boats kept to the center of the wide channel and the deepest part of the river, forging upstream against the slow current. The sails were furled, for now the ships were driven by the crystal-powered engines carried in the outrigged pods which had been attached to either side of the boat. These propelled the ships cleanly and quietly upriver.

Bemused hill creatures inhabiting the thickets and groves along the wide banks halted their foraging to watch the grand procession pass. The Fieri hailed the animals, watching the banks and pointing out each new species to one another. Yarden hung over the rail with the rest, enjoying the scenery and the fauna, quite forgetting her agitation of the night before in the beauty of the day.

At first glance desolate, the hills were actually swarming with wildlife once one learned how and where to look for them. There were creatures that looked like fluffy, long-legged antelopes, floating like tawny clouds as they grazed the rolling hillsides in scattered herds. Lower, among the frilly trees along the riverbanks, scuttled small orange bearlike animals with shaggy golden manes. Larger, darker shapes moved among the shadowed backgrounds, and stout gray-blue water beasts with long necks and rotund bodies plied the shallows, diving and surfacing with water pods in their toothless jaws.

Besides the ubiquitous rakkes, there were avian battalions of swooping, diving fishers with pointed beaks and brilliant green and red banded wings that sliced the air in sharp maneuvers to the delight of their captivated audiences, snatching tiny striped fish out of the water on the fly. Their less pretentious cousins strolled the river's edge on pink stilt legs, stepping carefully through the turquoise forests of long-bladed watergrass, their bright yellow heads cocked, great round eyes scanning the silted bottom for the jade-colored lizards on which they fed.

Yarden was enthralled with all she saw, and never tired of

looking as each new bend in the river revealed a panorama of fresh beauty. The slow, steady progress of the boats, marked by a lulling chorus of bird and animal calls, worked on Yarden like a delicious elixir, and she drank in every brilliant moment.

Gerdes also inspired her, too, but in a different way. Each afternoon the Fieri teacher gathered her brood of eager young artists beneath the ocher canopy on the aft deck of the barge. There she led them through exercises. "A limber body is often the companion of a limber mind," she told them. "The body is the bridge between the mind and the emotions, just as the emotions are the bridge between the mind and spirit."

Of the eight students Gerdes had gathered for the journey, Yarden was the oldest by far, and found herself slightly envious of their youth, wishing she had embarked upon her career earlier. An absurd thought, she told herself on reflection, since there was no way she could have come to Empyrion any sooner, and in her other life—her life as an executive administrator to one of the most powerful men in the known universe—the idea of becoming an artist had never occurred to her. Seriously, that is. She had sometimes felt artistic yearnings within her, and thought she might like to do something creative, but always dismissed the urges as inappropriate or impractical.

But here on Empyrion all things were possible. She was not subject to the tyranny of the practical. In fact, her previous life seemed to her now to have been largely a waste of precious time. A waste she would have resented if it did not now seem so remote and inconsequential. In fact, she had to think very hard about it in order to remember her life with Cynetics at all.

Together the eight would-be artists and their instructor filled the afternoon hours with exercises in body awareness and movement, and sessions of mental conditioning. Through all of the exercises, Gerdes imparted nuggets of her artistic philosophy: "Art is thought as well as feeling. An artist's abilities, mind, and spirit are brought to the act of creation."

"Why do we spend so much time in movement exercises?" asked one of the Fieri, a stocky young man with black curly hair and a ruddy complexion, full of exuberance and high spirits, but definitely not inclined to patience.

"Because, Luarco, my restless one," Gerdes said, and the other Fieri laughed, "we already know how to think. We think all the time. The mind controls all we do, sometimes inhibiting motion. The body was made to move, not to think; therefore, we must learn to free the body to do what it knows how to do."

"But doesn't that contradict what you just said about the role of the artist's mind in the act of creation?" asked a young woman sitting next to Yarden.

"Ahh, Taniani, you are always running far ahead. I was coming to that. Once we have learned to move freely, without unnecessary restriction, we can reintroduce the mental aspect in its proper place. Here is the key: *balance*. In art there must be a balance of the physical, mental, emotional, and spiritual."

"The Preceptor calls that the key to life," Luarco pointed out—with just a touch of belligerence, Yarden thought.

"Oh, it is, Luarco, it is. It is also the key to great art. Think now! What is the most important component of the work?"

"Skill," replied a young man sprawled out full-length on the deck, his sandy hair ruffled in the breeze.

"I'm not surprised you would say that, Gheorgi. Your skill is admirable." Gerdes asked the others, "Is he right?"

"No," said the girl next to him. "Technical skill by itself means nothing. The thought the artist is trying to communicate is the most important. If the artist has nothing to say, it doesn't matter how great his skill."

"It's the artist's *expression*," said another. "Without the right expression nothing is communicated, no matter how well conceived or executed."

Gerdes smiled with self-satisfaction. "Do you hear yourselves? You have proven my point. Who sees it?" Her gaze swept the group. "Yarden?"

Yarden had been engrossed in the discussion, and was startled to hear her name called. "Because," she said slowly, "any element elevated to the exclusion of the others . . . ah, works against the piece."

"Precisely!" Gerdes crowed. "Do you see it? Balance! As in life, all elements are equally important. It is self-evident: exclude one and the work is flawed. Without the physical, there is no substance; without the emotional, it has no heart; without the mind, it has no direction; and without the spiritual, the work has no soul. All elements are necessary. All must be maintained in balance."

The rippling of water and the clear keening of the rakkes punctuated the silence as the students turned these things over in their heads. At last Gerdes said, "Make this a part of your meditations for tonight. We will begin with brush and ink tomorrow."

Noting Luarco's pained expression, Gerdes added, "Yes, *black* ink, Luarco. Color will come later. First, I want to see your brush strokes live."

The students broke up, most drifting off along the decks in pairs, continuing the discussion; others stretched out beneath the canopy, now golden with the afternoon sun full on it. Yarden got up to leave and Gerdes came to her, taking her arm and steering her toward the stern.

Fieri sat on benches along the rail, quietly talking, or napped in colored cloth deckchairs. Several youngsters had made paper boats which they floated from the ends of long strings. It was, Yarden thought, a typical tourboat scene from the last century. They found a place on a nearby bench and sat down together. "A very perceptive answer, Yarden," began Gerdes.

Yarden smiled, but shrugged off the compliment. "You said yourself it was self-evident."

"Certainly, but we do not always see the obvious—rarely, in fact. Anyway, it showed you were thinking."

"I am doing a lot of that lately, it seems."

Gerdes' kind face puckered in concern. "Not all of it about painting, I would guess."

She gave her teacher a sideways glance. "I know, think no negative thought. But—well, I just . . . I've had a lot to think about. I didn't know it showed."

"When the heart is troubled, the body responds in its own way. I noticed your exercises were stiff, tentative. You were not centered in yourself."

"It's true. I did feel awkward this afternoon. But I'll do better tomorrow."

Gerdes smiled gently and took her hand. "Dear Yarden, do you really suppose that's why I wanted to talk to you? I care about you far more than I care about your lessons. I merely thought that if something was troubling you, and if talking would help, we could talk."

"Thank you, Gerdes; you're kind and thoughtful. But this is something I need to work out alone."

"You're sure?"

Yarden nodded, and squeezed her teacher's hand.

"As you say. Still, if you think it might help—"

"I'll remember."

Gerdes rose and moved off. Yarden remained by herself on the bench. What am I going to do? she wondered. Just when I think I've made some progress, someone comes along and tells me I'm unhappy. I've got to pull myself together.

• • • • • •

The rain pattered down upon the forest floor, filtering through layer upon layer of leaves until it percolated down to the ground to soak the fertile soil and transform forest pathways into gurgling brooks. The man and his great dark feline companion waited out the rain, listening to the water sounds and napping beneath a low, umbrella-shaped bush whose broad, frilly leaves kept them perfectly dry.

The bond between the man and the wevicat had deepened since the combat with the behemoth, and Crocker had begun talking to the cat, haltingly at first, but with increasing fluency. The cat gazed at the man with golden calm in its great eyes, now and then licking its paws with its deeply grooved tongue, prepared to listen to the man-sounds indefinitely.

"Rain, rain, go away," muttered the man.

The wevicat rolled over on its side and laid its head down on the dry leaves. In a moment a rumble like mountain thunder sounded as the animal began to purr. It was the sound of pure contentment and soon Crocker, too, had stretched out, his head resting against the cat's warm flank. "Rain, rain, go away," he said again, like a child enthralled with the sound of its own voice. "Crocker come back another day."

*THIRTY
FOUR*

Jamrog was beside himself. "He doesn't look like much. Are you certain this is the Fieri? Perhaps you have captured a Jamuna wastehandler by mistake." The Supreme Director walked slowly around his prisoner, prodding him roughly with the butt of the bhuj. Diltz and Mrukk looked on. "Why, he looks just like an ordinary Hageman. I must say I'm very disappointed, Mrukk. I expected much more."

"Look at his teeth, Hage Leader," suggested Diltz.

"Open your mouth, Fieri," commanded Jamrog, grabbing Treet by the chin. Treet did not cooperate, so the Supreme Director called the Mors Ultima standing at attention nearby. "Open his mouth," he ordered.

Treet's jaws were forced open. Jamrog came close and poked a finger inside his mouth. "Ah, yes! I see what you mean, Diltz. Those teeth have never been touched by Nilokerus physicians. They are perfect. But can he speak with those perfect teeth in his mouth?"

Treet said nothing. His initial shock at being apprehended had worn off, and now he was simply sullen. Oddly, he was not at all afraid. Instead, much to his own surprise, he was merely disgruntled by the necessity of having to deal with the inconvenience of being a prisoner once more.

He had not yet worked out in his own mind how he was going to respond to the situation. There were a number of options: he could become the indignant emissary and make subtle threats; he could remain unresponsive, refuse to play along; or he could put on a harmless demeanor, pretend he was friend to one and all.

None of the options appealed to him. For one thing, he didn't like Jamrog. The man was creeping slime from what Treet could see. Sirin Rohee had been different; at least with Rohee there had been a scrap of humanity in the old man that Treet felt he could appeal to. Though he'd never met Jamrog, he'd heard from Tvrdy that the man was filth, and dangerous filth at that. The moment he set eyes on the new Supreme Director, Treet knew Tvrdy's assessment had been only too accurate.

The heavy, bulging forehead; the dull, empty eyes and lusterless complexion; the full, sensual lips curled in a perpetual sneer; the easy, open stance that spoke of indulgence and authority; the smooth, milk-fed flesh: all combined to create a portrait of cool, malignant debauchery.

Treet recognized Jamrog for what he was, and shrank away from the recognition. Not from fear did he recoil, but from revulsion. The reaction was so strong, it surprised him. Treet, a man of tolerance, a man accustomed to taking life as he found it and witholding judgment, felt a genuine and powerful disgust for the man mocking him. And he felt something else as well: pity.

He saw Jamrog as a petty, pathetic poser, drunk on power and sinking beneath his own ballooning megalomania even as his appetite for greater and greater atrocity grew. Treet looked at him and saw a poor, crabbed creature, stunted and shriveled. A being with a soul so wasted it could no longer be called human, could no longer even be feared, merely pitied.

He had no doubt whatsoever that Jamrog should be stamped out. But there was no vengeance in the thought, just a little sadness—as much as a man might feel upon realizing that a rabid dog has to be put out of its misery.

These were new thoughts for Treet, new sensations. He seemed to be seeing all before him with unaccustomed clarity—a trick he chalked up to his heightened awareness. It was as if he were viewing events through new eyes.

"The question now is what to do with him. Any suggestions?" Jamrog babbled on. "We could let him go, I suppose. But what mischief would that cause? No, too risky." He rumpled his brow in mock thoughtfulness. "I know," he said gaily. "We could persuade him to divulge the secrets of the ages." He put his face close to Treet's. "What do *you* say, Fieri? What should we do with you?"

Treet made no move.

"Your refusal to speak wearies me. Speak, Fieri. What do you think we should do with you?"

Treet returned the Supreme Director's gaze calmly.

"Answer me!" Jamrog screamed, a thick vein standing out on his forehead.

"You won't like what I have to say," said Treet, who didn't really know yet what he had to say.

"See? I told you, Mrukk, he does talk. What's more, I understood every word." He leaned close, placing a hand on Treet's shoulder. "I'm not your enemy, Fieri. I can help you. Yes, I want to help you."

"Then let me go."

"But I want you to be my guest here and stay with me. You'd like that. I could make you very comfortable. I could take good care of you."

"Like you took care of Sirin Rohee?"

That rocked the Supreme Director back. "You must not listen to idle Hage gossip while among us, Fieri." He darted a glance at the chief of the Invisibles. "Mrukk, take him. Reason with him, and bring him back in a more receptive mood."

With that, Treet was hauled from the kraam and marched off into the convoluted heart of Threl High Chambers.

● ● ● ● ● ●

The Preceptor met them at the door to her stateroom below deck. The early evening sky still held the afternoon light. Pizzle entered first, remembered his manners, and pulled Starla from behind him, ushered her ahead, then came in himself, closing the door.

"I'm glad you could see us so soon, Preceptor," Starla said, completely at ease.

"Yeah, it's real great of you," remarked Pizzle. He walked like a puppet whose strings were fouled.

"Let's sit down here." The Preceptor directed them to three cushioned chairs. They sat, and there followed a moment of thoughtful silence into which Pizzle blurted, "This is a real nice room you have here, Preceptor. Looks very cozy."

She smiled graciously. "I am very comfortable here. Are you enjoying the journey?"

"It's outrageous, it really is. I mean it's simply fantastic. Super-fantastic! Did you see those gazelle-things? And those fuzzy orange lion-bears? Incredible." Pizzle realized he was making a fool of himself, but was unable to stop. His face felt tight.

His hands were flying all over the place, and his voice cracked with excitement. He forced himself to take a deep breath. "Yes," he said as he exhaled, "I guess you could say I'm enjoying the trip very much."

Starla came to his rescue. "Asquith and I need your guidance, Preceptor."

"How may I help you, Starla?"

Starla turned to Pizzle with encouragement in her glance. "We are thinking—that is, Starla and myself want to know if you can tell us if . . . is there any reason that we ought to know about . . . I mean, is it all right with you for us to get married?"

The Preceptor did not smile this time. She studied both of them for a moment before replying. When she spoke, her voice was gentle but firm. "I have known since the beginning that this question would arise. Now that it is here, I must speak frankly."

"Please do, Preceptor," said Starla. Pizzle, whose mouth had suddenly gone dry, bobbed his head.

"You may find my words hard to accept." She looked from one to the other of them. Pizzle licked his lips.

"We wish to hear them, Preceptor," Starla said and turned to Pizzle.

"Right! Sure. Oh, yeah," he managed to say.

The Preceptor placed her fingertips together and raised them to her chin. "It is my opinion that marriage would not be beneficial for you."

Pizzle saw the light go out of Starla's eyes, felt his heart go lumpy in his chest. A startled "What?" passed his lips.

Starla regrouped quickly. "Could you explain, Preceptor, so we may better understand?"

"As you wish." The Preceptor inclined her head. Turning to address Pizzle directly, she said, "Empyrion has not yet traveled one-half of its solar cycle during the time you have been with us. That is very little time when one is considering the commitment of a lifetime. There are differences between your people and ours, Asquith—"

"I appreciate those differences," put in Pizzle.

"Perhaps in time you may come to appreciate them. The distance between your race and ours is not measured in billions of kilometers; it is a distance of hearts and minds, which in its own way is just as profound as the distance between our stars."

Pizzle could not speak; he did not have the words to counter this unexpected argument. He turned hopeless eyes on his beloved.

"Forgive me, Preceptor, are you saying that we should not be married?" Starla asked, her voice tense and quiet.

"You have come to me for my advice. I have thought about this matter for a long time, and I am persuaded that a marriage between you would be a sad, perhaps tragic, mistake." The Preceptor regarded them both lovingly. From the open porthole came the gentle sounds of the river at play against the hull and the cry of the rakkes as they soared overhead.

Pizzle was still trying to make himself understand what he had heard when Starla rose to her feet. "Thank you for your guidance, Preceptor. We will abide by your decision."

"Wait a minute!" Pizzle was on his feet. "Is that all? Can't we talk about this? I mean, really. Huh?"

Starla looked stricken. She'd never heard anyone speak to the Preceptor so. "Asquith! Please, don't—"

The Preceptor accepted Pizzle's outburst with aplomb. "Speak, Traveler Pizzle."

Pizzle ran a hand through his hair and began to pace. "It's just that . . . I mean . . . Look, is this advice of yours final, the last word? I mean, can't we do anything about it? It seems to me we ought to have the chance anyway."

"What would you do if granted such a chance?" the Preceptor asked, her violet eyes keen in the fading light of the stateroom.

"Make you change your mind."

"How would you do that?"

"Well, shoot, I don't know. What would it take?" He nodded vigorously, his ears waggling. "Name it, I'll do it—we both will. Anything! Just you name it."

The Preceptor rose from her chair and came to stand before them. "It will be a most difficult trial for you. Are you willing?" Both nodded silently, looking at each other for encouragement. "You must not see one another again until the end of the solar cycle."

"Not at all?" Pizzle's voice whined.

"In the presence of others only; you must not be alone together."

Starla nodded, her expression grim. Pizzle frowned, but nodded too. "That's all?" he asked.

The Preceptor held up a long finger. "I also ask that you, Asquith, undertake a period of instruction from one of the Mentors."

"Sure. No problem. That's it? Then you'll change your mind?"

"We will see what time brings; then we will talk again."

"**L**et the Fieri go, Mrukk," a strangely muffled voice commanded from the shadows. The Invisibles halted at the sound. They were two levels below Threl chambers in a dark and disused corridor, leading their prisoner to one of the many kraams throughout Dome that the Invisibles had recently converted for special interrogations.

The Mors Ultima commander whirled toward the sound, his hand already on his knife. "Show yourself."

A dark mass moved within the darkness of a blacked-out entryway leading to a connecting tunnel.

Treet peered into the darkness and recognized the bulky shape.

So did Mrukk, who barked a sharp laugh. "We don't need you yet, physician."

"Let him go now if you care for your lives." Again the muffled voice, as if the speaker were wearing a mask.

Mrukk took a step closer to where Ernina stood. "Come, we will talk. I'll share the reward with you."

There came a tiny pinging sound, and Mrukk stopped. "What was that?"

To Treet it sounded like a glass bead dropped onto concrete.

"Release the Fieri now." Another ping. A small round pellet dropped to the floor, bounced and rolled into the darkness.

"We could ta—" began Mrukk.

Another pellet dropped. Treet stood still, relaxed but ready to dive toward the tunnel instantly.

"What are you doing?" Mrukk demanded.

"Send the Fieri to me now!" At that, two more pellets fell and bounced.

"Stop it!" ordered Mrukk. "What is that?"

"Release him." A whole handful of pellets rattled onto the floor. Treet saw them bounce and scatter like marbles.

Mrukk signaled one of the Invisibles to advance on the

physician. He inched forward as if he were walking on live coals.

A few more pellets cascaded onto the floor of the darkened corridor, each ping echoing in the empty corridor.

"Do not step on one of those capsules," warned Ernina.

"Get her!" shouted Mrukk. The Invisible took one more step. There was a hollow crunching sound, as if he had stepped on a light bulb.

In the darkness Treet saw the man raise his foot to take another step, totter, and stagger back gasping for breath. He made a gurgling sound in his throat as he pitched forward onto his face. A second later Treet tasted almonds on his lips: cyanide.

"You will die for this, you stupid old mother!" swore Mrukk.

A whole hailstorm of pellets fell, pinging and bouncing into the corridor, some of them rolling to the Invisibles' feet. Everyone stood paralyzed. The odor of almonds was strong in the corridor now. The Invisible holding Treet coughed. "I could kill him right here!" Mrukk growled.

Ernina's reply, though muted, was calm. "What would Jamrog say about that?"

Mrukk ground his teeth and spun on Treet. In the dim green light of the single overhead globe, Treet could see Mrukk's face twisted into a snarl of impotent rage. "When Jamrog is finished with you, Fieri, you are mine! I will have you both before the day is out."

Then he turned to where Ernina stood in the darkened tunnelway. He laughed and said, "Take him, old mother. I give him to you. Let's see how far he gets."

"Come forward, Orion," she said. "Carefully."

Treet raised his foot and lowered it as if expecting the floor to explode. He felt nothing beneath his foot, so trusted his weight to it. He took another equally nerve-stretching step, and then another.

He was now three steps from Mrukk, and one from the Invisible collapsed on the floor. This was certainly the slowest getaway in the combined history of two planets. He doubted whether anyone had ever escaped from the Mors Ultima less speedily.

"Stop there," instructed Ernina. "I'm going to throw you something." She moved to make the throw.

Treet heard a rustle of cloth behind him. "Down, Ernina!"

The knife whizzed by his head, and he heard it clatter in the tunnel beyond, followed by Mrukk's stifled curse.

Treet straightened. "I'm ready." A moment later he felt something rubbery land in his outstretched hands.

"Put it on," said Ernina. "You'll be safe."

"I'll find you!" shouted Mrukk, his voice raw with hate.

Treet turned the floppy object over in his hands several times before he found the opening and pulled the mask over his head. The mask fit snugly over nose and mouth, but left eyes and ears free. He could breathe easily, but the air tasted flat and heavily metallic.

He took an experimental step and crunched a pellet under his heel. He smelled and tasted nothing but the stale, filtered air of his mask. Treet dashed forward quickly, his feet scattering pellets and crunching them willy-nilly. Then he was standing before Ernina and felt her hands on his arm, tugging him back into the tunnel.

"Follow us if you will," called Ernina over her shoulder, as she dumped still more pellets into the tunnel.

Gasps and coughing filled the corridor as they dashed off. They came at once to a turn, and Ernina pulled Treet around the corner. She paused to scatter another handful of the mysterious pellets. "Pray to Cynetics that these will slow them down," said Ernina into her mask, and they hurried on.

• • • • • •

Tvrdy did not like yielding to Bogney in the matter of planning the raid, but knew that the Dhog leader was his only hope of getting in and out of Hyrgo Hage undetected. Bogney had taken Tvrdy's decision with great good humor, roaring at the invitation to lead the sortie. "Tanais needs the Dhogs. Giloon not being useless, seh?"

"No one ever said you were useless," replied Tvrdy. "We all have our expertise. Moving through Hage unnoticed is your expertise. We must all learn from each other."

Bogney roared still louder. "You watching then and learn, Tanais. Giloon be teaching you good."

The plan had been discussed from all angles and the route, including two alternate escape routes, approved by all. Then, as soon as darkness had come to the Old Section, they set off, moving into the complex labyrinth of long abandoned corridors and tunnels known as the Isedon Zone.

The Dhogs knew this mazework intimately, knew every turn and every blind avenue, knew each tunnel junction and intersection. Many of the streets they passed through were choked with rubble but for a narrow footpath winding around the debris. Most of the tunnels had collapsed completely, or had been filled in—whether by the Dhogs or by Hagemen, Tvrdy couldn't say. Bogney led the party expertly, keeping a good pace, even through the worst of the ruin.

Tvrdy marveled at the speed with which the Dhogs could move—never hesitating, never making a wrong turn—covering the same distance in minutes that had taken him hours to navigate that first day. But then this was, after all, the Dhogs' domain, and much of their protection lay in their ability to move quickly and quietly. As they went along, Tvrdy began to feel he'd been right to include Bogney when he had.

The raiding party, thirty-five men in all, made its way along the Isedon Zone toward the border between Chryse and Hage Jamuna. There, the Kyan swung out nearest the Zone, and they could pick their way carefully to the river and along the River-walk to the boat Rumon had left for them. By boat they would follow the river through Jamuna and into Hyrgo Hage.

The trip was accomplished without incident, although they had to skirt a checkpoint on the Chryse border which they had not known about. Once in Hyrgo, Piipo took charge, saying, "Now I'll show you Hyrgo efficiency."

To Tvrdy's surprise, Bogney merely shrugged and fell back to wait at the head of his Dhog troops. Tvrdy had expected a confrontation, and was glad he did not have to intervene. He began to feel that the raid would succeed without incident.

Piipo ordered the boat into a small cove just west of the granary wharf, and the party disembarked. With movements just as certain and decisive as the Dhogs had shown in the Zone, Piipo led them directly to the great ribbed mounds of the Hyrgo granaries, avoiding open areas and the Nilokerus checkpoints.

"There is a door on the third level," Piipo explained as they gathered outside the granary nearest the river. "The climb is not difficult, and the door will be open. Wait here until you hear the signal. I'll need help opening the doors."

"You're not to go," protested Tvrdy. "That isn't in our plan."

"No one is going to plunder this storehouse but me."

"Piipo, think what you're doing."

"Wait. I will return in a moment."

Tvrdy didn't like this development, but allowed Piipo to go without further comment. In a few minutes the party, huddled outside the huge granary doors, heard a distinct clank, a pause, and then three solid knocks on the fibersteel doors. Grabbing the rings, the Dhogs hauled the doors open and then stood staring at the wealth of food stacked within.

"Move, Dhogs!" whispered Bogney urgently. "Drool later." He pushed by them and ran inside to where Piipo's Subdirector, Gorov, had arranged the granary stock to make it easier for the raiders to load onto the waiting warehouse wagons.

Piipo smiled broadly when he saw that and said, "See? The Tanais and Rumon are not the only ones who know how to plan."

The Dhogs leaped to the bulging grain sacks, a dozen to a stack, and began heaving them onto the first wagon. When it was full, they began hauling it out of the warehouse. Ordinarily tractor ems were used to pull the wagons, but these were too noisy. So the wagons had to be disengaged from their tracks and pushed to the boat.

The first wagonload arrived at the boat and was stowed on board within minutes. The plan was working perfectly. But Giloon Bogney commented, "This being too slow. Wharf being near for fast big loading."

"We follow the plan." Tvrdy's tone left no room for discussion.

On the second trip to the boat, two teams of Dhogs disappeared and Bogney as well. Tvrdy, arriving at the boat with the third load, discovered the second wagon waiting at the cove, still loaded. "Where are they?" he demanded of the Tanais he'd left to guard the boat.

"I tried to stop them, Director," said the man, none too happy himself. "They brought the wagons and then left. I thought to signal you, but I did not want to jeopardize the operation."

Tvrdy smashed his hand against a grain sack. Whap! When

he could speak again he said, "Did they say where they were going?"

"No, but they went that way," replied the Tanais, pointing toward the wharf.

"I'm going after them." He turned to those behind him. "Start unloading the wagons. When the next wagon gets here, empty it and then get the wagons on board. Tell Piipo if I do not return by the time the wagons are aboard, he is to leave without me. Understand?"

The Tanais mumbled and began unloading the wagons. Tvrdy turned and followed the Riverwalk to the wharf. The walk was dark most of the way, and he covered the distance quickly, arriving at the waterfront just in time to hear a startled cry.

Tvrdy ducked down beside the Riverwalk wall and crept forward in a crouch, keeping out of sight of the Nilokerus checkpoint. There, directly ahead in the center of the waterfront where the wharf and the Riverwalk met, he saw three Nilokerus struggling, their weapons flashing dully in the ring of lights around a checkpoint booth swarming with Dhogs.

THIRTY
SIX

They were deep in Saecaraz, somewhere in the confusion of galleries and passages below Threl High Chambers. They rounded a corner; Treet felt cool fresh air on his face, and a moment later they were standing at a rimwall overlooking the great barren expanse of Threl Square on their flight to the river. Pressing a hand to his side, and wheezing like a leaky bellows, he gasped, "I—ha-ave to . . . rest . . ."

Ernina halted and pulled her mask off and Treet's as well. "Is the pain bad?"

"N-no . . . I can make it," Treet gulped, head down. "Just need . . . rest a minute."

"Over here is better," she said, leading Treet to a clump of flat, fan-shaped trees growing at the edge of the rimwalk. "Take shallow breaths. Relax. The pain will go." She looked behind them and saw the globe-lit rimwalk bending away out of sight into the darkness. "We must hurry on soon."

In a moment Treet was indeed breathing easier. "Thanks for coming back for me. What were they—cyanide pellets?"

Ernina's sober face wrinkled in a smile. "No, just an anesthetic—and fear. The Invisibles are so used to such cruelty, they easily imagine the worst. Their own fear paralyzed them."

"You had me fooled," replied Treet. "Where did you get those things?"

"I have been making these," she dug into a bag at her side and held up a pellet the size of a marble, "since Hladik took my first Fieri. I foresaw the day when I might need an escape."

"It worked, and I'm glad. But you had me going for a while."

"I'm not proud of that. I hope you weren't distressed."

"When I calmed down, I figured that it was just an act. Hollering about your reward—that was good." Treet straightened; the pain in his ribs had eased. "Where do we go from here?"

"We must get to the river. There is an entrance to the Old Section between Jamuna and Chryse." She appraised Treet with a practiced eye. "Can you make it?"

"I'm not staying here. You know where this entrance is?"

Ernina looked grave. "I don't. But some of Hladik's prisoners I have treated over the years have told me about it. I'm no guide, but perhaps we can find it."

"Will the Dhogs take us in?"

"A physician is always welcome. And you, a Fieri, will be worshiped."

"Is that so?" Treet had to give her credit. She was made of stern stuff. Standing up to Mrukk like that, outwitting him, cutting him down to size with bluff and nerves alone—that took plenty of cool courage, and a good knowledge of the human psyche, as well as just plain old backwoods cunning. "Well, I'm ready. Let's get moving. I think we've worn out our welcome."

They hurried off again and were soon making their way across the dark expanse of Threl Square, two small figures scuttling over the stone flagging toward the line of spire-shaped trees marking Kyan in the distance. They had just reached the far side of the square when the shouts began. Treet threw a glance over his shoulder to see the black shapes of Mors Ultima boiling out into the square behind them.

● ● ● ● ● ●

Tvrdy could not believe his eyes. Unarmed Dhogs had attacked the Nilokerus checkpoint. Apparently their uncanny stealth had allowed them to get within striking distance, for the Nilokerus had not had time to draw their weapons. Perhaps the guards had been asleep. At any rate, the struggle was decidedly one-sided. The Dhogs, due to superior numbers, had the Nilokerus subdued in short order, and Tvrdy stepped out from hiding.

"Ah, Tanais!" cried Bogney when Tvrdy came up. "Now we loading faster, seh?"

Tvrdy did not strike the Dhog leader, but came very close. He fought down the impulse to lay into the grubby Bogney— causing the Dhog leader to lose face in front of his men would be a grave tactical error, especially at the moment of their first success. They *had* taken a checkpoint; that, for the Dhogs at least, was a real triumph.

"Take some men back to the boat. When you have finished

loading what is there, tell my man to bring the boat around. We will have the other wagons ready to load from the wharf." He cocked an eye skyward to the enormous vault of the dome, still showing the faint glimmer of stars in the firmament beyond its transparent panes. "We've got to hurry if we're going to make it back to the Zone before sunrise."

Bogney chose a few of his men, and the Dhogs raced silently away. Tvrdy looked at the Nilokerus unconscious at his feet and wondered what to do with them. He had not planned on taking any prisoners and hated the thought of killing them outright. But if they regained consciousness before the operation was finished, he'd have no choice. He stooped and retrieved the three Nilokerus weapons. "You stay here with them," he ordered the remaining Dhogs. "Do not let them get away, and do not let them signal for help."

Tvrdy made his way back to the granary, where two more wagons were ready to go. "Take them to the wharf," he told the men. "The boat will be there soon."

The wagons rolled out on their tracks and down the slight incline toward the wharf. "Come on, get moving!" Tvrdy yelled. "There are still two wagons left."

Piipo came up puffing. "What happened down there? I heard a shout."

"The Dhogs changed the plan. They attacked the checkpoint on the wharf."

"Anybody killed?"

"No. The Nilokerus must have been asleep. They didn't even get their weapons out. It was clean."

Piipo let out a sigh of relief. "Two more wagons and we're free. When the priests find this tomorrow, there will be Trabant to pay, of course. But Gorov will thunder and shout and demand an inventory. That should keep them busy. There's a chance Jamrog may not even hear about this."

"You're forgetting the Nilokerus down there. They'll talk."

"What do we do?"

"I don't know. Nothing, I guess. Jamrog will find out. We can't help that now."

"Then let's take the Nilokerus with us."

Tvrdy's eyebrows arched up. Piipo explained, "Of course, if we leave them they will talk; but if we take them, no one will know precisely what happened. They may even think the Nilokerus had something to do with it. Also, if we take them back with us, we can force them to tell us the arrangement of the checkpoints and how they are manned."

"Piipo, I underestimate you. Who knows, after they have told us what they know, they may even wish to join us—considering the alternatives."

A group of men came dashing up from the wharf just then, sweating from their night's exertion. "Just two more loads," Tvrdy told them, "and then we start back."

The men fell to, hefting up grain sacks and heaving them onto the wagons. They were joined by others up from the wharf, and the wagons were loaded in minutes and pushed out on the tracks down to the waiting boat, pausing at the checkpoint booth to pick up the groggy Nilokerus, who were tossed atop the load. Tvrdy and Piipo walked behind the last wagon to make certain nothing went wrong.

"We're going to make it," said Piipo as the last wagon, its wheels emitting a gritty squeal on the track, was pushed up to the side of the boat.

The words were no sooner out of his mouth than a bright, jagged tongue of flame streaked out of the night and the nearest grain sack exploded in a shower of bright orange sparks, flinging grain like tiny shrapnel in all directions. The next blast strafed the front of the boat, melting the fibersteel where it touched.

"Get aboard!" cried Tvrdy. "Leave the rest!" Piipo scrambled aboard, and Tvrdy climbed into the boat behind him. "Cast off! Let's go, you men! Get aboard or we'll leave you," he shouted to the Dhogs still heaving grain sacks over the rail.

He signaled to the pilot, and the engines growled. The boat slid backwards in the water. Still the Dhogs did not give up. They continued piling the grain sacks into the moving boat as the fire flashed around them, striking the dock, the boat, sending up steaming showers of water where a blast impacted on the surface of the river. Tvrdy shouted, "Leave the grain! Get aboard!"

He grabbed one of the Nilokerus weapons he'd confiscated and, jumping on top of the sizable pyramid of grain sacks, began returning fire. He was joined by two of his lieutenants, and the Nilokerus swarming down to the wharf from the granaries were momentarily shocked to find themselves exposed and under fire.

The boat pulled away from the wharf. The Dhogs, who had not so much as peeked over a shoulder during the attack, threw the last grain sack aboard and then flung themselves over the rail just as the boat swung into the bay. The last Dhog aboard was Giloon Bogney, who picked himself up and began pounding his men on the back.

"We got it all!" he crowed, grinning through his tangled mat of beard. The water around the boat erupted in steaming geysers as the Nilokerus on the wharf, having scrambled to cover, opened fire once more.

Tvrdy gave his weapon to one of his men and stomped back to Bogney. Towering over the shabby Dhog, he glared down and, with a voice as cold and sharp as ice, said, "Get your men below deck, and stay there with them. I don't want to see any of you until we reach Jamuna." He walked away, leaving the Dhog with a quickly fading grin on his greasy face.

"**H**ead for that Hageblock," said Treet. "If we can outrun them we have a chance." There were, as near as Treet could count in the dark while running, only eight Invisibles pursuing them. But he had little doubt there would be more soon. Without a word Ernina took off; Treet followed on her heels.

Threl Square was bounded on all sides by a band of tree-lined greenspace. Saecaraz Hageblocks, squat gray slab-and-pillar structures, stood along this border. Treet and Ernina made for the nearest of these, flying over the darkened lawn, darting and dodging in an erratic batflight through the trees.

They reached the block and dashed into the first entrance they came upon. The block was built around a courtyard, and the fugitives fled through the open entry and into the yard. "It's blind!" Treet whispered harshly. There was not another exit to be seen.

"Hurry!" said Ernina. "Over there!" She pointed to a line of doorways facing the courtyard.

They ran across the yard, the footsteps of the Invisibles sounding in the short passage behind them. Ernina slipped into the fourth doorway; Treet followed her, and together they shrank into the shadowed depths. An instant later Invisibles pounded into the courtyard.

The Invisibles spread out and began combing the court-yard, those on the perimeter checking each door as they passed . . . the first door . . . the second door . . .

Treet heard the footsteps outside the doorway next to theirs. Silence. Then the footsteps paused outside their door. Treet held his breath and pressed himself flat against the rough wall, mentally readying himself to fight.

The Invisible stood framed in the doorway. He took a slow step forward.

Treet's hands balled into fists, his heart lunging against his ribs.

The Invisible advanced, and Treet, remembering the pellets

in Ernina's pouch, felt at his side. He found the pouch and pulled out a handful of pellets, took a deep breath and held it. Ernina did the same. The Invisible heard the movement and swung around, his weapon arcing toward them. Treet threw himself forward and put his hand into the Invisible's face, crunching the pellets in his fist in the same motion. The Invisible backpedaled, gasped, and then wobbled uncertainly on his feet. Treet kept his hand before the man's face, laid him down, and then tiptoed to the entryway to peer out across the courtyard. There was not an Invisible to be seen. Treet did not linger to analyze the situation, expelling his breath and tasting almonds on his tongue. "This is our chance," he said. Ernina staggered forward and Treet grabbed her, pulling her forward with him as he raced out into the courtyard once more.

They fled back through the entryway and into the greenspace beyond. Then, step by careful step, they worked their way through the trees and around toward the river once more. But between them and the river stood block upon block of Hage dwellings and, at the center of the main thoroughfare, directly ahead, a Nilokerus checkpoint.

"Well, what do we do now?" said Treet. He was tired. The exertion was beginning to tell on him. He felt limp and wrung out. "We can't go that way."

"We'll have to go around, but keep working toward the river." She raised a hand to his damp forehead. "How are you feeling?"

"Okay. Lead on," said Treet as he fell into step.

When they reached the first of the dwelling blocks, Treet gave a quick backward glance to see the dark shapes of Invisibles once again on course behind them. Although he didn't count them, it appeared that the original eight had picked up a few reinforcements along the way. From the way the Invisibles were approaching—slow and deliberate with a lot of side-to-side movement—Treet guessed they had not yet discovered them, but were stalking. "Our friends with the crummy sense of humor are back," whispered Treet.

He and Ernina ducked into the nearest entrance, a covered gallery leading into the interior of the block. The tunnel curved sharply to the right, and after passing dozens of kraams, each sealed with opaqued unidors, the gallery teminated at a plaza formed by the backs of the Hageblocks. In the center of the plaza, yellow lights blazing, sat another Nilokerus checkpoint.

Treet took one look at the booth, and his heart sank. There were five Nilokerus at attention talking to three Invisibles; each of the Invisibles wore the shimmery black yos of the Mors Ultima. "It doesn't take them long to—"

"Shh!" Ernina said sharply. "Listen."

In the distance came the pattering of footsteps in the gallery.

"We're in it now," Treet said. "Trapped."

"Perhaps we could work our way around the plaza."

"Not with the men in black out there."

The footsteps in the tunnel behind them grew louder.

"We've got to do something," Ernina pointed out.

"How many of those goofballs have you got left?"

"The anesthetic?"

"Yeah, how many?"

Ernina dug into the pouch and brought out a handful. "Not many. Two or three handfuls."

"That might do it. Give me a handful, and you take the rest."

"What are you going to do?"

"See if we can burn these bozos three times with one match."

Treet pointed Ernina back down the tunnel. "Scatter them evenly and then come back here." She nodded once and hurried away.

Treet crept to the mouth of the gallery and laid down the pellets one-by-one just inside the entrance. Then, stepping through the carefully arranged trap, he took a deep breath and stepped out into the plaza.

Treet proceeded along the side of the Hageblock. To his dismay, none of the Nilokerus or their Mors Ultima helpers saw him. A few steps ahead he saw a stack of metal rods leaning against the wall. Treet put his foot against the stack and shoved. The rods clattered to the ground and rolled.

Treet jumped back and looked surprised. The heads of the Nilokerus swiveled around. The Mors Ultima were already racing toward him. Treet pretended indecision and then flew back to the gallery and disappeared inside. He rounded the curve of the tunnel and nearly collided with Ernina. "Put this on," she said, thrusting the mask into his hands.

Pulling the mask on, Treet felt his stomach tighten into a hard lump—as if he'd swallowed a cast-iron grapefruit. Either his plan would work or they'd be captured right here. They waited.

There were a few sharp coughs, some gasps and a moan or two, and then silence.

"It worked!" Treet shouted, the mask garbling his voice.

They ran back to the plaza entrance to find bodies sprawled helter-skelter just inside. "Uh oh," said Treet, "there's one missing."

Ernina confirmed his body count as she stooped to retrieve several untrampled pellets. "Five Nilokerus and two Invisibles."

"The other Invisible's still out there someplace." Treet peered out into the plaza. "I don't see him anywhere."

"Maybe he went to signal the others."

"We can only hope." Treet paused and considered the alternatives and then shrugged. "Well, we can't stay here."

They picked up two of the Nilokerus weapons and left the tunnel, reaching the other side of the plaza moments later. There was still no sign of the missing Invisible, so they hurried on into the warrens of the Hageblocks, making their way to the river.

The Saecaraz Hageblocks were old and had been allowed to spread over the centuries as kraam was added to kraam and building thrust upon building until they resembled nothing so much as the ancient gypsy ghettos Treet had once visited in old Budapest. Picking their way through the narrow, winding streets and meandering boulevards crowded with kraams and market stalls and kiosks was slow work. Treet felt his strength going; he was light-headed and woozy.

At one point Ernina stopped beneath a yellow glow globe, turned to him, and placed her fingertips against the side of his throat. "Your pulse is fast." She gazed deeply into his eyes. "Treet, are you all right?"

"I'm a little tired," he admitted.

"Here—" The physician reached into her yos and pulled out a flat, puck-shaped biscuit. "Eat this—it'll give you strength."

Treet raised the biscuit to his mouth and nibbled. It was dry and tasted of herbs. "What is it?"

"It's a stimulant."

Treet chewed slowly, wishing he had something cold and

wet to wash it down. Ernina watched him for a moment and then said, "The river is just beyond here, I think. Saecaraz is very logical—not like Chryse or Rumon—and I've been here often enough on health inspections."

"And then?"

"There are boats along the waterfront."

"I wouldn't mind a ride."

They moved off, and Treet did begin to feel revived. The stimulant worked, but he wondered how long he could keep going. The deeper into the warren they went, the more twisted and convoluted their path became until it seemed as if they were following a meandering creek bed through stone canyons. They passed beneath towering cliffs of jumbled kraams and Hageworks stacked layer upon layer. Whenever there was a choice of direction, Ernina took the route that moved them closer to the river. Winding through the empty byways made Treet think of touring the bombed out shell of a city: any one of a dozen or so Irani-Syrian-Lebanese settlements gutted during the Middle East holocaust of the last century.

But these streets were empty, whereas any other city on Earth, no matter how desolated, literally crawled with life— beggars and scavengers certainly, wandering armies of orphan pickpockets usually, packs of yapping dogs and vermin if nothing else. In Saecaraz at least, the citizens were sealed tightly in their kraams until dawn's early light.

"It sure is empty," said Treet as they paused at a deserted crossroads to consider the best direction. "I've never seen a city shut down so completely."

Ernina raised her finger to her lips and looked around.

Treet heard the scuffle of a footfall. It stopped abruptly.

"Our tail is showing," said Treet.

"The missing Invisible," replied Ernina. "But the waterfront is just down there." She pointed through an open archway overgrown with hanging vines, orange in the light of a single globe. A stone pathway angled down through the arch into the darkness beyond.

They struck off for the arch, and the footsteps started again. At the arch Treet paused to listen; the shuffling steps paused, too. Treet ducked under the archway and stepped to the side. Ernina took up a position on the other side, and they waited. Treet did not intend on ambushing the Invisible—he doubted whether he could go hand-to-hand with one even if he were in peak condition, and he was far from being in the best of shape. He merely hoped that by hiding among the hanging vines they could throw the Invisible off their trail long enough to find a boat.

Long moments passed. Then, as Treet was about to risk peering around the corner to see what had become of their tracker, he heard the soft scuffing footfall again, closer. He froze.

The Invisible came through the arch and then hesitated. He stopped and looked around as if perplexed. Treet noticed that the Invisible was a good deal shorter than he was and slighter of build. Also, he wore the banded silver of the Saecaraz.

This was no Invisible. Treet decided to take a chance.

The man was only a step and a half away, and, even granted the element of surprise, Treet nearly lost him.

Treet stepped from his hiding place, and the vines rustled. The Saecaraz turned at the same instant, saw him, and bolted away. Treet stretched after him, snagged the corner of his yos, and held on. The grab yanked the stranger off his feet, and he landed with a thump and a whimper on the pavement where he squirmed, throwing his hands over his head to protect himself.

Ernina ran up and took one look at the Hageman cringing at Treet's feet and said, "Get up!" Her tone was authority itself, and the man jolted as if he'd been struck. But he lowered his hands and peered fearfully up at the two standing over him. A look of recognition lit Ernina's eyes.

Treet saw it and remarked, "You know this clown?"

Ernina bent to help the man to his feet. An expression of relief erased the fear from his pinched face. "I know him," said Ernina. "It's Nilokerus Subdirector Fertig!"

THIRTY
EIGHT

"*I* am Fertig," the Hageman replied, "but no longer Sub-director."

"I gather there's a lot of that going around," offered Treet. "So what are you doing following us?"

"I have been hiding—many days it is now—trying to find the Old Section." He spread his hands wide. "But I can't find it. There is no entrance in Saecaraz—perhaps at one time, but it no longer exists. I decided to wait and watch for Dhogs to come into Hage and then follow them."

"You thought we were Dhogs?"

"No." Fertig shook his head, a wisp of a smile on his lips. "I knew you were not Dhogs, but when I saw the Invisibles chasing you, I guessed Jamrog was up to something. I decided to follow you."

"Can you get us out of here?"

"It depends on where you are going."

"Chryse," explained Ernina. "The entrance to the Old Section is in Chryse on the Jamuna border." To Fertig's look, she replied, "A physician of many years learns many things; not all concern medicine. Now we will need a boat."

Fertig shook his head. "An em would be better. Faster."

"Great! Where can we get one of those?" asked Treet.

"Rohee had many of them placed around the Hage. It fell to Hladik to maintain them. It is one of the things I was responsible for—making certain they were always ready. If Jamrog hasn't moved them . . ." He stared out into the mottled darkness, eyes scanning the shadowed jumble of the waterfront before them. Kyan lapped the pilings and riffled in the shallows. "This way," said Fertig, starting away. "I think there is one near here."

Treet and Ernina followed the former Subdirector along the waterfront and came to the Saecaraz dockyard. Row upon row of boats chained for the night to fibersteel rings set in the dock let Treet know that they would have had a very difficult time getting a boat here. But Fertig led them away from the dock, turning back toward the Hageblocks for a short distance until he came to a flat-roofed building with a double-wide unidor.

Fertig went to the door and pressed the code into the lighted tabs. The unidor snapped off with a crack as an interior light blinked on. There before them was a silver em with two rear seats. "Our spirit guides are with us tonight," called Fertig as he leaped into the driver seat. "This one Rohee used to take him to and from his boat."

The em rolled out of its nook on squashy tires. Ernina climbed into the seat beside Fertig, and Treet piled into the one behind. "Home, James," he said.

"Can you get us to Chryse?" asked Ernina.

"Yes. We could follow the riverwalk, but I know a better way."

"What about checkpoints? The Nilokerus have been alerted; they will be looking for us by now."

"Don't worry. There will be no checkpoints."

The em jerked away and they were off, rolling soundlessly along the riverwalk. Treet watched the blurred shapes of trees ripple past and the occasional light across the river dance over the silent water. The air in his face felt good; he slid down in the seat and closed his eyes.

He awoke again as the em jolted to a stop. They were sitting in a narrow street with tiered kraams pressing in on either side. Ahead was a deserted arcade with a few empty kiosks. The place had a gritty, stained appearance. Clearly, they were no longer in Saecaraz. "What is it?" asked Treet, his voice hoarse with sleep.

"Invisibles," whispered Fertig. "I saw three of them cross just ahead of us."

"Where are we?" He swiveled his head around. The dome overhead showed dull charcoal, and there were few stars showing. He had slept a good while then, but it seemed only an instant and he was still exhausted.

"We're in Jamuna Hage," replied Ernina, "near the border of Chryse. It's only a little way now."

Treet sat in the back and rubbed his face. He felt as if he had been pulled apart and reassembled backwards, every joint out of place and wrong. They waited a few minutes, and then Fertig said, "I think we can go now."

The em rolled out into the arcade and headed for a street

angling off into deep Hage. They reached the street and heard the shout simultaneously. A split second later a portion of the pavement sprouted flame, and rock splinters scattered. Fertig raced ahead and turned off the street at first opportunity. Treet, white-knuckling the handgrips and watching their rear, saw two Invisibles appear in the street behind them, raise weapons—and then they were taken from sight by Fertig's quick turn.

"We're at the border," said Fertig as they raced down narrow, twisting streets. "There is a checkpoint just ahead—"

"Go right on through," said Treet. "Don't even slow down."

"But—"

"They know we're here now. And it's close to dawn. We've got to find that entrance soon. I say run the checkpoint."

Fertig nodded and grimly pressed his foot to the floor. The em was not built for speed, and with three passengers it would never set any land speed records, but Fertig coaxed the little vehicle to a respectable pace and they whisked through the empty Jamuna streets and out into a section of terraced fields of brown sludge overset with dingy towers. "Oohh! Smell that," said Treet, tears rising to his eyes. "Ammonia!"

Past the fields rose a wall of stone brick topped by a high curtain of fibersteel panels. A great arch was cut in the wall allowing the road to pass through. Directly ahead was a Nilokerus checkpoint with a gate. Two Nilokerus stood by the gate and one inside the booth, all three apparently asleep on their feet.

The em whizzed toward the gate and the oblivious guards. The fugitives were barely ten meters away before the first guard awoke and sounded the alarm. The em crashed through the gate, shoving it into the booth as the two gate guards stood gaping. They yelled and then ran after the em, but it was too fast, and they stopped. As an afterthought they pulled out their weapons to fire halfheartedly at the receding vehicle.

"We did it!" crowed Treet. Fertig grinned glassily, his hands tight on the steering bar. "Masterful job, Fertig old stick! We're rolling now."

They were rolling, but not for long. The entire front end of the em started rattling, and then vibrating, and then shaking as if it would fly to pieces. Fertig allowed the machine to coast to a stop, got out, and stared at the left front tire.

"I knew it was too good to last," sighed Treet as he surveyed the flat tire. "We must have picked up part of the gate."

"It doesn't matter," replied Ernina gazing at the landscape. "The entrance is near."

Treet followed her gaze. Chryse was as different from Jamuna and Saecaraz as Fierra from Dome. Even in the gloom Treet could see that Hage Chryse had a symmetry of design that set it apart. He remembered his last and only visit to the Hage when Calin, his magician guide, had brought him here. A double-barbed pang of guilt and grief pierced him at the thought.

"We should get this thing off the road," said Treet.

Fertig climbed back in and drove away, limping down the hillside to a clump of droopy-limbed trees. He drove the em into the trees and emerged a moment later, hurrying back up to the road. Ernina strode away in the opposite direction, climbing the nearest hill. Treet and Fertig followed, and soon they were walking parallel to the towering border wall.

The dome above grew lighter, graying with the sunrise. The hills of outer Chryse took on shape and definition; color seeped into the landscape. White moundlike structures emerged out of the murk away to the left. On the right, green hemispheres of hills met the wall, which stretched in a long, slow curve toward deep Hage.

Ernina pressed ahead at a nimble pace, and soon they came to a place where the sculptured hills ended and Chryse Hageworks began. Picking their way among the scattered structures, the three paused often to allow Ernina to study their position. "They say there is an old air conduit beneath a broadcast antenna—from before the Old Section was abandoned," she said, gazing around her at the huddled conglomeration of buildings crammed together in the carved-out bowl of the hillside.

"Why was the Old Section abandoned?" wondered Treet.

"No one knows," said Ernina. "It was many Supreme Directors ago."

"Some say it was destroyed long ago and no longer exists," offered Fertig. "Others say it was taken over by the Fieri and they sealed it. They were left alone, and no one went there after that."

"Hmmm," Treet said. Doubtless there was something in what Fertig said, although most likely he had it reversed. The

Fieri were probably driven back or quarantined in the Old Section and the section sealed to prevent their escape or to keep them separated from the rest. Then again, the Old Section may have had some lingering bad associations with the Red Death and had become psychologically uninhabitable. "Are you sure this is the place? I don't see any antenna."

"Here somewhere, yes," replied Ernina. With that, she moved down the hill and entered the Hageworks, keeping the border wall to her left as she pushed deeper into the Hage. Chryse appeared as if it had been designed by inebriated gnome architects. Squat mushroom-shaped structures, large and small, sprang from the scooped-out grassy bowl. The streets were pink, paved footpaths winding through arches and walls and around the smooth, white-stuccoed buildings in almost whimsical fashion, making it difficult to proceed with any kind of haste. The dome grew brighter as dawn came on; the fugitives' efforts became more desperate.

"Maybe we should find a place to hide out," offered Treet at one point. "We could lay low until nightfall and take up the search again." He looked around at all the Hageblocks and imagined Chryse pouring out of them at any moment to start the day's work. "We don't want to be caught out here."

"It's near," insisted Ernina.

"Sure," agreed Treet. "But it might take a little more time to find than we dare spend right now. I still don't see anything that looks like an antenna. We should have seen it long ago if it was close by."

Fertig stood a little way off, listening. He broke in, saying, "Shh! Someone is coming."

Due to the ensnarled pattern of arches, pathways, and walls, it was difficult to tell where the sound was coming from, but Fertig was right: the shush of many feet on the pink stone pavement told them someone was coming quickly their way.

"Invisibles," muttered Treet. "We've got to get out of here."

"This way," said Fertig, leading them through the nearest archway into a narrow street lined with round kraam entrances like mouse holes.

There they waited, peering around the smooth white arch to see a ragged man, the tatters of his clothes flying as he came.

He paused, glanced around quickly, and then signaled to others behind him. Then there came a creaking sound, as if a heavy machine were being pulled along with leather straps.

Presently a troop of men, each as disheveled as the next— like deserters of a bedraggled army—came into view pushing Hyrgo wagons loaded to bursting with sacks of grain. The wheels of the wagons were wrapped with sacking.

"Dhogs!" whispered Ernina, her eyes lighting up. "We can follow them."

Treet watched as one grain wagon disappeared down the next street, followed by another, and then another. With the fourth wagon came a rear guard—two Dhogs and two others. One of these turned toward them, and Treet jumped out from behind the arch. "Tvrdy!"

It was a foolish move. Instantly the procession froze. Weapons whipped around, and he would have been flash-fried if the quick-thinking Tanais Director had not intervened.

"Wait!" Tvrdy cried, throwing wide his hands.

Treet gulped. What have I done, he thought? I'm wearing Nilokerus colors. He doesn't recognize me.

Tvrdy approached. The Dhogs stared. No one moved.

The Tanais came to stand directly in front of Treet; he stared into his eyes. Recognition came slowly. "Traveler!" Tvrdy said, breaking into a wide grin. "You have returned at last. I thought you dead."

"It's good to see you, too," replied Treet.

Tvrdy turned and signaled to the others to move on quickly. "There are Invisibles after us," Tvrdy explained. "We cannot talk now. Come with us."

"We'd be glad for the escort. The Invisibles are after us, too. We're looking for the entrance to the Old Section."

"We?" A light leapt up in his eyes.

Treet motioned for Ernina and Fertig to come out of hiding. "It's all right," Treet said. "They're going our way."

The stocky physician stepped confidently out from behind the arch, followed by Fertig, looking none too certain about his reception. Tvrdy eyed them both, disappointed. "Ernina, sixth-order Nilokerus physician, I believe." She inclined her head, and Tvrdy glanced at Fertig slinking up. "Ah, another Nilokerus! Defection makes our numbers swell."

"They helped me," said Treet. "Ernina saved my life, and Fertig kept us out of reach of the Invisibles."

Tvrdy nodded curtly. "Perhaps he can do the same for us one day." He waved, and the wagon creaked into motion once more. Treet and the others fell in behind the wagon, and the Dhogs led them through the still silent streets. At one point, the procession surprised a Chryse, sleepy-eyed and yawning, who was just stumbling out of his kraam. The man stood gawking for a moment before it dawned on him that he was seeing something highly illicit, then closed his eyes and scuttled back into his kraam.

Before the raiding party could encounter any more Chryse, they reached the further edge of the bowl and a deserted district where a cluster of gutted shells of buildings formed a boundary to the Hageworks. And there, behind this boundary, lay the long, collapsed skeleton of the antenna.

They pushed between two of the empty hulks and found that the Dhogs had rolled their wagons up to the foot of the antenna, which at one time stood atop a low embankment. On one side of this embankment was a large oval louvre panel. As Treet watched, the panel was pried open and the first of the wagons hauled inside the giant air duct.

Ernina, Fertig, Treet, and Tvrdy were the last to go in. Fertig and Tvrdy tugged the louvre down and secured it from the inside. And then Tvrdy hurried to where Treet and the others waited in the darkness of the conduit. "A night's work done," he said. "I hope not wasted "

THIRTY
NINE

For Yarden, the days settled into a routine of pleasure. She awoke to silver mornings of tranquil meditation and convivial breakfasts with her shipboard companions. Then she spent the next hours totally absorbed in her painting exercises, standing with her easel at the rail, face scrunched in concentration as she labored to achieve fluidity of motion in the controlled line. Her afternoons were taken with Gerdes' classes under the orange canopy on the aft deck of the ship. Evenings found her alone, watching night sweep over the fair landscape, talking with Ianni, or taking in Fieri entertainment under the bright Empyrion stars.

And always, the wide enchanting countryside slid by the rail: hills alive with exotic wildlife; thick, luxuriant vegetation blanketing the land and encroaching on the river's edge; mountains, blue-misted in the distance, rising up to crown the tumbling hills with cool supremacy. Empyrion was paradise—a vast, unspoiled paradise.

She slept well at night and emerged fresh in the morning to begin another day just like the one before. And each morning as she came on deck to greet the day, she felt born anew. Such was life among the Fieri. They were, Yarden was learning, not only gentle, peaceable people, but they were also nimble-witted, and possessed of an insatiable appetite for jokes and humorous stories of all kinds.

Still, their humor was just as gentle as they were themselves, never unbecoming, never cynical. Yarden began to believe that the Fieri did not have it in them to mock or jeer; cruelty of thought or word was as far beneath them as cruelty of action. There was joy and wisdom in their frivolity—a soaring lightheartedness that was an expression of genuine Fieri goodness. And it came through their humor as in everything they did.

Wherever two or more Fieri gathered for very long, there would be laughter, and Yarden found she could listen to the sound of it for hours, though at first she did not always understand the jokes—many of which depended on a clever observation of a world with which she was, in many ways, still unfamiliar. The stories, though, she understood well enough; and in the evenings, wrapped in starlight and the warmth of one another's company, the Fieri would cluster on deck to hear a tale.

Everyone told stories—the supply was apparently limitless. But the best Fieri stories were the province of certain designated storytellers—men and women who had gained reputations as skilled and inventive orators. Typically, the storyteller would have prepared a story for the evening, although tradition demanded that he be coaxed into telling it. The listeners would gather sometime after the evening meal and begin talking about how it was a beautiful night for a story (any night for the Fieri was a beautiful night for a story), and how they missed hearing the old stories, and how it had been such a long time since they had heard a really good tale (even though in all likelihood they had heard one just the night before), and how they longed for a storyteller like the storytellers of old . . .

The call would go up for a story, and the call would quickly become a chant. Then, to a crescendo of cheers and applause, the storyteller would stump up in feigned bewilderment, usually saying that he didn't know if his stories would please or not, but with the audience's indulgence, he'd try. The audience would draw close—children right down in front, their parents and other adults pressing in behind. When everyone was settled, the storyteller would climb up on his stool; when all was quiet, he'd begin. Some stories had set beginnings, but ordinarily the teller would start by connecting his tale to some recent event or an observation he'd made that very day.

This preamble would stretch out as long as he could sustain it, building tension while inexorably working toward the place where he'd say something like: "which reminds me of the time that. . . ," at which point the audible sigh of relief would go up from the audience and he'd be off on his tale.

Yarden enjoyed the stories as much as any Fieri child. The storytellers were as much actor and actress as tale-spinner, breathing life into their characters with vocal inflections, gestures, and facial expressions, especially at moments of high drama. The Fieri would sit and listen raptly, catching every nuance of the performance, savoring it, showing their approval with their "ohs" and "ahs" in the appropriate places. Each Fieri knew the stories so well that it was something of a game to try to catch the teller in a slip or omission. The tellers, on the other hand, knew their audience was waiting for a bungle, and kept them vigilant by refusing to tell their stories in precisely the same way as before.

Thus the stories were always the same, yet always different, and the stories had a fresh familiarity about them that Yarden found appealing and comforting—though she had not been among them long enough to have heard all the stories once, let alone twice.

When at last the evening's tale came to an end to universal acclaim, the group would disperse reluctantly or, in typical Fieri fashion, finish a singular entertainment with a time of singing.

Fieri songs were rich, mellifluous creations with innumerable verses and haunting melody lines that wandered, lapsing and recurring almost at will, Yarden thought—although every Fieri knew exactly where the tune went. The songs were difficult to learn, but a joy to hear, and Yarden would sit amidst the singers, arms wrapped around legs, chin on knees, drifting in delicious rapture. Fieri singing was exalting, stirring, and somehow always poignant—as if the music bubbled up from a fountain at whose deep roots seeped a sadness that mingled the music with traces of pain.

This pain, Yarden suspected, stemmed from the Burning— the nuclear holocaust visited on their noble race by the monsters of Dome centuries ago. It was a scar the Fieri bore, a pain that would never heal.

As playful as the Fieri could be, Yarden often wondered whether the humor was not alloyed of feelings of profound grief. She asked Ianni about this one evening, and Ianni's answer surprised her. "You are very perceptive, Yarden. Perhaps our merrymaking does spring from the hurt of the past."

"But wouldn't it be better to forget the past, to let it go so the wound can heal?"

"Time will not heal it; nothing can. The hurt is too deep."

Yarden didn't understand this, so pressed the question again. "But that doesn't make sense. You say the Infinite Father cares for you. Can't He do something?"

Ianni only smiled and shook her head. "You see, but do not see yet. Look around you, Yarden." She lifted a palm upward. "All of life is pain. We are born to pain and death, and there is no escape from it. Every living thing must bear the pain of life."

"That sounds very pessimistic," snapped Yarden. "What's wrong with you? You're the one who's always telling me, Trust, believe, have faith. What good is any of that if there is no escape from pain and death?"

"Ah, but we do not attempt to escape from the pain."

"No?"

"No. We know it for what it is; we embrace it. We take it to ourselves, and through the Infinite's love we transform it into something else. In the end we transcend it."

"What is the suffering transformed into?"

"Love, compassion, kindness, joy—all the holy virtues. Don't you see? As long as one tries to escape, the pain will consume and destroy. But if it is accepted, it can be transformed."

"I don't know if I want to accept it," said Yarden. "You make it sound so . . . so hopeless."

"Never hopeless. Hope is born of grief, Yarden. Without the suffering, there can be no striving for something better. Hope is the yearning for a better place where pain can no longer hurt."

"Is there such a place?"

"Only with the Infinite. He has promised us His presence in this life and the life to come. He helps us bear the pain of our creation—it is no less His pain, after all."

They spoke of other things after that, but Yarden remembered and thought about this part of their conversation often. It had affected her deeply, although she didn't know it at the time. The idea of hope springing from the basic pain of life was foreign to her. Not that Yarden was naive—she knew that life was tough, that one was born to hardship, that strife was the nature of things. But she had always believed that only through struggle could one overcome the pain and hardship.

The notion that pain must be embraced was difficult for her to accept. But the more she saw of the Fieri, the more she began to understand. The Fieri professed that the creation of the cosmos had cost the Infinite Father something; He had paid a tremendous toll to bring His beloved universe into existence. He had labored, and suffered the pain of His laboring. In this suffering, love itself was born.

"What else is love," Mathiax had asked her one day, "but

671

taking the pain of another as your own—especially when you are not obliged to?" Thus, pain was woven into the very fabric of the universe—because there could be no love without it, and because the Infinite Father had set love as the cornerstone of His creation.

These were heady thoughts, but Yarden found herself returning to them again and again as she tried to understand the Fieri and their God, whom she wanted very much to accept as her own.

So the trip upriver to the Bay of Talking Fish became for Yarden an inner pilgrimage as she wrestled with these thoughts and felt the struggle changing her, slowly, gently as understanding grew.

Each day the sweeping line of barges drew nearer the vast wrinkled highlands of the Light Mountain range, and at night the passengers could see the faint glow in the sky above the peaks—each night a little clearer than the night before. But earlier in the day the nautical procession had passed beyond the green-wrapped foothills and into steep-sided, red-rock canyons. Ahead lay the bare, wind-whipped crags and peaks of the Light Mountains.

This night, Yarden sat with Ianni and others on the foredeck watching the sky give forth a splendid display as the Light Mountains lit the heavens with a shifting aura of colors—an earthborn borealis, known to the Fieri as a sunshower.

The light began at dusk when the sunstone began giving up its stored solar energy, glowing brightly as the sky darkened. The colors were soft, opalescent blues and greens and golds with wisps of red and violet, corresponding to the various types of sunstone—the same sunstone used to build Fierra. The shifting color was brought about by a combination of common atmospheric conditions: minute sunstone particles in the air, turbulence caused by layers of warmer surface air rolling against cooler upper air, reflection off high clouds.

The effect was stunning. It was like watching slow motion fireworks, Yarden thought dreamily as she gazed up into the shimmering sky. The evanescent color formed softly spectral patterns—shifting ribbons of light, transparent streamers that lit up, swirling and blending, then vanishing, only to reappear again and again in continually changing shapes.

Yarden found herself mesmerized by the brilliant aerial

performance, transported beyond herself and into a realm of pure light and color. She looked at her surroundings as if gazing down upon the world from the rarefied heights of a region absolutely alive with peace and beauty and joy. All this she saw mirrored on the upturned faces of the Fieri gathered around her.

After a while one of the Fieri—a Mentor named Elson—got up and addressed the rapt watchers. Speaking softly, he said, "We are now following the way of our ancestors. In the Wandering our fathers found Taleraan and sailed long ships up the deep water into the Light Mountains. Perhaps they too lifted their eyes to the sky one night to see the first sunshower and discovered the secret of the shining stone.

"We do not know their thoughts, but we can imagine what they must have felt at that time of great discovery when, looking into the darkness, they saw the very rock of the mountains begin to glow with unaccustomed radiance.

"When the time of wandering came to an end, they built the bright cities with this same shining stone and named it sunstone. They lived in splendor both day and night . . ."

Although the recitation went on, Yarden's thoughts drifted in another direction. She remembered the Preceptor's words the night Treet had declared the growing danger from Dome. "On that day, our bright homeland became the Blighted Lands, a desert where no living thing could ever survive . . . All that we knew passed away; all that we loved died. The treasures of our great civilization fell into dust . . ."

All at once, Yarden felt the ache of that loss as she remembered those words and that night. She had just been reunited with Treet, and then he'd gone and made his ridiculous pronouncement: "The horror is starting again!"

And that had put an end to their burgeoning relationship. Rather, *she* had put an end to it by refusing to follow him back to Dome. For the first time since that night, the tiniest barb of doubt pricked her conscience: What if he was right?

FORTY

There was nothing to do but weather the storm and hope to repair the damage later. The three members of the Supreme Director's inner circle stood stoically and took the full brunt of their superior's fury. Jamrog was livid. Since the night of the raid, information had been trickling in, and now he could assess the full extent of the debacle. Which was not, as first thought, one failure only, but a whole series of disasters—apparently all linked together.

The ceremonial bhuj swung in short, swift, murderous arcs as he paced, his teeth grinding between clipped words. "So! The Fieri has escaped again—taken right out of your hands, Mrukk. And with the help of one of your physicians, Diltz. Meanwhile, checkpoints are overrun by force and guards carried off, never to be seen again." He stopped to glare at his silent audience. The Invisibles behind him kept their eyes riveted on the ceiling, not daring to witness the dire proceedings. "Does anyone have an explanation?" Jamrog challenged. He thrust the bhuj at Osmas.

The Saecaraz Subdirector swallowed hard and said, "The Dhogs are becoming more brazen, Supreme Director. They—"

"Dhogs! Yes, surely, blame the Dhogs. But doesn't it seem strange to you that Tvrdy and Cejka disappeared—and Piipo, too, for all we know—and suddenly the Dhogs become more *brazen?*"

Osmas winced at the bite of Jamrog's sarcasm.

"They were well organized," offered Mrukk. "The raid was well planned and perfectly staged. There is little doubt it was Tvrdy's doing."

"Thank you, Mrukk," Jamrog said sweetly. "I'm so glad for your keen evaluation. You who had your captive stolen from you by an old mother and failed to lift a finger to prevent it. None of your men were killed? No? In fact, no one suffered so much as a scratch, I believe.

"What about it, Diltz?" The bhuj swung toward the emaciated Director. "She was one of your physicians."

"Yes," he replied, his tone even more sepulchral than usual. "She was a Nilokerus."

"That's all you have to say? She was a Nilokerus?"

Diltz remained silent.

Jamrog spun away angrily and continued pacing. "And this morning Hyrgo priests tell me there is grain missing from the stores. It seems they were reluctant to say anything about it before, but in light of the general disarray we find ourselves in these last days, they thought better to mention the incident in case something could be done about it."

"Supreme Director, how much grain is missing?" asked Mrukk.

"Oh, enough. Enough to feed a whole Hage for several weeks!"

"They had to have help," observed Osmas.

"What makes you say that? With guards asleep at checkpoints and Invisibles unable to follow even an old woman, they had all the help they required."

Jamrog spun the bhuj in his hands and with a swipe that indicted them all, he said, "I tell you, Hagemen, I will tolerate no more failure. Do you understand me? I find myself forced to take emergency measures for the good of Empyrion."

"Emergency measures?" asked Osmas.

"These will be announced shortly. I have convened a special session of the Threl this afternoon, and I will present my plan then." He paused and stared into the distance momentarily, then tapped the bhuj on the floor. "But I have something for you three, too, never fear. I want every Invisible involved in the fiasco punished. I want the guard doubled at each checkpoint. I want the entrance to the Old Section found, and I want the Dhogs routed out and slaughtered. I want Tvrdy and Cejka apprehended and brought before a Threl tribunal to answer for their crimes before they face execution."

His eyes narrowed as he gazed at his coterie. "Oh, yes, and I want the Fieri found. I want him found and brought back to me at once."

Diltz, ignoring the consequences of affronting the Supreme Director, asked, "Why is this Fieri so important to you? How do we know the Fieri even exist anymore?"

Jamrog allowed himself a fierce smile. "Don't you see it, Diltz? It should be obvious to all of you. The Fieri are behind the disruption we are experiencing. The Fieri are fomenting rebellion; they are inciting the Dhogs."

The three shifted uneasily.

Jamrog continued, "I imagine that when we get to the bottom of this, we will find the Fieri have been involved from the beginning. Rohee was a fool. He believed they had come in goodwill, believed he could learn something from them. But it's clear that they want only what they have always wanted: Empyrion's downfall.

"History repeats its lessons from time to time, Hagemen. We are witnessing the first attempts by the Fieri to establish themselves once more within our midst. This time, however, we will be ready. This time we will be vigilant. We will strike before they can gain their full strength. We will search them out and destroy them before they destroy us." Jamrog, who had been momentarily carried away by his speech, came to himself and concluded, "I want the Fieri found before he can do any more harm. I want him, Hagemen."

With that, Jamrog left the kraam, taking his bodyguard with him and leaving the three chastised followers glowering at one another.

Osmas was the first to speak. "This is your fault, Mrukk. If you—"

"Watch your tongue, little man."

Diltz spoke as if to himself. "These Fieri interest me. I must find out more about them."

"Fieri!" Osmas snorted. "There are no Fieri. They are something Rohee imagined in his dotage."

"You're wrong," said Mrukk. "I saw him. He was like us, but unlike us."

"A Dhog."

"No. He was no Dhog."

"One of Tvrdy's agents then, or Cejka's."

Mrukk shook his head. "I was there the day they arrived."

"They?" wondered Diltz.

"There were four. With my own eyes I saw the airship. I saw the scorch marks on the platform. I gave the order to take them."

"Airship?" wondered Osmas. "I never heard anything about a Fieri airship."

"Rohee demanded secrecy. He had the airship destroyed, and the Fieri were given psilobe to deaden their memories. Then

676

he stupidly had them hidden in Hage—all except one. He kept one for himself."

"What happened then?" asked Diltz, fascinated.

"Tvrdy got them. He hoped to use them to take over the Threl. But Jamrog intervened, and we moved in before they could mount their attack. They were forced to retreat. They escaped through the Archives doors to the outside."

"Outside?" Osmas reeled in amazement.

"Extraordinary," said Diltz. "Where did they go?"

"To the southwest. We lost sight of them in the hills."

"You didn't pursue them?"

"What was the point? They had no weapons and were fleeing for their lives. They could do nothing."

"But now one of them, at least, has returned," said Diltz. "They seem most insistent."

Mrukk shrugged. "We will capture him again. And this time he will not escape."

· · · · · ·

Treet's first impression of the Old Section was that he had entered a life-sized, three-dimensional representation of a Heironymus Bosch painting: a chaotic postapocalypse world—fire-gutted and crumbling, vermin-infested ruins through which scrabbled half-naked creatures that may once have been human.

Refuse moldered in reeking mounds piled high in the center of the main square surrounded by charred and twisted trunks of trees. Pale, sickly weeds squeezed up through cracks in the wildly tilting paving stones. The air was rank and stale, the yellowed light weak. The few desolate facades still standing were blackened by soot and time.

The Old Section was clearly older than the rest of Dome. The architecture was different—more like contemporary utilitarian architecture back on Earth: permastone slabs and fiber-steel girders, plastic sheathing over industrial foam—all of it arranged in the standard honeycomb fashion of interlocking square boxes. The only variation Treet could see was that here and there the design had been augmented by native stone. A few wrecks showed signs of a developing indigenous architecture quite different from the stark, no-nonsense constructions around them.

Treet realized he was seeing back in time to the earliest days of the Cynetics colony. He imagined the young colony alive and thriving, building a glorious future on a paradise planet. The hope these people must have felt, the dreams they must have had for themselves and their children were now ruined and sinking into filth. The ruins had the stink of age, that oppressive sour smell of a thing too long removed from fresh air and sunlight.

Here the Red Death had forever changed the destiny of the colony. No, he reminded himself, not the Red Death alone. That had been a factor certainly, but there were others. A massive failure of nerve perhaps chief among them. Where had the men of vision gone, the men of bold ideas? Why had the voices of wisdom and intelligence been silenced? What had become of the courageous women who with their gentle, steady hands anchor all around them against the chaos? Were there no young people burning with impatience and idealism to challenge the status quo?

The ruins knew, and Treet could guess. In a word: fear. Paradise had turned against the settlers—apparently through their own carelessness—and the resulting disaster had so demoralized the survivors that they were paralyzed by fear. They had become afraid to dream again, afraid to act, afraid to trust their own best instincts and those of their fellow survivors. Afraid to live again.

Empyrion's bright promise had faded, and darkness rushed in to crush out the trembling light forever.

Now all that remained of the original colony was a blasted shell inhabited by the subhuman nonbeings. As Treet passed through the Old Section, Dhogs, their tattered remnants of clothing fluttering like feathers, flitted among the refuse heaps like great scavenger birds scrounging for scraps and morsels. Scruffy, malnourished children bawled like stray animals, their tears making muddy rivulets down stained cheeks.

The Dhogs were a noisome bunch, and Treet could hardly stand to be near them. The odor was such that a few whiffs could make his stomach unsteady. He recoiled from contact with the Dhogs and tried to avoid them without giving offense, which was difficult because, as Ernina had predicted, among the Dhogs he was revered to the point of outright worship.

The first day the rumor had spread that a Fieri was among the newcomers. That night hundreds of Dhogs had gathered silently outside the building where he'd been given a room. The crowd waited all night, hoping for a glimpse of him.

The mad flight to the Old Section had sapped most of Treet's strength. It took a couple days of bedrest for him to recuperate enough to feel like getting up and moving around again. On his first venture out, he discovered the uncanny effect he had on the masses. People followed him wherever he went—politely, at a distance, murmuring to themselves. But if he stopped long enough, they would become bold and put their hands on him, touch his skin, pinch his flesh as if to reassure themselves of his corporeality.

As uncomfortable as that made Treet feel—being worshiped by a rabble of reeking scavengers—he accepted that it was necessary, even desirable for the time being. After his first encounter, Treet had spoken to Tvrdy about it. "Shouldn't we tell them I'm not a Fieri?" he had asked.

"Why? It does no harm, and it might be a useful thing when the time comes."

"When the time comes for what?"

"To stir these people to action."

"The Dhogs? You're not serious. You don't mean—"

"Mean to use them? Certainly I do."

"But they're hopeless. Look at them—they can hardly feed and clothe themselves. What could they do against Invisibles?"

"Don't misjudge them. They are shrewd and capable within certain limits. They have survived for centuries in this festering pesthole. Besides, we have begun training the more able-bodied—that is what the food is for. And soon we will begin feeding the rest."

"Fattening the lambs for the slaughter, is that it?"

Tvrdy did not understand the metaphor, so Treet explained, "I mean, I don't see how you can ask them to fight for you."

"Not for me, for themselves. Do you think Jamrog will forget what happened? For years he has been laying plans to attack the Old Section and exterminate the Dhogs. Now there is nothing to stop him. He will come. Sooner or later we will all have to defend ourselves or be killed." Here Tvrdy stopped and grinned unexpectedly; he placed a hand on Treet's shoulder. "Besides, I won't be the one to ask them to fight."

Treet stiffened. "Who then?" He already had a pretty good idea who.

"The Fieri will ask them."

So Treet had grudgingly become the resident Fieri, and tried to keep a low profile, staying out of sight as much as possible. But then something happened to make him more sensitive to his delicate position.

The morning of his fifth day among the Dhogs, he had attended the morning briefing session with Tvrdy and the others. There he and Ernina had been introduced to the mechanics of the rebellion; he had then related what had taken place on his mission to the Fieri. Although it hurt him to tell it, he had ended by saying, "We can expect no help from the Fieri. I tried very hard to convince them, but they are prevented by a sacred vow of nonaggression from entering this struggle—even for a good cause."

Treet did not say that this vow had come about because Dome had wiped out the Fieri cities with nuclear weapons, reducing their fair civilization to radioactive waste, and therefore the Fieri were understandably shy about involving themselves in the perverse machinations of Dome politics. He did not say that the *only* reason he himself had returned was to try to prevent it from happening again.

Treet's unhappy news had been greeted with calm acceptance, and he guessed that no one had really expected any help from the Fieri. It had been a long shot, after all. No one knew that better than Treet—just surviving the desert had been remarkable enough in the Dome dweller's eyes.

After the briefing ended, a swarthy little hobgoblin had come up to Treet, thumped himself on the chest, and said, "Giloon Bogney."

"Orion Treet," he replied.

"Come, Giloon show you Old Section."

Tvrdy had been looking on and nodded his encouragement, so Treet had agreed. Bogney led him out, and they were quickly surrounded by Dhogs. The Dhog leader waded through his people, pulling Treet along with him, and they struck off across the refuse-piled New America Square. The tour became a parade—more people joining the procession as it wound through the jumbled, beaten-earth pathways.

They stopped from time to time for Bogney to point out some item of local interest. The Dhog's speech was so deteriorated that Treet caught scarcely any of what was said. He nodded a good deal and looked bemused. Finally they stopped before a wall—most of which was lying in collapsed sections under the low roof of dirt-and-smoke filmed crystal.

The wall was made of gray Empyrion stone, cut and fitted into place without mortar. It stood to just over Treet's head, though the top row of capstones was missing. In all it was fairly unremarkable, except for the feature Bogney indicated with his grubby hand.

Carved into the stone was the image of a winged man with his hair tied back in a long braid and wearing a flowing robe. The man's wings were stretched wide on either side of his body, with broad feathers radiating out behind him. A mysterious amulet hung on the thick chest. The head was in profile, and with a blinding shock of recognition, Treet remembered where he'd seen those same straight, angular features:

On a door nearly eleven light-years away, back on Earth, in Houston. The door to Chairman Neviss' office suite.

Treet gawked at the chiseled image. It was rather crudely done, but clearly recognizable and the subject so unique there could be no mistake. The artist whose hands had created the likeness had seen the very doors Treet had seen—three thousand years ago by Empyrion reckoning.

He reached a hand to the stone and traced the work with his fingertips, marveling at the mix of emotions roiling inside him: awe, despair, loneliness, and other feelings too obscure to decipher. I am the only one who knows what happened, he thought. I am the only one. He felt immensely old and burdened just then—as if the knowledge he held inside him was an enormous weight he had carried a lifetime.

He gazed at the carved image, and it occurred to Treet that both he and the nameless sculptor had stood in the same spot and admired the Chairman's doors back on Earth—a place Empyrion's present inhabitants did not even remember.

This seemed incredibly significant to Treet, until he thought about it. What did it mean really? What did it tell him that he did not already know?

In the end, nothing.

A sense of hoplessness stole over him. What was the use? Dome's problems were legion. What could one man do?

"Cynetix," said Bogney, fingering the image.

"Huh?" Treet stirred.

"Cynetix," Bogney repeated, and the Dhogs pressed closer, muttering the name softly.

Treet nodded. "Yes, Cynetics."

Bogney raised a hand and patted the air, as if to flatten it. The Dhogs understood the gesture and sat down on the ground. Pointing to the image once more, Bogney said, "Cynetix. Dhogs hearing Fieri man telling now." He then sat down cross-legged with the rest, and they all looked up expectantly at Treet.

Treet gazed around him. What can I tell them? he wondered. They think this winged man is Cynetics, a god. They think *I'm* a god of some sort. How would they ever understand?

Looking at their earnest eyes, Treet again felt the strange, burning-face sensation he'd felt in Ernina's hospital. The Infinite was still with him, within him. The presence stirred, and the hopelessness vanished. In its place appeared a word of comfort: It's not up to you to solve Dome's problems—only to do your part, and do it as well as you can.

Very well. Here then was one thing he could do. He could tell the Dhogs about their history and what was happening in the world outside the Old Section; he could sow the seeds of truth. He had no sooner framed the thought than the words began making their way to his tongue; so, adopting the mythical language of the storyteller, he began.

"In the old time there were giants who lived far away beyond the stars. The biggest giant of all was Cynetics, and he was very big. The world where he lived, Earth, grew too small for him, so he turned his eyes to the sky one night and he saw this world."

The Dhogs murmured at this and nodded, hunkering down like children to better hear the story. Treet didn't know how much they understood of his speech, but figured the sound of his voice was what mattered most anyway.

"Cynetics said to himself," Treet continued, "I will send my sons there to make a new place for me to live. So, riding in a— ah, sky em—the sons of Cynetics came to Empyrion and flew over the land until they came to this place, and they said, 'Here we will make our home.' And they built a city and named it Empyrion. They filled their city with people, and the city prospered.

"One day, when the city was still new, the Red Death came, and the sons of Cynetics died. Men and women, young and old alike, everyone died, for nothing could stop the Red Death. The people struggled; they fought for life and a few survived, but the city was broken." The Dhogs were hushed, taking in the story in awed silence. "The city was broken into two pieces. Both were Cynetics' children, but they quarreled over how to rebuild the city.

"In the heat of the quarrel, the sons who had taken the name Fieri were cast out. Those who remained here raised high walls and sealed the city with crystal, forever shutting out their brothers. They became Dome.

"The Fieri wandered the world and grew strong in the

683

open air. The day came when they stopped wandering and built their own city, called Fierra. It was a magnificent city, a city of wonders untold. And the Fieri grew great in the land.

"Many long years passed, and the people of Dome saw the greatness of the Fieri and grew jealous. Their jealousy turned to hate, and they rose up against the Fieri and killed them with a fire that burned even the stones.

"The dome dwellers rejoiced, believing they had rubbed out all the Fieri, but a few lived on, even as the Old Ones lived on after the Red Death. The Fieri who survived the all-consuming fire traveled far away and built another city by the sea—that is, a great water. They renamed their new city Fierra and said to themselves, 'Nevermore will we go to our brothers in Dome, for we will not forget what they have done to us.'

"In time, the Fieri grew strong once again and became very wise, and the new Fierra became greater even than the first city." Here Treet paused, uncertain of where to go with his tale. He looked out on the upturned faces, alert, intent. He saw the flicker of hope in the dull gray eyes and understood the power he now held. The Dhogs trusted him. Their trust gave him unquestioned authority over them. The next words he spoke would determine how he used that authority and power.

"Many long years have passed," said Treet slowly. "And once again the rulers of Dome are preparing to make war on the Fieri. I have come to try to stop them." He turned and regarded the winged man carved into the gray stone. "Cynetics is far away. He does not hear his sons anymore, and he cannot help us. It is up to us to help ourselves."

From the astonished stares of his hearers Treet saw the revolution these last words had stirred. He decided he'd said enough for the moment, so stepped from the wall and made his way through the crowd still seated on the ground.

· · · · · ·

The afternoon light through Dome's great crystal panes shimmered over the green fields as, their day's work done, the Hyrgo began descending from the terraces to make their way back to their kraams. The workers wound down the zigzag path between the tiered fields leading to the broad boulevard at the bottom of the valley, heading back to deep Hage and their suppers, talking quietly among themselves in the slow, patient Hyrgo way.

A group of about thirty workers reached the lower field and proceeded along the boulevard. They had not gone more than a hundred meters when they were met by a band of Invisibles.

The Hyrgo fell silent, moving ahead hesitantly. As the first of the Hyrgo approached, the Invisibles fanned out across the boulevard. "Halt!" shouted the Invisibles' commander, a Mors Ultima in glistening black.

The Hyrgo stopped at once, looking fearfully at one another.

"What is the trouble, please?" asked the foremost Hyrgo, a fourth-order tender.

"Shut up!" yelled the Invisible. "Against the wall!" He shoved the foreman toward the rimwall.

Weapons appeared in the Invisibles' hands and the Hyrgo backed to the wall, eyes wide, mouths quivering in mute protest. "What is this?" cried the Hyrgo foreman. "We have done nothing. We are field tenders."

The Mors Ultima stepped up and slashed the man across the mouth with the butt of the weapon in his hand. The Hyrgo workers gasped. Blood dribbled over the injured Hyrgo's chin and down the front of his yos. He fell back with a whimper.

"Get moving!" ordered the Invisible in charge. The stunned Hyrgo did not move, so his men leapt to action and began driving the Hagemen back along the boulevard.

"Where are you taking us?" demanded the Hyrgo foreman through bleeding lips.

The Mors Ultima stepped close and struck him against the side of the head with the weapon. The Hyrgo went down. Two Invisibles sprang forward, hauled him to his knees, and dragged him away. Other Hyrgo coming down from the fields appeared along the rimwall. "Go to your kraams," shouted the Mors Ultima, "or else follow your Hagemen to reorientation."

The frightened Hyrgo hurried away, letting their Hagemen go without a word.

At the Hyrgo checkpoint, the group was held until large multipassenger ems arrived; then they were pushed aboard, and the vehicles whisked them away to the reorientation center on

Cavern level deep in Hage Nilokerus. There, along with prisoners from other Hages—they saw the turquoise-and-silver of Chryse, the blue hood and hem of Bolbe, and the red stripes of Rumon—they were crowded into newly constructed holding pens. Women were crying hysterically and men stood dazed, wringing their hands and staring.

"What is happening here?" asked the Hyrgo foreman of a fourth-order Chryse.

"Reorientation," replied the Chryse flatly. "What else?"

"I don't understand. We were taken from the fields. We have done nothing."

The Chryse shook his head and spat. "Haven't you heard? The Supreme Director is angry with the Chryse and Hyrgo— you for letting the grain be stolen, us for letting the thieves pass through our Hage."

"But it was Dhogs. We had nothing to do with it."

The Chryse lifted his shoulders. "Does that matter?"

"I see Bolbe here—what of them?"

"I don't know. They claim they have done nothing, but it's clear they must have violated the Clear Way or they wouldn't be here."

Just then Nilokerus security guards came to the holding pen and began pulling people out—the Hyrgo foreman among them. He was taken into the central admitting area, a huge cylindrical room aswarm with people. He was made to stand in a long line before a desk behind which sat four hooded Nilokerus, their faces green in the light of data screens.

When his turn finally came, he was prodded to the desk by a guard with a long, flexible rod. "Name," said the Nilokerus at the terminal. He glanced up from the screen. "Give me your name."

"Grensil," replied the Hyrgo.

"Cell N-34K," said the Nilokerus. "Next."

"Wait!" shouted the Hyrgo. "What have I done? You must tell me what I have done."

"Take him away," grunted the guard. "Next!"

The rod jabbed him in the ribs, and the Hyrgo foreman was prodded into one of the long corridors radiating out from the central admitting area. The corridor was crowded with guards and prisoners, and they shoved their way through to the cell. When the unidor snapped off, the Hyrgo was pushed forward. He threw his hands out and gripped the stone, holding himself back. The rod smashed his fingers again and again until he let go and, to a chorus of curses, tumbled into the cell.

Inside there were six men—six men in a space designed for only one. No one could stand upright, and there was not room for them to sit down. So they squatted against one another, shifting their weight painfully and cursing. The air was foul with the odor of vomit and urine. One of the men, a Rumon, at the back of the cell was bleeding from facial wounds; he muttered incoherently, his head lolling back and forth.

Grensil settled into the crush of bodies and was elbowed sharply as he tried to fit himself into the too small space. Light-headed, reeling with the horror of what was happening to him, the Hyrgo closed his eyes, muttering, "Trabant take me, I am dead."

FORTY TWO

The night's dispatch had brought a thick file of information. Upon arrival, Tvrdy had awakened to spend the early hours deciphering it. Now, as the others gathered for the morning briefing, the Tanais Director sat gray-faced, hair disheveled, dark circles under his eyes, waiting to begin.

Cejka was the first to arrive, followed by Piipo with two of his aides, and Kopetch. Treet shambled in, greeted everyone, and sat down in a corner by himself. Ernina arrived, spoke a few words to Tvrdy, and took her seat. Giloon Bogney strutted in last, two odious Dhogs on his heels. They sat down front and center, and Giloon craned his neck around, saying, "All here now. We begin."

Tvrdy raised himself slowly to his feet, passing a hand through his hair. "This came in during the night," he said, thumping the file reader in his hand. "It isn't good."

"Tell us everything," said Cejka. The others mumbled their assent.

"The retaliation is worse than we expected. At last count, upwards of eight hundred Hyrgo have been arrested and taken to reorientation—"

"No-o," Piipo groaned.

"Nearly as many Tanais," Tvrdy continued, "and about a hundred Bolbe have been taken as well."

"Rumon?" asked Cejka.

"There are two hundred Rumon missing—although no rumor messengers, so far. Seventy-five Chryse have been taken. Numbers are not available for the other Hages, but all are presumed to have been affected. There are reports of Nilokerus and Saecaraz being tortured—probably for failure to apprehend us in the raid. Also, Jamuna have been killed outright by Mors Ultima; Jamuna Director Bouc is in hiding. These are unsubstantiated reports at present, but it appears Jamrog is being very thorough in his retaliation."

"The monster," muttered Ernina. "How can he justify this—this outrage?"

"The official explanation," Tvrdy replied, "is that the Fieri have infiltrated Empyrion and are determined to seize power. This is what Jamrog has ordered the Directors to tell the Hages. Before the retaliation started, he convened a special session of the Threl and bullied them into approving his emergency security measures. The checkpoints have been strengthened and an official curfew imposed. Invisibles are patrolling the main entry and exit routes between Hages during curfew hours, and they have set up interrogation cells throughout.

"Also, he has granted priests authority to act as informants for reward. Predictably, they are quick to accuse and collect for any imagined crime."

"It isn't hard to see where this will lead," said Cejka. "No one will be safe from their greed."

"We could use that," pointed out Kopetch. "Don't we have a priest or two we might persuade?"

"Yes," confirmed Tvrdy. "See me after the briefing." He glanced down at the file reader and thumbed the scanner window. "Invisibles are searching Hage Chryse for the entrance to the Old Section. We'll have to seal that entrance and use the others from now on."

"That's to be expected," offered Cejka.

"Here is something unexpected: food rations are being cut, and work hours extended to meet increased production quotas. The Archives have been opened to Nilokerus and Saecaraz magicians—"

"I ran into them," put in Treet.

"What does it mean?" asked Piipo.

"Jamrog is readying himself for a fight," explained Kopetch. "He is attempting to create a surplus from which to stockpile supplies. When he feels he has enough to sustain a protracted battle, he will strike."

"But—the Archives?"

"They're searching for weapons," said Treet. "From the old time."

"He's probably right," affirmed Tvrdy. "They may succeed."

"We can't let that happen," said Cejka. "We would be defenseless."

"Obviously he is moving faster than we anticipated," said Tvrdy. "We're going to have to become active sooner than we planned."

"That, or use our Hage forces," said Kopetch.

"We must not endanger our Hagemen," said Piipo.

"They are already in danger," snapped Kopetch. "All of Empyrion is in danger."

"But if we don't anger Jamrog again," began Piipo, "perhaps—"

"Didn't you hear?" said Cejka, his voice shrill. "Eight hundred Hyrgo and Tanais—and who knows how many others! Jamuna killed and Saecaraz tortured! That's just the beginning."

Treet felt the tension rise in the room as fear frayed taut nerves and tempers escalated. He glanced at Tvrdy and saw that the Tanais Director felt it too. Tvrdy roused himself. "All right!" he shouted. The room fell silent. "Yes, we feel deeply for those who suffer Jamrog's wrath. But we must not let this divide us or draw us from our task. Let it instead provoke us to greater determination."

"He's right," said Cejka, and the tension dissipated at once.

The briefing resumed matter-of-factly, and Treet did not again sense the crippling fear. Tvrdy had, like the adroit leader he was, acted with quick efficiency to defuse a potentially disastrous situation. "Now then," Tvrdy continued, "in view of the information we have received, I suggest we begin planning another raid."

As the others turned this unexpected idea over in their heads, Kopetch leaped up. "Yes!" he said. "It is exactly what we need."

"Wait," said Piipo cautiously, "we should discuss this first."

"Of course." Tvrdy motioned for Kopetch to be seated. "I merely wished to put forth the suggestion. I have no specific plan at this time."

"But it makes sense," offered Cejka. "It will keep Jamrog off balance."

"Forgive me, but I am new to this way of thinking. What would be the aim of this raid?" asked Ernina.

"That remains to be determined. But the effect of the raid would be at least twofold: harassment, as Cejka has suggested; and a demonstration of our ability to move at will throughout Empyrion."

"This demonstration is important? Important enough to justify the probable loss of life?" asked the physician.

"I believe so. Jamrog must know that he is not in total control."

"Wouldn't this drive him to further atrocities?"

"Perhaps," answered Kopetch. "But his anger would also cloud his reason. An angry man makes mistakes—mistakes we could use to our benefit."

Ernina did not appear convinced by this line of reasoning, but said no more.

"I'm with Ernina," put in Treet. "I think it's a costly enterprise. Maybe too costly—unless the stakes were raised significantly." The blank looks of his listeners let Treet know he'd used an obscure figure of speech. "I mean, unless the aim of the raid were of greater importance."

Cejka joined in. "I agree. The purpose must justify the risk."

"Your concerns are mine, Hagemen, precisely," said Tvrdy.

"Would this raid take place soon?" wondered Piipo, who had been whispering to his aides.

"That I can answer with certainty," Tvrdy replied. "The Trabantonna—"

"The Feast of the Dead!" cried Piipo, "But that's—"

"Not much time," said Tvrdy calmly. "I know. But it must be during the Trabantonna feasts. We will not have a better chance. The confusion will be a natural cover for our movements."

"It's the perfect time," said Kopetch, "to work maximum havoc with minimum risk."

The briefing ended; the participants filed silently from the room, each preoccupied with private thoughts. Treet, who had promised to help Ernina begin setting up a medical center, watched as the others hurried away to their duties, one thought drumming in his brain: two thousand people are right now suffering for the rebels' actions, and the Fieri are being blamed!

I was right, Treet thought bitterly, seeing the cruel irony of the situation. I came back to try to save the Fieri, and it's through my actions that the Fieri have become involved.

How swiftly had the complexion of the struggle changed. It wasn't a question of personal survival anymore . . . it was war.

• • • • • •

Except for two brief and somewhat furtive meetings, Pizzle had not so much as set eyes on Starla for a week. The deprivation was killing him. He moped around the deck of the ship all day and grew distant and morose at night. When he wasn't talking to Anthon, his Mentor, Pizzle was absolutely disconsolate. Nothing short of the thought of an impending visit with his beloved could cheer him up. And since Starla had moved to another ship—ostensibly to keep from torturing Pizzle with her presence, although her absence tortured him just as much—Pizzle was miserable a good deal of the time.

Even the nightly spectacle of the sunshower failed to lift his spirits very much. He lost his appetite, his sense of humor, what little native dignity he'd possessed. He wallowed in his self-pity as if it were a balm to his forlorn soul.

Anthon chose not to notice Pizzle's misery, but diverted him as much as possible with stimulating monologues and discussions pertaining to Fieri life and thought. During these episodes, Pizzle was able to forget himself a little and enjoy the mental exercise. Mentor Anthon was a wise instructor. He spoke as one who contemplated life from a pinnacle of years, although in appearance he seemed only slightly older than Pizzle himself. And despite the sagacity of his thought, from under the dark ridges of his brows glittered bright brown eyes as quick as any delinquent youngster's. In all, he reminded Pizzle of Mishmac the Mahat, a character from Papoon's immortal *Orb of Odin* series.

Pizzle made the most of his opportunities to talk with his Mentor. And they enjoyed one another's company for hours on end. Still, as much time as Anthon gave him, there were too many empty hours. Preben, too, noticed Pizzle's predicament and tried to help by assigning him more duties aboard the ship. But try as he might, Pizzle could not muster more than a lackluster enthusiasm for sailing.

"You must think us very cruel," Anthon said one day when Pizzle came for his catechism.

"Cruel?" The word took Pizzle aback. He shook his head until his ears wobbled. "Never. No way. Why would you say that?"

"Separating you from your beloved is a painful charge."

"Yeah," Pizzle agreed. "I guess so."

Anthon looked at him for a long moment and then said, "Tell me the Prime Virtues in the order of their ascendancy."

So began the day's lesson, but at least Pizzle knew that his Mentor understood what he was going through. That helped a little. Seeing Starla helped more. Unfortunately, he could only see her when the boats made one of their infrequent landings, and the next one was not scheduled for another five days.

Early the next morning he found Yarden sitting by herself on deck, wrapped in a scarlet blanket. He slumped down beside her and put his hands behind his head, closing his eyes, feeling the warmth of the polished wood on his back. "I don't think I'm going to make it," he said glumly.

"Welcome to the club," she said.

Her reply was so uncharacteristic Pizzle jolted upright. "You, too?"

Yarden didn't answer. She gazed steadily out at the water and at the ragged roots of the mountains gliding by.

"You want to talk about it?" asked Pizzle.

She turned red-rimmed eyes on him. "If I wanted to talk about it, would I be sitting here by myself all night?"

"You sat here all night?"

She nodded, raising a hand to rub her eyes and smoothe back her hair.

"What's wrong?" Pizzle's misery had made him a shade more sensitive to others' feelings.

"Everything," she snapped. "I thought this trip would be something special. More and more, I'm sorry I came."

"You can say that again."

She gave him a look he could not read. "I heard about your little trial."

"You make it sound like I deserve it or something," Pizzle whined. "I didn't do anything to deserve the way I feel."

"Calm down. At least you still have Starla."

"Yeah, and last time I looked, you were all hot on this art stuff."

"Go away, Pizzle. I don't want to talk about it."

"Sheesh! Every time I come around it's 'Go away, Pizzle! Go away, Pizzle! I don't want to talk about this, I don't want to talk about that.' How come you're the only one on this planet that gets to have any private feelings? You're always delivering these

693

ultimatums to everybody. Well, I for one am getting tired of it."

Yarden softened, smiled. "Your ears get pink when you're mad, you know that?"

"Hmmph!"

"I'm sorry, Pizzle. I apologize, okay?"

"Okay," Pizzle allowed grudgingly. "Us Earthlings ought to stick together."

"Fair enough," said Yarden. She was silent a moment, then sighed and said, "It's just that I'm afraid I've made the most dreadful mistake."

"Treet again?"

Yarden nodded, chin pulled in.

"Pshoo—" Pizzle let air whistle over his teeth. "I don't know what to tell you there."

"It's all right. I have to work this out for myself."

Pizzle didn't say anything. The two simply sat together and listened to the rippling water and the canyons echoing with the keening cries of the ever-present rakkes sailing the wind currents among the rock peaks high above. The white sunlight struck the angled cliffs, scattering silvery light off the rocks. The deck rocked gently as the boats, strung in a long, sweeping line, slid relentlessly upriver toward the bay.

"I should have gone with him," said Yarden softly. It was the first time she had admitted it to herself, but once the words were out she felt the truth in them.

Pizzle took his time responding. "How could you know? I mean, he was far from stable. It sounded so . . . so theatrical. Crackpot—you know? I liked the guy, and I still thought the idea was nutso."

"*Liked*. Past tense."

"Sorry, bad choice of words."

"You think he's dead, too."

"Dead?" Pizzle's head swiveled around. "Golly, Yarden, you shouldn't think anything like that."

"Why not? It's possible, isn't it?"

Pizzle swallowed hard. "Possible," he allowed cautiously, "but highly improbable."

"All to probable. Which is why none of us would go back with him."

"He knew the risks."

"Yes, he knew the risks and he still went back." Yarden

dropped her head to her updrawn knees. "I've been so incredibly selfish."

Pizzle watched her for a moment. "Preben says the bay is only a week away," he said, trying to change the subject. "The last few kilometers, however, are overland through the mountains. But there's a pass, so it's an easy climb."

"I've lived my whole life without regret," Yarden replied. "Now this."

"Would it help if you knew he was okay?"

"What are you suggesting?"

"Well, you could find out easy enough, couldn't you? I mean, with your mental thing you could find out." He studied her expression for a moment and added, "You never thought of that?"

"I—no, I couldn't do that to Treet."

"Why? Afraid of what you'll find?"

She dropped her eyes.

Pizzle climbed slowly to his feet. "I'm hungry. Are you? I smell something cooking below. Want to come down and get some breakfast with me?"

"Ah, no. No, thank you, Asquith." Yarden raised her head and smiled. "I appreciate what you're trying to do for me. Really. But this is going to take a little time."

"Sure." He turned and started away, then paused and turned back. "Look, if you want me for anything I'm here. I mean, if you should want to try contacting him or something. Okay?"

Yarden accepted Pizzle's offer. "Thanks, I won't forget. Us Earthlings ought to stick together."

"Darn right."

"**W**e can't do it this way. It's wrong." Treet was adamant.

Tvrdy gazed at him with an exasperated expression. "I don't understand you. Jamrog is our enemy—remove him and the Purge is over. It is as simple as that."

"It is never that simple," Treet retorted. He looked around the ring of grim faces, yellow in the foul light of a smoking lamp. They were going over the newly revealed details of the Trabantonna raid. It was late, and everyone was tired.

"It's a good plan," Cejka put in gently. "Tvrdy and Kopetch have spent every minute of the last two days working on it. It's brilliant."

"It was you," said Kopetch, "who insisted the purpose of the raid must justify the risk."

"I wasn't suggesting that we assassinate Jamrog."

"What else is there?" demanded Tvrdy. "We cannot fight the Invisibles and the Nilokerus security forces; we are not ready."

"It is most expedient," added Kopetch, fatigue making his voice sharp. "In terms of risk against feasiblity and potential reward, it makes perfect sense. Besides, the timing is extremely advantageous."

"In the whole history of humankind, assassination has never solved anything. It just doesn't work." Treet growled. "I won't be a part of it."

"That cannot be helped," Tvrdy snapped. "The plan is set. Trabantonna begins in two days. Our Tanais and Rumon Hagemen have been informed. Everything is ready. Kopetch is right—it is the best chance we will have for a very long time. And it is the one thing Jamrog will not expect."

Treet clamped his mouth shut and sat down. The briefing continued, but he was no longer paying attention. There was something very wrong about the planned assassination. The trouble was, he couldn't articulate exactly what made it wrong. As Kopetch maintained, the plan made sense in several solid ways that made Treet's feeble objections seem grossly irrational.

It's a curse, thought Treet, to be suddenly afflicted with a good conscience so late in life. One felt the pangs of righteousness, but was unable to give proper voice to them for lack of the long history of careful, reasoned thought and self-examination necessary for persuasive argument. Without that, all one had left was the emotional discord caused by ruffled scruples.

What was so wrong, really? Removing one man made infinitely more sense than engaging in the slaughter of thousands. In terms of human suffering alone, it was no contest; given a choice between all-out war and the simple assassination of one depraved ruler, assassination won every time.

And yet the idea repulsed Treet. He found it morally repugnant. Assassination was a dirty business, the domain of terrorist subversives and scheming anarchists warped by ideological misanthropy and too cowardly to stand up in the light of day and support their beliefs, however perverse, in honest combat, intellectual or otherwise. No matter how well justified, assassination always tainted its practitioners with its own reeking corruption. And yet, in this particular case perhaps . . .

So he sat and fumed, furiously trying to determine why he felt the way he did, and how to put it into words. The effort came to nothing. And by the time the briefing was over, Treet was no nearer an answer.

"It is a good plan," Tvrdy said as the others trooped from the room. "We should all be united in its support."

"I know how you feel, Tvrdy. I'm sorry. I can't tell you why, but I know this is wrong. It won't solve anything."

Tvrdy appeared about to object, but changed his mind. "You will remain here with Ernina. The raid will take place as planned."

"Fine." Treet rose stiffly and stumped from the room.

In darkness, he walked across the bare compound toward the building where he had his room. As he was about to enter, he saw a light shining from the low semiruined structure Ernina had commandeered for a medical center, and where she planned to begin treating the Dhogs for parasites and toxicity as soon as she could get her hands on a few basic supplies.

Treet moved toward the light and entered the building to find the physician busily arranging large floppy mats on the floor by the light of a single lamp whose dirty flame produced more smoke than illumination. The smoke stank.

"The briefing is over?" She watched him with concern in her sharp green eyes.

"It's over."

Ernina laid the mat down and indicated for Treet to take a seat. He dropped onto a mat and leaned on his elbow. "You look terrible," she observed.

"I feel terrible."

"Perhaps you are not recovered fully from our escape. You were very weak. I feared you would not make it."

"It isn't that. It's the raid."

"Oh? You are not happy about the decision?"

"It's wrong. I don't know why, but it is."

The physician regarded Treet for a few moments. "I agree."

"You do?"

"That's why I did not come tonight. I will not come to any more briefings—I have no time for planning death."

"Even if it's an insane tyrant like Jamrog?"

She frowned. "I have enough to do trying to keep people alive."

"I tried to convince them to abandon the idea. I tried—" He looked at the physician's kind face earnestly. "But I don't have the words. I don't know what to say to them. Their reasons all make perfect sense. Kill Jamrog and the Purge will end. The insanity will stop. Thousands of people will be spared. The torture, the death—remove Jamrog and it will stop. And yet . . ."

"You don't believe it."

"No," answered Treet sadly. "It doesn't matter how I justify it, I can't make myself believe it. At first I thought I was just being squeamish, scared. I don't know—maybe I am just scared. I don't know what I expected."

"The suffering must stop."

"Yes, but not this way."

"There is a better way?"

"No. I don't know. There must be." Treet lay back and put his hands under his head. "It's just that this is so—so dirty, so cowardly, so cold."

"All the same, Jamrog does not shrink from it—it put him in power."

Treet stared at the physician for a moment, then jumped up. "That's it! Ernina, that's it exactly. If we use assassination we're no better than he is. Once we stoop to using our enemy's tactics, *we* become the enemy."

He reached out and took Ernina by the shoulders. "That's it! That's what's been gnawing at me. I've got to tell Tvrdy."

"Do you think he will listen?"

Treet stopped. "What he does about it is up to him, I guess. I have to tell him, though." He took Ernina's hand and gripped it tight. "Thanks for understanding." Then he was gone.

Treet found Tvrdy in his room, sitting on a cushion poring over the maps of the Old Section. He looked up as Treet came in. "It is amazing how many secrets the Dhogs have guarded over the years. I never guessed there were so many entrances and exits linking the Old Section to the Hages. We will be able to strike in four Hages at once! Think of that. The confusion will be complete."

"We can't do it," replied Treet. He sat down beside Tvrdy and tapped the map with a forefinger. "All the planning in the world won't make it right."

Tvrdy's features clouded with anger. "If you have come here to weary me further with your irrational misgivings, save your breath. I have more important things to do."

"Tvrdy, listen to me. Please, just listen, and then I'll go. If we assassinate Jamrog, we're no better than he is. Do you see that?"

Tvrdy turned away. "No."

"By taking our enemy's weapon and using it against him, we become *worse* than he is. Yes, worse; because we have a choice. We don't have to use it. If we do, we become the enemy—we perpetuate the evil. You can't fight evil with evil, Tvrdy. You must see that."

"Who is to say what is right and what is wrong? In war, good and evil have no meaning. You do what must be done to win. There are no rules. There is only expediency."

"You don't believe that. You can't."

"Unless we kill Jamrog first, he will kill us. That is a fact. Where is your good and evil then? If we lose, good will also die."

"What will that matter if we win and lose ourselves in the process? We will be just as bad as Jamrog."

Tvrdy stared at Treet, eyes hard, mouth pressed into an implacable line. "You argue nonsense," he said softly.

"I'm right, and you know it." Treet stood slowly. "I leave it with you, Tvrdy. I'm not going to say anything more about it." He walked to the doorway, paused, then added, "Think about what I've said. It's not too late to change the plan."

Tvrdy shook his head and returned to his maps. "It is too late. To change now would place our Hagemen in danger."

"Cancel. Call it off."

"The information has gone out. Using the network again before the raid would jeopardize the entire operation. I won't do that."

Treet turned and walked back to his room. I've done what I can, he thought. It's out of my hands.

FORTY
FOUR

*D*anelka hurried across the plaza, skirting the lake. He entered the central tower and smiled to himself. All was in place for the coming raid. He'd seen to the last and most delicate details himself and sent the ready signal. No more communication would take place until after the Trabantonna . . . and then? And then there would be no need for stealth.

One more day . . . just one more day . . .

He dashed across the empty hall. Upon reaching the Director's lift, two figures stepped from a nearby alcove.

"What do you want?" Danelka said. The two men at the lift entrance wore Tanais gold.

"Please, we need your help." The man on the left stepped close, glancing quickly around to see if they were observed.

"Yes?"

"You must come with us."

Danelka looked at the men more closely. "Who are you? You're not Tanais."

The man on the right moved nearer. "There is a problem."

"What problem?"

"Only you can help."

"I don't understand. What sort of problem?"

"Security," answered the first man. He put a hand on Danelka's arm.

The Tanais shook off the stranger's hand. "I'm not going anywhere with you." He turned back to the lift.

"We have authorization." The first man raised his voice.

Danelka spun back around. "What sort of authorization?"

The second man pulled a packet from his yos. "Charges have been made."

"What sort of charges?" Danelka demanded angrily.

"Very serious charges," said the man with the packet.

"It's probably a mistake," replied the first. "But you must come and help us straighten it out."

"I'm not going anywhere until I know what this is all

701

about." Danelka glared at the two men and crossed his arms across his chest.

"We should go now," said the second man, the more reasonable of the two.

"What are these charges? If someone has been making accusations against me, I have a right to know what they are."

"You have been charged with treason," the first man told him.

Danelka blanched. "Let me see that!"

The man pulled the packet away. "It's probably a mistake," said the first man. "If you come with us, we can get it cleared up."

Danelka hesitated. "I'm going to call my Subdirector. He must be notified."

"It won't take long."

"Treason . . . that's ridiculous." A sick look skidded across his face.

"A mistake, surely," said the man on the left. "We will clear it up now, and you can return to your kraam and to your supper."

The man on the right took Danelka firmly by the arm and pulled him away from the lift. "Let's go quietly. It does not look good for a man of authority to cause trouble."

"It is a mistake," said Danelka harshly. "And you will soon regret your part in it, I promise you."

The interim Director was taken to an interrogation kraam in one of the Hageblocks near the Tanais border with Saecaraz. There he was made to stand before an Invisible who was sitting behind a portable data screen. The Invisible read a long list of charges, then looked up at the prisoner for the first time. "Do you confess to these charges?"

"Lies! All lies!" Danelka shouted. "I confess to nothing. I want to call my Subdirector."

The Invisible remained silent, but motioned to the two who had brought him in. Danelka resisted and was dragged bodily into the next room, where he was shoved into a large metal chair. His yos was stripped off, and loops of thin wire were fastened around his wrists and ankles and around his neck.

"You can't do this to me!" shouted Danelka. "I am the Tanais Director. I demand a Threl hearing."

The Invisibles left then, Danelka's angry shouts ringing in the empty room. A few moments later two more Invisibles entered the room. One took his place behind the console which controlled the chair, and the other came to stand before the prisoner. Danelka took one look at the Mors Ultima yos and quailed.

"We know you are in contact with your former Director," said Mrukk. "I can have the charges against you dropped now if you tell me where he is."

Danelka glared back at the Mors Ultima commander, but kept his mouth firmly shut.

"He will be caught and executed for the traitor he is." Mrukk put his face close to his victim's. "But you don't have to share his fate. You can go free. I can arrange it for you to continue as Director. I can even see to it that you are rewarded: ten thousand shares. It's all yours if you speak up now."

The Tanais Director pro-tem squirmed in the interrogation chair. The wire thongs bit into his flesh at wrists and ankles. "I won't be bought," he uttered through clenched teeth.

"Too bad," sighed Mrukk. "Ten thousand shares—a man could do something with ten thousand shares." He gave a nod to the Invisible behind the console, and the wire thongs jerked tight. Danelka stifled a scream. Sweat beaded up on his forehead and trickled from his armpits.

"Your loyalty is admirable," continued Mrukk as if nothing had happened. "But do you not have a greater loyalty to the Supreme Director? That's worth thinking about. Shall I leave you to think about it?"

Danelka stared at his blue, swollen hands. His feet felt as if they were about to burst. Sharp needles stabbed his flesh. "I will come back in a few hours to see if you have changed your mind."

"I won't tell you," Danelka hissed. "Kill me now."

"No, not yet," replied Mrukk, pressing his face close. "Already you ask for death, and we have just begun. It can get much worse. Believe me . . . much worse. You'll be amazed to discover how much you can take. I'll be back and we'll talk again."

"Trabant take you!"

Mrukk strode from the room and heard his victim's

screams sharp in the air. There was still much force behind the cries, but a few more hours under the wires would see them weaken.

When Mrukk returned, Danelka was unconscious, his flesh pasty and damp, his breath coming in shallow gasps. The Mors Ultima chief smiled to himself. It was too easy, really. These bloodless wretches had no stamina, no endurance. The first twinge of pain and they crumbled.

"Wake him up," Mrukk ordered. The Invisible monitoring the pain sensors stepped from behind the console with a probe in his hand. He applied the probe to the side of the victim's neck, and the body jerked spasmodically. Danelka's eyes fluttered open, and he moaned.

"Now then," said Mrukk, "this can stop at once. Tell me where your master is and what he plans, and I will release you."

Danelka made no reply. His head rolled limply on his chest. Mrukk leaned forward, grasped a handful of hair, and snapped the head up. He gazed into the clouded eyes.

Taking the probe from the Invisible standing by, Mrukk inserted the probe in the victim's mouth. A strangled scream tore from Danelka's throat; front teeth shattered as rigid jaw muscles clamped tight.

"That's better," observed Mrukk, peering into his victim's eyes again. The fresh pain had revived Danelka somewhat. "Now then, tell me and this will end. Where is Tvrdy?"

Danelka opened his mouth, hesitated. Mrukk brought the probe close once more. "N-n-o! I—I'll tell you."

"Tell me then."

"He is with the Dhogs in the Old Section."

"We already know that!" shouted Mrukk. "What are his plans?"

Anger shook the young man's frame. "Y-you said . . . only . . . where he is . . . you said—"

"That was before. But you've kept me waiting. I want more. What are his plans?"

"I don't know."

"You're lying." Mrukk placed the probe against the soft flesh of the Tanais Subdirector's belly. The man writhed in the chair, cords standing out on his neck, facial muscles etched in a rictus of agony.

"What are his plans?"

Danelka gasped. "I don't know."

Mrukk's hand flicked out from under his yos. He held the knife blade before Danelka's horrified face. "His plans?"

Danelka, sweat streaming from his face, shook his head weakly. The blade dropped, and the Subdirector's index finger tumbled onto the floor amidst a spray of blood.

Mrukk raised the stained knife blade again. "You have many other fingers, Hageman. We will try again. What are Tvrdy's plans?"

Danelka grimaced and spat out, "I don't know his plans. He did not tell me."

The blade slashed down, and another finger rolled to the floor. Mrukk stooped to retrieve it, held it up before Danelka's ghostly face. "Perhaps he did not tell you precisely what his plans were," he said, turning the severed finger around. "But he told you something. What did he tell you?"

Mrukk lowered the razor-sharp blade slowly onto Danelka's little finger. The hand, held firm by the wire at the wrist, twitched, but could not evade the knife. The blade pressed down.

"The Trabantonna!" Danelka yelled. "The Trabantonna . . ."

"What will happen?"

Danelka squeezed his eyes shut as tears streamed down his face. "Assassination."

Mrukk straightened, grimacing fiercely. "You stinking Tanais filth!"

Danelka's eyes flew open. "I—I told you . . . release me!"

Mrukk's hand blurred in the air, and the knife sliced through the soft flesh of his victim's neck. Danelka's scream died bubbling in his throat.

• • • • • •

Mrukk entered Jamrog's kraam, was met by Osmas, and passed quickly through to Jamrog's private bedchamber. There Mrukk found the Supreme Director in the company of three comely young Hagemates. The girls giggled as the Mors Ultima commander came in.

"Ah, Mrukk," said Jamrog, rolling out of bed. "I expected you much earlier and grew tired of waiting."

"The subject was quite unresponsive, Supreme Director. He required extensive convincing."

"And was he convinced?"

"In the end."

Jamrog laughed. "You can be most persuasive, Mrukk." He held out his arms for one of the girls to drape a hagerobe over him. "Leave us for the moment," he told them. The girls tittered, and Mrukk's eyes followed their easy movement as they flounced from the room. Jamrog saw the look and said, "Yes, they are beautiful, aren't they? But you don't like women, do you? What do you like, Mrukk? I wonder."

The Mors Ultima stiffened.

"Ah, well, what did your inquiries produce?"

"It is as we suspected, Supreme Director," Mrukk replied tersely. "Tvrdy and the others have fled to the Old Section. They have formed an alliance with the Dhogs."

Jamrog nodded, walked to a table, took the flask from the warming cradle, and poured two cups of souile. He handed one to Mrukk and downed his cup in a single swallow, poured another, and sipped slowly. "Yes, it is as we suspected. Continue."

Mrukk stared at the cup in his hand. "They are transferring information freely from the Hages to the Old Section."

"Yes, yes," said Jamrog impatiently, "do go on."

Mrukk glanced up and eyed the Supreme Director.

"What is it?" demanded Jamrog. "Why do you look at me like that?"

"There is to be an assassination."

"An attempt on my life? When?"

"During the Trabantonna."

"During the Trabantonna!" Jamrog cried. "Wonderful!"

"We don't know where."

Jamrog sipped the warm souile and said, "It doesn't matter. We'll be ready for them. This will be a triumph, Mrukk. A triumph!" Jamrog downed his cup in a gulp and poured another. "We must make special arrangements for our unexpected guests. You'll see to it, Mrukk."

The Mors Ultima nodded slowly. "I will see to it."

"Tvrdy has overreached himself at last, and will be destroyed!" Jamrog spun and smashed his cup down on the table. The cup shattered, and glass fragments scattered over the floor. Jamrog raised a bleeding finger to his mouth and sucked it. "I don't want him killed, Mrukk. Instruct your men; they can kill the others, but not Tvrdy."

"They will be instructed."

Mrukk turned and made his way to the door. "Remember," Jamrog called after him. "I want him alive. Alive!"

FORTY FIVE

The night before Trabantonna the Hage priests hold vigil in the temples of Empyrion. Black tapers of rendered human fat with wicks made from the braided hair of children are burnt through the night, while the priests pour libations over themselves and submit their bodies for ritual cleansings.

As dawn draws near, the priestly revel reaches its climax as the Hage priests, having chosen the corpse of a recently deceased Hageman, strip the corpse, paint it red, and bind it to a thronelike chair. In an elaborate ceremony the cadaver is consecrated to Trabant Animus. The chair and its grotesque occupant are then lifted high and marched around the temple.

As morning's first light strikes Dome's massive crystal panes, the painted corpse emerges from the temple borne on the shoulders of the Hage priests. The procession is greeted by the people who have gathered before daybreak to await the spectacle. The priests push through the crowd and move slowly down the ramp and into the temple square now thronged with onlookers. Those closest to the priests press themselves closer still in an effort to touch the lifeless celebrant as the chair passes.

The chair is carried in this way to the center of the Hage where, in the largest square or plaza, it is established at the head of a table set up on a stage or scaffold. The corpse is officially welcomed and the title Chairman of the Feast conferred upon it. The populace then engages in rites of mourning: men shout and curse and pound the stones with their fists; women wail and throw themselves to the ground, tearing at their clothing and hair.

When the ritual mourning reaches a fevered emotional pitch, a Hage priest, dressed in a scarlet yos, moves through the crowd, scattering warm blood (from freshly killed sacrificial animals) over the mourners. Upon receiving the spattered blood on clothing, faces, and hands, the people leap up and begin dancing hysterically, throwing themselves into wild and unnatural contortions. They scratch themselves and claw at their flesh, they writhe and squirm, they shake with convulsions—all this to the accompaniment of a ghastly chorus of howls and shrieks.

The mad dance continues until exhaustion overcomes the participants. Gradually the screams die and the people lie still. The priests then move through the cataleptic throng touching the people on the back of the neck with a ceremonial bhuj. At the touch, each unmoving Hageman rises slowly and goes to the table where, taking up a bowl and filling it from the mounds of food piled in the center of the board, he sits down to eat.

So begins the Trabantonna, the Feast of the Dead.

• • • • • •

Jamrog looked out on Hage Saecaraz from a rimwall overlooking Threl Square, where the Saecaraz Trabantonna celebration had just commenced. The squares, filled to overflowing with bellowing, gyrating Hagemen, were ringed with gigantic banners bearing the Supreme Director's likeness. Mrukk stood beside him, restless, wary, tense.

"Relax, Mrukk," Jamrog cooed. "It is early yet. The Feast is just begun. He will not strike so soon. He will wait until the evening, when the chaos is complete. Then Tvrdy will come. And then we will spring our trap."

"Underestimate Tvrdy today, Supreme Director," replied Mrukk stiffly, "and you will pay with your life."

"Have you no faith in your own Mors Ultima to protect me?" Jamrog's smile was fierce and rigid.

Mrukk did not answer. Instead he said, "I have posted men in every Hage. We will be in continual contact with them as we move from Hage to Hage. Any unusual activity today will be met with extreme force."

"Pity the celebrant who drinks too much souile and wanders off to puke in the river." Jamrog's laugh was a sharp bark.

"We are not playing tuebla. Let Tvrdy outsmart you and tomorrow Empyrion will have a new Supreme Director."

"You would like that, Mrukk, would you?" Jamrog laughed again and turned to gaze out over the square where the celebrants writhed and flailed, their screams ringing off the stone. "Listen, it's the music of misery," said Jamrog. "This will soon be Tvrdy's song as well."

"You wish to join the feast now?" asked Subdirector Osmas, deep lines of anxiety etched across his forehead. He and several underdirectors stood back among the Invisibles; they knew of the impending assassination attempt and were trying to remain inconspicuous.

Mrukk stood with arms folded across his chest, black yos glistening in the morning light, narrow eyes sweeping the scene below, watching for any unusual detail: a figure too aloof, an eye too watchful, a shadow out of place.

"It's a long day. There's no need to hurry it along. We can wait here a few more minutes. I will make my appearance when the feast has begun."

They watched as one by one the celebrants grew still. When all the square lay covered with unmoving bodies, the Saecaraz priests began moving among the silent populace, touching each celebrant on the neck and passing on. When all the people had been thus resurrected, Jamrog turned to Mrukk and said, "Now I will go down to them."

Jamrog turned and, with Mrukk at his right hand and his close bodyguard of handpicked Mors Ultima right behind, made his way down to the square. There, to the loud acclaim of his Hagemen, he climbed to the high table where the grinning corpse sat overlooking the feast. The Supreme Director gazed benevolently out upon the proceedings and spoke a few words of license to the revelers. He was presented with a bowl of food, which he accepted and immediately passed to one of his bodyguards. Jamrog then walked among the celebrants for a time.

So caught up was he in the drama of his own presence, Jamrog did not notice that their greetings were perfunctory and subdued—as if the people were afraid to address him at all, yet feared not addressing him even more.

When he had tired of the Saecaraz, Jamrog and his entourage left Threl Square, boarded waiting ems, and were whisked away to Hage Nilokerus. There they were greeted by Director Diltz, who welcomed them warmly and led them along to the feast site. "As you have ordered, Invisibles are scattered among the celebrants, and the perimeter is under hidden patrol. There have been no reports of anyone leaving the feast, and all who arrive are searched."

"Have you found anything?" asked Mrukk.

"Nothing."

"You won't find anything," said Jamrog. "Tvrdy will not attack here. He will choose a neutral place. Hage Nilokerus is too hostile for him. He needs a place where he can manuever more easily—Hyrgo, Rumon, or Tanais would suit him best."

"I'd say Tanais," offered Diltz. "There his network, if he has one, will be ready."

"It would suit Tvrdy's arrogance," said Osmas. He shrank back as soon as he had spoken, remembering his plan to stay out of sight.

"Enough," Jamrog said. "I have come to participate in a feast, not a funeral. We'll stay with our plan and trust to Mrukk's invincible efficiency."

Mrukk grunted, and they moved off. A few hours later the party moved on to Chryse Hage, arriving by boat. They disembarked and were greeted by Director Dey and his underlings, who escorted the growing entourage to the feast site where the Chryse, in an effort to outshine the other Hages in an extravagant show of loyalty, had constructed a huge, octagonal tower in the center of the feast square and scores of long poles around its perimeter. Each side of the tower, as well as every pole, wore Jamrog's huge portrait framed in Saecaraz red.

The gesture was not wasted on the Supreme Director. "I'm impressed, Director," he whispered. "I did not expect the Chryse to respond so warmly."

Dey caught the insinnuated reference to the imprisonment of the seventy-five Chryse and replied, "My Hagemen would not have you think that all Chryse are suspect. They want you to know that they are forever loyal to their beloved Supreme Director. This . . ."—he gestured to the massive display—over a hundred gigantic banners in all—"is but a small token of Chryse sentiment."

"I'm sure it is," Jamrog replied. "I am flattered. What is more, such a demonstration requires a response of equal magnitude. Once their reorientation is completed, Director, I will personally see to it that your Hagemen are returned to Hage Chryse rather than being reassigned elsewhere."

"You are too gracious, Supreme Director," bubbled Dey. "But the Chryse seek no special favors. We are only happy to serve." He inclined his head toward Jamrog in a gesture of submission, but did not take his eyes from the Supreme Director's face.

"You have earned this favor, Dey. It is a feast day, and I can afford to be generous. And since I am in a generous mood, I invite you to join my party." Thus, several more bodies were added to the number surrounding the Supreme Director.

• • • • • •

As the afternoon drew on, and the Hage celebrations continued, Tvrdy, Cejka, Kopetch, Piipo, Bogney, and all those chosen to join the raid readied themselves and their equipment—most of it retrieved earlier from Tvrdy's private stockpile—for the trek through the Isedon Zone to the Hages they would strike. When all was ready, the leaders went through the details of the plan yet once more.

"This is the last time we do this," said Tvrdy gravely. "If there are questions, ask now." He looked at Bogney as he said this, but the Dhog leader did not respond. "All right, Cejka, you first. The Nilokerus temple is furthest from the feast site. That is where we will stage our first deception. Cejka, you must make certain the flames are seen before you leave. Sound the alarm yourself if you have to, but we must be certain that the Nilokerus know the temple is on fire. At the same time, four of your men will set fire to two Hageblocks," he pointed to the map, "here and here. They are enough distance from the temple that you will not have any trouble getting away safely. The temple is the crucial distraction; let them find the Hageblock fires on their own. It will produce more panic if discovered separately. Once the fires are lit, get away. Make your way to the rendezvous place in Isedon and wait for us. We will signal you if we need you."

Cejka nodded solemnly. "I understand."

Tvrdy swung to Piipo. "You and Bogney will go in with Cejka, but wait until the flames are sighted and the alarm given. You know where the Starwatch level is—" They both nodded. "So get there as quickly as possible. Ernina has given you a complete list of the supplies and equipment we need. Get what you can and get out. In the confusion, it will not be difficult to pass yourselves off as security. No one will question you if you shout orders and insults along the way. Meet Cejka at the rendezvous and wait with him. We will reclaim the supplies later." He paused. "I wish Pradim were here for this, but we don't have a guide, so you'll have to trust your own eyes and senses."

712

Piipo replied, "I have memorized the map; I believe I could find Starwatch in my sleep."

"It will look different—count on it. And don't be fooled." Tvrdy looked intently at Bogney. "Do you have any questions?"

The Dhog tapped his temple with a grubby finger. "Giloon understanding everything."

"Fine." Tvrdy turned to Kopetch. "Your mission in Tanais is of highest importance. Its execution must be perfect. Jamrog will visit Tanais last, and security will be tightest there. Mrukk will have Invisibles seeded throughout the Hage; they'll be alert for anything suspicious. It is imperative that you accomplish your goals without arousing the interest of the Invisibles. You'll be alone; there is no backup."

"I can do it," said Kopetch. "It will be a pleasure to outwit the Invisibles in plain sight."

"Just get close to Danelka. He'll tell you how Jamrog will be traveling back to Saecaraz." Tvrdy glanced at each of the others, drew a long breath. "That leaves the assassination itself."

"My rumor messengers are already in place. The weapons were hidden yesterday, and they only await Kopetch's signal."

"They'll have it in plenty of time."

"Nevertheless, use your shoulder set if you have to. The Invisibles will be monitoring all frequencies, so keep it short and in code. By the time Jamrog reaches Tanais, he will be informed of the fires in Nilokerus and will assume that we have bungled our plan. Or they will think it a distraction and expect the attack in Tanais. Either way, the Tanais visit will be perfunctory. He will be anxious to return to Saecaraz—this will help you, Kopetch."

Tvrdy continued, "Upon receiving the signal, I will get in place." His face lit briefly in a tense, tight smile. "Hagemen, I will not fail."

713

FORTY
SIX

Cejka and his men crept from the disused drainpipe and made their way quickly, quietly through deserted streets, passing between the walls of Hageworks and blocks of kraams. Behind him, one minute later, came Piipo and Bogney with their team. Upon reaching the temple, Cejka and his three firestarters crouched in the growth at the edge of the temple square and waited until the second team had disappeared across the square and were well into the Hageblocks beyond.

"Now!" whispered Cejka. Instantly four figures were racing across the square, up the long ramp, and into the temple itself. The pyramid was empty, but the smutty black candles still burned. As they made their way to the altar at the front, each man lifted his yos and untied the bundle secured around his waist. Then each took up a candle and ran to the heavy hangings behind the altar.

Cejka took his bundle—a plastic bladder filled with a volatile liquid—and aimed the nozzle at the enormous hanging before him. He touched the candle to the damp spot, and the fabric burst into flames. In seconds fire streaked upward along the slanting ceiling. Then, walking backwards, Cejka began pouring the contents of the bladder over the floor. The others, candles in hand, went from one hanging to the next along the further aisles, igniting them as they went. All met at the temple's entrance and paused to view their handiwork.

Each floor-to-ceiling hanging had become a sheet of flames. Smoke rolled up in thick billows and spread like a black fog toward the entrance. All emptied the remaining contents of the plastic bladders in a pool at the door and tossed them aside. "Well done," said Cejka. "Now for the alarm."

They ran back across the temple square and hid once more in the dense growth at the edge of the square. There they waited. Smoke poured out of the open entrance, then flames, following the trail Cejka had left behind. Soon the temple square was lit up in garish orange. The sound of the fire became a roar, but there was no one around to hear it.

"Go back to the drainpipe. Wait for me there. If I do not

return, go back with Piipo and the others." The three crept away, and Cejka raced off toward the feast site.

He had not run far, however, when he was apprehended by two Invisibles on patrol. "Where are you running?" asked the nearest, weapon drawn.

"Fire!" Cejka bellowed as loud as he could. "Fire! The temple's on fire!"

The two Invisibles looked at him closely. "There have been no reports of a fire."

"Four men . . . just now," Cejka panted. "See for yourself." He turned and pointed behind him. "I must sound the alarm."

"Stop!" growled the first Invisible. He stepped close, and his hands played expertly over Cejka's body. "No weapons," he told his partner.

"Weapons?" gasped Cejka. "There's a fire! Go see for yourself if you don't believe me."

The two Invisibles hesitated, uncertain what to do. Cejka saw his chance. "I'll sound the alarm. You go see what you can do at the temple. Maybe you can catch them." He made to take off.

"Not so fast!" shouted one of the Invisibles. Cejka's heart faltered. Did they guess he was somehow involved? Should he try to get away?

He stopped, turned around. "All right," he said. "*You* go sound the alarm. I will stay here." The two Invisibles looked at one another. Just then there came a whoosh, and a brilliant red orange fireball lit up the night as it flashed skyward to flatten itself against the dome high above.

"Fire!" screamed Cejka again. "The temple's on fire!"

The two Invisibles dashed away, leaving Cejka alone. He wasted no time hurrying back the way he'd come. The quavering blare of a fire siren sounded as he reached the rendezvous point. "We've done our part," said a breathless Cejka as he hurried into the drainpipe to meet his men. "Let's hope the others succeed as well."

• • • • • •

True to his word, Piipo did not have any trouble finding the medical center on Starwatch level. He and Bogney and their team of ten encountered no one on the way and entered the physicians' domain unobserved. Once inside, they easily found the supply kraam and began filling the packs each one wore beneath a new Nilokerus yos with the articles Ernina had requested.

When all the packs were stuffed full, they went into the recovery kraam, where, to the astonished stares of the few Hagemen lying there, they took empty suspension beds, threw off the bedding, and began loading larger pieces of equipment onto the floating bed frames. The three physicians on duty heard the commotion and came running in. They were immediately seized, bound, gagged, and pushed into a corner.

The raiders took the beds and shoved them out of the kraam and into the corridors beyond, fleeing back down to the main level. When they reached the lower rimwall outside, they were met by a crowd of frightened Nilokerus Hagemen who had been stopped by security men. The Nilokerus security guards eyed the equipment suspiciously; the guard in charge barked an order, and weapons appeared. "The Hage is on fire!" someone shouted.

"Out of the way!" hollered Piipo, shoving people aside. "Can't you see we're physicians! We're needed elsewhere!"

The security men stepped back as Piipo pushed by. The others followed, and they rushed on. Bogney kept his head down and hurried along, not daring so much as a quick look around. By the time they slipped back into the drainpipe, the smell of smoke hung heavy in the air and flames could be seen darting above the trees in the distance.

"We did it!" cried Piipo when they reached the rendezvous point in Isedon. Cejka and his fireteams greeted them with jubilant hoots, and they all pounded one another on the back. "Anything from the others?" asked Piipo when the sound died down.

"Nothing," replied Cejka. "It's up to Kopetch and Tvrdy now."

• • • • • •

Tanais born, Kopetch had no trouble making his way unobserved to the place where Danelka would meet and offer an official greeting to the Supreme Director. The success of his assignment would depend on getting close enough to see Danelka's signal. If no signal were forthcoming, Danelka would lead the party close to the place where Kopetch waited, and a pre-arranged distraction—some souile-soaked Hagemen stumbling over one another, perhaps—would allow the agent to slip in unobserved.

Kopetch, secure under the protection of Jamrog's own Invisibles, would then go along with the official party until either Danelka found out Jamrog's return route or Kopetch himself discovered it by simple observation. Then he would relay the information to Tvrdy. His signal would allow Tvrdy to get into position for the kill.

He waited in the shadow of a boathouse near the wharf, listening to the cacophony of the feast from nearby Tanais square. The simple two-word Rumon signal he'd received earlier indicated that the Supreme Director left Hage Jamuna by boat, and that the official party had grown to nearly sixty people. With that number he would have little trouble blending in—*if* he could elude detection by the Mors Ultima.

The boat was late, but Kopetch, alert at his post, was soon rewarded by the sound of engines rumbling over the water. A few minutes later he could make out the craft, rounding a bend in the river, lights blazing.

I should be the one to do it, thought Kopetch. I could take him as he steps onto the dock. It would be suicide, but worth it for the privilege of killing the twisted tyrant. Why didn't we plan it that way?

Because, he told himself yet once more, if the attempt failed, the reprisals would destroy Empyrion; thousands of Hagemen would die. It was too chancy for a lone assassin. They had only one chance and had to maximize the possibilities for success. Yes, it was better that Tvrdy, backed up by two dozen Rumon, make the attempt. This way, they could manage more of the variables. By the time Jamrog returned to Saecaraz, they would know the exact place and time of his arrival. And, more importantly, Jamrog would believe himself safe from attack. Having visited each and every Hage without incident, he would think he had survived the day. At any rate, he would definitely not expect attack in his own Hage.

The boat came gliding into the Tanais cove. The engines

were cut as the heavy craft slid to the dock. Kopetch noticed that those aboard were strangely silent. Ordinarily, the Supreme Director's boat was the best place to enjoy the Trabantonna. In Sirin Rohee's time, those invited aboard were fed and entertained splendidly. But Jamrog's party was markedly subdued.

It is as Tvrdy said, Kopetch thought. Jamrog guesses something will happen here, as do all the rest. Their visit here will be cursory. The first passengers disembarked—Jamrog was not among them.

At the same moment the Tanais welcoming party arrived and proceeded to the boat.

What's this? wondered Kopetch. Only four? Where's the fifth? He looked closer.

Danelka! Where's Danelka? A jolt of fear quickened his pulse. Danelka was not with the Tanais party. There could be no signal.

Kopetch's mind whirled through his list of limited options and decided that to join the party in an effort to learn the information on his own would be dangerous without Danelka and his prearranged diversion, but possible.

He steeled himself for his task.

Jamrog was on the dock now, surrounded by his bodyguard. The Tanais were making him welcome. Now they were leading him into the Hage. The party—bodyguard and official guests included—gathered around the Supreme Director, and all moved off at once, leaving four Invisibles to guard the boat. The party went into Hage by a different way, passing far from where Kopetch waited.

Kopetch shrank back into the shadows, touched the switch at his side, and, turning his head to his shoulder, whispered, "Old mother, Trabant has taken our Hage Leader. Trabantonna proceeds without us."

FORTY
SEVEN

Kopetch's message was clear enough: Danelka had not appeared, and there had been no signal. Without Danelka to guide them along the prearranged route, Kopetch had not been able to join the party himself and now remained on the waterfront, awaiting further instructions.

Tvrdy had two choices: abort the operation, or take a chance on where Jamrog would reenter Saecaraz. If he guessed wrong, there would be no assassination. He had to decide now. In a few minutes Jamrog would be informed of the fires in Nilokerus, and he would leave Tanais.

The plan hinged on knowing ahead of time where Jamrog would arrive back in Saecaraz, because Tvrdy needed every possible second to get himself and his men into position or the attempt would never succeed. He had to know when Jamrog could be intercepted.

Danelka's part had been to supply that crucial bit of information sometime before the Supreme Director left the Hage. But all was not lost. If Kopetch remained in place, and if Jamrog left the Hage by boat, Kopetch would see and give the signal himself. On the other hand, if upon learning of the Nilokerus fire, Jamrog left by em, Kopetch would not know when or even where they had gone.

There were too many ifs in the equation to suit Tvrdy. To make any kind of intelligent guess, he'd have to have more information. He decided to risk another message. "Hagemate," he said into his shoulder mike, "can we cruise?"

There was a moment's silence, and then Kopetch's voice crackled, "No . . . too crowded on the dock."

Kopetch's answer meant that Invisibles guarded the Supreme Director's boat. Tvrdy made up his mind at once. Since the boat was guarded, there was a very good chance Jamrog meant to use it again. He was already on his way to the Saecaraz waterfront when he gave the signal to his backup team. "Hagemen, Trabant is thirsty."

• • • • • •

The Supreme Director, tired now from his long day of official duties, walked among the Tanais, bored by the wild revel around him. The orgiastic rite was now at its frenzied peak. Food and drink had long ago obliterated all normal inhibition, and the Hagemen, having given themselves over to the celebration, now indulged every desire. For Jamrog, however, the excess of the day had quickly jaded his experienced palate, and he longed for the piquant pleasures awaiting him back at his kraam.

Yawning, he reviewed the feast site and saw his magnified image displayed in every quarter. He shunned the Tanais delicacies prepared especially for him, but drank souile—which he had brought with him—with the underdirectors, who appeared anxious and ill-at-ease.

"I expected your Subdirector to meet me," said Jamrog as he sipped the warm liquor. "I hope he is not indisposed."

Underdirector Egrem heard the intentional slip. Danelka was pro-tem Director following Tvrdy's disappearance; his Directorship had not yet been ratified by the Threl, so technically he was still only the Subdirector. "He will regret missing your visit, Supreme Director," replied Egrem. "Too much food and drink have laid many low this day."

"Too much of anything when one is unused to it can be torture," Jamrog sniffed. "Oh, well, I am not one to hold the weaknesses of a man against him. Still, you strike me as one who could handle a Directorship."

Egrem blanched. Was Jamrog offering him, an underdirector, the Tanais Directorship? Here? Now? It didn't make sense unless, as they all suspected, Danelka was dead. "I count it an honor to be so highly considered, Supreme Director," Egrem answered.

"Yes," said Jamrog, as if thinking of it for the first time. "Come to me, and we will talk more about this. What with the trouble Tanais has had lately with its leadership, I believe a term of stability would greatly improve relations between Saecaraz and Tanais. Am I right?"

"Of course, Supreme Director. And I am flattered you think me capable of helping achieve this stability." Egrem smiled warmly, much more warmly than he felt. All the time thinking, So Danelka *is* dead; the Hage is without a Subdirector.

"Good," said Jamrog flatly.

Just then Mrukk, who had been conferring with one of the Mors Ultima in the bodyguard, interrupted saying, "A message, Supreme Director." Jamrog inclined his head, and Mrukk stepped close and whispered something into his ear.

Jamrog's smile transformed itself into a scowl. "When?" he asked sharply.

"Only minutes ago," Mrukk said.

The Supreme Director turned away from the Tanais delegation and spoke with the Mors Ultima commander. The official party stood looking on, whispering among themselves. When Jamrog turned back, he announced to the group, "Events take me elsewhere. I must return to Saecaraz at once. I'm sure you all understand." There were murmurs throughout the party. "My boat will return you to Saecaraz," he told his guests. To Egrem he said, "I require an em at once."

"Certainly, Supreme Director." Egrem nodded to one of the other underdirectors and the man disappeared, two Invisibles dogging his footsteps. Moments later the em appeared, moving slowly through the crowd, the Invisibles clearing a path for it through the mass of Tanais celebrants.

When the em arrived, Mrukk slid into the driver's seat with one of his Mors Ultima beside him; Jamrog climbed in the back with three more—one on either side and one behind, riding on the back of the vehicle. More Invisibles cleared the way in front of the em, and it rolled away. The remaining Invisibles then began herding what was left of the Supreme Director's party back to the waiting boat.

FORTY EIGHT

"I don't like this," said Cejka. Piipo and Bogney nodded grimly in the torchlight, their teams of raiders sitting quietly along the curved sides of the conduit. "Kopetch should have responded by now."

The frequency monitor between them was silent. The last transmission had been the Nilokerus message to the Invisibles regarding the fire. They expected Kopetch's signal at any moment relaying Jamrog's movements to Tvrdy. The seconds, stretched by anxiety, ticked away slowly.

"Come on . . . come on," said Piipo under his breath.

Bogney stared at the monitor as if willing it to crackle to life. His lips remained pressed firmly into a straight line.

"Something's happened to him," Piipo said, his voice pinging off the fibersteel walls. "The Invisibles have—"

"Shh! Listen!" Cejka pressed his ear to the ancient machine's speaker. "There it is!" He held up his hand for silence. The others held their breath.

A row of tiny red lights on the monitor's control panel lit up. The speaker crackled. "Old mother, Trabant sails . . . but where is Trabant?"

Cejka's eyes flicked to Piipo, who stared at the monitor, a perplexed expression on his face. "What does it mean? 'Trabant sails, but where is Trabant' . . ." the Hyrgo said.

"It means," replied Cejka slowly, thinking, "that the boat left the Hage, but Kopetch did not see Jamrog."

"That must be it!" agreed Piipo, then looked stricken. "But this is not foreseen—what are we to do?"

"We go to Saecaraz." Bogney said it so matter-of-factly, the others blinked at him for a few seconds before understanding dawned.

"He's right," said Cejka at last. "We have to go to Saecaraz. Tvrdy may need help. We won't go into Hage unless we're needed, but we'll be there and ready."

He turned and described the situation to the waiting raiders, and they all hurried off together, Bogney and his Dhogs in the lead, guiding the way.

• • • • • •

Tvrdy received Kopetch's message halfway to the Saecaraz waterfront. He stopped and waited for the trailing Rumon to catch up with him. With lookouts posted, they huddled in an empty passageway, and he explained the problem: "We don't know whether Jamrog is on the boat or not. He might be, but Kopetch couldn't see him. We can't be sure."

The Rumon took in this information silently. "I think we should abort," Tvrdy continued. "If we strike and miss Jamrog, none of us will get out of Saecaraz alive."

"Director," said one of the Rumon, a slim young man with a cool, thoughtful gaze, "permit me to make a suggestion."

Tvrdy checked his first impulse to gainsay the suggestion at once without hearing it and instead answered, "Yes? You have something?"

"You have planned this operation well. It will still work. Only let us divide our number. Fifteen will go to the boat yard; the rest will go to the nearest border checkpoint."

The Cabal had originally considered doing just that—covering two or more Hage entrances—but had scrapped the plan as requiring too many people, people who had to be armed and moved through the Hage, thereby increasing the risk of discovery. Instead, they had opted for precise information. Now that had broken down.

"There are enough of us," added the Rumon, "to cover each place."

Tvrdy frowned.

The young Rumon pressed his argument. "If Jamrog comes by em, he cannot have his entire bodyguard with him. We could be at the checkpoint as planned. If he arrives, we take him and escape into Tanais."

"What you say is true," Tvrdy said slowly while his mind feverishly examined the idea from all angles. The only flaw that he could see was that dividing the force would leave those covering the dock shorthanded if Jamrog happened to be among his entourage after all—but not seriously shorthanded . . .

His head snapped up, eyes shining in the darkness. "It could work. We know that most of his bodyguard will be on that boat, even if he is not. All right . . . ." The Director had made his decision. "We will do it."

The em careened through Tanais Hage toward the border checkpoint. Mrukk coaxed the maximum speed from the vehicle, the headlights swinging right and left as they wound through empty streets and deserted roadways. But as they approached the checkpoint, Mrukk slowed, his killer instincts pricked by some sixth sense.

"What is it?" demanded Jamrog impatiently.

Mrukk made no answer, but his eyes narrowed as the booth came into view.

The em rolled closer.

The lights of the checkpoint booth shone brightly, creating an island of brilliant white light in the darkness. Five guards stood at attention around the booth. They turned casually as the em came toward them, one of the guards stepping into the center of the road, weapon leveled.

Mrukk coasted nearer.

"Tell them to let me through," said Jamrog. "I'm in a hurry."

The Mors Ultima commander touched the switch on his chest and spoke into his shoulder mike: "The Supreme Director will come through."

"Welcome, Supreme Director," came the reply. Ahead, the guard in the center of the road moved off to the right. The em proceeded, still losing speed.

"Well?" Jamrog waved them ahead. "They've cleared us."

Mrukk stared at the scene ahead, his senses quickened. Something was not right; he could feel it. Mrukk looked again and saw that each guard still had his weapon trained on the approaching vehicle . . . *after* having given clearance.

Mrukk suddenly jerked the wheel to the side and pulled on the brake, sending the em into a sideways skid, crying "Ambush!" at the same instant.

The air around the em convulsed as five thermal weapons discharged simultaneously. The heat-flash reached the skidding vehicle an instant later, blistering exposed flesh. But Mrukk's precise reflexes had saved them. The em took the full force of the blast, which lifted it and rolled it onto its side.

The Invisibles leaped from the still rolling em, weapons

drawn, firing, their clothing scorched and smoking. Mrukk threw himself from the vehicle and pulled Jamrog out, throwing him down on his face behind the em.

One Invisible racing for cover at the side of the road folded up in midstep and thudded to the pavement, his torso neatly creased in the middle. Another took a hit in the chest that flung him backward a few steps to drape himself over the side of the em, the front of his black yos sporting yellow flames.

The other two Invisibles reached cover and laid down a blanket of fire. The guard booth wilted under the blast and exploded, taking two raiders with it; another went down under Mrukk's expert marksmanship.

Mrukk touched the switch at his side and shouted, "Checkpoint under attack—Saecaraz/Tanais border! Supreme Director in danger!"

Shadows quaked and lightning sizzled around them while the air shuddered with a continuous ear-splitting shriek. Jamrog kept himself flattened to the pavement as blast after blast shook the burning em, rocking it back and back, raining sparks and hot metal debris down on the Supreme Director.

Then, just as suddenly as the firefight had begun, it stopped.

The two remaining Invisibles seized the chance and dashed forward. Mrukk jumped up. The raiders were nowhere to be seen.

"It's a trick!" Mrukk shouted.

But too late. The Mors Ultima were cut down before their commander's warning reached them. One moment they were sprinting for the flaming booth; an instant later they were tumbling through the air, bundles of blazing rags.

Mrukk, still standing in the open, marked the place where the raiders fired from, and directed a withering blast over the bodies of his men. The blast tore a flaming gash in the shrubbery; trees shriveled and burst into fireballs. At the same time a streaking bolt raked the ground at Mrukk's feet.

The Mors Ultima dove behind the burning em once more. "Do something!" cried Jamrog.

"Invisibles will be here any second."

"We'll be killed any second! Go after them! Kill them!"

A voice sounded over Mrukk's shoulder set. "Squad in position, Commander. Awaiting orders."

Mrukk turned his head and said, "They are in the ground cover to the left of the burning booth. I will draw their fire."

With that Mrukk jumped up, firing a bolt into the smoldering shrubs. Hot sparks showered over him as the expected return fire smashed into the nose of the em. He flung himself down again as his hidden Invisibles loosed a blazing volley into the roadside thicket.

There was a choked scream and then silence, save for the tick of hot metal. Moments later, the advancing Invisibles gave the all-clear. Mrukk stood and helped a shivering Jamrog to his feet. The Supreme Director—face blackened, hair and eyebrows singed—shook with fear and rage. His fine hagerobe hung in smoking tatters, full of holes where hot shrapnel had burned through. He looked as if he'd been set upon by incendiary moths. The air was sour with the smell of ozone.

"They meant to take us upon reentering the Hage," Mrukk growled.

"Tvrdy!" Jamrog spat, the word a curse on his tongue. "I will have his head—"

Before he could finish, Mrukk was barking orders into his radio. "Emergency! All Invisibles—Supreme Director's bodyguard will be attacked. Saecaraz boat yard! Emergency! Unit heads two, three, and four move your squads into cutoff position in sector eight. Unit heads five and six advance squads to the boat yard."

The Mors Ultima glanced up, smiling grimly. "We have him now. Tvrdy will not escape."

FORTY NINE

The Supreme Director's boat was a floating bonfire. Bodies lay sprawled on the dock and floated in the flame-tinted water. Tvrdy's only thought was to disengage and retreat. He knew that within minutes more Invisibles would be swarming down on them.

They had been waiting for the boat, hidden among the boathouses and equipment on the dock near the Supreme Director's mooring place. A squad of Invisibles had appeared and begun searching the boat yard. The Invisibles were thorough. Moments after their arrival on the scene, one of the Rumon had been ferreted out and killed on the spot. Tvrdy knew then that their plan had been discovered, and he opened fire on the Invisibles.

The enemy squad was cut down in seconds. The raiders had then fled back toward the feast site and had been waylaid by another squad of Invisibles. Tvrdy lost six of his fighters before he managed to break away and flee back to the docks. They arrived just as the Supreme Director's boat came gliding in, canceling any hope of escape over the water. Overanxious, Jamrog's bodyguard opened fire on them—a foolish thing to do since the boat was such an easy target. Pinched between the river and the Hage, the raiders attacked the boat, easily destroying it.

But now they were pinned down on the docks, the blue-white bolts of thermal weapons searing the air around them.

"We cannot stay here," Tvrdy told his men. "There are more Invisibles on the way. We'll be surrounded. We've got to mount a counterattack at once. Concentrate your fire on the right—they appear weakest there. If we can break through, maybe we can reach Threl Square and lose ourselves in the celebration."

The raiders put their heads down and, under a withering barrage, advanced from the dock to the boat yard. Each meter they gained cost them, however, and upon reaching the boat yard the counterattack floundered. They simply could not break the Invisibles' line.

"This is it," said Tvrdy, panting. He and the five remaining Rumon crouched behind the overturned hulls of unfinished boats. "We dare not let them take us alive. We have two choices." He did not have to say what the choices were.

"I say we take as many with us as we can." The Rumon spoke with bold determination.

"I was about to suggest it," said Tvrdy. "We'll spread out, hold fire, and force them to come in and get us . . ." He paused and added, "You'll all know what to do."

"Director," said one of the Rumon, "you could get away." He nodded toward the river behind them. "We could cover your escape."

"No," replied Tvrdy. "I won't abandon you."

"The rebellion needs you," said another. "It is your duty to save yourself if you can."

"My Hagemen are right," put in a third. "Go now while you still can."

"We will die anyway, but our deaths will aid our Hagemen if they allow you to escape," added another.

Tvrdy looked at each of them. Yes, it would be most expedient. But something inside him struggled with the notion. "We can all escape," he said.

"If we all go, they'll catch us," replied the first Rumon. "But if you go alone, you have a chance." The others nodded their agreement, eyes hard, jaws set, faces earnest in the flickering light of the burning boat.

It's true, Tvrdy considered. There is a chance. What will happen to the rebellion without me?

"Old mother—" The voice startled Tvrdy. "Trabant is looking for you."

"Cejka!" He hit the switch. "Trabant has found us in the boat yard." He looked at his men. "We hit them as soon as Cejka opens fire. Be ready to move the instant the line breaks."

A long minute passed. Then another.

The Invisibles, suspicious of the lack of activity, began blasting the boat yard. The raiders hunkered down and covered their heads. "Hurry, Cejka," whispered Tvrdy.

The Invisibles, intent upon destroying the boat yard, did not see Cejka, Bogney, and the Dhogs slipping in behind them. The instant Cejka and his team attacked, Tvrdy and the Rumon opened fire. The Invisibles, crushed between the hammer and anvil of a dual attack, succumbed in seconds.

It happened so fast that it took Tvrdy and the Rumon a moment to understand that the way was clear. They crept cautiously from hiding and then scrambled over burning wreckage to join their comrades.

"Can we get back?" asked Tvrdy.

"I think so," answered Cejka, "if we hurry. There are more Invisibles on the way—we can count on it."

"Talk later," grunted Bogney.

They made their way slowly back to Threl Square using the escape route Tvrdy had designed, avoiding open areas and better-traveled byways. Bogney led the way, using his Dhog's finely honed sensitivity to detection. They saw no one until, skirting Threl Square, they encountered a Mors Ultima squad making a sweep through a row of Hageblocks.

"Deathmen coming this way," whispered Bogney.

"We'll have to leave our route, go around," Tvrdy replied. "Can you get us back on the other side?"

"Dhogs get Tanais and Rumon back." With that, he struck off in the opposite direction.

If not for the fact that the Dhog apparently possessed an uncanny sense of direction, Tvrdy would have said they were becoming hopelessly lost. But just when Tvrdy decided he must stop Bogney now before it was too late, the Dhog's unerring sense proved itself, and they emerged from an obscure passage into a close behind the Hageblock they'd been heading for when the Invisibles forced them off the path.

"Well done!" said Tvrdy, clapping the squat leader on his broad back.

They hurried off again, and eventually reached the Saecaraz refuse pits, which in times past had been built over the remains of the ductwork that at one time fed air to the Isedon section. At the bottom of one of the pits lay a grate which opened into the ancient duct.

The refuse pits were surrounded by a high fibersteel grid fence, which the Dhogs had long ago adapted to their own purposes. But between the Saecaraz wall and the fence lay a no-man's-land—a razed strip of moldering rubble.

The exhausted raiders stood in the mouth of a broken

sewer conduit and looked out across the strip. "We're almost there," said Tvrdy. "Cejka, you and your team go first. We'll cover you from here."

They struck off across the strip. Tvrdy and the others fanned out in front of the sewer conduit, scanning the surrounding Hageblocks and streets for any signs of approaching Invisibles. Cejka reached the refuse pits and gave the all-clear. "You're next," said Tvrdy to Bogney, and the Dhogs rushed out into the strip.

There must have been at least five squads of Invisibles already hidden in the rubble because lightning struck from every direction at once. The Dhogs, caught in the open, shriveled under the terrible blast, cut down as they ran.

Tvrdy attacked the Invisibles from behind, and Cejka's men, finding themselves suddenly exposed to hostile fire, scrambled for cover.

The Invisibles turned their attack on Tvrdy's team, now well hidden in the ruins around the sewer. The resulting fight was fierce and fast. The Invisibles, having divided up the raiders nicely, now sought to crush them by dint of superior numbers. They advanced without regard for life or limb, throwing themselves into the fight with a ferocity Tvrdy had never witnessed before.

The rebels fell one by one to the horrific onslaught. The Invisibles pressed the attack, bearing down relentlessly, forcing the rebels to give ground beneath a sheet of searing fire.

Tvrdy saw what was happening, and realized that if his men broke and ran, the Invisibles would butcher them in a killing frenzy. Their only hope was to stand against them and somehow withstand the force of the attack.

Above the shriek and crackle of the thermal weapons, the rebels heard a voice, Tvrdy's voice, crying, "Stand your ground! Stand! Stand!" And they saw their commander standing fast with his weapon on his hip, firing bolt after blistering bolt into the onrushing Invisibles.

Cejka's team, having survived the initial attack and regrouped, now laid into the Invisibles from behind the fibersteel grid of the refuse pits. The Invisibles' attack, broadsided even as they pressed for the kill, faltered.

Tvrdy saw the momentary confusion—the Invisibles' divide and conquer tactic had turned on them. He dashed forward, shouting, "Attack!" His men jumped up, and they ran to meet the Invisibles, screaming, weapons crackling, orange flames bursting the night into a million shadows. The Invisibles fell back upon themselves, stumbled, tripped over one another as the foremost ranks collided with those behind.

In seconds the Invisibles were reduced to chaos, and Tvrdy, still firing into the swarming ranks, broke off the attack and headed out across the strip. He reached the place where the Dhogs had gone down and found the few survivors struggling to pull their dead and dying out of the rubble.

"Leave them," shouted Tvrdy. "Save yourselves!"

"No leaving Dhogs behind," replied Bogney, swaying under the weight of a body slung across his shoulders.

There was no time to argue about it, so Tvrdy ordered his men to help get the casualties out while the Invisibles regrouped across the strip behind them, Cejka doing his best to hold them off. A moment later the raiders were fleeing to the refuse pits, the Invisibles charging hard after them.

The raiders reached the gridwork around the pits just as the Invisibles, seeing their prey escaping, rallied and broke out of Cejka's containment, their black shapes flying over the broken strip.

They came rushing in, heedless of the wilting return fire. Invisibles fell in clusters as Tvrdy's men labored to hold them off. But the Invisibles were too many and too quick. Their Mors Ultima commanders had decreed a suicide attack in a last-ditch effort to stop the rebels and, despite fearful casualties, were leveling the full force of their attack on Tvrdy's group, trapping them outside the grid fence.

Hemmed in on every side, men dropping all around, the rebel team made a desperate last stand—weapons blazing, throw-probes glowing white hot, overheated handgrips searing the hands of those who held them—and kept on firing.

The Invisibles bore down, wave after wave of raking fire strafing the stranded rebels. In seconds it would be all over.

Then, with a flash and a roar, the strip erupted, hurling debris and dirt high into the air as one long continuous explosion ripped the ground. The Invisibles, frozen in the terrible cataclysm, were blown back by the force of the explosion, their bodies broken and flung like so many bundles tossed through the air.

"Piipo!" Tvrdy cried, turning to see the Hyrgo and his squad racing to their aid, the blunt barrels of their old-fashioned weapons smoking.

"Get moving!" yelled Piipo. He waved the gun overhead. "We'll hold them off until you're inside."

The rebels scurried to safety, taking their casualties with them as they fled down into the refuse pits. Once inside, they passed the bodies of their comrades through the grate at the bottom of the pit and then followed them into the duct. More explosions thundered above, and then Piipo's team came pouring through a gaping hole in the grid fence and down into the pit.

"They'll . . . follow . . . us," said a breathless Tvrdy when Piipo had joined him. "Get the injured . . . out of here." His voice rang in the ductwork with a harsh metallic sound.

Cejka and his men were already dragging the injured and lifeless deeper into the great curving corridor. Piipo brandished his weapon. "I saved two rounds for them."

"Good," said Tvrdy. "Seal the duct. That will slow them down."

"We can never use this entrance again anyway," said Cejka. "Now they know about it."

"Give us as long as you can to get clear and then destroy it," ordered Tvrdy. He turned to leave, saying, "And give yourself plenty of time as well."

"Get going. I'll join you soon."

They hurried off down the snaking ductwork, hands pressed against the smooth metal sides, feeling their way in the darkness, for the old duct was lit only at rare intervals by smudge pots placed along the floor.

They felt the rumble of the detonation before the concussion pummeled them like a giant fist, laying them out in one devastating punch. The shockwave rattled the duct with a deafening clatter as the walls convulsed.

And then all was silent.

Tvrdy and Cejka picked themselves up, choking in the smoke and dust raised by the explosion. Both peered fearfully into the churning blackness behind them, "Piipo?" Cejka called. "Piipo!"

Hearing a cough and another and then footsteps staggering toward them, they reached out their hands and caught the floundering Piipo as he lurched toward them.

"Are you hurt?" asked Cejka.

Piipo looked at them with a dazed expression. "I'm all right," he shouted. "I can't hear so good."

They took him by the arms, and together the three threaded their way back to the Old Section.

FIFTY

"We heard on the monitor that you were in trouble," said Piipo, speaking slowly and a little overloud. He sat with his head in his hands, his right ear bandaged, both eyes black from the concussion of the bomb he'd used to seal the entrance. "When Cejka went to find you, he told us to stay there in case we were needed. I remembered the old weapons Tvrdy had showed us in the arsenal, and I thought they might be useful if the Invisibles found us. So I sent men back to get them."

"You sent men back?" wondered Tvrdy. "All the way back to the Old Section for those weapons?"

Piipo smiled proudly. "The Hyrgo are sturdy. It was nothing." Then he remembered the dead and added with a slow, sad shake of his head, "But we might have been quicker."

"You did well," said Tvrdy. "We all owe you our lives." He looked at Cejka. "And I thank you, too."

The mood in the briefing room was subdued. Treet had seen the raiders return, had seen the dead and dying carried into the Old Section, had seen the haggard, beaten expressions on the faces of the men . . . and knew that the raid had failed.

Now, a few brief hours later, Tvrdy was leading a much dejected group through an autopsy of the miscarried mission. "That is something at least," continued Tvrdy, "to still be alive this morning when so many are not."

The others in the room remained silent.

"I take responsibility for the failure of the raid," said Tvrdy, speaking softly. "It was my idea. I gave the order. I was wrong, and others paid for my mistake."

"Not your mistake," said Cejka. "We all agreed. We did what we thought right. Besides, the raid was not a total failure. We succeeded in every other objective. We wiped out Jamrog's bodyguard—the best of the Mors Ultima—and several squads of Invisibles." He raised a fist to shoulder level and smashed it into his palm. "And we would have had Jamrog, too, if not for Mrukk."

"The fact is," Tvrdy said, "that we did not meet our primary objective—to remove Jamrog. This morning he is alive, and his hatred burns against us. We have succeeded only in making him more furious than ever."

"Also a minor objective," Piipo reminded him.

Tvrdy gave a snort of displeasure. "But at what cost? Too many men died for that success to have any value."

Treet remembered it was Kopetch who had suggested that Jamrog's anger might be useful. He glanced around the room and saw that Kopetch was not among them. Had he been killed, too?

He also noticed that Bogney and his two Dhogs sat in stony silence. Knowing the Dhogs had taken the brunt of the beating at the refuse pits, he supposed they were hurt and angry about the results, and were demonstrating as much by their aloofness.

Fertig, who had stayed behind with Treet and Ernina, entered the room and took a seat. All eyes turned toward him.

"You might as well tell us now," said Tvrdy. "Waiting won't make the news easier to hear."

"We lost forty-three in the raid," Fertig replied. "Seven more died of their wounds during the night. Fifty altogether."

"The wounded?"

"Sixteen. Most should recover, but three or four may not. Time will tell."

Tvrdy nodded. Treet had never seen him so despondent, so beaten. "We have lost over half of our ready force."

"And the Invisibles now know one of our entrances," pointed out Cejka.

"It is sealed," offered Piipo.

"How long do you think that will stop them?"

"He's right," said Tvrdy. "We've got to destroy the rest of the duct. We'll do it today."

"Not enough," said Bogney, speaking up. "Deathmen now be coming for us here." He turned around again, away from the others.

"We don't have enough supplies to hide here indefinitely," said Piipo.

"Getting our men back in fighting shape will take time," Cejka said.

"We weren't ready," replied Tvrdy, mostly to himself. "I was too anxious . . . too arrogant . . ."

"We all wanted it as badly as you," Cejka said. "We couldn't know Danelka would be taken. We underestimated Mrukk."

"It will not happen again," said Tvrdy. "I can promise you that." He paused and drew a hand over his face. "We're all tired. I suggest we get some rest and meet back here tonight to begin picking up the pieces."

Treet shuffled out with the others, feeling particularly useless and overlooked. Is there nothing I can do to help the cause? he wondered. Why am I here?

• • • • • •

The forest had been thinning for two days, becoming less dense with every kilometer. The big cat walked easily beside the man, both as soundless as the shadows they passed through. They had awakened early a few days ago to a restlessness, a tingling sense of necessity to be moving, traveling. Taking up his spear, Crocker left the sheltered bower, following the cat, and they began walking.

They ate when hungry, satisfied their thirst in cool forest pools and muddy streams, slept when they grew tired. But hour by hour they pushed deeper into the forest, moving further westward, following the nameless urge.

With every step, a long-forgotten sense of anticipation quickened in Crocker. He felt as if he would see something very important around the next turn, or the next.

There was no frustration in the expectation when, as he rounded the next bend, only more blue forest presented itself to view. Instead, Crocker experienced a continual sense of assurance: when he reached his journey's end, he would be rewarded. It was not a thought, but a strong undercurrent of the same expectation. So he continued on, unhurriedly, even as the anticipation grew moment by moment.

From the jerk of the wevicat's tail, the man knew his feline companion sensed the growing anticipation, too. From time to time, as the cat ranged further ahead, it would stop and look back at the slower human, then watch him with large, luminous eyes full of sly intelligence as if to say: Hurry! There is little time. Something's going to happen. We must not miss it.

FIFTY ONE

The boats reached the headwaters of the Taleraan at sunset. The Fieri disembarked to spend the night on shore—a rock shelf cut between two sheer canyons. Tomorrow they would make the journey by foot up through the mountain pass and down again to the lowlands and the Bay of Talking Fish, reaching it by dusk.

On shore Pizzle walked with his Mentor, Anthon, gazing at the canyon cliffs high above and at the sky beyond, taking on the color of iron. As they passed along the long line of boats moored in the shallows, Pizzle kept one eye peeled for a glimpse of Starla while Anthon instructed his charge in the protocol of approaching the talking fish.

"The fish really talk?" Pizzle inquired.

"Oh, yes," Anthon assured him. "But you must know how to listen, and you must be ready."

"How? How do you get ready?"

"Their speech is of a delicate, subtle kind—not really speech at all, since it has no words. Naturally, since this faculty is shared between two entirely different species, it is not at all strange to expect it to be so."

"But what do they say—however they say it?"

Anthon laughed. "They don't *say*, they *communicate*."

"Pure communication—is that what you're telling me?" Pizzle accepted Anthon's nod. "But communication must be about *something*, or it's not communication at all."

"Precisely, or we would never have called them talking fish." Anthon's brow wrinkled in an effort to put words to the enigma of the talking fish—something the Fieri had long ago given up trying to do, preferring simply to accept the phenomenon. "They communicate . . ." Anthon said, straining after words, "sense impressions; they communicate their experience of the world. The talking fish communicate themselves. That's why you have to know how to listen, or you'll never hear it."

Pizzle shook his head. "I still don't get it. What am I supposed to do? Meditate?"

"Precisely!" said Anthon. "You meditate, fill your heart with thoughts of goodness, of truth, of joy. You draw the fish to you by the quality of your thought. You prepare a place for the fish to come to you."

"I see. So I'm sitting there thinking all kinds of beautiful thoughts, and this fish swims up, and if he likes what he sees we have a chat. Is that it?"

Anthon laughed again. His laugh, like his manner, was gentle, understanding. "Yes, that's the sense of it."

"But do I say anything? Or do I just listen?"

"Whatever you feel," Anthon told him. "Most people prefer just to listen. That is enough."

"Hmmm." Pizzle frowned in concentration. "I think I'm getting it now. Forgive me, I'm not usually this dense."

"It's more difficult to explain than it is to do," admitted Anthon, placing a friendly hand on Pizzle's shoulder. "It's the same with so many things in life. We hinder ourselves with our fears and concerns when all that is needed is trust and faith."

"Believe that the fish will speak and they'll speak—something like that?"

"Something like that."

"When will the fish come? Will we have to wait long?"

"Not long. A day perhaps. At most, three." Anthon saw Pizzle's involuntary grimace and added, "But you won't mind waiting. The bay is beautiful. You will enjoy yourself. Besides, since everyone will be together on the beach, I don't see any reason why you and Starla should be apart."

"Terrific! You mean it? Wow, this is tremendous! Thanks, Anthon. You're aces!"

Anthon shook his head in bemusement. "The things you say, Asquith. Earth must be a very strange place indeed if everyone talks as you do."

They walked along a little further, and Pizzle gazed at the wide river stretching out before them, calm and deep, now shimmering with the reflected light of the sunstone cliffs, like captured sunset. The Fieri around them readied the evening meal, and smoke began drifting along the water's edge as music, light and tinkling like delicate cut glass, lifted into the darkening sky.

"It's so peaceful," remarked Pizzle. "I love this life."

Anthon heard the wistfulness in his voice. "Your life was very different on Earth?"

"*Very* different."

"Do you miss it?"

"Miss it?" Pizzle glanced at the Mentor quickly. "No, not at all. I never even think about it. Why would I? Back on Earth I was nothing—a cog in the corporate wheel, a nameless drone. All I did was shove printouts from one side of a plastic desk to the other, siphoning numbers off and putting them on other printouts. It was hell."

He sighed at the futility of it. "No, I don't miss it. Everything I ever dreamed of is here—it's paradise. I'm surprised you even understand an emotion like longing, you know?"

"How so? Are we so fullfilled we cannot long for ultimate perfection?"

Pizzle shrugged. "I don't miss it at all. Should I? I mean, I'm happier here than I ever was back there. Here . . . it's like a dream I never want to end, you know? I want it to go on and on forever."

"You speak of paradise," said Anthon. "This isn't paradise, Asquith. The life you speak of is found only in the Infinite Father. If Empyrion is good, its goodness is only a reflection of the greater goodness of the Creator."

"I don't care where it comes from," replied Pizzle. "I just know that's what I want." They were silent for a while. Upon reaching the last of the Fieri ships, they turned and started back. "Anthon?" said Pizzle. "Tell me something."

"Anything."

"Is it true—all you say about the Infinite Father?"

"There is a truth greater than we know, Asquith. This greater truth is the Infinite. We cannot know it; we can only get snatches, fleeting glimpses of it. But it is there. It exists. In fact, all that exists moves and lives in it." He paused, and added, "However, I can offer no proof for this assertion."

"I believe you," said Pizzle, "but not because of anything you could say."

"Oh?"

"No. That's all good stuff, you understand. But it makes sense to me because I know I'm a better person now, believing it, or trying to, than I ever was before. You know?"

Anthon put his arm around Pizzle's shoulders. "You have a freshness about you that does this old soul good. Yes, I know what you mean. Experience does often reflect its source. It is proof of a sort."

They walked back along the river and came to one of the large fires that had been made at intervals on the bank. Fish roasted on spits arched over the shimmering pyramid of flames. In the coals, wrapped in bundles of wet leaves, fresh-gathered vegetables steamed. The aroma melted into the air, piquant and tantalizing. Pizzle and Anthon sat down among the others gathered there as the first spit was taken down.

Pizzle ate, enjoying the close kinship of the Fieri, feeling very much a part of it himself. But after he had satisfied his hunger, he excused himself and got up to wander back to the boat.

There would be no sunshower tonight; the air was too clear and still. Instead, the Light Mountains gave forth a steady warm glow that reminded Pizzle of the lights of a city seen from a distance on a clear night.

He went up the gangplank and stretched out on the empty deck to watch the stars come out. Tomorrow they would reach the Bay of Talking Fish, and he would be with Starla. But tonight he wanted to be alone with his thoughts—to let himself wander in his mind toward the truth Anthon spoke of. This night he felt closer to it than ever before, and he wanted to savor that closeness, and to increase it if he could.

Mostly, he just wanted to be alone and experience the sensation of solitude devoid of loneliness—something quite rare for him. The experience reflects its source, he thought. You can tell the tree by its fruit. Now where had he heard that?

• • • • • •

When the boats reached the mooring place, Yarden did not stir. She remained below in her berth. In fact, she did not attend the last of the art classes that day either. And when Ianni told her that Gerdes had asked about her, she merely shrugged and said she hadn't felt like going.

"You've been withdrawn the last few days," Ianni told her. "I've noticed. Would you like to talk about it?"

"Not particularly," said Yarden. "It's something I've got to work out myself."

"You look as if you are in pain, Yarden. Perhaps I could help."

"No . . . thank you, no. I'd rather be alone."

Ianni had left her then and Yarden had stayed there, listening to the voices of the Fieri as they left the ships and began preparing for their last night on the river. Tomorrow they would begin the trek through the mountains and down to the bay—a prospect which should have filled Yarden with excitement.

But she lay on her bed in the dark, listening to the clear, happy voices, watching the circle of sky growing dim through the porthole, feeling cut off from what was happening around her. Adrift on a troubled sea.

Over and over she asked herself the same questions—the same questions she'd been driving herself crazy with for days: Should I try to contact Treet? What if I don't like what I find? What if he's dead or in trouble? What then? Oh, God, what am I supposed to do?

She rose, went up on deck, and watched the activity on shore. There was an urgency about it—the coming of night made the Fieri move a little quicker in their preparations. They were aware of the fading day and did not wish to lose the light.

I've got to decide, Yarden said to herself. I've got to decide right now. If I wait any longer, I too will lose what little light I have.

She turned and walked back along the deck to the stern, as far from the bustle on shore as she could get. She sat down cross-legged on the polished wood and drew a long deep breath. God, help me, she thought. I don't know what to do.

"The Dhogs have blasted the ductwork, Supreme Director." The Invisible commander held himself stiffly and stared straight ahead. "It will take time to reach the Old Section through the refuse pits."

"You *will* reach the Old Section," intoned Jamrog menacingly. "I want those responsible brought before me at once. Do you understand me?" The bhuj flashed back and forth in the Supreme Director's hands as he sat in the thronelike chair he had had placed in the center of the Supreme Director's kraam. His face was puffy and blistered, his scalp mottled gray and patchy where clumps of hair had been burned off. His flesh was red and painfully swollen from the scorching he'd taken on the night of the failed assassination.

"The duct is destroyed, Supreme Director," explained Osmas, realizing he was dangerously near the flashpoint of his superior's vile temper. Jamrog had been raving mad since the Trabantonna attack; it didn't do to argue with him or gainsay his whims, however unreasonable they might be. "I don't see what anyone can do."

The Saecaraz Subdirector motioned toward the door, and the Invisible backed gratefully toward it. Jamrog had killed three of them in the last two days, and Osmas wanted to save the man if he could. What with the demise of the Mors Ultima bodyguard, upper echelon Invisibles were getting scarce. "We'll find another way in," Osmas said hopefully.

"How?" roared Jamrog. "Searching is impossible, and guides are less than useless!"

It was true. For some unknown reason, guides had never been able to locate the hidden entrances and exits of the Old Section. There were many theories to explain this, but it remained a mystery why the blind wayfinders could not discover the Dhog's secret pathways—even with the help of their psi entities.

"Nevertheless, I'm told that the interrogations are proceeding successfully. We will uncover useful information soon."

At that moment Diltz, the cadaverous Nilokerus Director,

entered the kraam and crossed the floor in quick, confident strides. His sunken eyes gleamed in his skull. "I bring good news, Supreme Director," he said with a deferential nod of his long head.

"The Fieri have been located?" Jamrog half rose out of his chair.

The corners of Diltz's mouth drew down. "Ah, no, Supreme Director. But I can report that we have located what appears to be a navigational tower. I have brought a map to show you."

He produced a thin roll of yellowed plastic from the folds of his black-and-white yos, stepped close, and unrolled it for Jamrog. Osmas pushed in to see it, too. "Here," said Diltz, pointing to a newly drawn circle on a flat expanse of plain beyond the river that ran near Empyrion. "The tower is located in this area—called, I believe, a desert." He pronounced the unfamiliar word carefully.

"Desert," repeated Jamrog. "And just what is this desert?"

"Nothing—literally. The word, I am told by my readers, is an ancient mapmakers' term for *void*."

"I see," said Jamrog, looking askance at the map. "And how will examining a void help us find the enemy?"

"The tower is of Fieri design," explained Diltz, the enthusiasm draining out of his voice. "We are searching the area now. If we find another such tower, we may be able to fix a direction to the Fieri settlement."

"Or away from it," said Osmas, snapping the brittle plastic map with a fingernail. Since adopting the Supreme Director's questionable notions of finding and exterminating the Fieri using the old weapons, Diltz was enjoying a rapid ascendancy in Jamrog's favor. Osmas resented it.

The Saecaraz Subdirector thought they should concentrate solely on eradicating the Dhogs. He disliked seeing Diltz win favor through the continued support of an idea he personally considered dangerous. Moreover, he disliked the fact that the Nilokerus had been given control of the Saecaraz magicians assigned to the Archives. Diltz seemed to be making steady progress in his assignments, while he, Osmas, met with nothing but setbacks in digging out the Dhogs.

Jamrog, ignoring Osmas' remark, asked, "What of the weapons?"

"Ah, yes." Diltz smiled. "The weapons have been removed and examined." The smile turned wicked. "I am assured that there will be little problem reactivating them. Readers are working on deciphering the technical material now."

"Excellent!" cried Jamrog. He turned to Osmas and pointed a puffy, red finger at him. "You see? This is what can be done with some effort."

Diltz grinned smugly, but said nothing.

"The Fieri settlement still remains to be found," observed Osmas sourly. "Meanwhile, the Dhogs are here among us."

"And remain to be found," said Diltz.

"With more help—"

"You have all the help you need," barked Jamrog, flinging himself from the chair. "Mrukk tells me you have not been making full use of resources."

Chagrined to find himself on the defensive, the Subdirector sputtered, "Until the interrogations turn up some useful information—"

The Supreme Director thrust the bhuj in Osmas' face. "Are you questioning my directives?"

"Never! But perhaps the Mors Ultima are somewhat overzealous in carrying out their orders. Reorientation cells are crammed beyond capacity—six, eight share a space designed for one. Four of five die under the questioning. Corpses are being stacked in Hage squares—the Jamuna cannot render the bodies fast enough. The smell of death is everywhere."

"Let it be a warning to the rest!" yelled Jamrog. "I will *not* have my directives questioned!" He swung the bhuj at Osmas, missed him, and then threw it at the Subdirector. The ceremonial weapon clattered across the floor.

Osmas, already backpedaling toward the door, tripped over his own feet and landed on his backside. Jamrog, standing over him, lashed out with his foot, screaming, "Get out! Get out!" Throwing his hands up to protect his face, Osmas rolled away from the vicious kicks, gathered his feet under him, and sprinted toward the door, leaving a livid Jamrog bellowing in rage.

Diltz watched the scene with unconcealed pleasure. Here was an opportunity to consolidate his advantage: he would see to it that Osmas would no longer pose a threat to his ambitions. He approached the seething Jamrog.

"His loyalty wavers, Supreme Director. But is he danger-ous?"

Jamrog turned, the veins bulging on his neck and forehead. "Is no one to be trusted?"

"Trust me," said Diltz softly. "Allow me to deal with this problem for you."

"It's yours." Jamrog whirled away, retreating back into his bedchamber. "I want nothing more to do with him."

• • • • • •

The walk up through the mountain pass was more exhila-rating than exhausting. Over the years, Fieri engineers had carved out a generous pathway over an easy route of gentle inclines amidst towering cliffs and plunging gorges threaded with rushing freshets and reckless cascades crossed by graceful cantilevered footbridges. Long tunnels bored through solid rock laced the route—cool and damp, and echoey with the sound of pattering feet and whispered voices.

At the summit of the pass, the travelers emerged from a tunnel to view their descent winding down through blue-green moss forests shimmering in silver mists. The moss flourished on spindlelike rock spires and columns in the cool-air heights, nour-ished by the mineral-rich spray of a hundred dashing waterfalls.

The Fieri, delighted with the beauty of the scene, ran down through the hanging mists, laughing to feel the tingling splash on their faces, soaking their clothing in the spray. The children ran to gawk at each waterfall, shouting above the crash and roar as they followed the tumbling water down and down to the plain below.

The day was fine and bright; wonder lurked around every corner, and glory loomed on the near horizon. Joy was conta-gious, infecting young and old alike with a most virulent strain that broke out in luminous smiles, songs, and laughter. Pizzle, walking hand in hand with Starla—Anthon strolling an amiable distance behind—felt drunk with happiness.

He chattered happily away, describing his long, lonely days and even longer, lonelier nights to a sympathetic Starla. For her part, his beloved appeared content merely to be in his presence. She smiled and nodded and squeezed his hand, luxuriating in his unflagging attention.

In this way they came down the mountainside, passing by tunnel through one last stone curtain to emerge blinking on the other side, dazzled by the spectacular vista of Talking Fish Bay—a great golden sweep of sand cradling a bowl of jade-colored water.

The bay was enormous—making the whole of Prindahl look like a duck pond in a park—stretching from horizon to horizon. The ragged tops of mountains formed a boundary on the right; on the left the deep blue-green of the Blue Forest smudged the distant skyline like a low, dark cloud bank. Directly ahead, jade water danced under the white sun as far as the eye could see.

The Fieri hurried down to the bay, the young ones racing ahead, abandoning themselves to headlong flight. "Magnificent!" breathed Pizzle. "I never dreamed it would be this—this wonderful." He paused, grasping for superlatives. "It's like something out of *Lord of the Rings!* I feel like Frodo coming to the Grey Havens."

"It's even more beautiful than I remember," said Starla.

Those still lingering over the view voiced similar sentiments. Anthon came to where Pizzle and Starla stood with their arms wrapped around each other. "It inspires me anew each time I see it," he sighed. "The Creator is indeed extravagant with His beauty." Then he turned and eyed the lovers. "Well, come on, we'll find our places."

"Places?" inquired Pizzle as they started off.

"For our tents—" Starla began to explain.

"And also to meditate," added Anthon. "But tonight—tonight we all come together—"

"Songs and stories," said Starla, tugging Pizzle along now. "And swimming."

They overtook Anthon, who waved them on, saying he would be along in his own good time, and hurried down to join the first ranks of Fieri now spreading out over the beach below.

● ● ● ● ● ●

At the rear of the long procession making its way down to the golden beach walked Yarden, last but for those guiding the supply train—a train made up of miniature balons whose gondolas were laden with provisions and camping equipment. Bobbing and weaving through the mountain course, the long string of balons resembled a giant centipede wobbling down to the sea, flanked by attendants carrying poles and tether ropes to steer it.

Ianni walked beside Yarden, troubled for her friend, but respectful of Yarden's silence. Her attempts at conversation along the way had elicited only vague, halfhearted responses, and Ianni had given up trying to draw Yarden out and had contented herself with lending comfort by her presence. They stopped at the overlook to take in their first sight of the bay, and Yarden stirred from her reverie. "Oh, it is wonderful," she said reverently.

Ianni, glad for any response, pounced on this pronouncement. "Yes, it is. It's always been one of my favorite places. Wait until the fish arrive—that's something to see as well. The first thing I want to do is go for a swim, and then—" She broke off. "What is it, Yarden? Tell me what's wrong."

At first, Ianni thought Yarden wouldn't answer. There was a long silence in which Yarden merely stared out across the enormous bay, as if taking in the majestic sight, but Ianni saw that Yarden's dark eyes were unfocused, her gaze directed inward. The balon centipede bobbed past them. Several of the Fieri walking with it looked at the women concernedly, but Ianni gave them reassuring glances and they continued on.

"It's nothing," Yarden replied finally. She turned and smiled, and Ianni saw her force down whatever had been troubling her, and noticed that the smile was strained. "I'll be all right," insisted Yarden. "Come on, let's get down to the beach. A swim would do me good, I think."

FIFTY
THREE

Spirits improved somewhat when the missing Kopetch returned to the Old Section. He had been gone three days and was considered a casualty of the operation. But, tired and hungry, he appeared at the Chryse entrance, presented himself to the sentries there, and was brought safely in.

Now, after some food and a few hours rest, the rebel Cabal sat before a gray-faced Kopetch, listening, worry lines etched on every brow, eyes staring at a bleak, hopeless future filled with pain and death.

"I stayed as long as I could, to gather information. Invisibles were everywhere . . . I had to get out," said Kopetch, sipping from a cup of water. "I knew the raid had failed, but I could not believe the speed of the retaliation."

"He already knew what he would do," suggested Fertig. "Jamrog had it planned. Hladik helped him before he was killed."

"Likely," agreed Tvrdy. "Go on."

Kopetch gulped down some water and resumed his dire recitation. "Every Director is under Mors Ultima guard—"

"Mors Ultima *arrest!*" snorted Piipo.

"And Jamrog has disbanded the Threl," continued Kopetch. "Each Hage is under the direction of a Mors Ultima commander—except Saecaraz and Nilokerus, of course. There is talk of a quota; five thousand from each Hage must be interrogated."

"Tortured, you mean," said Cejka.

"The Invisibles have been given a free hand to question Hagemen. Work must continue, but everyone is afraid to leave the Hageblocks—although anyone discovered hiding in a kraam during work time is immediately arrested. Hagemen are pulled off the streets at random and herded into ems. Invisibles roam the walkways with lists; if one is on the list, he is taken. Or, if one is *not* on the list he is taken. It doesn't matter; the lists are meaningless—they make the arrest appear more official, that's all. If it appears official, the people don't question it; they go along quietly."

"How are the lists made?"

"During interrogation, the Mors Ultima offer a Hageman a chance to save himself further agony by giving the names of fellow traitors. If he gives them names, they might stop the torture. They get lots of names.

"Women go to special interrogation kraams where they are raped before being questioned. Often their Hagemates are forced to watch. The Invisibles get many names."

"Those who resist?" asked Tvrdy.

"Few resist," said Kopetch sadly. "Corpses are fished continually from Kyan's coves—these are said to be Hagemen who dared question their arrest or made interrogation difficult."

"What of the Hage priests?" wondered Cejka. "How can they continue to accept their rewards? Don't they see what is happening?"

"The Hagemen say the priests insist that it is a political problem and they must not take sides."

"Not take sides!" shouted Piipo. "They inform on Hagemen and say they cannot take sides. They will pay with their lives for that lie!"

Tvrdy waved him silent. "What of security?"

"It's nearly impossible to move around. If not for our Tanais on the network, and a ready escape route, I would not have made it back. The Hage borders are sealed to all—goods only may pass through. Invisibles patrol the streets. They confiscate anything a Hageman may possess, or arrest at will."

"The attitude of the Hagemen?"

"Baffling." Kopetch shook his head in dismay. "They act as if it is not happening . . . as if to admit something is wrong will turn the insanity upon them. Their Hagemen are taken from the next kraam, and they stand looking on. They say, 'He must have done something. He deserves what he gets.' " Kopetch halted, disgust choking him. "I—I wanted to kill them for their stupidity."

"Incredible," observed Cejka. "They see their Hagemen taken away to be tortured and yet think they can be safe themselves."

"The cowards!" cried Piipo.

"What reason is given for the arrests?" Tvrdy asked.

"The Supreme Director has issued a statement saying that the Fieri have infiltrated Empyrion. He says many of our people have gone over to them, that treason runs deep and must be cut out."

"He blames the Fieri?" wondered Piipo.

"There was a rumor—some time ago—of a Fieri invasion," put in Fertig. "Mors Ultima caught some people outside. No one knows what they were doing. Rohee tried to cover it up, but Hladik and Jamrog knew about it and were making plans, although the Fieri disappeared before they could get at them. They were furious over it—it's why Rohee was killed, I think."

"We know," said Tvrdy, a ghost of a smile touching his lips.

"We were the ones who removed them from under your noses," Cejka added. "And you're right—Jamrog used it as an excuse to murder Rohee."

"I should have guessed," said Fertig.

"It doesn't matter now." Tvrdy looked to Kopetch. "Anything else?"

"I heard that a Mors Ultima squad is again searching outside," the Tanais replied.

"Searching for what?" asked Piipo.

"Fierra."

"Does Jamrog actually believe the Fieri are involved in the rebellion?" Cejka shook his head slowly. "It makes no sense. He knows we are responsible. He knows . . . and yet—"

"Yet behaves otherwise," remarked Tvrdy. "He is shrewd and dangerous."

Treet, grieved and angered by Kopetch's recital, roused himself to declare, "He will not be content with ruling Empyrion unopposed. Jamrog means to destroy the Fieri, too. He's using us as an excuse to go after them."

"If he can find them," said Piipo.

"He'll find them," Fertig warned. "Saecaraz magicians are searching for maps in the Archives. Diltz has become very interested in the Fieri, and he is commanding the search himself. They will find what they are looking for."

"Jamrog means to destroy everything," Treet said. "And I'd say he's got a pretty good start."

"That is not our worry," snapped Tvrdy. "We have to save ourselves before we can save anyone else. Right now, that's all I care about."

The meeting was dismissed and, hands thrust into the folds of his yos, Treet stumped off across the empty compound toward Ernina's makeshift hospital to relieve the physician. He couldn't understand Tvrdy's reaction. The Tanais had acted as if Treet's simple observations were out of place, ill-considered, and unwanted. What was the matter with him anyway?

He was halfway across the compound when he heard a sound like a kettle drum and the ground vibrated beneath his feet. He stopped, looked around.

Earthquake?

He started forward, walked a few more steps, and the ground rumbled again. He turned and glanced back at the decrepit buildings round about. The creaky structures rattled and loose rubble fell, but they didn't sway or pitch forward.

Just then three Dhogs appeared, racing across the compound from the direction of the Isedon. Treet stopped them. "What is that? What's going on?"

The Dhogs, sweating, out of breath, gulped air and looked at one another fearfully. "Deathmen . . ." one of them managed to utter. "They be coming!"

"**I**nvisibles? Where?"

Another rumble, louder this time, shook the ground. The Dhogs looked down as if the earth might part and swallow them. They made ready to bolt once more.

Treet grabbed the nearest Dhog and spun him around. "Where are they?"

The man's eyes rolled in his head, and he pointed behind him. "Saecaraz—"

"The ruined duct." Treet held the man and forced him to listen. "Okay, we haven't got much time. You go find Bogney. Hear me?" The Dhog nodded, terror in his eyes. "Tell him to come here. Fast. Got it?" The man nodded again. "Go! Hurry!" The three raced off, rags aflutter.

Treet turned and hurried back to the briefing room, nearly colliding with Cejka and Piipo as they came flying out the door, their faces taut, anxious. "What is it? What's happening?" asked Cejka, indicating the Dhogs whose backs were just disappearing behind the wall of the command post.

"Invisibles," Treet explained. "They're blasting out the ruined duct from Saecaraz."

"Trabant take them," muttered Piipo.

Just then Tvrdy and Kopetch joined them, and Treet explained the situation. Tvrdy was silent for a moment, and Treet had the awful feeling that the Tanais was going to crack; but when he spoke, his tone was crisp and commanding. "Take some men and get down there," he told Kopetch. "We've got to know how much time we have. Keep monitor channel 3 open."

Another explosion rumbled the ground—this one louder, closer, more violent. The Invisibles were not wasting a second. Treet had bizarre visions of a whole squad of specialized subterranean Invisibles bursting up through the ground like oversized black mushrooms, thermal weapons blazing in their moleflipper hands.

He turned and followed the others back into the building.

● ● ● ● ● ●

They huddled over a crude map in the briefing room, staring at the place Tvrdy had marked—the exit shaft leading from the Isedon Zone to the refuse pits of Saecaraz. No one spoke, although the nervous shift of eyes around the table told all.

"We can't keep them from blasting through," Tvrdy was saying. "So I suggest we don't try. Let them come in—in fact, we let them come all the way through Isedon and then take them here—at Annerson Spike." He stabbed a finger at the map.

"They'll expect an ambush. They'll be ready," said Cejka.

"Yes, but I propose to offer them a first ambush before they reach the Isedon—a false ambush. We have men here and here," his finger moved over the map, "and we wait until the Invisibles get into position. We hit them, give them a fight, then break and run, leading them into New America Square and the real ambush." Tvrdy glanced up to see if everyone was following him.

"They'll still be very cautious—suspect a trap."

"Perhaps, but it won't matter. I talked this over with Kopetch, and he agrees. Once attacked, they'll have to give chase. They don't know where else to go. The secret lies in making the first ambush appear genuine. To do that, we'll have to make the attack quick and sharp. It must not appear that we're holding back our true strength."

"What happens to the men here?" asked Piipo, pointing to the other place Tvrdy had specified.

"They wait. Once the Invisibles have moved off in pursuit, they will destroy the entrance once again and then follow the enemy in, cutting off the retreat.

"Bogney," Tvrdy continued, "you will lead the first ambush and then lure the Invisibles in. You must be careful not to go too far ahead. We don't want to lose them or give them time to think. If they believe they can overtake you and finish you off, they will try it before regrouping and moving in." He paused. "Of course, move too slowly and they *will* overtake you and finish you off." Tvrdy glanced across the table. "Fertig will go with you."

"Dhogs knowing how to trick deathmen." Bogney's face

was set in a dirty scowl. Anger burned in his small, close-set eyes.

"Piipo, you will join Kopetch and his men at the entrance. You will be responsible for sealing the entrance once the Invisibles have moved off. Then follow them in, but at a fair distance. They must not see you or even suspect that you're there."

"How will I seal the entrance without alerting the Invisibles?"

"Wait until the first ambush starts. They won't hear you then."

"Cejka, you and I will take our positions here in the Isedon. We'll hit them from two sides at once. Bogney will circle back around and hit them on the blind side. The resulting crossfire should finish them. Any who try to flee back to the entrance will be met by Piipo."

There were nods and grunts of agreement all around. It was a good plan on short notice. Tvrdy glanced around the ring of faces. "Any questions?" No one said anything. "Then we go."

Treet felt as if he should say something, give a pep talk, remind them that the future of the planet was riding on this battle, but decided that no one needed that kind of pressure. Still, the thought nagged him.

"What about me?" he asked as the others hurried off to join their squads of men, already assembled and waiting in the compound field.

"You stay here," Tvrdy said curtly. "There's nothing for you to do now."

"I could help; I could fight."

"No." Tvrdy's face remained impassive. "Stay here."

Tvrdy's order struck Treet as bullheaded. Just because he and Tvrdy had had words moments before the blasting started, did that mean Treet couldn't fight by Tvrdy's side? "If you're still upset about what I said before, I'm sorry," said Treet. "But I think I should come with you now."

"You are not trained with these weapons," replied Tvrdy. Outside in the yard, the men moved off, their shouts of victory ringing hollow in the stale, unmoving air of the Old Section. "And I do not want anything to happen to you."

"You're using me as some kind of figurehead," said Treet. It suddenly dawned on him why Tvrdy was so insistent on protecting him. "You want me safe so I will look good on the platform when the time comes."

Tvrdy rolled up his map and stuck it in his yos. "I have to go."

"That's it, isn't it, Tvrdy? What for? I want to know." Treet stepped up to him. "Answer me."

"The people respect you," replied Tvrdy hastily. "You've seen how they watch you, look at you. They believe you know how to save them. We need this hope if we are to survive. Stay here, and let us handle this."

The Tanais hurried away. Treet picked up the radio monitor and went in search of Ernina, thinking they'd hold vigil together.

Upon arriving at the ruined exit, Kopetch had reported that the Invisibles were, by his best estimation, six to eight hours away. That had been an hour ago, Treet reflected. Figuring it would take another couple of hours for the squads to get into position, the main ambush might not take place for another three or more hours . . . plenty of time for Treet to get to the ambush site and find himself a place to hide.

He had no sooner thought of it than he was hanging back in the doorway, watching Tvrdy and Cejka lead their men off to their positions. As soon as they disappeared behind a ravaged wall at the far end of the field, Treet made his move, taking up the trail behind them.

• • • • • •

The comforting shadows of the Blue Forest lay two days' journey back. The man and cat walked in the bright daylight, uneasy in the open spaces, wary of the uncluttered distance around them. Since sunrise this morning, when they resumed their trek, they had been ascending a gradual incline, climbing the broad back of a rock shelf that lifted the earth in an easy tilt. Tan rock poked through the shelf's thin crust. Unable to hold the moisture, the soil was dry and dusty, the sparse ground cover withered white by the sun.

The huge black wevicat padded along, its sleek midnight coat gray with the dust that puffed up beneath its great paws.

Crocker, too, was covered in fine powder from crown to sole, except where sweat made muddy trails down the sides of his face and below his armpits. He still carried his spear, but used it now as a staff to help pull himself along.

They walked for hours watching the sun scale the eastern sky wall. By midmorning they had reached a rocky promontory that bulged up above the surrounding landscape; they climbed the mound and stopped there in the shade of a solitary fan tree to rest. The man squatted in the dust and sniffed the fitful breeze blowing from the east. "Water," he announced. The cat gazed at him with its lemon eyes and yawned, its big pink tongue curling backward behind jagged rows of clean white teeth.

There was not a sound to be heard except the breeze sliding over the rock and ruffling the wispy leaves at their feet. To skins used to the shadowed dampness of the forest, the naked sun felt hot and the air unnaturally dry. The man looked back at the bluish smudge of the forest in the distance, felt a tug: to return would be comfort, safety.

But the force that moved them onward was stronger. Ahead, just over the next rise, or the next, lay their destination. What would happen when they reached it?

It didn't matter. Reaching it was all that mattered.

When the sun stood directly overhead, the man rose and took up his spear again and began walking, his long legs swinging into the loose, ground-eating stride once more. The cat got up, shook itself all over, and stood motionless for a moment, sampling the wind-borne scents for anything of interest—warm-blooded or otherwise. There was water not far ahead, and something else.

The wevicat's nostrils worked the dry air and soon caught the human scent—very faint. The cat's tailtip jerked back and forth quickly as it put its head down and trotted ahead.

Their shadows had begun stretching out before them as they reached the edge of the cliff. The rock shelf ended in a series of bluffs overlooking a vast bowl of cool green water. The bluffs tumbled down onto the strand, and there, spread out upon the sand like colorful geometric flowers or grounded silken kites, lay a thousand tents, glowing in the afternoon light.

The sight filled Crocker with wonder . . . and fear. He looked at the strange, asymmetric tents—and at the people moving in and out of them—and his mind reeled. People! So many of them!

His first impulse was to run away, back to the hidden depths of the Blue Forest. But the voice in his head, which he had not heard for many, many days, came back instantly. *Stay!* the voice told him. *It's all right. They won't hurt you. Stay. Sit down. Rest. Watch them. You have come for this purpose.*

Crocker nodded to himself. "Stay," he told the cat and dropped to his knees at the cliff's edge, hugging his spear as he gazed out over the Fieri tent city. As they watched, cooking fires sprang up on the beach and smoke began drifting up the cliff face, pushed by the breeze.

The smoke was sweet scented, smelling of roast meat and savory spices that brought the water to his mouth. He leaned on his spear, licking his lips and thinking of what it would be like to taste such food. The wevicat beside him lay down on its stomach, head erect, feet stretched out in front of it, tail slapping the dust into little ridges. Together they gazed down at the scene below them, drawn to it, but held back at the same time.

The stars found them still sitting there, immobile, watching the firelight sparkle on the sand, and listening to the faint tinkling sounds of music and laughter drifting up to them from the beach. Waiting.

FIFTY FIVE

The next morning, after a long, luxurious swim, Yarden began feeling almost normal again. The day was bright, and as fresh as the breeze across the clear jade water. She ate a splendid breakfast with Ianni and some of her artist friends, then sauntered back down to the water's edge to take her place with the rest of the Fieri assembling there.

All along the strand, stretching both ways over the wide arc of the bay, Fieri settled themselves to await the coming of the talking fish. Ianni had told her that the best communication was achieved when one emptied oneself of all negative thought, all anxiety, and made oneself ready to receive the fish.

"Think only good things," Ianni instructed her. "Invite them. Ask the fish to join you, to share the joy of life with you. They respond to pure thoughts."

Yarden understood what Ianni was getting at and did not press for details. She wanted the mystery of the event to lend excitement to the wait, which Ianni warned could be several days.

Yarden dropped easily into her customary meditation pose, a modified lotus position: ankles crossed, arms resting easily on the inside of thighs, hands open, empty. She closed her eyes, emptying her mind of extraneous thought, centering herself in the moment, turning her sight inward.

The sound of waves gently lapping on the sand formed an aural background for her meditation. She pictured herself at peace, perfectly calm, a beautiful robe of glowing white, symbolizing joy, draped across her shoulders.

As she concentrated, she felt the peace she imagined flowing over her and through her, felt the calmness spreading out from the center of her being to the extremities, as if a stream of contentment ran over her, around her, through her. She drifted in its gentle waters . . . drifted . . . drifted . . .

• • • • • •

The murmur of voices roused Yarden from her meditations. She opened her eyes slowly and saw her own long shadow stretching out across the sand to the water. She realized she must have fallen asleep, for she was not aware of the passage of time. It seemed she had just closed her eyes and now opened them, feeling refreshed and at peace.

She stretched languorously and looked around. Most of the Fieri remained in attitudes of meditation, but some were on their feet staring out into the bay while others talked softly among themselves. This was the murmur she had heard. She closed her eyes again, to savor once more the sweet, drifty drowsiness, but the image of the Fieri standing, looking out over the bay intrigued her. What were they staring at?

She opened her eyes. A second later she was on her feet, too. There far out on the horizon she saw them. The fish were coming in! Yarden could see the water shimmering and breaking as the school skimmed the surface, fins slicing the sparkling water.

The westering sun glittered on their backs as they surfaced and dove, swift as torpedos, breaching and swerving, each graceful stroke multiplied by thousands. In the middle distance, Yarden could see their flashing sides dart through green-gold water. She looked down and saw that she, like all the others gathered on the shore, was striding through knee-deep surf, wading out to welcome the fish.

Yarden felt excitement ripple over her. There were shouts of joy all around her, and she added her voice to the merriment, her heart beating wildly. "Welcome!" she cried, picking up the chant from those around her. "We greet you in joy!"

The creatures slowed as they came closer, and the school separated, each fish proceeding alone to a waiting human, emitting squeaks and clicks of pure pleasure. The Fieri furthest out were met first, and the fish leaped in the water or swam circles around their human friends, who laughed and plunged after the playful animals.

Yarden laughed, too, to see the joyful play and then looked and was surprised to see one of the creatures regarding her, its head lifted out of the water, its large, clear eye watching her with bright amusement.

The animal was much larger than Yarden had anticipated, and bore a passing resemblance to the pilot whale of Earth. It had the same smooth, streamlined shape and rubbery-looking skin. But it had no dolphinian snout and sported not one, but two large dorsal fins on its powerful back. Its forebody was large, with a swelling mound atop its head over two large, disturbingly human eyes the same color as the sea.

The creature was a beautiful deep sky blue at the tips of its great dorsi and along the spine ridge of its back. The color faded gradually, however, so that its underbelly was white—it looked as if the fish had been held upside down and dipped in blue ink. The male of the species, Yarden learned later, had two brilliant parallel yellow stripes running the length of its stomach from its lower mandible to its ventral slit.

Instinctively, Yarden held out her hands, murmuring soft sounds of welcome. The fish twitched its broad, fluked tail and slid closer. Yarden lowered herself in the water and floated toward it. Her hands reached for the gleaming skin and found it warm to the touch. Warm-blooded! The animal was mammalian. She caressed the beautiful skin and said, "You're no fish; you're almost human!"

With nimble movements the creature circled her body, brushing against her, bumping her playfully, exploring her with long, jointed front flippers. Yarden dove and swam with it, holding the forward dorsal fin like she'd seen divers do in pictures. The creature swam with easy strokes of its powerful tail, propelling both of them through the water. Yarden felt the tremendous life-force of the animal engulf her, and her heart soared. She felt like a child in the great, calming presence of a wise and gentle giant.

She regained her feet in the chest-deep water and the fish swam close, nuzzling her. She put her hands on the mound of its head, and stared into the very human eye. It was a natural enough gesture, and although she knew the creatures communicated, she was unprepared for the result.

Instantly, a feeling of tremendous warmth and serenity inundated her. It was as if she had touched a live current and received a most unusual jolt. Yarden jerked back her hand, and the contact was broken.

She floated in the water and gazed at the creature wonderingly. Beneath that swelling mound of its forehead was a brain—a wonderful, intelligent, and extremely powerful brain. She reached out to the animal once more, using both hands this time and concentrating on sending a message—much as she would employ the sympathic touch—to the talking fish.

Her message was a simple greeting: *Hello, I am Yarden. I'm glad to meet you.* The words were secondary, however; the primary communication was in the emotional charge she delivered with them—welcome and acceptance.

Placing her hands on the smooth blue skin, Yarden sent her message and waited. All at once, as if rushing up through her fingertips, she felt a tingle of wonder and then excitement as the creature recognized what she had done. The excitement subsided almost as quickly as it had risen, but was replaced at once with a strange emotion, utterly alien to Yarden: a feeling of vast, boundless energy and equally expansive pleasure—an infinity of restless delight.

In a flash of understanding Yarden realized what she was sensing: the ocean! The ocean as seen through the fish's eyes. But there was more, too—a breezy, buoyant cheer combined with a sense of winsome audacity which Yarden did not understand at first.

Her puzzlement must have been communicated instantly, for the series of emotional impressions was repeated. Extraordinary! thought Yarden. It's very like the sympathic touch, only emotion-oriented rather than image-oriented.

The affect phrase was repeated yet again, and Yarden understood that the aquatic creature was giving her its name, its sense of self.

Yarden projected understanding, replaying, as far as she was able, the affect string she'd received, and was rewarded with a flourish of glee. That's what I'll call you, thought Yarden: Glee.

She concentrated for a moment, deciding how best to interpret herself for Glee, then sent an affect phrase that went: elation/hope/amity/wonder/zest and also, after a moment's hesitation, a touch of disquiet.

Glee played back understanding which was followed by a moment of fleeting uncertainty and the same disquiet—as much to say, *Why uneasy?* This was accompanied by a long, lingering, brushing stroke of a flipper against Yarden's side.

Yarden stared in disbelief. The animal was asking her about the source of the restlessness in her soul. Would it understand?

Indeed it seemed to be an extremely understanding creature. She gazed into the deep green eye closest to her and projected fear/anxiety/depression in roughly equal proportions.

Glee was silent, and Yarden thought she'd broken the delicate contact between herself and the animal by projecting a negative emotion. But Glee replied with an outpouring of sorrow and sympathy which took Yarden's breath away. It was pure empathy, powerful, undiluted by any sense of self.

Yarden, misty-eyed at the unexpected response she had received, gave back heartfelt gratitude and, in a spontaneous gesture, threw her arms around the beast and hugged, pressing her face against the warm, wet, pliant skin. Glee presented Yarden with a sensation of peace and acceptance such as Yarden had rarely felt in life.

Then, abruptly, Glee turned and swam away. The action was so sudden Yarden opened her eyes and glanced around for her friend. With more than a twinge of regret, Yarden watched the triangular blue dorsal fins racing away from her. Apparently the meeting was over.

Yarden treaded water for a moment, looking at the spot where she had last seen the fin before it disappeared beneath the easy swell. Then, feeling sand under her feet, she turned and started back to shore.

She had not gone far, however, when she heard a squeak behind her. She turned to see Glee streaking toward her, and counted three other sets of fins speeding in her wake. Yarden waited; the fish slowed as they approached. Glee nuzzled her and clicked something to the others, who came close and stroked her with their flippers.

Yarden sank down among them and caressed each one in turn, projecting welcome and acceptance. They surrounded her then, and pressed close. Glee nudged Yarden's hand and with a mewing squeak indicated that she wished Yarden to reestablish contact. Yarden placed her hand on the bulging cranial mound and received once more the affect phrase for inquiry.

Without additional prompting, Yarden understood that Glee wanted to tell the others what she'd shared with Glee. So Yarden sent the fear/anxiety/depression string while flippers continued to stroke and caress her.

The animals went still in the water, as if stunned. Then without any of them having moved a muscle, Yarden felt herself rising up out of the water. The sensation was so strong, it took a moment for Yarden to realize it was not physical; they were buoying her up emotionally. She felt as if she were riding the crests of a rolling sea as wave after wave of consolation and kindness washed over her. The tears rose up, overflowing the barriers of her eyelashes to spill down her cheeks as Yarden allowed herself to float on the ineffable charity of the wise creatures.

The emotional tide gradually subsided, and one of the newcomers rolled over on its back, showing Yarden the two parallel yellow stripes. He repeated the action twice, leading Yarden to name him Spinner. He put his head forward, and Yarden placed her hand on his cranial mound. The fish sent welcome and acceptance, and then empathy. *I understand.*

The quality of Spinner's speech, while quite similar to Glee's, was different in some respects. There were nuances of secondary emotions interlacing the primary, making his communication feel more abstract. Before Yarden could respond to the initial string, Spinner sent a complicated string which had to be repeated twice before Yarden could make sense of it. Its main component was a feeling of vast darkness and brooding menace: danger and lurking disaster.

When Yarden responded with understanding, Spinner gave the affect phrase for inquiry, repeated the danger/disaster string and added Yarden's designation of herself. Again Yarden found herself staring at the remarkable animal. Spinner had not been anywhere near when Yarden had given her self-sense to Glee; yet Spinner knew it. Perhaps the constant interplay of flippers among the whales served to link the others to the conversation, creating a communication network.

Spinner repeated the string and waited while Yarden deciphered its meaning. He seemed to be asking whether Yarden felt the same sense of impending doom, and whether the awareness of its presence was what caused her depression.

She sent puzzlement/inquiry, and Spinner backed away; he slapped the water impatiently with his flukes. When he came up under her hand, Yarden received the sensation of threat with a virulence behind it that shocked her. The threat was powerful, all-consuming, ultimate in its expression. She pulled back her hand, and Spinner raised his head from the water to look her in the eye, as if willing her to understand.

Yarden placed her hand back on his head, and he sent the grim danger/disaster string once more, adding a soft note of hope at the end. This time, Yarden experienced a completely different reaction. The hope, however subdued, seemed to overshadow the danger/disaster motif and offer the suggestion that the menace was not certain. It was real and palpable, but not inevitable, or at least not indomitable.

Spinner gazed at Yarden with his intelligent green eyes, and slowly his meaning became clear. With a clarity that chilled her, Yarden understood what Spinner was trying to communicate to her: Dome.

Spinner's triple barrel roll in the water let her know she was right.

Dome was on the move. Treet's prophecy was coming true.

FIFTY
SIX

*T*reet lay inside a piece of old fibersteel pipe, part of a smokestack, no doubt, now nearly buried behind a collapsed bank of permastone bricks which formed a slope down to the broad plain of the Isedon below. It was a good vantage point and safe; the fibersteel formed a turret around him and the permastone a bulwark.

Safe and sturdy it might be, but comfortable it wasn't. He had spent the night in the pipe, dozing fitfully, waking at intervals to listen and look out on the night-dark plain. Now, as dawn tinted the filthy scales of the Old Section's translucent roof a sickly yellow, there was still no sign of the invaders, and Treet had begun to think that perhaps the invasion had been canceled. The blasting had stopped hours ago, and there was no indication of movement around the ruined duct.

If the ambush went according to plan, however, it would be a massacre. The Invisibles would be surrounded in the open to be picked off at will by the hidden rebels. The site was well chosen from that perspective; Tvrdy had shown his genius once again. Treet found himself feeling a little sorry for the hapless Invisibles.

The radio monitor lay at his feet; he had brought it with him so he could hear any communication between Kopetch and Tvrdy. He surveyed the battlefield. It was roughly rectangular, the burned out shells of buildings forming the sides of the rectangle, which was open at the back end where the Invisibles would enter. At the far end, two big mounds of rock and debris formed the fourth side; the faces of these mounds were covered with straggling bushes and wispy thin trees. It was behind these and in the rubble at the foot of the mounds that Cejka and Tvrdy waited with their men. Treet could not see any trace of them, which was good. They were well hidden.

Treet yawned and rose to stretch himself; he did a few torso twists, windmills, and overhead arm pulls to loosen the kinks. He was in his fifth deep knee bend when there came a muffled rumble in the distance. He stopped to listen, and a few seconds later the monitor at his feet whispered with Kopetch's voice: "The duct is open."

Treet imagined Invisibles boiling up out of a still-smoking hole in the ground, blasters between their teeth. He waited, holding his breath, listening for the far-off sound of battle. But he was too far away. He slumped back down into his turret to wait, balancing the monitor on his knees, but the box remained silent. Most likely, Kopetch and the others were too busy to report. At any rate, it wouldn't take long. Even now the Dhogs were probably attacking the first of the Invisibles.

God help them, he thought—and then wondered if praying for an enemy's death was kosher. He amended his prayer to, God help us all.

The ambush began sooner than expected. Treet was sitting in his foxhole wondering how long it would take for the Dhogs to reach them when he heard the sound of thermal weapons echoing from across the Isedon.

He raised his head to look down upon the battlefield and saw Dhogs already running into the rectangle. They scattered as they came in, spreading out and heading for the nearest cover. At first Treet thought their actions very convincing. Too convincing. Something about the way they were running—headlong, flat-out, without looking back—let him know that something was wrong.

The first wave of Dhogs had entered the Isedon, a squad of Invisibles hot on their heels. Where were the rest? There should have been more Dhogs—at least twice as many.

Then he saw the reason for the Dhogs' severely decreased number. Clattering slowly onto the battlefield came a large, heavily armored em, spitting lightning from at least four ports as Invisibles crouched and dodged around it, laying down a blanket of deadly fire.

A tank! The infernal Invisibles have a tank!

Treet's heart sank to the pit of his stomach. We're going to lose, he thought. There's no way we can fight a tank. They've already cut down half of Bogney's squad—they'll wipe out the rest of us just as quick.

Why was there no warning? Could it be that Kopetch and Piipo had been killed before they could send the alarm?

As Treet looked on, horror-stricken, the improvised tank moved into position in the center of the battlefield and began unleashing its terrible firepower. Bolt after bolt of blue lightning streaked from its ports, screaming through the air to shatter the mountains of debris. Cejka's men are down there, he thought desperately; they're getting murdered!

The Dhogs began fighting back tentatively. But each time someone managed to get off a good shot, the tank retaliated and took the sniper out.

Where was Tvrdy? How could he stand by and watch the slaughter? Why didn't he do something?

If only I had a weapon, Treet thought. I'd . . . I don't know what I'd do, but I wouldn't sit here and wait for them to blast me to smoldering jelly. Somebody's got to do something!

His palms were wet; he glanced at his hands to see blood weltering up where his fingernails had dug into the soft flesh. Help us! Please, God! Help us now if You're ever going to!

Under the scream of the thermal weapons, Treet heard a low droning noise. Glancing at the far end of the battlefield, he saw another tank lumber into view, and behind it another and yet another. Four tanks! And each with a contingent of Invisibles hovering around it.

We're lost! he thought. They have us outmanned and outgunned. We've had it!

As the last tank came in, the others rolled forward, spreading out across the field, each taking a quadrant to scour.

In a few minutes it would be all over. There was nothing left to do now but roll over and die.

Why didn't Tvrdy act?

What could he, Treet, do? The Tanais Director was pinned down with enemy fire bursting over his head. If Treet showed himself now, it would be swift and certain death. But someone had better do something, and quickly. The Invisibles would have the whole battlefield secured in a matter of minutes. The only resistance came from the few Dhogs still foolish enough to risk popping off at one of the tanks.

But soon enough even that activity ceased. The Invisibles kept firing for a few seconds and then, seeing no further resistance, stopped. A stifling silence claimed the battlefield. The air stank of ozone and hot metal.

Treet peered from his perch. Could it be over? So soon?

The Invisibles began moving out across the field toward the mounds of debris where the Dhogs had hidden. They searched the still-smoking rubble, pulling bodies out. The corpses were lined up out in the open where, lest there be any doubt, they were scorched once more for good measure.

The stupid, sadistic scum! Treet's clenched fists pounded his thighs. Where was Tvrdy?

• • • • • •

Yarden sat cross-legged on the sand, hands resting on knees, palms upward in the classic meditation pose. She had disciplined herself to sit this way for hours at a time, without making the slightest movement, without breaking concentration. She had spent most of the flight to Empyrion in her cabin aboard the *Zephyros* in just this way: sitting immobile while her mind practiced the exercises of the sympathic art, keeping the pathways open, the process sharp.

Now, here on a different world beneath a different sun, she sat facing the dark green water as the foaming surf flung itself upon the shore before her. She had been sitting this way through the night, and now dawn broke the gloom in the east, stripping night from the horizon and peeling it back to reveal a new day.

Yarden had spent the night thinking, praying, searching for answers inside herself. There was so much to think about, to sort out, to find answers for. The familiar posture of meditation comforted her, made her feel as if she was in control once more—although, as she well knew, her life was out of control, careening for a crash.

So she sat out on the beach under the alien stars, examining the pattern of her life in the hope of finding the clues to unravel the mystery of what had gone wrong.

Before coming on this journey, she was happy, her life in Fierra full; she'd had definite plans and the sense of a future bright with promise. Somewhere along the way, however, that changed. She couldn't pinpoint the exact place or time, but she felt the effects acutely. Things had just generally fallen apart— apparently without any particular turning-point or major catastrophe. One day she was happily sketching away, developing her burgeoning artistic skills; the next day she was stumbling through ashes.

She lost sight of the bright future; her happiness leaked

away like a rare gas through the sides of a porous container. As the weeks of the journey went by, Yarden felt her grip on her life slipping, and it had slipped so far that she now no longer knew which way to turn, where to go, what to do.

That was bad enough. But worse, she could not shake the feeling that her life had become inextricably bound up with the person of Orion Treet.

It was a mystery to her how a human being could, in his absence, dominate life more completely than he ever had with his presence. Even the talking fish seemed to be talking about him—or, to be a little more accurate, talking about the same things he was talking about, which was disturbing enough in itself.

Everywhere she turned: Treet. And again: Treet.

Did she love him?

It was more than that, of course. Her anxiety and confusion were not merely the result of an inability to make up her mind whether she loved the lout or not. The roots of her dilemma went deeper. Far deeper.

As she sat there, hour upon hour, the sound of the wind-driven rollers droning in her ears, she patiently sifted the tangled thoughts and feelings that had brought her to this brink. And she began to feel as if Pizzle's remark last evening might have hit closer to the mark than she at first suspected.

She had sought out Pizzle to tell him about her experience with the fishes earlier in the day—about the warning. She found him walking along the strand at sunset, arm in arm with Starla. They walked together for a while—awkward in each other's company, Yarden feeling her intrusion with every step—until Starla excused herself and returned to camp.

After Pizzle got over being miffed at Yarden for butting in, they had a good talk. They walked along the beach, and as the lowering sun touched the water and turned it to quicksilver, Pizzle told her about his experience with the talking fish. "It was kinda weird," he said. "At first I didn't get anything from them—just a sort of lift, you know? Just being in the water with them is a blast. They're beautiful animals—a lot like those pilot whales back on Earth. Anyway, after a while I started to get something; I could tell the fish was trying to tell me something."

"Anything in particular?" asked Yarden.

Pizzle lifted his shoulders slightly. "Beats me. All I got was a warm feeling and . . . how should I say this?—a feeling of real peace and contentment. They seem to be happy creatures all right, no doubt about that."

Yarden told him what she discovered about how to talk to the fish and then, out of the blue, Pizzle asked her what was bugging her.

"What makes you say that?" she asked.

"You never want to talk to me unless something's bugging you. We're not the closest of buddies, you know. Besides, you've been chewing your lip like it's beef jerky. I figure something must be worrying you."

"I don't know what's wrong with me," she'd told him. "Honestly, I don't. I can't seem to get in sync—everything's off kilter somehow. I don't know what it is . . .

"I feel drawn and chased at the same time," she concluded.

"Then stop running," he'd said.

Stop running.

How? She wasn't even aware that she *was* running.

"The Seeker won't rest until all men know Him," Pizzle had said. "That's what Anthon tells me."

Now, as she sat watching night loosen its hold on the land, those words came back: the Seeker won't rest . . .

Fine, but didn't I *welcome* the chance to learn about You? she demanded of the Infinite. Didn't I do my best to learn, to understand? What else is there? What do You want from me? What more could You possibly want?

Stop running.

Am I running? What am I running from?

Surrender.

What an old-fashioned word: surrender. Giving up, giving in, giving yourself to another. Relinquishing control.

Yarden bristled at the notion. Ah, there was the rub. I feel drawn and chased at the same time, she thought. Drawn by a presence she did not want to give in to—so she ran. And she was pursued.

Now that same probing presence drew near once more. The Infinite . . . the Seeker. She could run, push the presence aside, and run. Or she could simply sit there, wait—whatever would happen, let it happen.

Something inside her did not want to let it happen. There was a knotty lump of defiance within her, born of equal parts fear and self-will. She'd gotten where she was in life by feeding this defiance. Would I have survived without it? Would I have gotten anywhere by giving in?

Look where it's got you, Yarden. Look at you. You're falling apart. You're sitting out on a damp, drafty beach all night mumbling to yourself. You don't know what you want or where to go. You're lost. You've lost control, because this is something that can't be controlled by you.

Your sympathic abilities are the most important thing in your life, yet they have never brought you a moment's happiness. Ever wonder why? Why? Weren't they just another way to control things around you?

Control, Yarden. That's what this is about. What do you fear most? Losing control. But tell me, who is in control now?

FIFTY SEVEN

Tell me, who is in control?

Yarden heard herself asking the question. It was her voice, the voice of her conscience, and yet it wasn't

I am in control! she answered, and instantly felt shame wash over her in waves.

You see? Your heart knows better. Yarden, surrender.

Again, the old-fashioned word. *Surrender.*

What will I get if I surrender to You? she demanded.

Something you don't have now: peace.

Peace. Yes, that would be worth having. To shed the weight of her imperfectly borne burdens and walk away, rest, find sanctuary. But could she trust the Seeker, this Infinite so intent on winning her? Could she trust the Seeker not to crush her, not to leech away her personality and make her a drab, unthinking zombie?

Yarden, the voice chided, wake up and look around. What do you see? Are My people unthinking zombies? Are they crushed by their devotion to Me?

I am the Infinite, Yarden. I have taken infinite pains to make you who you are. Why would I now destroy what I have made? To prove a point that doesn't need proving?

You run because you fear losing yourself, losing control. Yet I tell you that you are already lost, and that the control you thought you had was just an illusion. You are just now discovering this because you have hidden the truth so well for so long. But you see the truth now, and it scares you.

Control is very important to you. But can you now see that striving after it has given you more pain than pleasure all your life? Your desire for control has thwarted you most often when you were closest to giving in to better things.

This is why you could not love Orion Treet. He had the audacity to suggest that you love him as he was. But you demanded that love should be on your terms or not at all. You gave him an ultimatum that he rejected; so you rejected him. He was a threat to you because you could not control him.

Was? Is he no longer a threat? she wondered.

We are talking about *you*, Yarden, not Treet. It is you I want now, at this moment. The choice is yours.

What choice do I have? Her inner voice was shrill, near breaking.

You can always remain as you are.

How can I? Yarden fired back. You have given me a taste of what it's like and now demand I choose. I'm not ready. I need more time.

Listen to yourself, Yarden. *A taste of what it's like* . . . First you say you fear I'll crush you, then you admit you've had a taste and want more. Yes, you tasted and found it good. Why do you hesitate? Do you think you will learn more by waiting, that the decision will become more clear? I tell you no. No. You have been given everything you need to decide. You have even been given the taste you asked for.

That I asked for? When did I ever ask for it?

Think for a moment. Who was it that pleaded to become an artist?

Artist? What's my becoming an artist have to do with this?

You yearn for truth, and burn to create beauty. Then why do you resist the source of all truth and beauty, the One who has given you your heart's desire?

There was no answer to that.

Come to Me, Yarden. Give Me the gift of yourself, and I will give you a gift far greater than you can imagine. Yarden, trust Me and believe.

All eternity vibrated in that moment. Yarden imagined that time had stopped and would remain stopped until she answered. The stars, the sea, the wind, the blood coursing through her veins—everything would wait, frozen in that instant, while she decided.

Yes, I'll trust You, she thought. *Yes!*

She expected something then. A sign of divine approval, a rush of emotion—a response of some kind. But there was only the sound of waves on sand, the breeze blowing gently, the first rays of sunlight tinting the horizon, and the sound of her own heart beating in her ears.

It is done, she thought. It's over. The running is over.

There was relief in the thought. Yarden slumped, allowing her muscles to move now; she brought her hands to her neck and rubbed gently. She rose, coming out of her trance position like a flower unfolding itself slowly.

For a moment she stood looking out across the dawn-lit water, molten green in the faint morning light—seeing it for the first time, although she'd stared at it all through the night without noticing it at all—then yawned and stretched, feeling tired and a little lumber-headed from lack of sleep. But there was something else, too—a warm place deep down inside, small but spreading outward; she was at peace within herself.

Smiling to herself, she turned and started back along the water's edge toward the Fieri camp. She had not gone more than a few steps when she saw, far off on the strand, approaching her from the direction of the line of cliffs opposite, a figure—no, two: a man and the dark, fluid shape of a wevicat walking beside him. The ghostly figures emerged out of night's quickly fading gloom.

Strange. Who would be awake at this time of the morning for a stroll? There were no wevicats in camp. Who could it be?

Yarden continued walking, and the figures drew nearer. The man appeared naked, except for a loin pouch, and carried a long staff. The cat loped easily along, stopping now and then to pounce on a wave or roll in the surf, playing in the water.

Closer now, there was something familiar about the figure. Something she recognized, but could not place. Her pulse beat faster. What? Who was it? She quickened her pace.

Closer.

No! Oh, no! It can't be.

She froze in midstride, her hands flying to her face. No! Dear God, no!

But it was.

Crocker!

• • • • • •

The Invisibles, satisfied that the Dhogs had been exterminated, now began disengaging. The tanks backed away slowly as the men on foot fell in behind, weapons at the ready, wary.

They're getting away! Black rage bubbled up like scalding pitch inside Treet as he watched the enemy retreating without so much as a single singed uniform.

Futile tears stung his eyes. It was over. The Invisibles had won. Now they would scour the Old Section, searching out all the hiding places, executing the survivors by twos, by tens, by hundreds. And nothing, nothing would stop them.

Even as these hopeless thoughts filled his mind, Treet felt the inner presence stir. Once again he felt the uncanny assurance, the strange peace that had no objective source. The despair thickening around him dissipated. The fear and frustration melted away.

He looked out on the battlefield through hanging streamers of smoke. The first of the tanks had reached the narrow entrance to the field and was turning to move into the Old Section. But as the death-dealing machine swung around, it appeared to raise slowly off the ground on a puff of gray smoke.

The levitating tank then proceeded to fly to pieces as the explosion ripped its undercarriage to slivers, scattering jagged chunks of metal in a lethal rain. The roar reached Treet a split second later as Invisibles, blown backward by the blast, tumbled loose-jointed through the fire-drenched air. Others nearby were cut to ribbons by flying shrapnel.

The two middle tanks halted at once, but the tank at the rear of the procession ground ahead, faltered, and tried to reverse. Too late. The second explosion took off its front half in a shearing sheet of red flame which billowed out of its ports. The Invisibles crouched behind the tank dropped dead to the ground, felled by the heat wave of the explosion.

Before the two center tanks could back away from the scene, however, rebels appeared from out of nowhere. A shout went up across the battlefield, and Tvrdy's squad swooped down upon the two stalled vehicles. The Invisibles, pinched between the burning wrecks of two tanks, scattered to the mound of debris behind them, where they were mowed down before they knew what had happened.

Cejka was simply not there one moment, and very much there the next—along with a squad brandishing flame-sprouting weapons.

The Invisibles wilted before the onslaught. The tanks made feeble efforts to turn the battle once again, but the attackers were too close and the clumsy vehicles were easily outmaneuvered.

The battle was over in a moment. Treet stared at the carnage, feeling numb and empty. The ferocity of the fight, the concentrated violence had deadened his senses, even as the booming shock of the explosions had stunned his eardrums.

It is over. I should feel relieved, happy, he told himself. We won.

But there was no joy in the victory. It had cost too much. Treet climbed from his bunker and began picking his way down to the battlefield to join Tvrdy and the others. He was halfway across the field when he saw men flying into the rectangle from the direction of the duct. Kopetch, Piipo, and their men reached the place where Tvrdy, Cejka, Fertig, and Bogney, who had somehow managed to come through the battle unscathed, waited amidst the wreckage. As Treet came up, he heard Kopetch saying breathlessly, ". . . too many . . . couldn't hold them . . ."

"The duct?" asked Tvrdy. He gave Treet a frown of reproach, but didn't say anything. His mind was on other matters.

"Still open," replied Piipo. "Couldn't seal it. We tried . . ."

Tvrdy cursed and began shouting orders. But before anyone could move, they heard again the menacing grumble of a heavy machine approaching from the direction of the duct.

"We can't stay here," said Tvrdy. "Too risky. We'll have to make them chase us and try to take them on the run." He shouted an order and they all started off, but not before the Dhogs finished separating a few of the dead Invisibles from their weapons.

FIFTY
EIGHT

Yarden stared in disbelief at the man who had once been Crocker.

The former pilot leaned on his spear, gazing at Yarden with an odd expression, innocent and wary at the same time. The great black wevicat sat on its haunches, licking sand from a huge paw, regarding the woman with keen disinterest.

Her hands fluttered as she reached out toward him. "Crocker?"

The man did not acknowledge the name, but merely gazed back with a vacant, animal look in his eyes.

She took a step toward him. The cat's head snapped up; its lips curled back. She hesitated. "Crocker," she said, trying to control her voice, "it's me, Yarden. Remember me? Yarden . . . your friend."

He raised his hand and began scratching his stomach.

Tears misted Yarden's eyes. "Oh, Crocker . . . what's happened to you? What . . . ?" Just then the implications of what she was seeing detonated in Yarden's cerebral cortex, sending shock waves through her central nervous system. Her knees went spongy, and the horizon tilted wildly.

"Oh, no . . . Crocker—tell me what happened. Where's Treet? Where's Calin? Crocker? What happened? Can you talk?" Ignoring the cat's low growl, she stepped up to the man and put her hand to his face. Tears streaming from her eyes, she said, "Crocker, can you hear me? Can you speak? Oh, please, say something."

The man stared dumbly at her. She bowed her head, and the tears fell into the wet sand.

They stood that way for some time before Yarden drew a sleeve across her eyes, sniffed, and said, "Come on, I'm taking you back to camp. I'm going to get you some help." She put her hand on his arm. He did not resist and allowed her to lead him away. The cat watched them depart and then moved off along the strand.

• • • • •

Jaire awoke from a disturbed sleep. She glanced around her room as if she might find the source of her disquiet in its shadowed corners. She rose and went to the curtain, then drew it aside to stand gazing out over the dark water of Prindahl.

The dream was still fresh: black, malformed shapes boiling in the seething darkness; in the center, standing in a shaft of white light, pinioned there, stood Orion Treet, his hands upraised in an attitude of prayer or supplication . . . or defeat. And then, with a terrible ripping sound, the light went out and Treet was swallowed by the roiling darkness.

That was all. But the image carried with it an emotional charge, a feeling that persisted even though the dream had ended: futility, hovering doom, despair.

Jaire shivered in the predawn light and, drawing a robe around her shoulders, hurried off to find her father.

Talus, pulled from his bed by his daughter's quiet touch and the intense, worried expression on her face, listened as she related her disturbing dream. They sat in the jungled courtyard of the great house Liamoge, drinking herbal tea as pearly daylight slowly claimed the sky.

When he had heard the dream, Talus said, "I see why you awakened me, Jaire. It is a most distressing sign." His voice rumbled in the empty courtyard like small thunder.

"You think it is a sign?"

His eyebrows went up. "Oh, yes. The Protector is trying to warn us. The dream is a warning."

"I agree," said Jaire, then looked puzzled. "But what am I to do about it?"

"That is for us to discover."

"If Orion is in trouble, we must help him."

She spoke with such conviction, her father looked at her closely. "You have a feeling for the Traveler."

Jaire smiled briefly. "I always have."

Talus nodded absently. "Well, we must consult Mathiax first thing. As acting Preceptor, he may have some suggestions. He will want to be informed in any case."

Jaire rose. "I am ready."

Talus smiled as he climbed to his feet. "We can wait until the sun is risen, I think." He hugged his daughter and planted a kiss on the crown of her head. "Don't worry. We will have the time we need."

FIFTY
NINE

Mentor Mathiax nodded gravely as Jaire told her dream. When she had finished, he said simply, "I knew something like this would happen."

"The dream?" asked Jaire.

He glanced up, held her eyes with his for a moment, smiled faintly. "The dream? Yes, I suppose—although I wasn't certain what form the warning would take."

Talus spoke up. "Then you consider it a warning, too?"

"Definitely," he agreed. "A warning. What else?"

"We have to do something," said Jaire. "We have to help him."

"Oh, yes, I agree," said Mathiax. "What to do—that is the question. Helping him may not be easy."

"Was returning to Dome easy for him?" snapped Jaire.

"No, no, child," soothed Mathiax. "I only meant that given our vow of peace, we may be limited in the kind of help we can offer."

"You are Preceptor. You could send help. Authorize—"

"Acting Preceptor, if you please." He smiled as he shook his head. "I do not have such authority. Even the Preceptor herself does not have that power. The question will have to go before the College of Mentors."

Jaire jumped from her chair. "That will take too long! We must act at once!"

"We will certainly do what we can." Mathiax looked thoughtful. "Leave the matter with me." He rose and took Jaire's hand in both of his. "I know you care for the Traveler. Can you believe that I care as much?"

• • • • • •

Since Osmas' most timely demise, Diltz had proceeded with his plans unhindered. Jamrog began to think he'd found the perfect subordinate in the sly Nilokerus Director—smarter than the dull, officious Hladik, stronger than the weak-willed Osmas, more pliable than the inflexible Mrukk. Each had had their uses, to be sure, but the power-hungry Diltz was a tool made for Jamrog's hand.

The attribute that made him most attractive to the Supreme Director was that Diltz seemed to anticipate his moods and thoughts. Removing Osmas, for example, at the precise moment the worm had outlived his usefulness—and without the slightest hint having been dropped—what more could a leader want?

Diltz's rise to prominence had not gone unnoticed, however. Mrukk—busy putting down the rebellion, as well as overseeing Jamrog's massive reorientation campaign—still found time to keep himself apprised of the happenings in the Supreme Director's kraam. He had marked Diltz from the beginning as a quietly devious, ambitious schemer whose loyalties could be bought by the highest bidder, and was not at all surprised when Osmas' bloodless body was fished out of Kyan lacking a throat.

Mrukk entered Jamrog's kraam now and paused in the vestibule, looking out over the polished floor. Jamrog's torches—a foolish affectation from some imagined past—burned in their wall sockets, casting more shadow than light, Mrukk thought, making the kraam seem alive with insubstantial movement, as if the oversouls of dead Directors flickered among the potted greenery and hovered around the black-and-silver Bolbe wall hangings.

And there was Diltz, practically lying on the Supreme Director, leaning over him as he presented a much creased map for Jamrog's inspection, his nasal voice crooning as he described some feature there. Mrukk grimaced to see Jamrog's expression: gloating, greedy, self-satisfied, and arrogant, eyes narrowed in smug contemplation of his latest conquest.

Mrukk knew what that was: Fierra.

Mrukk had heard the reports. The devious Nilokerus had apparently discovered the fabled city of the Fieri. Out there across a near endless expanse of white nothing lay a deep lake; beside the lake was the city of their ancient enemy.

It was not proven, of course. Not yet. But Diltz had exploration teams searching outside Empyrion, while Nilokerus and Saecaraz magicians searched the Archives. This latest map had come from the Archives—from some captured Fieri artifacts. Saecaraz readers had authenticated the find. The map was genuine, if old.

Mrukk stepped from the entryway and proceeded silently across the floor to the throne. Neither of the others looked up until he was practically upon them. How easy it would be, thought Mrukk. The fools! I could have their still-beating hearts in my hand before they could open their mouths to scream.

"Mrukk!" said Jamrog, glancing up as the Mors Ultima commander came to stand before him. Diltz did not raise his head from the map. Mrukk noted the slight and filed it away for future reference. "We are to be congratulated."

"How so, Supreme Director?" Mrukk kept his tone civil, but flat.

Diltz grinned, stretching the flesh of his lips across his teeth. His head came up slowly and he said, "The Fieri, at long last, are ours."

"Are they indeed?"

"Of course," explained Jamrog. "We must dispatch an expeditionary force at once—as soon as the weapons are ready."

"You are speaking of the old weapons found in the Archives, I assume," said Mrukk.

"Yes, what about them?" Diltz's ghastly grin faded.

"I would have thought the problem obvious to a man of your intellect, Diltz."

The cadaverous Nilokerus stiffened. "I am a Director. My stent is higher than yours. You will address me as your superior."

Now it was Mrukk's turn to grin. He'd pricked the rancorous parasite where it hurt. "As you say," replied Mrukk placidly.

Jamrog chose not to notice the sparring between the two and said, "Well, mighty Mrukk, are you going to tell us? What's wrong with the old weapons?"

"They are dangerous, unstable. They will not work."

"Oh? The magicians say they will. They all agree."

"Then they are blind as well as ignorant."

"What do you know?" snapped Diltz. "You can't even subdue a handful of malcontents."

"Perhaps our leader would not dismiss them so lightly." Mrukk inclined his head toward Jamrog.

"*Dangerous* malcontents," corrected the Supreme Director,

who still felt the sting of his burns. "Still, I remain unimpressed with your success thus far, Commander. I had hoped for more immediate results."

"Which is why I have come, Supreme Director—to inform you personally that after two days of brisk fighting, we have the entrance to the Old Section secured and supply lines in place. The Dhogs have been forced to retreat."

"But they are not yet exterminated," sneered Diltz.

"Not yet," replied Mrukk. "But soon. Very soon"

"Yes, yes, of course." Jamrog yawned. "In the meantime, you will increase the interrogations. The Saecaraz and Nilokerus are to be spared no longer. I have reason to believe the treason has spread even into our own Hages. It must stop. We must eradicate all opposition." He glanced at Diltz, and Mrukk saw the look that passed between them. "If you will excuse us, Mrukk, we were in the middle of planning the attack on Fierra."

Diltz produced his grotesque smile once again and went back to his map. Mrukk offered the Mors Ultima salute, fist over heart, then backed away from the throne, turned on his heel, and walked quickly from the room.

"He resents me," murmured Diltz when Mrukk had gone. "I believe he disapproves of my success."

Jamrog sniffed. "Mrukk resents everyone and disapproves of everything—a quality I am beginning to find very annoying." He looked at the place where Mrukk had been standing. He tapped his teeth with the tip of his bhuj. "He may be taking himself too seriously of late. A very bad habit, don't you agree?"

Diltz smiled and nodded.

"Now then, where were we?" asked Jamrog.

"Fierra," replied the Nilokerus. He pointed to the map. "We were planning its destruction."

SIXTY

The breached air duct from the Saecaraz refuse pits had been secured by the Invisibles, as Kopetch reported. They had quickly fortified the position and now guarded it with a vengeance, affording themselves a small base of operations and a vital supply link with the Hage. There was nothing the rebels could do to staunch the hated flow of men, weapons, and equipment into the Old Section.

What was worse, the Invisibles did not wait to consolidate their position, but pressed forward immediately, putting the rebels on the run and forcing them to fight a moving battle. The rebels fought viciously, exacting a heavy toll in every confrontation, but still came away a little weaker each time.

The Invisibles pressed them relentlessly back and back, giving them no time to rest or regroup. At the end of the second day, the rebels were forced to abandoned the Isedon. They retreated into the Old Section's maze of ancient ruins to reorganize themselves to fight a defensive war.

Treet, ordered back to the command compound early in the struggle, watched as the exhausted fighters returned, defeat rounding their shoulders and bending their backs. He and Ernina had prepared food, and he took it to the briefing room. While the captains assembled, Treet served them and hoped the hot food would revive their spirits.

"It's bad," said Tvrdy, rousing himself after his meal. He stood and began to pace slowly in front of the others. "I won't try to tell you otherwise. In losing the duct, we've lost our best advantage. They can now strengthen themselves at will, while we can only grow weaker."

"We have already lost half our ready force. It will take weeks to get more men trained," said Kopetch. "Even then, we're grossly outmanned. Dhogs against Invisibles! We don't stand a chance."

Bogney, his hair a matted and sweaty cap plastered to his skull, frowned mightily. "Let them come. Bogney don't care. Dhogs taking care of our own."

Yes, but who takes care of the rest of Dome? wondered Treet.

The thought caused Treet to reflect on just how much of an outsider he was: the war, his war, was proceeding without him; Dome's inhabitants regarded him as either an enemy of the state, or some sort of demigod, or a propaganda tool to be applied sparingly.

He merely floated around observing events as they unfolded—which was, after all, just what he'd spent the last thirty years of his life doing. Apparently, that's what he did best: talent will out.

However, he had returned to Dome not to be a spectator, not to hover at the fringes of life with notebook in hand, not to observe dispassionately the tilt and sway of power's precarious balance. He had returned specifically to prevent Apocalypse II.

Instead, it was beginning to look suspiciously like he'd caused it.

Treet hadn't thought about it before, but his presence had somehow focused the irrational forces of Dome, thereby bringing about the current state of affairs. Now, not only were they no closer to derailing Jamrog's death machine, but it seemed as if they would soon be ground beneath its wheels.

Perhaps, he reflected, the Fieri were right—the laissez-faire approach was best. What a time for second-guessing. Now, as the tramp of enemy feet could be heard in the empty corridors of the Old Section, and enemy weapons spilled the blood of brave, foolish rebels . . .

But no. It was a trap to think that way.

The rebellion would have begun without him—did, in fact. Jamrog did not come to power through any action of Treet's. The sides were chosen long ago, and he had nothing to do with it. Ah, but whether Jamrog would have turned his cold eye toward the Fieri . . . that was another question. One that Treet could not so easily lay aside.

Treet looked at the leaders huddled together in the room, then at Tvrdy—haggard, fatigue sitting heavily on his shoulders, dark hair showing gray—and he remembered the Tanais saying to him, *Your presence here among us is a catalyst for action.*

That's me, thought Treet, the ever-faithful catalyst. Doom and destruction at your service. Treet's the name, Armageddon's the game. Have notebook; will travel.

What am I doing here? What is my purpose? Why me anyway?

"We can hold out two, perhaps three months—*if* we do not allow the Invisibles to come this far into the Old Section."

"How do we keep them out?" wondered Piipo.

"We keep them going around in circles. We make them chase us, and make certain that we stay well away from here."

"And in the meantime?" asked Cejka.

"In the meantime, we try to find a way to close the air duct. There must be a way."

"If there isn't?"

"We be fighting face to face," grumbled Bogney.

"No, we cannot afford to do that. Even when we win, we lose too much. They would eventually pare us down to nothing. They could win the war while losing every single battle."

"Without a way to close that duct," said Kopetch, "it doesn't matter what we do. They'll just keep coming at us until we can't hold them off anymore."

Fertig, the former Nilokerus Subdirector, spoke up. "Now that they know about this entrance, they'll do everything in their power to keep it open."

"He's right," added Piipo. "Even if we somehow managed to close it, they would open it again. We'd be helpless to prevent it."

Treet listened to the tension in the voices and heard the fear creeping in. It was as if an unseen hand had closed around the group and was slowly crushing out what little hope they were able to generate. He could feel the futility spreading, and looked to Tvrdy to see his reaction. Tvrdy stood before them exhausted, drained, his features blank.

He can't stop it this time, thought Treet.

The same instant he felt his face grow hot and a prickling sensation over his scalp. The presence was stirring within him again. Then he was on his feet.

"Listen to yourselves," he said quietly. The others turned, and Treet looked at their faces as if seeing them for the first time. They all looked so helpless he wanted to cry for them.

"There is fear in this room. You feel it growing," he continued, talking quietly. "You think it is fear of Jamrog, of losing against him, of death, but you're wrong."

Cejka started to object, but Treet silenced him with an

upraised palm. "What you feel comes from a different source—
It is from the source of darkness itself. It is the fear your own
ancestors felt, that crippled them and then stripped them of
their humanity. It is the ancient mindless fear that paralyzes and
consumes, that destroys first the will and then the heart."

All were silent, watching him intently.

"Listen to me!" His words, spoken earnestly, were a shout
in the room. "You think to pull down a dictator to save your
Hagemen, but the danger is greater than you suspect. We have a
world to save."

"A world," scoffed Cejka. "Right now I'd settle for saving
the Old Section."

Treet turned on him. "Do you doubt me? Jamrog does not
fear us. He believes it's only a matter of time before he catches
us. He believes that no one inside Empyrion can pose a serious
threat to his rule. At best, we are but a minor annoyance to
him."

There were mutters of agreement. "But what about outside?" Treet gestured beyond the walls to the greater world
beyond the dim crystal panels of Dome. "What about out there
across the great blight of desert? What about the Fieri?"

The others looked at Treet strangely, but said nothing.
"Don't you see it? Jamrog fears the Fieri. And what he fears, he
destroys.

"Kopetch told us, remember? Right now Jamrog has Saecaraz magicians ransacking the Archives, searching for information and weapons—the atomic weapons of old. He will find
them and rebuild them. He will send out search parties to find
Fierra, and they will find it . . . and then he will strike.

"He will plunge this world into another cycle of agony and
death that will last thousands of years."

Treet's voice had risen steadily as he spoke. He stopped so
abruptly, his words still rang in the air. The others watched him
warily, as if any moment he too might explode.

Treet continued more quietly. "We must not give in to the
fear. Our position is far from hopeless. The future of Empyrion
depends on us. We can rebuild. We can overcome; we must. We
can fight Jamrog, and we can win."

Seeing that no great upsurge of confidence met his words,
he pressed on. "Listen, the great battles of history have always
been won by shrewd generals who used their advantages, few or

many, while neutralizing their enemy's, advantages or even turning them into disadvantages. So what advantages do we possess?"

"None," murmured Kopetch.

"All right, I'll rephrase the question. What advantages do the Invisibles have? Greater numbers, superior firepower, better training, and supplies. Yes?" What else did an army need? Ooh, this was going to be tough—but not impossible. Individually, none of those advantages were insurmountable.

"Greater numbers? Under the superb leadership of Leonidas, a handful of Spartans held off the entire Persian army, the greatest fighting machine Earth had ever seen, in the Battle of Thermopylae in 480 B.C.

"Superior firepower? Fragile British Spitfires scrambled to meet the might of the terrible German Luftwaffe in the skies over England, not only once, but time and time again, until the German airforce gave up.

"Better training and supplies? A ragtag army of Afghan mountain tribesmen made do with antique rifles and pitchforks to outflank the best military minds of the vastly superior Soviets and bring the Red Giant to its knees.

"Don't you see? There is always a way." He looked around the room at the uncomprehending stares. "All we have to do is find it. We can't give up until we do."

In the hush that followed his words, Treet sat down. Tvrdy stared at him for a moment, then looked away and said, "That is all for now. We will meet tonight to begin planning our survival." At that, everyone rose and filed out silently.

Treet shuffled out, head low, shoulders slumped. Why did I shoot off my mouth? he wondered. It didn't do any good. The timing wasn't right. No one understands.

He'd walked only a few paces when Bogney approached him. Treet acknowledge the Dhog's presence with a nod and the twitch of a nostril.

"Dhogs being ready now," Bogney said cryptically; his two filthy companions gazed at Treet steadily.

"Ah—" Treet replied, "ready for what?" He studied the swarthy dog carefully. The greasy countenance appeared resolute, and a strange light burned in the normally lackluster eyes. "Are you talking about the raid?" asked Treet, knowing that wasn't it.

The Dhog shifted from one foot to another. "Dhogs not raiding no more. Giloon be thinking Fieri man taking us to Fierra. Dhogs ready—we living here no more."

Here was a problem. Apparently the Dhogs, having had a taste of war, wanted nothing more to do with it; they wanted to pull out, were ready to go, in fact. Treet looked around; Moscow Square was empty. It occurred to him that he hadn't seen many Dhogs since the ambush. Apparently they had been busy packing up and getting ready to leave.

But how could he explain that he couldn't lead them to the promised land? He had to stall them until he could find a way to talk them into staying. "What about your dead?"

Treet pointed to the triple row of covered bodies lined up outside Ernina's makeshift hospital, most of them Dhogs.

Bogney glanced at the bodies. "We be sending them on this night," he said firmly, turning back to Treet, his jaw set. "Then you be taking us to Fierra."

Treet decided it would be unwise to lie to Bogney. He replied simply, "I won't do that."

Giloon Bogney stared at Treet, the wheels of his mind grinding slowly, his expression one of defiance and challenge. Treet expected him to throw a punch any second, but the Dhog merely stood fingering his filthy beard, staring.

"Giloon showing you something," Bogney said finally. "You come tonight."

"All right," agreed Treet. "Tonight."

SIXTY
ONE

By the time the mourners reached the cremation site deep in the Old Section warrens, daylight had abandoned them. Night came swiftly, deepening the putrid half-light of the ancient shell. While the Dhogs set about readying the funeral pyre, Treet gazed at his surroundings. A more depressing place would be difficult to imagine: sun-starved trees, long dead, lifted leafless branches to the smoke-dark dome; limp, wasted weeds cast clinging nets of pale tendrils over reeking piles of debris; black moss draped the stone and hung from the lifeless limbs like tattered shrouds.

They made their way to a great heap of tumbled stone which lay in the center of this dismal scene, and there they stopped. Bogney surveyed the hill and said to Treet, standing beside him, "Bogneys always burn dead. For a hundred many years and more, Bogney men always."

Nice family business, thought Treet. Lots of trade to keep you busy, I'll bet.

"You saying Dhogs afraid." The squat leader spat on the ground to show what he thought of that notion. "Dhogs not being afraid of death—it take us from *here!*" He lifted his hands.

Good point, thought Treet. "Welcome release, is that it?"

They watched while the dead, carried so carefully through the labyrinthine byways of the Old Section, were stacked atop the flattened crown of the man-made hill. Torches which the women had brought with them were set in crevices around the pyramid of dead bodies, and a huge effigy, fetched from a keeping-place nearby, was trundled up the hill on the backs of some of the men.

Treet recognized the effigy as that of the strange winged man the Dhogs called Cynetics. Made of fibersteel crudely patched together, the thing was erected on the summit amidst the carefully arranged bodies. The rest of the Dhogs gathered at the foot of the hill, murmuring in agitated voices as Giloon Bogney ascended the hill with a lighted torch and began lighting the ring of torches while men poured the contents of plastic containers over the pile of bodies.

The murmurs became wails and rose in volume. The name Cynetics could be heard in the rising tumult. Then Bogney, having ignited the planted torches, stood on the hilltop holding his torch in his hand, gazing down at those below, his face shiny in the furtive light. He waved the torch in a circle and the Dhogs grew silent, joined hands, and circled the hill.

"Dhogs," he shouted, "why we be coming here?"

The Dhogs below answered in chorus, and Treet made out the words: "We coming to set free the dead."

"Where we be sending them?"

"We send them Home."

Home. It was the first time Treet had heard the word used on Empyrion. In the mouths of the Dhogs it sounded impossibly remote.

"We be sending them Home," confirmed Bogney. "We sending them Home to Cynetics."

Treet felt his flesh tingle at the realization that to the Dhogs "home" was a sort of heaven where their souls went after death, and Cynetics the welcoming deity. It made sense, but struck Treet as unutterably pathetic.

Once their ancestors had longed for a place called Home where a benevolent entity called Cynetics would receive them and care for them, grant them the pleasures so long denied in life. The Old Ones must have yearned for it, dreamed about it—those who remembered probably even told stories about what it was like, stories that grew to legend and slowly became myth—and they passed on to infant generations the dream of one day returning home.

The dream never dimmed, although it must have become painfully clear at some point that it was impossible, that they would never again make contact with Cynetics, that they could never go home. But the human spirit is a remarkably tenacious thing; it does not easily give up its dreams. So, home became *Home,* and the physically unreached became reachable in spirit: in death their souls, so desperately homesick, could travel there. Cynetics, so powerful, so remote, and so aloof, could be re-joined, if not in temporal life, then in the afterlife.

Thinking these things, Treet watched the sad spectacle unfold around him. In their profound naiveté the Dhogs still clutched at the bare threads of a tradition they could no longer understand. He felt the tears rise in his throat; he swallowed hard, and passed a hand over his eyes. The hand came away wet.

"Fire set them free!" cried Bogney, leaping with the torch.

"Fire set us all free!" rejoined the Dhogs.

"Where they going?"

"Home!" cried the Dhogs. "Home to Cynetics."

Bogney turned, took the torch to the pile of bodies, and ignited the pyre. The other Dhogs with him on the hill took up their torches and touched them to the stack of corpses. In seconds the pyre was awash in streaking red flames. In the center stood the grotesque metal effigy, its outspread wings glinting dully in the firelight, its harsh face solemn, cold, distant in the white smoke rolling up to the high arched dome.

Treet stood aghast at the cruel trick time had played upon these simple people. He felt the yearning of the blind, ignorant souls around him.

Tears fell from his eyes, and he wept.

• • • • • •

Yarden lay in her tent in the dark, listening to the clear, happy voices of the Fieri, watching the pale slice of sky growing dim through the tent flap. In the midst of a most festive atmosphere—the arrival of the talking fish raised the ordinarily jovial Fieri into a mood of high jubilation—she felt distant, cut off from the celebration around her.

Crocker's unexpected appearance on the beach that morning had thrown her into a tailspin. She would not have been more surprised if the ghost of her greatgrandmother had taken flesh before her eyes. Seeing the lanky pilot striding up, spear in hand, wevicat beside him, had shattered the delicate peace of mind she had won as a result of her long night's vigil.

She had brought him back to camp and gathered the Mentors. One look at Crocker, and the Preceptor was summoned. The Preceptor came, and Yarden witnessed an act of touching kindness and tenderness as the Preceptor knelt down beside the naked, dirty man and took his hands in hers. The Mentors gathered round and put their hands on Crocker, and they all prayed for him quietly—with not a few of the onlooking Fieri joining in as well.

Crocker bore the experience without so much as a twitch

of acknowledgment. When they had finished praying, they painstakingly examined the man and then bathed and clothed him—all under the Preceptor's watchful eye. Crocker seemed not to mind their ministrations; indeed, he accepted the probing and poking amiably and without comment.

The examination over, the Preceptor consulted with the Mentors and, upon charging them with Crocker's care, departed once more. Yarden watched the proceedings with growing distress. The pilot was clearly not himself, and yet no one appeared concerned over this fact. Nor did they seem concerned at all with the implications of Crocker's presence.

"We can find nothing physically wrong with him," Anthon told her when the Preceptor had gone. "At least, nothing a few good meals won't put right. He's a bit sunburned, of course, but then he's been living in the forest—"

"Nothing wrong? How can you say that? Look at him. If nothing's wrong, why won't he talk? He just sits there looking at us. Why won't he tell us what's happened?"

Anthon gave her a fatherly look and patted her shoulder. "I said *physically*. He has undoubtedly sustained a severe trauma which has affected his mind."

All of which was painfully obvious to Yarden; she'd known it the second she saw him. And she saw the implications immediately, too: if Crocker was here, he couldn't very well be with Treet and Calin.

Pizzle had come by, frowning and shaking his head sadly, saying, "This is bad news. I don't like this at all. From the looks of it, I'd say the show closed on the road."

Yarden was in no mood for his analysis, so drove him away with a few barbed words and a fistful of sand.

But Pizzle was only articulating Yarden's own fears, and in doing so unleashed all sorts of grim scenarios—all of which tended to resolve into the bleak prospect that Treet, Crocker, and Calin had never reached Dome.

That's when the questions had started—the same questions that had been whirling inside her head all day: Are they all right? Should I try to contact them? What if I don't like what I find? What if they're dead or in trouble? What then?

Oh, God, what am I supposed to do?

She rose, stepped out of the tent, and stood watching the warm, convivial knots of people mingling among themselves, freely, joyously, but with a little urgency, it seemed to her, as if the fading of the daylight would steal the happiness from them.

I've got to know, Yarden said to herself. I've got to know right now.

She turned and walked slowly down to the water's edge, as far from the bustle as she could get. The setting sun had polished the bay to resemble a gleaming bronze mirror reflecting the early evening stars. She sat down cross-legged on the damp, smooth, wave-packed sand and drew a long deep breath, clearing her mind.

What she would do now was different than accepting the fleeting thought impulses she'd received before. Those were unbidden; unavoidable, actually. But the intentional, calculated drawing of another's thought into her mental awareness was something else again. Most people, especially men, resented it, considered it spying—which in a way it was; hence the reprehensible term "brain dipping."

The sympathic "touch," misunderstood though it so often was, could bring great benefit when used skillfully and responsibly. What Yarden proposed was, she hoped, responsible and not merely selfish.

Yarden exhaled slowly, drew another breath, held it, exhaled, placed her hands together, fingertips touching lightly. She cleared her mental screen—an imagined area of space right behind her closed eyelids—emptying her mind completely, concentrating her consciousness, focusing it down and down, drawing it thin as wire until she could feel it sharp and fine within her.

When she was ready, she formed the image of Calin on her mental screen. She pulled another long breath deep into her lungs, held it, and exhaled slowly. As the air flowed from her mouth, she released her rarefied consciousness, sending it out from her, a laser beam to thread the finest needle.

She waited.

Ordinarily she would begin receiving thought impressions immediately, but nothing came. She concentrated harder, probing with her consciousness, forcing it further afield, questing.

Where was she?

There was no sign, no spark, no vibration of being. Calin was not there; she had vanished. Yarden knew then that she was dead.

Fighting back the impulse to break concentration, to give in to her worst fears, she replaced Calin's image with Treet's and forced herself to continue.

Instantly a vague, flickering image floated onto her mental screen: a man with wings standing before a fire with white smoke rolling up. No, not standing before the fire . . . standing *in* the fire. Burning with it, but not consumed.

A strange image. What did it have to do with Treet?

She cleared the image from her mind and concentrated again, sending her awareness out like searching fingers.

Then she found him. Her touch vibrated with his presence; she knew it, recognized it as Treet's, but it was distant, external—as if he were covered by a thick, impenetrable shell or membrane.

He was alive, yes, or there would be no trace of him at all. Yet, something was blocking her attempt to reach him directly. Like a lead sheet shielding a body from X rays, something stood between her and Treet, something that either absorbed or deflected her probing consciousness.

Yarden forced the probe deeper, trying to pierce the membrane, all her being concentrated at the rapier-sharp tip, thrusting like a surgical needle. She felt the membrane part, slipped in through the narrow rent, and was overwhelmed by a sudden sensation of doom, of death and despair roiling fiercely, ugly and menacing. And Treet was there—somehow caught in it, enveloped by it.

And then she felt a presence, quick and incredibly strong, moving toward her through her contact with Treet. It reached out for her as if to pull her in, to envelop her, drag her down. Hate radiated from this maleficent presence like the rays of a dark star. Or a black hole which sucked all living matter into its gaping maw, vomiting lethal radiation in return.

Yarden recoiled from the contact, but tried to hold on to Treet. She felt him receding, slipping away. Then the membrane closed and she was expelled. On the outside again, she could sense Treet, but received no impressions from him. He was alive. Beyond that?

The effort at maintaining the touch was exhausting her; she felt her energy draining away.

Yarden came to herself with a shudder. She raised shaking hands to her face. Never in her sympathic experience had such a thing ever happened. And yet, as horrible as it was, it seemed familiar.

She had encountered a force of incredible strength—the merest contact had left her shaken and spent. But there was more to it than strength. There was a will, mindless and insensible, but grasping, tenacious, holding fast to all that came beneath its sway as if with countless writhing tentacles—so strong, so possessive that it could shield a human mind from her seeking touch.

It was a long time before Yarden could move again. When she finally struggled to her feet, she felt unspeakably old, weary, tired in her soul. But she remembered where she'd encountered the dark presence before: Dome . . . the Astral Service . . . Trabant Animus.

SIXTY
TWO

"Just what am I supposed to tell them?" asked Treet, exasperation making his voice brittle. "Why won't you talk to me?"

Tvrdy glowered and waved his hand in the air as if to dismiss the question. "Tell them you can't do it, of course. Tell them it's impossible. Tell them we need them here. Tell them anything you like." Tvrdy turned away.

"I've told them all that. They think I am a *Fieri*—remember? They believe I can lead them to the promised land, and they want to go *right now*. Haven't you wondered why it's been so quiet around here since the ambush? They think they're leaving. I've put them off as long as I can. We've got to talk to Bogney— explain to him exactly what's going on here—" Treet paused, looking at the Tanais' rigid back.

"What's wrong, Tvrdy?" he said more softly. "You've changed. What's eating you?"

Tvrdy turned on him, eyes flashing. "You ask what's wrong? You really want to know? I'll tell you: *we can't win.*"

Treet had never heard defeat from Tvrdy's lips. He stared, unable to speak.

"Do you hear?" Tvrdy's voice jumped several registers. "We can't win against Jamrog. He is too strong."

"We lose one skirmish and you're ready to toss in the towel?" Tvrdy's puzzled glance let Treet know he'd used another obscure figure of speech. "You're giving up after one battle?"

"I will never give in to Jamrog. But I know now that we cannot take him." Tvrdy paused, looked away again. "Maybe the Dhogs are right. Maybe we should leave the Old Section . . . go to Fierra."

"I can't believe it's you saying these things, Tvrdy. Look at me! Look me in the eye and tell me we're lost."

Tvrdy kept his face averted, said nothing.

"See? You can't do it. You don't believe it yourself. Besides, if we left now, it would only be a matter of time before Jamrog hunted us down. You know that."

"We could go to the Fieri—"

"I *tried* that, remember? Besides, there's the little matter of about ten thousand kilometers of nothing but nothing between here and there. Even if we were all up to a nice long stroll, where would we get the supplies? How would we carry them?"

Tvrdy's head dropped.

"Look, we'll find a way to beat him," said Treet. "Our hit and run raids aren't going so bad. We just have to hold on until something turns our way." He took a deep breath and let it out through his teeth. This was hard work, keeping all the ends from unraveling. "In the meantime, we have to figure out what to tell the Dhogs. They're waiting."

"Tell them the truth." The resignation in the Tanais leader's voice cut at Treet like a razor.

"Okay." Treet nodded. "I'll take care of it."

He went out and walked across the empty training field, trying to frame the words in his mind. The truth, yes—but what was the truth exactly? That he was not a Fieri?

That was easy enough. But if not a Fieri, what was he?

I'm a traveler. I'm from another world, another time. I'm the Ghost of Christmas Past . . .

The truth?

You think Cynetics is a god. It isn't. It's a bloated, blood-sucking corporation. (What's a corporation? Look it up in the dictionary.)

You think the Fieri are your saviors. They aren't. In fact, for all their angelic goodness and righteousness, they wouldn't give a rat's hind end to save this stinking hellhole. And I don't blame them one bit.

See, they're human beings, too. And they have long memories. They tried for peace with you bubbleheads once upon a time and paid the ultimate price for the attempt. As it happens, they aren't particularly anxious to repeat the experience. They'll leave us to die our miserable deaths without lifting a finger.

Running away across the desert won't help, either. There's a madman on the throne of this little cess pit, and he won't be happy till he's incinerated the entire planet. So even if we could run, which we can't, there's really nowhere to run to. See?

This is reality, folks. Get used to it. We're in the brown soup up to our rosy red cheeks, and it's getting hotter by the minute.

"I tried to contact Treet and Calin," Yarden said at last, her voice sounding strained. "Sympathically."

Ianni scanned her friend's features minutely. Yarden had sustained a severe shock, there was no question about that; her eyes were dull and her expression slack, drained. "You don't have to tell us—" she began, leaning toward Yarden with her hand extended. But Gerdes, with a quick shake of her head, silenced her, and Ianni withdrew the hand.

In a moment Yarden continued. "I couldn't find Calin . . . I think she's dead. There was one horrible moment when I thought Treet was dead, too. But I forced the touch, and I reached him . . ." She raised her eyes and focused on the two women for the first time.

"I'm listening, Yarden." Ianni spoke softly, her tone full of compassion and reassurance.

"Go on, daughter," Gerdes said.

"There was . . . something—I didn't know what—like a shell. It covered him, would not let me touch him. I sensed Treet's presence, but could not touch him. When I persisted, the thing turned on me, forced me out. I—" Yarden's jaw worked silently as she lost the words for a moment.

She searched Ianni's eyes for understanding, and reached out a hand to take her friend's arm. "Ianni, I have never felt such hate in my life. It was ugly. Hideous! I got the feeling that if it could have killed me through my contact with Treet it would have—instantly, without hesitation . . . and then I remembered . . ."

Ianni grasped Yarden's hand. She could sense the great struggle taking place within, a war in which Yarden fought valiantly to remain stable and rational. But there was desperation growing in her eyes; the fight was taking a toll on her strength. Soon she would buckle under the strain. She looked to Gerdes for help.

"What did you remember, Yarden?" Gerdes asked, pressing Yarden to continue. "Say the words. Release their power over you."

A spasm of fear squirmed over Yarden's face. "Trabant . . ." She whispered the name. ". . . it wanted to kill me."

"But it didn't kill you," said Gerdes. "It couldn't harm you at all. You're safe now." Gerdes spoke soothingly, but her words had the opposite effect.

"No!" shouted Yarden shrilly. "You don't understand. I'm not worried about myself. It's Treet! He's in trouble and I can't . . . I don't know what to do."

Ianni thought for a moment. "The Preceptor will help us," she said, looking to Gerdes for affirmation. Gerdes nodded her approval. "We will go to her at once."

The three were silent as they walked to the Preceptor's tent, which looked like a large, multisectioned orange, white, and blue blossom—inverted and dropped onto the sand. Ianni and Yarden waited outside while Gerdes sought audience for them within.

They were admitted and entered. Globes of pale yellow sunstone rested in sconces in the sand, bathing the interior in soft illumination. Mentors Anthon and Eino were seated on cushions on either side of the Preceptor; Preben was in attendance as well. Anthon jumped up as soon as he saw Yarden. "Come in, please. Sit down," he said, offering his place next to the Preceptor.

The Preceptor gazed at Yarden, concern and compassion mingled in her eyes. She lifted a regal hand and helped Yarden down to the cushion beside her. Yarden felt healing power in the touch as her heart calmed, and a measure of peace returned.

"Don't be afraid, Yarden," said the Preceptor. There was strength in the simple words, strength Yarden could lean on. She settled down gratefully beside the Preceptor and looked at the faces ringed around her. She could feel the kindness and sympathy flowing out to her, and relaxed a little.

At a glance from the Preceptor, Anthon leaned forward and said, "We have been discussing the appearance of your friend Crocker. We would like to hear your thoughts."

"Yes," offered Mentor Eino, a dark-bearded man with an easy smile and large hairy hands. "We are concerned, as you must be, and seek guidance in this matter. You could help us a great deal by speaking candidly."

"I'll try," said Yarden softly. Music floated into the tent from outside, along with the sound of Fieri voices, a happy evensong rippling on the evening breeze. The sound was at once comforting and remote, as if taking place in a separate and distant sphere of existence, while what was happening in this tent at this moment was all that was real.

"I am afraid," Yarden began, "afraid for my friends—I fear

that something terrible has happened." She paused, and Ianni, sitting directly opposite, urged her with her eyes. "I tried to contact Orion Treet sympathically—that is, with my extrasensory abilities. After some effort I found him, but was not able to establish contact—something prevented me, opposed me."

She explained about her attempt to reach Treet and her encounter with the evil spirit of Trabant Animus, and how just the briefest touch had left her drained and frightened. "Treet is alive," she declared, "but he is in trouble. We've got to do something to help him."

The Preceptor nodded slightly, accepting Yarden's story. "Is there anything else you would like to tell us?"

"Why, yes," said Yarden, "there is something else. The talking fish—"

"The fish?" Anthon darted a glance to Eino and leaned forward. "Tell us."

"It may have been my imagination, but I believe they were trying to warn me of danger." She then told them of the strange "conversation" she'd had with Spinner and Glee.

Her listeners were silent, their faces grave when she finished. Preben, who had followed the story carefully, spoke up. "This is precisely the matter that brought me here tonight. I have been hearing similar stories these last two days."

Mentor Eino nodded thoughtfully. "I, too, received such a warning from the talking fish, although I could not interpret it half so well." He nodded in deference to Yarden's ability.

"Exactly what I was thinking!" Anthon interjected. "A remarkable telling."

It had not occurred to Yarden that her sympathic ability might have given her a special facility for understanding the talking fish. Although she had recognized at the time that the creature's "speech" was quite similar to the sympath's touch, she did not imagine that she would prove to be a first-class interpreter.

The Preceptor, who peered over interlaced fingers at Yarden, asked, "What do you believe to be the nature of this warning?"

Yarden paused to gather her thoughts. She wanted to be as precise as possible—Treet's life might depend on her answer. Closing her eyes to aid memory, Yarden thought back—was it only a day ago?—to her time with the fishes. She could feel the remarkable presence of the wise and gentle creatures, and once more experienced their pure and uninhibited expression.

The affect string came back to her with terrible clarity, magnified by her own still fresh experience with Trabant. She felt again the swarming, pestilential darkness; the mindless hate and unreasoning malice; the all-consuming malevolence of the hideous, twisted thing; the stifling threat of creeping doom.

Yarden shivered and began to speak. "There is darkness, a seething, potent darkness, and hate—such unbelievable and total hate; it wants to destroy us, to poison us with its evil, exterminate us." She opened her eyes slowly to find the others watching her, frowning deeply, thoughtfully. "I believe the fish were warning us about Dome," she concluded.

The word seemed to freeze them all for a moment. All except Yarden.

She looked triumphantly from face to face, thinking, There! I've said it. It *cannot* hurt me. Its only power is fear, and I have conquered that here tonight. I am free of its malignant influence, and I refuse to give in to it again. I am free!

SIXTY THREE

Giloon Bogney stared at Treet with murder in his eyes. The bhuj in his hand flicked back and forth, the discolored blade glinting dully in the dirty light. "Giloon could kill you, Fieri man," he growled.

"What would that solve? You'd never get out of here then." For the last two hours Treet had been explaining all the reasons he could think of why he couldn't lead a Dhog exodus out across Daraq, the Blighted Lands. Now he was tired and wanted to sleep.

"Huh!" Bogney grunted, rubbing the bhuj against his hairy cheek. Then he pushed the weapon into Treet's face. "Maybe Giloon be killing you now, seh?"

Treet pushed it away angrily. "Look, I don't want to play games with you. I want to go to sleep. So, unless you have any further—"

"You taking Dhogs to Fieri," Bogney insisted.

"I've told you twenty different ways: n-o—no! It's impossible. We'd never make it. I can't. I won't. Kill me if it will make you feel better, but we are *not* going to Fierra. Not now. Not tomorrow. Not ever. Get used to the idea. We are not going!"

Bogney stared at him with his good eye, his zigzag scar puckering angrily. "Dhogs don't needs you, Fieri man. We be going lonely anyhow."

Treet sighed and rolled his eyes. "We've been through this, Bogney. You have no idea what a desert is, what it's like out there. In fact, you don't even have the slightest idea of what it's like to breathe fresh air! Let me tell you, words can't describe how painful it is. That's what it's like. Real air would wipe you out in a second."

Bogney listened patiently. When Treet was done, he remarked in exactly the same stubborn tone as before: "Dhogs be going lonely anyhow."

"Okay! Fine! Go! Bon voyage! Vamoose!" Treet crossed his arms over his chest and flopped down on his bed. "You're the boss, Bogney. Happy motoring. Don't forget to write. Good-bye and good luck and good riddance!"

Bogney stared at Treet for a moment longer, turned, and walked slowly out, his much-stained cloak—the one Tvrdy had given him—sweeping the floor behind him, leaving only a residual reek in the air.

What a day! thought Treet. Tvrdy's giving up, Bogney wants to leave, and everyone else is just comatose from exhaustion. If that isn't enough, the Invisibles are systematically tearing the Old Section apart brick by crumbling brick. What can happen next?

Treet knew he should not have asked that question. He didn't really want an answer. But he got one anyway—in the form of a ripping blast that raked the compound outside, spattering rocks and dirt clods against the trembling walls of the building.

Treet rocketed straight up off the bed and reached the door without touching the floor. He was outside a split-second later as people came spilling out onto the field.

"Get back! Get back, you fools!"

Treet spun around to see Tvrdy racing toward him in a crouch. He saw the flash and saw Tvrdy throw himself to the ground, but before he could do likewise, the shock wave hit him and flattened him. Brick fragments and bits of debris pelted into him, followed by a rain of hot gravel.

Wriggling on his stomach, Treet inched over to Tvrdy. "I thought they weren't supposed to be this far in," shouted Treet, his voice lost amidst the roar still echoing in his ears.

"Those were long-range seekers." Tvrdy jerked his head up, looked around. "The Invisibles will follow them in, but we still have a little time to get out."

"I know a place—the Dhog cemetery. Bogney took me there. It's safe—hey!—where're you going?"

Tvrdy was already on his feet, dashing away, shouting at the top of his lungs. "Save the supplies and weapons! Everyone carry something! Supplies and weapons! Leave the rest!"

Two more blasts shook the compound, but they landed wide of the arsenal and supply buildings. Despite the rising panic, the evacuation got under way speedily and efficiently. Treet gathered himself and ran for the ramshackle hospital.

"What's happening?" Ernina asked as he came in, her square face floating in the light from a hand-held lantern. The moans of the injured filled the darkness.

"Invisibles—they've found us. We still have some time. We're getting out."

"I can't leave the wounded." She made to turn away.

Treet caught her arm and held on. "We'll take them with us. Get all your equipment together. I'll find Bogney."

He hurried out again into the confusion. Flares burned outside the supply buildings, casting the scene into garish relief. Treet made for the far end of the compound and struck off for the Dhog leader's lair. He met Bogney and several of his underlings flying toward him along the narrow street with torches in their hands.

Treet halted. "Bogney!"

The Dhogs ignored Treet, pushing past him without a word. "Bogney! I have to talk to you." He began running after them.

"Giloon be finished talking," The Dhog leader called back over his shoulder.

"Listen to me!"

The Dhogs ran on without looking back.

"I'll lead you to Fierra!" screamed Treet. "Do you hear me? Fierra! You win. I'll take you."

Bogney stopped and turned around. Treet ran to him, and the Dhog shoved a torch into Treet's face and glared at him. "Fieri man be lying big to Giloon?"

Treet shook his head, his breath coming in gasps. "No . . . I mean it. I'll take you, but you have to help me first—help me get the wounded out of the hospital. I'll need all the men you can get; we have to carry them to safety."

"Then you take us?"

"I don't know how, but I'll take you." Another blast lit up the night. A tottering ruin several blocks over tumbled, spilling its rubble into the street behind them. "We've got to hurry. Make up your mind."

"Lie to Dhogs, Giloon killing you dead."

"If I'm lying, you can kill me all you want later. Only come on, we've got to move now!"

Bogney whirled and sent two of his companions racing off in the opposite direction. Then he and the two remaining Dhogs followed Treet back to the compound.

• • • • •

"It will take too long to assemble all the Mentors," protested Yarden. "We must do something now."

The Preceptor smiled, but said firmly, "We will have the time we require. The Protector will look after your friend. The Mentors must be assembled, for wisdom is multiplied when many wise come together." She rose, signaling an end to the interview.

Yarden glanced around the ring of faces and saw that pressing the matter further would gain nothing; she had done all she could for one night. She rose and said, "Thank you, Preceptor, for hearing me out. If I have spoken more frankly than I might have, it is because I believe time is short."

The Preceptor went to Yarden and put her arms around her. "Think no negative thought, Yarden. Trust in the Infinite Father to care for His own. He will provide a Deliverer."

"I will try, Preceptor. It's hard, but I will try."

The Preceptor released Yarden and stood for a moment holding her at arm's length. "I detect in you the kindled flame of belief. I sensed it earlier when you entered this evening, and it is stronger now."

Yarden bowed her head. "It's true," she admitted shyly, then raised her head, face beaming. "And it feels wonderful!"

"Feed the flame, Yarden." The Preceptor squeezed her hands. "Feed it with all that is in you."

With that, Yarden said good-night and followed the others out. Anthon was waiting for her a few paces up the beach. The campfires were mostly out, and the songs had died away. The Fieri were turning in for the night. "Walk with me a little, would you?"

"Of course," replied Yarden and they fell into step with one another. She breathed in the night air and glanced at the hard, bright stars burning in the deep heavens. Empyrion didn't have a moon, but she didn't miss it—except at rare times, like now.

When they had walked a little way, Anthon said, "It went well tonight. You were very persuasive."

"Hmmm, I am convinced that trouble is coming," replied Yarden, uncertain what Anthon was trying to say.

"I don't doubt it at all. The Preceptor is right, however, in convening the Mentors before suggesting any action—if action is to be taken, since this will likely affect all Fieri."

"Why are you telling me this?"

Anthon gave a slight shrug and made a dismissive gesture with his hands. "I have been in contact with Mathiax and Talus," he said simply.

"You have? How?"

"The Mentors' crystal."

Of course, thought Yarden, I should have remembered. Each Mentor has one. "What did they say?"

Anthon stopped walking and stood for a moment facing the great, restless shadow that was the sea. "Jaire—Talus' daughter, you remember—"

"I remember."

"Jaire had a dream—very much like the warning you received from the fish. In fact, in describing the warning for the Preceptor tonight, you used almost precisely the same words Jaire used in describing it to Mathiax. Disturbingly precise."

"So you think there may be something to the warning."

Anthon gave her a sharp look and resumed the pace. "I said I did not doubt it, and indeed I do not. But the matter is more complicated than that. There are those among us who have become persuaded that perhaps the time has come to try reestablishing contact with Dome. You have to understand that to change the course we have followed happily for many centuries is no easy thing." He looked at Yarden curiously. "In your world, change is more quickly accomplished, yes? I gather it's considered something of a virtue in itself."

"Often it is." Yarden looked skyward and sighed. "But you make it sound as if it will take centuries to do something to help Treet—and to save ourselves. If the warning is genuine, and we all agree that it is, time is running out for all of us."

"This is why I wanted to speak to you now. You can help us change, Yarden. Perhaps it is the very reason you were sent to us in the first place. We need your spark, your dynamic energy. We need you to show us the way."

Show them the way? I'm just barely crawling yet myself, she thought. I can't show anybody the way.

Anthon continued. "It's true. That's part of the reason Mathiax and Talus allowed Orion Treet to return to Dome."

"You mean they *used* him."

"No, not at all. They sensed the Infinite was working in him and argued for his return, hoping he would somehow show

806

us how we were to proceed in this matter of approaching Dome."

"We're talking about life and death here. Treet was right: Dome is out to destroy us. Surely you understand self-defense."

"We understand that self-defense is a most subtle trap. Was there ever a time when aggression was not called self-defense?" Anthon shook his head sadly. "Those who worry overmuch about defending themselves build walls instead of bridges."

"Granted," said Yarden. "But you said you hoped Treet would show you how to proceed. Has he?"

"We believe he has. And we believe you are helping, too."

"Anthon, forgive me, it's late and I'm not thinking clearly. Just what is it you want from me?"

"Only your understanding. For us, it is not so important whether Dome destroys us—believe me. We would welcome our own destruction sooner than lift a hand against our destroyer if in destroying him we become like him.

"But a few of us—Mathiax, Talus, Eino, and myself, along with a few others—have come to believe that by leaving Dome to itself, we may actually be guilty of encouraging evil."

"You're serious?"

"Very serious. You see, evil left to itself breeds only evil. By separating ourselves, we have ensured that evil would grow."

Yarden nodded slowly, finally grasping what Anthon was trying to say to her. "I understand. How will they ever find the light if there is no one to show them?"

"Yes, that's it. By withholding the light we possess, we have condemned Dome to darkness."

"But that's not your fault. They chose it for themselves."

"Did they? Take away the light, and there can only be darkness. We were the light among them and we left, taking the light with us. Only a madman blames the darkness for being dark when he has withdrawn the light."

Yarden thought about this a long time and Anthon watched her closely. They stopped walking and faced each other. "Tomorrow," said Anthon, "we will confer with the Mentors. You will have an opportunity to speak, and I wanted you to know that you are not alone."

"Thank you, Anthon." Yarden took his hand and held it. "I think I know what to say now."

A few minutes later, Yarden approached Pizzle's tent. Starla and Pizzle were sitting in front of the tent, arms wrapped around each other. As Yarden came up, she heard Pizzle saying, ". . . so after Gandalf tangled with the Balrog, and the orcs got Boromir, the Fellowship just fell apart, scattered."

"What of the Ring-bearer?" asked Starla, eyes wide with wonder.

"Oh, Frodo and Sam escaped and went on by themselves. Gollum followed them and when . . ." Pizzle glanced up. "Oh, hi, Yarden, what's up?"

"I'm sorry to disturb you," she began, glancing at Starla.

Starla rose quickly. "Please excuse me, I will leave you two to talk."

"Hey, wait a minute! You don't have to—" Pizzle protested.

Starla smiled and put a hand to his face. "It is getting late, and I must go anyway. Yarden wishes to speak privately with you. We will be together again tomorrow."

"Thank you," said Yarden. "That's a very nice young woman," she said, watching Starla walk away.

"Yeah," admitted Pizzle. "So why'd you run her off?"

"I have to talk to you."

"So talk."

"Pizzle, how much do you know about atomic bombs?"

SIXTY FOUR

The last Dhogs carried the last wounded man from the compound ten minutes before the first Invisibles arrived. The rebels were struggling through pinched alleyways and dark corridors not two hundred meters from New America Square, each one laden with as much as he could possibly carry, when the explosions streaked the darkness behind them.

"It looks like they found Tvrdy's surprise," Treet muttered.

"That might slow them down," said Cejka, who was leading a platoon to cover their retreat. He turned to watch the torchlight procession wind through the desolate streets. "You go on, and keep them moving up ahead. I'll stay here and watch for a little while."

Treet jogged heavily on, urging those ahead of him to hurry. Ernina, bent double by the weight of the medical instruments and supplies she carried, labored alongside the line of wounded. The few that could walk tottered along weakly; the rest were slung in blanket-contrived hammocks carried by Dhogs. Treet came up beside her. "Are you going to make it? Or should I send someone back to help out?"

In the wildly flickering light her eyes glinted with determination as she glanced up at him. "I'll make it—might take all night, but I'll make it."

"If you get to lagging behind, sing out. I'll get you some relief."

Treet hitched up his own heavy packs and trundled off. Evacuation was no picnic, and the place they were headed for was no garden spot. He only hoped it would not turn out to be needlessly symbolic: making their last stand in the Dhog cemetery. At least it had two strong points to recommend it. One, it was difficult to get to if one didn't know precisely where one was going. And two, it was close to a secret exit which led to Bolbe Hage.

Still, being run out of their base was a stroke of bad luck, to put it mildly. They had counted on being able to stay there, rest, and get reorganized in their own good time. Now it appeared as if they would have to do it on the fly, if at all.

Up to the moment when the enemy began bombarding the training field, Treet had believed that a miracle would happen and that they would, by some genius masterstroke, deal Jamrog the *coup de grace;* or, if not, that they would be rescued. The chances of either thing happening grew more remote by the minute as Treet sensed time running out. If there was going to be any saving, it would have to come soon—while there was still something to save.

The evacuation was divided up into three stages or groups. Group One, under Tvrdy's direction, was in charge of weaponry and supplies necessary for survival; they had gone ahead to lead the way. Group Two was the wounded and injured, helped along by the Dhogs Bogney had provided and anyone else Treet had been able to commandeer for the task. Group Three was the Tanais and Rumon soldiery defending the rear to ensure a successful evacuation.

They reached the gloomy cremation site without incident. Piling their burdens on the ground around the massive burning mound, now studded with flagging torches instead of flaming corpses, exhausted people dropped where they stopped and sank into sweat-drenched slumber.

Treet and Ernina worked to make the casualties as comfortable as possible under the conditions, while Tvrdy moved like a ghost through the silent encampment, taking a mental inventory of what they had been able to save. Cejka, Kopetch, and Fertig, having arranged for a nominal watch between them, settled down to rest. Bogney disappeared somewhere into the Dhogs' labyrinthine fastness with a few of his assistants.

When he had done all he could for the wounded, Treet found himself a flat spot to stretch out and sank down gratefully among the stacks of gear. He was asleep as soon as his head touched the ground.

• • • • • •

Diltz examined the huge carapace with exacting care. Three Saecaraz magicians hung back uncertainly, exchanging nervous glances and fidgeting in their black-and-silver striped yoses. At a nearby workbench several Nilokerus magicians pored over an old plastic-bound text, murmuring as they vocalized the words written there.

His inspection completed, Diltz straightened and put his hands on the metallic skin. He closed his eyes and spread his thin lips in a sick smile. "I feel its power," he whispered. "Listen!" He pressed his ear to the smooth surface. "It speaks! 'Death to Fieri!' it says—'I am death to Empyrion's enemies.' "

He cocked his head to peer at the magicians. "You have done well. The Supreme Director will reward you personally." His lips twisted in a paroxysm of joy. "How soon may I inform our leader of the demise of his enemies?"

The foremost magician stepped cautiously up. "The text, Director—" He indicated the Nilokerus scanning the ancient document.

"The text, yes. What of it?"

"The text is, shall we say, vague on several points. It is . . . ah, our feeling is that . . . perhaps—"

"Speak, man! What are you trying to say? Is the weapon serviceable?"

"Oh, yes. We believe it is. The power beneath its metal shell is not, as far as we can determine, diminished by time."

"Then what is it?"

The magician hesitated and looked to his comrades for support. "We do not yet know how to . . . the word—what's the word, Geblen?"

One of the red-hooded Nilokerus raised his head. "Eh, *launch,* I believe is the word you require."

"Launch. It only remains to discover how to launch the weapon."

Diltz peered at the magician skeptically. "What is this launch?"

"The, ah—" He made a pushing motion in the air with his hands. "The sending forth of the weapon."

"The sending forth? How is it sent forth?"

"Why, through the air, Director. Or so we believe."

Diltz looked at the man as if he'd lost his mind. "Thrown through the air? By what means?"

"Engines, Director." He pointed to the rear of the weapon, the flaring exhaust ports of three huge rocket engines.

Diltz waved a hand impatiently. "Well, how long until you learn to operate these engines?"

The Saecaraz shook his head sadly. "As you see, we are reading the texts even now. Several passages look promising."

"Get more Readers. I want this weapon operational as soon as possible—two days! I'll wait two days and no more."

The magician inclined his head and went back to the others. Diltz took a last look around the Archives, and at the odd-looking death machine with its stubby, knife-thin protrusions along its narrow flanks, its snub nose and bulging engines, gray skin gleaming under a row of grid lights. He rubbed the long body with his hand and then departed, rejoining his Mors Ultima bodyguard at the door.

Most of the Fieri had gone down to the sea to meet the talking fish once more. But a few, the Mentors among them and designated leaders such as Gerdes and Preben, had stayed behind to sit in council with the Preceptor.

After her talk with Anthon, and her session with Pizzle, Yarden had returned to her tent where she lay awake most of the night composing in her mind the argument she would use in helping persuade the Fieri to abandon their age-old policy of nonaggression and nonintervention and go help Treet.

They assembled in the clear morning air out beside the Preceptor's tent. The bright, white sun was warm on the sand as Yarden joined the group, taking her place in the large circle beside Gerdes and across from Anthon. Pizzle was nowhere to be seen; neither, for that matter, was Crocker.

The beauty of the day would work against her, she thought as she knelt down, digging her bare toes into the sand, feeling the cool, moist layer just below the warm, dry stuff on top. The sound of laughter and splashing water drifted across the beach. The blue backs and fins of the talking fish flashed in the jade-green water as the Fieri sported with the playful creatures. How does one take seriously a description of hell when surrounded by heaven?

Preben worked his way around the circle, distributing what appeared to be clothing tags to each person in attendance. He stopped before Yarden and handed her one of the tags. She saw that it was a flat, triangular card with a crystal affixed to the front. A thread-thin wire hung from the back of the card, and on the end of the thread was a small plug.

"You can hear with this," he explained. "It's tuned to the Preceptor's crystal."

Gerdes helped Yarden fasten the tag to her chinti and showed her how to place the plug in her ear. Anthon caught her eye across the circle. He smiled and lifted his hand in a gesture which imparted confidence. Yarden returned his smile and settled in to wait, using meditation calming techniques.

When she opened her eyes again, the Preceptor was taking her place. A large green-flecked crystal was placed on a stand in the center of the circle. Yarden put the earplug in her ear. There came a pleasant chiming sound and Mathiax's voice said, "Good morning, Preceptor. The Mentors are convened as you requested. We await your pleasure."

The Preceptor acknowledged those in the circle. "The importance of our discussion this morning is not to be underestimated because of the informality imposed by circumstance," she began, speaking slowly, solemnly.

"We understand," answered Mathiax; his voice was so distinct, so present he seemed to be standing in the center of the circle. "Your instructions have been reviewed, and we agree that a timely examination of this matter dictates such necessity."

"Then we may proceed."

"Very well, Preceptor. Mentor Talus has prepared an opening statement. As Clerk of the College of Mentors, I recognize his seniority."

"We will hear Mentor Talus' statement."

"My friends," began Talus, his voice a small aural earthquake. "I will be brief.

"It is now over eleven centuries since our fathers in their wisdom terminated all relations with Dome, leaving them to their evil. I don't need to remind you that the great riches and blessed life the Fieri have enjoyed in the intervening years are but a foretaste of the Infinite's intent for His people.

"However, less than half a solar cycle ago, Travelers were found alive in the Blighted Lands. Certain of the Mentors and myself have come to look upon the arrival of the Travelers as a signal that the time of our isolation from Dome is ending.

"We believe that the Infinite is speaking to us through the presence of the Travelers and that we must listen very carefully to learn what direction we must choose."

Talus hesitated, and it seemed to Yarden that he had been about to say something else and instead said, "Please, my friends, I urge you to open your hearts and minds to the voice of the Teacher."

There was a little silence and then the Preceptor said, "Thank you, Talus. Your words are well chosen. Since we are reminded that time is critical, I think we will be well served to hear from one of the Travelers now."

Yarden glanced around to discover every eye on her and realized the Preceptor meant her. Anthon nodded encouragingly. She took a deep breath. "Thank you, Preceptor," she said, and swallowed hard.

"I am Yarden." Her voice quavered slightly. "Although I have lived among you only a short time, I have been enriched and blessed. I have learned of the Infinite Father's love for His people, and for me.

"I have also learned something of your past, and the reason why you have chosen to allow Dome to go its own way. Rightly, you remember the grief of that terrible day—the day you call the Burning.

"Yes, you remember the grief; it is with you still. But you do not remember the horror. That too should be remembered. Let me remember for you now."

Yarden closed her eyes and began to speak in a hushed voice. No one moved or made a sound.

"The morning sun shone down on green fields around the sparkling cities on the plain. Children played, lovers awakened in one another's arms, students returned to their lessons, workers to their jobs, and the Fieri began a new day of living.

"As the sun climbed higher into the sky, you paused to eat your midday meal. Some of you took food outdoors to enjoy the beauty of your world from the shade of fine old trees. The breeze ruffled your hair and bathed your limbs. You napped and dreamed, or laughed with your families and friends around the table.

"The sunlight dimmed momentarily as a shadow passed in front of the sun. It was nothing; a cloud perhaps. But a moment later you heard the roar of engines and the whistling scream of the missiles as they fell. You looked up.

"The blue flash—brighter than ten thousand suns, yet only one hundred meters in diameter—blinded you instantly as the bomb exploded eight hundred meters above the ground. In that split second when the flash was still traveling earthward, the hypocenter reached a temperature of over three million degrees—many times hotter than the surface of your sun.

"On the ground below, stone buildings melted into pools of glowing lava, metal bridges burst into flame, as did the rivers under them, and ceramic roof tiles boiled. Your people, still looking skyward, the first intimations of terror just beginning to register in the cells of their brains, simply vaporized, the fluids of their bodies turning directly into steam and gas—leaving their shadows etched on walls and pavement.

"Due to ionization, the churning air filled with the pungent, electric smell of ozone as the blue, sunlit sky flashed to yellow and green and then red-brown as the massive fireball spread, roaring skyward on a lethal plume twenty kilometers high. The vile mushroom cloud rose so high that its intense heat condensed water vapor, and a viscid black rain began to fall—sticky wet lumps of hot radioactive mud sluiced from the skies to pelt down on the survivors.

"In the first tenth of a second, every living thing in a radius within nine kilometers of ground zero was incinerated, and every building, tree, and shrub, anything standing above the ground level, was blasted into oblivion.

"A little further out from the epicenter, the damage was more shocking. At a radius of thirty kilometers, people were charcoalized. Mothers fleeing with their babies in their arms, men running to protect their families, everyone standing in the open air when the heat flash swept by was turned into a charcoal statue.

"Winds of one thousand kilometers per hour followed the heatflash. The terrible winds lifted lighter objects right off the ground or sucked them out through doors and windows of buildings. People were picked up and hurled through the air with incredible force; they became missiles traveling at ferocious speeds to smash into walls and solid objects. Skulls, vertebrae, and long bones were pulverized on impact.

"Those safe from the winds did not escape the tremendous overpressures that accompanied them. These overpressures produced instantaneous rupture of the lungs and eardrums. Windows were extruded from their frames by the overpressure and then burst into millions of needlelike shards which sliced through the air, penetrating human flesh and producing hideous lacerations.

"At about fifty kilometers from the epicenter, the heat from the explosion spontaneously ingnited trees and vegetation. People were turned into human torches where they stood, and every building became a crematorium.

"Miraculously, however, some of you survived to wander dazed and bewildered through the glowing ashes, looking for loved ones, lost in a featureless landscape. All landmarks, all orienting points had vanished. Nothing remained but a flat, burned-over prairie.

"You felt little pain at first. The greater shock of the desolation left no room for normal human suffering. You walked around naked, your clothing having been blown off or burned away. You felt no shame or immodesty, for it was impossible to tell men from women since every sizzled body looked alike.

"Friends and family members could not recognize one another. Everyone had lost hair and eyebrows; most had their facial features burned off. A man might have the imprint of his nose 'photographed' on his cheek, or the remnant of an ear grafted to his neck. Little was left but nondescript indentations for eyes and nose, a lipless slit for a mouth.

"You reached out to help the more severely injured and drew back hands filled with skin and flesh that slid off bare bone in charred gobbets. Your wounds smoked when dipped in water, and you walked like scarecrows with your arms outstretched to prevent raw skin surfaces from rubbing and sticking together.

"The lakes and reservoirs were choked with swollen red bodies—victims who had been boiled alive when the water turned to steam. Anyone who happened to witness the flash was instantly blinded, their eyesockets burned hollow. You staggered through the wreckage as the fluid from your melted eyes ran down your cheeks.

"In the days that followed, many survivors died horribly, retching blood, skin peeling away in sheets. Within twenty-four hours, even those survivors who had escaped serious injury began dying by the thousands. Their brain cells were damaged by radiation, causing their brains to swell inside their craniums and producing severe nausea, vomiting, diarrhea, followed by drowsiness, tremors, seizures, convulsions, and finally, massive internal hemorrhages and respiratory failure.

"Fallout and radiation continued to take a toll as the weeks passed. At first you felt merely weak or tired; then you began to notice that your hair was falling out, your teeth hurt and your gums bled, you lost your appetite, vomited, and developed bloody diarrhea, you bled under your skin, painful mouth ulcers formed, infections set in, producing fever and coma. Death came slowly, a result of fluid loss and starvation.

"You died and watched your loved ones die: by the thousands, instantly, and then with agonizing slowness, one by one. Amidst the ruins of your fair homeland, you experienced the ultimate suffering that hate can devise."

When Yarden finished, she opened her eyes. The Fieri sat in stunned silence, eyes closed, each face shimmering with silent tears. The day seemed to have grown colder, the sun more distant. The wind and waves had stilled.

"This happened long ago," said Yarden simply. "But it will happen again soon. My fellow Traveler, Orion Treet, predicted it and he was right. I know that now. The evil of Dome is growing. Even now its hatred burns against us; soon it will reach out for us.

"Treet went back to Dome to try to stop his prediction from coming true. He is there now giving his life to prevent the madness from consuming us once more. But time grows short, and Treet needs help.

"The Protector has sent His messengers, the talking fish, to warn us. Crocker, who returned to Dome with Treet, has appeared in our midst a broken, pathetic husk: another warning of the malicious intent of Dome. We have been forewarned."

Yarden paused and looked around the council ring. What were they thinking? Were they with her? Only Anthon appeared supportive, gazing at her directly. It only remained for her to make the appeal.

"We have been forewarned," she repeated. "Now we must decide what we will do. As for that, I have no suggestions. I only know that somehow I must go to Dome to add my life, my light, to that of those who struggle against the growing darkness.

"That's all I have to say. Thank you for listening to me." She bowed her head in a fervent prayer that her words had done their work.

The Preceptor drew herself up. "Yarden has spoken most persuasively. Is there anyone to challenge her argument?"

The voice of Mathiax sounded over the earplug. "The Clerk acknowledges Mentor Linan."

Mentor Linan cleared his throat. "My friends, I am deeply moved by Traveler Yarden's words, as are we all. I wish to remind this assembly, however, that our response to Dome was chosen from the first. We cannot intervene and still remain Fieri.

We have chosen our path and must not abandon it at the first hint of danger. Whatever happens, our strength is not in ourselves, but in the Infinite. By Him we stand or fall."

Mentor Bohm answered him at once. "Mentor Linan speaks for many, no doubt. But I would remind him that before abandoning Dome to its evil, our 'first' response was to reach out to our brothers. We did not choose our path; it was forced upon us, for there seemed no way to be reconciled to such a hard-hearted and deadly enemy.

"The agony and horror of the Burning, so vividly rendered for us by Yarden, was fresh when we devised our plan. And while it is true that we live only by the Infinite Father's light, does it follow that we must continue on a path that has come to an end?

"We can no longer allow Dome to breed its darkness and destruction. We are responsible if we withhold the help we could give. We all know that he who commits an evil, sins against the Infinite. But he who permits an evil he could prevent is guilty of the same sin. Is this not a precept among us?

"We are guilty of that sin, my friends. Too long have we hidden our light from those who labor in darkness, thereby permitting evil to flourish. I believe the time has come to seek a new way. I acknowledge Yarden's appeal. We must go to Dome. We must find a way to arrest the evil before it destroys again."

Bohm had no sooner finished speaking than another Mentor took the floor. "Mentor Bohm is right to remind us of a most apt precept," the speaker said. "But how do we really know what Dome intends? The presence of the Travelers, remarkable though it is, does not equate with danger. For all we know, Dome is simply living out its perverse destiny. There is no cause for alarm here, surely."

And so it went: one Mentor agreeing with Yarden, and another disagreeing, the arguments seesawing back and forth, opinion swaying first one way and then the other. Yarden became weary of the talk, and disheartened. Only Anthon, Talus, and Bohm appeared to support an expedition to Dome outright. Mathiax also supported Yarden's appeal, but as Clerk of the College, he could not speak for one position or the other. The majority seemed against making any radical changes in policy regarding Dome.

As the arguments went on and on, Yarden left the circle

and went down to walk along the water's edge. She walked far up the strand, and when the Fieri encampment was small in the distance she sat down and gazed out across the shining bowl of the bay toward the chalk-colored cliffs.

Beyond those cliffs, and beyond the arid uplands lay the deep sanctuary of the Blue Forest, and beyond the forest rolled the stark and empty hill country where Dome sat brooding.

I tried, Orion, she thought. God knows I tried. I did the best I knew how. I'm sorry if it wasn't enough.

Then she put her head down and cried.

SIXTY SIX

A dismal daylight awakened the rebels to the task of finding a new home among the reeking ruins of the Dhog cemetery. The prospects were not promising. The place was even more desolate and depressing than Treet remembered; besides the cremation mound, there was not another standing structure for a kilometer around. The wasted trees and rock heaps scattered over the area offered little cover and no protection.

Tvrdy and Kopetch paced off the perimeter and returned grumbling. "It's little more than hopeless," announced Kopetch. "Indefensible from any tactical point of view."

"We'll move as soon as we can find a better place," Tvrdy replied. "I will have scouts begin searching at once."

Piipo spoke up. "The Hyrgo fields are not far from here, I believe—unless I am much mistaken. Were we to go there, we would be close to our food source."

"It is not far," Cejka said, "but access is a problem. The Invisibles could reach us easily there."

"They'll find us anywhere we go," remarked Fertig. "It's only a matter of time now." He stared around the group helplessly. "It's over," he muttered softly to himself.

Treet ignored Fertig's comment. "What about the Bolbe exit?"

Tvrdy considered this for a moment. "It has possibilities."

"Isn't it a corridor?" asked Cejka.

"A tunnel," said Tvrdy. "Originally used for drainage."

"A tunnel, yes," Kopetch nodded, working it out in his head. "Even if they found us, they couldn't cut off our escape unless they somehow discovered its exit. And we'd only have one front to defend."

"An excellent idea!" Tvrdy beamed. "We'll check it out at once."

"Anywhere would have to be better than here." Treet winced as he looked around. "I've got a bad feeling about this place."

The rest of the day was spent taking stock of the supplies and arranging things for the next move. The camp was silent—depressed, thought Treet, by the dreary surroundings. By mid-morning the scouts Tvrdy had sent out returned, and also Bogney, whom no one had seen since the night before.

He came with six Dhog women dressed in frayed shreds of clothing, each one bearing a rag-wrapped burden on her back. They came into camp a few minutes after the scouts. "I wondered where they had hidden the women and children," said Kopetch as he watched the women enter warily.

Bogney and his entourage proceeded to the center of the camp where Treet, Tvrdy, and the others waited. The newcomers stared uneasily at the Tanais, Rumon, and Hyrgo gathered around. "Dhogs bringing some fine gift," Bogney explained, motioning for the women to put down their burdens.

"A gift?" wondered Tvrdy. "Why a gift?"

"Dhogs leaving soon. We be sharing goods with friends, thinking never see no more again."

Tvrdy shot a dark glance at a stricken Treet. "Oh? Where are you going, Bogney?"

"Fierra," he announced triumphantly. "Fieri man here be leading us." He grinned hugely at Treet and held out his hands. One of the women unwrapped her burden to bring forth a large plastic bladder filled with a dark liquid. "Tonight we sharing good drink. Tomorrow we gone."

"Is that so?" Tvrdy swung to face Treet directly.

Treet's mouth worked before the words came tumbling out. "Wait a minute here, Bogney. I didn't say *when* we would go. I only said I'd take you."

"No making big noises now. Giloon decides. Dhogs ready."

Tvrdy smiled suddenly. "We accept your gift," he said, picking up one of the bladders. He opened it and raised it to his nose. He coughed and shut his eyes, thrusting the bladder from him. "It is most thoughtful of you."

"We be drinking tonight. Tomorrow be going to Fierra."

Treet stared at Tvrdy as if the Tanais had parted company with his senses. As soon as the liquor had been carefully put away, Treet took Tvrdy aside. "What do you mean by encouraging this ridiculous idea?"

"What do you mean by making irrational bargains with him? You know Dhogs are like children."

"I had to do something. It was the only way I could get him to help us evacuate the wounded. We couldn't leave them for the Invisibles to find."

"Why not?" Tvrdy fixed Treet with a hard, implacable gaze. "Thanks to you, we have saved our wounded. They require food and constant attention; they are a drain on our limited resources. They will die here anyway because we cannot care for them properly. Why not let the Invisibles solve the problem quickly and easily?"

Treet listened, horrified. "You don't mean it. Do you hear what you're saying? You sound like Jamrog!"

Tvrdy made a face. "It is the voice of reason."

"Reason? It's insanity. This is exactly the kind of coldhearted expediency that loosed the monster in the first place. Tvrdy, listen to me. I know. I've read the records. When the Red Death broke out, the survivors fought back with everything they had; but when it looked like they couldn't win, they began cutting their losses. They abandoned the dying and sealed themselves into survival cells. They began systematically reducing civilization to base utilitarianism."

Tvrdy frowned. "It was life or death."

"And they chose death, Tvrdy. Don't you see? Whenever some lives become expendable, whenever some are written off for whatever reason—this one is nonviable, this one nonproductive, this one nonfunctional, this one nonconforming to the party line—when the weak or disagreeable lose their humanity—it's death, not life."

"It was necessary," replied Tvrdy sullenly. "Inevitable."

"True human beings do not make deals with death, Tvrdy. It may well be inevitable, but civilized people do not give up on life; they do not embrace death just because life becomes too hard."

"What do you know about it?"

"I told you. I read the records," said Treet. "Feodr Rumon wrote it down. I know what happened."

"You would have done the same thing. Anyone would."

"No, Tvrdy. Some would, it's true. But not everyone. They had a choice—there's always a choice. They chose wrong, Tvrdy. The ancestors of Dome chose death rather than life. It was wrong, and you've been paying for it ever since."

"It can't be undone now."

"No, it can't be undone, but we don't have to repeat the same mistake. We can choose differently. If we're ever to be free of the madness, we have to choose the right way."

Tvrdy glared at Treet in silence. It was difficult to tell what the Tanais leader was thinking. "I don't see what a few wounded have to do with this. They will die anyway."

"If you really believe that," said Treet softly, "then there's no hope for us."

With that, Treet walked off. "Think about it, Tvrdy," he said turning back. Tvrdy stood where he'd left him, staring at the ground. "You know I'm right."

• • • • • •

Jaire walked back and forth on the curving crown of the hill. The towering obelisk, with its ring of smaller obelisks throwing long afternoon shadows down the green hill, pointed heavenward as if poised for imminent flight.

She stopped when she heard the chime, and turned toward the amphidrome. Talus emerged with Mathiax close behind him, the dismissal chime still ringing in the air. "Don't be angry, Talus," Mathiax said. "It is more than we had a right to hope for."

Jaire hurried toward them. "What is the decision?" She glanced from one to the other of them hopefully, saw their expressions, and asked, "What's wrong? Will they not allow us to go?"

"One fleet only," replied Talus tersely. "And Mathiax is to stay."

"We will be in constant communication," said Mathiax. "I will be as close as your own skin."

"It isn't the same." Talus stood woodenly, arms folded across his massive chest—like a tree taking root on the sculpted green lawn of the amphidrome.

"Accept the wisdom of the College," soothed Mathiax. "It is for the best."

"The best? The best? It is too little and too late."

Mathiax closed his eyes and shook his head gently. "It is in the Protector's good time. You are upset or you would agree."

Grim-faced Mentors began streaming from the amphidrome and passing silently around them. Bohm approached and joined them. "I have spoken with the crew. We are clear to depart as soon as you are ready, Talus. The others will leave in the morning."

"Come," said Mathiax. "I'll go with you to the airfield."

"We're leaving at once?" Jaire glanced around expectantly.

Talus took his daughter's hands. "I am sorry, Jaire. I should have told you straight away. You are to stay here as well."

She pulled her hands away. "Is Preben going?"

"Yes. Preben, Anthon, and Yarden will be picked up at the bay."

"Who else is going?"

"Besides myself, only Bohm and his fleet crew."

Jaire smiled defiantly. "Then I will go, too. I am part of Bohm's crew." Her expression dared anyone to gainsay her.

Mathiax and Talus looked at one another. Bohm explained, "She is part of the emergency medical support group."

"The College did not say anything about medical support," said Mathiax. "It's your decision, Talus."

He gazed at his daughter. "No, Jaire. It will be difficult and dangerous. I can't allow it."

"Since it's dangerous, you may need medical support. I am going." Jaire gazed steadily at her father and saw him weaken. She laid a hand on his arm. "It was my dream, remember. I am part of this. You cannot deny me."

Mathiax watched them both. "Talus," he said stepping close, "Jaire is right. The dream was given to her. She has been called. It is in the Infinite's hands; trust in the Protector."

Talus assented. "I am overruled by a higher authority. Go say good-bye to your mother, collect your things, and meet us at the airfield. We will leave as soon as you return."

Jaire smiled slyly. "I have already anticipated your decision, Father. Mother knows, and my things are in the evee. I am ready now."

Bohm clapped his hands once and started toward the waiting vehicle. "Then we leave at once."

• • • • • •

It was near sunset when Anthon came to her. Yarden was sitting with her chin on knees, eyes closed. She heard the gritty squeak of his tread on the wet sand and stirred.

"Did I wake you?" he asked as he came to stand over her.

She opened her eyes slowly, and lifted a hand. Anthon took it and helped her to her feet. "I wasn't asleep," Yarden answered. "I was praying."

"Ah, yes." He paused, gazing raptly at Yarden. "You know, as I came up to you just now you looked just like my wife. From a distance, that is. She was another one who loved her solitude. I would find her like this—out alone somewhere—and I'd ask her what she was doing. 'Praying,' she'd say, exactly like you did just now. Or, 'Being alone with my thoughts.' That was another one."

They began to walk back to the encampment. "I didn't know you were married, Anthon. Were you very much in love?"

"Yes, yes. It was a good marriage. I loved her as much as any man could, and maybe more."

"What happened?"

"It was an accident. She was with our son on a boat; they were out for the day sailing on Prindahl. A storm came up, and they were too far out. I think the boat swamped, and they drowned. We never found the boat or the bodies. They just sailed off one morning and never came back."

"How tragic! I'm sorry, Anthon—I wouldn't have asked if I'd had any idea—"

"Please, it's all right. I don't mind. I have nothing but good memories. I get lonely for them sometimes, it's true, but it only serves to make our eventual reunion the more joyful. I know that we'll be together again one day. In the meantime, there is much to do. I am needed here."

"I'll say," said Yarden, taking Anthon's arm. "I have a feeling I'm going to need all the friends I can get."

"You know how the council decided?" He cocked an eyebrow quizzically.

"Well, let's just say I have a feeling my speech didn't sway the masses."

"Sadly, no. We could have hoped for a better response, there's no denying that. But we did gain something—perhaps more than you suspect."

Yarden looked up sharply. "What? Tell me," she said. "You must!"

"I thought you knew everything."

Yarden stopped. "Please, don't joke about this. It's too important."

"You're right. Forgive me; I was taken by your b—" He hesitated, turned, and looked out across the bay. "I forgot myself for a moment."

Yarden felt a warmth envelop her. "It . . . it's all right, Anthon," she said softly. "What did you come to tell me?" She let her hand slide away from his arm. They began walking again.

"The Preceptor has decided to allow a balon fleet to travel to Dome to assess the situation."

"Really? That's wonderful!"

"It is a beginning. Talus and Bohm argued most eloquently, and I did what I could, of course. But in the end the College remained unconvinced of the threat. It was all we could do to get them to agree to one fleet—six balons. They only consented because the Preceptor supported the idea—it was her suggestion, in fact. A compromise. Talus wanted six fleets; the Mentors were against sending any. The Preceptor suggested a fleet in case there were people to bring out, and the Mentors relented."

"But still, it's a victory. How soon can we leave?"

"You can believe Talus and Mathiax were already prepared. A balon is probably on the way to pick us up now."

"That'll take weeks!" exclaimed Yarden, suddenly realizing just how far away from Fierra they were. "Can't we leave for Dome now?" The notion was absurd, and Yarden admitted it as soon as the words were out. "Forget I said that. It's just that . . . well, isn't there a faster way?"

Anthon chuckled. "A balon can travel quickly. It won't take them as long as it took us. Two or three days. Anyway, you don't want them to go without you, do you?"

"You'll go, too?"

"Yes, and Preben has volunteered. Talus is going, as you know, and Bohm also, with his regular balon crews. That's all."

"Mathiax?"

"In the Preceptor's absence, he must stay in Fierra."

"Maybe I could get Pizzle to come, too. He might be useful in the clinch."

Anthon stopped and took her by the shoulders. "Yarden, this is to be an observation tour, not an invasion. We do not go in force—the Fieri have no weapons in any case."

Yarden glanced at her feet. She nodded. "I understand. I got a little carried away." She raised her eyes hopefully. "But whatever we can do to help Treet, we'll do, right?"

"Whatever we can do to help, we will do. Beyond that . . ." Anthon shrugged. "We will have to wait and see."

He stared at her for a moment without speaking. Yarden became self-conscious under his gaze and looked away, feeling that strange warmth again. "The Preceptor," he said finally, "would like to see you now. We'd better get back."

SIXTY SEVEN

From the suddenness of the attack, Treet guessed the Invisibles had been in position and only waiting for daylight to commence the slaughter. At sunrise the rebel camp lay in sodden sleep, having dosed themselves to the point of numbness with the Dhog's rough, bitter liquor. Shared out among the men, there had not been enough to actually liberate anyone from his senses. Still, the attack caught them asleep—disaster for a soldier.

The first blasts brought the rebels to their feet. They dove for their weapons and began returning fire while the echoes still boomed from Dome's crystal shell. The rebels understood that if they did not win, this would be their last fight. They fought with dire ferocity, driving the Invisibles' assault force back by the sheer force of their fury.

When they saw their hopes for a quick victory evaporate under the rebel's blistering defense, the Invisibles withdrew to surround the cemetery mound and dig in.

Tvrdy, standing atop a stack of weapons cases, shouted orders to his men. Cejka and Kopetch dashed here and there around him, organizing the equipment for transport. "What's going on?" asked Treet as he came running up.

"We're going to try to reach the Bolbe tunnel," yelled Cejka as each blast showered smoking clods and rock dust over them.

"We'll never make it," said Treet. "It's too far. There's nothing between here and there but dead trees and broken ground."

"Treet!" shouted Tvrdy. "Help or get out of the way. We're going. We can't stay here."

"What about the wounded?" Treet demanded, hands on hips.

Tvrdy glared at him and then turned away, saying, "We take them with us—of course."

The next few hours were a nightmare of death and searing fire. The rebels—Dhogs and Hyrgo loaded like pack animals—

retreated en masse, their exit covered by Tanais and Rumon marksmen. The Invisibles sensed victory close at hand and pressed the retreat hard, hoping to divide and scatter the rebels. Casualties on both sides were heavy.

Treet, laboring alongside Ernina, assisted the wounded and helped keep up the flagging spirits of those around him as, meter by meter, they fought their way to the safety of the Bolbe tunnel. Each meter cost them dearly. When a man fell, not only did they lose a soldier—they lost the supplies he carried.

But Tvrdy, displaying superhuman leadership and tenacity, kept them all together and moving ahead, while the marksmen put down a blanket of fire behind them. This way, the Invisibles were unable to move into position ahead of them and cut off the retreat.

Firebolts streaked through the crackling air as the rebels pushed on. The Dhogs, caught in camp when the attack started, had no choice but to join the fight. They had planned to be away at daybreak, heading for Fierra with Treet leading the way.

Giloon Bogney cursed and gnashed his teeth, and worked himself into a purple rage at the Invisibles for stealing his chance to leave Dome forever. But he also put his head down and applied himself nerve-and-sinew to the task of getting himself and his people to safety.

It seemed to take an eternity to reach the Bolbe tunnel.

In actual fact, it took forty minutes to travel a distance slightly more than two kilometers. Treet was among the first to reach the tunnel. He saw the tunnel's mouth yawning from a low earthen bank covered with dry shriveled brush. He ran ahead and ducked inside. The interior was dark and cool, with a fetid, musty odor.

He took a quick look around and dashed outside again as the Invisibles, now comprehending the rebels' destination, redoubled their effort. The shriek of their weapons filled the air like a scream of rage.

The Rumon and Tanais marksmen, limping from hillock to ditch to rubble pile, dug in to face the attack while their comrades scurried to safety.

Treet helped herd the wounded inside the tunnel, and then went back to help the Hyrgo carry equipment and supplies while the Tanais and Rumon formed a semicircle around the tunnel mouth to cover them. Tvrdy stood in the center, directing the fire and urging on the struggling carriers.

Treet saw one Tanais crumple and fall, and Kopetch appeared in the gap, snatching up the man's weapon before it touched the ground, firing away.

The Invisibles gathered their forces together and charged the rapidly dwindling defenses. Treet, sweating and panting from his exertion, muscles throbbing, lightened the burdens of others, pulling the heavier articles from their packs to carry himself, dashing back and forth to the mouth of the tunnel.

Above the frizzling whine of thermal weapons, Treet heard the shouts of the Invisibles as they rushed the defenders. He turned to see a formidable wave of black-clad Mors Ultima surging toward them, the throw-probes of their weapons white-hot and spitting lightning.

The line of defenders buckled as the rebels shrank back. Treet was bent over a fallen Dhog when a Rumon marksman cried out, spun backward, and collapsed; his weapon clattered to the ground. Treet hoisted the Dhog to his feet and rushed to the Rumon, whose body twitched on the ground. The scorching discharge of the weapons around him was deafening.

The Rumon had taken a glancing hit; the side of his neck was a shriveled red welt and the flesh along the top of his shoulder was burned away, revealing a length of fire-blackened clavicle. Treet bent over the man, heard a sizzling crack, and dropped flat to the ground as the air convulsed over his head.

The wash of air that hit him stank of ozone and the retchingly sweet odor of burning flesh.

He saw the Rumon's weapon steaming on the ground, rolled to it, and scooped it up. He pointed it in the direction of the oncoming Invisibles and hit the pressure plate with his palm.

The weapon jolted in his hands as the blast discharged in a blinding flash with a sound that pierced his skull.

Treet fired again and again, heedless of his aim—his only intent to discourage the Invisibles in their assumption of him as an easy target—sliding backward on his belly over the uneven ground.

Tanais and Rumon were falling around him. The cries of the wounded rang in the air between blasts. He choked on the stench of hot metal and charred meat.

Somehow he reached the mouth of the tunnel once more. He felt a tug on his left hand and discovered that he still gripped the arm of the wounded Rumon and had pulled the unconscious soldier back with him.

Smoke stung his eyes, and he became aware of a tingling sensation in his right hand. He glanced down and saw his hand burning where it gripped the throw-probe of his weapon. He released the gun and stared in disbelief at his hand. There was no pain, but the palm was seared and his fingers burned bloody.

A blast ripped the dirt beside him. He felt the heatflash pass over him. The battlefield grew blurry, and his head buzzed. Treet gritted his teeth and crawled backward to the tunnel, still clutching the body of the soldier and dragging it with him.

He reached the tunnel and pulled the soldier in. People rushed by him, and he heard Tvrdy yelling for reinforcements. Then the daylight began to flicker and the tunnel to spin. Treet flung out his arms and tried to hold on.

· · · · · ·

"Please, Asquith, I wouldn't ask you if I didn't think it very important. We need you."

Pizzle scowled at Yarden in the fading twilight and said, "How come when you want something its 'Asquith, please. Asquith, we need you,' huh? The rest of the time its 'Shut up, Pizzle,' 'Get lost, Pizzle.' Just leave me out of it this time, okay? I mean, I gave at the office."

Yarden's eyes flashed. "That woe-is-little-me act won't work this time, mister! You've used it once too often with me. Now, here's the deal: we're going back to Dome to pick up Treet. I want you to come."

"You make it sound like a promenade in the Easter Parade. It isn't a Sunday fete we're going to."

"Then you'll come?"

"I didn't say that. Why do you need me anyway? You said the Fieri are sending a whole fleet."

"They're sending the balons, yes. But they're mostly just for backup and in case we can bring any people out. We're going to be a little short of manpower."

"A *lot* short it sounds to me."

832

"Pizzle, quit being such a baby. You're going, and that's that."

"Sure, you get to make the grand magnanimous gesture—play Florence Goodheart. All I get is orders, aggravation, and ulcers."

"Ulcers my eye! Nothing penetrates that colossal selfishness of yours. You wouldn't know a magnanimous gesture if it slithered up and spit in your eye." Yarden rolled her eyes in disgust. "This is just like you, Pizzle. I give you a chance to do the decent thing, and you throw it back in my face. I should have known better!"

She stomped off. Pizzle shouted after her, "Don't worry about hurting my feelings."

"You don't have any!" Yarden disappeared behind one of the tents.

Pizzle looked around, feeling ashamed and foolish. The whole camp probably heard the ruckus, he thought. Now they'll all think I'm a coward. He ducked into his tent and flopped down on his sleep mat.

It isn't that I'm afraid. It isn't . . . not really. It's just that now that I have Starla, I've got something to live for. I mean, I don't want to die before I really get a chance to live.

Is that so selfish?

If it is, it's just too bad. Treet made his own decision to go back to Dome. He knew what would happen, and he took his chances. I don't see why we all have to throw ourselves into fits now just because Yarden gets all excited. She didn't care all that much when he left.

But things can change. Hearts can change.

Yarden has had a change of heart, he thought. Would Starla also have a change of heart if she thought he was a coward?

The idea chilled him. Would Starla think less of him if he stayed behind? Would she think him a hero if he went?

Pizzle tossed on his mat. This is all your fault, Treet! Why can't you leave people alone?

SIXTY
EIGHT

Treet heard the sound of voices talking above him and pushed himself up on his elbows. The movement brought pain which cleared the cobwebs from his head. He was lying in the tunnel, far back. He could hear the muted roar and rumble of thermal weapons in the distance. There were bodies lying around him, some disturbingly silent and others moaning softly in the darkness.

He sat up gingerly and took a quick physical inventory. Except for his hand, which throbbed mightily but numbly, he was not hurt anywhere that he could tell. He climbed to his feet, careful not to step on anyone near him.

Someone was moving down the tunnel with a hand-held lantern. He crept toward the light.

"Does your hand hurt?" asked Ernina, holding the light to his face. She examined the pupils of his eyes, and then gave him the lantern and took up his bandaged hand.

"No, it's okay. I feel fine. Do you need help?"

"I'll manage. Some of the Dhog women have come. They're ignorant, but they do what they're told."

"Just tell me what to do. I'm here to help."

She shook her head wearily. "Tvrdy wants to see you. He told me to send you as soon as you woke up."

"What happened to me? Besides the burn, I mean. I didn't feel a thing."

"Concussion." She reached up a hand and touched his head. "Tender?"

Treet winced. "A little."

"Thermal shock wave. You were fortunate. Any closer and you would have been burned."

"How long have I been out?"

"Not long. Two hours, maybe three." She took the lantern from him and made to move off. "Tvrdy's waiting for you down there."

Treet gripped the physician's shoulder with his good hand. "Thanks, Ernina."

"I did nothing. Worse wounds than yours demanded my attention."

"And I suppose this bandage just wrapped itself around my mitt?" He gave her a hug and stepped away. "Anyway, thanks; I appreciate it. I'll come back when Tvrdy's finished with me."

He hurried off down the tunnel toward the sound of the fighting, following the curve of the large conduit with his good hand outstretched. He arrived a minute later at the improvised command post a few dozen meters inside the mouth of the tunnel.

Bright globe lights burned from the ribbed ceiling. Tvrdy stood in the center of a group, bathed in white light. He acknowledged Treet when he came up. The others shifted to allow Treet a place to stand. Treet did a quick mental roll call: there was Kopetch, and Cejka, several Tanais and Rumon commanders, Piipo, and next to him the squat Bogney, looking disgusted and angry.

In fact, now that he noticed it, everyone wore the same expression: as if they were holding something old and rotten on their tongues and didn't like it one little bit.

"Where's Fertig?" he asked.

"That's what we'd like to know. Did you see him this morning?"

"My day got off to kind of a rocky start. I don't remember much of anything."

"No one saw him," said Kopetch. "He sneaked out last night."

"Maybe he got killed in the attack," offered Treet without much conviction.

"It's possible," Tvrdy allowed, although his tone implied that he thought the possibility exceedingly remote. "No one recalls seeing him before the attack or at any time after."

"But if he died early on, that would explain it."

"It doesn't explain the Invisibles finding us so fast," replied Kopetch acidly.

The bile rising in his throat told Treet that Kopetch was right. He forced down the bitter taste. We trusted Fertig, he thought. He saved my life. Was it just so he could turn traitor?

The shock of the betrayal stung like the smack of a brick between the eyes.

"The point is," Tvrdy was saying, "we must assume he told

them where the exit of this tunnel lies. They will have begun searching for it, and they will find it."

That's it then; we're trapped like rats in a sewer pipe, thought Treet. He felt sick to his stomach at the duplicity, the treachery, and the futility of their position.

"I have sent men to the other end of the tunnel in Bolbe. They should return shortly with a status report." Tvrdy continued the briefing matter-of-factly, although to Treet it sounded as if the heart had been gouged out of the man; he spoke in a strained and hollow voice. "I doubt if the Invisibles will have had time to locate the exit in Bolbe. If it is still open, we can escape into Hage."

"And then what?" asked Piipo. "Wait for the Invisibles to pick us up? There's a Purge going on. We'll be arrested for interrogation as soon as we set foot in Bolbe."

"He's right," said another. "It would be the end of the rebellion. We'd have to split up our forces and go underground."

"Maybe that's just what we need to do," shouted Tvrdy angrily. "We have not been successful in any other way. If the rebellion is to live, we must also survive."

"How long can we hold them off at this end?" Cejka asked.

"A day. Perhaps two." Kopetch shook his head slowly. "We are well protected here, but powerless to mount an attack. We can only defend. Meanwhile, the Invisibles are strengthening their position. If we stay here, they will eventually overrun us."

Talk continued like this for some time as options were examined and discarded. When the briefing broke up, Treet started back to offer the help he'd promised Ernina. He felt a tug on his arm and turned to see Bogney glowering at him.

"Fieri man promised Giloon to be taking Dhogs to Fierra," the Dhog leader said.

"That's right. But there's not a lot I can do about it now."

"You promised!"

"What do you want me to do—walk through walls? I can't take you now. And believe me, if I had my choice right now the desert seems a better bet. But in case you hadn't noticed, we're stuck here for a while. No one is going anywhere."

Bogney spat, and his face twisted into a greasy sneer. "Dhogs going," he announced, and stomped off.

• • • • •

Yarden could not get over the blandness of Crocker's expression, the blankness in his empty gray eyes. She had never seen an amnesiac, but Crocker came close to fleshing out her mental picture of one, right down to the fleck of spittle gathering in the corner of his slack mouth.

"Crocker, it's me, Yarden. Do you remember me?" she asked as she came into the tent where he sat, freshly groomed and clothed in a brown shirt and trousers. The pilot appeared not to notice her at first, then, as she sat down across from him, turned his head and looked at her without interest.

"Yarden," he said. He might have been a bird mimicking a new sound.

She turned to Anthon, who had followed her in, and gripped his hand as he sat down beside her. "I don't think I can do this," she whispered.

"He's making progress," Anthon said. "You'll see. Go on."

"Crocker, I brought you something." She unfolded a cloth she carried and held out a piece of sweet herb bread. "Here, taste it. I think you'll like it."

The man took the bread and looked at it, raised it to his mouth, and took a bite. He spit the bite out at once and put the cake aside—all without the slightest reaction or expression.

"Now what do I do?"

"Just talk to him," Anthon urged. "Eino says that his periods of lucidity come and go, but mostly they come when you force him to respond to you."

"Crocker, look at me," Yarden said. "I have something important to tell you." She spoke slowly and with exaggerated care, as if speaking to a child too young to comprehend a grown-up problem. "I am going away for a little while. There is trouble, and I must go see what I can do to help. Do you understand?"

Her question brought no response. She looked helplessly at Anthon. "Make him respond," he told her.

"Do you understand what I said? Answer me if you understand."

She saw a tiny glimmer of recognition in Crocker's dead eyes. His features quickened. It was as if the man was surfacing from a deep sleep underwater and resuming consciousness. "Yarden," he said softly. "Good to see you."

"Good to see you, too, Crocker. We've been worried about you. How are you feeling?"

837

The man's lips drew back from his teeth, and a noise like creaking bones came from his throat. Yarden realized it was meant to be laughter. The sound sent a chill through her heart. "Feeling good. Feeling fine. Crocker's feeling all right."

Yarden shivered. Anthon slipped his arm around her shoulders and gave her a squeeze. "Go on, you're doing well."

She drew a deep breath. "Crocker, I'm going away—"

"You just got here."

"No, I mean soon—tomorrow. Treet is in trouble, and we're going to help him."

Crocker shook his head, and a vague expression of confusion passed over his features. "Treet."

"You remember Treet. He was with us, one of us. He went back to Dome, and we have to get him out."

"Dome," said Crocker. His face contorted in a ghastly smile. "Do you remember Dome?"

"I remember, Crocker. Why don't you tell me what you remember? I'd like to hear it."

He stared at her.

"What do you remember, Crocker?"

"Dome was a very big place. Very old."

"Yes, it was. But what about the people? What happened when you and Treet and Calin went back? Do you remember going back?"

"It was night. I saw them sleeping there. I should have done it then, gotten it over with." Crocker seemed to be speaking to someone else. His eyes were unfocused and hazy. "I knew there would be trouble with that girl along." He paused and then growled out, "She was trouble. I should have done it then when I had the chance."

Yarden kept her voice level. "Done what, Crocker?"

"Killed them, of course. What do you think I'm talking about? I was supposed to kill them both—would have, too. But that stupid slut of a magician interfered. She made me miss." He laughed creakily while Yarden covered her face with her hands. "I fixed her though. I shoved that thing in her throat, and that fixed her."

Yarden stifled a cry and turned away, sobbing. Anthon comforted her. "Now you know what happened. The worst is over. You're doing fine."

Presently she dried her eyes. "Crocker, listen to me very

carefully." Yarden leaned forward and put her hand on his arm, gripping it hard as if willing him to understand what she was about to say. "Anthon," she indicated the Mentor with a nod, "believes that you will get better. I believe so, too. You *can* get better, Crocker.

"You've had a bad experience, and it has upset your mind. You're safe now, and no one can hurt you anymore. You can get better if you want to. Do you want to get better?"

He nodded, watching her closely.

"Good. I want you to get better, too. It is going to take time. But mostly it's going to take a lot of work. Very hard work. No one can do it for you. If you want to get well, you'll have to work at it. Do you understand?"

"I understand."

"We will help you all we can. But it's going to be up to you. If you want to get well, *you're* going to have to do the work, Crocker."

"I'm tired," the pilot said and laid down, placing his head on his arm. He closed his eyes.

Yarden glanced at Anthon, who rose quietly and said, "It's enough for now. We'll go."

"We're going now, Crocker. But I'll come back to see you tomorrow before I leave. All right? Good night."

They crept from the tent to the sigh of Crocker's deep, rhythmic breathing. They walked a few paces away. Stars glittered in the high, wide sky and shimmered in the mirrored bay.

"He's asleep already. Out like a light"—she snapped her fingers "—just that quick. Simply talking to me exhausted him."

"The trauma was severe. It will take time to heal."

"He looks so fragile. Can he really come back?"

"Yes; it's entirely possible. Eino and the Preceptor have examined him, and they agree. But it is as you say. Recovery will take hard work, and it will be up to him to do the work. There is no other way."

Yarden thought about this. Yes, it did sometimes seem the hardest work of all to impose order on the chaos of thoughts and emotions, to think clearly, rationally. Sometimes it took all the strength of will she possessed.

Yarden shivered and rubbed her hands over her arms, feeling goose bumps. "Poor Calin. I keep thinking about her, and I can't believe it—it's like a bad dream." They walked along a while in silence and came to Yarden's tent. "Isn't there anything we can do for Crocker?"

"Oh yes," replied Anthon. "Encourage him, try to make him understand what he must do, support him. You'd be surprised how much that can help. But you must realize that ultimately he will have to make the decision to get well for himself. No one can make the decision for him."

"Thank you, Anthon." Yarden smiled wanly. "I'm glad you're here. I don't know what I'd do without you."

SIXTY NINE

The balons took on color as the sun rose: royal blue, red, verdigris, saffron, violet, and bronze. They tugged at their tether lines, anxious to leave the great green field for their true home, the clean, empty skies of Empyrion. As the sun climbed above the horizon, the first airship broke free and drifted silently upward.

As if this was the signal they had been waiting for, the others rose as one, floating heavenward in slow, dignified procession, like so many puffballs rising on the wind. They ascended in silence, their bulbous shapes ghostly in the fresh light.

Fierra, the glowing sunstone of its gracious buildings fading now with the coming of day, lay peacefully below, surrounded by fields and fruit groves on three sides and the great silver bowl of Prindahl on the fourth. When each balon had gained sufficient altitude above the sleeping city, the massive engines sparked to life and with a deep, throaty purr pushed the graceful aircraft into the early morning sky.

Under power, the ships turned and headed west, their spherical shadows going before them, gliding over the hills. Only one person saw them go. Mathiax stood alone on the edge of the airfield and watched the balons rise, take power, and purr swiftly away. He watched until the huge spheres were mere colored flecks in the sky and then held up his hands, saying, "Go with all goodness and return in peace. I send you in the power of the Infinite Father, Creator of us all."

● ● ● ● ● ●

Away to the north, another balon was making its way across the ragged peaks of the Light Mountains. The sharp, red-brown spires and pyramids, flattened by the balon's altitude into a dull, featureless rumple, took on a measure of its actual shape as the shadows cast by the rising sun threw the mountainscape into knife-sharp relief.

Aboard, the crew and the passengers—Talus, Bohm, and Jaire—still slept, except for the pilot and navigator on duty. They monitored the flight and marked their hourly progress on the large projection of their destination on the flightboard.

"The wind is with us," remarked the navigator as he returned to his station beside the balon pilot. "We're making good time. I've estimated our ETA—we should reach the bay early tomorrow afternoon."

"Good," answered the pilot. "That means we can catch the others en route and arrive at Dome together."

There came a chime, and presently the relief pilot and navigator appeared to take their places. They logged in, saying, "Go get some sleep, you two. We'll take over from here." And the balon pushed on, its engines booming in the rock canyons of Taleraan far below.

• • • • • •

As the sun flamed the ocher bluffs, whose reflections shone like gold in the dark olive-tinted water of the bay, Crocker slipped from the tent. He padded silently down to the water's edge and stood for a moment gazing at the bluffs. He saw a familiar shape perched on the rim of the nearest cliff, watching, waiting.

The man's head swiveled toward the Fieri encampment. The sun's first rays were reaching across the sand as the mountain's indigo shadows receded. Soon people would be waking and stirring. They would come to the bay to swim; the air would fill with the sound of their voices. The fish would come near once more before taking their newborn young back out to the deeper waters of their ocean home.

Now, before anyone will see. Do it now.

Crocker untied the cloth belt at his waist and shrugged the brown shirt from his shoulders. He let the trousers fall and stepped out of them. He waded into the water of the bay to his waist and cupped water in his hands, drank, and splashed handfuls of water over his body. He walked back to shore and stood for a long moment, looking at the tents spread over the sand.

"Too hard," he muttered to himself. He turned his eyes

away to the west and began running toward the bluffs and the wevicat waiting for him atop the seacliff.

• • • • • •

A sharp kick in the ribs brought Fertig awake. He moaned and rolled over weakly. "On your feet. The Supreme Director wants to see you now." The guard raised his foot to kick again. "I said, on—"

"No! No! I'm getting up. See? I'm getting up."

Fertig was taken from the filth-encrusted cell and half-pushed, half-dragged through the corridor to a waiting em. Two Mors Ultima stood beside the vehicle; he was shoved in, and they drove off.

The journey went by in an anxious blur, and when Fertig roused himself from his stupor, they were stopping in Threl Square. A stupendous Jamrog stared down at him from the enormous banners ringing the square. He heard the shush of feet on the stone and saw a platoon of Invisibles marching in double time across the empty square. Then he was hauled from the em and pushed toward the immense gray columns of the Threl Chambers entrance.

They passed between the columns—and a double row of Nilokerus security men—and entered the gigantic ground-floor chamber. At the far end of the vaulted room, red streamers hung down from the ceiling over the crystal bier of Sirin Rohee. They swept past the transparent coffin, and Fertig glanced at the ashen corpse within. The shrunken, waxy remains little resembled the former Supreme Director whose life had so dominated his own.

It was just a glimpse, and they were past. They rode a lift up through the core of the building to the Supreme Director's kraam, paused outside, and waited to be announced. A moment later, the unidor snapped off and Fertig was propelled inside.

Jamrog stood on a riser in the center of a room much changed since Fertig had last seen it. In the shifting light of torches he saw sumptuous furnishings, fine Bolbe hangings, great standing jars of greenery, and tables laden with fruit and food. The Supreme Director himself was dressed in an opulent hagerobe of blood-red with designs worked in shimmering silver. It was open from neck to ankles and he stood with legs splayed, twirling a bhuj in his hands. Beside him on the riser stood the wasted Diltz, whom Fertig recognized as one of the coterie of grasping underdirectors he'd overseen as Nilokerus Subdirector and Hladik's rightful successor.

Jamrog bent his head to catch a whispered word from Diltz as Fertig was brought forward. The Supreme Director held up his hand and beckoned the guards closer. "Bring him to me; I want to see him."

The guards yanked him closer. Jamrog lowered the bhuj and pressed its point into Fertig's chest. "That's close enough." Jamrog smiled viciously. "Welcome home, Subdirector. We have missed you."

Fertig threw a dark look at Diltz. Jamrog saw it and said, "I see you remember Diltz. Yes, *Director* Diltz. What did you expect? Hladik departed life so quickly, he left a void in the Hage hierarchy. The Hage had to have a Director, and you, unfortunately, were not to be found."

Jamrog spoke so calmly, so reasonably, Fertig began to hope that he would succeed after all, that the value of the information he held would buy his life. "I am sorry, Supreme Director. I was frightened. Confused."

"Yes, and you forgot who your friends were. Didn't you, Fertig?"

"I did forget, Supreme Director. It's true."

"But now you have remembered. Is that so?"

"That's so, Supreme Director." He could feel sweat dampening the palms of his hands.

Jamrog turned to Diltz. "There, you see, Diltz? A simple misunderstanding. Nothing so sinister as you suggest. He was frightened and ran away. And now he has come to his senses and returned. Just so."

Fertig's heart leapt in his breast. This was better than he could have imagined. Jamrog must be in a supremely generous mood. Perhaps the rebels had already been subdued. The thought gave him a momentary pang. But after all, the situation was hopeless; it was every man for himself.

"Perhaps he is still frightened, Supreme Director," suggested Diltz in his sepulchral voice. "Frightened enough to withhold valuable information."

844

"You're not frightened anymore, are you, Fertig?" The prisoner shook his head. "There, you see, Diltz? He's not frightened anymore. And he knows what would happen to him if he withheld information that could help us crush this untidy rebellion."

Jamrog stepped down from the riser and came to stand before Fertig. "You would have to go to interrogation. Unpleasant things can happen to a man during interrogation, I'm told. The Mors Ultima are very persuasive, but tend to be somewhat overdramatic."

"They are most effective," said Diltz.

"Bah! Listen to him, Fertig. I believe he wants you taken to interrogation. You don't want to go there, do you? You'd prefer to talk to us here and now. Isn't that right?"

As Jamrog was speaking, Mrukk stepped from behind the riser and came to stand facing him a little to the left. At the sight of the Mors Ultima commander, Fertig blanched. "Answer me, Subdirector. You'd like to tell us what you know."

"Y-yes, Supreme Director, I'll talk to you now. I'll tell you everything I know . . ." He hesitated, his mouth dry, sweat starting to seep through his clothes. "Everything. But my information is worth something." He cringed as he said it. "I've already demonstrated its value—I told your commander where the rebels were hiding."

Jamrog smiled and put his face close. "Of course. A very valuable piece of information, too. And you shall be repaid. Now, tell us where the tunnel exit is."

Fertig licked his lips. "In Bolbe. It's near the material stores in deep Hage, I think."

"You'll have to be more precise than that," said Diltz, "if you expect us to believe you."

"The scouts did not say precisely."

"Are there connecting tunnels?" asked Mrukk, cold eyes glinting in the torchlight.

"No—none that I know of."

"He doesn't seem to know very much," remarked Diltz.

"I told you where you could find the rebels."

Jamrog dismissed the matter with a jerk of his hand. "We have already discussed that. Besides, we would have found them eventually. Isn't that true, Mrukk?"

"We were very close to finding them when Fertig was captured."

Fertig smiled weakly. "I—you did not capture me . . . I came to you—brought you the information."

"Is Tvrdy still in command?" asked Mrukk.

"Yes," replied Fertig warily.

"What of the Fieri?" said Jamrog.

"He is there as well. He was to lead the Dhogs to Fierra. They made a bargain."

"Does he command?" Mrukk moved closer.

"No." Fertig gave a quick shake of his head. "He tends the wounded mostly."

"Extraordinary!" exclaimed Jamrog. "Did you hear that, Diltz? The Fieri tends the wounded."

"Remarkable."

"Why does he do this?" asked Mrukk. "Do the other leaders not trust him?"

"They trust him. But he prefers to help the wounded. The others wanted to leave them behind, but he wouldn't allow it."

The three inquisitors were silent.

Fertig glanced around him. "That's all I know. I've told you everything."

"It isn't much," replied Diltz.

"Nevertheless," said Jamrog, "I agreed to pay him what he deserves." He raised the bhuj, and Fertig saw that the ornate ceremonial blade had been honed to razor sharpness.

"What are you doing?" demanded Fertig. "I—told you . . . my information . . . I gave you . . ."

Jamrog nodded, and Mrukk swiftly stepped behind the prisoner and jerked Fertig's arms back, pinning them behind his shoulders. "No! Please no!" he pleaded. "Send me away. Send me to reorientation."

The two Mors Ultima seized Fertig's yos and tore it from his shoulders, baring his chest. Jamrog placed the blade against the soft flesh over Fertig's heart.

"No! No!" he screamed. "Don't kill me!"

The bhuj bit into the skin, and blood oozed out around the blade. "I'll go back to the rebels. I'll spy for you. I'll find the tunnel exit. I'll work for you. Please, let me go."

"You're a traitor, Fertig. We could never trust a traitor."

"Don't kill me!" The bhuj sliced deeper. "No!" Fertig struggled feebly, but was held fast in Mrukk's iron grip. Blood trickled freely down Fertig's stomach. His features twisted in agony.

Jamrog laughed and forced the thick blade deeper. Fertig writhed. His head arched back, and he gasped. Jamrog saw the head go back and put his weight behind the blade, driving it in and up. The bhuj ripped upward, and Fertig went limp. Mrukk stepped away, and the body slumped to the floor.

The Supreme Director gazed merrily down at his handiwork. He put his foot on Fertig's chest and grasped the long shaft, gave it a twist, and withdrew it. "Did you hear, Mrukk? The tunnel connects with Bolbe; begin searching the material stores."

"You should have no difficulty," added Diltz. "We have done your work for you."

Mrukk inclined his head in a stiff bow, turned on his heel, and walked out. Neither Jamrog nor Diltz saw the thin, mirthless smile.

SEVENTY

The balon sat waiting on the beach where it had touched down several hours earlier, drifting down out of the clear azure sky as lightly as a bubble. After conferring with the Preceptor, the passengers would begin boarding and the balon would continue on its journey. Yarden took advantage of the wait to have a last walk on the beach. The talking fish were nowhere to be seen; they were birthing their young and would not come near shore for a few days. Yarden wished that Glee and Spinner were there now to comfort her.

She had not thought leaving would be this hard. True, she still felt the urgency of her mission—if anything, that was more acute—but she was beginning to have qualms about going, not so much for herself, but for the Fieri involved.

I've talked everyone into this endeavor, she thought—what happens now? What do we do exactly? What happens if we fail? We have no weapons, no protection. What if someone gets killed—what if we all get killed?

Failure had not occurred to her before. Now it seemed a very likely outcome.

We're not prepared. We're lambs headed for slaughter, she thought. And yet, we have to go. *I* have to go. Staying here and doing nothing would be worse.

She saw a wad of brown cloth lying at the water's edge just ahead; she stopped when she came to it and stooped to pick it up. It was a shirt, and nearby lay the trousers: Crocker's shirt and trousers.

She stood and looked off toward the seacliffs to the west. Anthon found her standing there. "He was getting better," she said, shaking her head sadly. "He was safe here. Why would he leave?"

Anthon followed her gaze. "He made his decision, Yarden. And we have made ours. Come, it's time to go."

They turned and walked back to camp. Ianni and Gerdes were waiting for her when she returned. "I guess this is goodbye," Yarden said as she joined them. "I'd planned it differently."

"Not good-bye," said Ianni. "We want to give you a farewell blessing."

"Trust in the Infinite and let Him guide your steps," said Gerdes, raising her hand over Yarden's head. "Go in peace and in peace return."

"Thank you," said Yarden, reaching for their hands. She drew them both into a hug. "Thank you both very much."

"The others are boarding," said Anthon, and they turned and walked across the sand to the balon, passing among the Fieri gathered there to see them off. Yarden craned her neck as she moved through the crowd. "Looking for someone?" Anthon asked, pausing to glance over his shoulder at her.

"No, I guess not. I was only hoping . . ." She scanned the crowd, searching for Pizzle. Up to this moment she had believed Pizzle would come around. But it appeared that he, too, had made his decision. He was nowhere to be seen.

Without another word they continued on to the balon. Upon reaching the boarding ramp, Yarden turned to steal a final look back at the Fieri who had gathered to see the balon on its way. She searched the somber faces of the crowd. There would be no warm send-off, no sung farewell. They were going to Dome, and that was a matter of extreme gravity.

A chime sounded from within the balon. "They are ready to lift off as soon as we are aboard," said Anthon, moving up the ramp.

Yarden took the guide rope and started up the ramp. She reached the top, took a last backward glance, sighed, and went inside. There was a whirr of machinery as the ramp began to rise.

"Hey! Wait a second!" A high reedy voice rang out behind her. "Wait for me!"

Yarden whirled around. "Lower the ramp! We have another passenger."

As soon as the gangway touched the sand once more, Pizzle came bounding up and into the balon. "Well, what are you grinning at?" he demanded. "You're not the only one who knows how to make a magnanimous gesture."

Yarden threw her arms around his neck and planted a kiss on his cheek. "What's that for?"

"I'm proud of you, Pizzle. Thanks—"

"Whoa there, sister. You don't think I'd let you take this

849

luxury cruise without me? Us Earthlings stick together, right?"

"Right."

• • • • • •

The Invisibles pounded the rebels' meager earthwork defenses through the night, using three of the improvised tanks. The ditch was hastily dug and shallow, its breastwork made of dirt and rubble heaped around the mouth of the tunnel. The rebels stayed low and fired back when they could, risking as little as possible.

But the Invisibles' superior firepower made it impossible for the Tanais and Rumon marksmen to retaliate effectively, and each strike punished the rebels severely. The hours crawled by, and the rebel return fire became more random and spotty as the enemy's strength hammered the defenders down.

By morning it became clear that the Invisibles intended to grind the defense down to nothing and then rush the tunnel. Four enemy battalions were massed on the bumpy, broken plain across which the rebels had fled a day earlier.

Tvrdy appeared briefly to reconnoiter the enemy's position, gave a few brief instructions to the men, and then came back to the tunnel. Cejka met him and said, "How much time?"

"A few hours. They believe us to be trapped. They'll wait until they're reasonably certain of victory before moving in for the kill." Tvrdy rubbed his eyes with fingertips. "For now, they wait."

"We'd better begin moving into Bolbe." Cejka did not look at his friend, but gazed past him into the thin yellowish light slanting into the tunnel mouth.

Tvrdy nodded.

"I'll give the order if you prefer. You should get some rest while you can."

"No, Cejka. I'm all right. I'll give the order."

Tvrdy moved off down the tunnel. Cejka watched him go, and then went to speak with his men.

Treet came up as Tvrdy and Kopetch were talking. The occasional thunder from the tunnel entrance swamped their words as it rumbled along the ribbed walls. They turned to regard Treet as he approached, both appearing haggard and drawn. Neither had slept for over twenty-four hours. "I hear we're visiting Bolbe," Treet said.

"I've given the order."

"What happens then?"

Kopetch answered. "The tunnel will be destroyed so we cannot be followed. By the time they come searching for us, we will be hidden in deep Hage."

"Will the Bolbe agree to hide us?"

"They have no choice. They will do what we say."

Treet faced Tvrdy. "Not like that. We can't do it like that. If we just come in and start pushing people around, giving orders, and taking over, we're no better than those Mors Ultima thugs out there." He waved in the direction of the tunnel entrance.

Tvrdy nodded absently. "He's right, Kopetch. Not that way. What do you suggest?" he asked Treet.

"Well, I don't know if this means anything or not. But Bogney told me the Dhogs were leaving. I thought he meant he still wanted me to take them to Fierra when we got out of here. And then I got to thinking about something Ernina said when I woke up after my little escapade on the front line."

"Yes?"

"Well, just after I woke up, I met her in the tunnel. I asked her if she needed any help, and she said some Dhog women had come and they were helping."

"Dhog women had come? That's what she said?"

"Her exact words: 'Some of the Dhog women have come. They're ignorant, but they do what they're told.' I figured she meant the same ones that had brought the liquor the night before, so I didn't think about it again until Bogney confronted me." He peered apologetically at Tvrdy and finished by saying, "I haven't seen Bogney or any of the other Dhogs for hours."

"Another exit!" said Kopetch, his eyes alight with the discovery. "The Dhogs know about it."

"Why didn't they tell us?"

Treet shrugged. "They're unpredictable. Maybe they're trying to get even with us for refusing to take them to Fierra."

"I'll find out if anyone has seen Bogney," said Kopetch. He made to dash off.

"That can wait. First send me all the men we can spare. Get them lanterns. Hurry! We may not have much time."

• • • • • •

Mrukk stood beside a table set up in the center of a deserted plaza deep in Bolbe Hage. Squads of Mors Ultima searched among the long ranks of the material stores—the huge storage bins of highly prized Bolbe hagecloth—searching for the tunnel exit. Every few minutes an Invisible appeared, conferred with his commander, and then disappeared again. Mrukk would then move to the table and consult the map spread out there. He would make a mark on the map and return to his place to wait.

He had just finished marking off one entire section of the map when another of his lieutenants approached quickly, offered the Mors Ultima salute, and said, "Commander, perhaps you would like to come inspect what we have found."

"Where is it?" Mrukk stepped to the map and pointed. "Show me."

The Invisible placed a finger on a place already marked off. "I was returning to move the squad to a new quadrant, and I noticed a godown in the main hoarding. It is not visible from the forward approach. I went in and found a grate. Air moves through the grate. I put my ear to the opening and heard weapons discharge—indistinct, but audible. Very far away."

Mrukk slowly raised his head from the map, gray eyes narrowed. "Enjoy the fleeting moments of freedom that remain to you, Tvrdy," he murmured to himself. His hand came up and made a fist. "Soon I will have you in my grasp."

SEVENTY ONE

Treet had never felt more useless in his life. After intense, brain-numbing sessions of contemplation, he could not come up with a single idea that offered even a glimmer of hope. He ransacked his mental files, recalling every detail of every historical battle he had ever studied, dredging up every stray military fact he had ever learned.

Nothing he could come up with suggested even the remote hint of a solution to their dilemma, and he was faced with the heartbreaking conclusion that his mission had failed and that he was absolutely powerless to change the situation: the Invisibles had found the tunnel's exit and now waited to attack. It was over but for the shooting.

Curiously, he did not mind for himself. Although his failure meant death for him just as surely as for his friends, he had, upon reentering Dome—weeks? months? years . . . how long ago?—considered himself abandoned to his task, an instrument in the hand of whatever power moved him. Apparently, he had proven a poor instrument, or that power had other plans.

If anything could save them now, it was up to the Infinite. Treet had done all he could with the cards that had been dealt him, and he had no regrets—except that he would not be able to save the Fieri from the impending slaughter. The gentle, loving Fieri, so good, so pure, so vulnerable before evil's destructive power.

What did it matter if he were caught and crushed in the teeth of the doomsday machine he hoped to stop? The whole idea had been to save the Fieri from a second holocaust by interposing himself between gears. He had accepted that it might end badly for him. But he had hoped that some good might be accomplished by his presence—or if not, that some gain might be secured by his death.

Now it appeared that his death would count for nothing. This realization—growing stronger with each passing minute—filled his mouth with the taste of ashes.

And death was certain now. For while every able body

searched for the Dhogs' secret passage, the Invisibles had discovered the tunnel's exit to Bolbe. Fighting had not begun there yet, but according to Kopetch the Invisibles only awaited the arrival of additional platoons. Tvrdy had dispatched troops to secure the exit, but held little hope of holding it. When the enemy reinforcements arrived, the pinching operation would commence. The rebels would be caught in a deadly crossfire with no place to run, no way to hide. The tunnel would become a tomb.

In the meantime, every millimeter of the tunnel from the Old Section to Bolbe had been scoured in search of the Dhogs' secret passage—to no avail. There was no seam, no opening, no break that had not been minutely examined and reexamined, the search yielding nothing but frustration.

The Dhogs had vanished—Bogney, the women, the few remaining soldiers. No one recalled precisely when, but they were gone, taking the secret of the tunnel with them. And knowing that there was a way to escape from the tunnel, and not knowing how or where to find it, multiplied the agony. Nothing the Invisibles could devise by way of torture could have been worse.

The last few hours were spent feverishly inspecting the length of the tunnel yet again. Treet knew they would not find the secret, but went through the motions anyway, thinking the exercise better than sitting around waiting for the Mors Ultima to cut them down.

Tvrdy had both ends of the tunnel fortified and manned, but the narrow width mocked maneuverability and reduced movement to absurdity. A skinny tunnel was no place to fight a last battle. The rebels' only consolation was that the Invisibles would have to come in and get them one by one.

It was late when the Invisibles pulled into position. With victory now a mere matter of execution, Mrukk consulted his commanders and then left to return to Saecaraz. The Invisibles were to wait until sunrise to begin the attack. This would minimize confusion and any mishap caused by darkness, and it would also allow Mrukk time to reach the Supreme Director's kraam. He planned to be with Jamrog when the tunnel fell, and to personally announce the rebels' defeat.

• • • • •

In the Archives, lights blazed into the night as Saecaraz and Nilokerus magicians and Readers slouched over the ancient texts. At one end of the long table, a sixth-order magician and Reader from both Hages huddled together, their heads bent over the diagrams they had deciphered.

"It is time," announced the Saecaraz magician. "We have reviewed all available lore. It is apparent that the machine responds to number impulses called 'coordinates,' which must be implanted in this device called 'systems guidance.' Are we agreed?" The others bobbed their heads and pulled on their chins in agreement.

"The coordinates for Fierra have been calculated according to the lore formula. We have adhered to the Clear Way and followed the Sacred Directives regarding the revival of machines. We must trust our lore and the psi of this place to aid us."

The others muttered approval. The ranking Nilokerus said, "My Hagemen and I are ready to proceed. Once the missile is returned to the launch cradle, the launch may progress as planned."

"I will notify Director Diltz," the Saecaraz said. He rose from the table. "Begin the procedure. The Director will wish to give the order himself."

• • • • • •

The Dhogs, arranged by family, each of the sixteen families grouped together with their essentials and provisions, stood waiting to begin their exodus to Fierra. Since abandoning the war with the Invisibles, Giloon Bogney and the family heads had worked their hardest, scraping together every last morsel of anything edible, and filling every available container with water. When all was ready, the Dhogs put on their best articles of clothing, trussed up their livestock, and assembled by family to await the order to move out.

Bogney took his place at the head of the great procession. "Dhogs," he said, waving his bhuj to get their attention, "this here being a great day. We starting off traveling. We now going to Fieri like Giloon promising."

With that the Dhogs moved off, clattering like an army of panhandlers. They lumbered through the long-deserted avenues of the Old Section, the sounds of battle ringing off the curved sections of the skyroof above them. Like noisy ghosts, they left the familiar haunts of their ancient home, leaving for a better place they had been told lay out there, somewhere beyond the barriers of the time-fogged crystal.

SEVENTY
TWO

In the clean light of the rising sun, Dome's enormous crystal shell glittered and winked like a faceted jewel mountain, its clustered peaks distinct in the early light. A multitude of giant spires protruded from its skin, each lifting an immense webwork of thick support cables, bearing up the weight of the sealed shining shell with its insane jumble of steeples, turrets, rotundas, and cupolas bulging, swelling, bellying out, one atop another as if springing from a cancerous growth. The colossal range of bulbous mounds reached skyward, hill heaped upon hill, all of them outtopped by tremendous tuberous humps and knobs and gibbous mounds.

"There it is," said Pizzle, gazing down on the sprawling mass, "somebody's idea of modern architecture run amuck."

"This isn't funny," said Yarden. It had been a long trip and a tense one for her, staring out the balon's ports at the barren hills—a deadeningly monotonous landscape, all of a uniform, unvarying soft turquoise green—watching while the interminable hours crept by, wondering, despite the many assurances that they would arrive in good time, whether there would be anything worth saving when they reached their destination. Now here it was, and she was in no mood for Pizzle's smart-aleck observations.

Talus stood like a rock, fingering his beard, staring at the glassy mountainscape of Dome. Pizzle asked him what he thought, and he replied in a strangely hushed voice, "It is arrogant and unnatural. I can feel its evil reaching out to us."

"You think it's bad now," quipped Pizzle, "wait'll you get inside."

"Will you stop!" Yarden snapped.

"He raises a pertinent question," said Bohm quietly. He, like all the other Fieri on board, was reticent and subdued as they watched the gleaming monstrosity slide silently beneath them. "How *are* we to get inside?"

"There is a landing platform on the far side," Yarden pointed out. "And large doors below it. That's where we came out."

857

"You know what happens to anyone who lands on that platform," said Pizzle. "I'm not about to try that again."

"But we must find a way in," said Jaire. She spoke with such intensity that all heads turned to look at her. She blushed, crimson rising to her throat and cheeks.

"I agree," said Anthon. "We must find a way in—and find it quickly."

"I will instruct our pilots to circle at the present altitude until directed otherwise." Bohm went to the command center and spoke to the pilot. He returned a moment later and said, "We will remain in this formation while we entertain ideas."

"Okay," said Pizzle, "don't everybody speak at once."

• • • • • •

With the rising sun came the Invisibles' assault on the tunnel. As expected, they attacked both ends at once, but with a vengeance that was completely unexpected. Their armored ems were moved in close, and under the cover of a fiery barrage, the first squads rushed in.

Heedless of the scorching resistance, the Invisibles were cut down in waves as the rebels, fighting for their lives, threw all they had at the reckless onslaught.

For one optimistic instant, it appeared that the rebels would stem the murderous tide. But rank on rank of Invisibles, advancing over the bodies of the fallen, began, by sheer pressure of numbers, to push their way inside. They gained the mouth of the tunnel, and then one meter of its length, and then another, driving the rebels back and back.

The fighting was vicious. The interior of the tunnel began to fill with smoke and fumes. Treet, having elected to stay with the wounded, tending them to the end, heard the shriek of the thermal weapons relentlessly drawing closer, and knew that the final battle would soon belong to the past—a brief footnote in a history that would never be recorded.

Crouched in the darkness of the tunnel, while around him the wounded began to moan and cough as the acrid fumes touched their lungs, Treet tried his hand at calming those disturbed by the wild shouts close at hand and the sound of thunder cracking ever closer. "Rest easy," he told them. "It will soon be over."

Ernina swept by him as he made his way among the wounded. "I'm going to see to what I can do up there," she told him. "Stay here and keep them quiet."

"Be careful," he called after her and wondered whether he ought to go to the front, too—not to help the wounded, but to fight. Part of him ached to be in the thick of the battle, to give some account of himself, to make the enemy feel his death. The bandage on his burned hand made that a ludicrous proposition.

Ironically, the one time he had taken up a weapon, he had incapacitated himself and had nearly lost the man he was trying to save. Yes, he reflected, it was better this way. He would wait here and do what he had determined to do since coming to the Old Section, to save life rather than waste it. There was enough killing in Dome without adding to it.

The air was thick with the stink of blood and death, the tunnel hot. The raking scream of the Invisibles' weapons echoed and reechoed, reverberating along the walls of the tunnel. The answering fire of the rebels became hesitant and less frequent. The Mors Ultima ground the resistance down, driving the rebels further and further into the tunnel.

At one point Treet heard the sound of running feet and thought the Invisibles had broken through at last. But Tvrdy appeared, leading what remained of his troops and shouting, "Now! Down! Everyone down!"

Treet obeyed. A second later the tunnel bucked under him as if it had suddenly taken life. The shock of an explosion rattled his bones in their sockets.

Tvrdy leaped up at once. "Get these supplies stacked up here!" he shouted. "Make a wall!"

Treet fell to with the rest of them and began stacking all the remaining crates and bundles in the center of the tunnel to make a wall and seal themselves in. "It won't take them long to dig through out there," Tvrdy told him. "But we'll seal this end and join Cejka and Piipo at the other end. We can hold out longer that way." He paused and looked at Treet, an expression of sorrow flitting across his smoke-blackened face. "I'm sorry it ends this way."

"It isn't over yet," said Treet.

"Come with us."

"Thanks, but someone has to stay here." Treet indicated the wounded.

Tvrdy nodded and pulled Treet to him in a brusque hug. "Good-bye, friend," he said and then was hurrying away with his men as they ran to join the fighting at the other end of the tunnel.

SEVENTY THREE

"Look, I don't know if this'll work. It's only an idea," said Pizzle. "We could try something else, you know? Yarden? C'mon, talk to me. Say something."

Yarden stood gazing at the image of Dome projected onto the map table, her fingers steepled and pressed against her lips. She did not respond.

Just then, Talus returned to where the others stood bent over the map table. He shook his head slowly. "Mathiax has consulted the Preceptor, and both agree there is no precept to cover this situation. We are to proceed according to our own judgment."

Bohm nodded and raised his head. "What do the builders say?"

Talus shrugged. "Not enough is known about the structural qualities of the materials to answer precisely. They would have to make tests. However, the principle is well known."

"We have nothing to lose," said Anthon.

"Only time," said Jaire grimly. "We could lose valuable time."

"That is a risk," Anthon assured her gently. "I only meant that if it doesn't work, we are free to try something else."

Abashed, Jaire clamped her mouth shut, glanced around at the others, and left the table.

"We need a decision," said Pizzle. "I say we go for it and see what happens."

Preben was quick to second the motion. "I agree. It is an inspired plan." He looked to his father.

Talus stared at the slowly revolving image on the table, and then nodded. "Yes," he said slowly. "We have no better plan. I say we try it. This is Mathiax's thinking as well. He points out that if it succeeds, we will all be very busy in the hours to come."

"It is settled." Bohm smacked his hand down in the center of the projected Dome. "It is time to end the madness. I'm going to give the order." He beckoned to Pizzle. "Come along. I will need you." He returned to the balon's command center.

Pizzle moved around the table to join him. Passing by Yarden, he paused and said, "Go ahead and do it."

She looked up sharply. "You know what I'm thinking?"

"I've seen that look before. Do it."

Her gaze drifted back to the gray projection. "You don't know what you're asking."

"You'll feel better. Besides, I don't see how else we're going to warn him."

Pizzle moved off, leaving Yarden transfixed before the image on the flat octagon of the table. Anthon came near and put his arm around her shoulders. She covered his hand with hers. "What should I do?" she asked. "I need guidance. Help me."

"Sometimes the itch is supplied by the Infinite, but we must scratch it ourselves," he replied.

Yarden threw him a dark look. "What is that supposed to mean?"

"We are meant to find our own way in many of life's difficult moments."

"In the doing comes the knowing—that's what Gerdes told me once. I guess it applies." She wrapped her arms around herself in a hug. "I feel so alone."

"The Comforter goes with you, Yarden. Always."

She gave Anthon a weak smile and turned to climb the stairs leading to the crew quarters. She went up and found Jaire sitting on a bench, her back against the rail of the circular balcony. She sat down on the bench and touched the young woman on the arm. Jaire stirred and looked up, her eyes wet with unshed tears.

"I know you care for him," Yarden said, and realized as she spoke the words the reason for Jaire's uncharacteristic behavior. It was obvious: Jaire had been displaying all the signs of a distraught lover. "Is there anything I can do?"

"I have been praying that he will be rescued safely. . ." Her voice trailed off.

"I know." Yarden nodded. "Sometimes it doesn't seem like it's enough. Wait here." She got up slowly. "I'm going to try to reach him, warn him."

She went to her cabin and sat down cross-legged on the floor. She took a deep breath and released it; drew another, emptying her mind of all thoughts, clearing her mental screen. She placed her hands together, fingertips touching lightly, and began focusing her consciousness into the fine, sharp probing instrument her sympathic touch required.

She gathered her awareness and sent it out from her, releasing it like an arrow from the bow.

Once again she felt the awesome oppression of the power that held Dome in its unrelenting grasp. She found herself hard against the thick membrane she had encountered before. She steadied herself and pushed through. As before, it yielded and admitted her.

There was howling darkness and the icy numbness of death. She framed Treet's image in her mind and instantly felt a shudder of rage course through the darkness. The response surprised her, but she did not retreat and did not allow herself to be unnerved or distracted. She steadied herself, pushed ahead, and a moment later Treet was there—his presence weak, distressed, shifting wildly, but alive.

• • • • • •

Treet knelt over a thrashing soldier as the sounds of battle boomed in the tunnel. The young Rumon, hysterical with fear, was intent on tearing off his bandages. Treet calmed him and was about to move on to the next casualty when, as he rose, he caught a whiff of a familiar scent. Just the barest suggestion of a fragrance—faint, but unmistakable . . .

Yarden.

He stood rock-still. The sense of her presence was irresistible. It was as if she had suddenly distilled out of the air beside him. Her nearness was almost tangible.

In the dim smoke-filled tunnel, Treet closed his eyes and opened himself to her touch, shutting out the noise and stink and pain around him. Concentrating, bending his will to the effort with every gram of strength he possessed, he gathered the frazzled shreds of his awareness and projected himself to her. He was rewarded for his effort by a violent wrenching sensation, as if a giant hand had reached into his skull and given his brain a twist between thumb and forefinger.

The sympathic touch weakened. He felt Yarden receding from him and reached out for her, strained after her, but could not hold her. Before the touch faded completely, even as it slipped away, he received a clear and distinct infusion of hope. His spirit leapt up inside him.

Help is coming, she seemed to say. Lay low and hold on.

· · · · · ·

On Skywalk level of Hage Saecaraz, the Supreme Director strolled the shaded garden walkways of his pleasure grounds. Nilokerus Director Diltz walked beside him, enjoying the greenery and the sunlight shining through the huge crystal panes directly overhead, basking in the praise of his superior.

"You are to be congratulated," Jamrog was saying.

"Not at all, Supreme Director," replied Diltz. "I remind you that it was your idea. I merely oversaw it's implementation."

"As you wish." Jamrog nodded solemnly. "I accept the triumph. I am, after all, the generative force of my people. I am the blood and spirit of Empyrion. I am life and beyond life." He turned to regard Diltz, his eyes glassy from flash. "Do you understand what I am telling you, Director?"

"Of course, Supreme Director, I—"

"From now on, I will be addressed as Father."

"Of course, Father." Diltz gave him a sidelong glance. "The magicians await your order. Will you give it now?"

Jamrog's eyes closed, his lips curled lazily. "My breath gives life or takes it. My word is law and death." He stopped and raised his hands to the sun, which was shining through the enormous panels of the dome above. "I am light; I am becoming one with the sun. My mind is racing far ahead. My enemies seek to trap me, but I know their plans before they are conceived. I am filled with thoughts incomprehensible to lesser beings.

"Behold me—I am advancing through spiritual realms. My incarnations fall from me and are borne away by the oversouls of my predecessors. Trabant Animus speaks to me. I will be purified in the blood of my enemies."

He stopped and lowered his hands. A fierce, wicked light shone in his eyes. "The Fieri will be destroyed. Their hateful memory will be erased forever. I give the order."

A shadow passed over them just then, and they heard a mighty booming sound that throbbed in their ears. They

glanced up in time to see the curving bulk of a balon glide by
overhead.

"Behold!" shouted Jamrog above the noise. "The Seraphic
Spheres! Do you see, Diltz? They have come to transport me to
the Astral Planes. It is a sign: I am to be made immortal!"

SEVENTY
FOUR

"The fleet is in position," said Bohm, turning from the flight board.

"Then let 'er rip!" shouted Pizzle from his place at the projection table, and the airship's engines, normally audible as a distant, burring hum, suddenly filled the cabin with a virtual avalanche of penetrating, bone-vibrating sound.

The others, clustered around the projection table, watched Dome's revolving image, their teeth clamped tight to keep them from rattling in their jaws. Talus, barely able to make himself heard over the droning thunder, shouted, "How long?"

Pizzle shrugged and shook his head, mouthing the words, "Don't know. Wait and see."

• • • • • •

The people of Dome heard the resounding boom of the Fieri airships and looked to the heavens. Far above, beyond the gigantic vault of crystal, they saw great spherical shapes gliding over the translucent roof-shell, and they stopped to stare in wonder.

Mrukk strode into the Supreme Director's pleasure garden. He found a flash-jagged Jamrog and an extremely apprehensive Diltz standing in the center of the grounds. Jamrog had his arms outspread, face upturned in the sunlight, a beatific expression on his face.

Diltz saw him and came to him. "What is it?" he demanded, glancing toward the sky as another balon passed overhead. "What's happening?"

Mrukk glared with disgust at the emaciated puppet. "Afraid, Diltz?"

Diltz drew himself up. "I am concerned for the welfare of the Supreme Director," he huffed. "As you are responsible for the Supreme Director's safety, I demand to know what is happening."

"Nothing to concern you." He moved to Jamrog, who seemed oblivious of his presence. "Supreme Director—"

"He is to be addressed as Father from now on," Diltz informed him.

Mrukk's eyes narrowed, and his lips curled in a silent snarl. "Supreme Director," he repeated, "I bring word that the attack on the rebel stronghold is effectually complete."

"Your disrespect has not gone unnoticed, Mrukk." Jamrog opened his eyes slowly and gazed at the Mors Ultima commander. "I have been made immortal. You will honor my physical manifestation with all respect."

Mrukk crossed his hands over his chest and inclined his head in a short bow. "Father, the rebels are subdued."

"That is nothing to me." Jamrog said airily.

"But—"

"Silence! You are in the presence of deity." Jamrog scowled, and then raised his hands to his head. He closed his eyes once more and intoned, "My mind sees events before they happen. All secrets are revealed to me." His eyes flew open, and he stared at Mrukk accusingly. "You imply that this disturbance means something to me. Your very presence mocks my power."

Mrukk stiffened and stared.

Jamrog continued imperiously, "This is the day of my awakening. The innermost secrets of men are laid bare before me. My words are alive, and I speak of realities beyond reality. I am radiant. Feel the power streaming from me. This is the day of my triumph." He turned to regard Diltz fondly. "Director Diltz honors this sacred day by delivering my enemies into my hands."

"The rebels are your enemies."

"The Fieri are my enemies!" screamed Jamrog. "I have given the order to destroy them."

Mrukk whirled on Diltz. "What have you done?"

Diltz fell back a step. "The weapon is ready. It has been activated—"

"You fools!"

"You have failed, Mrukk." Jamrog stepped toward him. "Your failure must be atoned. Atone to me, Mrukk. By your death you will be purified." He turned to Diltz and motioned him away. "Call my bodyguard."

There was a flash in the sun, and the knife appeared in

Mrukk's hand as if from nowhere. "Stay where you are!" hissed Mrukk. "We will see whose orders are to be obeyed."

•••••

"Nothing's happening," shouted Pizzle. "Can we increase the power any more? And maybe make the circle a little tighter?"

Bohm nodded and spoke into the transceiver, then made an adjustment on the flightboard. The din of the engines, already deafening, doubled in volume. "Maximum threshold!" Bohm called back.

Through the port, Pizzle watched the airship descend toward the hills and valleys of a rumpled, crystal landscape until they flew only a few meters above the undulating contours of Dome. Pizzle gazed onto the scene, watching the shining surface slide by beneath them, staring as if entranced. All at once he whirled away from the port.

"I've got it!" he cried, racing back to the flightboard. "I've got it! It's phase!"

"What?" shouted Bohm. The others looked up from the projection table to see the two of them yelling noiselessly at one another; the boom of the unmuffled engines drowned their words.

"Phase!" screamed Pizzle. "The engines are out of phase!" He made wavy motions in the air with his hands—one hand high when the other was low. "We've got to bring them into phase—make the sound waves reinforce each other!" The wave motion came together as his hands moved in unison.

Bohm frowned and rubbed his hand over his grizzled head, squinting in concentration. He stared at the flight instruments and began adjusting the controls, listening to the timbre of the engines. After a moment, he looked up. "We'll try it," he said. He flipped a switch and began shouting instructions to the other balon pilots.

Pizzle yelled, "This is it!"

•••••

The sound penetrated Dome, thrumming through the twisted mazework of its corridors; rolling through Empyrion's elaborate labyrinths of avenues, streets, and tunnels; echoing down the terraced hillsides, and into the walled valleys; pealing through the Hages like endless thunder from the hard crystal sky.

Diltz cast a frightened glance skyward as the great sphere of a balon passed by the transparent roof. The sound seeped into his skull and vibrated up through Empyrion's superstructure and into the soles of his feet. "What is happening?" He started to back away.

"Shut up!" snarled Mrukk. "Stay where you are."

Diltz froze.

The Supreme Director spread his hands magnanimously and moved toward Mrukk. "Your unbelief has blinded you, Mrukk. Turn the knife on yourself, and gain enlightenment."

As Jamrog spoke, the skydome shuddered. The immense panel above them—but one tiny scale among millions in a reptile's skin—gave forth a tremendous crack, and he looked up to see fissures streaking through the crystal.

"What's the matter, Immortal Father?" Mrukk asked sweetly. "It is just the Fieri. Even your enemies have come to pay homage to you on your most auspicious day."

"I have no enemies," Jamrog said grandly. "The fire of my being has extinquished them."

The cracking sound grew louder—as if an entire forest of trees were being snapped off at midtrunk, as if the rock cores of mountains were splintering.

"They've come to destroy us!" shouted Diltz.

Jamrog advanced, arms outstretched. "I am immortal, and all I touch is transformed. All is laid waste before me. Death is my ultimate transformation."

"Immortal? Let's see how immortal are you!"

Mrukk held his knife level while Jamrog stepped into it, the blade piercing the Supreme Director's body just below the heart. Jamrog's eyes went wide; an astonished expression appeared on his face. Mrukk threw an arm around the Supreme Director's waist, twisted the knife, and slid it up toward the sternum. Jamrog gasped and looked down in horror at the crimson rivulet streaming from his body. He clasped the knife blade as Mrukk rammed it home.

Jamrog staggered, making little mewing sounds deep in his throat as the sky panel overhead splintered and groaned.

With a terrible rending crash, the crystal ceiling high above them shattered.

SEVENTY
FIVE

The battle raged on in the Old Section. The rebels, fighting with a ferocity born of desperation, had pushed the Invisibles out of the tunnel and across the ditch and then dug in, stubbornly refusing to retreat.

The Invisibles regrouped and brought in their makeshift tanks to finish the fight. As the armored vehicles advanced, Tvrdy rallied his men to face the final assault, shouting for them to stand their ground.

The tanks bumped slowly forward over the rough terrain, Invisibles spread out behind, grinding closer and closer.

"Hold fire!" Tvrdy cried. "Make them come get us."

When they reached kill range, the tanks opened fire, laying down a blistering barrage. The air writhed with the streaking fire of their weapons.

Back in the tunnel Treet heard the awful screech of the guns—growing louder as they drew nearer. His heart sank. Whatever help Yarden could bring now would come too late. "God, help us!" he whispered to himself. "This is it!"

The guns stopped.

The silence brought Treet to his feet, and he was running toward the tunnel entrance before he knew why. He pounded along, wondering what he would find when he reached the opening. Surrender in progress? The sizzled corpses of his comrades?

Presently he saw the tunnel entrance looming ahead. After the numbing shriek of weapons, the silence roared. He reached the mouth of the tunnel and slowed, stepping hesitantly from the tunnel into a scene of suspended animation. The rebels were all standing frozen, weapons lowered and eyes skyward. Across the battlefield Invisibles stood in the same posture: still as statues, weapons at their sides, and faces raised, gazing up through the hanging smoke to the filth-dark canopy of Dome far above.

Tvrdy stood nearby. "Wha—" began Treet. Tvrdy waved him silent with a chop of his hand.

It was then that the sound Treet had been hearing for some moments registered—the sound that had stopped the battle in its final, furious throes: an awful snapping sound, awesome in its enormity—as if the very foundations of Empyrion were shifting and giving way at once.

With this sound came the howl of rushing wind. Then the sky-shell of Dome began to seesaw.

Huge rifts appeared in the enormous panels, widened, spread like stop-action lightning.

"It's coming down!" cried Treet even as the man-made heavens buckled and chunks of crystal began to fall.

Tvrdy was the first to react to Treet's warning. "Into the tunnel! Run!"

The men stood transfixed, mouths open, watching in disbelief as the only sky they had ever known collapsed upon them.

"Run!" screamed Tvrdy. Cejka and Kopetch snapped to life and began hurling men toward the tunnel entrance. "Into the tunnel! Save yourselves!" they yelled.

Treet grabbed the arm of a Hyrgo soldier and pulled him into the tunnel, returned for another, and was then pushed back by a sudden crush of bodies streaming into the narrow opening as everyone charged in at once.

They all surged forward. The floor of the tunnel shook beneath their feet as one horrendous crash after another—whole cities of glass toppling, sliding, and smashing—echoed through the conduit.

And above the tremendous din, Treet heard the raw whistle of wind rushing toward him. A second later, a blast of cool fresh air struck him, tore at his clothing, and raced on. Without considering the consequences, Treet gulped a deep breath.

A split second later he remembered only too well, remembered with every atom of his being the incendiary torture of breathing Empyrion air for the first time.

It sliced at his windpipe and spread like liquid fire into his lungs, as though his esophagus had been scoured with an industrial corrosive and the wound cauterized with a blowtorch. He reeled blindly forward.

Men around him halted in their headlong flight, gasped, clawed at their throats, and fell screaming to the tunnel floor. In seconds everyone was convulsing in agony.

Everyone except Treet. He leaned against the tunnel wall, head down, forcing himself to breathe normally, remembering a time when he, too, rolled in anguish while his lungs ignited:

872

The escape from Dome—Yarden, Pizzle, Crocker, Calin, and himself—traveling by skimmer over the bleak hills. Three days into the journey, Yarden had insisted that they all take off their helmets. Treet had done it, accepting and suffering the necessary pain.

And now, having once experienced sudden exposure to the rarefied air of Empyrion—with its dramatic side effects—having breathed the air and survived, Treet's pain subsided rapidly. It was nowhere near as bad as the first time. In a few moments his vision cleared, and he was able to stand upright and walk again.

The Dome dwellers were not so fortunate. Untold generations of life inside the closed and controlled atmosphere of Dome rendered them absolutely helpless in the free air. They lay unconscious in moments.

Panting just a little, Treet retraced his steps back to the tunnel's entrance, carefully threading his way over and around the still-quivering bodies of the stricken.

Upon emerging from the tunnel, he stood blinking in utter disbelief at the scene that met his astonished gape.

Clear light from the unfiltered sun streamed into the shadowlands of the Old Section, stripping away the pall of gloom. The battlefield was a glittering plain of shining crystal. It looked as if a winter ice storm had dumped frozen rain in sheets upon the land—as if Dome itself had been transported to the Arctic and set down upon the frigid silver floes.

Everywhere he looked, he saw the rainbow shimmer of broken crystal. Dome was buried in a thick layer of the stuff—like a plate-glass snowfall, making it appear eerily open and brittle. The landscape gleamed with such harsh bright light that Treet had to squint and cup his hands around his eyes as he surveyed the wreckage.

Most of the Old Section's tottering ruins were erased, flattened by the fallen remains of Dome's vast sky-shell. Broken spars jabbed up from the debris trailing snapped support cables, or lay like felled sequoias entangled in fouled fishing line.

Off to his right, he could see the ragged skyline formed by the few structures still standing in the Hages. To his left, beyond the tumbled walls, was the green rolling sea of the barren hill country, startling in its nearness.

Above, and this surprised him more than anything he'd seen so far, was the glowing blue sky of Empyrion—scintillating, radiant, so bright that Treet had to turn his eyes away. And hanging soundlessly in that infinite, empty blue sky was a multi-colored fleet of Fieri balons.

• • • • • •

Pizzle was beside himself with joy. He jumped up and down, embracing Bohm and Talus and Preben all at once. He hooted and screeched in utter ecstacy. "We did it! We did it!" he cried. "Look at that, will you?" He pointed out the observation window at the collapsed mess of Dome, which from above looked as if someone had dropped a tray of crystal bowls and stemware onto a slab of concrete.

Unlike smashing dinnerware, though, Dome's destruction took place in slow motion. First, cracks had appeared in the smooth shell of the large central dome—cracks which shifted and widened, snapping support cables and fracturing huge panes, which in turn unbalanced the gigantic supporting pillars, causing more crystal sections to break and the support poles to give way altogether.

The crazy rippling motion of the heretofore solid structure reminded Pizzle of a holofilm he'd once seen in which a circus tent had had its centerpoles yanked out from under it. The great expanse of fabric held its shape for a split second and then began to sink—not all at once—but in sections, the higher sections plummeting more rapidly, dragging the lower sections down with them, plunging from the center and working out to the edge in undulating waves.

Dome fell like that.

It was a solid shape defining an absolute space one moment, and the next a fluid mass, rippling, churning, and sinking under its own weight. One section went, pulling down another and then two more, all of them sliding, toppling, tumbling, crashing down—all of them, every cupola and mound and bubble, breaking up and falling.

Pizzle's inspired idea of using the Fieri balon engines to set up crystal-shattering sonic vibrations had succeeded. Dome was an immense fragile crystal bubble waiting for the right touch to break it. The Fieri had provided the precise touch required.

"We did it, Bohm! Did you see that? Kerplooey! Humpty

Dumpty had a great fall! Splat! Now you see it, now you don't! Fantastic!" He danced from window to projection table and back, hugging all the others in jubilation.

The Fieri shared his relief and joy, if not his enthusiasm. Talus beamed and Preben laughed out loud, while Bohm just shook his head in wonder. The women were more subdued. Jaire gazed out the window at the dreadful destruction, biting her lip. Yarden stood by her saying, "When I reached him, I had a brief image of a tunnel. He was inside it, kneeling." She looked at the awful destruction they had wrought below and said, "I think he'll be all right. I know it."

"Well, what are we waiting for?" exclaimed Pizzle. "If I'm right, our Dome friends are enjoying some fresh air, which means that we have about a half hour or so to get established before people start to come around."

"We've got to locate Orion first thing," said Jaire, turning away from the window.

"Fine," said Pizzle, "but that's not going to be easy. He could be anywhere." He turned to Yarden. "How about it, Madame Mindreader?"

Yarden closed her eyes and touched her forehead with the fingertips of her right hand. She stood motionless for a few seconds and then announced, "It's Saecaraz! I couldn't hold him; he's scared, and his awareness is shifting all over the place. But there's a huge square right in the center and this massive pyramid—all these tiers stacked atop each other—Threl High Chambers. I think he's heading for Saecaraz. I'm almost sure of it."

"That makes sense—he must be doing okay breathing-wise. Now where is Saecaraz?"

The Fieri looked at one another, and at the Travelers. "Don't look at me," said Pizzle. "I spent most of my time down there knee-deep in, ah . . . effluent. I don't know where Saecaraz is."

Yarden scrunched up her face in thought. "I went there once with the Chryse. I think I'd recognize it if I saw it again. From this vantage, the square and the pyramid should be fairly obvious."

Bohm said, "I will instruct the fleet to remain suspended in formation. We will go down for a closer look."

"We'd better find him fast," warned Pizzle. "It's going to be chaos down there once people start coming around."

Treet made his way as quickly and carefully as possible through the debris and wreckage of the Old Section. He had only one hope: to reach Jamrog as swiftly as possible and take him prisoner. Then he would force the Supreme Director, on pain of death, to call off the Invisibles and stop the war. Toward that end, he had secured a large and extremely lethal-looking weapon from one of the dead Invisibles on the battlefield.

His first thought was that every one of the enemy troops had been killed by falling chunks of crystal—some of which were fifty meters or so on a side. But upon investigation, he was amazed to discover that many had survived. His next thought was to disarm the survivors so that when the rebels came around they'd have the upper hand. The only problem with that idea was that it would take far too long to find each and every Invisible survivor and collect all the weapons—what if they started waking up before he got finished? Also, it was highly unlikely that all the Invisibles were on the battlefield when Dome collapsed. There was sure to be a central command post close by with reinforcements waiting to go into battle. And what about all the other Invisibles scattered throughout the Hages?

Then Treet hit on the solution of reaching Jamrog before the effects of free-breathing Empyrion's atmosphere wore off. Bypass the chain of command and go right to the top. Jamrog, he guessed, would be found in the Supreme Director's kraam.

How to get to Saecaraz in time, though, was the problem. The devastation was almost certain to be worse in Dome's interior: whole buildings and Hageblocks demolished, galleries, commons, and arcade areas crushed beneath tons of rubble, wreckage choking the streets . . .

But he didn't have to go overland—he would go *under*: the tunnel leading to the Saecaraz refuse pits. That would take him very close to his destination, Threl High Chambers.

He scrambled as quickly as possible over the battlefield,

which was littered with jumbled slabs of crystal tossed in an infinity of angles. He kept calm, telling himself that if he broke his neck hurrying, Jamrog would have the last laugh. So he went quickly, but cautiously enough to keep from impaling himself on the jagged shards.

Once, as he was clambering over a heap of fallen brick-work, he heard the throb of a balon's engines and caught a glimpse of a Fieri airship plowing past, too far away to notice him. It disappeared among the ruins to the north, stirring up the old frustration of watching salvation drift lightly and casually by, a reminder of the bleak hopelessness he'd felt in the desert when the balons had sailed right over him and his companions without stopping.

He reached New America Square, although he had to take a good look around in order to be certain that was indeed where he was. The nearly collapsed buildings were gone, and the entire area was covered by a single flat pane of crystal over which one of the gigantic support poles had fallen. Treet grappled to the top of the pole and proceeded on. The pole was grooved, so his feet didn't slip, and he was able to run easily along the top—like jogging on a giant redwood log or tubetrain conduit.

A few minutes later, owing to the fact that he was able to travel in a straight line above the wreckage, he arrived at the entrance to the Saecaraz tunnel. Don't let it be caved in, he muttered between clenched teeth as he climbed down the side of the fibersteel pole.

It was not caved in, but the entrance was blocked by a vehicle which had been caught halfway out of the tunnel; the whole back end was smashed flat by a section of wall. Treet squeezed by the junk and was able to edge in. Once inside the tunnel, he found another vehicle—this one intact, with four unconscious Invisibles inside. He hauled them out, jumped behind the wheel, put his foot to the pedal, and sped off. The tunnel had been repaired since the rebels destroyed it so the Invisibles could bring vehicles through. Treet had very little difficulty in navigating the conduit, although it was pitch dark most of the way.

Upon reaching the Saecaraz refuse pits at the other end, however, he almost despaired of ever making it to Jamrog's kraam. He emerged from the refuse pit to look upon a scene reminiscent of the Great Tokyo Earthquake: an entire city shaken, stirred, and ground to tiny pieces fit only for landfill.

But ahead, rising from the wreckage like a building-block pyramid that had somehow escaped being toppled when all the other building blocks fell, stood Threl High Chambers, massive and gray and looking distinctly shabby in the dazzling light of day.

In fact, the whole of Dome—that is, those few structures remaining at least partially intact—had taken on a decidedly declasse appearance. While it was never a cheery place to begin with, true, unfiltered daylight revealed its flaws. Treet was struck by the incredible dullness and sameness and meanness of its architecture. Dome appeared, as never before, what it truly was: a place designed by petty, brutish men in whom the love of life, of goodness, beauty, and vitality had long since vanished.

Funny, he thought, it had always been so well hidden before. Now, however, as pure light washed over the exposed interior, the baseness of Dome was revealed in all its perverse grandeur.

Treet puzzled over this as he made his way to Jamrog's kraam. Off in the distance he could see several sections of Dome's roof that had not caved in. They arched over the ruins, ragged edges glinting in the sun, looking very fragile—as if one touch, one breath might bring them crashing down to make the destruction complete.

The Fieri balons still hovered above. What were they waiting for? he wondered.

Threl Square lay buried under a solid mass of splintered crystal, fallen with such force that it had pulverized the stone beneath. Several of the great banners bearing Jamrog's imposing image remained upright, although they were shredded beyond recognition. He hurried across the square and ducked under the columns, glancing apprehensively upward. The lower tiers of the building had caught the most damage, many of the upper terraces having been torn away to fall on the ones below.

Once inside, however, he forced down his fear of the building's collapse and made his way to the lift. He remembered the Supreme Director's kraam as being on one of the upper levels, but didn't remember which one. It took him a few minutes, and a few false tries, to find it, only to discover that it was empty.

Now what? he wondered. Time was running out. Everyone

would come to any minute. He couldn't count on being able to move around freely much longer.

Jamrog must be nearby. If not in his kraam, then where?

Treet decided to take the lift to the top and start down from there. The minute he stepped out of the capsule onto the uppermost level he knew he'd guessed right. The garden looked as if a hurricane had swept through. The miniature trees were broken, the shrubbery tattered, the grounds strewn with anomalous junk. But there, in the center lay two bodies—and one of them was Jamrog's.

He approached cautiously.

The Supreme Director was quite dead. Even without the knife handle sticking out of the chest, Treet knew at a glance. The filmy, blank stare, the slack, open mouth, the utterly vacant appearance—like that of a birdcage whose feathered inhabitant had flown—the look he'd come to know so well in the last weeks, told all. Wherever Jamrog was, he was no longer among the living.

He sighed and tossed aside his weapon. How do you threaten a corpse?

Treet was so immersed in the quandary of what to do next, he failed to notice the shadow creeping toward him over the broken ground. But he heard the rustle of clothing and the whistling sound of something flying through the air toward him, and ducked.

The meter-long splinter of crystal sliced by him and dug a furrow in the grass. Treet rolled to his knees to face his attacker, and his heart went cold with fear. Mrukk stood but three steps away, red-eyed, panting heavily, blood trickling at the corners of his mouth.

Treet took in Mrukk and his own discarded weapon in the same glance. He threw himself toward it, falling awkwardly over Jamrog's body, reaching the gun just as Mrukk scooped it up.

The Mors Ultima leveled the weapon at him, sneered wickedly, and said in a low, raspy voice, "You'll have to do better than that, Fieri, if you plan to take over Empyrion."

Treet sat up slowly. "Look around you, Mrukk. It's finished. The Fieri have already taken over." Treet wished he could have said the words with more conviction, but his heart was beating so fast, he was lucky to be able to speak at all.

Mrukk glowered at him, shook his head as if to clear it,

and spoke again with pain. "You think that matters to me? Ask Jamrog." He indicated the body beside Treet. "Now, Fieri, you will join him."

With that he pressed the gun's pressure plate. Treet saw Mrukk's palm flatten and closed his eyes. There was a faint fizzling sound, and a plume of smoke issued from the throw-probe. That was all.

Mrukk shoved the useless thing barrel-first at Treet and then dove for him. Treet pitched forward and rolled to the side, landing once more on Jamrog. Mrukk's fingers were around his throat before he could squirm away.

He grasped Mrukk's hands and tried to dislodge them from his windpipe, but Mrukk's thumbs pressed down mercilessly. Treet tried to scream and could not; his air was cut off. His vision blurred, and he felt his mind growing fuzzy. It seemed as if he was drifting away from the scene, losing touch with his body—except for the fact that something hard was digging into his back, under his left shoulderblade.

Using all his strength, Treet shifted his weight and managed to slide off the hard thing a little so that it was only digging into his side. He could feel himself slipping, consciousness fading. But the thing jabbing him in the side was uncomfortable. With his good right hand he felt for the cause of his discomfort so as to pull it away.

His hand closed on the handle of Mrukk's knife.

Treet didn't know what happened next. His vision cleared, and he saw an extremely surprised Mrukk rise up and fall backward. Air rushed into Treet's lungs in long, raking gasps. He rolled off Jamrog's body and discovered the gun, his gun. He picked it up.

Mrukk squirmed on the ground, his hands clutching at the knife which had somehow become embedded in his left shoulder.

"That's enough," wheezed Treet. "Lay still. I don't want to kill you."

Mrukk cursed and looked up, saw the faulty weapon in Treet's hand, and laughed. The fog had lifted enough by now for Treet to realize that he'd made a very silly, yet very fatal mistake: the gun was a dud.

Mrukk laughed again, a short, sharp bark that brought tears to his eyes, and then flung himself at Treet's legs. Treet staggered backward, his right ankle firmly in Mrukk's grasp. He landed on his rump and the gun in his hand discharged, sending a blazing bolt skyward.

Mrukk stopped laughing.

Treet aimed the weapon carefully at Mrukk.

"Fun time's over," rasped Treet. "We've got a lot to do, and I don't have time to mess around. You're going to cooperate, or you'll be one sorry buckaroo, *comprende?*"

He edged close and plucked the knife from Mrukk's shoulder. A spasm of pain contorted the Mors Ultima's face. "Feel better now?" Treet asked, tucking the knife into the waistband of his yos.

Just then he heard a gravelly groan and noticed that the body lying next to Jamrog was moving. Keeping his eye on Mrukk, he rolled the body over with his foot. "Director Diltz, isn't it? Why yes, I remember you. Welcome to the party."

Diltz moaned pitifully and cringed away from the gun.

"That's right," said Treet. "I'm not too good with one of these things, so you'll want to go easy. We've all had enough excitement for one day."

"What do you want?" asked Mrukk flatly.

"Stop the Invisibles," stated Treet. "That'll do for starters. Then we're going to go down to Cavern level and open some cells. We're closing down the torture shops. Like I said, it's over. Kaput. Finis."

"Kill me," rasped Mrukk. "I won't do it."

Evidently the Mors Ultima did not intimidate easily, and Mrukk had called Treet's bluff. He had no plan for stopping the assault of the Invisibles without Mrukk. They were deadlocked.

"Killing you would be too easy, too quick," said Treet. "Get on your feet. We're all going for a little stroll."

Treet felt no hope of getting back before the fighting resumed, but there was no better option but to return to the Old Section and force the Invisibles to stop the battle or forfeit their leader's life. Keeping the gun on Mrukk he shouted, "Diltz, get up. Take off your yos and tear it into strips. Hurry! We don't want to miss the opening credits."

Diltz stripped off his yos and began tearing it. When he had a few long strips, Treet said, "That's enough. Wrap one of those around his shoulder so he doesn't bleed to death before I've had my fun. Then tie his hands." He waved the weapon at

Mrukk. "Tie them good, because I'm going to check your work."

The Nilokerus did as he was told, bandaging the bleeding shoulder and binding Mrukk's hands behind him while the Mors Ultima glared death and cursed. Treet was saved from having to figure out how to tie Diltz's hands without taking the gun off Mrukk by the sound of balon engines droning nearer.

He looked up to see the huge red sphere of the Fieri craft gliding over them. He fired another blast into the air as a signal, and a moment later the airship spun on its axis and began its descent. The balon landed in the center of the garden, bouncing lightly as it kissed the earth. Before the craft has settled, before the ramp was fully down, there was Yarden, running toward him, with Pizzle a close second, and Jaire, Preben, and Talus scarcely a step behind.

Yarden took in the situation at a glance. "We saw your signal and came as quickly as possible. Are you okay?"

Treet nodded, his throat suddenly constricted by a very big lump. "I'm fine."

SEVENTY
SEVEN

"**H**ow can we help?" Yarden asked, her eyes straying to Jamrog's whitened corpse. "It looks like this situation is under control."

"I promised these boys a ride in the balon if they behaved," said Treet, handing the knife to Preben. "Watch the big one— he's got an attitude problem." He turned to Pizzle. "You'd better tie up Diltz there. He's bound to think of trying something slick."

Talus said, "Tell us what you want us to do."

"Gladly. But first things first; we've got a pressing engagement elsewhere. I'll explain on the way."

They arrived in the Old Section a few minutes later and landed on the battlefield in the midst of a handful of very distracted Invisibles. Treet pushed Mrukk down the ramp ahead of him and called to them. "We have your commander. Throw down your weapons."

The Invisibles glanced uneasily at one another. Despite the shock of seeing a Fieri holding their commander prisoner, they made no move to disarm themselves. "Tell them, Mrukk," insisted Treet. "No more killing."

Mrukk steadfastly refused to open his mouth. "Jamrog is dead," Treet continued, calling to the Invisibles. "Dome is under new management. You are ordered to throw down your weapons and surrender."

The Invisibles paid no attention to his speech, and instead began advancing slowly toward him. Treet wished he had thought of a better plan.

"Halt!" The word was raw, but forceful.

Treet swiveled his head to see Tvrdy, Cejka, and Kopetch coming around the near side of the balon. Behind them were thirty disgruntled rebels, each with a weapon trained on an enemy. The Invisibles needed no more convincing. Hardware clattered to the ground, and the rebels wasted no time gathering it up.

Tvrdy approached, his eyes full of questions, looking at Treet as if seeing him for the first time. "I don't know how this has happened," he said in a voice that sounded as if he had been gargling acid, "but I think you are responsible." He embraced Treet with the arm that wasn't holding a weapon.

"Thank you for saving our lives," said Cejka in a rough whisper.

Treet beamed at them both. "I was afraid I wouldn't get back here in time." He glanced at Mrukk—who was currently wearing the classic expression of a man who has suddenly remembered an important appointment elsewhere—and told Tvrdy, "Here, I brought you a present. Maybe you can think of a way to make him talk."

"What do you want him to say?" asked Tvrdy, squinting with pain as he spoke.

"He has a lot of people locked up. How about letting him talk about that?"

"Good," Tvrdy said. "Anything else?"

"Take Diltz here to the Archives. If I'm not mistaken, the magicians are up to some funny business there. He'll want to help you all he can, I'm sure. Pizzle, you go with him."

"Right, Chief," said Pizzle.

"I'll see to it," promised Cejka.

Treet turned and waved to the balon.

Inside the airship, Yarden saw him and said, "There's his signal. It's over!"

Bohm flipped a switch on the panel before him and said, "All balon pilots: you are free to land. Begin establishing aid stations in the designated areas."

At his word, the Fieri balons began descending into the ruins. The siege of Dome was over.

● ● ● ● ●

Giloon Bogney saw the balon coming toward him; he gathered up his bhuj and strode toward the alien craft purposefully. The last few hours had been extremely trying for him. Leading an exodus of eleven thousand Dhogs out of Dome wasn't as easy as he thought it would be.

In getting to the old exit, it had proven all but impossible to keep the families together. There were stragglers among the elder members, and children slowed the procession down so that it took much longer than he had planned just to reach the old airlock.

The airlock was set in the great, curving wall of the Old Section's outer rim. It was huge, and although they had known about it for hundreds of years, the Dhogs had never attempted to use it. But Bogney was determined to use it now.

He had the Dhogs gather before the outer door—the inner door of the lock had long since been dismantled and carried off for scrap—and with great ceremony lifted his bhuj into the air and waved it in a circle over his head. Two dozen of the bulkier Dhogs fell upon the opening mechanism at once. The ancient works resisted their best attempts; so the Dhogs took up long fibersteel struts and began levering the door open.

They worked themselves into a sweat with the effort, and in time heard a great sigh as the door's brittle seals cracked and gave way. The portal fell outward with a tremendous crash, its upper wheels sheared off.

What happened next could only be described as disaster. The Dhogs were treated to a rude revelation as they met Empyrion's volatile atmosphere. For Bogney it was doubly worse, for not only was it excruciatingly painful, but rolling around on the ground made him lose dignity in front of his people, not that anyone noticed.

Eventually the effects of the nasty surprise wore off. And no sooner had they regained their composure than they heard a most unsettling sound: an ominous, droning thunder which seemed to pervade all of Dome. Frightened and still groggy, the Dhogs scooped up their belongings and hustled through the portal out into the green hills of Empyrion.

They had not trooped far, however, when they were arrested by the sight of the Fieri fleet circling high above them, skimming the uppermost peaks of the crystal mountain range. That, combined with the fact that they actually had ventured outside and lived to tell about it, and the mind-boggling reality of unlimited vistas and far-distant horizons, combined to halt the exodus. They were overcome.

The Dhogs stood flabbergasted and watched the colored balons circle, their engines roaring with power, thunder booming down to them from crystal canyons.

Then it happened. Dome collapsed.

There was a horrific cracking sound and terrible rifts appeared, streaking down from the topmost peaks and mounds. The entire edifice wobbled for an instant, and then plunged inward upon itself.

The Dhogs' first reaction was to run back into Dome, which was familiar to them. But Bogney was successful in preventing this; he forbade them entrance to the crumbling bubble, turning them instead to the valleys beyond, where they watched the destruction from a safe distance. When it was over, they crept from their hiding places to look upon the shattered remains of their former home.

Bogney was at a loss to explain what had happened, but figured that the mysterious airships had to be of Fierran origin. He called the family heads together and explained to them that they no longer had any need to walk to Fierra. He pointed to the hovering spheres and declared, "Fieri be coming for Dhogs. We now be going to Fierra."

The Dhogs accepted this as reasonable, and they all went back to explain to their families, whereupon the multitude sat down and waited for the second stage of their exodus.

That was how the balon found them, sitting with their bundled belongings and livestock, ready and waiting to be taken to Fierra.

Bogney approached the craft as the ramp slid down. He stationed himself at the foot of the ramp to greet the Fieri. When the pilot appeared, Bogney held up his bhuj and said, "We being great glad to see you, Fieri man. Big thanks you coming here for us to get us. Dhogs ready. Let's go."

Tvrdy and a contingent of armed Tanais conducted Mrukk to Nilokerus Hage and proceeded to the Cavern level security cells. The groggy Nilokerus stared in disbelief at Mrukk and his captors. One word from Tvrdy, however, and they began opening the cells and setting their prisoners free.

"Now then," said Tvrdy, pushing Mrukk toward the communication console, "you're going to contact all those interrogation kraams of yours. Tell your men it's over. Any attempted reprisals will bring death."

Mrukk stood immobile. "Tell them!" yelled Tvrdy. "Tell them now, or I'll turn you over to your own prisoners."

The Mors Ultima grimaced and leaned over the console. Tvrdy flipped some switches, opening all channels. Mrukk spoke gruffly into the microphone. "All Mors Ultima squad leaders, release your prisoners. This is a special directive from Commander Mrukk. All prisoners are to be released at once." He straightened and stepped back from the console. "Satisfied?"

"No. Now we're going to begin closing down your network. We'll visit each Hage and make sure your orders are obeyed."

"My orders are always obeyed," sneered Mrukk.

Just then, the first of the prisoners began emerging from the corridors. They saw the Nilokerus standing in a clump with Tanais guns on them, and Mrukk with his hands tied behind his back and a bloody bandage on his shoulder.

One of the prisoners, a Jamuna with a battered face and eyes swollen nearly shut, fearlessly approached Mrukk and spit in the Mors Ultima leader's face. Other prisoners witnessed the act and rushed forward.

Tvrdy quickly intercepted them. "No more!" he told them. "It's over. The killing is over."

The prisoners, revenge gleaming in their dull eyes, muttered and stepped away. "Put the Nilokerus in the cells for now," Tvrdy ordered several of his men. "The rest of you come with me." He pushed Mrukk before him, and they left the cells to begin their tour of Jamrog's torture chambers.

Pizzle and Cejka, along with several Rumon soldiers, made their way to the Archives. Diltz remained silent the whole trip, staring sullenly ahead as the ems made their way through the lower-level streets and corridors.

They arrived at the Archives level and forced Diltz to open the succession of sealed doors. Upon entering the Archives, they found the stubby missile already aboard its carrier and crawling toward the Archives' huge outer doors, which were open. The magicians, wearing atmosphere helmets and oblivious to the destruction visited on the rest of Dome, were trundling the aged weapon toward the doors.

"I don't believe this!" shouted Pizzle. "They're getting ready to launch that thing!" He rushed across the floor which had been cleared to accommodate the missile, and grabbed the first magician he came to by the throat. "Stop it!" he screamed. "Turn it off!"

The magician made a movement with his hands, and Pizzle was thrown backwards through the air. The Rumon rushed forward to Pizzle's aid. The other magicians, Nilokerus and Saecaraz, turned to stare at the scene. They raised their hands, and the Rumon went down in a heap. One magician advanced to stand over them, putting out his hands to keep them pinned down.

Cejka fired his weapon at the foremost magician, who averted the blast but was slammed back into the missile by the force of the blow. Pizzle regained his feet and dashed for the missile. He reached it and tore open the hatch on its side before he was again lifted off his feet and flung back.

"Stay back!" cried Cejka and loosed another volley at the magicians, pushing two more back before the weapon was jerked from his hands by the psi force the magicians wielded.

Diltz saw his chance and hit Cejka with a body block that shoved him down the steps to the Archives floor below. "Launch the weapon!" he screamed. "Launch it at once!"

The magicians looked at one another blankly.

"No!" hollered Pizzle. "Don't do it!"

Diltz flew down the steps and scooped up Cejka's weapon. "I am Supreme Director!" he yelled. "Obey me. Launch the weapon."

The magicians, wearing their atmosphere helmets, could not understand what Diltz was raving about. They simply stared at him and exchanged puzzled glances. "Don't you understand?" he screamed. "I am Supreme Director now. I order you to launch the weapon! What's the matter with you? Do as I say."

Pizzle saw what was happening. "Ha!" he shouted. "They're deaf with those helmets on. They can't hear a word you're saying."

Diltz frowned. "Shut up!" He strode up and slapped a magician's helmet. "Take off those helmets! Take them off! I order you!"

The magicians hesitated. Diltz put down the weapon and took the helmet in his hands, gave a sharp twist, and lifted it off.

The others pulled their helmets off as well, and Pizzle watched the surprised expressions appear on their faces. Eyes starting from their heads, they clawed at their throats and sank to the floor to thrash in agony.

"Now!" yelled Pizzle. The Rumon scrambled to their feet. Pizzle ran to the missile, which was still creeping slowly toward the open doors.

"You tricked me!" screamed Diltz. He stooped to recover his weapon and, raising it, leveled it at Pizzle and pressed the pressure plate. The blast went wide as Diltz's knees buckled and he pitched forward. Momentum carried Cejka over the top of his victim. His hands found the skidding weapon, and he whipped it around.

"I should kill you, Diltz," growled Cejka.

Diltz groaned and writhed on the floor.

"How do we disarm this thing?" called Pizzle. "Hurry! I don't think we have much time."

Two Rumon hauled Diltz to his feet and dragged him forward. "You heard him," said Cejka. "Disarm it!"

Diltz stared back defiantly. "Disarm it yourself!"

Cejka slapped the Nilokerus across the mouth. "Disarm it now or I *will* kill you."

"I don't know how," Diltz spat. "*They* do." He jerked his head to indicate the unconscious magicians. "Tell *them*." He laughed, a creaking sound from the tomb.

"We've got to stop it," said Pizzle. The missile had reached the threshold and was moving out under the landing platform. "My guess is that it's set to go off once it clears the platform."

There was a grinding sound, and the missile began raising slowly up in its cradle. "It's going into firing position! We've got maybe two minutes." He raced to the missile again and peered into the hatch at the welter of blinking lights and dials. There was a row of buttons, all lit green. As Pizzle watched, one by one, they all blinked red. He heard the whir of the internal timing mechanism inside.

Cejka joined him, saying, "I know nothing of this type of weapon."

"Get one of those magicians over here," said Pizzle. "Hurry!"

Cejka signaled to the Rumon, who began trying to rouse the magicians.

"It will be a few minutes yet," said Cejka. "We can't wake them."

Diltz put back his head and laughed—an evil, hateful sound.

"I'm not going to let this thing launch," said Pizzle grimly. "I won't."

"What then?"

Pizzle drew a hand over his sweating forehead and, still gazing into the hatch, his face lit by the blinking lights, took a deep breath and said, "I'm going to start pushing buttons. I might get lucky . . . Then again, I might set the thing off right here."

Cejka did not flinch. "Do what you must do, Traveler."

"Here goes nothing," said Pizzle. He whispered a prayer and reached into the hatch. With a quivering finger he pushed first one button and then another. The lights continued blinking and the dials pulsing. "It's a sequence arrangement, I'm sure, but I don't know the sequence."

The missile had crawled far out beneath the platform. Pizzle could see the far edge of the upper canopy coming nearer as they approached. He began pushing the buttons and flipping switches indiscriminately, but to no avail. The missile with its atomic warhead, now in launch position, moved ever nearer the predesignated launch site.

Pizzle dashed back inside and went to a magician. He picked the insensate form off the floor and shook it. "Wake up!" The man's head lolled and his tongue bulged from his mouth. He let the body slump back to the floor. "It's no use. I can't stop it."

Diltz laughed hysterically.

Pizzle raced back to where Cejka stood watching the missile as it cleared the edge of the platform. The carrier stopped.

"It's going to launch!" yelled Cejka.

"Here, give me that thing!" shouted Pizzle, snatching the thermal weapon from Cejka. He ran to the missile, raised the weapon, and aimed at the hatch. He closed his eyes and pressed the pressure plate with his palm.

Sparks and hot metal shrapnel erupted around him. He stood his ground and kept firing into the missile. There came a rumble, and the missile shuddered.

"It's going to launch!" cried Cejka.

"No it's not!" Pizzle threw himself forward and reached into the blasted hatch. He grabbed a handful of wires and pulled. There was a sizzling noise, and the missile rocked in its cradle twice and was still.

"You did it!" yelled Cejka, running up to pound him on the back. Behind him the Rumon burst into cheers. "You stopped it!"

Pizzle staggered back as relief burst over him. He rubbed his dripping face with his hands and sighed. "Man alive!"

SEVENTY
EIGHT

The next three days were, as Mathiax had predicted, extraordinarily hectic. There was aid to be administered, order to be established, and a whole new epoch in Empyrion history to be inaugurated.

Sadly, there were a multitude of casualties, scores of which were beyond hope of recovery—although not as many as Talus and Bohm had feared. Most of Dome's inhabitants, it seemed, had been huddled in their kraams in deep Hage, hiding from Invisibles who were seeking victims for their interrogation and torture quotas. Or they were near enough to a sturdy Hage-block to run for cover when the sky-shell began to shatter and break up. Still, there was great sadness amongst the rescuers as they buried the bodies of innocent Dome dwellers who had been killed by the shattered crystal.

When the natural, vital air of the planet came roaring in, replacing the eternally recycled sterile air of Dome, the effect, while terrifying and unspeakably painful, was not actually harmful in any lasting way. The populace was instantly rendered helpless, if not altogether docile.

At first, survivors wandered dazedly through the ruins of their world, muttering incoherently, lost and forlorn, dazzled by the light of an unfiltered sun. But when they finally understood that the Fieri had come to help them, that Jamrog's nightmare reign was over, and that their lives could only get better as a result of the collapse, their spirits improved radically.

On the fourth day, reinforcements arrived from Fierra: three more balon fleets filled with Fieri volunteers led by Mathiax. The new arrivals came with supplies and heavy equipment to begin tackling the monumental cleanup operation.

For the architects of the new order, the days sped by, every minute crammed with emergencies large and small and with decisions of all kinds about nearly everything. The whole society of Dome—which wasn't really *Dome* at all anymore—had to be reorganized. There were innumerable positions of leadership to fill, and countless functionaries to appoint. Not to mention a herculean rebuilding project to orchestrate.

But by the end of the second week, the wheels of the newly formed provisional government were firmly on track, and the rescuers were able to relax somewhat. Talus announced that they would celebrate their victory with a dinner where they could all sit down together.

They assembled in Tvrdy's kraam, which had come through the apocalypse most intact, and shared a simple meal, prepared and served by the Fieri. After dinner, and a succession of souile toasts, they mingled and talked about the future.

When Talus, Tvrdy, Mathiax, and the others began discussing, as they had been all week, various options of organization for the new government and the kind of ongoing aid its leaders would require, Treet excused himself and joined Yarden, who had wandered off to sit by herself in a far corner of the room. It was the first real opportunity he'd had to talk to her alone since her arrival.

"Here's to the future," he said, raising his glass. He sank down onto a cushion beside her.

Yarden regarded him over the rim of her cup. "The future," she said a little wistfully.

"What's the matter? Having second thoughts about saving me?"

"It isn't that. I'm happier than I've ever been."

Treet laughed. "You certainly have a unique way of showing it."

She bent her head. "You're right. I'm sorry. It's just that . . . well, I've got a few hard decisions to make."

"Such as? Tell me. Maybe I can help."

Yarden took a deep breath. "A few of the balons are going back to Fierra day after tomorrow. I think I'm going back with them."

"So soon? I thought you'd stick around a while."

She shook her head gently. "I'm not needed here. What I came to do—it's finished. I'd only be in the way from now on. Besides, I've got my own life to rebuild. I've got my art, and—" She hesitated, glancing up quickly. Treet saw the light come up in her eyes and knew that it wasn't for him that it shone. "There's no way you could have known about that—so much has happened . . ."

"You're right. I've missed out on a lot."

There was a small, awkward silence then, and Yarden changed the subject. "You know we found Crocker?"

"Pizzle told me."

"And Calin—how did she die?" Treet looked away. "It might help to talk about it. She was my friend; I'd like to know."

He was silent for a few moments and then said, "We were just a couple kilometers from Dome on our way back. Crocker had started acting strange that morning, and the closer we got, the stranger he grew." Treet took a deep breath and let it out between his teeth. "He attacked us . . . he smashed Calin's throat, ripped it open with a metal bar—"

"Oh, no!" murmured Yarden.

"She never made it back. I almost didn't make it, either. Crocker was crazy, like an animal. He meant to kill us both."

"You're sure?"

"Without a doubt. He would have succeeded, too. Only Calin saved my life. She protected me somehow with her psi. She was concentrating so hard on me, she didn't see it coming."

"What happened then?"

"To Crocker? I think something snapped inside his head. He just ran off. I didn't chase him—never saw him again after that."

Yarden shook her head. "What made him do it?"

"Hladik's conditioning—that's my guess."

"The same thing they tried to do to you?"

"Probably. Only I was luckier than Crocker, that's all."

"No," she said firmly, "not luckier—stronger maybe."

Treet lifted a shoulder ambivalently. "Who knows what they did to him? I don't know if I could have lasted much longer."

"But that's just it. You stuck it out. You had the will to survive. You endured. Crocker was weak; he gave in."

"How can you say that?"

"Because I know. When Crocker came to us, we offered him the chance to recover. We gave him the opportunity to begin helping himself. All he had to do was say yes. Instead, he chose to run away again rather than endure the hard work of getting better."

Treet nodded silently. "Still," he said after a moment, "I can't blame him for what happened. It wasn't his fault. To tell you the truth, I probably wouldn't be here now, but . . . I know this is going to sound crazy, but when I was in the tank I tried to contact you and got something else instead."

Yarden's glance quickened. "What was it, Orion?"

Treet looked into his cup as if he might find the answer written there. "The Comforter," he said. "The Infinite. At least that's the only explanation I have." He bent his head and silence fell between them. When he spoke again, his eyes were focused far away. "After it was over, I carried Calin's body back to Dome and buried her outside."

"I'd like to see her grave. Would you show me?"

"Sure. She deserves a headstone or marker of some kind. I've been thinking of fixing something up when things calm down around here."

• • • • • •

The next morning Treet led Yarden to Calin's grave, and they knelt together while Yarden paid her final respects. Treet placed a simple stone marker at the head of the grave and stepped back. "That'll do until I can find something better," he said, then looked at Yarden. "You're going to be an artist; maybe you could make something. I think sunstone would be nice."

"You're right; sunstone would be perfect. I'll do it."

They turned away from the gravesite and began walking around the perimeter of Dome. The day was bright, as always, the breeze fresh, the air full of the sounds of industry as the cleanup continued full swing.

"Figured out what you're going to do, Orion?" Yarden asked after they'd walked a while.

"I've thought about it some. I guess I'd like to do what I came here to do—write Empyrion's history."

His answer brought a sharp reply. "You can't think you still have any obligation to Cynetics? Not after all that's happened. They used you, used us all."

"Easy, Yarden," Treet soothed. "No, it's not for Cynetics. It's for . . . well, for everyone really, but for the Fieri maybe most of all. The Preceptor gave me a note when I left Fierra. She reminded me that the Fieri are a people without a past, and she said, 'I ask you to remember for us who we were . . .' I guess I'd like to give them back their past." He shrugged, "Beyond that, few historians ever have the chance to view firsthand the kind of upheaval I've seen; fewer still live through it. Witnessing the birth of a new civilization is an opportunity I'd never get at home."

"Speaking of which, do you think we'll ever go home again?"

"Not much chance. Pizzle and I have talked about it. He points out that even if Cynetics sent a rescue ship—which in itself is an astronomical longshot—the chances are at least five hundred quadrillion to one that it would reach us. It could end up anywhere in Empyrion's time spectrum—like we did."

"Oh, well. I won't miss not going back. I don't think I would even if I had the chance. I'm happy here, and there's a whole world of things to learn and do. It's the adventure of a lifetime, and I plan to take a lifetime to enjoy it."

"You sound like Pizzle," Treet said. He looked at Yarden and felt her pulling away from him. Nowhere in anything she'd said so far was there a hint that she was considering a future with him. He stopped walking, and turned to her. "Last night you spoke about having to make some hard decisions. Was I one of your hard decisions?" he asked. There—now it was out in the open.

She dropped her head. "The hardest of all."

"Yarden—" He stepped toward her. "You don't have to—"

"It's no good, Treet. We don't love each other, not really. If you think about it, you'll see I'm right."

A bewildered expression worked its way across his face. "What was that we felt before? If it wasn't love, it sure fooled me."

"We'd just survived a terrible ordeal and were grateful to be alive—an absolutely normal response under the circumstances. We were in love with life, Orion, not each other."

"I love you, Yarden," he said.

"I love you, too. I hope we'll always be the very best of friends."

"It's cruel to tell a guy in love that you want to be his friend."

"I'm sorry. The last thing I wanted to do was hurt you."

Treet stared at Yarden—she was so beautiful, so alive. It

hurt to end it like this. She stepped close and put her lips to his cheek. "For friendship?" he asked.

"For friendship."

They walked some more and rounded a pile of debris to see what looked like a sizable refugee camp spread out on the hillside. "What is that?" asked Yarden. "Where'd they come from?"

"You haven't met the Dhogs? Well, you're in for a rare treat, because here comes Giloon Bogney—top Dhog himself."

Yarden stared as a grotesque little man dressed in the filthiest, most ragged clothes she had ever seen came waddling toward them. His beard was plastered to his grimy face, and a livid scar divided his forehead, warping his countenance and twisting one eye upward so that he seemed to be appraising the weather. He waved a bhuj before them and smiled broadly.

Yarden cringed at the sight. A wafting breeze carried his aroma to her, and she rocked backward.

"Steady," whispered Treet. To Bogney he said, "Greetings, Bogney. I see you managed to survive."

Irony was lost on the Dhog leader. "You no looking much dead yourself, Fieri man. Giloon be saying good-bye here now. Dhogs being gone to Fierra soon, very soon."

"You'll love it there, I know. Good luck."

Bogney leaned forward on his bhuj in a confiding way. "We no more making big stinking noises since you leaving us lonely. Giloon knowing you bring air machines to take us, so we still being big friends."

He scuttled off then, leaving Yarden agape.

"A friend for life." Treet turned to Yarden. "Well, what do you think? Will Fierra ever be the same?"

"The Fieri may have survived the atom bomb, but I'm not sure they're ready for the Dhogs."

EPILOGUE

*I*n due time Dome became Sildarin, after the nearby river, and with the steadfast help of the Fieri, sweeping changes were made. The Hages were disbanded and a new economic and social structure introduced. The Fieri opened schools and began teaching the people. The temples were closed and the priesthood defrocked. Worship of the god of Old Dome, Trabant Animus, lingered on surreptitiously for a time among the older Hagemen, but most people turned gratefully to the Infinite Father of the Fieri.

Others, however, could not accept the new era. Mrukk was found dead in his cell, a victim of suffocation, having stuffed the better part of his own yos down his throat. Most of the imprisoned Invisibles, after the example of their leader, committed suicide rather than face the justice of the new order—a pathetic and wholly unnecessary exercise since the Fieri had no thoughts of revenge. Diltz, having lost the only thing he cared about: power, lost the will to live and simply wasted away.

Tvrdy became the first Governor of Sildarin. He was installed with due ceremony by the Mentors, and immediately began working to effect the reforms he had so long envisioned for his people. Cejka took his place as Secretary-General of the new government and served with great distinction. Kopetch was appointed First Secretary and was placed in charge of redesigning and rebuilding the new city-state.

Ernina undertook the study of Fierran medicine, eventually returning to Sildarin to establish a training hospital of her own. As a result of the dramatic upswing in the Sildarinian birthrate following the collapse of Dome, *Ernina* became a favorite name for little girls whose mothers came under the care of the wise and kindly physician.

Talus established an official liaison program, a sort of Fieri embassy, for the ongoing betterment of relations between the Fieri and the Sildarins. Mathiax took on the task of overseeing the development of the new school system, which led to his becoming an extremely popular holovision personality by way of his educational programs. One of the first new projects was an airfield for the balons carrying materials and equipment from Fierra to aid the reconstruction; hence Bohm became Director of Transportation and Trade.

After the prescribed waiting period, Pizzle and Starla were married in the finest Fieri style. Pizzle grew two inches and lost most of his pudginess. Starla was credited with the remarkable accomplishment of taming his obnoxious nature, and he eventually developed into a gentle, loving, and strikingly thoughtful spouse. He also gave Empyrion its first publishing concern: a press devoted to preserving in writing all the Fieri classics of wisdom, learning, and storytelling—and also, incidentally, a few science fiction and fantasy creations of his own.

Yarden returned to Fierra as planned and applied herself to the study of art, eventually becoming a well-respected artist for her wonderfully atmospheric and intuitive paintings. She developed a unique style, which led to her taking on students of her own who wanted to learn her techniques. In Anthon, Yarden found a soulmate, and the two became inseparable friends.

The first volume of Treet's masterwork, *Darkness and the Light: The History of Empyrion,* was published by Pizzle's Empyrion Press, and was greeted with great acclaim. Work on the second volume was delayed, however, for a lengthy honeymoon cruise which Treet and Jaire undertook following an ardent, if leisurely courtship. The two divided their time between Fierra and Sildarin, and did their level best to keep Mathiax and his school system busy teaching successive editions of little Treets.

On numerous occasions Treet went to the Blue Forest to look for Crocker. He never found the pilot, but left preserved food, clothing, and simple tools and implements behind. These items were always gone when he returned the following year, and a crude present—a spear or a pair of sandals made of bark—was left in their place. In time, Treet accepted that this was how Crocker wanted it, and the yearly pilgrimage became less a manhunt than a mission of mercy for a fallen friend.

Giloon Bogney and the Dhogs found in Fierra everything they had ever imagined paradise to be. Cleaned up and fed regularly, they quickly acquired the rudiments of civilization. From the first they were fascinated by sunstone, and were delighted to learn that it came from far-off mountains. Bogney was taken to a quarry there, and upon viewing the work declared that henceforth the Dhogs would learn to work the marvelous stone and become quarriers and builders. Although they loved Fierra dearly, the Dhogs loved the Light Mountains more, and chose a place for themselves in the Star Cliffs region where with the patient expertise of the Fieri they would eventually build a shining city of their own overlooking the unlimited expanse of the jade green ocean.

Also from Lion:

SONG OF ALBION

Stephen Lawhead

Book 1: *The Paradise War*
Wolves prowling the streets of Oxford.
A Green Man haunting the Highlands...
Lewis Gillies is face to face with an
ancient mystery.

Drawn from the dreaming spires of
Oxford to the misty moors and glens of
Scotland, Lewis expects little more than a
pleasant weekend away. But the road north
leads to a mystical crossroads, and he finds
himself in a place where two worlds meet,
in the time-between-times.

The ancient Celts admitted no
separation between this world and the
Otherworld: the two were delicately
interwoven, each dependent on the
other. In *The Paradise War* this balance is
disturbed – a breach has opened between
the worlds and cosmic catastrophe
threatens.

'In a style reminiscent of Tolkien,
Lawhead presents a world of vivid
imagery. This book is a delight.'
Bookstore Journal

ISBN 0 7459 2466 2

Book 2: *The Silver Hand*

The great king, Meldryn Mawr, is dead
and his kingdom lies in ruins. Treachery
and brutality stalk the land. Prince
Meldron, prompted by the cunning and
grasping Siawn Hy, now claims the throne.

Kingship, sovereignty and the making
of a true king lie at the heart of this second book in the *Song of Albion* trilogy.
Herein lie passion and power, heartbreak
and hope – the fate of Albion and the destiny of the long-awaited champion: Silver
Hand.

'An epic struggle between Light and
Darkness... well paced, exciting and
well researched.'
Mick Norman, *Forbidden Planet*

ISBN 0 7459 2510 3

Book 3: *The Endless Knot*

Fire rages in Albion: a strange, hidden
fire, dark-flamed, invisible to the eye.
Seething and churning, it burns, gathering
flames of darkness into its hot, black
heart. Unseen and unknown, it burns...

Llew Silver Hand is High King of
Albion and the Brazen Man has defied his
sovereignty. Llew must journey into the
Foul Land to redeem his greatest treasure.
The last battle begins.

Celtic myth collides with modern life
in a timeless story. With *The Endless Knot*,
Lawhead strikes the final resounding
chord in the *Song of Albion*.

'Celtic twilight shot with a brighter,
fiercer light, and tinged with modern
villainy... savagely beautiful.'
Michael Scott Rohan, author of
the *Winter of the World* trilogy

ISBN 0 7459 2783 1

THE PENDRAGON CYCLE

Stephen Lawhead

A magnificent epic set against the back-cloth of Roman Britain and the legends of King Arthur and lost Atlantis.

Book 1: *Taliesin*
Atlantis is extinguished in a monstrous holocaust, out of which three ships bear the survivors to the isle of Ynys Prydein. Here Celtic chieftains struggle for survival in the twilight of Rome's power. One hero-ic figure towers over all: Prince Taliesin, father of Merlin.

ISBN 0 7459 1309 1

Book 2: *Merlin*
Merlin's story is the story of the Island of the Mighty – of warring battlechiefs and bloody Saecsen invaders, of the hidden Hill Folk and the waning power of Rome. It is
a tale of love, savagery and madness; an all-consuming vision of the Kingdom of Summer, of treachery and death, of the saving of a babe, and of a sword in a stone.

ISBN 0 7459 1310 5

Book 3: *Arthur*
'It is the eve of Christ Mass, and the noblemen have come to Londinium to hold council – to essay who among them might become High King. Fifteen years have come and gone since the sword was first placed there. A young man stands grim-faced, gazing at the sword thrust deep into the stone... hesitant, uncertain. "Take it, Arthur," Merlin tells him...'

So the story begins – a tale of high hope and bitter endeavour, of loyalty and treachery, of spiritual quest and the winning of a kingdom – a story whose end, like its beginning, is shrouded in mystery.

ISBN 0 7459 1311 3

Book 4: *Pendragon*
'I, Myrddin Emrys, was with Arthur from the beginning. I stood beside him on his darkest day. A day unlike any other in the long history of our race – a day of deceit, and great glory. For on that day Arthur won the name he treasured above all others: Pendragon. That is a tale worth telling.'

ISBN 0 7459 2763 7

Book 5: *Grail*

Following his miraculous healing by
Christ's cup from an apparently fatal
wound, Arthur sets his heart upon
establishing a shrine to the Grail as a
symbol of the Summer Realm he has
introduced to Britain. But, in this account
by Gwalchavad (Galahad), Myrddin's
(Merlin's) old enemy Morgian concocts
a devastating betrayal by one of Arthur's
dearest companions. Arthur's dream is
soon in tatters and the newly won peace
and promised prosperity in Britain are
threatened with great evil.

ISBN 0 7459 3883 3

All Lion books are available from your
local bookshop, or can be ordered via our
website or from Marston Book Services.
For a free catalogue, showing the complete
list of titles available, please contact:

Customer Services
Marston Book Services
PO Box 269
Abingdon
Oxon
OX14 4YN

Tel: 01235 465500
Fax: 01235 465555

Our website can be found at:
www.lionhudson.com